BELLA POLDARK

The twelfth Poldark novel

By the same author

Ross Poldark

Demelza

Jeremy Poldark

Warleggan

The Black Moon

The Four Swans

The Angry Tide

The Stranger from the Sea

The Miller's Dance

The Loving Cup

The Twisted Sword

Night Journey

Cordelia

The Forgotten Story

The Merciless Ladies

Night Without Stars

Take My Life

Fortune is a Woman

The Little Walls

The Sleeping Partner

Greek Fire

The Tumbled House

Marnie

The Grove of Eagles

After the Act

The Walking Stick

Angell, Pearl and

Little God

The Japanese Girl

(short stories)

Woman in the Mirror

The Green Flash

Cameo

Stephanie

Tremor

The Ugly Sister

The Spanish Armadas

Poldark's Cornwall

WINSTON GRAHAM

Bella Poldark

A Novel of Cornwall 1818–1820

MACMILLAN

First published 2002 by Macmillan
an imprint of Pan Macmillan Ltd
Pan Macmillan, 20 New Wharf Road, London N1 9RR
Basingstoke and Oxford
Associated companies throughout the world
www.panmacmillan.com

ISBN 0 333 98923 6 (HB)
ISBN 0 333 98923 6 (TPB)

5 7 9 8 6

A CIP catalogue record for this book is available from
the British Library.

Typeset by SetSystems Ltd, Saffron Walden, Essex
Printed and bound in Great Britain by
Mackays of Chatham plc, Chatham, Kent

To
Max and Joan Reinhardt
For many years of loving friendship

Contents

Note from the Author: The Poldark Saga

This is the twelfth and last Poldark novel. New readers may like a short account of the characters and what has gone before, and, since the eleventh Poldark was published some years ago, even former readers who remember a great deal may appreciate a brief résumé.

W.G.

SIR ROSS POLDARK. Belongs to the small Cornish gentry, created a baronet by Lord Liverpool on his being sent on a mission to Paris on behalf of the government during Napoleon's exile in Elba. Owns Nampara, a small estate with two operative mines and some farm land.

DEMELZA (née Carne). Daughter of a Cornish miner. Ross marries her when she is seventeen and they have five children: JULIA, who dies of diphtheria when a baby; JEREMY, who is killed at Waterloo; CLOWANCE, now the widow of Stephen Carrington, who has died in a riding accident; ISABELLA-ROSE, who possesses a fine voice; and HENRY (almost an afterthought), who through his brother's death is heir to his father's baronetcy.

CUBY POLDARK (née Trevanion, of Caerhays Castle) is the widow of Jeremy Poldark. NOELLE is their daughter, born after Jeremy's death.

CLOWANCE CARRINGTON continues to run the small shipping line set up by Stephen in Penryn before his death. They have no children.

SIR GEORGE WARLEGGAN, knighted by Pitt in return for political support. Son of the founder and now head of Warleggan & Williams' Bank. Marries, first, ELIZABETH POLDARK (née Chynoweth), widow of Francis Poldark, Ross's cousin, and previously affianced to Ross.

Elizabeth has a son by Francis, called GEOFFREY CHARLES, now a veteran of the Peninsular War and living at Trenwith, the family home of the Poldarks, which is four miles from Nampara. He and his Spanish wife AMADORA (née de Bertendona) have one daughter, JUANA.

Elizabeth had two children by George Warleggan: VALENTINE, who is married to SELINA (widow of Clement Pope) and lives with her at Place House, Trevaunance, which is about three miles further along the coast from Trenwith and near the village of St Ann's. There is bitter enmity and suspicion about Valentine's parentage. Elizabeth's third child – the second by George – is URSULA, whose birth causes Elizabeth's death.

George's second wife – married ten years later – is LADY HARRIET CARTER, sister of the Duke of Leeds, and by George she has twin daughters. They live at Cardew, a mansion bought from the Lemon family by the Warleggans about thirty years ago, and situated over the spine of Cornwall in the gentler part of the county, looking towards the Restronguet Valley.

Nearest neighbours of like standing to the Poldarks of Nampara are the family of TRENEGLOS, who live at Mingoose House.

A mile beyond Sawle Church in an inland direction live the ENYSES, at Killewarren. Thirty years ago DWIGHT ENYS came as a young doctor, and his friendship with Ross has been deep and abiding ever since. So has Demelza's for Dwight's wife, CAROLINE, (née Penvenen). They have two daughters.

JINNY CARTER, one of the brood of Martins living in Mellin Cottages, lost her first husband, Jim, who, sent to prison for poaching, died of a gangrenous arm. She later married Whitehead Scoble and ever since has kept the only shop in Sawle. Her son – by Jim – is BEN CARTER, who is captain of Wheal Leisure, the only profitable Poldark mine.

Demelza has five brothers, of whom two have close connections with the story: SAM, who has become the leader of the Methodists in the district; and DRAKE, who has moved away to Looe, where he lives with his wife MORWENNA (née Chynoweth) and their daughter LOVEDAY.

VERITY BLAMEY (née Poldark, sister of Francis and Cousin to Ross) lives at Flushing with her husband, a retired sea captain.

BELLA POLDARK

Book One

VALENTINE

Chapter One

The evening was loud and wild. Black clumsy clouds were driving up from the north, lit at their edges by light from a sliver of moon. A few hazy stars speckled the patches of sky. But it was not dark. Even when the moon was quite gone there would be some luminescence from the restless sea because the longest day was still only a month past. Yet it did not seem like late summer. The sea drift was cold, the air was cold and noisy, the waves melancholy as if waiting for autumn.

A man was climbing down the cliffs half a mile east of Wheal Leisure. He was long-legged, and firm-footed like a cat. It was not an easy climb, for though the rocks were of granite and would never break away, they were greasy in places from the morning's rain. He was bare-headed, and wore some sort of tight black jerkin, rough barragan trousers and light canvas shoes. He carried a bundle tied to his back.

The last bit was the most difficult. If he jumped from ten feet a large sea pool barred his way. No doubt the water would break his fall, but he would be completely soaked and the wind was cold for the ride home. And was the pool deep enough? A broken ankle would not be welcome. He decided to inch his way round the edge and if he fell on his back in the water the pool's depth would not be so important.

He edged round, missed his footing, found it again, squirmed round a big projection, slid down two feet, jumped and landed on soft sand.

Satisfied, he got to his feet, moved to harder ground, took the bundle from his back and untied it. It was a riding cloak and a rolled-up black felt hat. As he put these on a voice said: 'Good eve to you.'

A tall, older man, taller even than he was. The climber dropped his hat, swore and picked it up, shook the sand from it.

'Judas God! You gave me a fright! What are you doing here?'

'It's always wise, isn't it,' said the older man, 'to get in the question first. What are *you* doing here? You are much further from home than I am.'

'Did you know I was here?'

'No, just strolling.'

'At midnight? You were not sleepwalking, Cousin?'

'I was strolling. Then I saw your horse.'

'Damnation! I thought I had well hid him. But you could not recognize him: I only bought Nestor last week.'

'Well – it was a nag of some quality and not many people leave their mounts untended in the middle of the night.'

'So you concluded it was me?'

'. . . I thought it a possibility.'

'And what led you to this particular piece of the beach, Cousin? My footprints were washed away.'

'I know there's a path from here up to Mingoose House. Coming down, you lost your way.'

'I suppose I did. Judas God. Don't tell Demelza.'

'I might agree to say nothing if you stopped using her special swear word.'

'What? Is it? Why is it?'

'Because as far as I know no one else has used it before.'

'I rather fancy it.'

'Maybe.'

'It's not ladylike.'

'I agree. Are you walking back to your horse?'

'Yes.'

'Then I'll walk with you.'

The clouds had lifted a little, and as the wind bullied the men along it was possible for them to discern more of each other. Although there was a similarity between them – in height, in colouring, and sometimes in the voice – there were greater areas of difference. The older man had broader shoulders, an altogether bonier face, heavy eyelids not quite hiding direct, unquiet eyes. The younger man had mischievous dark eyes, but they were a blue like his mother's, and closer together.

They talked for a moment or two about the new horse, then Ross said: 'It was an unusual way to call on the Tregenloses. Can I assume you were up to no good?'

After a pause while they negotiated another pool. 'Why should you assume that, Cousin?'

'Isn't it most likely? The direct route to Mingoose, as you well know, is via the upper lane that takes you to the front gates.'

'Yes. You are entirely right.'

'And in the last two years you have given no indication that you were likely to mend your ways.'

'Mend my ways. A quaint phrase. It might come from Sam's church.'

'It doesn't. It means in this instance being considerate and neighbourly. The Tregenloses are neighbours of mine.'

'Ah, yes. Quite so.'

The wind continued to buffet them, and they staggered like drunken men. The conversation so far had been on a bantering level, but there was a hint of iron in Ross's voice.

'Nearly there,' said Valentine. 'I'm surprised you spotted the nag.'

'He neighed . . . Had you gone to Mingoose to steal something?'

'Dear Cousin, I do not like being accused of theft.'

'Since I helped you out of that scrape last year, I think I am in a privileged position.'

'Perhaps you always were. But I have called a man out for less.'

They stopped. Ross said: 'Your horse is still there. I can hear him. Goodnight.'

'I suppose,' Valentine said, 'I might as well confess, lest I be suspected of worse. It has been a sort of theft, though of the gentlest sort. Do you know a kitchenmaid, Carla May, whom Ruth recently engaged?'

'Why should I?'

'Indeed, why should you? Perhaps I am younger and more susceptible, but last week calling on Frederick for a morning's shooting I espied such a sweetly pretty smiling face under a muslin cap that I had to make further enquiries. Her name is Carla May. I'll swear I stole little from her that she was not willing to give.'

Ross considered this. 'How is Selina?'

'Six months forward.'

'Well?'

'In blooming health.'

'She will not bloom so handsomely if she knows you have been seen climbing into the back bedrooms of Mingoose.'

'That is why I took such care not to be seen! . . . But, seriously, Cousin—'

'Have we not been serious so far?'

'When I married her she assumed I was a saint. In spite of my affair with her while her first husband was alive, she apparently believed I had to be faithful to her unto death. That hope has long since gone. I told her that I crossed my fingers in the ceremony when it came to "forsaking all others". I believe we do not get along too badly now. So long as I exercise a little discretion. So long as she is not privy to it.'

'This is a very close-knit community. Do you think I shall be the only Paul Pry?'

But Valentine had not quite finished what he wanted to say. 'D'you know, my dear Cousin, I don't really think women so very much mind if their husbands stray, so long as they know nothing about it and so long as others know nothing about it. It is not love that is so much injured, it is *pride*. It is self-esteem. It is vanity. Love plays a small part in their sense of outrage.'

'Maybe it is the same for men. Some men. Ultimately it surely comes down to the characters of the people involved?'

'Well done! You are learning fast.'

'Insolent puppy.'

Valentine laughed. 'Now I know I am forgiven.'

'I have nothing to forgive, except your impertinence. Make sure you don't meet others less amenable.'

'Give me a leg-up, will you? It's a job to get any springboard on this soft sand.'

Demelza was in bed when he reached Nampara, but not asleep. She was reading a book by the light of three candles. They smiled at each other.

'Did you get wet?'

'No, the tide was ebbing quickly.'

'I thought there was a shower.'

'I missed it.'

In the candlelight she looked unchanged. In the daylight the laughter lines round her eyes and mouth had become more noticeable, but even that detracted very little from her fine looks. Only the glint of zest had gone from her eyes since Jeremy's death.

Her hair, which had developed pronounced streaks of grey, was now back to its original colour. For some years, knowing Ross's dislike of hair dye, she had dabbed surreptitiously at various strands appearing around the ears and temples, believing he did not notice. But last year he had returned from London with a bottle of hair dye which had been matched to perfection because he had stolen a lock of her hair while she was asleep. When he gave her the bottle he had said simply: 'I don't want you to change.'

'Did you see anyone?' Demelza asked.

'Valentine.'

'Dear life. What was he about?'

'Paying attentions, I gather, to some maid in the Treneglos household called Carla May.'

'He is – impossible.'

'Yes.'

Ross regretted he had said so much. Valentine had become rather a bone of contention between them. Not that he felt he had broken his pledge to Valentine, for Demelza never gossiped.

'He was on the beach?'

'Yes.'

'Dear life. On the prowl, I s'pose. And Selina six months forward.'

He sat on the bed and began to unfasten his neckcloth. 'Bella safely in bed?'

'She went up soon after you left. Ross, she thought you'd gone out because she was practising her high notes.'

'I thought she might. I must tell her it was not so. You know how I get these impulses to take a long walk.'

'It truly was not so, then?'

He half laughed. 'She knows I am not partial to her voice. Truth to tell, I am perhaps not very partial to women's singing at all. Except yours, because yours is low and so easy to listen to. People say she has a good voice—'

'Far, far better than mine.'

'It is certainly *louder*!'

'It is much admired, Ross. In Truro they thought most highly of it.'

'I know. And when Christopher comes he flatters her.'

'I don't know if you happen to have noticed, but they are in love.'

He patted her hand. 'Sarcasm does not become you. But it is a condition in which one tends to exaggerate the talents of the person one loves.'

'I don't suppose I have often exaggerated your talents, Ross.'

He half laughed again. 'There have been times, but we won't go into that. In fact that could be taken two ways ... I must say, though ...'

'Well, say it.'

'I do not think Bella needs to start singing at nine o'clock at night. She'll disturb Harry.'

'When Harry is asleep it would take a thunderbolt to wake him. And, as another point, he *admires* his sister.'

'Admires her? Well so do I! *Very* much. She is – is the most *engaging* of our children. She's the most like you, except that she lacks the gentleness.'

He went to the table, opened a tin box, damped his forefinger and began to rub his teeth with his favourite red root. Then he filled a mug from the pitcher and rinsed his mouth out.

'Talking of daughters,' he went on when he had finished, 'we have not had our usual letter from Clowance. I hope nothing is amiss.'

'If I don't hear I will go this week. She was well enough last time, though still committed to her ships. Or perhaps you should go, Ross, for a change.'

'I might if I could persuade her to sell up and come back here.'

'She seems – as I say – committed.'

'She made a loss last year.'

'That was chiefly because of the weather.'

'Hm.' He pulled on the short nightshirt that Demelza had made for him and then slipped into bed beside her. She blew out two of the candles and put her book on the floor beside the bed.

'I heard the first cricket tonight,' she said.

'Did you? Yes, I suppose it's about time.'

'Do you want to talk?' she asked.

'You choose.'

'Then I think I'm ready for sleep.'

He kissed her and snuffed out the final candle. Except when there was temporary war between them – and the last time was years gone – theirs was never a perfunctory goodnight kiss: it was the resealing of a partnership, a restatement of a sexual friendship.

Ross lay back on his pillow and took a deep breath of something not far from satisfaction. Despite the tragedies and traumas of life – far away the greatest among them the death of his elder son at Waterloo – he felt he had a deal to be thankful for. It was of course his nature to be restive; but he often found when an attack of what Demelza called the lurgies was pending, a long fast walk, preferably across the beach at low tide, and preferably alone, helped to drive it away. This had happened tonight – temporarily at least.

He put his hands behind his head and tried to think about his mines and his farm and his interests in boat-building, rolling mills and banking. He was close to becoming a warm man – though if the truth be told it was Wheal Leisure that made him warm. Wheal Grace kept going mainly as an act of social conscience – and the other interests were peripheral.

The curtains were drawn, but as his eyes got used to the total darkness he found it as usual not to be total. The curtains were stirring from an inch-open window and allowed a faint slit of light to creep into the room. One of the sash windows was trembling slightly as the wind too tried to get in. It had in fact been trembling for years, and he always meant to have it seen to. But perhaps if it was stopped now they would both miss it. The sound had become part of their sleeping lives.

Demelza said: 'Carla May.'

'What?'

'Carla May.'

'What of it? I thought you were asleep.'

'I don't know any May family in this district, do you, Ross?'

'Come to think of it, no. I knew a Captain May in America. He came from the south-west, but I think it was Devon.'

Silence fell. Ross decided that the sash window should be attended to. He would tell Gimlett in the morning.

He touched Demelza's shoulder. 'Why suddenly ask me this when we were just going to sleep? What's in your mind?'

'I was just thinking, Ross. Why should Valentine volunteer the name of the maid he was – was visiting at Mingoose?'

'I suppose he thought it added a little verisimilitude.'

'That's a silly word. But exactly . . .'

'What?'

'Do you really think if Valentine had been paying a love call on a maid in the Treneglos household he would have bothered to tell you her name? He might not even know it himself! To me it does not add very – whatever you call it – to the story. Is it not more likely that he invented the name just to convince you that there was such a person?'

'I'm not sure that I – oh, yes, I see what you mean, but can you think of any other possible reason why Valentine should be making an illicit entry into a neighbour's house? Especially being Valentine. He's hardly likely to be stealing the silver!'

'I was wondering if perhaps – just maybe – he was perhaps visiting someone else and – and told you, invented a name, to put you off.'

'Visiting? With the same purpose?'

'Tis possible.'

Ross's mind travelled quickly over the known inhabitants of Mingoose and which inhabitant could be the object of his desire.

'I don't see there is any possibility among the Treneglosses . . .'

'There's Agneta.'

'*What*? Agneta? Never! Why should he – how could he? She's – she's peculiar, to say the least!'

'Not that peculiar. I saw him eyeing her at the Summer Races.'

'She has fits!'

'Dwight says she has grown out of them.'

'All the same, she is not like the rest of us. Ruth was very worried about her at one time. If you were to have said Davida . . .'

I know. But we were all at Davida's wedding, and she is safely living in Okehampton. And Emmeline has recently joined the Methodists.'

Ross struggled with his thoughts. As sometimes happened, he remembered with a sense of grievance, Demelza was capable of pricking him with a little thorn of disquiet just when he was preparing to compose himself for sleep. That this was his own fault for breaking his word to Valentine did not disperse his displeasure.

'Do you always think the worst of Valentine?'

'Not *think* the worst, Ross; *fear* the worst perhaps.'

'God, if he fathers a brat on her there'll be Hell to pay!'

'Something Ruth said to me once makes me think that is unlikely . . . But I may be altogether in the wrong – I mean about Valentine and Agneta. Twas a speculation I should maybe have kept to myself.'

'Maybe you should.'

Ross seldom saw Agneta Treneglos, but he remembered she was the only dark one of the family: tall and sallow and a good figure but with errant eyes and lips that told you she had too many teeth waiting to be exposed.

His irritation moved from Demelza to Valentine, where it more properly belonged. Confound the boy. (Boy indeed: he was twenty-four.) Valentine was the unquiet spirit of the neighbourhood, one who could become regarded as the scourge if he continued on his present way. Ross uncomfortably remembered that his own father had had somewhat similar characteristics.

He did not notice any such wildness in the Warleggan family, to whom Valentine technically belonged. And Selina six months forward, producing a child after three years . . . There were rumours, which Dwight refused to confirm, that she had slit her wrists after one of her husband's love affairs.

Ross could tell that Demelza had gone to sleep. You could hear the regular tick-tick of her breathing.

He was peevishly tempted to dig her in the ribs and demand that she continue the conversation.

But, on the whole, he decided not.

Chapter Two

Clowance had no good reason for not having written, but she had been busy all week, and on the Saturday, which was the day on which she usually wrote, Harriet Warleggan had pressed her to go to Cardew for 'a little party'.

Since Stephen's death and the bitter disillusion that had come to be a part of her grief, she had concentrated her mind on keeping his little shipping business – literally – afloat. Tim Hodge, the fat, middle-aged, swart seaman who had become Stephen's right-hand man in the last adventure, had stayed on and now managed that part of the business which it was less appropriate for a woman to become involved in. He also commanded the *Adolphus*. Sid Bunt continued to be in charge of the *Lady Clowance*, and was entirely efficient in his little coastal runs.

This May Jason, Stephen's son, had returned to Bristol. With his share in Stephen's lucky privateering adventure, and part of Clowance's larger share, he had a modest amount of capital and thought to go into partnership with friends in Bristol. Clowance missed him but at heart was glad he had gone. Some of his ways reminded her too much of Stephen, and his presence, every time she saw him, was a reminder of the fact that she had never been legally married to Stephen because his first wife had been alive at the time. Although the bitter taste of Stephen's bigamy, the flavour of his betrayal, had grown less rancid as the months turned into years, it was still there. Yet the person she of course most greatly missed was Stephen himself. Whatever his faults, his personality had been strong and pervasive, at times engagingly frank and at times fiercely loving. With Jason no longer in Penryn she found it easier to ignore the memories of Stephen's faults and to remember him with loving grief.

She had remained living in the cottage where she and Stephen had spent all their married life. The big house Stephen planned had been only part-built at the time of his accident. It still remained unfinished, waiting for someone else to buy it, a monument to the vagaries and the uncertainty of life.

In the time since Stephen's death she had seen only a few of her family and friends, and of the latter she saw most of George Warleggan's wife. Clowance was certain that it was under Harriet's pressure that Sir George had come to an agreement with Hodge for the regular shipping of cement from the Warleggan quarries in Penryn by *Adolphus*. This was one of the contracts Stephen had angled for but never achieved. It was a great help for a tiny shipping line to have a regular commission.

So on a rainy afternoon in September Clowance went to the little party. She found as she had rather expected that Harriet's idea of a small party was relative, there being about thirty guests.

Harriet gave her parties when hunting was out of season, and Clowance's only surprise was that this was not quite the typical gaming group. True, there was a backgammon table and a roulette table, but three smaller tables were set out for whist, and at least half the guests Clowance had never seen before.

The one who made the most impression on Clowance was a Mr Prideaux, a fair-haired man probably in his late twenties, scrupulously dressed, tall and thin, and holding himself very erect, with small spectacles which he took on and off constantly to play cards. He had been in the West Indies, she learned during early refreshments, had been ill and sent home.

By some fell arrangement it turned out that she was to be partnered by Mr Philip Prideaux at the whist table. Their opponents were Mr Michael Smith and Mrs Polly Codrington, whom Valentine had once had an affair with.

Things went fairly well for a while; then at the end of one hand Mr Prideaux looked over the top of his glasses and said: 'If you had returned my lead, partner—'

'I did not have any more clubs,' said Clowance.

'But you followed—'. He stopped.

'Once. No more. I led a diamond, hoping that you might have the ace.'

'I had the king, which was taken by Mr Smith's ace.'

'It established my queen.'

'But you never made it.'

'No. As it happened, no. They were too strong in trumps. I had a lot of useless diamonds.'

'Wish I had, darling,' said Polly Codrington, looking at her ringless fingers, and laughing.

Philip Prideaux glanced at the speaker in slight distaste, as if it were an off-colour joke. Then he said to Clowance: 'Did you not have two clubs?'

'No.'

The game proceeded. After a while the tables broke up and were re-formed. It was a sultry afternoon, and when the rain stopped the windows were opened to give more air. Clowance went to one and looked out at the hedges of topiary and the sweeping lawns. She had lost four guineas. She hoped the odious Mr Prideaux had lost the same.

Dusk was now falling. A cluster of deer was scarcely visible against the darkening woods.

'Mrs Carrington.'

She turned.

'Mr Prideaux.' He had taken off his glasses.

'Mrs Carrington, I thought it was incumbent on me to apologize.'

She looked her surprise, but did not speak. He had quite large brown eyes which were unusually deep for such fair hair.

'It was inexcusable of me to reprimand you on the play of a hand.'

'Was that a reprimand? I did not take it so.' Not quite true, but for the moment she was prepared to temporize.

'Whether you had two clubs or one—'

'I had one.'

'Just so. It was not courteous of me to draw attention to your mistake—'

'It was not a mistake.'

He coughed. 'I am expressing this badly. Perhaps I should start again. I wanted to explain that in Jamaica I was accustomed to playing in all-male company, and the remark – my remark – slipped out. Genteel card parties such as this are – are unusual for me. A delightful change, I may say. I hope you will allow me to express my regret.'

'I hope you had better fortune with your second partner.'

'She was not so young or so charming. But yes, I came out the winner on the afternoon.'

14

What a pity, she thought. What a great pity.

'May I take it that you will accept my apology?' he asked.

'Your apology for rebuking me or for rebuking me wrongly?'

He swallowed something. 'For rebuking you, Mrs Carrington. In any case it was something that ill becomes a gentleman.'

'If you think it necessary to apologize, then I am happy to accept it.'

'Thank you.' He did not move away.

'Lady Harriet tells me you are a widow, Mrs Carrington.'

'Yes.'

'And do you live near?'

'In Penryn. And you, Mr Prideaux?'

'I am staying a week or so with the Warleggans. Lady Harriet's eldest brother is a friend of my father.'

George had just put in an appearance. At fifty-nine he had lost a little of the excess weight which had threatened him in his middle years. His face had thinned and become more like his father's, though granitic in colour rather than red. Coming in, he was gracious to all, but without altogether dissipating the formidable impression of his character and nature. The two great boar hounds looked up, silently inspected him, came to the conclusion that regrettably he was part of the household, and then went to sleep again. When some two years ago twin daughters had been born to him some cynic had remarked that if they had been boys they would more properly have been christened Castor and Pollux.

'Mrs Carrington.'

'Yes.'

'I believe supper is about to be served. Would you do me the honour of allowing me to take you in?'

As they went in Harriet was talking to George, but as Clowance passed by on the arm of Mr Prideaux Harriet closed a conspiratorial eye at her.

A monstrous suspicion formed in the breast of Mrs Carrington. Whenever they met Harriet urged Clowance to go out more, to see new faces, to mix among her friends, not to spend all her life organizing and scheming for her potty little ships. Was this some infernal machination to embroil her with a new *man*? If so, she had a fat chance with this one.

Just then Paul Kellow came by. 'Clowance!' He squeezed her hand. 'I have lost my wife. Have you seen her?'

'Yes, I think she just went upstairs.'

'How are you? You look as bonny as ever.'

Paul had not changed, though since his marriage to Mary Temple his circumstances had. The Temples owned property near Probus, and Paul was living in the dower house with his wife and managing the estate, which contained profitable slate quarries, for his father-in-law. Paul was ever smart, ever sleek, with lank but carefully trimmed black hair, slim, elegant, detached. No one, certainly not George, would ever have guessed that Paul was the one surviving member of the trio who had robbed Warleggan's coach six years ago. Of the three, only he had prospered. Yet his prosperity, though tangible enough, hardly seemed to have touched his personality. He was a difficult young man to know.

She enquired after his sister.

'Daisy? She's well enough in her hectic way. Coughing lightly.'

'Don't say that!'

'True, my dear. First Dorrie, then Violet. Next Daisy. The curse of the Kellows.'

'You are joking.'

'I hope so. But a few years ago I had three pretty sisters. Now one only – whom I tried to link up with Jeremy, and failed. She hasn't been quite the same since he was killed. And she coughs.'

'I – haven't seen her since the summer.'

'I go over once a week. You know my father has sold his coaching business?'

'I'd heard; but—'

'It wasn't practical to carry on without me. We got a very good price, sold just at the right time . . .'

Clowance glanced past him and saw his wife coming down the stairs. In the flickering candlelight she seemed to bear a striking resemblance to Paul's dead sister, Violet. Then as the candles shaded, Mary came towards them and Clowance saw how wrong she was.

Wrong? Yes. But there was a similarity of figure, of colouring. Did men sometimes marry women who looked like their mothers? Their sisters?

Clowance knew that Harriet thought she was grieving too long for Stephen, and since Harriet did not know the whole story – the sad

16

mixture of disillusion that went with Clowance's grief – that was understandable.

Few also knew of, though a few suspected, her distaste for Jeremy's widow, Cuby. The relationship between Jeremy and Clowance had been very close – much closer than an ordinary sibling friendship – a deep affection and affinity almost always disguised as banter. Jeremy had tried to protect her from Stephen until he was completely convinced of Stephen's sincerity. Then he had met Cuby, and Clowance thought only she had been fully aware of his total commitment, an absorption compared with which no one else in the world mattered. Well, that was all right as far as it went.

But she had seen his utter distress, amounting sometimes, she felt, almost to collapse, when Cuby had cold-bloodedly accepted the fact that her family desired her to marry Valentine Warleggan. It had almost changed his nature and in the end induced him to join the army to get away from Cornwall and forget Cuby Trevanion. What Clowance could not forget was that had it not been for Cuby Jeremy might still be alive. She often wondered how her mother and father could continue to accept her. Was it on account of Noelle, their granddaughter?

Philip Prideaux had said something as they sat down at the dining table.

'Please?'

'I was asking you, ma'am, whether you frequently go to card parties?'

'Very seldom. As a child I used to play whist with my brother. Then more lately I took it up again to please my husband, who was very fond of it.'

'Am I right that he was in the Oxfordshires and fell at Waterloo?'

'No, that was my brother. My husband died less gloriously – in a riding accident.'

'Oh, I *am* sorry. Clearly I did not attend properly to what Lady Harriet told me.'

Clearly he had not. 'Why should you be interested?'

'I was not *then*. I am now. So you have suffered a double blow. I am – very deeply sorry.'

'Thank you.'

Clowance picked delicately at the chilled lemon soufflé. She said more lightly: 'I was pleased to play whist with my husband because it kept him from the other gaming tables where more might be won or lost.'

'He was a gambler?'

'Are not all men?'

He smiled. It was more genuine than the polite curling of the lips she had seen before. 'I have known many women who have gambled just as rashly as men.'

'Your experience of the world, Mr Prideaux, must greatly exceed mine.'

He coughed his little cough. 'That I should rather doubt, ma'am. I have led a restricted life. From school I went straight to the Royal Military College at Marlow and thence into the King's Dragoon Guards. After Waterloo I was sent to garrison Jamaica with a regiment of the line, until I was discharged in disgrace and so came home.'

'Disgrace?'

'A fever is a disgrace if you cannot throw it off.'

'Were you at Waterloo?'

'Yes. It was a great occasion – something to recall all one's life – though too many good men fell.'

'Yes,' said Clowance fervently. This was a new view of Waterloo – a great occasion! Merciful God! 'Do you intend to return to the army when you are better?'

'No. As I mentioned, I find the life very limiting, narrow.'

'How shall you broaden it?'

'I hope—'. He broke off as venison pie was served. Clowance sipped her French wine.

'You hope—'

'Ah,' he said, putting on his ridiculous glasses. 'Yes, but I am talking too much about myself. What of your life, Mrs Carrington? Have you children?'

'No. My husband started a small shipping business. Mainly coastal trade. Since he died I have tried to keep it going.'

'Successfully, I'm sure.'

'It is not easy. Trade has been so uncertain since the end of the war. And what do you hope, Mr Prideaux? Or perhaps it's not Mr Prideaux?'

'I was a captain. But am no longer.'

'Do you not wish to retain your rank?'

'It is immaterial. I told Harriet I would prefer to drop it.'

'That seems strange to me. Is it not something to be proud of?'

'A captaincy. Possibly. I think I struggle with undercurrents in my own nature.'

'Before he was knighted,' Clowance said, 'my father was always known as Captain Poldark. But that was not so much because he had been a captain in the Army as because he was captain of a mine. That ranks as more important in Cornish eyes.'

The young man smiled. 'I am part Cornish. I have cousins at Padstow. I fancy I should like to stay in the county for a year or two.'

'You are a free agent?'

'I have parents in Devon and two sisters. But I want to make my own way in the world.'

He had long bony fingers to match his long bony frame. Now and then they trembled.

'But not in the Army?'

'Not in the Army. There are more interesting ways of living one's life.'

Clowance's attention was drawn away by the man on her other side, and for a while no more was said between them.

Then he said: 'Your father is a Member of Parliament, Mrs Carrington?'

'Was. He resigned last year.'

'But still, I believe, a man of affairs.'

'I don't know how you would define a man of affairs. He has certainly led an adventurous life.'

'I should like to meet him sometime.'

After a moment she said: 'You spoke of more interesting professions.'

'Er . . . You mean for myself? Well, I have an intense interest in archaeology. Cornwall is full of prehistoric remains. My father has a small property near Penzance. It is at present unoccupied and I thought I might be able to persuade him to rent it to me for a year or two.'

At the door as she left Harriet patted her arm. 'I see you found much in common with my young Mr Prideaux.'

Clowance said: 'Harriet, you are a monster.'

'Why ever? It is time you found somebody else.'

'Heaven forfend that I should look kindly on Mr Prideaux!'

'He is not at all a disagreeable fellow. He grows on one.'

'I don't think he would grow on me, dear Harriet.'

'He's unmarried. He appears to be clean-living and house-trained. He is a cousin of the influential Prideaux-Brune family. My brother, who knows his father, sends a good report of him. I do not find him unattractive.'

Clowance kissed her hostess. '*Chacun à son goût.*'

'Don't you like those long limbs?'

'I am not taken by his arrogance. I am not taken by his condescension. And those glasses. Sorry, my dear. Your intentions, I'm sure, were strictly honourable.'

'So would his be, I've no doubt, if given the chance. Will you come again next week?'

'Will he be there?'

'I can't guarantee that he will not be.'

'I'll think on it. But thank you. You're so kind.'

'And you are a horrible girl. I don't know why I bother ... Seriously, I think good comes of this sort of meeting. It is a challenge, abrasive or seductive. When you get home you will no doubt think of him.'

'Possibly.'

'It's good to have someone new to think about – if not with loving thoughts, then with irritation.'

The next morning Valentine Warleggan called to see her. It was a great surprise. She had been about to leave for the little office in the Strand at Falmouth where she conducted most of her business affairs, and Valentine, almost as lean and bony as Philip Prideaux, raised his eyebrows when he saw the case of papers she was carrying.

He kissed her.

'You are on your way out, Cousin? I am come at the wrong moment.'

'The right moment,' said Clowance, 'else I could have missed you. Pray come in.'

They went in, and she explained her mission to meet Sid Bunt sometime in the forenoon, the *Lady Clowance* having berthed last night. Valentine answered questions about Selina's well-being. She thought: perhaps it is because his eyes are just a little too close together that he is less than good-looking. Yet many women found him irresistible.

He said: 'You're sure your business with Bunt can wait an hour? It is in a sense a little business that I have come to see you on, cousin. Or it might be. It concerns a certain vessel called – or potentially called – the *Lady Carrington*.'

'It is still on the stocks,' said Clowance.

'I gather so.'

'And a long way from being finished. At least, finished in the way Stephen wanted it finished. The hull is complete, and the cabin and bulwarks, though the cabin is just a shell. Stephen had ordered Canadian red pine for the masts and yards – he said it was the best – they had come before he died, but I don't think they have ever been raised. Whether Bennett's still have them or whether they've been used for some other vessel I don't know.'

'Did you pay for them?'

'I – I think so. I haven't had the will to go down to the yard myself. I'll ask Bunt to go, if you want to know.'

'I'm sure if you paid for them they will still be there. The Bennetts are Quakers.'

Clowance stared out at the sunlit day, then turned to look at Valentine sprawled in her best chair.

'Is this of some special interest to you, Valentine?'

'I thought if you were not wishing to proceed with it I might like to buy it.'

'Oh?'

'You're surprised at this new interest of mine? Well, it is not altogether a new interest. I have had a part share in a vessel for some time. She is called – was called – the *Adelaide*. A clinker-built lugger, two-masted, smaller than the ship Stephen planned, but sturdy enough for most seas and shallow-drafted for the coastal trade.'

She still felt it was a new interest for her cousin. His long legs were stretched out and the tight twill trousers he was wearing showed the curvature of the left leg, legacy of the rickets he had had as a child.

'What happened to her?'

'Who?'

'The *Adelaide*. You spoke of her in the past tense.'

He grimaced. 'She ran aground on Godrevy and became a total wreck.'

'The crew?'

Valentine yawned. 'They got ashore.'

'Were you aboard?'

'Merciful God, no! I don't *sail* in these things.'

Clowance smiled. 'So you – you want a replacement?'

'Yes.'

'The *Lady Carrington* is only part-finished. I would not know what to ask for her.'

'Could be settled. If you cannot find the receipted bills among Stephen's effects, the boatyard will know. Total these up and add twenty per cent for your profit . . .'

Privately Clowance had been eking out the prize money that Stephen had left, but giving Jason a large part of it had reduced her capital. The house remained unfinished and no one seemed to want to make an offer for it. The boat, which had been half-built, had similarly attracted no interest.

'Are you going to go into competition with me?'

'No, Cousin. I have no such thoughts.' As she did not speak, he went on: 'I am a north coast man these days, and landfalls among all those cliffs are hard to find. There is virtually nothing between St Ives and Padstow. Trevaunance Cove, which I look down on, is a death trap, and St Ann's has its harbour wall breached every second year . . . Basset's Cove, a little further west, is better than many suppose. Coal has been brought in there from Wales for years without serious mishap.'

'And you wish to go into the coal trade?'

'No.' Valentine wrinkled his nose at the thought. 'I want to cut in on the trade with Ireland. At present Padstow has a monopoly.'

She got up. The room was too small to pace up and down in, but she felt the need for a moment or two to think.

'Stephen said once that there were more Irishmen in Padstow than in Rosslare.'

Valentine laughed. 'Ask your friend Hodge to work it out on your behalf with Bennett's. I hope it will not come to more than about three hundred guineas because I estimate it will cost me about another two hundred to get her finished and ready for sea.'

'Yes,' said Clowance thoughtfully.

Valentine eyed her for a moment or two. 'I seldom see you at

Nampara these days. You seem addicted to your little home in Penryn.'

'Oh, I come sometimes.'

'Tell me, is your reluctance in any way bound up with the possible presence there of Jeremy's widow?'

She flushed. 'I do not think there is any reluctance on my part. It is just that I am very busy looking after the two vessels.'

Valentine continued to eye her. 'Cuby is quite an agreeable young woman, you know. Once upon a time I nearly married her.'

'Did you?' said Clowance, using irony for a change. 'Well, well.'

'But it's all so long ago, isn't it? What, four – five years? It seems much longer. Anyway, all that time is long past. Bygones be bygones etcetera.'

Clowance said: 'Valentine, I cannot see any reason why I should not sell the lugger to you if you wish to buy it. The extra money would not be unwelcome.'

'Good.'

Then she decided to take the attack to him for a change. 'I confess I am surprised.'

'Why?'

'Well . . . you are married to a lady of means. I did not know you would be interested in owning a vessel. You have your new mine. Have you discussed all this with Selina?'

'So far she knows nothing of it.' When Clowance raised her eyebrows, 'Cousin, I have an active mind. And although you say Selina has means, she has two stepdaughters to launch in the world, and her means are not inexhaustible. Anyway I prefer to make my own way in the world.'

A laudable sentiment which would have carried more conviction if his expression had been less ironical.

'Very well,' said Clowance. 'Hodge is at sea, but is due in tomorrow. As soon as I see him I will ask him to go and discuss it with Bennett's. Will you want to employ them to finish the boat to their specifications?'

'I might want some alterations, but they can do the job if we agree what they would charge me.'

Clowance rose again, and he got up too and went to the door.

'One thing, Valentine. I do not think *Lady Carrington*, if you don't mind. Why not *Lady Selina*?'

'I'll think on it,' said Valentine.

Chapter Three

The following week an unexpected visitor arrived at Nampara – that is to say, he was unexpected to everyone except Isabella-Rose.

By this time Isabella-Rose was sixteen – or nearly seventeen, as she preferred to say. In the three years since Waterloo she had grown taller and come more to resemble her father, with a strong nose and high cheekbones. Yet in general looks and in her person she was as feminine as ever and had a slim sturdiness of figure that was particularly becoming. She had lost some of her girlish habits but none of her enthusiasm or relish in life, and, contrary to general expectation, none of her interest in Christopher Havergal.

They had seen each other quite rarely since their separation at the end of 1815, but in April of this year she had seen him an additional time when Ross had gone to London on business and taken her with him. Their correspondence had continued almost weekly.

As the visitor got down from his horse, careful to disentangle his artificial foot from the stirrup before dismounting, Bella came scuttering out of the house and embraced him. Demelza, looking up from talking to Harry, observed through the window that there was no hesitant formality on either side.

Christopher's blond moustache was still much in evidence, but he was wearing his hair shorter than he had in the Army. He had found employment in the City with Nathan Rothschild, which suggested he was financially in a comfortable position, but the fact that he was not a Jew would be a likely bar to his promotion.

Looking at him, Demelza knew she had to keep her maternal instincts in check. In spite of his dashing looks and his sophistication he always seemed to her to be alone in the world. She knew his mother was dead and that he was estranged from his father; he never spoke of his family and, with the handicap of his artificial foot, one had to be careful not to look on him as the little boy lost.

It was a surprisingly quiet supper, and Demelza with her acute perception was aware of an element of tension. The only talkative person was Harry, who was now nearly six and had been allowed specially to stay up because his friend Christopher had arrived. Ross had just returned from an encounter with Valentine, and tended to be absent-minded. The two young people looked at each other a lot but were unusually unconversational. Then, towards the end of the meal, Demelza's perceptions were justified. Christopher asked if he might have a serious talk with his hosts – after he had fulfilled his promise to see Henry to bed.

Demelza glanced at Ross, who said: 'Of course. Nine o'clock?'

'Thank you, sir.'

Soon after nine they were in the parlour. Ross poured a glass of brandy for Christopher and himself, a port for Demelza, an orange juice for Bella, who for the last half year had been taking no spirits.

Christopher sipped his drink then took a large gulp, as if, Demelza thought, he was seeking Dutch courage. His glance as he put the glass down met Demelza's and he half smiled.

'Sir Ross. Lady Poldark. I do not know how to begin, but it cannot have escaped your notice that for more than three years I have been in love with your daughter.'

'No,' said Ross. 'It has not.'

'When she was so very young I knew – Lady Poldark made this clear – that an attachment, a formal engagement was out of the question. I have accepted that. Until now I have accepted that. But I would like to ask now for your daughter's hand in marriage. I would like you to be so very kind as to consider it. But before you answer,' he hastened on, 'I have something else to say. I – I have always had a tremendous admiration for her singing voice. I know she is taking lessons twice a week in Truro. A – a Mrs Hudson, I think—'

'Hodgson,' said Bella.

'Hodgson. Twice a week. This is probably the best tuition available in Cornwall. But as she approaches seventeen she would greatly benefit from more intensive tuition from a better qualified teacher. Now I have to tell you – with apology – of a little subterfuge that took place when Bella came to London—'

'I must tell this, Christopher,' said Bella. She turned to her

25

father. 'Papa, you must not blame Miss Armitage, whom you employed to companion me. I pretended to her that I wanted to go to Oxford Road, so we walked up that way and by design met Christopher. Miss Armitage was indignant, but when she heard we were only going to Marlborough Street to try out my singing voice she reluctantly came with us . . .'

Christopher said: 'I took her to a Dr Fredericks. You may have heard of him? He has coached many of the best singers of the day. He only takes a pupil who, in his view, may become a top singer. He has high charges and he picks and chooses with great care.'

'This was all rather deceitful,' said Demelza, but interested in spite of herself.

'I know, Lady Poldark. And I ask your pardon again. If – if there is any excuse for the deceit perhaps it lies in Dr Fredericks's opinion. He says Isabella-Rose has an exceptional voice.'

'Indeed.'

'Yes, sir. He says he would accept her as a pupil at any time.'

'But in London?'

'Yes, sir, in London. His school is in London.'

Ross finished his brandy, poured another, offered the decanter to Christopher, who hesitated, then shook his head. He was susceptible to drink and at the moment needed a very clear head.

'What are you suggesting?'

Christopher coughed into his fist. 'Bella will be seventeen in February. If she were betrothed to me, it would be a privilege to take care of her in London. I would be happy to pay her fees at the school. Of course you would decide where she would lodge. But I know two highly respectable ladies who keep a lodging house in St Martin's Lane, and possibly . . .'

He paused and looked at his listeners.

'Go on,' said Ross.

'Well, sir, that is my proposal. I shall be happy to elaborate on it, but I did not want you to feel that I was attempting to have everything cut and dried, without first having your permission to discuss it.'

Demelza glanced at her daughter and knew at once that in Bella's mind, at least as far as the proposition went, everything was indeed cut and dried.

Ross finished his second glass of brandy. This man, this Dr Somebody or Other, did he *really* have such a high opinion of

Bella's voice? It was fine to sing out at a party and have others join in. Even as a small girl she had had this very strong singing voice (sometimes Ross called it privately her shouting voice). Lots of people enjoyed it: they were impressed by its loudness and clarity; but they were *friends*, it would come natural to praise such a precocious talent. Dear Bella. Such fun. How she sings! 'Ripe Sparrergras' and 'The Barley Mow'. Remarkable.

But a top professional? Was this doctor as much of a leading teacher as Havergal claimed? If he were not he might need pupils, and how better to gain an extra one than by exaggerating her talents?

Isabella-Rose was a lovable but headstrong girl, and gullible. No doubt Havergal was sincere in all he said, but she could not be allowed to do all this simply on his assurances. If Bella were allowed to swallow the bait she might make a partial success of a singing career, in a couple of years become a member of some shoddy touring company, appearing for a week in Glasgow, a week in Newcastle. Even if she had as much talent as they thought, she would have to begin that way. Ross knew that seedy actors and their touring companies were not a thing he wanted his daughter to become involved in. This perhaps was too sour a view: Christopher had a little money and, if he truly loved Bella, would not permit her to live the life of a second-rate mummer. (But what of the heartbreak of expecting to be a star – and failing?)

What if she *were* a success?

'You speak of betrothal,' Ross said. 'Betrothal leads to marriage.'

'Indeed, sir. But that could wait on events. I have waited three years. It would depend on how her singing career progressed. Obviously marriage is what we should want, but consideration of it could be delayed for a while.'

Ross hesitated. Then he looked at Demelza. Oh, wisest of women, what would she say now?

Demelza said: 'I would like another glass of port.'

That morning Ross had been to call on Dwight and Caroline. He had taken one of a new batch of cheeses Demelza had made; this was only an excuse, but it served. They had chatted amiably for an hour or so; he had refused an invitation to dinner and left about noon. On his way home he had met Valentine.

Well shod, well mounted, well dressed, Valentine had raised his crop in salutation.

'Well met, Cousin. I was thinking of coming to see you later today. May I join you on your way home?'

Their horses ambled together.

'I visited Clowance last week,' Valentine said.

'How was she?'

'As pretty as ever. I think she has almost got over her bereavement.'

'Her double bereavement.'

'Indeed. I notice Demelza has not yet.'

'Not yet. I doubt if Clowance has, but you're right; she is better.'

'I went to see her, Cousin, to propose that I should buy from her the part-finished vessel that Stephen had laid down the month before he met with his accident.'

'Oh?' Ross looked at his blue-eyed young relative. 'You surprise me.'

'I think I surprised her. Nevertheless she agreed to the sale. Work will commence next week; the boat should be ready soon after Christmas.'

Ross said: 'The *Adelaide*, I'm told, was a total wreck.'

'Ah, so you know about my interest then. There is little in this district that goes unremarked.'

'I'm told it carried illicit goods.'

'It did in part. Only in part. A few tubs of brandy now and then, a roll or two of silk, a box or two of tea.'

'And tin?'

'What?'

'Tin.'

'Well, yes, now you mention it. The vessel could hardly sail from these shores in ballast.'

'It sailed to Ireland?'

'Yes. It was convenient for us and convenient for them.'

'For the French?'

'Yes. The Irish make little that we need.'

'Whiskey?'

Valentine laughed. 'Of a sort. Smoky stuff. But the French do not mind coming that far if there is profit in it. And although there is some Custom watch on our north coast, it is mainly concentrated on the south.'

'Not all,' said Ross, remembering well.

'So,' said Valentine, 'as we have lost the *Adelaide*, I thought it would be a simple matter to replace her with the *Lady Selina*.'

'Advertisement of your connection?'

'It was just a thought. If you think of a better name, pray suggest it.'

'Valentine, why are you telling me all this?'

'You have experience of the trade.'

Ross smiled grimly. 'That was all before you were born. And it was chiefly when I was in some financial need. You can hardly say that of yourself.'

'I have precious little money, except Selina's, which of course is now mine. And into that I have already made far too many inroads.'

'So you want to make money?'

'Who does not?'

'By acting beyond the confines of the law.'

'If necessary.'

They passed Sawle Church. A few women were about, heads bent, dark shawled, chiefly round the well.

Ross said: 'I am in no position to preach, Valentine. But from what you have said I take it that your exports could be more valuable than your imports – they clearly carry the greater hazard.'

'Why?'

'You must know half Cornwall is waiting to buy your brandy, your silks, your tobacco. In following that trade you have almost everyone on your side. But in shipping raw tin out of the county you are stepping on unpopular ground. The Society of Associated Tinners is not to be overlooked. And there are a number of influential figures in the county connected with the Coinage Halls of Truro, Helston and Penzance.'

Valentine shrugged. 'It is the outgoing cargo where lies the profit. Did you care for the risk when you needed money?'

'I did not need money for women or to pay off gambling debts. But no . . . the risk was worth taking. And we did not export tin.'

'Ten tons of the crude stuff will fetch seven hundred pounds. That shows a massive profit.'

'I can believe.'

The horses had come to a stop. From here you could see Fernmore, where Mr and Mrs Kellow and Daisy still lived in a sort of poverty-stricken gentility. (It was rumoured that Paul helped them.) You could also see the chimney of Wheal Grace, and in the distance that of Wheal Leisure. Nampara was still out of sight in the valley.

Valentine pushed his hat back to allow the wind to cool his forehead.

'D'you remember when you and your cousin Francis went into partnership to develop Wheal Grace?'

'Indeed. But you cannot. It's thirty-odd years ago.'

'My mother told me about it once. It was a great success.'

'In the end. But Francis died in it.'

'I know. But it was, I would have thought, a very suitable sort of partnership.'

'While it lasted, yes.' Feeling he was being a little curt, Ross added: 'Francis and I had a friendly relationship. We had played together a lot as boys. Then he married the girl I was in love with, your mother, and that soured our friendship. Later we – came together again. But you must know all this. It is part of our family lore. Have you some reason for bringing up Francis's name?'

'I simply meant that we too have a – friendly relationship. If different . . . It occurred to me that you might fancy joining me in this new little adventure with the vessel that is about to be launched.'

Ross stared. 'You can't be serious.'

'Why not? You have had a somewhat lurid past. Do you not find your too respectable life nowadays a small matter tedious?'

Ross laughed, but grimly. 'I am fifty-eight – an old man. The last time I had any connections with the trade was when I sanctioned the use of Nampara Cove for the traders to use. Even then I only played a passive part in it. And that was – let's see – that was '93, twenty-five years ago.'

Valentine was not to be deterred. 'Yet your life, my dear cousin, has been full of action, vivid adventure, even since then. I envy you. And although at fifty-eight many men are stertorous, pot-bellied, dropsical sots with no further interest than to sit by the fire like flatulent pug dogs waiting to be fed, you are still lean and long and strong, and at heart longing for adventure. Are you not? Be honest. I thought it might be appropriate if we joined forces, just as you and Francis did.'

'And what, may I ask, is there to be gained – I mean, gained by you – in this extraordinary suggestion?'

'Money, financial backing, the benefit of your wide experience, and the advantage of working with a close relative, and a man of my own class.'

'Had you not better invite your half-brother, Francis's son? You are nearer of an age.'

'Geoffrey Charles? No. Nor would I.'

'You grew up together – at least in the same household. He's at a loose end.'

'Not now. He's studying law. When we were young together there was too much of a difference. And you speak of being nearer of an age. Ten years when you are growing up is an enormous gap. Then when our mother died he hardly came home at all.'

'You are neighbours now.'

'Indeed, and he has a handsome little Spanish wife I would be happy to get my hands on . . . But his long time in the Army has changed him. Nowadays he would always, most tiresomely, be on the side of the law.'

They had ambled as far as the decline leading to Nampara Combe. You could hear the thin hissing of the wind like running water through the wheat stalks, under the black clouds and the hot sun peering.

'Well,' said Valentine, 'this is as far as I shall come.'

'Where do you intend to operate from?'

'What? Oh, my little shipping activities?'

'Yes.'

'Officially, Padstow to Rosslare and return. As we have been doing with the *Adelaide* until she foundered. Straightforward, and all above board, as you might say.'

'And below board?'

'Ha. We call in on the way there and back. Basset's Cove, chiefly. Isolated, and a moderately safe haven on this damned inhospitable coast.'

'I wondered what you were doing running aground near Godrevy. But have a care not merely for rocks. Basset's Cove is not entirely unpopulated. There are a few cottages. And whispers sometimes get to the wrong ears.'

'It's a chance one takes, Cousin. This county thrives on whispers.'

Ross hesitated. 'Talking of whispers, are you by any chance becoming over-friendly with Agneta Treneglos?'

Valentine bent to pat his horse's neck. 'Where did that come from?'

31

'The whisper? Does it matter? If it is not true.'

'How can one judge what is over-friendly? I have seen quite a little of the dear girl of late. She misses Horrie. She lacks young company.'

'She has younger sisters.'

'Male company. I find her interesting.'

'The other night when you were returning from Mingoose House . . .'

'Oh, that was my little kitchenmaid. Can't recall her name for the moment . . .'

'Carla May?'

'How brilliant of you to remember, Cousin.'

'So long as you do not confuse that name with the name of Agneta.'

'It seems unlikely, don't it?'

'It is for you to say. Her father is an unagreeable person if crossed. Years ago Francis, when a young man, used to fight with John, and often enough I was drawn in. They were not malicious quarrels, but when it came to John and Richard against Francis and me there was little quarter asked or given.'

'Should this concern me?'

'Agneta is the apple of her father's eye – in spite of her handicap. With Horrie married, John finds his family dispersing and prizes the more those he has left. Anyway he is not a man to be trifled with.'

Valentine pulled at his bottom lip.

'Agneta needs fresh company. She responds to it. Because nature has been a trifle casual with her intellectual equipment, it does not follow that she is not capable of enjoying life. If she does not understand a joke when you first tell her and if she then sees it when you have explained it to her, she will laugh more loudly than anyone. Her sense of taste and smell are as acute as any animal's. Why should she not enjoy herself in any way she can? I must confess I find her interesting.'

Ross looked at his companion. 'You are a strange young man, Valentine.'

'And of course,' Valentine said, 'she's so *grateful*.'

*

32

Christopher left on the Thursday. His mission, if not accomplished, was progressing.

It had been provisionally agreed that before Christmas, if the weather remained open, Demelza should take Bella to London, in the company of Caroline Enys, who was quickly drawn into the plan. There they would see Dr Fredericks. In the meantime Caroline had said she would invite her aunt, Mrs Pelham, who seemed to know everything and everybody, to discover for them how famous Dr Fredericks really was and what other teachers might be consulted before any positive step was taken.

Demelza found herself in a cross-current of emotion. (Perhaps she would have felt something in common with John Treneglos.) To 'lose' Isabella-Rose – which was almost what it amounted to – only two and a half years after Jeremy's death was something that all her instincts cried out against. With Clowance obstinately remaining in Penryn, there would only be little Harry to be a companion to (apart from the monthly visit from Cuby and Noelle to break the pattern of the days).

But all this, Demelza knew, was often the lot of the mother: to lose her children, by illness, by the tragedy of war, or the lottery of marriage. She could not, she said passionately to herself, deprive Bella of an opportunity that she was overwhelmingly eager to take. Safeguards, all sorts of safeguards, must be written in to ensure that this was not some romantic scheme of Christopher's, aimed chiefly at marriage to the girl he loved.

Bella must be given a fair chance.

As for marriage, it had been a principle of hers and Ross's, that their children should have free choice, but it *was* really like a lottery ticket whom their children would draw. Clowance had sincerely loved Stephen – obstinately, passionately – and still mourned him, though something sour seemed to have crept into her memory after his death.

But although most of the family, including Jeremy, had come to have an appreciation of Stephen's many good points, it could not be said that anyone except Clowance had become genuinely attached to him. This was not true of Christopher; everyone in Nampara liked him.

Then there was Cuby, of whom everyone was fond except Clowance. To Demelza she was of course a poor substitute for Jeremy –

even with little Noelle thrown in – and on dark windy hollow nights, of which there were many for Demelza, no more than Clowance could she forget the sequence of events that had led Jeremy to join the Army. Yet Demelza from the first had felt a kind of affinity with Cuby, and no one, Demelza reasoned, could estimate the pressures which had existed on Cuby to do what she did.

As for Bella, she would soon be seventeen! Demelza had known long before she was seventeen whom she loved and would always love. (It wasn't the same, the other side of her argued. She and Ross had been living in the same house and seen much of each other, albeit as master and servant. Was Bella being enchanted by the glamorous ex-soldier without having any chance of seeing whatever obverse side of the coin might exist?)

Ross did not tell Demelza about Valentine's proposition. He had intended to mention it amusedly, but the conversation with Christopher the same night had rendered his encounter unimportant. His wife at the moment only had the problem of Bella in her head and heart.

Once or twice his thoughts roamed over the proposition Valentine had put to him. No one but a perverse, slightly unstable character like Valentine would ever have suggested it. It was true that since Jeremy's death Ross had lived quietly, but at no time had he considered it 'tedious'. His chief aim had been to bring Demelza back to normality, and in this to a large extent he thought he had succeeded. Her long spells of silence had gone. He had tried to take her out to supper parties or for weekends in the county. With that he was content in making her content.

Had he had ideas of resuming a more publicly active life, it would certainly not have led him to the illegalities of tin smuggling. If there was one disturbing aspect to his present retirement, it was the thought of unfinished business at Westminster. When the war ended he had felt that, whatever the value of his activities over the previous ten years, they had now been justified by the defeat of France. It had been his only reason for remaining Lord Falmouth's representative in the Commons. That and Jeremy's death had led him to resign his seat. He had no further use for it.

He had expected – as had many – that the end of the war would bring not merely peace to Britain but a wave of prosperity. It had not happened. The fall in government spending from its wartime levels had meant a drastic drop in the demand for British manufactures. Then the sudden demobilization of soldiers and sailors had thrown thousands of extra men upon the labour market. Many factories in the north and Midlands had closed down, and agriculture too had fallen into a deep depression. Much agitation and rioting had led to the burning and smashing of machinery, so that the government, instead of introducing at least some of the reforms planned by Pitt, had brought in more repressive measures. Canning was back in England, had become MP for Liverpool, and often wrote to Ross. Ross sometimes thought the letters contained a hint of reproach.

The only serious content in the encounter with Valentine had been his near admission about Agneta.

If Valentine were to antagonize the Treneglos family it would be too close to Nampara to be comfortable.

Especially as the Trenegloses were known to believe the local gossip that Valentine was Ross's son.

Chapter Four

Clowance did not see the over-attentive Mr Prideaux for nearly three weeks. Then one Wednesday, having ridden into Truro to order some supplies, she saw him coming towards her in Church Lane.

She had only just turned into the lane from Boscawen Street, and briefly contemplated a hasty turnabout; but he was only three yards from her and there was no escape.

'Mrs Carrington! What a fortunate meeting. I trust you're well, ma'am. Though in truth I do not think you can be so well as you look!'

Not used to double meanings, Clowance charitably took this to be a compliment. He was in a dark blue cut-away coat and fawn twill trousers caught under the instep with black elastic. Fortunately he was not wearing his spectacles.

'I would have called upon you before this, but Lady Harriet seemed uncertain of your exact address. You must give it me, pray, before we separate. I did not think you lived in Truro.'

'I do not. Now and again I come to shop here.'

He felt in his fob and gave a shilling to a beggar who was importuning him. 'Last week I met a Major Geoffrey Charles Poldark, who lives on the north coast. It is an unusual name, but I did not at first connect you. He tells me he is your cousin. Is that so?'

'Oh yes. His father and my father were cousins.'

'Go away,' said Mr Prideaux to the beggar who, having bit the coin and found it good, was now being overwhelming in his thanks.

'We never met because we were in different regiments; but of course there was Waterloo to talk about.'

36

'I'm sure.' Clowance looked after the beggar, who, unable to believe his luck, was cavorting across Boscawen Street. Then he tripped and fell flat on his face in a puddle and had to be helped up. They could still see the shilling he held firmly between finger and thumb.

'You should not be so generous with your alms,' said Clowance with a half-smile.

He was affixing his spectacles. 'Giving a little to a poor creature like that is a form of self-indulgence. Besides, it is nice to be called "Milord" now and again.'

'Yet you do not wish to be called captain?'

'It is whatever you please. Captain if you so desire.'

'But not milord.'

'Not yet. I am still young.'

She could not tell whether he was joking or serious.

'Well,' she said, making a move. 'I have to do a little more shopping yet—'

'Please do not go. I have just been taken with a perfectly splendid idea. I have an appointment to take tea in the Red Lion with a friend. The friend, I am sure, is well known to you. Would you do me the honour of taking tea also?'

She hesitated. For the first time he did not seem quite so impossible. 'Is it Geoffrey Charles?' she asked.

'No. But I am sure you will be pleased. It cannot, I think, delay you more than half an hour, and the hotel is but ten paces down the street.'

Hodge was not due until five, and the chances were he would be late.

'Thank you,' she said.

There were two dozen inns in the town, but the Red Lion was the largest and the most important. It had a pleasant large room on the first floor, which had become in recent years something of a meeting place for the social minded. As she mounted the stairs Clowance realized she was rather thirsty. But who was this eccentric man taking her to meet?

The room was quite full, it being market day, and at first Clowance did not see anyone she recognized. Then she saw a table by the window with a solitary young woman at it. She was clearly waiting for them. It was Cuby.

'I knew this would be a present surprise,' said Philip Prideaux, rubbing his hands together. 'Mrs Poldark, Mrs Carrington. Eh? Eh? Sisters-in-law!'

Clowance had first met Cuby at Trenwith when she had come with her sister Clemency to Geoffrey Charles's and Amadora's big party. She remembered then registering surprise that this idol, this icon of Jeremy's, was not better looking. Then rather reluctantly she had acknowledged that Cuby had wonderful skin and eyes. They had spoken scarcely at all, for the breach between Cuby and Jeremy seemed then unbridgeable, and Clowance had resented her on sight – as Demelza on the same evening notably had not.

When the plans for Cuby's marriage to Valentine had fallen through and she and Jeremy had eloped, they had, according to reports, been 'blissfully happy' in Brussels, but, while accepting that, Clowance still felt that the tragedy of Jeremy's death at Waterloo need never have been.

Now they were facing each other across a small tea table, thanks to the blundering good will of the egregious Mr (Captain) Prideaux.

Cuby had coloured. One could not be sure how much she knew of the other girl's enmity, though some of it must have been made reasonably plain by the fact that whenever she went to Nampara Clowance was not there.

Philip ordered tea for himself and Clowance, but Cuby said she would have coffee.

There was one subject which could not add to the chill. 'How is Noelle?'

'Passing well, thank you. She has been slow to talk, but now it is beginning.'

'You do not have her with you in Truro?'

'No, Clemency is caring for her. They are great friends. It is long since you have seen her, Clowance. I'm sure you would find her engaging.'

'I'm sure,' said Clowance.

Mr Prideaux glanced from one to the other, and took off his spectacles.

'Do you know what I have been doing this week, ladies? I have been to Chysauster.'

Both looked blank.

'Where is that?'

'Near Gulval. There are the remains – the very splendid remains – of a "beehive" hut. It is of early date, if not actually prehistoric. And a subterranean passage, part fallen in. Roman-British times. Probably third or fourth century. I believe a man called Borlase has written about it.'

The two ladies listened courteously while Philip told them some of his activities of the week. In friendlier circumstances they might have smiled understandingly at each other, but Clowance did not meet Cuby's eyes.

Tea was finished, and what little casual conversation there had been dried up. Philip beamed at them both, impervious to mood or atmosphere.

Then suddenly Cuby said: 'Clowance, I know how busy you are, but would you spare the time to come to Caerhays and spend an afternoon with us? It is, I know, quite a long journey, but if you took the King Harry Ferry it would cut several miles from the trip.'

Clowance hesitated, and to her annoyance knew herself to be colouring.

'Very kind,' she said. 'If you are sure your brother would welcome me?'

'Why should he not?' Cuby asked indignantly.

Clowance glanced at Philip Prideaux and wished him far away. Well, he was not, so . . .

'Before you married him, was not Jeremy several times turned from the door?'

Cuby looked daggers at her sister-in-law.

'That must have been when I was affianced to Valentine Warleggan. I did not know of this. I suppose John thought he was acting for the best.'

'I imagine so. All the same, Jeremy was profoundly upset.'

Cuby said: 'But in the end I married your brother. Do you remember that? I was at fault before it came about. But I had in the end six months of life with him that were so full of happiness that I shall never forget them as long as I live.' There were tears in her eyes now.

Clowance said: 'I'm sorry. I should not have said that. If we had not met so unexpectedly perhaps I should have spoken less ill—'

'It is better you should say what you feel.'

'I don't know if I have the right. I don't know all the circumstances of your refusal of him. My love for Jeremy went so deep that it warps my judgement. I could only see his almost manic distress—'

'Ladies, ladies,' said Philip Prideaux, aware at last of the battle that was beginning before him, 'this is clearly a distressing subject for you both! Could we not discuss something brighter?'

Her eyes full of tears, Clowance turned to him and said: 'Captain Prideaux, will you please go away.'

Selina was delivered of a male child on the thirtieth of November 1818. On the third of December Valentine went to see George Warleggan at his bank in Truro.

George could hardly believe his ears when Valentine was announced.

'Mr *Valentine*, did you say? . . . Where is he?'

'Downstairs, sir.'

It was on his tongue to say he was not in, but angry curiosity got the better of him.

'Show him up.'

When Valentine came in George was studiously writing. After a couple of minutes he lowered his pen and said: 'Well?'

Valentine was as usual well turned out, but not flamboyantly in the way Ossie Whitworth had once been. George was irritated that he could find no fault in the young man's attire.

'Good day to you, Father. Some years since we met. You're well?'

'Well enough. What do you want?'

'What do I *want*? Well, less than nothing, so far as I know. May I sit down?'

George gave no indication of assent, but Valentine sank into the black-studded leather armchair that Cary occupied when he came into the room. It was the least uncomfortable seat this side of the desk.

'I came to tell you, Father, that my wife Selina gave birth to our first child last Thursday. This mayhap you will have heard?'

'I know nothing of your family, and care less.'

'A pity. I came to tell you that mother and child are doing well.'

'Indeed.'

George remembered the insults that had flown between them in their last quarrel. He was not a man who easily forgot. But *years* had passed since they had spoken or even seen each other. There was little obvious change in the young man. The same narrow good looks, the same arrogance, the same insolent bearing. Rumours had reached George that in the intervening years Valentine had been up to no good in the county. Carrying on with this woman and that. Using his wife's money in various semi-nefarious ways. But *he* had spent a lot of money on this young man too, the only one to bear the name of Warleggan. What was this news the young puppy was bringing?

'So?'

'I have a son. And you a grandson. I thought you might like to know. Harriet I'm sure will be pleased to know. The christening is to be on Sunday next, just after morning prayers. Very quiet. No fuss.'

'Indeed,' said George again, from under lowering brows.

Valentine brushed a dab of mud off his highly polished riding boots. 'How are the twins?'

'What? Oh . . . So-so.'

'I'm sorry, I have temporarily forgot their names.'

'Rachel and Anne.'

'Of course . . . Well, yes, on consideration there is one extra point to my coming. The question of a name for my son. Selina and I have given careful thought to the matter. Would you object if we called him George?'

Someone was shouting in the street outside, selling eels. There was a tap on the door, and a clerk put his head in. He recoiled like a wounded snail when George looked at him. The door closed. Valentine looked out of the window. It was streaked with stains of yesterday's rain, and the iron bar across it did not add to the cosiness of the room.

George said: 'Is this some attempt to curry favour with me?'

'Why should it be? I have money of my own.'

'You mean Selina's.'

'Not altogether.'

'Well, your mine is not paying,' George said spitefully. 'I happen to know that.'

'The Duchy of Cornwall, as I'm sure you know, has leased its duties for collection to Mr Edward Smith. He has been very exacting, as I am sure you also know, and two of the smaller mines in my district have closed this month. Others will follow . . . *You've* closed Wheal Spinster. But I have other sources of income.'

'I would like to hear them.'

'I don't think this a suitable matter to disclose in open court, if you follow me.'

'Illegal, you mean. I urge you to take care.'

'I did not say they were illegal, Father. But sometimes I indulge in a little gamble, with satisfactory results.'

'Have a care that you do not get involved with John Permewan. Or with the United Copper & Zinc Company. Or Wheal Seton. Their investors are up-country people who know nothing of mining and less of finance.'

'Of course not,' said Valentine, who in fact was already doing business with two of the names mentioned. 'But in my view few ventures that make money are made without an element of risk.' Then, feeling the words hanging in the air, he added: 'The smaller the risk naturally the better.'

George grunted. 'If you are bent on having some interest in mining, avoid tin. Copper's doing well. If you meddle in tin you'll get into a mess like the Gundry family have at Wheal Vor. Bankrupt after three years!'

Valentine said: 'I have a notion that was mismanagement, Father. From reports, there is nothing amiss with the mine.'

George looked up. 'You are well informed.'

'I do my best. But of course you know so very much more. I doubt if there is anyone who knows more about the mercantile prospects of Cornwall.'

Silence fell.

George said: 'How d'you get on with your neighbours?'

'Which neighbours?'

'The Poldarks, of course.'

Valentine stretched his legs. 'I see very little of 'em. Geoffrey Charles is up and down to London. It is said he is reading law. His little Spanish wife keeps much to herself. I don't think she feels quite safe among the Cornish folk when Geoffrey Charles is away.'

'I was referring to the Ross Poldarks.'

'You said neighbours, Father. It is at least five miles between us. I see nothing of them. The loss of Jeremy has hit them hard. I prefer more cheerful company.'

'Are you to have a big christening?'

'I told you. Very quiet. Just a few of the household. Would you care to come?'

'No, thank you.'

Valentine let out a slow breath, which George did not notice.

'Well, I must not take up more of your time. May we call your first grandson George?'

'I cannot stop you.'

'You can deter me.'

George hesitated. 'Give it him as his second name if you wish.'

'I could give him a second name so that if he chooses when he grows up he may use it instead. I do not see why he should wish to do that, though. George Warleggan is a name to conjure with.'

George picked up his pen and looked at the quill. Some fool had not sharpened it this morning.

'I have three daughters. All their dowries must be secured. I have no money to leave to a grandson.'

Valentine got up. 'I should prefer my son to make his own way.'

'By marrying money,' said George, with a slight sneer.

'Just so, Father. We all have different ways.'

'Then call him George,' said George, 'if it pleases you.' And be damned, he added, but under his breath.

Chapter Five

It was more than three years since Demelza had been in London, and she had rather hoped she would never see it again. She liked the great city, but twice had been terribly unhappy in it. On her very first visit there had been the enmity and then the duel between Ross and Monk Adderley. Never a more anxious time in her life. Then on her last visit she had had to leave Ross in France, where he was being illegally held as a prisoner-of-war, and no knowing how long before they saw each other again – if ever. Before he came back he had had to send her the news of Jeremy.

This time she had Caroline and Bella for company on the tedious coach trip, and this time, which was to be a short stay, they would stop with Mrs Pelham, Caroline's aunt, who insisted they should do this.

The little house where Dr Fredericks lived was just off Chancery Lane, three-storeyed, and leaning to one side as if receiving support from the warehouse next door. Christopher Havergal had brought them, and they were ushered by a rather shabby maid into a rather shabby front room with pot plants in the window and diplomas on the wall. A walnut piano in a corner. The quartet were invited to sit down. They did so, but when the door closed Isabella-Rose was on her feet again studying the diplomas. From upstairs came the sound of another piano striking only one note, a middle C. Then a female voice joined in. Starting quietly, it grew to a crescendo and then faded away to a delicate pianissimo. The piano sounded the next note of the scale, and the exercise was repeated.

'Look, Mama,' said Bella. 'It says here—'

'Shush,' said Demelza, who had picked up the sound of footsteps.

A man came in. He was very short, not more than five feet, tubby, with a mass of grey curly hair cut to the shape of his head, clean-shaven, in a loose collar with an untied white cravat half hanging, a stained purple velvet jacket, striped trousers, small feet in patent shoes.

Christopher introduced his guests, though Dr Emanuel Fredericks had met Bella before. He acknowledged this at the end of the introduction by saying, 'And my little Donna.' At which she dimpled.

Christopher said: 'Of course you know the object of our visit, Dr Fredericks. Her mother and Mrs Enys have come to discuss with you her daughter's talents and future.'

Dr Fredericks nodded. 'Lady Poldark, I tested Miss Isabella-Rose's voice in a number of ways at her last visit, and I have to congratulate you on possessing a daughter of remarkable talent.'

'Thank you,' said Demelza, wishing almost for the first time that she had lost more of the Cornish accent from her voice. 'Mr Havergal has told me that you think highly of her. I am not sure what that means in – in terms of her future.'

'I am the most exclusive teacher in London. That without immodesty I can certainly claim,' Fredericks said. 'I assure you, my lady, I can pick and choose whom I have as a pupil. I restrict my numbers to ten. I teach only the essential mechanics of the voice. The words larynx or glottis, or other such technical terms, are used sparingly in this house. I seek a natural voice and to enhance musicality. I divide my instruction into three main areas: rhythm, diction and phrasings, and ornamentation. My tuition involves hard work and the utmost dedication. It will take in all about two years for the basic course.'

'And at the end of that time?' asked Caroline.

He spread his small white hands with their spatulate finger ends.

'No one can tell. I believe this young lady to have the most natural talent of any of the last fifty pupils it has been my privilege to teach.'

Greatly daring her daughter's displeasure, Demelza said: 'Some people – a few people – find her voice rather, well, hard.'

'Ah, yes, I can understand that,' Fredericks said. 'The vocal cords are magnificent and surprisingly mature. At times she may even seem to shout. But that is all latent tone, latent talent, an expression of the vigour of youth. That can be trained out of the voice so that the top registers are as sweet as the lower ones.'

'And she is – is what is called a mezzo-soprano?'

'That is so.'

Caroline looked at Demelza, as if aware that hers was not a major role but . . . 'Dr Fredericks, have we your assurance that Miss Poldark has an exceptional voice – or one of exceptional promise? Suppose she comes to you for two years, and at the end of that time she has fulfilled her promise, what then? What might her future be?'

Dr Fredericks again spread his hands.

'A pupil I had last year began with sponsored recitals; then recently she has been engaged as the principal soprano by the Bristol Oratorio Society. Another whom you may have heard of, Christine Smythe, has already sung in opera and is now in Paris, singing there and receiving further tuition from the great Bernard de Vries. A third has been in Milan in a new opera called *Norma.* For a young lady with a supremely good voice the world is open.'

Caroline said: 'You refer to ladies. How many of your present ten pupils are in fact ladies?' (Only Caroline would have asked that, Demelza thought.)

'Er – three, no, four. The other six come from relatively humble backgrounds.'

'And these high fees you charge? Are all your pupils charged the same?'

'I have awarded two girls scholarships because their parents are quite unable to find any money at all. They have great promise, and I feel I am paying my own debt to society by giving them free tuition. Only one of these is a singer, the other is a student of the piano. Miss Poldark, if she comes, will no doubt make their acquaintance.'

After a thoughtful pause Demelza said: 'Lieutenant Havergal will have told you we live in Cornwall. It is many miles from London. I think about three hundred. It takes two to three days by coach, and you cannot be certain sure by sea, sometimes shorter, often longer. My daughter is not yet seventeen. She goes to Mrs Hemple's School in Truro and is taught singing by a local teacher, Mrs Hodgson. May I ask the – the ages of your other pupils?'

'Seventeen to thirty-one.'

'My husband and I are not – not anxious to stand in Bella's way. If she really has such a fine voice we do not wish to prevent her from developing it. But in our view she is still so young, and although she boards with Mrs Hemple during the week she has never lived anywhere else but at home—'

'Oh, Mama,' said Bella. 'I have lived in Paris!'

'Yes, yes, but then that was our home. When you – if you were to live in London you would have to face it alone – or nearly alone. Do you board girls in the house?'

'Yes, my lady. We have accommodation for four, but all these bedrooms are taken at present. Mrs Fredericks would I think be able to recommend someone nearby.'

'I do not think that will be necessary,' said Caroline. 'I think my aunt would be willing to accommodate her, and a groom would escort her daily.'

'I had not thought of such a thing,' said Demelza, in surprise, pleasure and panic. She felt she was on a slope which was getting steeper and on which it was difficult to call a halt. She would dearly have loved Ross to be there to offer some more common-sense observations. Or did she mean objections?

'Mozart,' said Christopher. 'I think—'

The piano upstairs was suddenly clearer, as if someone had opened a door.

'It's a sonata,' he said, 'but I'm not sure which one.'

'Number One in C,' said Fredericks approvingly.

'Do you play the piano, Christopher?' Caroline asked.

'Alas, no.'

'I believe that Miss Poldark does,' said Fredericks.

'Well, a little.'

'That is something you must do if you come here. There must be many rests from singing so that you do not strain or tire your voice. And breathing lessons – that before you ever begin. And languages. You must know three or more languages at least well enough to understand them and to pronounce them. And deportment. And acting . . .'

Demelza looked at her daughter, sturdy and slender at the same time, her eager expression, her clear blue eyes, her luxuriant hair. There were two standards to be passed, not one. If indeed she had an exceptional voice, had she the mental stamina, the determination, the resolution to develop under some stern taskmaster? Had she any real *idea* what she might be undertaking?

Aware of her gaze, Bella looked at her mother and winked. This was the same young lady who during their flight from Paris had charmed a potentially dangerous group of Polish dragoons by playing an old harpsichord and singing the 'Marseillaise' in an old inn in France. It was equally easy to underestimate her. At that inn in St Quentin Demelza had watched her through the bars of the landing stairs, furious at her recklessness and half beside herself with anxiety as to what Bella might have plunged herself into. In long retrospect some of the fury had turned into pride. That her daughter, not yet fourteen, had had the courage to do such a thing: one's heart beat faster even today at the thought of it. She and Ross had bred a girl of exceptional talent, exceptional courage, exceptional self-reliance. She deserved the best. Was this the best?

In the afternoon of the same day they went to see two other experts recommended by a musical friend of Mrs Pelham. The first was a Mr Peter Reumann, who was musical director of the King's Theatre in the Haymarket. They were taken to the back of the theatre to meet him, where a rehearsal room was empty except for half a dozen chairs and a concert grand piano. He was another small man, but slight of build and with an obvious authority.

He took Bella to the piano and asked her to accompany him in a few simple tunes.

After fifteen minutes he said: 'A quite distinctive voice and noble in one so young. It needs training, of course, and we do not have the teacher or the facilities here for such training. Here you could take small parts very soon – but, yes, I understand you are not seeking that – next summer we are considering productions that could offer her an opening. That way she would pick up a great deal; sometimes one can learn so much from others. I know of two young women who have prospered that way. Both of course took private lessons as well. If you change your mind and care to write me in about six months I will be willing to see you again. Can you act, Miss Poldark?'

'I think so,' said Isabella-Rose, all agog at being behind the scenes in one of the great theatres. 'I would want to.'

'Of course, of course. Acting is always an integral part of singing, whether in simple glees or in grand opera. You must appeal to the eye as well as to the ear.' He added to Demelza: 'She has not perhaps got *your* looks, madame, but she is the right build and already has presence.'

Caroline said: 'You think her voice might be – exceptional?'

Reumann hesitated, then decisively: 'Yes, I do.'

'Ideally, where should she go for the best tuition?'

'There is talk of opening a Royal College of Music. At present: Falconer, Fredericks, Alesi, Lotti Schneider. Perhaps those are the best four. If you are aiming merely for operetta, then you could not do better than go to Paris, where there are several excellent people.'

Caroline said: 'We have an appointment with Madame Schneider at five.'

Madame Lotti Schneider, a fair-haired, buxom, handsome woman, said: 'Com' 'ere, *meine liebe.* Let me look into your mouth. Your throat, my little, it is the instrument on vich you must play all your life. No? It is 'ere, 'ere and 'ere vence comes the tone, the quality. Come over 'ere to der piano. I see you breathe vell. Now let me 'ear this voice. Gently, gently at first in answer to ze piano, just as if you were soothing a little baby to sleep.'

This was a quiet street, not like the King's Theatre, where even through closed windows one could hear the rumble of carts and carriages. Listening to her daughter's voice following the piano up a note, up an octave, and gradually increasing in volume, Demelza thought: if Ross could hear her now he would realize what an *intelligent* girl Bella was. She seemed to know exactly what Madame Schneider wanted even though she was being spoken to in a thick German accent.

When it was over Lotti Schneider patted one of Bella's hands. 'Dat is very good. Lirico-Spinto is what you may become. You have a daughter of great talent, Lady Poldhu. She should 'ave a splendid future. I would be 'appy to take her – and will *do* so, but I 'ave to say I am shortly to embark on a concert tour of Europe: Rome, Milan, Vienna, Berlin. When this 'appen my pupils do not 'ave the best attention. Natural, I give exercises to fill up their time with careful study. Do you have foreign languages? French, Italian? I leave London after Christmas and shall contemplate to return at Easter. She could gain much in working with a professional mezzo like me, but dere are drawbacks too.'

Demelza said: 'But you think, madame, dat – that my daughter should go on with her studies?'

'Of a certainty. Oh yes. Oh, yes. Oh, *yes*. But the voice needs careful 'andling. You must avoid wear and tear. The slower one progresses, the more surely one progresses. Many leap too soon. Of course in my vorld there is much competition. But dere is always room for another if the talent is dere. I personally, venever I can, sing Mozart. This can be a top singer's salvation – it helps to stay on der right path.'

'Do you have many pupils?' Caroline asked.

'Two, three only. But dey are not quite pupils. Dey are already singers. But Lady Poldhu, could you come back, return, after Easter? I can teach your daughter a great deal. A year mit me is worth two year mit anyone else.'

In the evening, after a quiet supper, when for once Mrs Pelham was entertaining no other guests, they went into the choices thoroughly: Demelza, Bella, Caroline, Christopher, Mrs Pelham.

Demelza said: 'Caroline, you are my oldest friend. Tell us, please, what thoughts you have.'

Caroline rubbed her long patrician nose. 'First, I suppose you have to say that Christopher was right. Not only the teacher of his choice but two others, nominated by Aunt Sarah, have confirmed his opinion. This seems to prove that Isabella-Rose has exceptional talent. They would – could not be generous without good cause. Therefore, if you can afford the fees – and I know Ross can – the likely decision is that she should have a year or more's training to see what progress she makes.'

Christopher said: 'I have already offered to pay the fees.'

'We could not accept that,' said Demelza. 'Thank you all the same. We can meet them.'

'Let us agree then that the expense is not a hindrance. Do we agree on the rest?'

After a pause Demelza said: 'I think so . . . yes.'

'Then for that year – or several years if all goes well – the question is . . .'. Caroline stopped. 'No. It is good of you to give me the floor, my dear, but I should not be talking like a judge dealing with the custody of a child. She is *your* child. I must not take over your role.'

Demelza said: 'But do you not see, Caroline, that it is *because* I am her mother I cannot see this detached. So please go on.'

Silence fell. Caroline sighed.

'Well, if that is the provisional decision, some other important decisions or choices will need to be made. Of the three highly placed professionals we have seen today I know Bella would choose Mr Reumann—'

'I never really said that!' exclaimed Bella.

'I heard you whispering to Christopher, and I know why you fancy Mr Reumann, my dear. It is because he inhabits a *theatre*. And one of the finest in London. You came over visibly faint at the sight of stepladders and panels of scenery and the smell of cosmetics.'

'You must not pull a face like that, Bella,' Demelza said, 'you must be polite to your aunt.'

Caroline laughed. 'Aunt in name only.'

Christopher said: 'But did not Reumann say he could not take Bella at present? He surely meant – in fact he said – come back in six months.'

'True.'

'Of course I was not with you,' Mrs Pelham said, 'but Madame Schneider sounds the most romantic to me – and perhaps the most practical! Indeed, I have heard her sing more than once, and her help would be invaluable. She is performing at present? Otherwise I might have invited her to sup with us before you returned home.'

'Duke Street, St James's, is much further from here than Chancery Lane,' Caroline remarked. 'It is worth thinking of in the winter.'

Demelza thought of that other side of London, of which they had seen plenty today, the endless beggars, some of them ex-soldiers lacking limbs, the pigs rooting free in the gutter, the crush of traffic, the smell of drains, the pie sellers, the quacks, the knife grinders who crammed the edges of the pavements, the ragged boys and barefoot children.

She said: 'Mrs Pelham, is it true – I only heard mention of it this forenoon – is it true that you would allow Bella to live here for a very short while until she found her feet? Tis really good of you—'

'My dear,' said Mrs Pelham, looking benevolently at Isabella-Rose. 'That was not quite what I said. My meaning was that I should be pleased – indeed happy – to invite her to live here, not for a short time but for just as long as ever it may suit her.'

Mrs Pelham had not met Demelza's second daughter before this week and was clearly much taken with her.

Bella beamed at her, and when she smiled like this it was as if all her face lit up. It could not have been a more suitable friendship for all concerned. Mrs Pelham was wealthy, well supplied with servants, constantly entertaining but personally lonely, knew most of the best people in London, had a private carriage (which she seldom used), lived in this big, handsomely proportioned house, often went to the theatre, had no children of her own.

Demelza wriggled uncomfortably in her chair to try to rid herself of a curious stab somewhere in the breast or upper stomach. She refused to recognize it at first, but after settling down again and murmuring her most profuse thanks to Mrs Pelham, she had to acknowledge that the uncomfortable stab was a feeling of jealousy. Not of course jealousy of Bella, for whom this visit was turning out more favourably than she surely could ever have dared to hope; but jealousy of Sarah Pelham, who, henceforward, if this plan now went ahead, would see far more of Bella than Demelza could ever hope to do.

Somewhere in the depths of her soul a solitary miserable creature was weeping. 'I lost my first daughter Julia years ago when she was scarcely more than a baby; and then it is only three years since Jeremy my elder son, at the height of his charm and youthful maturity, was killed at Waterloo; now I have to part with my youngest daughter, gone three hundred miles away, to live in this beautiful house with this elegant elderly lady, in pursuit of a singing career. What a tragedy it is that she ever met Christopher Havergal. How much happier Nampara would be with her at school in Truro and singing for fun. How much happier Bella herself might be in the end!'

She swallowed and said: 'I b'lieve Madame Schneider would take her. *And* Dr Fredericks, I'm sure. You – you would advise Madame Schneider, Mrs Pelham?'

'When I first heard of Dr Fredericks as the best teacher in London,' said Christopher Havergal, 'and took Bella to see him in July, I had no certain idea where she would be able to stay. As you all know, I hope to marry her, but have willingly agreed to a postponement, and I have been much exercised in the matter of finding somewhere suitable for her to board. But of course Mrs Pelham's magnificent offer makes this all unnecessary. Ma'am, I shall consider this the greatest favour you could offer us. Thank you.'

Mrs Pelham smiled.

He went on: 'Mrs Enys has raised the question of the distance the two teaching establishments are from here. Dr Fredericks is little more than half a mile, Madame Schneider is nearly two miles. I have been measuring it on a map. This perhaps should not be the main factor in a decision, but it might be taken into account.'

'Perhaps,' said Caroline, 'we should ask Bella how she feels.'

Bella smiled one of her irradiating smiles. 'I am – enchanted.'

'With either?'

'With either.'

Chapter Six

While her mother and Isabella-Rose were away Clowance went to Nampara to keep Ross company and to be an extra companion for Harry. As the cross-country route was slightly more risky in the winter, she decided to take the coach road to Truro, where Matthew Mark Martin would meet her to escort her the rest of the way.

Halfway to Truro she made a short detour to tell Harriet that she would not be at home for a week. Harriet of course was out with her hounds, so she went into the house and wrote a brief note for when she returned.

As she sanded the paper a footstep creaked in the hall, and she turned to see the lanky figure of Philip Prideaux bearing down on her.

'Mrs Carrington. How good it is to see you. I fear Harriet is out.'

'So I have discovered. I should have known. You are not hunting this morning, Mr Prideaux?'

'No. I thought to stay in and read. Sometimes I think I have had rather too much to do with horses in my life.'

He wore the usual stiff collar, a silk stock, a fine white cambric shirt under a bottle green jacket, tight black trousers. He had just put his glasses on.

The footman who had let her in was waiting by the door.

Clowance said: 'I am going to see my father on the north coast, so I must make haste.'

Prideaux said: 'I will see Mrs Carrington out, Parker.'

'Very good, sir.'

As the footman left Philip said: 'I wrote to you, Mrs Carrington.'

'Did you? I did not receive it.'

'No. I put it in the fire.'

'Oh? Why?'

'I could not – I did not feel my apology was well expressed.'

'Apology?'

'For taking you to meet Mrs Poldark, your sister-in-law. I had no idea of course that there was a coldness between you.'

'I am sure,' Clowance said, 'that the apology should be mine. To ask you to leave in that way was quite unpardonable. Your intention was perfectly civil and proper.'

He smiled stiffly. 'Someone wrote the other day that "It is more wittily than charitably said that the road to hell is paved with good intentions." That was why I destroyed the letter I wrote.'

'I don't understand you.'

He took his glasses off and stuffed them in his pocket. His eyes were always a darker brown than she expected. They looked temporarily absent-minded as they adjusted to a new focus.

'I thought the letter, read in cold blood, might compound the offence I had given you. I seem far too often in our short acquaintance to have done or said something that you deemed inappropriate. I did not wish to add to my sins when trying to expiate them.'

'I think we should excuse each other,' said Clowance, smiling too. 'Waterloo – I suppose Waterloo still casts a long shadow. It must answer for a lot, mustn't it. Perhaps I should say that my meeting with my sister-in-law helped to clear the air.'

'I'm so very glad. I think young Mrs Poldark is a charming lady. I confess I do not so much take to her family.'

'Oh?' Clowance looked up with interest. 'Why do you say that? She is very attached to them.'

'I know. Her brothers are too hubristic.'

'I scarcely know either of them. A third was killed in Holland.'

'That great castle they have built. I am told they do not have sufficient funds to complete it.'

'No, that has been the trouble all along,' said Clowance, remembering afresh Cuby's duplicity.

'My cousin has an over-large house at Padstow,' said Philip Prideaux. 'But he inherited it. Perhaps I am splitting hairs in thinking that ostentatiousness in one's ancestors is more excusable than in oneself.'

Clowance said: 'And perhaps your ancestors could pay the builders?'

'Quite so. Quite so.' He extended his hand and bowed over hers. 'May I write to you again sometime?'

'Of course,' said Clowance, and went down the steps. He followed her and helped her to mount.

Nampara was uncannily quiet without the presence of its two most ebullient inhabitants. (Even though Demelza was not as talkative as she used to be, she was still the centre of the house and in her absence a hollow existed.) Little Harry seemed to grow every time Clowance saw him. He would be six in a week's time, and Mama would be returning specially for his birthday. He was the sturdiest and most easy-going of all the Poldark children. He had the same flashing smile as his second sister and used it more frequently. In fact Ross and Demelza had come to the joint conclusion that he had already discovered it to be his handiest weapon – to charm, to excuse, to avoid blame and to get his own way – and he would probably be able when adult to use it in a finer-honed form to make his way in life. He had already shown himself to be lazy when learning to read and write and not at all studious or thoughtful; but in no way lacking in intelligence or the ability to use his brain when he felt like it.

They decided not to worry. He was young yet and easy company and good to be with. Ross instanced as an example not to be followed that of a professor he met in London whose son could not read the *Morning Post* at the age of three, so he took the child to a brain specialist.

Clowance saw Ben Carter a couple of times. He was still unmarried and greeted her with a mixture of admiration and respect on his black-browed, black-bearded face. She knew she was very fond of him, but it never amounted to more. She wondered if she would ever again feel that deep personal involvement with anyone else now Stephen was gone. Why did her memory still gag at the deception he had practised on her? He had lied to her to get her. What was so unforgivable in that? He had not *deserted* her. Not for the first time she wondered if she was becoming a widow with a 'grievance'. But it is hard to argue with your heart.

On the second night Dwight, who had also become a temporary bachelor in the furtherance of Bella's career, invited them to sup at Killewarren, and Clowance was surprised and pleased to find Geoffrey Charles and Amadora there. Geoffrey Charles was still enamoured of his pretty Spanish wife and she with him. The religious difficulty had been accepted, though not ignored, and Amadora's wish to have Juana brought up in the Catholic faith was an extra stumbling block. Neither Geoffrey Charles nor Ross, now the senior member of the family, had very strong feelings on the subject, so Amadora was having her way. But at Ross's suggestion they were keeping quiet about it, for there would be strong feelings in the neighbourhood if it came out. Demelza's brothers, Sam and Drake, were deeply shocked, though sworn to secrecy. Most of Ross's aristocratic friends would also look askance, having been brought up to hate and fear Catholicism.

Amadora and Clowance had a long talk about Juana; though Clowance had no children of her own she was interested in them, and her emotional clash with Cuby in Truro had ended on a much more peaceable note after they had begun to discuss Noelle.

While they were so talking Clowance heard the name Prideaux mentioned by Geoffrey Charles, and after supper she brought the name up herself.

'Captain Prideaux?' said Geoffrey Charles. 'Philip Prideaux? I do not know him well, for we were in different regiments. But he's well thought of. Interesting fellow. Wonder he's alive.'

'D'you mean at Waterloo?'

'Yes. He was in the King's Dragoon Guards. One of the crack Household Cavalry regiments. It was on the Sunday morning of Waterloo when the bloody skirmishing was almost over and the real battle about to begin. Some of our infantry got into trouble and were losing ground and losing men. Lord Uxbridge saw what was happening and ordered six brigades of Dragoons and Inniskillings and Scots Greys to charge.' Geoffrey Charles paused a moment to exercise his part-crippled left hand. 'Uxbridge led the charge himself. But you will have heard all about this? There have been pictures painted, ballads sung.'

'I do not believe I have.' Clowance had not been interested in the heroics of a battle that had cost her her brother.

'Well, they totally routed the French, scattered them like chaff, running for their lives, cleared the whole valley. I saw a part of it: it was magnificent. But no one took any notice of commands to rein in and regroup. They drove on and on deep into the French lines, and when the wild charge finally came to a stop and they could hear the bugles still blowing for the retreat they had no reserves to cover them. So they were cut to pieces. Only about a quarter returned.'

They listened for a moment to Horace III yapping at the door to come in.

'And Captain Prideaux was in that?'

'Very much so. Quite the hero. He rescued Colonel Fisher, brought him back across the saddle of his horse. He was wounded himself four or five times.'

Horace III was allowed in, and went snuffling round the room looking discontentedly for his mistress.

Geoffrey Charles said: 'I lost sight of him for a while then. I believe he was in hospital for six months. Then they sent him to the West Indies. He had some sort of a breakdown there.'

'So he has resigned from the Army?'

'Did he tell you that?'

'I think he did. I assumed it.'

'Well, yes. But it was not voluntary. He was discharged for killing a man.'

'I did not know that.'

'Perhaps I should not have told you. Clearly he would prefer it not to be known.'

'How did it happen?'

'I have no details – or at least reliable details that I would pass on – but it was during the period of his breakdown. That's all I know.'

'Did he go to prison then? For killing someone . . . Or was it a duel?'

'It was not a duel. I think he was considered of unsound mind. These black fevers can very quickly have that effect.' Geoffrey Charles studied his cousin. 'Those glasses he wears nowadays. I believe he can see well enough without them. They may be a symptom of some sort. Probably he will be better now he is out of the Army altogether.'

The shadow of Waterloo, Clowance thought again; even after three years, it lay over them all. Jeremy killed, leaving his family bereft, and a widow and an unborn daughter, Christopher Havergal, with an artificial foot, Philip Prideaux apparently a nervous wreck, Geoffrey Charles with a part-paralysed left hand (though that in truth was a relic of the Peninsular War). Four young men.

All over England people would still be licking their wounds. And in France too. And in many other countries. All because of one great man's vaunting ambition.

'I should like to meet him,' said Ross.

'Who?'

'This Prideaux man. I heard much of the cavalry charge but never saw it. I was on a mission to carry a message to Prince Frederick of Halle. It was well on in the afternoon before I . . . returned . . .'

Deliberately changing the subject, Dwight Enys said: 'Was anyone invited to the Warleggan christening yesterday? Were you, Ross?'

'No.'

'Katie said there were only a dozen there; just servants from the household. He's a healthy boy of eight pounds. I advised Selina not to go. Whether she did go I know not. But she is not of robust constitution, and one would not want her to risk a prolapse.'

'A strange household altogether,' said Geoffrey Charles. 'It was a mystery what induced her ever to marry that Pope fellow in the first place. Now I wonder why she married Valentine.'

'She 'as two daughters already?' asked Amadora. 'I 'ave never seen them.'

'They're her stepdaughters by Mr Pope's earlier marriage. They seem to have been more or less permanently farmed out somewhere in London – Finsbury, I believe. Is it true that they have christened the new baby George?'

'I don't know,' said Dwight shortly. 'I heard so, but it may be only a rumour. Or one of Valentine's sick jokes.'

Everyone waited for Ross to speak, but he said nothing, and his expression gave nothing away. Clowance wondered whether her mother would be so self-contained at the news.

Mingoose House was part medieval. Built shortly before Trenwith, it had few of Trenwith's airs and graces, and like Werry House, six miles inland, it had large gloomy rooms, a multiplicity of corridors and staircases and doors that opened unexpectedly into smaller rooms and cupboards. The Trenegloses had lived there since the early 1550s when one Edward Treneglos with a group of camp followers had spoiled two Spanish ships with cargoes of velvets laden for Antwerp. This was off Mount's Bay, and they had landed at Ilfracombe with their spoils. Some months later, with a doxy of his choosing, he had settled on this desolate area of the north coast and begun to build.

The house was half-finished when he died of drink, but his son, having found some tin deposits on the newly acquired land, had completed the house after his own fancy. Since then generations of Tenegloses had lived out their lives there, on the whole noisily but minding their own business and taking no part in the religious and political traumas which had racked the county. The fifth-generation eldest son had married a Joan Trevanion, who had brought them land and property in Plymouth Dock which had cushioned the family against the worst economic winds ever since. Their mines were long since played out – except for Wheal Leisure, in which, thanks to Ross and Jeremy, they had shares, and from which they regularly had, as owners of the land, a 'dish' or percentage on the ore raised. For the rest they hunted madly on all possible occasions, went shooting with friends on the more bird-prolific south coast, got drunk when they had the mind to, and played interminable hands of whist. Old Horace, a contemporary of Ross's father, had been something of a Greek scholar, but none of his family had picked up this disagreeable habit. What fields they troubled to cultivate yielded amazingly well, considering the ranting winds and the shallowness of the soil.

It was here that Valentine Warleggan found himself at the time he was being discussed by Dwight Enys and Ross Poldark.

The gaunt house was quiet and almost empty, except for the servants. John and Ruth had gone to visit Horrie, their newly married son, at Minehead. Emmeline was away, and the youngest daughter Paula was in bed with a light fever. So Valentine was in bed with Agneta. Early in the evening was not without risk. He could have met a maid in one of the corridors, or might do still when he left. But an element of risk added an element of spice to the adventure.

And he was beginning to need a little spice to sustain him. One of the joys of his life was discovering a new woman. Although the cynical streak in his mind told him that in the end all women were alike, his constant need was for conquest. Nothing matched the savoury sweetness of the courtship and the first consummations. Alas, it did not last.

Agneta had first taken his interest because of her utter innocence. At twenty-nine life had passed her by. Because she was what
the Cornish called 'half-saved', her father and mother had kept a
closer watch over her than over her sisters. All through her adoles-
cence and early twenties she had had a maid-companion to keep
her company, so even if she had had the normal impulses of a girl
to kick over the traces, the opportunity had not been allowed to
exist.

And she was not unattractive. With her lank shiny hair and
startling brown eyes and dark skin, she might have been a half-
caste. There was a legend in the family that when Edward Treneglos
had settled here all those centuries ago the woman he had brought
with him and bred from had been a Creole. If so, a slight touch of
the blood continued to exist, as some of the portraits in the hall
seemed to bear out.

At the moment Valentine, having had his satisfaction with her,
was stroking her long, pale, fawn-coloured back, and she was
giggling. He knew that she was expecting him to come again, and
he might well do so soon, but he was recognizing the feelings of
satiety within himself which told him that this affair was nearing its
end. Not quite the end. He had no one else in view. He wished she
did not giggle so much.

She rolled over on her back and folded her arms to conceal her
fine breasts.

She said: 'Do you love Neta?'

After a few moments he nodded his head. 'Yes, I think I do.
Quite a little bit.'

She displayed a huddle of front teeth as her full lips parted.
'Neta wants to know what is a little bit?'

He pinched her nose. 'Neta should know it is improper to ask
too many questions.'

'What is proper?'

'Not what we are doing now.'

'When will Vally see me again?'

'I am not sure. I have been having a new ship built in Falmouth,
a lugger, a small brig. Do you understand that?'

'Up and down, up and down. Yes.'

'Well, it is ready and I shall be taking delivery of it with three
men I know, and we shall sail it from Falmouth to Padstow. That is
perhaps tomorrow or Tuesday.'

'What?'

He repeated his statement slowly. 'So I shall not be back for several days.'

The teeth disappeared. 'You come again?'

'Of course.'

'You come again now?'

'Soon.'

'My Mama and Papa come again too.'

'What do you mean? You said tomorrow.'

'That is right. Tomorrow, Sunday.'

'Today is Sunday!'

'Oh? Yes. Perhaps it is Monday. Perhaps Mama said Monday.'

Valentine listened. The house was deadly silent. Of course he had often been here when all the family was here. But if they returned this evening it would be natural for Ruth to come upstairs to see her daughter. He looked at the door. It was of solid oak, and he had himself turned the great key.

Oh, well. An element of risk added pleasure to any pleasure.

'Agneta.'

'Yes, Vally?'

'If I have you again tonight I do not want you to cry out.'

'Neta *wants* to cry out.'

'But you know I have told you—'

'They will think she is dreaming. She often cries out in her dreams!'

'Agneta, it is only eight o'clock. You should not be a-bed at eight o'clock. If you cry out, someone will come knocking thinking you are having one of your – thinking you are not well.'

She giggled. 'You locked the door. Agneta will tell them to go away.'

The rain was pattering on the lattice windows. It would be a dreary ride home for him. His horse was hidden in a coppice nearby, so he could hardly return by way of the cliffs and the beach. He wondered why he went to all this trouble. And a sulky wife to greet him when he reached home. Would Agneta be difficult to uncolonize? That was always the tricky part of any affair, the tears, the anger, the recriminations. In this case perhaps just absence would be sufficient. Over six miles separated the houses. He could, in fact, with his new ship to play with, have a genuine reason to absent himself. He looked at Agneta and wondered if because of her simpler reactions she would be easier or more difficult to shake off. The latter probably. Maybe he would dally about her for a time, let his visits become slowly less frequent. He did not want to break the girl's heart.

Chapter Seven

The day before they left London for their long trek back to Cornwall, a red-haired lady in her late forties called at Mrs Pelham's house in Hatton Garden. With her was a tawny young man, clean-shaven but with fine wavy hair escaping from under his silk hat. When Demelza came into the upstairs drawing room they were already talking to Mrs Pelham.

On seeing Demelza the red-haired lady sprang up: '*Ma cherie!*'

'Jodie!' They embraced. 'What a surprise! Judas God, I thought I was seeing a ghost!'

'So you might, for we could give you no notice and alas we hear you are leaving tomorrow. And my darling Bella! What joy!'

Presently the young man was introduced. He was Maurice Valéry, whose home was in Lyons, but who was at present living in Paris.

'How did you know?' Demelza asked.

'I saw Christopher this morning in a coffee house. He said you were here on a fleeting visit, and if I wanted to see you I must make haste.'

'Yes, we leave at seven. It will take at least two and a half days before we are home. Ross will be some sorry not to have seen you.'

'He is – well? You are well? I heard of course of your great loss. And of course I wrote. My darling, you have suffered much. War is *vile* and *terrible*. Your loss is – still raw and fresh. Peace has come at last and the usurper is locked away. Far away, where I pray he may do no more harm . . .'

Maurice Valéry was looking about the room, appreciating its elegance.

'Are you a Bonapartist, young man?' Mrs Pelham asked abruptly.

He smiled and shook his head.

'There is still much Republicanism in France,' said Jodie, 'but very few want Bonaparte back. This time the Bourbons seem to be securely in place, and it may be that the forces of occupation may be persuaded to leave France before 1820, as it was agreed in the treaty. That can only help us the more.' She leaned forward towards Mrs Pelham. 'Did you know, Madame, how Lady Poldark helped in my escape from Paris? And little Bella – not so little, *ma petite*, not even then – risked her life by diverting attention from the man Sieur Menieres who was escaping with us.'

'For me it was just a prank,' said Bella, blushing. It was not like her to blush, and Demelza wondered if the presence of the handsome young Frenchman had brought on this unusual display of modesty.

'Perhaps you will stay and sup with us, Madame de la Blache?' said Mrs Pelham. 'Christopher Havergal will be here. And also my niece, Mrs Enys, whom I would like you to meet.'

Jodie glanced at the young man, who smiled in acquiescence.

'Thank you,' she said. 'We shall be enchanted.'

Ross said: 'So you decided it was right for her to go?'

'I wish you had been there.'

'I did not want to – overload the delegation, so to say. You are her mother, with perhaps the greatest interest of us all in keeping her home. Caroline has a wise and sophisticated head. If you have decided, I am not in a position to criticize it. And Havergal's recommendation was the one you finally chose?'

'When we got there, after we had been there two days, it seemed I was on a slope. You know I do not really like London – I am a little afraid of it – but it was at its best this time. And things seemed to move in only one direction once we were there. Mrs Pelham was that warm and welcoming, and she took the greatest of a fancy to Bella – and Bella to her . . .' Demelza sighed. 'But the most important part is that there don't – doesn't seem any doubt that all three teachers think highly of Bella's voice. Dr Fredericks said it was one of the best he had heard for years. Mr Reumann said he would be happy to have her, and so did Madame Schneider. I thought much of Madame Schneider, for she was a tip-top singer herself. But we chose Dr Fredericks because twas the nearest to a normal school, and he is very – what is the word? – dedicated. She will get full tuition there, and it is much nearer Mrs Pelham's house.'

They were lying in bed and talking by the light of a single candle. A half gale was booming, and the windows rattled as usual at each particular gust. A wearisome ride back from Truro, where Matthew Mark Martin had been waiting for them. The end of a long day in a jolting coach. It was nine when they reached Nampara, and they had supped lightly – Bella passing on the glowing news to her father between bites at a rabbit pie – and then she had shot off with Farquahar at her heels, no doubt taken him to bed to tell him the story all over again.

Demelza said: 'This business of Mrs Pelham wanting Bella to live with her. It was some nice of her, for I could see she really truly meant it and it made all the difference to my feelings. It made *all* the difference, Ross. She will be in a *home* not in a cheap rooming house, and Mrs Pelham even says she will send one of her footmen to take her and fetch her each day. It is such a lovely house.'

'I remember,' said Ross. 'And of course coming from such a house gives her an added importance in the scheme of things. One side of us may deplore that, but it is a fact.'

'And also,' said Demelza, 'being the daughter of a baronet.'

'Faugh! I suppose so.'

She stretched. 'Oh, I'm glad to be home. That coach jolted and lurched so much.'

He put his hand in hers. 'No more now, then. Go to sleep.'

'Just a little more, Ross. Who do you think came to sup with us the night before we left? You will never guess. Jodie de la Blache!'

'My God. How is she? And what is she doing in London?'

'She said just a holiday. Of course she has many friends in England. But you never know with Jodie, do you?'

'How do you mean?'

'What is the word she used so often about herself? *Une espionne.* She was so long a conspirator that now you have to wonder . . .'

'Happily there is little to conspire about now the wars are over.'

'She had a young man with her. Much younger than she was. I do not think . . . But he was handsome and he said he played the fiddle in an orchestra in Paris.'

'It seems we cannot get away from music.'

'Do you want to?'

'I like the sort of music you play.'

Her hand closed on his. 'That is not music proper. That is tunes. Anyway I have invited Jodie to come and stay with us.'

'The Devil you have.'

'The Devil I have. Oh, not now. They are off back to Paris on Monday. But sometime. If she is over again.'

'I hope you told her we did not have a house like Trelissick, where she stayed years ago.'

'I told her we lived in a farmhouse which had had some improvements.'

He yawned. 'Shall I douse the candle?'

'Please.'

He did so, and there was silence between them, though there was no silence in the room. Hail struck the windows like fistfuls of gravel hurled by a petulant child.

'It is growing worse. You were just home in time.'

'Have you finished the Long Field?'

'Yesterday. We ended by moonlight. The sea was so heavy we knew bad weather was on the way.'

'So all is safely gathered in.'

'*You* are. That is rather important, you know. As for the seed, some of it will be washed or blown away . . . Even Sam and Rosina called.'

'That is uncommon good of them. Was they both well?'

'I think so. They stayed to help but, I imagine, Brother Sam thought you would be home yesterday. He asked me if we had come to any decision about Isabella-Rose.'

'He – being of his persuasion – will think we are casting our daughter to the Beast by considering she might go on the stage.'

'Not sure I don't think that myself.'

'Oh, Ross.'

'I swear the jest be laughable.'

After a minute Demelza said: 'Well, there is still time to withdraw.'

'That time is not yet. We must play fair with Bella.'

'I am glad you feel that.'

They had a house party for Christmas at Cardew, but it was of Harriet's arranging, not George's, so he suffered it but did not too actively participate. Parties that *he* arranged were not undertaken solely for the pleasure of laying out large sums of money to give his friends entertainment; they always in some greater or lesser degree had a purpose, an end, a reason, in view. If the guests he invited did not actually *give* anything in return, they contributed to his plans: either to impress an important guest with the extent of his own possessions, or because his guest's profession or business was interesting to George, or because the guest was a large investor in Warleggan's Bank or might be persuaded to become one. People like Sir Christopher Hawkins of Trewithen, who had put the pieces together to enable him to buy the rotten parliamentary borough of St Michael, were always welcome, as were a few other such scattered about the county.

Harriet, on the other hand, had a disappointing habit of having people to stay for whom, without regard to their standing, she had developed a sudden liking – like this young fellow Prideaux who always seemed to be staying, or if not staying, visiting, or if not visiting, appearing and disappearing at unexpected moments. Of course he seemed a decent enough fellow, and well connected in the county, and there was no personal reason to object to him; but one wished for and had expected something different. Her brother, the sixth Duke of Leeds, for instance, had *never yet* been down, and when they were staying in London he always seemed to be abroad. Harriet, with a lazy chuckle, said she had never got on too well with George William; they were too much alike, she supposed, and rubbed each other up the wrong way. Besides, his wife was ineffably tedious and never hunted.

'Nor do I,' said George.

'Oh, come. I sometimes see you bringing up the rear.'

'It is a matter of courtesy, as my wife always leads the field.'

'You stand my teasing better than you used to, George. Anyway, George William is not at his best on a horse. Dear God, why are there so many Georges in the world?'

'Another George has recently been added to it.'

'Oh?'

'Valentine has christened his new brat George.'

'No! . . . How do you know? Has—'

'I heard before Christmas, but there has been such a to-ing and fro-ing, and looking to my own extensive affairs and observing the haunches of your horse as you ride away . . . And then this party . . .'

Harriet took a small gold watch from her jacket pocket. 'Ursula should be home soon.'

'They said six. It wants fifteen minutes.'

'Did you *see* Valentine?'

George hesitated. 'Yes. He came to the Bank.'

'Has he changed?'

'As usual very self-possessed. No hint of apology for the way he behaved.'

'As you know, my dear, I have always had a feeling that we reacted too ferociously at the time.'

'You mean I did.'

'Yes, if you put it that way. Valentine, whether we like it or not, is a young man of spirit. You arranged a marriage for him. He clearly did not fancy Miss Trevanion as much as you supposed. It upset your plans. But did you ever think you may have driven him into Mrs Pope's arms?'

'What on earth d'you mean?'

'He was about twenty at the time, wasn't he? You are rather an intimidating man for Valentine to tell to his face that he won't fall in with your plans. You might even have over-drove him, over-drove him trying to marry him to Cuby. His one security was to do what he did do – seek the protection of the law by marrying someone else – in this case Selina Pope. Once he had done that you were powerless.'

'And does it please you to reflect that Valentine rendered me – powerless in this way?'

'Oh, la, George, do not put it into such dramatic terms. I am merely suggesting to you that the unfortunate event should not be looked on as the end of the world.'

He stirred restlessly. 'So you think it is some small matter that had best be ignored and ordinary relations between us should be resumed.'

'My dear, he's your son, not mine. Do whatever you have the fancy to. I rest easy in this either way.'

George picked irritably at a few bristles under his chin which Hingston had missed when shaving him that morning. Feller was getting careless: it was the second time this month.

'And the insufferable insults he paid me during the last quarrel, when I turned him out of the house?'

'I was not privy to them. But most insults, I believe, go curled and yellow at the edges after a number of years.'

George eyed his distinguished but irritating wife. Still only thirty-nine, she had lost few of her looks, her skin still very good, her hair still shiny and raven-black. (No white hairs.) If she would only take more care for her dress during the hunting season. Striding about like a man, dropping mud on the carpets, smelling of dogs.

He had never mentioned or even hinted to her of the jealous thoughts that had constantly poisoned his first marriage, and the vile doubts as to whether Valentine was his true son. It had all turned upon whether Valentine had been an eight-month child; and when Elizabeth lay dying after giving birth to an eight-month daughter he had sworn to himself that never, never again (even though so far as Elizabeth was concerned it was too late) would he doubt that Valentine was his son. And so it had been. The doubts were gone – or had been locked like poisonous snakes in some dark cellar of the subconscious – and he had come to regard Valentine as truly his. He had planned everything, disregarding Valentine's looks, his sarcasms, his casual misdeeds, and arranging a fine marriage to a fine young woman of aristocratic but moneyless family, a fine castle – the most beautiful in Cornwall – all, all, all would have been Valentine's, Valentine Warleggan of Caerhays – and the young puppy had thrown it all back in his face, with insolence, abuse and – one suspected – naked dislike. It was the expression on Valentine's face more than his words which remained most vividly in George's memory.

Then, only then, had that dark cellar been opened an inch or two and some of the malodorous suspicions resurfaced. Valentine was very *unlike* Elizabeth or himself. Not that he was particularly like Ross Poldark, except for his height and colouring. But, although George did not remember him, one or two ill-intentioned people had whispered that he was like Joshua, Ross's infamous father.

There was therefore this other enormous obstacle, of which Harriet knew nothing, to any sort of reconciliation. And Valentine's manner when he came to the Bank was anything but contrite. He had lounged in a chair, his long, elegant bent leg over the arm, casually asking George's permission to name this so-called grandson after him. The strangest move on Valentine's part. Inexplicable except as a move towards a reconciliation. But to what end? There seemed to George to be only one answer: money.

He said: 'I shall take no notice of his visit. If he expects to be invited here with his wife and son he will be much mistaken.'

'I have never once seen him in Falmouth or Truro,' Harriet said. 'He has become very much of a north-coast man. I wonder how his marriage is making out.'

'His marriage? Why?'

'Well, I would think him far too free with his favours to be content to bestow them on only one woman.'

George eyed her suspiciously. 'Has he – did he ever . . .'

She laughed. 'Make approaches to me? Think again. But a woman does not need to be seduced by a man to know how he feels about women in general.'

George was about to say more, but was prevented by the arrival of Ursula, his daughter by Elizabeth. She had been spending Christmas with the Rashleighs of Luxulyan. George had willingly sanctioned this, as he knew Sir Colman Rashleigh was an important man in the county.

Ursula was now just nineteen. She was still stoutly built with thick legs and a noticeable bust. But because of the alchemy which begins to work on girls of this age she was less dumpy, less unattractive than she had been earlier. Her skin was good and mercifully unmarked by pox, her grey eyes, though frequently masked by sullen lids, very sharp when seen. Her straight flaxen hair was curled and dressed.

Not a vivacious girl, and when asked how she had enjoyed Christmas her appreciation was expressed in short sentences and simple monosyllables. George had early taken her away from Mrs Hemple's School in Truro – partly because Isabella-Rose Poldark had arrived – and sent her to Madame Blick's Finishing School for Young Ladies at Penzance. He was now about to move her on somewhere else – Exeter or London – where she could be taught the niceties of society life and behaviour. But he hadn't decided where. In truth, he was a little baffled by her attitude. Was no child of his ever going to conform to expectations? She was only mildly interested in clothes; (Harriet, when she could find the time, would give advice to her dressmaker). She was only mildly interested in boys. She was only mildly interested in horses and foxes and the countryside. What she *was* interested in was metals and mines: tin stamps, copper smelting; the side products of Cornish mining such as gold, silver, zinc, iron, lead. George sometimes blamed himself for ever buying her that clever reconstruction of a Cornish mine, built by an out-of-work and crippled miner, which she had played with endlessly as a child. True it was not an inappropriate or unwelcome hobby for one living in the centre of the Cornish mining areas, but not quite the thing for a woman, a young girl of quality.

'Oh,' said Ursula at supper that evening. 'Erica Rashleigh knows Bella Poldark.'

We all live too close together, George thought between his mental teeth, Cornwall is just a big village.

'Indeed,' he said discouragingly.

'I hardly knew her,' said Ursula; 'she was among the juniors. I know you don't like them, but she seemed to have sufficient agreeableness. They say she sings.'

'Walter, you may bring the port.'

'Very good, sur.'

'Bring the '87,' said Harriet. 'Last night's was over the top.'

'Very good, m'lady.'

'I thought it was well enough,' said George snappily, after the butler had gone.

'Uh-huh,' said Harriet. 'Did they give you port at the Rashleighs, Ursula?'

'No, Mama. Erica is only eighteen, and not treated yet as if she were quite grown up.'

'Well, taste this tonight. I'm sure your father will not mind.'

'Bella Poldark,' said Ursula, 'is going to London to school.'

Harriet raised her eyebrows. 'Who told you that?'

'Erica.'

'Where is she going?' asked George after a moment.

'It is to be to a special school where she is to be taught singing.'

'That will cost them a pretty penny. Her father is still largely dependent on his mines.' George shrugged his shoulders as if his jacket were becoming uncomfortable. 'No doubt his other small investments pay their way.'

Chapter Eight

Ross was in the silversmith's in River Street when the bell jingled and Valentine came in, stooping, as Ross had stooped, to avoid the rafters.

'Why, Cousin,' Valentine said. 'Well met. What brings you here?'

'I might say the same. As we have agreed before, the point really is who gets the question in first.'

'Indeed you might. Afternoon, Penarth. I am after a bracelet to please a vain woman. I see you are among the candle snuffers, Ross.'

'As you say. This is a new kind of snuffer which does not let the dead wax fall on the table but stores it to be deposited later in the fire.'

'Excellent idea. Thank you, Penarth, I'll just look around your little shop.'

'Ais, sur.'

'I'll take three of these,' Ross said.

'It puzzles me,' Valentine said. 'Men are always finding some mechanical improvement to make life easier. But they never find anything to improve themselves.'

Ross glanced at the fat young shopkeeper. 'Penarth, I believe, is of the Methodist persuasion. He might take a different view.'

Penarth grinned awkwardly. ''Tis not for me to differ from my betters, sur. Especial too when they are my customers. I d'think young Mr Warleggan was speakin' of more practical things.'

'Tact,' said Valentine. 'Tact is what I think you have. Tell me, is this bracelet good silver?'

'Oh ais, sur. You'll see the mark just near the clasp.'

Valentine dangled it in his fingers, holding it up. 'Does that please you, Cousin?'

73

'You are not buying it for me. You must consider the lady's tastes. Do you know them well?'

Valentine closed his eyes in thought. 'Not very well. She's my wife.'

Ross paid for his candle snuffers, and Penarth took them into the back of the shop to wrap them in tissue paper.

Ross said in a low voice. 'And how is George?'

'George?'

'Your son.'

'Oh. That George. Lusty and full of life.' Valentine's sallow face had coloured slightly.

'And Selina?'

'Dwight Enys is not well satisfied with her. D'ye know, Cousin, women are strange creatures after recently giving birth. Instead of being full of joy at having come to her time and produced a fine healthy baby, she is mopish, under-spirited, indolent, subject to tears. I think she needs rhubarb, but Dwight has other ideas.'

Penarth could be heard rustling paper in the back of the shop.

'A strange name to give your son, was it not?'

Valentine sucked the handle of his riding crop.

'It is a very common name. I gave scarcely a thought to my – er – ex-parent. I have seen neither sight nor sound of him since the almighty sparring that took place between us when I told him I was married to Selina. How many years ago is that? It seems half a century. I never think of him nowadays.'

Penarth came bustling back with his parcel, but seeing his important clients engaged in conversation, he went behind again and began to polish some candlesticks.

'In fact,' said Valentine, 'if I thought of anyone when I chose the name I thought of George Canning. He is one of your heroes, is he not?'

Ross said: 'Do you remember Aunt Mary Rogers? Pally Rogers's wife?'

Valentine stared. 'No.'

'No, I suppose you are too young. Aunt Mary was a fat, jolly woman who smelt strongly of camphor. She had one weakness, which was a high level of gullibility. She would believe almost anything you told her. So when I was young, if you were confronted with some obvious untruth, you would say: "Tell that to Aunt Mary."'

Valentine nodded. 'Just so. And you are not Aunt Mary Rogers. Just so. So, Cousin, I will unveil the facts. We all know the scurrilous rumours which circulate in our neighbourhood about my parentage. Whatever the truth or the untruth of them, it is your known and expressed wish that they should be ignored or, where they cannot be ignored, denied. What better could I have done to play my prescribed role in this matter than by christening my son George?'

It was not often that Ross got the worst of an argument with Valentine, but he found himself nonplussed and illogically resenting it.

'Here we are, sir,' said Penarth, producing the carefully packed candle snuffers. 'I've made a loop of strong twine if so be as you wish to tie it to your saddle.'

'After all,' Valentine said, 'would you better prefer it if I had called him Ross?'

Near home Valentine called in to see Henry Cook, the grass captain of the Wheal Elizabeth mine, which had come into existence close to Place House. The site had been the object of speculation before Valentine had married into the property and when Unwin Trevaunance and Michael Chenhalls had lost interest he had taken it up, called it after his mother and engaged twenty men to explore it. It had borne some fruit, but as George Warleggan had pointed out maliciously to Valentine it was not yet paying its way. No engine had been installed because the site was on a slope beside the track leading to Place House and all early workings would drain easily onto the moorland and thence to the sea. Five shafts had been dug, each with its separate name: Diagonal, Western, Central, Moyle's and Parson's; but of these only the first two had brought a return, and it was not enough. At a tin ticketing in Truro Valentine had met a Mr John Permewan, who had the reputation of being able to raise money for mining, a man with many connections up-country. So he had commissioned Permewan to write a prospectus for Wheal Elizabeth to see what interest was aroused. There was money about, Permewan said, and often the North Country speculators, if presented with a well-written prospectus, would take up shares 'sight unseen'.

As he approached Place House he saw there was a more than

usual number of lights on. Selina often went early to bed. Strange if she had decided to entertain in his absence. He had only been away a day.

Music came to take his horse. 'Is your mistress up?'

'Yessur.'

'Nothing wrong?'

'Notsino, sur.'

He went in, took off his cloak and, seeing no servant about, hung it on the baroque hatstand in the hall, then went into the sitting room on the left which had been Sir John Trevaunance's study. Unerringly he had located the cause of the trouble. His wife sat at one side of the fire, and perched on an armchair on the other side was Agneta.

Valentine went across and kissed Selina on the cheek as she turned her face away.

'Greetings to you, m'dear,' he said. 'I am later than expected because I stopped at the mine . . . Agneta! This is quite a surprise, so far from home, and late at night.'

She was still in the black cloak in which she had come, and her hair, blown about by the cold January wind, was hanging in lank strings about her face. Blood and bones, thought Valentine, does she not look a freak! What did I ever see in her?

'Neta came to see Vally,' said the girl, wiping her nose with the back of her hand. 'Why has he been away so long?'

'I said I was much occupied,' he replied in a quiet soothing voice. 'You should not have come here disturbing my wife with your complaints.'

'Neta wanted to see you. You promised to see Neta. It is weeks since you saw Neta. The last time—'

'Has she been here long?' he asked Selina.

'Too long.'

'That tells me nothing.'

'Twenty minutes.'

Selina's narrowed eyes were gleaming, more than ever like a Siamese cat's in the candlelight. Valentine fingered the silver bracelet in his pocket, aware that the gift would be worse than useless tonight. What a tedious business this all was!

He went across and pulled the bell rope.

Agneta said: 'All through Christmas. Never seen Vally all through Christmas. Neta went to church on Twelfth Night. Mama took her,

76

along with Paula. Neta thought she might see Vally there. When we came out there was snow in the wind.' She began to cry.

As it happened, it was Katie who answered the bell.

'Has Music gone home yet?' Valentine asked sharply.

'No, sur. We was besting to go 'ome together.'

'Agneta, have you a horse?'

She looked up wet-eyed at the thin, dark, angry man. She shook her head.

'You *walked* here? . . . Katie, tell Music to saddle a pony for Miss Treneglos. And Katie!'

'Sur?' She swung round.

'You and Music take horses – doesn't matter which – not Nestor – and I want you both to escort Miss Treneglos home to Mingoose House and see she is safely with her family. *Understoood?*'

'Yes, sur.'

'Very well, that is all.'

This time Katie stood her ground. 'Beg pardon, sur.'

'What is it?'

'I was 'elping Maud see for your supper. Cook's abed with the cramps and Elsie 'ave gone off.'

'Damn my supper! I will have whatever Maud can give me cold. Now be off. Miss Treneglos is ready to leave.'

'Neta is thirsty,' said Agneta cunningly.

'I'll give you a glass of wine, m'dear,' said Valentine, his voice softer when he was speaking to her.

Selina got up. 'I shall retire to bed.'

Valentine opened the door for her, and his wife swept out. Then he went to the cupboard and took out a bottle of Canary, found a glass for Agneta and one for himself.

As he handed the glass to the snivelling young woman, he said: 'Listen, Agneta. Are you listening? Listen carefully. You must never, never, *never* come here again.'

They had slept separately for some time, but he crossed the corridor and tapped at his wife's door. There was no answer, so he went in.

Selina was lying across the bed, the curtains part drawn. Her night-rail was rucked up so that her pale slender legs were exposed to well above the knee. He sat quietly on the edge of the bed.

'Get out of my room,' she said.

After waiting for a few moments he said: 'What did that woman want?'

No reply. He put a hand on her foot. She withdrew it as if his hand had been a hot iron. Then she dragged her nightdress down. Her face was still buried in the pillow.

'Selina,' he said quietly, 'what have I done wrong this time?'

No reply.

'Look,' he said. 'A half-witted girl escapes from her parents' clutches and comes over here asking to see me. I am sorry for a poor creature like that. Sometimes I try to talk to her. So she thinks I am fond of her and constructs her own wild fancies around what is a mere friendly pity. Do you think I am so perverse, so desperate for a woman's company, that I have to dredge among the mud flats and pick out the witless, nashed, screw-eyed daughter of John Treneglos for my favours? Blood and bones, what do you think I am? Where will your insane jealousy lead you next?'

No reply.

He said: 'Doesn't she have fits?'

Selina moved her ash-blonde head. 'She said you kissed her knees.'

He laughed. 'Really, m'dear, this is a jest. All right, all right, very good. Granted that I have not been as faithful to you as you have wished. But give me leave to show a little taste in these matters. Why did I marry you? Why do I love you? Yes, just as much as I ever did. Now also we have a lovely baby . . . Where is he?'

'In the next room with Polly.'

'As well to keep our voices lowered, then. Now Selina, if you promised not to kick my teeth out, I should be very happy to kiss your knees at this very moment. Your disorder when I came into the room was mightily seductive. Your legs are very pretty, you know; quite flawless, the skin so fine it might be without pores. An enchanting woman like you almost by instinct can assume the most attractive attitudes.'

He put his hand gently on her ankle. She kicked it away.

'Do you believe that girl? That half-crazed woman? You would believe anybody against me, would you not. If some wizened hag off the streets came in and said she had received my favours you would assume she was telling the truth and I was lying. What has come over you, Selina? You have married a rake? Yes, I admit it.

But if this were true, why should I not admit it also to you? Can you not believe that this rake tells you the one big important truth when he says that he truly loves you?'

He waited then. Over the years of their marriage he had come to know her. You could appeal to her reason, but her sense of outrage would not allow it to respond. He fingered the bracelet in his pocket again. Tomorrow at the earliest. God damn that Treneglos creature for coming here tonight. He was tired and aware that any supper Maud had laid for him would be congealing on its plates. But this could not be left until the morning.

'Selina.'

'Get out of my room.'

'Have you ever been raped?'

She opened an eye. '*What* did you say?'

'It is rather a nasty business, but it can be quite amusing overall. I once had to learn some damned Shakespeare at school: "To take her in her heart's extremest hate . . . tears in her eyes . . ." How does it go? I cannot remember.'

'I told you to leave my room.'

'And I am not going while you continue to disbelieve me. After all, the law says that a man cannot commit rape upon his own wife. We should have to pretend we were unmarried for the occasion.'

'If you touch me I shall scream and wake George and Polly. And Maud is not yet a-bed.'

'Remember,' he said, 'when I visited you in this house – not this very room, but one down the corridor when your first husband was sleeping – how quiet we were in our loving. Can we not pretend it is that time all over again? I would like to be gentle. I should like to be stealthy.'

No reply. But the one glimpse of a Siamese blue eye told him there was hope.

'I have not had my supper,' he said. 'But I need you first.'

Chapter Nine

A month later, when the February winds were blowing over the moorlands of Cornwall and rustling the leaves of the evergreens, a woman was found stabbed to death close to the village of Angorrick near Devoran Creek. Her name was Mary Polmesk, a farmer's daughter with an illegitimate child, and it was thought that she had been sexually assaulted. The crime was reported in the *West Briton*, but raised no great stir except in the surrounding villages. Crime had increased noticeably in Cornwall since the end of the war. The point of interest was that she had been working as a part-time maid at Cardew, and was on her way home on a dark, cold evening when she was attacked.

George said it was partly Harriet's responsibility for employing a girl of bad reputation. Harriet said she had barely *seen* the girl, but passed on George's complaint to the butler, who it turned out was Mary Polmesk's uncle. He offered to give in his notice, but that was refused.

At the end of February, the weather not yet relenting, and two weeks after her seventeenth birthday, Isabella-Rose left home and travelled to London to begin her voice training and general schooling at the establishment of Dr Emanuel Fredericks. Ross asked Clowance to go with her, at his expense. On the Friday following their arrival on the Tuesday, Geoffrey Charles would be returning to Trenwith, so Clowance would have company both ways.

'Thank you, Papa, but do you not have business yourself in London, something that—'

'As it happens, no. And I shall have perhaps to go to Liverpool in a few weeks on this Base Metals and Mining Commission, so would prefer not to travel this month.'

'And Mama?'

'She thought to have a few days with Verity. Your aunt has not been quite so well of late.'

'I know, I know. I saw her yesterday. But she has taken some physic which appears to be helping.'

'Also,' Ross said, 'it will make the break easier between Bella and her mother, who does not greatly care for London. Besides, I thought – we thought you have scarcely been anywhere since Stephen died, except an occasional visit to Nampara, and the brief holiday—'

'Might do me good?'

'Might do you good. You and Bella are fond of each other, I know.'

'You think I need a breath of fresh air?'

'Of new air – certainly not fresh. Well, it could do you no harm, could it?'

Clowance nursed her chin. 'When would it mean leaving?'

'Next Friday.'

'I suppose Hodge could manage if I were away for ten days. He managed well enough when I had influenza last year . . . Don't think me ungracious, Papa. I am, as you suspect, in rather a rut.'

'Can we agree, then?'

'Thank you. If Bella does not mind a censorious and rather firm older sister as company.'

'Nobody here would recognize that description. Certainly not, I imagine, Philip Prideaux.'

'What's all this about?' said Clowance. 'Who has mentioned Philip Prideaux?'

'I have.'

'You do not know him. You said so at Dwight's.'

'I said I would like to meet him sometime.'

'And does that involve me?'

'Not necessarily. But Cuby mentioned him when she was at Nampara last week. She said it was clear that this Prideaux man is taking an active interest in you.'

'Considering that the only time I met him in Cuby's presence I dismissed him from his own tea party, that is quite a large assumption.'

'Apparently he came back after you had left.'

'I certainly must go to London now,' Clowance said, 'to escape the erotic temptations that beset me here.'

Ross regarded his daughter with quizzical amusement.

'At least, my dear, you are now on more companionable terms with Cuby, or so I hear. It's an ill wind.'

'What do you call the ill wind – Philip Prideaux?'

They both laughed.

So the sisters went to London together, and arrived at the Star & Garter Hotel in Pall Mall at four in the afternoon, four hours late, to be met by Lieutenant Christopher Havergal, who had been inside the hotel for four hours, desperately resisting the temptation to drink himself into a stupor while waiting.

Without regard to decorum Bella flung herself into his arms. When Christopher at length disengaged himself and bent over her sister's hand – they had never met – Clowance looked at him with smiling interest, this sturdy, blue-eyed, moustached figure with the limp and the military bearing and the long fair hair. He was a very attractive man. He would have little difficulty in charming women if he had the mind to. Yet spying Isabella-Rose in Paris three years ago when she was literally a child, he had apparently had eyes for no one since. Of course he might have had other ladies on the side, there would be no knowing, but his real love for Bella was plain to see. And she returned it, which to Clowance was less hard to understand. There could be no hidden motive on his part – Bella was no heiress, nor was she titled or came of an influential family. It had been love at first sight.

A pang went through Clowance's breast. Had it not been the same with her, the same with her and Stephen? Once they had met, exchanged glances, exchanged kisses, no one else would do. And at last they had come together and married and lived in harmony – a sort of harmony, until at the end it came out that he had lied to her continuously, had married her bigamously, after his son by his former marriage had turned up. Pray the gods that this love between her young sister and this charming soldierly man would turn out better.

What if she did *not* become a prima donna, but only climbed as far as back row singer? Or became a teacher? Were these high hopes worth the risk of disappointment?

That was Tuesday evening. On Wednesday Clowance went with Bella to the Fredericks Operatic School for Young Ladies in

Woburn Court, off Chancery Lane, and left her there, and met her again at five, this time with a footman to accompany them home in the dark.

Although still bubbling, Bella seemed slightly more serious as they walked home through the noisy pulsating streets. Something in that first day had opened up to her the enormity of the task.

On the Thursday Mrs Pelham took the two sisters and Geoffrey Charles, who, by arrangement, had just turned up, to a performance of *Iphigenia in Tauris* at His Majesty's. (Christopher was working late at Rothschild's in order to make up some of the time he had missed on Tuesday.)

It was not a good performance, the name part sung by a French prima who was well past her best, but Gluck's music was unfamiliar and tuneful, and Isabella-Rose drank it in with uninhibited zest. Clowance had never been to a London theatre before, and realized that in spite of its noise and smells and artificiality London had something to offer that Cornwall could not provide. Geoffrey Charles admitted to being tone deaf, but sat through it with polite good humour.

In the second entr'acte there was a tap on the door of their box, and a footman came and offered a card to Mrs Pelham. She peered at it short-sightedly, then: 'Of course, pray ask him in.'

Clowance was talking to Geoffrey Charles, and did not at first realize that she knew the heavily built young man who was shown in.

Then she got up. 'Lord Edward!'

'Please do not disturb yourself, Mrs – er – Carrington. It so happened that I was sitting in the box on the opposite side and I instantly recognized you. I felt I must come and intrude upon your hostess, whom I had not previously had the honour of meeting.'

'Pray sit down, sir,' said Mrs Pelham.

'Miss Isabella,' said Lord Edward, bowing over the girl's hand. 'We met once before, you will remember – or perhaps you will not remember – coming out of the theatre in Drury Lane. You were with your parents.'

'Of course I remember,' said Bella, dimpling at him just as she had done four years ago. 'Do you often go to the theatre, sir?'

'As often as I am able. Sometimes I make the excuse—'

'Would you care to stay here for the third act,' said Mrs Pelham, 'as it seems you are all such old friends?'

'I am with my brother and sister-in-law. I should be delighted to stay, and can send a man round with a note. Sir, you are Major Geoffrey Poldark? We have not met.'

Lord Edward Fitzmaurice had changed scarcely at all, Clowance thought, since he had proposed marriage to her. She wondered if *she* had changed. For an aristocrat, living a life of ease and plenty and with all absence of stress, probably the years would have slipped by easily and elegantly enough. For her it had been a lifetime – or seemed it. She wondered how much she had altered in his eyes. For this occasion she was very plainly dressed: she had not expected that Mrs Pelham at her age should be so much in society. No doubt to Lord Edward she now looked a dowdy country girl. Did it matter? Not in the least. She had never been in love with him. Certainly not now. Probably he was remarking to himself how fortunate that she had turned him down. What a lucky escape, he must think!

She looked up and met his eyes and did not see any such thoughts there. She looked away again quickly towards the stage, wishing the third act would begin.

During the rest of the opera he sat just behind her, with his face occasionally touching her hair. He smelt of some pleasing pomade.

'Miss Clowance,' he said at the end.

She withdrew herself to turn in her chair.

'Lord Edward.'

'Do you remember at Bowood you used to call me Edward?'

'That was a long time ago. But yes, Edward, I did.'

'And I called you Clowance. That is what I would like you to allow me to call you.'

'Of course.'

'It does away with disagreeable surnames.'

'I do not find my surname disagreeable.'

'Nor should you. I meant that they were disagreeable, like a fence, between friends.'

Isabella-Rose and Geoffrey Charles were laughing together.

'What is it, seven years?'

'It must be,' she said.

'I remember that visit with the greatest pleasure.'

'So do I.'

'You met my brother and sister-in-law, of course.'

'How are they?'

'Very well. They have two children now.'

84

'And you, Edward?'

'Not married – yet. I was grieved for you when I heard of your tragic bereavement. It was at Waterloo, was it not?'

'No, a riding accident.' Why did people always seem to get this mixed up?

'Do you live with your mother and father again?'

'No. My husband left a small shipping business and I am continuing to run that and live in Penryn.'

'It must be lonely.'

'I manage. And of course I have made many friends there.'

'I would like you to meet Henry and Catherine again, but we are supping with the Beresfords, who are sharing our box, and I cannot keep them waiting. Clowance.'

'Yes?'

'It would give me the greatest personal pleasure if you were to visit us at Bowood again sometime this coming summer. If your mother were free we should all be happy to see her too. She stayed, you know, at Lansdowne House while she was in London waiting for news of your father . . .'

'Thank you. It might be – a little difficult for me to get away, but it is a very kind thought. How is Aunt Isabel?'

'No longer mobile. But she is still able to enjoy life. Did you say you were going home tomorrow?'

'Yes.'

'Please give my respects to your mother and pray pass on the invitation. If she and you would consider it, I will send you a few dates from which you may choose your time.'

'You're very kind. Unfortunately, as I said, I own this small shipping line, and this is the first time I have been away from it for more than a week since Stephen died. It is only a very small affair, but I suppose I am continuing to operate it in memory of my husband.'

'I appreciate how you must feel. Perhaps you would permit me to write you a little later in the year?'

Clowance smiled at him. 'Of course. And thank you. I remember my first visit to Bowood with great pleasure.'

'So do I,' said Edward.

Chapter Ten

On the following day in the afternoon, while the coach was proceeding on its jolting leisurely way towards Marlborough, and while Demelza spent her last day with Verity, Ross had a visitor at Nampara. As soon as he saw him and saw the expression on his rufous face he knew this was not to be a pleasant interview. Could there be only one cause?

John Treneglos was now approaching his sixty-second birthday. Some of the powerful muscles in his arms and back had turned to fat, but he still made a formidable figure. Years of over-indulgence had left lines on his face and pits in his skin, but his red hair, now almost white, was as upthrusting as ever and his strong, heavily freckled hands looked capable of handling any miscreant who happened to cross him. Though Nampara and Mingoose were only a mile or so apart, they saw, and had seen through the years, very little of each other. This absence of neighbourliness had not been helped by the fact that John had married Ruth Teague, who had hoped to marry Ross on his rebound from Elizabeth and had found her place taken by an insolent miner's daughter who had worked in the Poldark kitchen.

'Well, John, this is a surprise. Do you come on business or pleasure?'

The visitor walked to the window and stared out, his hands clasping and unclasping behind his brown velvet riding coat. 'Neither,' he said.

'Well, copper has risen again,' said Ross. He had no intention of making it easier for this man. 'That is not bad news for either of us.'

'To Hell with copper,' John shouted. 'Your Valentine has been doing a mischief to my Agneta!'

So there it was. Trust John to express it with such elegance.

Ross went to the wine cupboard and took out a bottle of brandy. As he did so, he noticed that the contents of the bottle of port standing beside it had not gone down since Demelza left. Illogically a spasm of the need to see her again.

'Cognac?'

'To Hell with cognac! You heard what I said!'

Ross poured a half-glass for himself, sipped it.

'What are you talking about? What mischief?'

'He's been laying his greasy hands on her! Creeping in like the snake he is, putting filthy thoughts into her head – that delicate girl, whoring after her! Being rude with her! Defiling her! You know as well as I do – and he knows well too – that Agneta has a – a handicap; she has not got the equipment to decide everything for herself. She is a *gentle* creature. And then this evil lecherous goat of yours has the damned insolence – indeed brutality – to take advantage of her! It is damnable! It is outrageous! Christ knows what Ruth will say when she learns!'

'How do you know all this?'

'Know? She has *told* me! Agneta has told me!'

'Do you think perhaps she is making it up?'

John Treneglos swelled like a bullfrog.

'Devil take you, Ross! That girl could not *lie*! She does not know *how* to lie. She does not have the cunning to lie—'

'Is she pregnant?'

'No, thank God. She does not have the monthly menses. You are dealing with a *child*! And this devil has besmirched her! The shock may kill her! It may bring back the fits that Enys cured her of! And now he has left her, she says! He's no more than Hell's spawn to treat her like a – a street walker, like a strumpet! May he rot in Hell!'

'Have you spoken to him?'

'No! I've sent to his house, but the creature is away.'

Ross finished his drink. 'And so you come to me? *Why* do you come to me? Twice since you came in this room you have referred to *my* Valentine.'

'Well, is he not? Is he not? Why bother to deny it?'

'I deny nothing, for there is nothing to deny. You should not pay so much heed to the scurrilous rumours you hear.'

'*Rumours?* Everybody knows in this district that Valentine is your son!'

'*How* do they know it? *He* does not know it. *I* do not know it. *George Warleggan* does not know it. Then how in God's name do you and the gossipy scrofulous old women you listen to know anything *at all*?' Ross was getting angry now.

'Nevertheless everyone—'

'Listen to me, John. Just listen. Valentine was twenty-five two weeks ago. If by any extraordinary freak he *was* my son, how should I be responsible for his actions? Am I my brother's keeper? Still less am I my son's keeper? Valentine Warleggan is married and lives at Trevaunance. He has a son of his own, a wife of his own. Because you *say* – you only say – that he has misused your daughter, you come blundering in here like a bull on heat demanding of me a satisfaction for some alleged insult paid to your family by a young man who was never in my care, and who has long since passed out of the care of his putative father, George Warleggan. You come stamping in here not knowing or caring a curse whether my wife is at home. Fortunately she is not, for she would be greatly upset and affronted—'

'Oh, yes, I knew she would be upset and always will be upset by suggestions about Valentine's parentage—'

'Damn you, John, so she should be! And let me tell you this straight out. If you have a quarrel with Valentine, you have a quarrel with Valentine; take it to *him*; don't dare to come here bothering us with your sordid accusations. Valentine Warleggan is a separate entity, lives in a separate house, lives a separate life. Take your complaints to him, don't bring 'em here again!'

John thrust his big hands into the pockets of his breeches and stared at Ross. Since those days when John had been the elder, and a bit of a bully, their situations had changed. Ross had grown in stature, not physically but in the esteem of the county. John, by comparison, had remained a hunting squire without any special prestige. And of course Ross was a baronet.

'Yes, well, I suppose you may be partly right. But since Jeremy died you've made a special friend of Valentine. He has been in and out of here all the time. And I know you helped him last August when he was in a scrape.'

'If there is any truth in what you accuse him of, then you need not worry that I shall make any attempt to help him out of *this* scrape. And pray face *him* without making any further attempt to draw *me* in. Demelza is visiting my cousin Verity in Flushing, and I expect her home tomorrow. I would like your assurance that if anything of this matter comes to her ears it will not have come through you.'

John coughed and bent to spit in the fire. Spittle sizzled a few seconds on the hot coal.

'I don't know how it happened,' he grunted. 'For a long time, as you know, we had a personal maid to look after her. Then, when Enys started treating her and she seemed to improve, we dropped the maid. All the same, there were other servants always around. And Emmeline and Paula and she were good friends. Don't know how it began at all.'

'If it did begin. I know you will resent that remark, but the ways of young women are often hard to fathom. The fact that Agneta is handicapped may, as you say, make her incapable of lying. But it might not prevent her from seeing Valentine and perhaps liking the look of him – for whatever his faults you can't deny his charm, particularly for women – Agneta may have pondered and fancied what it would be like to have an affair with him – and come to believe her imagination to be the truth.'

John grunted and grumbled to himself. He did not like the way the interview had gone. Eventually, without saying anything more, he turned and went to the door, clumsily as if ready to shoulder aside any obstacle that got in his way.

There he stopped and said: 'You always stick up for your own.'

The following week a stranger was to be seen walking through the straggling village of Grambler.

It was a girl, on the tall side, very slim, in a faded scarlet cloak, a fawn bonnet, grey linen skirt, scuffed shoes. She looked about sixteen, pale-faced, blue-eyed, blonde straight hair shoulder length but tied back with a black ribbon. She carried a black purse.

Strangers were a rarity in the district, especially on a cold March day, especially a young female, especially alone. In the more inhabited part of the village, which she passed through first before coming to the ruin of the great Grambler mine, there were various signs of life: two women – one carrying a wooden pail with water in it, the other brushing the path and steps to her cottage door;

half-a-dozen children squatting in the dust playing some game with stones; two old men sitting at an open door, muffled to the eyes, talking and coughing.

The two women wished the girl a grudging good day, but one of the children playing with the stones saw a chance of entertainment and squealed and got up and fell in beside the stranger. The others stared and then followed. The thin girl proceeded down the rutted street with an escort trailing behind her. They made such a noise shouting and whistling that a half-dozen others came out of their hovels to join in. Then two mongrel dogs were attracted to the scene and leaped about, dirty tails beating the dust. The two women shouted to the children to stop, but were ignored.

The stranger was nervous. She had answered the first questions put to her pleasantly enough until she saw that the children were poking fun at her. The first girl to come up to her, Lottie Bice, was still the ringleader; she was fourteen, pock-marked and mischief-making like all her clan. She tried to take the girl's hand to slow her down, but the girl pulled away from the grubby paw and quickened her step. Then a ten-year-old boy, Luke Billing, gave her a shove in the back that made her stumble. The girl stepped into a deeper rut and twisted her ankle and nearly fell. She dropped her purse.

Then a great deal happened in a very short time. A man was there cuffing the children and they were off like terrified rabbits. She bent to pick up the purse, and one of the dogs got there first, pulled it out of her grasping fingers. She grabbed it in her other hand and the dog snarled and bit her wrist.

Then almost in a flash it was picked up by its tail, a rope twisted sharply round its neck and it was hoisted onto a projecting beam of the nearest cottage and dangled there choking to death.

The man was early middle-aged, dressed rough like a miner, but with a short carefully trimmed black beard, no hat, a grim face.

'No, no,' the girl cried, 'you'll – you'll kill it!'

'Mean to,' the man said. 'They're a mortal danger hereabouts. Little boy died last year at Marazanvose.'

Sickened, she turned away as the mongrel's struggles got weaker. 'Here's your purse.'

She took it from him with her left hand.

The children had all disappeared as if they had been spirited away, except for the black head of Lottie Bice peering round a door.

'Could as lief do with less of them too,' growled the man. 'The Bices and the Billings . . . Near as much nuisance as the curs. Ye can look now. Cur's dead.'

An old man came out of the cottage which had been used as a temporary gibbet, bent on a noisy protest, but when he saw who it was he went indoors again.

'Thank you,' said the girl, and coughed. 'Twas not reelly – I'm strange round here. I was just going . . . I been sent—'

'Your hand's bleeding,' said the man. 'Best go 'ave it seen to. Can't be too careful. That young lad at Marazanvose . . .'

'I was going to Surgeon,' said the girl. 'I was – my mistress said I'd best go see him. He lives hereabouts, they say. Kille-something . . .'

'Killewarren. Yes, not far. I'm going that way meself. I'll show ee the way.'

She stood looking towards the ruined mine while he cut the dog down. She heard a thud as the body was deposited into a noisome gap between two cottages. He came up beside her.

They began to walk in silence.

In the end she said: 'That dog took my purse. I should not have had it with me, only mistress give me a shilling to pay Surgeon.'

Another silence. He was not tall, she thought, but he was frightening.

'You're a stranger,' he said at last. 'What's your name?'

'Esther Carne.'

'And where d'ye live?'

'Trenwith. I'm new there. They wanted a second nursemaid.'

'Poldarks, eh? Major Geoffrey Charles. Married a Papist.'

'That's naught to do with me.'

They skirted Sawle Church.

'Is your 'and bleeding?'

'Nothing to talk about.'

'You'd best talk to Dr Enys about it whether or no! Cann't be too sure.'

'You know Surgeon?'

'I reckon. He's been 'ere twenty-odd years. Proper man. None better.'

'Do you live around 'ere, Mr . . . ?'

'Carter. Ben Carter.'

Long pause. 'I oft think tis funny,' she said, 'but I'm niece to Lady Poldark. Oft I can't believe it. But I owe everything to she.'

He frowned at her. 'How do that come 'bout?'

She did not feel she would like to suffer this man's displeasure. Nervously anxious to justify what she had told him, she went into detail.

'Lady Poldark's mother died young, and her father married 'gain, see. She was called Mary Chegwidden. Luke, the oldest brother, who is near as old as Lady Poldark, is my father: he wed Ann Hoskins, my mother, and I was born soon after. We dwelt in Lanner then but more recent we moved back to Illuggan, where father thought there was more work. But there's no work anywhere. My Uncle Sam – Sam Carne – is a good man and he come over to see us and he told Lady Poldark about us, and she came over; and after that she recommended me to Lady de Dunstanville at Tehidy, and they took me as a chambermaid.' Esther paused, short of breath, and coughed.

Ben grunted. 'How old are you?'

'Nineteen.'

'Should've thought you was youngerer than that. How come you're now at Trenwith?'

'Mistress Geoffrey Poldark, she's with child again and they needed an extra nurse look after Miss Juana, so Lady Poldark spoke up for me. I only been here four weeks.'

They walked on.

'That's Killewarren,' said Ben, pointing to a few chimneys showing above the laurels.

'Thanks.'

'Gates are a bit further on. Nigh unto Goon Prince.'

'You don't need come no further, Mr Carter. Thank ee.'

He took no notice until they came to the gates: granite posted, weather worn.

He said: 'No consarn o'mine, but you was coming see Surgeon anyhow. Someone ill at Trenwith?'

'No,' she said, 'no one ill.'

'Well, don't forget tell Surgeon of that bite.'

Dwight Enys was tired. Though normally in good health, his constitution still suffered from the extreme privations of his imprisonment in France. His stamina was a finite thing which reluctantly he had had to take into account, though relatively brief spells of rest could restore him.

He had just been called in by an apothecary called Lewis to attend on Elsie Vage, who lived at Chapel Porth beyond St Ann's. She was in her tenth pregnancy and had now contracted rheumatic fever in the damp hovel in which she lived. Dwight had been called in once before, during her sixth lying in: that child was dead, and later Dwight had seen the mother crawling about the village bent double and leaning on a stick, looking sixty though she was only thirty-two. Today was a hopeless case: Lewis had sent over for him as a last resort. Dwight had stared at the patient, an unwieldy lump of flesh, her pelvis diminished in age, her spine bent so that her head leaned permanently on one shoulder, the child still alive and the mother screaming. Dwight had delivered the child, but was certain it could not live, nor could Elsie. On the way home he had drawn in the fresh air to fill his lungs after the miasma of that filthy hut. These were the depressing cases, those in which there was no hope and no point in his being there. The quean would die anyway, and medical skill was useless. He wished he had been saved the trip.

There were fixed hours when patients could come to the house, and this was not one of them, but he had heard of the Carne girl having come to work at Trenwith and wondered if she had some news about Amadora.

She had not. Thin and blushing, she explained to him that she had been sent here because she had a cough and Mrs Geoffrey Charles was concerned that it might be serious.

'You've cut your hand too,' said Dwight.

'Oh, yes, sir.' Esther explained how it had happened. ''Tis really nothing.'

'Let me see ... I think we should take precautions, though. These stray dogs can be dangerous ...' He peeled her sleeve back. 'There is really only the one toothmark where the skin has broken, and that has bled freely. I'm afraid I may have to hurt you, Esther. But it will be little more than a nip.'

'Like another dog bite,' she said.

'That's it. That's exactly it. Come over here and sit down. Do you faint easily?'

'Never 'ave, sir.'

'Good.'

She cried out loudly enough when he made the incision, but it was over quickly, and very soon he was bandaging her hand just above the wrist.

'Good girl. You'll do well enough now. Would you take a small glass of brandy?'

'Thank you.' She coughed.

'If your skin should become excessively tender or you should lose your appetite, come and see me again; but I assure you that is unlikely.'

'He killed the dog!' she said. 'It hadn't meant to bite me. I've never seen nothing so quick – twas done in a minute.'

'Mr Carter does not like stray dogs. Nor does anyone who knows the risks attached. Now what did Mrs Geoffrey Charles send you to me about?'

She blinked at him, and pushed a strand of her blonde hair off her forehead. 'I got this cough, had it almost since I came. I think mebbe Mrs Geoffrey Charles don't want me to give it to her or her little girl.'

Dwight nodded. Phthisis and scrofula were endemic in these villages. 'Will you loosen your blouse, please. No, slip it off; I shall want to listen to your back.'

She did as she was told, eyeing him warily. He sounded her chest, his mind registering the difference between this young flawless skin and the mottled, wrinkled, flabby skin of Elsie Vage.

She said: 'Do Mr Carter live around 'ere, sur?'

'What? Yes. Quite near. He is the underground captain of Wheal Leisure. Take a deep breath . . . And again . . . And again.'

'Wheal Leisure?'

'The mine on the cliffs. Just beyond Nampara. You can see it from the church. Very good, you may put your blouse on again.'

'So he be quite an important man?'

'It is the only mine in all this area which continues in profit. Esther.'

'Yes, sur?'

'Tell your mistress your lungs are both perfectly sound. What you have is an infection of the bronchial tubes. I will give you a linctus which you should take after meals three times a day.'

'Yes, sur.'

'And take this prescription for brimstone and tartar, which Mr

Irby will make up for you . . . With or without these medicines you should be better in a couple of weeks. If not, come and see me again. How much do you have to do with Juana?'

'I take her walking. I tell her stories when she goes bed of nights. Sometimes I see for her food. I be only the second nurse.'

'Well, tell your mistress not to worry about this; you do not have a serious condition.'

'Thank ee, sur.' She got up.

Dwight stared out at the lowering day, then looked at the thin, shabby, erect girl putting on her cloak. More properly Amadora should have sent another maid to accompany so young a woman. Amadora was still genuinely nervous about going out of Trenwith by herself, but probably thought the English girls could manage on their own. So they could if they were local girls. This one was a foreigner, come all the way from Illuggan.

'I will get one of our maids to walk back with you.'

'Oh, nay, sur, I'm certain sure I shall be all right.'

He took no notice but pulled the bell, and when Audrey Bone came gave her his instructions. It wanted two hours to dark, and Audrey Bone, daughter of his long-time personal servant, was known to everyone and would be safe as houses.

Chapter Eleven

Ross was as glad to see Demelza back as if she too had been to London. At first he said nothing about John Treneglos's visit. They had sufficient to talk over, with Clowance's report of all that had happened in London and incidents to tell about the farm and the mine. He had thought of saying nothing at all, but he had the disagreeable feeling that the unpleasantness would surely out, and it was probably better that the account should come from him.

Cuby was due tomorrow, and for once they were sitting in the library. Without Bella here hovering round the piano the room seemed rather forlorn.

She heard him out and sipped her after-supper port. There was no wind tonight, and accordingly the six candles in the two candelabra burned without so much as a tremble.

'So it was true.'

'It appears so. I don't like to condemn a man in his absence, but I think there is too much evidence against him.'

'He *is* impossible, Ross. Imagine him going after Agneta!'

'It seemed, my dear, that you could imagine such a thing well enough because you alerted me to the risk before Christmas.'

'Well, I saw him *look* at her, when the hounds came this way. That was all. Only a glance. Judas, I am getting like the old wives who sit in their doorways and speculate lewdly about their neighbours! What do you think John will do?'

'Tell Ruth, I suppose. If Agneta hasn't already told her. Fortunately, I gather from John, that there is no risk of a child.'

'Ruth will be as unpleasant as she can be. She always wanted to marry you and thought I stole you from her.'

'So you did. Though I must admit Miss Teague was not high on my list.'

'List, eh. Have you kept it in some secret drawer out of my reach? There was that Margaret Vosper, I mind. And I suppose many others.'

'Margaret, I admit. But she was strictly not in the marriage stakes. In all my life I swear I only flirted with Ruth once.'

She sighed. 'All the same. Seriously, Ross, this is a horrid situation. I wish – I wish Valentine would go away, leave the district.'

'Little likelihood of that.' He looked at her. She was arranging some primroses in a dish, propping up their delicate yellow with greeny-yellow sprigs of willow which she had bought from a gypsy in Penryn on her way home. 'Do you wish Valentine would leave the district for some other reason?'

'Reason?'

'That perhaps you feel I am become too friendly with him?'

'. . . Not that. Not quite that. But I know that you lack Jeremy's companionship. He was our son, wasn't he. Our – our most precious son. We have another son – one more – but he is too young. You cannot make that sort of a companionship with Harry – yet. So you have turned a little more towards Valentine, who is Elizabeth's son. Whatever else, he is her son. Valentine has your look sometimes, hasn't he?'

'I don't know.'

'But he's not really like you *at all*. Perhaps he is – is a harking back. Verity says he is like your father. But I don't know. It is something different from that. Elizabeth's other son, by Francis, is lovable; Geoffrey Charles is *normal*. Valentine is not normal!'

'I'll give you that,' Ross said. 'And I ask myself how much I am responsible for it.'

'D'you mean . . .?'

'Well, yes. Whatever the truth of it all, my continuing – affection, call it what you will – for Elizabeth and however the suspicion first came to George – I told you about Aunt Agatha – that suspicion has poisoned Valentine's early life. To have a father who sometimes treated him with generous affection, and then within a few days treated him as beneath contempt, even with hatred . . . Valentine has told me this, and I know from other sources that is the plain truth, it is enough to warp any child's emotional upbringing, his very nature. So that now, admidst all the charm and courtesy of his manner there is malice, wickedness, mischief-making and a per-verse wish to shock, to hurt, to break anything within his reach. I

97

don't think this is always a conscious desire – it rises from impulses he can't, or won't, control.'

'Verity said to me once – I don't think I ever told you – she said that Valentine would lend anyone a smiling hand on the way to perdition.'

'Demelza.'

'Yes?'

'Come away from those flowers. You can't improve on the arrangement. Come and sit down opposite me, so that I can see you – we've suddenly gone into very deep waters. And we have no beer cask to foment tonight.'

She half smiled at a very old remembrance between them, sat on the chair he indicated, put a finger on the piano behind her. 'And we can't set it to music.'

'I wonder how Bella––. Well, no matter. I think we ought to have this out, so far as we can.'

'I doubt we can, for Valentine will not go away.'

He took a deep breath. 'It is true that I am drawn to Valentine. I like him in spite of his perverseness, and feel – at least hope – that he will grow out of his worst faults. He is young enough yet. You're right about how much I miss Jeremy. Even though upon times we were edgy together, this was but a surface spat, meant nothing at all. I *miss* him every day, as you do. It is *intolerable*. But you are wrong in thinking I overlook Harry––'

'Not overlook, but––'

'Of course he is so young – he cannot replace Jeremy. I talk to him and he talks to me, but the gap is so wide – yet. But if you think I care too little for him, you are utterly wrong.'

'I should not need to be told, Ross, but it is good to tell me. Indeed – on the other side – I like Valentine at times. And feel sorry for him. But I am always a small matter uneasy with him. I never really d'know what he is thinking, what he feels for this family, apart from you. For the rest of the people in this house. I cannot rid myself of the feeling that he thinks you belong to him, and that the rest of your family, while acceptable enough in their way, are a little bit – what is the word? – super something––'

'Superior?'

'No, no, far from it. Superfluous, that is the word! That we are – are on the side, so to say; that he is devoted to you and that we, the rest of us – are no part of your relationship with him.'

He mused for a moment or two, eased his painful ankle. 'Jealousy is a very strange thing, is it not? I—'

'Ross, how dare you!'

'Wait a moment: do not jump on me like that! I was not referring specially to any one of us. Certainly not to you. I was only saying that jealousy – or in its lesser form possessiveness – inhabits us all. It is like a microbe that lives within any family, touches all human relations. Perhaps it is the least admirable of feelings, but we all have these and . . .'

He tailed off, and she bit at her handkerchief to keep the words back. She wanted to say that *she* did not wish to possess *him*, not, that was, more than she had always done for so many years. She had not *advised* him to give up his parliamentary seat. He chose his own life and always had done. She did not wish to possess him more *deeply*. It was only a tragedy of the war that resulted in him paying more attention to Elizabeth's child than he did to the last of her own – the last male – because he was too young.

He said, as if half-reading her silence: 'I should much dislike it if I thought that your bereavement – our bereavement – should in any way lead to a difference of view between us over—'

'It is not just possessiveness, Ross,' she interrupted.

'I did not say that was what you were feeling!'

'Well . . . if I can explain. It is not because Valentine is inside or outside my family that I have this feeling. I am uneasy for you.'

'For me?' He half laughed in genuine surprise. 'For God's sake! Do you think he is a bad influence?'

'Yes!'

'On me? Do you suppose that a young man in his early twenties should influence a man of *my* age? Shall I take to drink? – or gambling? – or smuggling? I've done 'em all. Or is it wenching you fear?'

She got up and went to the mantelshelf and put a smaller pot of primroses on it. The grey woollen dress brushed beside Ross's chair and he put his hand on her thigh through the dress.

'I suppose,' she said, 'you are right to treat this in a lighter way than I do. Maybe it is possessiveness – jealousy – hiding behind superstitious feelings that did not ought to exist. But you have known me long enough. No one has known me longer or been closer to me, and I have these feelings sometimes. You yourself, you have accused me more oftener than I can say of being like Meggy Dawes.'

'I sometimes wonder whether she ever existed.'

'Yes, she did, Ross. She had yellow hair; I suppose twas dyed; and the deepest of black eyes. I sat with her a lot when I was a child, and maybe she did teach me something – or I caught something. I get feelings, sometimes, instincts I cannot always give reasons for in a reasonable way, to convince a solid, reasonable man like you—'

'Ecod!' he said. 'Now who's joking?'

'*Please* . . .' She turned to face him and smiled at him, but in a troubled way. 'Just say that I have a feeling about Valentine that brings a chill wind. You – are fond of him, and when I see him I like him well. But – d'you know what the shrims are?'

'Yes.'

'He gives me the shrims.'

One morning George Warleggan had another unexpected visitor.

Philip Prideaux he knew pretty well because Harriet had taken a fancy to him. So they had met at Cardew and passed the time of day, and sat at the same dining table and even breathed the same air, but had hardly ever exchanged a personal word.

George was not greatly taken with the young man. For one thing he thought Harriet made too much of him, for another he did not greatly care for war heroes. Perhaps they reminded him too much of Ross Poldark (Philip was not scarred and he did not walk with a limp, but there was something about the type). For a third, now that he was out of the Army he did not seem to pursue any useful profession. George, of course, was very familiar with the ways of the landed gentry; most of them did not *work* for their living, and they largely looked down – if they dared, and only a few dared – on people like himself who did.

'Sir George Warleggan,' Philip said, standing like a beanstalk in the doorway.

'Captain Prideaux, come in. Pray sit down.' But George did not rise himself.

'Thank you.' Philip nervously adjusted his eye glasses. Wearing them, he tended to have a patronizing look, as if he were looking down on the person he addressed. It was what had first prejudiced Clowance. 'We meet, as you know, when I partake of your gracious hospitality, but this – what I came to see you about – is perhaps more a professional matter, so I thought I would call on you at your Bank.'

'Do you bank with us?' George asked, knowing very well that he did and the exact amount his visitor was overdrawn.

'Yes. But it was with your chief clerk that I dealt when I called to open an account, so . . .' Philip tailed off. 'It was not exactly on financial matters that I called. But perhaps I should say first . . .' He folded himself into the chair that a few months ago Valentine had occupied.

'Go on.'

'Perhaps I should say first that from the first day of September last I accepted a position with the Duchy of Cornwall. I was appointed Assistant Secretary and Keeper of the Records. I told Lady Harriet last week, but she may not have mentioned it to you.'

'She did not. I am pleased to hear it.' George speculated to himself what influence had been used, and from what source, to obtain for this young man a comfortable sinecure.

'It will be part-time,' said Philip, as if reading the other's thoughts, 'but this will give me the opportunity to pursue my archaeological studies when the opportunity arises.'

'I'm very glad,' said George, not looking very glad. 'I trust the stipend will be sufficient.'

'For my simple needs, yes. It will mean that I am not likely for very much longer to need the accommodation that you have so kindly extended to me under my uncle's guarantee.'

George nodded. 'But you tell me this is not the reason you came to see me?'

'No. As you know, sir, I am taking a keen interest in the Cornwall of the Stone and the Bronze Age, and this week past I have been concentrating on Truro and the districts of Kenwyn and Moresk, where the earliest settlements took place. I have made one or two interesting discoveries; but I will not burden you with the details. Something else has come much to my notice. It is a somewhat distasteful subject, but after giving the matter some thought I decided to come to see you about it. In short, Sir George, I am referring to the smells.'

'Smells?'

'Smells, Sir George. Stenches. Living here, one cannot fail to be aware of them. If you opened this window—', Prideaux gestured towards the barred window beside his chair, 'the smells from the street below would make this room scarcely habitable.'

'Perhaps in your soldiering you have become too accustomed to the open air,' said George sarcastically. 'It is a condition common to all towns.'

'Yet, sir, Truro is uniquely positioned. It is built in a valley, on a confluence of several streams and with a great river at its feet. Streams run down, three in all, the Allen, the Kenwyn, and another still smaller. As you know, they all flow down the sides of the streets in open leats, and you would expect them to be full of beautiful clean spring water brought down from the hills. Instead they are virtually used as open drains, so that any filth, animal or human, is thrown into them, they choke up and spill over onto the streets; the refuse accumulates and dries and stinks to high heaven.'

George's stare was contemplative. 'Why are you coming to me? I am not the Mayor of this town.'

'No, sir, but you are one of the Capital Burgesses, the only one I know by name and—'

'You may not be aware that there is a town body called the Improvements Commission, which attends to these matters.'

Prideaux took off his glasses and rubbed them on a silk kerchief. 'I am told, sir, that they meet but rarely, and when they are called upon to meet hardly any of them bother to turn up. I thought . . .'

'Yes, what did you think, Captain Prideaux?'

'I thought that as you are one of the most eminent inhabitants of this town – perhaps the most eminent, and I am sure among the most enlightened – you might be persuaded to instigate some action. Why, even the corner of St Mary's Churchyard is piled high with animal and human excrement—'

'Carried there by salaried scavengers, who collect the waste in the streets and eventually sell it to the farms as fertilizer. Do you know that last year over two hundred cartloads of such animal waste was sold by auction for nine shillings a load? You do not know the economics of a small town, Captain Prideaux.'

It dawned upon Philip Prideaux that he was not winning this battle. But he had not charged at Waterloo for nothing.

'It may be, Sir George, that you do not think you can help in this matter; but I was hoping, if not for help, at least for your advice.'

'Are you a resident of this town?'

'I am at present staying with my cousins at Prideaux Place.'

'Then I would advise you to forget all about Truro and see if you can do any better with the town of Padstow. It is an imperfect world.'

Philip stirred restlessly at the rebuke. 'There are, I am told, sir, about thirty public wells in Truro; from them most of the people in this town draw their drinking water. Many of these wells are very shallow and polluted. The Forbra Hunt keeps its hounds – thirty or forty couple of them – at Carvedras, and these are mucked out into the leats. The Ferris Tannery has diverted a part of one of the streams into its pits, so that it has become a scene of indescribable putrefaction. Privies empty into the same watercourses, wool merchants wash their fleeces, pigs root everywhere; in the bad streets children defecate openly—'

'You make me wonder,' said George, 'how any of us survive.'

'Some do not, Sir George. In some of the worst districts of the town: Goodwives Lane, Calenick Street, the old opes in Pydar Street, cholera, the pox, typhus, measles, scarlet fever—'

'Is this part of your new-gained appointment? I did not know that the Duchy of Cornwall—'

'No, no, sir, not at all. I approached you entirely as a private person.'

'Is this even archaeology? Are you studying hygiene too?'

Philip affixed his spectacles to his nose again. 'I'm sorry, I feel I have been wasting your time, sir. I should not have come. But at a party on Wednesday I met a Dr Daniel Behenna, and we had a considerable conversation—'

'Ha! Behenna! He's getting too big for his boots—'

'I should regret it if you thought he had urged me to come and see you. Not at all. I was the first to comment on the stench in the town, and he gave me some of the information I have since tried to verify. I did not think to call to see you until I had done this.'

'Does my wife know you have come?'

'No, sir. I believe she has been out with the hounds most of this week. But although you live mainly at Cardew, you have this excellent house in town, and it simply occurred to me that I could perhaps solicit your advice.'

George regarded the young man thoughtfully. He supposed the fellow was worth knowing. He had never met the head of the family, the Reverend Charles Prideaux-Brune, who was, he believed, something of a recluse. And they were connected with the Glynns of Glynn, and the Sawles of Penrice.

'Sometimes,' George said, 'towns grow rapidly. Truro has. Towns and cities in any event are never planned before they come into being, they multiply and add to themselves in a piecemeal way. Enough foresight is never shown. Nor perhaps ever enough public spirit. Poor people particularly breed too fast. Disease is nature's way of limiting the population. It is not possible to put the world to rights. Perhaps it is not always even desirable—'

'Surely it is desirable to try.'

George scowled.

'In this world it is not enough just to be an idealist.'

'Then a practical idealist.'

'You have come to instruct me.'

'Far from it, Sir George. I will leave you now. And thank you for your time.'

Captain Prideaux got up, enormously tall and erect, enormously rigid.

As he got to the door he said: 'May I as a favour request that you should not tell Lady Harriet of my visit.'

'If you say so—'

'I fancy sometimes she laughs at me.'

For the first time a small stirring of empathy moved in the rich banker.

'She laughs at everyone.'

When he left the bank Philip Prideaux was full of a sense of frustration, so intense that it was almost overwhelming. He wanted to kick something, to break something. By now he knew the symptoms. A surgeon in the West Indies had told a court martial he was subject to 'brain storms' – that surgeon's views had resulted in an acquittal for him on the one occasion when his frustrations had become insupportable. Since then he had been able to stamp down these terrifying impulses. He hoped and believed they would decrease with time as the visions of the carnage at Waterloo faded.

He turned in at the Fighting Cocks Inn, which was down an alley near the bank, and ordered a large cognac. He drank it off almost at a gulp and could feel the strong spirit burning as it went down. He ordered another.

'Captain Prideaux, isn't it?'

A sallow, good-looking young man, expensively but quietly dressed, lank black tidily trimmed hair, a velvet cloak held in place by a gold chain.

'That is so.'

'You don't remember me?'

Philip put on his glasses and hoped his fingers did not noticeably tremble. 'I – er – recall we have met, but just at the moment my mind was far away and . . .'

'Paul Kellow. We met at a party at Cardew. Lady Harriet gave a card party.'

'Of course, of course. How d'you do.'

'Bring your drink to this table. We seem to share the same taste in liquor and I have a bottle of it, not yet half sunk.'

They moved through the low-timbered bar and sat down, Philip awkwardly, seeming to fold his legs and his neck at the same time. He did not welcome this meeting, but he had no wish to offend.

Paul refilled his own glass and then topped up Philip's. 'Seen the *Gazette* this morning?'

'No. I haven't seen a newspaper for a day or two.'

'You still staying with the Warleggans?'

'Dear me, no. I am living most of the time with my cousins in Padstow. But last night I lay at the Red Lion.'

'Not much in it,' said Paul, pushing the broadsheet across. 'You don't ask me where I live.'

'I assume you are a resident in Cornwall and have a home in this district. Was your wife not with you at Cardew?'

'She was.'

They eyed each other. The brandy was doing Philip good. But when the bottle was pushed towards him again he fumbled with his eye glasses and shook his head.

'Where *do* you live, Mr Kellow?'

'Tregony. My wife is a Temple.'

'I do not know Cornwall very well, in despite of being part Cornish. I was at school in Devon, where my father lives, but then went straight into the Army and have spent half my life abroad.'

'Do you know the Poldarks?'

'But slightly. The Captain Poldark who died. Was he not in the Oxfordshires? And Major Geoffrey Charles Poldark, who lives in the family home on the north coast.'

'You don't know Sir Ross Poldark, who also lives on the north coast?'

'No. I've heard much of him.'

'You know his daughter, I believe?'

'Mrs – er – Carrington? Er – yes.'

'Stephen Carrington, that was her husband. I was his best friend.'

'Indeed.'

'Killed in a riding accident. We were the greatest friends. And Jeremy Poldark. The one who was killed at Hougoumont. We did many things together. A great threesome. Broke the law a few times, I tell you. You ever broken the law, Philip?'

It occurred to Prideaux to think that this was not perhaps the first bottle of brandy that had been drunk.

'Once at least.'

'Miss them both. Both great friends. Both great men. I miss them both. Of course that was all before I married. Bit of a rake, I was. Bit of a blade, you know.'

'Indeed?'

'Jeremy was in love with my sister, Daisy. Going to marry her. It was all fixed up. Then he met Cuby Trevanion and everything was changed.'

'That's very sad. At least – you are, I trust, happy in your own married life.'

Paul laughed. It was not a mirthful sound. 'Perhaps we're all accursed. Do you think we are all accursed, Captain Prideaux-Brune?'

'My name is Prideaux. It is only my cousin who has the hyphenated name. Why do you consider yourself accursed, Mr Kellow?'

'Because my new wife . . . Could I – should I call her new after a marriage already lasting nearly three years? – Because my wife, whom both I and my father-in-law were expecting to produce for us a son and heir – for whom perhaps we might have arranged a hyphenated surname – such as Temple-Kellow – how does that sound?' Paul finished his brandy and poured another. 'Come along, man, stop fiddling with your specs and take your drink like a captain of the Dragoon Guards, which I believe you once were . . .'

Philip allowed his glass to be filled and stared at his slender but saturnine companion. 'What are you trying to tell me?'

'My wife complains of a pain in her hip and a swelling there, so in the end I send for a sawbones, one Daniel Behenna, who has the reputation of being an acceptable member of his useless profession. He tells me that this twenty-two-year-old woman is suffering from a scrofulous tumour, which will have to be excised!'

Philip had now taken off the offending eye glasses and laid them on the table. The small tense crisis in his own emotional life having subsided, he was able to pay more attention to this casual friend.

'I am – grieved to hear it. I do not know precisely what a scrofulous tumour is, but any form of illness in one's wife . . . Have you consulted any other surgeon or physician?'

'Not yet.'

'By chance I met Dr Behenna at a soirée the other night. He is clearly a responsible man. There must be others.'

'There are many others – all quacks like him.'

'Many people have boils on their legs, or abscesses. Did he give you to suppose it was likely to be a serious operation?'

'Everything is serious with Behenna,' said Paul. 'It is his nature to be pompous. But I have omitted to point out to you that two out of three of my sisters have died of pulmonary phthisis, so it is not unnatural that I should take this seriously.'

'Scrofula,' said Philip, 'is that not the King's Evil?'

'It is Cornwall's evil! Those who do not cough have putrefying glands. I tell you, I've had enough of it!'

There was a long silence. The bar was almost empty, but a noisy quarrel was taking place in the street outside.

'I must go,' said Philip. 'It's a lengthy ride, and I promised to be back for supper.'

'Don't let me detain you.'

'Enys,' said Paul. 'Dr Dwight Enys. He is perhaps the best of a bad bunch. And he attended on my second sister until she died. If I could persuade him to come as far as Tregony . . .'

Philip picked up his spectacles but slipped them into his pocket.

'I wish you well, my friend. It's an unhappy time for you. I hope this doctor you speak of will help. Will you be in touch with Lady Harriet or Mrs Carrington? Pray let me know through them how your wife fares.'

'Here,' said Paul, as Prideaux was about to leave, and thrust the

Royal Cornwall Gazette towards him. 'Take this and read what there is to read. I see another young woman has been murdered.'

'Oh?' Philip took up the paper. 'Another? You're referring to the one last year? Her killer was never found, was he?'

'This was at Indian Queens. Not so far from Padstow, is it?'

Philip read the newspaper. 'It says she was stabbed to death. Margaret Jenkins, aged twenty-two. The other, that other, if I remember, was a light woman . . . What, far from Padstow? Oh, ten or twelve miles, I would suppose. I shall pass through it on the way home this afternoon.'

'Take care how you ride then,' said Paul. 'Lest the murderer be still abroad.'

Book Two

AGNETA

Chapter One

The weather that summer was drier than usual over the country as a whole, but especially so in Cornwall, where the most rain was generally expected. The sunshine was often smeared and windy, the land dry, the blown sand prevalent on the north coast, dust in the villages and towns. This year the East India Company under Stamford Raffles established a settlement in Singapore, and liberty of the press was finally permitted in France.

George Canning wrote to Ross from Liverpool in April.

Dear Friend,

I dare to hope that the worst is over in the manufacturing regions of the North. Trade is picking up, prices are stabilizing, and though there is still 'widespread distress throughout the land', to quote you in your last letter, it is showing signs of easement, so that you will no longer have reason to reprove me for my government's hardness of judgement. Reform must come slowly. The heart of the nation is sound.

I have been much concerned recently with our affairs in India, and earlier this month I was asked by Liverpool to move a vote of thanks to the Governor General of India, Lord Hastings (formerly Moira, of course) congratulating him and his army on their successful operations against the Marathas and the Pindaris. But, in case you have not seen the speech, I would point out to you that I began by strongly emphasizing I was offering sincere congratulations on the military conduct of the campaign, *not* on the disposition of our confrères in Indian to stretch their limits ever farther. I congratulated Parliament too on its efforts to check this ambition. Would to God, I said, that we could long since have discovered a front –

111

a *resting place* in India – where it was possible to stand without advancing further. From the wildness of Bengal or the Maharashtra it may look different, surrounded as they are by rampaging bandits, and weak and corrupt Principalities crying out for assistance, but from this small island, which only three years ago finished spilling its blood to prevent a tyrant from becoming Emperor of Europe, it does not look to most sensible men – among whom I count the vast majority of my colleagues – that we should be attempting to build a new Empire of our own in the East.

Old friend. When can we next meet?

In August a great protest rally, held in St Peter's Fields, Manchester, to draw attention to the bitter plight of the poor, ended in the deaths of eleven of the protesters at the hands of a regiment of undisciplined yeomanry sent in by panicking magistrates to disperse the riot. The number involved in this rally was about eighty thousand. They carried banners with their demands: 'No Corn Laws', 'Annual Parliaments', 'Universal Suffrage', 'Vote by Ballot'. The initiator of the rally, a man called Henry Hunt, was arrested and charged with high treason.

Mary, Paul Kellow's wife, had greatly improved without the need of the knife. Dwight had been prevailed upon to visit the frightened young woman and had prescribed goat's milk, Theban opium, fresh air, cold water to drink, hot linseed poultices applied to the tumour, which presently receded and healed. Both Mary and Paul were deeply appreciative. Dwight smiled but warned Paul in private that though over a period of months this might seem a cure, over an extended length of time the lump might return. 'If there is an infection of the lymphatic glands, this may resurface in the hip – or abdomen. I trust it will not. Your wife seems otherwise a very healthy young woman. So far so good.'

Paul's thin face had hardened at Dwight's words.

'Most of your profession claim too much, Dr Enys. At least you could never be accused of false optimism.'

'Caroline tells me I see too much of the dark side.'

'Perhaps the dark side is often all there is to see.'

'Not in this case. But one thing I am sure of, Paul, is that you must not let her have any inkling of doubt. I speak to you as a

112

friend. In all disease the mind is as important as the body. Be with her a lot. Keep her spirits up.'

They paused at the front door.

'You should have stayed to sup,' Paul said.

'Thank you, Caroline is expecting me, and before dark.'

They waited for Dwight's horse to be brought round. Paul's lank hair lifted in the breeze.

'I don't know how you have the stamina to follow your trade,' he said, almost resentfully. 'That is, with a nature like yours.'

'One develops a good memory for failures.'

'And successes?'

'Oh yes. In making a diagnosis it is good to remember both.'

'And what diagnosis are you making for the prospects of my – our future married happiness, Dr Enys?'

'There you should go to the soothsayer. It is not in my field at all.'

The horse's hooves could be heard outside.

Paul said: 'I have the oddest premonition.'

'About your marriage?'

'About life generally. Its ultimate purpose – insofar as it has a purpose – seems to be evil, not good.'

Isabella-Rose returned at Easter, full of fun, life, talk, music, apparently unchanged. The only difference, Demelza thought, was that the Cornish burr in her voice had lessened.

And her singing voice – her instrument, as she now called it – had *improved*. It was rounder, much more controlled. Ross confessed that he could now listen to it with real pleasure. 'But it is still not as sweet as Cuby's in the middle register,' he whispered to Demelza, who replied: 'Cuby has nothing *but* a middle register. Nor any power.' 'I know, my love, I know. Well, Fredericks is working wonders.'

Christopher did not come down with her. Rothschild's would not spare him for so long, but by discreet enquiry he was able to discover a Mrs Carne – a banker's wife and no relative of Demelza's – who was travelling to Falmouth and was glad of a young lady's companionship. Bella had a month off.

One tried not to notice, but Nampara was much noisier, more

alive when she was home. Henry's voice went up an octave to make itself heard, and they ran about the beach together like two puppies let out of a kennel.

One minor irritation over the Easter period was the constant visiting of Agneta Treneglos. Whatever had happened between her and Valentine was apparently at an end, and since she had been forbidden by him to visit him at Place House she took to calling at Nampara in the hope of catching him when he was there. She always came alone, but one of her sisters usually arrived to fetch her home, so the inference was that she slipped away from Mingoose when no one was looking.

Demelza had seen Ruth on a few occasions, but Ruth had simply stared at her as at a servant and never uttered a word. John had seen Ross twice more, but the name of Agneta was not mentioned. He too had turned a cold shoulder.

Ross was determined not to send Agneta away, in spite of one or two complaints from Bella that she was cloying. He felt that at least eighty per cent of the blame rested with Valentine, and one could not take it out on a handicapped girl.

He had seen little of Valentine, who appeared to be making himself scarce until Agneta got tired and gave him up. He had been in Padstow for a week or more, staying, he let drop, with the Prideaux-Brunes, but this Ross took with a pinch of salt. When Ross spoke of him to Philip Prideaux at a concert of the Philharmonic Society of Truro, which he had been cozened into attending by his musical daughter, Captain Prideaux looked blank and a mite puzzled.

Ross had been introduced to Prideaux by, of all people, his elder daughter, who apparently was among Philip Prideaux's guests. Possibly a taste of the gay life in London had unveiled to Clowance what she was missing. The two ex-soldiers had a chat together in the interval, and Ross thought him an agreeable, well-meaning fellow, but taut and over-stretched. In time civilian life might induce him to relax. One certainly hoped so if there was any possibility – and it seemed far from an impossibility, noting the attention that Philip Prideaux was paying Clowance – that he, Ross, might be approached sometime by the other man and asked permission to become his son-in-law.

Geoffrey Charles rearranged his plans to enable him to escort

Isabella-Rose back to London. The weather turned bad, and the coach was stuck for six hours in the snow east of Exeter.

Esther Carne had long since lost her cough and so was allowed to take charge of Juana. She began to venture more out of the gates of Trenwith and occupied her time off by visiting her uncle, Sam, who pressed her to go to see Demelza; but she said she did not like to presume. She kept a sharp lookout for Ben Carter, but did not see him. She questioned Sam, and then Sam's wife, Rosina, and then two of his flock, who were more forthcoming, and so learned more about him. So she was told of the scar on his cheek, which so resembled that on Sir Ross Poldark's that it had to be hidden by his beard – and all about the bitter fight he had had with Stephen Carrington, Clowance Poldark's eventual husband, of his being Sir Ross Poldark's godson, and the brother of Katie, who was wed to Music Thomas, and that only a couple of years ago he had moved out of his mother's shop – the one that sold the sweets in Stippy-Stappy Lane – and now lived on his own in a tiny cottage near Killewarren.

Just before Whitsun Clowance had sent a letter to Lord Edward Fitzmaurice:

Dear Edward,

It is so kind of you to have written repeating your generous invitation to my Mother and myself to spend a week at Bowood with you and your Family in May or June.

My Mother is not quite the person she was before Jeremy's death; she does not seem able to summon up the initiative for new scenes and new pleasures. She is not by any means sad all the time – or obviously sad any of the time – but although she went once to London last year, it was under the compulsion to decide my young sister's musical future, and she was – it seemed – altogether relieved to be Home. She loves her house and her farm and her garden, in which she spends increasing time.

Nevertheless I believe I might have been able to bring extra pressure to bear on her were it not for the unfortunate position I happen to be in myself. As you will recall, I own this small sea-trading company which was begun by my husband. We operate from Penryn and Falmouth, and, since I am a woman, I depend on a Partner – a quite elderly man – who puts into practice the things I want to have done but am not exactly in a position to do myself. Well, Hodge last week slipped and fell down the hold of the *Adolphus* and broke his leg. There was fear that he would have to lose his leg, but they think now it may be saved.

In the event, he will be laid up for many weeks, and I must try to carry on alone – or look for a replacement. It means I may not stray from Penryn for as long as this situation endures; so I must regretfully write this to say I cannot come to Bowood this early summer.

If Circumstances should suddenly change for the better I will write you more.

Most sincerely yours,
Clowance Carrington

When she posted the letter she wondered why she had not told the entire truth to her old suitor. In the first place she had put the onus of refusal on her mother. Then she had sidled away and attributed the refusal to Tim Hodge's accident. What was wrong with that? Her mother *was* reluctant to leave Nampara in a way she had never been before. Hodge had broken his leg, but it was such a perfectly clean break that even Surgeon Charteris, who adored removing injured limbs, was persuaded to agree to splint it up and wait to see if it would set.

So where was the deception? It lay in the knowledge that if she went to Bowood Edward would resume his suit; and even though she could always have said *no*, her own feelings were in such confusion that while she had no intention whatever of saying *yes*, she sheered away from an outright decision. It could be no next year . . .

The letter posted, she would have liked to take it back and redraft it.

Ross had a further letter from George Canning.

Dear Friend
The catastrophe of St Peter's Fields offends us all. I was

travelling in Italy when this tragedy happened. Liverpool sent for me in great distress, which I can well understand.

Sometimes I am frustrate with man's attempts to impose order, fairness, justice, decency upon the world, when a few evil men, or simple angry men, or hot-headed fools, can overturn the good intentions, the sincerity, the honesty of the great majority, and undo all the work of a well-meaning government.

Now we must build again. I don't know if you know that the charge of treason has been dropped against Hunt and the other men arrested. The trial is not yet, but I expect they will get a year or two in jail to cool their hot heads. The alarm of the nation is understandable. It has been rumoured with some authority – can rumour ever have authority, I wonder? – that behind the moderate demands put forward on the banners of the mob were far more sinister and revolutionary ideas – the destruction of the Bank of England, the equalization of all classes by an agrarian division of the landed property of the country, the removal of the Hanoverian dynasty from the throne and the election of a President, the abolition of all titles, and so on.

Whether these are the true beliefs of the majority of the protesters, or are only the hot-headed fantasies of a few evil, covetous men, I know not. I strongly suspect the latter. But no man can forget what happened in France less than three decades ago. It is only twenty-five years since their king went to the guillotine. Outbursts like the one in Manchester could very easily lead to a full-scale revolution in England. Do not forget that Robert Liverpool claims he witnessed the storming of the Bastille. Is Wellington to feel that the great victory he gained only three and a half years ago is to be dissipated by the collapse of a stable England into fratricidal chaos and revolution?

These must be the thoughts of any true Englishman on hearing the bad news from Manchester. That cooler reflection may suggest these thoughts are an over-response to the news does not and will not prevent many in authority from taking repressive action. And at least for the time being I must side with them.

117

You may well argue that had the reforms you urged have come more quickly no such riot might have taken place. I half agree. But it has.

I envy you for getting out of the political scene when you did. Westminster is a muddy place in which to spend one's life. I may yet take some other post abroad.

Believe me, most cordially and sadly yours,
George Canning.

Bella was home for a month in the summer. She did not need any subtle tactical questioning from her parents: she told it all. Mrs Pelham (Aunt Sarah) was sweetness itself and never allowed her to feel a burden or a trouble. (Ross had written to Caroline's aunt in April offering, indeed almost demanding, to be able to pay towards Bella's keep, and Mrs Pelham had replied to Caroline, asking her to tell her distinguished friend not to be so silly.)

Dr Fredericks was a tyrant, Bella said, but a good teacher; and her friendship with two of the other girls had flowered and strengthened. Christopher was Christopher; need one say more?

Christopher was Christopher, and arrived at the end of her holiday to take her back to London. While she was singing a lullaby for Henry and Demelza on the last night, and singing it with a singular sweetness that brought tears to Demelza's eyes, Christopher was sitting smoking with Ross in the old living room of the house, to which the music floated in only as the lightest of airs.

Presently he said: 'Sir, forgive me for raising this matter, but I am trying to bide my time with what patience I can summon, and I have not mentioned the subject of marriage – not, that is, since last year, neither to you nor your wife, nor indeed to Bella, except that between her and me it is a wish that is so obvious that it need not be spoken.' He stopped and relit his pipe from a spill, taking its flame from the fire. (Bella on such occasions was always afraid he would set light to his moustache.) 'You, sir, and her mother are still legally in charge of your daughter, and I am eternally grateful that you agreed to my suggestion that she come to London to get the best teaching. Therefore – therefore I would like to put forward a suggestion about our marriage. I would request that you would give us permission to marry this time next year.'

Ross's long pipe was drawing well, but he took it from his mouth and inspected it to give himself time to think. He had rather anticipated that Christopher would want the marriage earlier, but he was not going to say so.

'Assuming that your feelings for each other remain the same then?'

'Certainly.' Christopher smiled mischievously.

'Do you have any special reason to pick this time next year?'

'I have, sir. Isabella-Rose will have had fifteen months under Dr Fredericks, and you will observe how much her voice has improved in two terms. It could be that by the end of next year she may feel she has learned enough and will have the ambition to give some public recitals.'

'Bella tells me that she already sings at small parties Mrs Pelham arranges from time to time.'

'Yes, sir. And these will be invaluable to her in the struggle to become known. These little soirées are giving her confidence and poise.'

'Since when did Bella need confidence?'

Christopher laughed. 'Indeed. Then poise, projection, the faculty to adjust one's voice to the occasion. Above all, presence.'

They could just hear her from the library on a high note. No hint of strain.

'You will have thought of the problems of marriage, Christopher?'

'Problems?'

'A young woman if she is dedicated to a profession may find a conflict of interest in following it and at the same time living the life of a young bride.'

'We have talked about it together and how these problems could be faced. But at least she would be marrying someone who is as ambitious for her as she is for herself. I would be no jealous husband, begrudging her dedication to her success. In all cases her profession would take priority.'

'She might find she did not want it to.'

'For reasons of self-esteem I hope that's true. And I hope I should be able to steer her back to music.'

Ross stretched his legs. 'And what would happen when the usual outcome of a marriage occurs?'

'Children? Yes, sir, that too is a hazard. But I am promised a move to the executive office of Rothschild – this should be next

October – and this should mean I will have funds enough to take a modest house and hire a sufficiency of servants. If there were children they would not depend solely on their mother for attention.'

'There is, however, still the anatomical necessity that women have to carry their offspring for nine months before they are born. That is a time when a coming child is at its most demanding and, from a concert point of view, disfiguring.'

'You must be aware, sir – or perhaps you do not go much to the theatre in London – you would know that audiences are well used to seeing their actresses gravid with child. They observe a convention to ignore the lady's condition and concentrate on her acting. So I believe where a singer is involved it does not seem to upset the singer that she is many months pregnant, nor upset the audience who see her and listen to her in this condition.'

The song had stopped. It was time for Henry to go to bed. Perhaps he was already asleep, lulled by that voice.

'I presume you have discussed all this thoroughly with Bella?'

'We have discussed it, yes. But we wait on your provisional assent. Yours and Lady Poldark's.'

'I cannot answer for her. But speaking for myself – provided Bella remains totally committed – I—' Ross stopped. 'I think I must first ask leave to discuss the proposal – with Bella's mother.'

Christopher stroked his moustache. 'Thank you, sir.'

Chapter Two

A few days later, in a fresh breezy September wind, Valentine was showing two of his new adventurers over the workings of Wheal Elizabeth – Mr Saunders and Mr Tucking, both substantial men in their fifties, the first with a beard, the second with a paunch, and both with North Country accents.

They had arrived unexpectedly at John Permewan's office in Truro yesterday evening, and Permewan, as soon as he was able, had sent a boy to warn young Mr Warleggan that he might expect a visit from all three of them about noon tomorrow. The 'sight unseen' investors had decided after all to see for themselves. It appeared that they had left Leeds together last week and were making a leisurely tour of the West Country inspecting the properties into which they had put some of their money.

John Permewan was a man of forty-four who wore a black wig to hide his total lack of head hair, was snub-nosed, small-mouthed, ingratiating, and had a skill with words, particularly prospectuses.

Valentine said: 'After dinner you may go down either Diagonal or Western if you have the mind, for as you will observe the amount of work you may see above ground is relatively small.'

'Aye,' said Tucking, 'you're right there.'

'As I say, I am negotiating for the purchase of a forty-inch beam engine from Pendeen Consols at St Just. I have offered them two hundred and forty pounds for an engine which cost them eight hundred pounds to install. It was built by Hocking and Son and is in first-class condition. If the deal goes through, the engine should be moved and reassembled and working in ten weeks. Perhaps, if you have time, you could go over tomorrow to see the engine for yourselves?'

Saunders looked at the sky and then at Valentine. 'Where is – St Just, is it?'

'Near Land's End. Thirty miles or a little less.'

'We was to be at Hayle tomorrow,' said Tucking.

'You will appreciate,' said Valentine, 'that the location of this mine is singularly fortunate, for the sloping ground drains naturally into the sea. It is only now that we are approaching the fifty-fathom level that we need artificial drainage, and this engine that we are going to buy, that we are all going to help to buy as venturers together – shareholders, that is – will perfectly supply the need.'

'That mine we was at yesterday,' said Tucking, 'had much more headgear. And there was things they call washing floors. And waterwheels.'

'What mine was that? West Chiverton? That has been in existence thirty years, and has made a mint of money for the owners. A mint of money. We are only just beginning. But after dinner let me show you some of the samples of the ore we have already brought up. I think it a mine of the highest promise—'

'Excuse me,' said Saunders. 'I believe there be a lady trying to attract your attention.'

Valentine looked back towards the house. Coming away from it, hand raised as if to call him, was a young woman, her hair blowing wildly in the sea wind. It was Agneta.

'Oh,' said Valentine. 'It is a woman from the village. She is simple – in the head, I mean. My wife has been very kind to her and now she trades on the favours she has received. Pray excuse me.'

He walked furiously back towards the house, holding his hat against the wind.

'*Vally!*' said Agneta affectionately, and then she saw his face. 'You must not be cross—'

'Cross!' he said. 'I am furious. How dare you continue to pester us like this! This is three – four times—'

'You said not go to the house. But I went and you were not there! What is wrong? Why are you always away? Why do you not love Neta?'

'I did. Agneta, I did. But no longer. I am too busy. I am *married*. I must stay faithful to my vows. It was just a happy time we had together. No more. It is over. D'you understand? *Over!* Finished! Done for. I do not want you any longer.'

She stared at him, her eyes wide and brimming with tears.

'You not want Agneta? But Agneta wants Vally. She wants him. She pines for him! She will never give him up—'

By chance Music Thomas was mooching round the house. At ordinary times Valentine would have snapped at him to get back to the stables. But now he was welcome.

'Music! Here!'

'Sur?' He came across at a lolloping trot.

'Miss Treneglos is to go *home*. *Take her home*. In any way you can! Do not let her out of your sight until she is back in Mingoose! Understand?'

'Ais, sur, but—'

'Vally! I am here to see you—'

But Valentine had turned his back and was smoothing his hair and walking towards his visitors to resume his conversation with them. Trying hard to smile, trying hard to look unruffled, as if this had been only a trivial interruption to their business talk.

A difficult time getting Agneta home. A six-mile walk, and, since he had not been instructed to take horses from the stables, Music did not think he dared.

Agneta's shoes were already badly scuffed, and soon she was limping. Every now and then a fresh flood of tears would stream down her cheeks, and her wild hair blowing in the wind stuck to her face like seaweed.

Music knew Agneta to be a 'poor soul'. This was a phrase chosen by him rather than 'half saved' because that phrase had been used against himself until Katie bludgeoned it out of existence in her presence. But he also knew that Agneta was one of the gentry, and since Mr Treneglos had once sworn and shouted at him for getting in the way of his horse Music tended to keep clear of the family. So he let Agneta precede him and followed at about a yard's respectful distance. Sometimes she would stop and feel at her shoe, sometimes she would sit on a wall and wipe her face with her cloak; then he too would stop and wait until, under gentle urging from him, she would start off again.

They at last came to Grambler village. The sight of two such addlepates following each other, stumbling among the cart tracks, brought faces to doors and windows, but fortunately the children were all on the cliffs looking for samphire. As they got near the end of the straggling cottages Agneta put her hands to her face and began to wail. Casting about for help of some sort, Music saw his brother-in-law coming out of Music's own cottage and called to him to come over.

It had taken all of three years for Ben Carter to come to any acceptance of Katie's husband. To Ben, Music always carried the stigma of being the village idiot, and he had been scandalized at his big black-eyed sister throwing herself into wedlock with such a diddicoy. But Katie's eventual happiness in the match and her ferocious defence of her husband against snide or sneer or catcall had gradually brought Ben round. They met sometimes at their mother's house in Stippy-Stappy Lane, and Ben could now bring himself to be just polite.

'What's amiss, boy?'

Music explained, making himself heard with difficulty over Agneta's sobs and wails.

'Now then, miss. Miss Agneta, isn't it, eh? Why don't ee want go 'ome?'

Agneta stared at Ben, vaguely recognizing him.

'Who are you? Go away and leave me be. I shall go home when I want!'

'Ben Carter. I been up your house 'pon times. Tis going to rain. You'd best go wi' Music here.'

'I'll do whatsoever I please.' Music put a hand on her arm, but she haughtily shook it off. Music looked appealingly at Ben.

'Twould be a favour to come 'long, Ben, 'long of us. Just so far as the door. Tis no more'n a mile or two, I reckon.'

Music had not ever before ventured to suggest that Ben should do anything. Ben looked at the sky, which was blowing up dark and threatening.

'I was going mine,' said Ben grudgingly. 'Tedn far out of my way.'

When they had finally led Agneta, only snivelling now, into the arms of Emmeline, recently returned from a visit to Bath, they turned away. From being a difficult anxious task, for Music this was now turning into a heart-warming achievement: the sorrowing girl was safely back in her home, and more important to his sense of well-being was the fact that he had done something in company with his brother-in-law. They walked away from the house *together*!

Presently Ben struck off across the field path that led to the sandhills. When he saw Music accompanying him he said: 'This edn your way home, boy.'

'No, Ben. I thought mebbe I could come with ee so far as Leisure? There's no rush for me to get back, 'cos they won't know how long it d'take, and I haven't been see the Bal, not since the new engine were fired.'

'Please yourself,' said Ben.

Ben had never had Music's company at the mine and he certainly did not want it now, but an element of contrariness in his nature stopped him from sending the other man scuttling home. Let the devil take any of his miners who exchanged sidelong glances or whispered behind their backs. Music was Katie's husband, and if there were any dottle still thinking to see the funny side they could go jump off the cliff for all Ben told himself he cared.

Nor did he think many would do this. He knew he had established his position and he was entitled to respect from the men. As for the Bal maidens, those who really were maidens knew he was unmarried and probably fancied their chances with him. In the last few years Ben had grown up, become a little more moderate in his views, had grown more formidable, a leader in a sense yet remaining resolutely solitary.

There were, as he expected, relatively few people about except for those working on the washing and sifting floors. He went at once to the coal bins directly behind the engine house, Music shambling behind.

Dan Curnow came out, wiping his hands on an oily rag.

'All goin' right, Dan?'

'Aye. Naught wrong that won't wait till cleanin' next month.'

'If we keep goin' till then.'

'Oh, aye, the coal. Twill come no doubt in a day or two. You seen Cap'n Poldark?'

Ben screwed up his eyes and looked at the tormented sea. 'Saw'n yesternight. He been over today?'

'No.'

'I'd best go see 'im. Not like 'im to forget.'

'Never known it,' said Curnow. 'What'd he say yesterday?'

'Our load be out there, waitin' for the weather. Cap'n Poldark says it's been sighted off St Ann's, but there's precious chance o' making that harbour. She'd be scat to jowds. And Basset's Cove purty little better. Don't envy them folk. She've been out a week from Swansea.'

'Poor weather for September,' Music volunteered, hoping to join in.

Dan Curnow looked at him. 'Damnation poor.'

Ben said: 'Reckon I'll go see Cap'n. Mebbe he 'as other things on his mind. Nothin' fresh from sixty fathom?'

'All goin' well, I blave.'

'I mind a time years gone,' said Music brightly. 'Can't mind when. Twas that year o' the rains. Lugger come ashore. Just over there twas. You mind it, Ben? Come ashore wi' a load. All beach were black for months. I mind Art and John come back leadin' mule wi' panniers full o' good nut! Kept we warm 'alf winter!'

Dan wiped his hands again and looked at Ben. Ben said: 'Time you was off, Music. Katie'll be grieving for ee, thinking you've fell off the cliffs. I be going Nampara.'

'I'll come with ee,' said Music. 'Tes right on me way 'ome.' Then seeing Ben's face he added: 'I'll just come so far as the stile.'

Ben found Ross in the stables. He was considering what to do with Bella's pony, which he had bought for her at the Truro races some years ago. Most ponies can be put out to grass and take easily to a pastoral life, munching and lying in the sun or sheltering placidly under a tree in the rain, but Horatio had become such a pet of Bella's that he seemed to go off his food when she was away and moped and sulked noticeably. Ross was coming away, having conferred with Matthew Mark Martin and found no solution.

'Ben,' he said. 'No trouble, I hope?'

'No, sur. Nothing amiss at all except for a shortage of fuel. We got 'bout four days' supply and I was wondering what we was to do if the weather don't take off.'

'It is surprising, the height of the sea, for the wind is no more than a stiffish breeze. But the *Magpie* will never hazard herself until the sea abates. I have been in to Truro this morning and ordered six carts from the merchant there—'

'Ah, I should not 'ave bothered ee—'

'Well, first I tried Wheal Kitty, but they too were in short supply and did not wish to spare any in case this weather lasted. I hope the rain won't come, for the ways are mired enough between here and Truro and will not be improved by a procession of coal carts.'

As Ross was speaking he led the way round the house, through the yard with the pump in it, under a granite arch into the garden. They found Demelza there, in the far corner, talking with two other people, Sam, her brother, and Esther, her niece.

It was Essie's half-day off, and when she had turned up at Pally's Shop Sam had taken her by the arm and said: 'Come you with me. I wish for you to meet your aunt.'

'I met her the twice, Uncle Sam, first when she come to see Arthur wed, and then early this year. She's done much for me. I don't wish to put myself forward.'

'Ye'll have the chance to thank her then, won't ee. Gratitude is a holy virtue. Gratitude to God comes foremost with us all. But gratitude between one person and another is also blessed under the Lord.'

Essie was still half protesting as they came down the shallow valley with its bubbling stream, saw the old grey house set beside the turbulent sea. And Demelza was in her garden tying up the hollyhocks.

There was no embarrassment. Demelza kissed Esther as if she had known her well for years, and Sam stood by and allowed his young-old creased face to move into an appreciative smile. They walked around the garden, the wind tugging and pushing at them.

On this came Ross and Ben, through the arch and so to meet them. There was some slight awkwardness here, but it came from the visitors. At sight of Ben Carter Esther went crimson to the ears. Ross, who had not seen Esther before, thought her a waif of a girl, and when she dropped a curtsy to him he could see the beads of sweat starting on her forehead.

'We've met,' said Ben inscrutably. 'Just in the village, like.'

They looked at Essie. She blurted out: 'A dog bit me and – and Mr Carter killed 'im.'

Ross said to Ben: 'Stray dog?'

'Yes. Mongrel. Thought twas best.'

'Safer,' said Ross, but Demelza shivered.

'I been meaning to see ee, Ben,' said Sam benevolently. 'Your mam be one of my flock, but I d'know you're not of a mind to change—'

'No. Fraid not.'

'Esther here is besting whether to accept the pure fount of the Holy Spirit and join the communion. But to begin to take a part, a full part, in our worship, which be to the greater glory of God as manifested in Jesus Christ, she would need mebbe one morning off per week, just to take hold of the teaching. So I asked Jinny, your beloved mother, if she would write to Major Geoffrey Charles, or to his wife, putting this to them and requesting that she be given that extra time away—'

'What my mother say?'

'She say she don't like t'ask. She say she specially don't like t'ask on account of Mrs Geoffrey Charles being a Roman.'

'An' what do ee want o' me?'

'I thought mebbe ye could persuade your mother when I could not . . .'

Ross thought he detected an element of opportunism in Sam's benevolent appeal. He had probably brought the girl here and been prepared to make such a request to Demelza or even to himself; but Ben's appearance had given him the chance of making the request to Ben, with his niece and brother-in-law standing by and listening. (Sam, Ross knew, was very unhappy at his niece being in the constant company of someone who worshipped at the tainted altar of Rome. To bring Esther into the safe keeping of his Connexion would safeguard her from contamination.)

As anticipated, Ben refused, though with less impatience than expected.

'If Mam don't want to write, why don't you? You're leader of your group.'

'I'll surely do that if all else fails—'

'And what do Esther think?' Ben said, frowning at the girl.

She flushed up again. 'My mother an' father, they was both saved. And mother was always on at me. But some'ow I didn't quite take to it then. I *tried*. But nothing moved in me. Since I come here though, Sam 'as been that kind an' that helpful . . .'

'Tes your own life ye must lead,' said Ben. 'Did ee have that dog bite seen to?'

'Oh, yes . . . I—'

'Oh, yes,' said Ben. 'Else mebbe ye wouldn't be 'ere.' A glint of humour crossed his face. 'Well, I must be getten back, sur. Reckon as we got 'nough fuel for four days.'

Ross said: 'It will be here before then.'

Chapter Three

Agneta disappeared.

The first intimation at Nampara was the arrival of the stout Emmeline, leading a spare horse.

Emmeline was the nicest of the Treneglos family, and Demelza asked her in for a cordial. October was almost here, and perversely the weather had turned warm.

'Paula went in to see her about seven, and the bed was empty. It looked as if it had been used, but she always makes her bed untidy however much the maids see for it. We thought she might have gone on the beach. She has done that a deal recently – you know how upset and restless she has been. But Papa took his horse and rode right along to the Black Cliffs, and there was no sign of her. He was nearly cut off and is in the greatest of a temper. He sent me here and after this, if this draws blank, he says I must go to Place House, Trevaunance.'

'You have drawn blank,' said Demelza. 'Before you go I will ask around, just to be sure. It is over a week – oh, it must be two – since we have seen her.'

They gossiped about local affairs for ten minutes – there seemed no reason to take Agneta's absence too seriously – then Demelza consulted enough of her servants to confirm that nothing had been seen of Miss Agneta.

'Maybe twould save you trouble to go home again first,' Demelza said. 'She may be home by now. Valentine and Selina are usually quick to send her back if she goes there.'

'Oh, I'll go on,' said Emmeline, rising. 'I rather fancy the ride in this weather. There's time enough before dinner.'

Demelza watched her clomping over the bridge, and stood in the autumn sunshine until she had disappeared up the valley towards Grambler. She thought idly that she should have apologized for being implicitly embroiled in Agneta's trouble, but Ross had told her not to. At heart she agreed entirely with him – what were Valentine's misdoings to them? All the same it might have been good neighbourly to be more sympathetic.

She went indoors and gathered a basket of late plums that she was intending to send over to Daisy Kellow, who was in bed with a chill. Then she looked at the clock and saw there was time enough before dinner to walk over with them herself.

Emmeline had promised to send to tell them when Agneta was found, but no news came during the rest of the sunny autumnal day, so when dark fell Demelza sent Matthew Mark over to enquire. He brought back a note which said: 'No sign yet. Papa has gone out with two grooms to visit the other houses. He has also told Constable Purdy. E.'

'I suspect she's hiding somewhere,' said Ross. 'Maybe to give her family a shock. Or maybe to alarm Valentine – if she believes he still cares.'

'Yes, or she has fallen. There are so many holes and hollows.'

'Did she take a horse, do you know?'

'No. If she isn't found by tomorrow d'you think we could offer two or three of our men? Old Dick would not mind going, for one. Twould suit him, and he's not fit for ordinary work.'

'I'd go myself if feeling were better between us.'

'Where is Valentine?'

'From home, I think. He has many devious irons in the fire. I haven't seen him for a week.'

Demelza said: 'D'you know, I have not set eyes on their baby yet. D'you mind years ago Selina came here after Mr Pope had died, to ask your advice on mineral rights?'

'Yes. I sometimes wonder if she feels about Valentine's friendship with me something the same as you do.'

'Too close? Bad influence? No, I think it is Valentine's friendship with women that upsets her.'

'That cannot explain why she does not come here.'

'I'll go and see her later this week, after Agneta has been found.'

Agneta was not found. The following day Valentine himself called. He found both Ross and Demelza walking with Henry on Nampara Cove. They were very surprised.

'Well, well, a family scene, eh? And parting summer's lingering blooms delayed. May I join you? How is little Henry?'

'Proper, thank you,' said Henry, picking up a flat stone to skim it on the sea. It did not get very far among the waves.

'I've been in Ireland,' Valentine said. 'And must alas go back again. What's this about Agneta? Is she playing hide and seek with us?'

Ross said: 'There's no news so far. Cobbledick and two others are helping in the search. But perhaps your report is later than ours?'

'Are you welcome at Mingoose?' Valentine asked.

'No.'

'I have just come from there. The house, except for Ruth, is empty! Ruth is only staying in in case Agneta voluntarily returns. She screamed in rage at the sight of me.'

'Not unnaturally,' Ross said.

'Well.' Valentine picked up a couple of stones, which were fairly scarce on this part-sandy beach, and handed them to Henry. 'Sea's too rough to skim 'em, boy. Just throw these and watch them make an almighty plop.'

'Thank you,' said Henry.

After a moment Valentine said: 'And you, Cousin Demelza. You are singularly silent. Do you also put the blame on me?'

'What can one think? Perhaps you did it without evil intent . . .'

'Not evil, no. But selfish intent, I dare say.' Turning to the little boy: 'More stones?'

'Please.'

Valentine came back with two more. 'You'd do better at the other end of the cove, Harry. It is pebbly there.'

'I know.'

'Actually, Cousin Harry, there's a saying in the Bible: let him who is without sin cast the first stone. Might apply now, mightn't it, eh?'

'I don't know,' said Henry, and looked at his mother for guidance.

'How is Selina?' Demelza asked.

'A small matter put out, as you'd expect. Ah well, no doubt it will all blow over.'

'And your son?'

'Brave. Too young yet to know of his father's misdemeanours. Why do you not come over and see him?'

Demelza said: 'Only a few minutes before you came up I was talking of it.'

They walked to where the stream came out on the beach.

Valentine said: 'This really is a pretty familial scene, isn't it. Henry is a lucky boy.'

Demelza looked to see if Valentine was poking fun and decided he was not.

'I expect when you were young . . .'

'I was never taken on the beach by my parents in my life. Only once or twice was I *allowed* on a beach . . . Perhaps when we all settle down again I shall make up for lost time . . .'

Ross said quietly: 'You have been in Ireland. Did you not say you left the sailing to your – employees? I remember your being rather dismissive when I put the question to you once.'

Valentine looked at Ross thoughtfully. 'Quite correct, Cousin. Clever of you to recall that. Unfortunately my skipper, Vic Paulton, has quarrelled with my clients, and at the moment I do not trust the trainee in charge.'

'Trust?' said Demelza.

'Trust, Cousin. In this case it is an animal with two heads. One head is trusting Mabe to navigate the ship. I am ignorant of such things, but the two other members of the crew are not and I think *pro tem* I should supervise them. The other head is whether I can trust Henry Mabe to deal honestly with the money that comes through his hands.'

'Henry!' said Henry. 'Henry. That's me!'

'Not in this case,' said Valentine, with an unexpected rasp in his voice.

By Friday the alarm had been raised throughout the district. Two people had had possible sightings of the girl: Paul Daniel, scouring Hendrawna Beach in the early daylight of Tuesday, had seen a man and a woman walking near the end of the beach just below the Holy Well, and had been surprised to see anyone abroad so soon. Before he could catch them up they had disappeared, possibly towards the well. They had been too far away to recognize, but the woman could have been Agneta. The other sighting had been by Dwight Enys. Returning from a late call on Monday evening, he had come close by the gates of Mingoose and had seen Agneta with a small candle lantern walking in the road. He had spoken to her and asked her if anything was amiss. She had replied that nothing was amiss but she was looking for her cat, who had not been home for his supper. The girl had seemed quite composed and had been walking towards the gates of Mingoose. He had hesitated whether to intervene by ushering her back home, but instead had watched her until she turned in at the gates and watched the bobbing lantern until it reached the door.

Constable Purdy, in his element at the notoriety, organized search parties. As Demelza had said, the countryside was pitted with holes and caverns, some of them gaping and unprotected, others half-filled up and overgrown with heather and brambles, the outcome of a century's searchings for precious minerals; all this apart from the mining whims, some still in operation, many abandoned and dropping sheer for two or more hundred feet with water at the bottom. Most were protected, or at least masked, by a surrounding low stone wall. But this was not difficult to mount if one was of a mind to end it all. And many an infant born out of wedlock had been so deposited. They were better than the cliffs for such a disposal, for unlike the sea they seldom gave up their dead.

Purdy, who had been appointed soon after Vage had retired, was slightly more attentive to his duties than his predecessor, but his was a formidable task were his resources ten times as great. It really depended on chance. Otherwise the girl's disappearance might remain a mystery for ever.

It cast a gloom over a golden October. Ruth began to wear black, as did her remaining daughters. Horrie and his new wife and baby came down from Minehead to companion the rest of the family. Davida arrived.

Then Geoffrey Charles returned from London, and he organized the searches in a way that John Treneglos had not the talent to do, and which Ross had been prevented from doing by John's expressed enmity.

But it was Ben Carter, walking on the cliffs not far from Kellow's Ladder, who eventually found the body. His attention was drawn by the swirling of gulls to a mound on the high ground just before the declivity running down to the cliffs. He fought his way through the brambles until he came to the body, then after the briefest inspection he turned away, grey-faced, to fetch Purdy.

The body was brought down on a bier and carried back to Mingoose to await burial. Dwight went to examine it, and said the girl's throat had been cut. The funeral took place two days later.

It was in the afternoon of one of Mrs Pelham's evening parties that Bella received a letter from her mother telling her of events in Cornwall. It was Mrs Pelham's birthday – no one dared to ask her which – but it was special for Bella too: not only in the distinction of the guests but because Dr Fredericks himself had been asked to accompany her on the pianoforte and he had actually *accepted*!

They had been over the songs together in rehearsal all yesterday, and Bella was perfectly confident of her ability to do well, but this did not prevent a tightening of the stomach muscles during the afternoon. It was a curious symptom. Lack of confidence did not cause the physical and emotional tension. She knew she could sing what she had agreed to sing, she was almost certain the evening would be a success, but still the wires were stretched.

The letter was delivered during the afternoon while she was discussing with Mrs Pelham and two footmen whether moving the piano three feet forward would be better for the acoustics and better for the voice. She opened it, excused herself, glanced at the first few sentences to see that everything was apparently all right, then stuffed it in her bag and returned to the discussions.

When she got up to her bedroom and took it out, the first page had fallen out of sequence, and she read:

so clearly Valentine is in very bad odour in the neighbourhood around. He moves about very defiant, seeming to take little notice of the slights and insults that come his way. So many tongues wag and so much venom do they drop that it is fortunate he was away in Ireland when this thing happened, otherwise there would be some who would maybe ask who stood most to benefit by Agneta's death. Your father was in fact so questioned by Horrie Treneglos. (No one else would have dared!) But you will well guess the answer he received back!

Naturally Selina has made things much worse by leaving

135

him. She wrote no note, just left with her maid and a nanny, taking little Georgie with her. Once again there was the beginning of a hue and cry until it was learned that she was staying at Cardew! No one seems to know how she was received or how long she intends to stay. The baby's grandfather, the older George Warleggan, has been long estranged from Valentine, as you know, and I do not conceit with what favour he regards Selina, but at least he has taken her in. Valentine has been frequently at Nampara since she left – he says he intends to continue to live at Place House on his own. Katie says the servants steal about the house when he is in, for fear of disturbing him.

It has been a lovely October in Cornwall, somewhat soiled by all this trouble, which luckily only affects Nampara in a glancing sort of way. I was that happy to learn of your singing progress . . .

A distinguished dinner party, as had been promised, including Lieutenant Christopher Havergal, the Hon. Charles Wynford, M. Maurice Valéry, from Paris: twelve in all. Charles Wynford was known to be a crony of the Prince Regent.

No doubt it was the promise of such company that had lured Dr Fredericks. Bella sat next to her beloved. With the concert in front of her, her intake of food was light. Christopher's was even lighter. He refused some courses altogether, but drank a lot of Canary wine. She likened it in her own mind to her mother's predisposition for port, but Christopher's consumption was much the greater. It was odd, she thought, that often for days on end he drank only cordials or even milk, but once in a while he donated all his energies to Canary. It seemed to make little difference to his behaviour, but had she been asked she would have preferred him not to have indulged himself tonight. It did not occur to her that perhaps he was more nervous than she was.

Dr Fredericks had chosen a fairly demanding programme for her (some of the songs, though she did not remark this, had specially dashing accompaniments). But he had chosen in such a way that the early pieces were the less exacting. 'I have kept the *acuti* for the last pieces,' he said. 'We will begin with Cherubini, go on to Schubert, Méhul, Spohr, Haydn. Remember the size of the room; you should not give full voice with Méhul; think you are at a rehearsal. If you are nervous, empty the lungs like a tube of paint, from the bottom upwards. I know you will do everything to perfection.'

And it seemed afterwards that she had done just that. The warmth of the applause was not restrained by an awareness that one was in a private drawing room. The Hon. Charles Wynford was specially complimentary and took down the name of the song by Campenhout she had sung as an encore. He thought the Prince would be interested.

A golden evening. Bella was in heaven, Dr Fredericks little less, for Wynford's recommendation would mean much to him too. As people were beginning to leave in their carriages, Christopher disappeared for a few minutes. When she could get away, Bella went in search of him. She found him in the dining room holding a glass and a newly opened bottle of Canary.

He got up awkwardly from his chair, put glass and bottle down and embraced her. 'My little songbird, my little songbird.' (It was not quite *shong.*) 'You have flown tonight. I never thought, even in my wildest dreams, that you would sing like that. At least not yet. So soon. So soon. I listened hard among the guests and heard nothing but praise. Nor did I suppose there could be. You have climbed a high mountain tonight, my sweetheart!'

'If I am a songbird,' said Bella, showing some of her mother's quirky humour, 'I should be able to avoid the mountain, shouldn't I? We must go back at once to Aunt Sarah. She must not feel we have left her alone when the guests are gone.'

He picked up the bottle, and the glass rattled against the neck as he poured some in, gulped at it.

'*Leave* it,' Bella said, conscious of conflicting emotions struggling to affect her happiness. 'When you get home, Christopher. There'll be time then.'

'Join me now. There's a glass here.'

She shook her head. 'I'm happy enough.'

He stared at her uncertainly for a moment. 'I drink to you. And only for joy.'

'Yes, yes. It has been such a – such a good evening. Oh, Dr Fredericks, I thought you had gone! I'm glad you have not. Have I thanked you enough? You were such a support all the way through. You have taught me so much.'

'I have also learned tonight,' Dr Fredericks said, trying to adjust his linen cravat. 'I'm going home a happy man.'

Bella linked arms with him, and they went to the dining-room door. There she glanced back and saw that Christopher was gulping another glass.

Chapter Four

The inquest on Agneta Treneglos was held in the Bounders Arms, the inn run by Ned and Emma Hartnell, which was not far from Sawle Church. Its upper room was sometimes used as a meeting place, being, apart from those in the houses belonging to the gentry, the largest in the neighbourhood. Even so, aside from the jury and the witnesses, there was little space available for interested spectators, of whom there would have been many if accommodation had permitted.

The coroner was a Mr James Carlyon, who had ridden out from Truro. The twelve jurors, chosen from among the more responsible members of the public, sat on two benches against one wall. Zacky Martin, his asthma fortunately abated, was the foreman. A chair behind a table on the opposite side of the room served as a witness box. There were about a dozen spectators crushed in the doorway to watch and listen.

The first witness was Mr John Treneglos, the father of the deceased, who gave evidence of identity and could hardly contain his tears. He was followed by Constable Purdy, who gave an account of the four days' search that had taken place, then Ben Carter, who told of how he had found the body.

Dr Enys was called. He described the vicious knife thrusts which had caused the girl's death. In reply to the coroner he said that he did not think she had been violated. Nor did robbery appear to be a motive, as a bracelet and a brooch were still on the body. She had, when found, probably been dead about twenty-four hours. The question of Agneta's mental capacities was skirted around. Dwight said that from time to time he had attended the girl for epilepsy, also for St Anthony's Fire, and a number of conventional ailments. In recent years she had been in better

139

health, and so far as he could tell she had been in normal health at the time of death.

Two witnesses were called to testify to the distress Agneta had recently suffered because of her romantic attachment for a young married man of the neighbourhood. Neither of them had any idea where she had spent the last four days of her life. The last witness was Mr Valentine Warleggan.

Noisy abuse greeted him, and the shout of 'Murderer!' came from John Treneglos. The coroner was quick to cut this short. 'If there is any further disturbance from any quarter I will ask the bailiffs to clear the room.'

'Damned if I'll sit here and—'

'Mr Treneglos, *please.*'

Valentine, in a sulphurous silence, was allowed to give his evidence, which was that he had known the deceased for twenty years, and that there had always been a neighbourly friendship between them. Recently he had noticed that Agneta had been seeking more of his company, but he was himself a happily married man, his wife having recently given birth to their first child, and in maintaining his friendship with other ladies in the district he had never given any of them reason to suppose that he was seeking anything more than a casual continuation of that friendship. Recently he had been very much away on the trading business he was trying to establish between Cornwall and Ireland, and he had not as far as he remembered seen the deceased since late September, which was about four weeks ago, when she had called at his house and he had been busy with two North Country investors in his mine, and he had asked one of his servants to escort Miss Agneta home.

'Did she appear distressed on that occasion?' the coroner asked.

Valentine frowned. 'To tell you the truth, I was very much preoccupied with the business in hand. But no, I do not think so. She was rather an eccentric girl . . .'

Mr Carylon nodded understandingly. Horace Treneglos stood up. 'May I ask a question?'

The coroner inclined his head.

'Warleggan,' said Horrie. 'Why did you seduce my sister?'

Cardew was a large house, but sometimes George felt it was not big enough for him. His own twin daughters were boisterous and demanding. Although there were nursemaids in plenty, Harriet would not let her children be too sternly disciplined and, taking their cue from their mother, they treated their father in a nonchalantly friendly way. He felt that he did not receive the deference that should have been accorded him. They frequently climbed on his knee, demanding he should read to them or tell them a story or had some story of their own to tell of what had befallen them during the day. While his first inclination had been to be brusque and stern with them, genuine and unforced affection had not been common in his life, and he was content to grumble only to himself about it or after they had gone to bed. Complaints to Harriet usually ended in his grudging defeat. Then of course there were the two damned boar hounds, grown older and greyer round the jowls but not an inch smaller in size, usually occupying the best position sprawling in front of the best fires. Ursula, when she was home, also showed signs of getting above herself.

Well, that was the life he led, and in many ways it was satisfactory enough. His mercantile businesses were all prospering. Sometimes Harriet spent money like water, but the well always filled up.

But now he – or at least Harriet and Cardew – were playing host to four strangers. (He had been staying in Truro when they turned up unexpectedly.) A mother, related to him only by a disapproved marriage and accompanied by a young baby, a nurse and a personal maid, had requested sanctuary here, and Harriet had unhesitatingly invited them in. There had been no mention as yet of the duration of their stay.

'Of course you must have her,' Harriet said when he had protested to her in private. 'Your son has behaved like a dirty rat. Of course we only have one side of the story, but for him to have an affair with a mental defective puts him beyond the pale. And then to have done away with her—'

'Now, there's no sort—'

'Oh, I don't know whether he actually cut her throat. But he is responsible whether or not. Clearly he so disturbed the balance of this dotty girl that she wandered about all over the country, even at night, a prime target for some maniac to accost her and cut her throat – just like Mary or whatever the girl's name was who worked here. So it's natural enough that Selina should leave him and, since he has spent all her money, to come on you for help and shelter.'

George could not remember having met his son's wife before. As he had a weakness for blondes – in spite of the shining darkness of his second wife – he could not fault her in that respect, nor in the startling forget-me-not blue of her eyes; but, being far from out of the top drawer himself, he was quick to recognize another such. No one knew *what* she had been before she married the elderly Horace Pope; since then her gentility had been so pronounced as to make it suspect. She was a pretty woman, and vaguely resembled Elizabeth, his first wife, but the resemblance was barely skin deep. He thought her a climber.

It was a Sunday in mid-November. Leaves fell like copper snow in every wind, but not enough had gone to spoil the autumn foliage. A peaceful afternoon scene. The shadows of the deer slanting in the sun, a touch of early chill in the air; bonfires were burning at a discreet distance, wood and coal crackled together in the main fireplaces of the house. They sat down to dinner: George and Harriet and Ursula and Selina. The twins, having been to church, were as usual taking their dinner upstairs with their nurses. George was feeling irritated that this was the third Sunday dinner which had to be shared with their uninvited guest. He had left it to Harriet to ask her how long she was likely to be staying, and Harriet had not yet done this. 'Carpe diem,' she had said, which had irritated him the more because he wasn't quite sure what it meant, and he wasn't sure she knew either.

Just as the first course was served the two great hounds set up a gaunt hollow barking from the drawing room, where they had been lying on the hearth rug in luxury. There was some to-ing and fro-ing, and Harriet sent a groom hurrying to quiet them. Then Simpson came in and bent to murmur a name into George's ear.

George's brows drew together, and he turned to Harriet.

'Valentine is here.'

Harriet took another sip of her soup. 'Castor and Pollux are being very naughty. I taught them not to bark casually at visitors . . . Well, it is your house, George, and your son. Why do you not ask him in?'

Selina got to her feet, screwing her napkin in her fingers. 'I will go upstairs.'

'No you will not,' said Harriet. 'Pray sit down. Simpson, ask Jones to set another place.'

Simpson looked at his master and, receiving no other directive from him, said: 'Very good, m'lady.'

'I do not wish to stay here!' said Selina, her eyes flashing. 'Excuse me.'

'You are in our house,' Harriet said. 'We are not willing to excuse you.'

Valentine came in. He was wearing a fawn frock coat, red waist-coat, twill trousers, riding boots, cream silk stock, and grey suede gloves, which he was peeling off as he came in. There were lines in his cheeks which were not usually there. He stopped a moment when he saw Selina, then he went across and kissed Harriet on the cheek. She made a little distasteful gesture.

'Harriet, how do you do? Good day, Father.' And then: 'Well, little Ursula. Blooming, I see.'

'What do you want?' George demanded.

'I came to see my wife. But it seems that I have come at an inappropriate time.'

Harriet said: 'I am of the opinion that any time would be inappropriate so far as your wife is concerned.'

'The only unforgivable thing is that I have come to disturb your dinner. May I wait in the parlour?'

'Since you are here,' said Harriet, 'you may as well break bread with us. I presume your father has no objection?'

'Provided discussion of the object of your visit is postponed until the meal is finished,' George said coldly.

There was a hesitation.

'Hare soup,' said Harriet. 'Fresh-water trout, venison, tarts and sweetmeats. We eat sparely.'

Valentine's face twitched, part grimace, part smile. 'Thank you.' He looked around. Simpson had drawn back a chair. It was opposite Selina. Valentine took it. 'Thank you.' Tight-lipped, Selina kept her eyes averted.

Dinner was resumed in brooding silence, the only sounds being of cutlery and crockery. Eventually these stopped. Ursula viewed her brother with malicious eyes. She thought he looked a bit pasty, not as if he had (supposedly) been voyaging in the November seas to and from Ireland. They had not hit it off when Valentine lived at home. He had teased her unmercifully, and she remembered the violent tempers she had got into.

'Do you have news of Isabella-Rose?' she asked him suddenly, breaking the icy spell.

'Who? – Oh. No. Why should I? She's in London, I gather.'

'Yes, she is taking a musical course. I heard from a schoolfriend, Erica Rashleigh, that she is already singing at soirées and the like.'

'Agreeable for her.'

'Yes, is it not. Papa has sent me for a year to Penzance, to Mme Blick's Finishing School for Young Ladies. I do not know if they will teach me singing there.'

'You have no voice,' said George.

'Thank you, Papa. I confess I would rather go to London.'

'All in good time. You are yet only nineteen.'

'Bella is two years younger than I am.'

Harriet glanced round the table, then at Simpson and the other footmen. She had been brought up totally to disregard what servants might hear or overhear of family affairs, but she knew how strongly George disapproved of such outspokenness. In this situation something could be said for his views, but the artificial nature of the present conversation was hardly to be borne. Valentine met her glance, then looked away.

He said lightly: 'I saw Bella's father this week, after the inquest.'

This was not a remark calculated to make the situation more relaxed.

George said: 'No doubt he's well.'

'Well enough, I believe. Not greatly concerned for me, I fear. Much more disturbed of spirit at the government's passing these Six Acts.'

'He'd be best occupied in joining the agitators of St Peter's Fields, then, instead of fuming in his shabby little house at Nampara.'

'What are the Six Acts, Papa?' Ursula asked.

'A very natural response of the government to the unrest and the disgraceful rioting which took place in Manchester and in other North Country towns. We were on the verge of revolution.'

Valentine said: 'Cousin Ross thinks the response is too repressive. That you should meet unrest with sweet reasonableness. He feels that the lack of understanding between the poor and the rich has been gravely widened this year.'

'Did you vote for these measures, George?' Harriet said. 'I forgot to ask you.'

'I was not there at the time,' George snapped. 'You should know that. My two Members did. So did Wellington, whom no one could

144

call a panic-monger. So did George Canning, Ross Poldark's great hero. In fact every reasonable man.'

'Or reasonable woman, I suppose,' Harriet said. 'The Acts are repressive, but considering the state of the country . . .'

Valentine said to Selina: 'I have come to take you home.'

No one spoke. The situation had now become intolerable. George took charge.

'Simpson, will you escort Miss Ursula upstairs to her room? Then close the doors and I will ring when you may return.'

'Papa!' said Ursula, in indignation. 'I have not finished! Look, I—'

'We will send for you,' said George. 'It is not suitable for you to hear what may shortly be said—'

'But I know all about it!' she shouted, as she was escorted from the room.

They could hear her protesting after the door was shut. 'I am his *sister*!'

George said thinly to Valentine: 'I wonder she admits it. You came here uninvited. State your business and go.'

'I have already stated it,' said Valentine. 'I have come to take Selina home.'

Harriet was the only one still toying with a little food. 'Did you kill her, Valentine?'

'Who? What?'

'The girl. I forget her name. Did you cut her throat?'

Valentine took up his wineglass and held it to the light. 'Yes, her blood was the colour of this claret.'

Selina took in a deep breath of horror. Valentine smiled at her. 'My stepmother has a very forthright brain. But sometimes she allows it to lead her into absurdity.'

'Well, did you?' said Harriet.

'What, from across the Irish Sea?'

'And you were across the Irish Sea?'

'I was.'

'How do you know when she died?'

'Dr Enys's testimony.'

Harriet frowned at him.

'The newspaper has not yet come with the report of the inquest. What was the verdict?'

'Murder, by person or persons unknown.'

'And were you able to produce witnesses that you were in Ireland?'

'Affidavits. From a Mr Leary of the Waterford Arms and a Mr Connor of Connor's Shipyard.'

'Well,' said Harriet, after a moment, 'that is good, so far as it goes.'

'Oh, I agree, Stepmother. I quite agree.'

'But you seduced her?'

Valentine took a deep breath. 'Seduction suggests an element of guilt on one side and innocence on the other. She was not exactly a blushing violet, you know. Nor was she a drivelling idiot, with one leg shorter than the other and a squint. She had had other lovers long before me. She had a raging appetite for eligible young men. Her family tries to present her as an innocent halfwit whose purity I traded on. I could tell them different.'

Harriet regarded him for a long moment. 'Are you sure she had other young men?'

'Oh, certain sure!'

'Can you name any of them?'

'Not offhand. She referred to them only by their Christian names.'

Harriet said to Selina: 'Did she give you that impression?'

'What impression?'

'That she was pretending to be subnormal, simple-witted?'

'No . . . I could not tell! She was depressed, nervy, full of tears. All the time. Every time we met!'

Harriet put down her fork. Valentine drank his wine.

'Is the inquisition over?'

Selina stirred in her chair. 'I must go to see for Georgie.'

'A moment longer,' said Harriet. 'Shall you return with Valentine?'

Selina looked startled. 'No . . . I don't know!'

George said: 'I have no excuses for you, Valentine. Whatever happened, it was shabby and disgraceful. You'll get no help from me.'

'I have not come for your help, Father. I have come for my wife.'

'I think, George,' Harriet said, looking at him bleakly, 'that this is the other side of the coin, which we have not seen before. If it is true what Valentine says, then he is shown up as just a feeble, errant character who has done very little worse than many another man. What marriage is not shaken by infidelities? If my mother had left my father every time he took an actress back to his rooms we should hardly have seen her at all! But,' she went on, as George was about to speak, 'but *if* this is only Valentine's side, and the truth is what we knew, or thought we knew, all along, and if Valentine is deliberately lying – if not about her death, then about the character and simple-wittedness of this Treneglos girl – chiefly to whitewash and justify himself, then I think he deserves to be kicked out.'

'Thank you, Stepmother,' Valentine said. 'Mr Justice Stepmother. Well summed up. But I have already been before one jury. Where is the jury you may now invite to retire and consider a further verdict?'

'He lied to me!' shouted Selina, her eyes suddenly blue fire as she looked up.

'I lied that I was not having an affair with the girl,' Valentine said evenly. 'As my stepmother sagely says, what husband does not lie to his wife at such a time? I told you, Selina, quite plainly – and honestly – that Agneta was no halfwit, she was a thorough schemer, a lustful schemer—'

'You – I don't recall it all, but of a certainty you never said *that*!'

'Yes, I did. And that she played on the sympathy of her family so as to be treated as simple and guileless—'

'She *was* simple! That night she came to see you! And you forget she came three or four times more! She *was* simple—'

'It was play-acting! Of course I won't pretend she was as intelligent as you are, nor as Mr Justice Stepmother here, but she knew how to put on a half-witted performance; she knew how to get what she wanted, chiefly the sensation of having a man between her legs. She was no innocent. Half the footloose men of the village, I'll lay a curse, knew her well. And no doubt it was while she was out with one of them that there was a quarrel of some sort and he lost his temper and used his knife on her—'

George stood up. '*Enough* of this. Have done with your domestic wrangling – I will have *no more* of it here. Understand!'

Harriet said: 'Agreed. Maybe we can get no further at this stage. If this *were* a court of law, which God forbid, there would be only one expert witness I would call.'

'Pray who would that be?'

'Dr Dwight Enys.'

'He gave his evidence at the inquest.'

'I know. But what did he say?'

'They all kept tactfully off the question of Agneta's wayward intellect. Perhaps they felt if they raised it there would be too many available to testify to her animal good sense.'

After a moment Harriet said thoughtfully: 'I believe, Valentine, that with a little tuition, you could talk your way out of anything.'

Simpson came into the room. 'You rang, sir?'

'Yes, the footmen may come back. Continue to serve dinner. And tell Miss Ursula she may return.'

Selina went back to Place House, with her retinue of baby Georgie and two servants. She stayed for a week and then left for London, taking Georgie and the nurse with her. Valentine had had to go to Padstow, and when he returned he found a brief note.

I am leaving you and shall live in Finsbury with Mrs Osworth and my two stepdaughters. I have taken a few personal things; those which are valuable so that I may sell them and maintain myself. Pray do not attempt to follow me.
    Selina

The day before she left she called to see Ross. Somebody had told her that Demelza went to dinner at Caroline Enys's every Thursday, so there was an element of contrivance in the hour and day she chose to arrive. Ross had been up at the mine going through the cost books with Ben, which also was a regular arrangement. It was another good day, with a corn-red sun glinting in and out of prison bars of cloud, and the sea very grumpy and very quiet. As he walked back across the beach, gulls and other seabirds clustered together in protest meetings which, Ross thought, had they been human beings, would now be legally forbidden them.

The horse was tethered to a branch of the old lilac. Ross did not recognize it. He went in, and Matthew Mark Martin whispered: 'Mrs Warleggan.'

Ross stared. 'Which one?'

'Mr Valentine's wife, sur.'

Selina was in the old sitting room. Neither Ross nor Demelza thought it strange that visitors should automatically be shown in here instead of into the much more elegant library.

She had taken some care with her appearance: a purple pleated riding habit with a divided skirt, which had a longer plum-coloured skirt under it, a peaked black cap, black patent half-boots, pale yellow lace at wrist and throat. Ross had forgotten what a handsome woman she was, with her slim figure, glazed cat's eyes, ash fair hair. He remembered there had been a time while Mr Pope was still alive, when there had been rumours that she and Jeremy were becoming too friendly.

'Sir Ross. Forgive me for this intrusion. Is your wife not here?'

'No, she is at the Enyses. Can I deputize for her?'

'Well, it is you I actually came to see.'

'Please sit down. Take some refreshment after your ride?'

'No, thank you.' She took a seat and looked through the sunlit window. 'Your wife has made a wonderful garden. We seem to be so blown to pieces at Place House that very little will flourish.'

'A protective wall has worked wonders. The soil is very shallow and what there is is not rich in humus, but if you can keep the wind out you can grow almost anything.'

'We have a part-walled garden, but it is chiefly for raising vegetables and fruit.'

The subject seemed to have exhausted itself.

Ross said: 'I am very glad anyway that you have decided to return to Place. I think it will—'

'Oh, but I have not,' she said.

He looked at her. 'You have not?'

'No. I am leaving for London tomorrow.'

'Oh? You mean – for a holiday – or to stay?'

'To stay.'

'Does Valentine approve?'

'He does not yet know.'

Ross thought about that. 'He will not approve. Will he allow it?'

'I shall be gone before he knows.'

'Oh . . . But you came to tell me?'

She looked at him slant-eyed. 'Do you remember after my first husband died I came to ask your advice on a number of things?'

149

'It was chiefly on a question of mining rights, I believe.'

'You advised me well, were generally helpful. Also, you are almost closest of anyone to Valentine. I thought you should know.'

'But you have already come to your decision. My advice can hardly be that important.'

'I should welcome your opinion.'

'On your actually *leaving* Valentine?' Ross fingered his scar. 'Is it not a wife's duty to stand by her husband when he is in trouble?'

'It depends what sort of trouble.'

'My advice, Selina, which clearly you have not come to seek, is that if, after a close weighing of the circumstances, you feel you can no longer live with Valentine, then you must leave him. But if you leave him now, at this present, you will be doing him a greater disservice than depriving him of your company.'

'You mean Baby Georgie. Yes, I—'

'I do not mean Baby Georgie. I mean that you will lend extra credence to the rumour that he murdered the girl.'

'But officers went across to Ireland and took the evidence of two witnesses. That all came out at the inquest.'

'Who believes the oath of an Irishman? That is what I heard only yesterday. Rumours will continue to circulate. Only he had the motive – or so it seems. If his wife then flees from him with their child, it will suggest that she agrees with them.'

Selina looked stormy. 'And do they not think that an excess of infidelities – ending in the seduction of a halfwit – do they not think that that of itself is a good enough reason to go?'

'His friends will. But not his enemies. And he has a sufficiency of enemies.'

'Whose fault is that? He has made them.'

Ross nodded. 'Even so. I think also, Selina, in his own peculiar way he is deeply attached to you and will greatly miss you.'

'I have made up my mind,' she said. Her jaw, he noticed, was quite tight.

'Have you resources to follow this intention?'

'He has my money, of course. Has spent most of it in various commercial adventures – that is, what he has not squandered on his wenching. I have some jewellery which has a value. And I have a property in Finsbury, not extensive but it will suffice. Letitia and Maud are there and my cousin, Mrs Osworth. No doubt this should have all been included under the settlement, but I never told Valentine. He thinks it belongs to my cousin.'

'Indeed.'

'I never told Mr Pope neither.'

'But now you are telling me.'

She said: 'You are not likely to become my husband.'

Chapter Five

Later in the month Geoffrey Charles found Demelza in the garden, which was at its damp November ebb. He kissed her breezily and asked if Ross was around.

'He's on the beach with Harry. Some driftwood came ashore with the last tide, and Paul Daniel and others from Mellin are picking it over. It seems there's tobacco and a few bolts of cloth.'

Geoffrey Charles craned his neck. 'Ah, yes, I think I can see them. And how are you, my dearest aunt? *Ma foi*, you never look a day older.'

Demelza said: 'Does *ma foi* mean excuse me for a fib most abominable?'

'It does not, and you know it does not. After dear Jeremy died you were much changed. We all feared for you. Now your looks are back, and your spirits. I remark it every time I come.'

'Come more often then,' she said, and also peered over the wall. 'I think Ross is on his way home now. Why don't you wait?'

'Of course I'll wait. I really came to see you both, with the latest news sheet.'

'What? Oh, you're teasing me. How is Amadora, and little Juana?'

'Bravely, thank you.'

'Do you wish for a boy this time?'

'Amadora says she does. I do not at all mind. I suppose it would be good to perpetuate the Poldark name at Trenwith.'

They walked together out of the garden, across the sandy scrubland to the stile.

'By the way, your niece is doing well.'

'Oh, I am pleased to know it.'

'Vera, Juana's nursemaid, is emigrating with her husband, who is a miner, to Australia, so Esther has been promoted. It will give her more responsibility and better pay.'

'Lovely. So long as we don't tell Sam.'

They both laughed.

'In fact,' said Geoffrey Charles, 'there's truth in jest. Essie and Amadora suit each other so well that when the new baby arrives I could well imagine that another nursemaid will be engaged and Essie reserved as a special companion.'

The group of men on the beach had drawn nearer. They were laden with flotsam. Demelza waved and several waved back. Henry broke into a run, intent on outstripping his elders.

'Amadora,' said Geoffrey Charles, 'is still very shy. She does not easily mix with new people. She and Morwenna are the best of friends, but Morwenna can't bring herself to live in Trenwith because of its memories for her. Also she is a Protestant vicar's daughter. And Drake has his shipyard. They come, as you know, twice a year ... You mentioned Sam, perhaps half as a joke; but religion is partly at the bottom of Amadora's reticence and shyness. Papist is still a term of abuse in England. She still thinks some of the servants regard her as different, an alien, even a suspect alien. We laugh together about it, but it is there ... Esther is quite different. Esther of course goes to church, but she has no special attachment for Sam's church. She has been twice with Amadora to Mass in this Roman Catholic place near Truro and says she has enjoyed it. God knows what Sam would think if he ever got to hear!'

Henry was almost upon them, shouting his news with the good lungs that all the family had. A terrible pang stabbed in Demelza's breast, as a memory struck her of a similar scene a dozen or more years ago, only then it had been Jeremy who had been running through the marram grass towards her. She wondered if there was marram grass in Belgium.

The men from Mellin made their jolly but respectful greetings. Respect was not easily bestowed among the miners, but one of these two men had been a part of their lives all his life and was now a baronet, the other was a major and a veteran of Waterloo. Demelza of course was one of themselves, but none would have dreamed of taking liberties.

When they had trooped off with their booty and Henry had bounded away into the house in search of something to eat, Geoffrey Charles said: 'I came to tell you I had a letter today to say my father-in-law and my mother-in-law are to visit us at Christmas. We have invited them before, but they have been reluctant to undertake the voyage. Now they are coming Amadora is in a panic, and I am bidden to remain in Cornwall to be ready to greet them whenever they arrive in Falmouth.'

Ross said: 'It will, I hope, prove to them that their daughter is not living in the Savage Lands. Have they been to England before?'

'Times have been too stormy. But he is a great admirer of England and the English, so I hope we shall not disabuse him.'

'What are they called?' Demelza asked. 'You have told me, but . . .'

'Amador de Bertendona, that is his name. He is of a very old family and is a member of the Cortes and speaks good English. She's Portuguese. Her first name is Jacinta. She speaks no English – or did not when I first met her – she is learning, and last Easter spoke a few words, but it is still elementary. When I first asked permission to marry their daughter, she was the explosive stumbling block. He was thoughtful but very gracious. I believe it is his nature to be gracious. She opposed it bitterly, but between us we overcame her horror.'

'When will they likely be here?'

'About the twelfth of next month.'

Demelza said: 'Shall you give a party for them while they are with you?'

Geoffrey Charles looked at her interestedly, then laughed. 'You *must* see Amadora. I suggested just such a thing, but she said oh no, oh no, she would be far too nervous – *far* more nervous than when we gave a party for ourselves. But I believe the seed has been sown. All it requires is a visit from you bubbling with enthusiasm, and we shall carry the day.'

'Go on,' Ross said to Demelza. 'If you water the seeds you will carry the day.'

Geoffrey Charles laughed again.

'With bubbles?' Demelza asked.

'With bubbles.'

*

That evening Ben Carter called to see Demelza. His brother-in-law, Matthew Mark Martin, let him in. Demelza was practising a few hymn tunes on the pianoforte that Ross had bought for her at the time of Henry's christening, so for this meeting the larger and more elegant reception room was the accidental venue.

Demelza her husband had gone back to Trenwith with Geoffrey Charles and had not yet returned.

'Yes,' said Ben, frowning. 'I watched him go.'

'Ah.' Demelza sat down again on the piano stool. Ben was in his working clothes and he carried his cap, which he screwed between his strong fingers.

'I am not certain sure I should bother ye, ma'am, but I've been a small matter troubled o' thought 'bout my inclinations, and I had the mind t'ask your advice.'

'Oh,' said Demelza. 'Well, we can talk quite private here. That's if it is something private you wished to discuss.'

'Yes, that is so.' He took a seat on one of their smart blue-upholstered chairs as if he were afraid he would soil it. 'I still am lost 'ow to begin.'

'Is it something to do with the mine?'

'Oh, no. All goes well there, so long as the lodes is keenly . . .'

'Then?'

'To tell the truth, missus – I know I should not call ye that but—'

Demelza smiled. 'Tisn't important what you call me. Tell me what you have come about.'

He shifted and screwed his cap again. 'To tell the truth, I have a taking for your niece.'

Demelza looked completely startled. 'My niece? But I . . . Oh, do you mean Essie?'

He nodded and stared across the room.

'But – but what is there wrong with that? . . . Essie Carne? Who works at Trenwith? . . . That is good news surely, Ben. But is she – does she not feel the same?'

'She don't know how I feel.'

'And is that the problem?'

'The problem is I wished to have your thoughts 'bout my taking for your niece. Ye d'know the feeling I have long had for Clowance. That does not move, that does not change. But she have long been lost to me. Even now, although she be a widow, I d'know she is not for me. She will marry again some day, but twill not be to the likes of me. She maybe will marry that Lord that proposed to her once before. That would no doubt please you and Sir Ross. Or there's others interested. I—'

'Ben, stop a minute.'

He stopped.

'Clowance was never for you, Ben. I don't know why, for you grew up together and was always good one with the other. But that is the way it is sometimes. Stephen came on us unexpectedly, you might say; he came on *her* unexpectedly and once they had met there was no one else in the world for her. But at the time I told you – you remember we talked of it at the time of their marriage – I told you that it was Clowance's decision. *Nobody else's.* Not mine. Not her father's. I told you this: that it was our way and our belief – mine and Ross's – that our children should choose the person they would marry, without being under influence or pressure from us. Do you doubt that?'

'No, ma'am. I'm sorry. The words slipped out.'

Demelza put her fingers on a chord on the piano. 'Then I think they should slip in again.'

'I'm sorry,' said Ben again.

Demelza took a few deep breaths to cool her own temper.

'So now?'

'I 'ave only met Esther a half-dozen of times, and 'ave felt a taking for her. Except for Clowance tis the first girl I 'ave felt for ever in such a way. But I thought first before I made my manner of approaching to her I should first ask ye—'

'Ask me what?'

He smiled, half-apologetic. 'Ye have given me the answer.'

Demelza studied him. 'But I told you all this years ago, when Clowance and Stephen was married. In the old parlour. I remember exactly what we said about it all.'

'Yes, ma'am, I know – I remember well. But when there's all those dark nights lying alone and thinkin' of them being together – and thinkin' and wonderin' and having no one to say a word to 'bout it all, some'ow the remembrance of what you said don't stay quite as clear as it did ought to be, and ye begin to think things. I d'know full well that I'm not good 'nough for your family. Clowance is too good for any man I ever seen her with – she deserve a duke or such like . . . So now . . .'

'So now?'

'I 'ave the thought that I done the wrong thing coming to you like this—'

'You've done the right thing, Ben, if those were your thoughts, so that they can be cleared away – thrown out. Did you come to me for any other reason? . . . Or is it also that you think, because her mother is far off, that me as her aunt should be asked or told about your taking for her, *in place* of her mother?'

'Yes, that's so. But also – and this you have already answered, like – I thought twould be more proper if I was t'ask your permission.'

Demelza played another chord. This was more in tune than the last.

'Dear Ben, how long have I known you? Ever since you was born? You are Ross's godson. You are always welcome here. If you do not know that then nothing I can say now can convince you. If Clowance had chosen to marry you we should have welcomed you as our son-in-law. If you care for Essie, and Essie comes to care for you, nothing would be more pleasing to us both than that you should wed and be happy together. Is that well understood?'

'Well understood now, ma'am. And *thank* ee. I blame myself for ever bothering you.'

'Do you want this kept secret for the time being?'

'Twould be helpful to me.'

Chapter Six

Philip Prideaux called at Penrice Manor, a handsome two-storeyed house with projecting wings on the south coast near St Austell, and was shown into a small withdrawing room with extensive views over the deer park and the sea. It was a sunny December morning and the slanting sunlight seemed to make the sea paler than usual and the land darker, as if each were waiting for the promised rain.

Presently he was shown in to see the owner of the mansion. Sir Charles Brune Graves-Sawle was in his early fifties, and as one of the leading luminaries of the county was serving his term as High Sheriff of Cornwall. He was a short, spruce man with a military bearing, and he greeted Philip Prideaux, whom he had not met before, with friendly courtesy, as befitted someone distantly related.

A footman came in, and Rhenish wine and Madeira cake were served.

The baronet said conversationally: 'I'm told you took part in the great cavalry charge at Waterloo, Prideaux. Well done!'

'Who told you that, sir?'

'Friend of mine. William Rashleigh.'

Philip nodded. 'Yes, sir. I did. Though if I may correct an impression, it was not well done.'

Sir Charles's face sharpened. 'Why do you say that?'

'There may have been good tactical reasons for ordering the charge, but it was undisciplined. It succeeded and then was allowed to go far beyond the limits of a tactical success, and turned into a failure.'

'Wellington described it as a success.'

'Oh, yes, but he was defending the reputation of Uxbridge. And by the time he said that the battle was long since over.'

Sir Charles chewed reflectively. 'I have also heard that you do not like talking about this immortal charge.'

'True, sir. Nor of any part of the battle, which was so bloody, so relentless, so—'

'Otherwise my wife would very much like to meet you and hear your account. As would other of my friends.'

Philip adjusted his spectacles. 'It is only three and a half years yet. Perhaps there will come a time when I am less susceptible to the memories.'

'Yes, well – yes. You are enjoying your stay in the county, Captain?'

'Very much. And now with my new appointment I shall hope to make my home here.'

'Just so. Just so. It was about that that I wanted to see you. More wine?'

'Thank you.'

While he was sipping it, Sir Charles went to an ornate French desk and sorted some papers through. Philip gazed round the room at the formidable array of family portraits. When he had received the letter of invitation he had never heard the name Graves-Sawle.

'I have been talking to Lord Vacy about you,' said Sir Charles in his staccato voice, and came back to his chair with a couple of pages of what looked like names and figures. 'It seems to us, if you are now going to make your home among us, your presence could be put to greater use than the position you are about to occupy with the Duchy of Cornwall. That is to say, not as an alternative to your secretaryship but as a supplement to it.'

'I am studying archaeology.'

'That too I have been told. Both are rewarding occupations, studies, pursuits, call them what you will. I was going to suggest to you a third.'

Philip took off his glasses, put them away, the click of the case was the only sound in the room. 'Pray go on.'

'As High Sheriff, it is my responsibility to maintain law and order in this county. As you will suppose, this is something of a formality. I attend the Assizes, I fulfil a number of formal duties throughout the year, I have a position on the Prince of Wales's Duchy Council. But the actual maintenance of good behaviour within the county, that is left to a few constables and watchmen who are appointed for each substantial village and town. You do not need to be told that they are ill-paid, ill-found, and in the main grossly inefficient. In London they are called "Charlies". You know in what contempt they are generally held.'

'I can understand that.'

'In London crimes are committed with impunity. It was estimated recently that in England as a whole there is one criminal to every twenty-two of the population. In London it may well be more. The borough of Kensington, I am told, has an area of fifteen square miles. To protect the law-abiding population they have three constables and three boroughmen. All decrepit, some of them themselves corrupt. In Cornwall we have in general a peaceful population, but crime is greatly on the increase. Since the end of the war there has been a wave of thefts, brigandage and even murder.'

Philip nodded, and stared again at the surrounding ancestors.

'Recently in London,' said Sir Charles, 'horse patrols have been introduced, and a few dedicated detectives are now abroad. Some of these have had a modest success. But we do not have even these in Cornwall.'

Philip waited, but his host said no more. 'I cannot suppose that you wish me to do something in this matter?'

'Yes, that was exactly what was in my mind.'

'But in what form?'

'That could be decided in consultation if we could come to an agreement in principle that you would help us.'

'May I ask why you should invite – choose me?'

'That's not a difficult question to answer, Captain. First, you are a Cornishman – all right, a part-Cornishman – you have relatives, distant or close, all over the county. Second, you are a war veteran, and a distinguished ex-Guardsman – with a reputation for bravery under fire. You saved your colonel's life! Were there a medal to be struck for such actions you would most surely be awarded it. Third, you are young and energetic and, I think, ambitious to begin a new life. You used these last words about yourself in your application for this post with the Duchy of Cornwall.'

'Yes,' Philip acknowledged, resisting the impulse to replace his spectacles. 'But I am still very much in the dark as to what you would expect me to do. Are you suggesting that I should organize the constables and boroughmen into some – some more effective

160

force? Were the county to double the number of such men and pay them less inadequately, it would still be the smallest improvement. Surely. And petty crime could hardly be touched unless there were a radical reform of the laws to coincide with a serious attempt to reinforce them.'

Sir Charles dismissed this with a wave of his hand. 'We all know of the capital offences that it can be argued should not be capital offences. I am thinking of the most serious crimes: robbery with violence, all serious crimes against the person, especially unlawful killing. These are offences that are on the increase throughout the country, and Cornwall is not exempt; indeed, in the last year there have been five unsolved murders in Cornwall, which is as much as for the counties of Devon and Somerset put together!'

'You surprise me, Sir Charles.'

'Yes, well. Mind you, I am speaking of *unsolved* murders. There were three murders in the city of Plymouth alone, but these were crimes easily resolved: a wronged husband shot his wife, two sailors quarrelling in a bar, one killed the other. That sort of thing.'

'And there have been five unsolved murders in Cornwall this year?'

'Yes, one a merchant, one a farmer, in which the obvious motives were robbery. Apart from them, three young women have been killed, all in the same way, all in their twenties, with no apparent robbery or rape. These murders took place mainly in central Cornwall. Whether they were committed by the same person—. What are you smiling at, Captain Prideaux?'

Philip corrected his expression. 'Was I? Well, it could better be described as a rictus, sir, at the strangeness—'

'What exactly does that word mean?'

'Rictus? It means a smile without any laughter, sir. Perhaps it could almost be described as a smile of horror. You must, if you know my history, be aware of the paradox of this invitation—'

'I still do not follow you.'

'You are asking me to accept a charge from you – that is, if I take you aright – a charge, an invitation to enquire into these murders, to attempt to discover who the murderer is, when it is less than a year since I was before a court-martial for killing a black orderly in Jamaica!'

Sir Charles Graves-Sawle got up and went to the tall window, stared out at his deer peacefully feeding in the slanting sun.

'You were found not guilty.'

'I was found not guilty of murder. I was found guilty of man-slaughter but discharged because at the time I was near to death with blackwater fever and therefore it was held that I suffered from diminished responsibility. I was not exactly cashiered from the Army, but after the verdict, by which time I had recovered my responsibility, I was advised to retire.'

'Yes, I know this, I know this,' the other said impatiently. 'Or at least I did not know the precise details – and I do not want to learn them now! – but I was aware of the general circumstances. Are you telling me that because of this you believe yourself unfit to be considered for the position I am offering you?'

'Not exactly. But you asked me why I was smiling, and I tried to explain the smile.'

Sir Charles grunted. 'Tell me, Captain Prideaux: in your life how many men have you killed?'

'Oh . . . in the course of my career as a soldier? It would be hard to count. Probably over a dozen at Waterloo alone. But those were in the line of duty. It is because it was such a bloodbath that I prefer not to talk about it. One's dreams are sufficient . . .'

Sir Charles pulled the bell, said something to the footman, who presently returned with a decanter.

'Here, take a glass of this. Better for the liver than the Rhenish stuff.'

He was aware that his guest's hands were shaking, and he bobbled some of the brandy into a fresh glass and put it on the table before Philip.

'Have seen some active service myself, d'you know. In Holland in the Nineties. Have killed a few men myself. I don't think it ever greatly upset me. But of course this last battle far exceeded any other in ferocity and bloodshed. I can understand, I suppose, it leaving a mark on you.'

'You may well feel, then, that I am not the most suitable man to pursue your murderers.'

'I should not say that. It is a matter to ponder, no doubt. I may say I have discussed this with Sir Harry Trelawny, William Rashleigh and Lord Vacy. They do not see any let or hindrance in your own record. It is up to you, of course, how you interpret that record. Possibly you would like to consider the offer for a few days – let me know, say, by next Thursday week. Would that suit?'

Philip drank the brandy. The temporary emotion had passed – as more and more it was inclined to pass nowadays.

'That would suit me well,' he said.

Señor and Señora Amador de Bertendona arrived in England, three days late, on the fifteenth of December, their vessel having had to run into St Nazaire to shelter from a Biscay storm. They had both survived the ordeal pretty well, and after a night in Falmouth they travelled in a specially hired coach escorted by Geoffrey Charles and Juana, their little granddaughter, to Trenwith. Since there was no possibility of hauling a coach over the riding track across the desolate hump of Cornwall, they had to take the turn-pike to Truro, thence via Shortlanesend towards Marazanvose, where they crossed the other turnpike beside Werry House, where the Bodrugans lived, and struck the cart track, which persisted with a few unwelcome breaks until they reached the gates of Trenwith.

Geoffrey Charles, while apologizing for all the jerks and bumps, reflected ruefully that almost nothing had been done to improve the road since his mother was married in 1784. Thirty-five years of neglect.

His mother-in-law, he felt, would by now be looking sour and ill were it not for the presence of her beloved granddaughter, who occasionally gave squeals of excited amusement when the coach seemed about to overturn. It had been a stroke of genius on Amadora's part that the little girl should accompany her father to Falmouth. Juana had had almost three days to wait in Falmouth and had greatly enjoyed having her father entirely to herself.

As they drove up towards the house the sky behind was lit by the afterglow, and this, together with the winking lights just appearing in the house itself, made an impressive picture. Although the sea could not be seen from here, its proximity gave space and character to the position of the house: it was an invisible presence. Geoffrey Charles could see that both Amadora's parents had been expecting something smaller and perhaps even a trifle shoddy. Trenwith, its bulk and its design, satisfied them both. And there at the open front door was their own beloved daughter to receive them.

Geoffrey Charles and Amadora had planned their party for the twenty-first. They felt they could not wait to fix a date until her parents arrived because they wanted it to have a Christmas feel, and the guests must be given adequate time to reply. But because of the delay in arrival there was hardly adequate time to prepare the de Bertendonas for the prospect before them. Señor de Bertendona caught a chill and was in bed for two days. As a result there was little opportunity for relatives and friends to meet the distinguished visitors before the day of the party.

Geoffrey Charles came over to Nampara to explain the position and to arrange for the loan of three servants to swell those already hired. On his way out Demelza said she wanted to ask a favour of him. Would he invite Ben Carter as an extra guest?

Geoffrey Charles stared, half smiling. 'Who? Ben who?'

'Carter. You know him well enough. He manages Wheal Leisure.'

'Yes, of course. His name had not come to mind, but I have no objection.'

'I doubt if he would come,' Ross said, who had returned at that moment. 'What is in your mind, my dear?'

'Well, ask him,' Demelza said to Geoffrey Charles. 'Would you?'

'Of course. He's a decent enough fellow. I'll send someone over.'

'I don't think he will be too much out of his element,' Demelza said. 'Drake will be there. And Sam, if we can persuade him. And one or two others you've known all your life, Geoffrey Charles.'

'The invitation will go as soon as I get back.'

When he had gone Ross put an arm round his wife and pinched her. 'What is this little game you are playing?'

'That's cheeky,' she said. 'Gentlemen don't behave like that.'

'By now you must know better how gentlemen can behave. Anyway I'll wager Ben will not come. He does not have the clothes, for one thing.'

'I have the thought that you have too many clothes, Ross. Too many *old* clothes. You could give him a suit of yours and would not miss it.'

'It wouldn't *fit* him,' said Ross derisively. 'You must see that.'

'I think it might fit fair about the shoulders. Of course you are a little taller. Six inches maybe.'

'Nearer eight.'

'Scissors could see to that.'

'And who, pray, would wield the scissors?'

'I thought his mother might help if I asked her. Jinny was always handy with a needle.'

'You have some weird idea of bringing the poor fellow into society. You are not trying to contrive something between him and Clowance – at this late hour?'

'Certainly not. Certainly not. That would never happen.'

Ross was thoughtful. 'D'you remember Julia's christening? How we tried to invite your folk one day and my folk the next.'

'You don't need to remind me of that! But that was a – a calamity entirely brought about by my father's wrong-headedness.'

'And Jud's, no doubt.'

'I am only trying to bring Ben out a little bit. After all, he is your godson and we have not done all that for him.'

'True. But after long, long years of being married to you I have developed a sixth sense when you are plotting something untoward.'

'Yes, what long, long years they have been,' said Demelza. 'I wonder what dress I shall wear. Should I have something fresh? Are they very grand people, Amadora's parents?'

'Not as grand as many you have met. I wonder if George will come.'

'Geoffrey Charles has invited him. He told me. He feels they have had many favours from Lady Harriet.'

'And George happens to be his stepfather. The last time we met at Trenwith there was rather a nasty scene between us.'

'In my memory I can hardly recall any occasion when you met George at Trenwith and there was not a nasty scene!'

'Well, have no fear; we shall not come to blows this time. Both far too old and far too cautious.'

'Mind you keep to that,' she said, content that she had steered him away from the subject of Ben. There was no reason whatever why he should not know of Ben's new taking; but she was happier plotting on her own. Manipulating a situation in which Ben and Essie had an opportunity of a closer meeting required a tactful delicacy of touch. If he knew, Ross, with the best will in the world, might accidentally upset the applecart.

Meggy Dawes had always told Demelza that winter began in Cornwall on the twenty-first of January. Demelza thought of this when the twenty-first of December dawned with still weather, a light cloud cover and a somnolent sea.

There were to be about fifty guests. Geoffrey Charles, having been in the Army so long and absent from Cornwall so much, did not possess a wide circle of local friends, but he had made a number of Cornish friends in the Army, and ten of them accepted his invitation. There was a John Trelawny from Trelawn, a Vyel Vyvyan from Trelowarren, a Harry Beauchamp from Pengreep, and Tom Gregor from Trewarthenick. He had talked over with Ross what other members of the county families might be invited, and they had agreed to ask some. But the dark days, the winter rain, the muddy lanes were against them.

Lord Falmouth sent a friendly letter to Ross asking him to explain to his cousin that he had 'almost a full house' himself and, much as he would like to, he could not desert them. Knowing Falmouth's rigid opposition to any form of Catholic emancipation, Ross wondered if this might be a tactical excuse. He had heard a rumour that when the old King died the Viscount might be made an Earl.

Two days before the party Drake arrived with his beloved wife Morwenna and their daughter Loveday, bearing a present for Amadora: one of Drake's special rocking chairs, skilfully fashioned by him on winter evenings, of beech and stripped willow. He had first made one for Morwenna, and then, when it was much admired, one for Demelza. Next day he headed an expedition into the more wooded hinterland of the north coast, near Werry House and beyond, in search of holly – especially berried holly – and ivy – especially variegated ivy – to bring back to decorate the house.

All these woods were stunted in growth, sheltering from the savage winds by flourishing only in shallow valleys or on slopes slanting down to desolate streams. But there was much to be found here even in midwinter: pockets of primroses already flowering, the sharp, spiked, grey promise of daffodils thrusting through a cushion of fallen leaves and hart's tongue ferns – once an ungainly apple tree hung with the remains of wild clematis and looking like an elderly lady in Russian sables. And here and there, especially in the Idless Valley, they found a few sprigs of mistletoe! This was brought home with special care lest the berries should drop off. Demelza, who could not be kept away from this expedition, said she had been told in Illuggan as a little girl that once upon a time the mistletoe had been a fine tree, but because its wood had been used to make the Cross it had ever after been condemned to live only as a parasite.

Christopher and Isabella-Rose arrived too late for this adventure, but took part in decorating the dining hall. A small band which had been hired to play in the minstrel gallery had called in a day early to test the acoustics of the hall and to see to the general arrangements. Once and again Bella could be heard raising her voice in a pure gentle trill, but she was careful not to impose herself on the scene.

Among those on the hunt for greenery were Paul and Mary Kellow and Daisy. Daisy now had a deep loose cough, which sounded menacing, but she made little of it and tramped with the best. Paul's wife, it seemed, had quite recovered from the scrofulous tumour, so the Kellow family was in a good mood.

The party began at one p.m. and dinner was at two-thirty. Among the other guests were Dwight and Caroline Enys, with their two tall daughters, Sophie, aged sixteen, and Meliora, fifteen; Philip Prideaux, who had wanted to accompany Clowance, but Clowance had crossed the county two days before; Cuby Poldark, with Noelle, and Clemency Trevanion to keep them company; and Emmeline Treneglos, representing her parents, who preferred to nurse their bereavement and resentment against anyone with the Poldark name.

Señor de Bertendona, now fortunately recovered, stood with his plump little wife in the smaller entrance hall to welcome the guests, and Geoffrey Charles was there to make the introductions, with Amadora beside him to translate for her mother.

Slowly the big drawing room on the first floor filled up, and some guests drifted into the great hall, where the table was set for dinner. Chairs had been a problem, and – with Place House and Mingoose House more or less out of bounds because of Agneta –

Nampara, Killewarren and Fernmore had been stripped of their dining chairs, and even of chairs which one could make believe were dining chairs only for a special occasion.

'There has never been so large a party in this house,' Ross told Geoffrey Charles, 'not even the wedding party when your father and mother were married.'

Because of de Bertendona's indisposition, Ross had not met them before, and Demelza had met only the Señora. They bowed to each other, clasped hands, murmured greetings in two languages, while Geoffrey Charles went into flattering details of his relationship with his cousins. They all smiled and bowed again and were about to pass on when Ross bent and kissed Señora de Bertendona.

It seemed to surprise everyone present, not least Demelza, who had never suspected her husband of extravagant gestures.

(Later, just as they were about to go in to dinner, Amadora exchanged a private word with her mother. The plump little lady was still looking slightly flustered. She said: 'What a grand party you are giving for us, Dora! . . . But that man! . . . Sir Ross, did you say? When he bent towards me, I thought, he is taking the *greatest* liberty! What an oaf! How ill-mannered! How typical of a clumsy Englishman to behave so! And then I looked up. And up. And I thought, what a man, how handsome! And oooh! My toes twisted and curled! And he speaks *Portuguese*. . .!')

Before they went in to dinner, Demelza whispered: 'Well, my dear, that was the first shock of the evening!'

'What was?'

'You embracing the important lady.'

'I did not embrace her. I implanted a gentle welcoming kiss on her powdered cheek.'

'Cheek? It didn't look like that to me. She was aghast. So was he. You might have started a war!'

'Perhaps I have now,' Ross said, squeezing her hand.

'If you behave like this when I am present, I tremble to think what you do when I am not!'

'I just *felt* like it,' said Ross. 'The poor woman is in a strange land, surrounded by foreigners. She can scarcely speak a word of English and does not much like us as a race. Would you begrudge her a friendly salutation?'

'And you were *chattering away*! I did not know you knew Spanish!'

'I don't. Or very little. That was Portuguese.'

'Judas!' said Demelza. 'What next?'

'You forget,' he said, 'that I was part of the delegation to escort the Portuguese royal family from Lisbon to Brazil in '07. On the voyage I used to play backgammon with the Prince Regent almost every night . . . He called it *tric-trac*.'

In fact Ross's sudden impulse had grown out of a sensation of cheerful rebelliousness which had come upon him during the last few days. There was no obvious cause for it, but it had never been in his nature to abide by the courtesies of strict good behaviour, and the life he was at present leading – as Valentine had once perceptively pointed out – was slightly humdrum – pleasantly so – but humdrum all the same. He felt he wanted to kick free from the many tiny restraints that beset him, agreeable though they usually were.

He missed his contacts with George Canning – and sometimes with those dissidents and known Radicals. (It was perverse and odd and perplexing, he thought, that although his sympathies were with Major Cartwright, Samuel Bamford, Robert Owen and the rest, circumstances had as often as not pushed him into the opposite camp and he had acted to preserve the stability of the status quo.)

Almost last to arrive at the party were Sam and Rosina, and with them was Ben Carter. Demelza by her choice of clothes, and Jinny by her cuts and hasty stitchings, had made a very presentable job of dressing this fierce young man. A cream-coloured muslin cravat tied so loosely that it was not greatly different from the knotted red scarf he usually affected, a blue velvet jacket with brass buttons, a cream-coloured waistcoat and black buckskin breeches, with his own best boots. The brass buttons would not comfortably fasten at the waist, for Ross, for all his age and height, was of the lean kind. And the mine barber, Parsons, had been called in to trim Ben's beard very short, so that it narrowed almost to an imperial.

When they finally sat down Demelza thought he looked in no way different from anyone else. It being almost Christmas, some of the other guests had arrived wearing what might be described as a jolly approach to fancy dress. In this great hall, with its enormous window, the whole festooned with holly and ivy and a dab here and there of mistletoe, sixty candles wavering in the warm and errant air, the long table fairly groaning under its weight of enticing food. Wine bottles, silver dishes, decanters, knives and forks in serried array, chicken and turkey and goose and lobster, and soups and a hashed calf's head and boiled bacon, and whole cauliflowers decorated with sprigs of holly, and baked and fried potatoes, and pigeon and rabbit pie and mackerel pie, and syllabubs and fruit and lashings of cream.

Esther Carne had told Amadora that she was astonished to be at the dinner party and that she would far, far rather work in the kitchen or even – horror of horrors – wait at table, than be treated as a 'guest'. Amadora told her that as a newly joined member of the staff and principal nurse to Juana she must take her proper place and be available to be called on at a moment's notice if she, Amadora, required anything during the meal. Since Amadora had long since grown out of her morning sickness, Esther was perplexed as to what use she might be at the dinner, but she did not argue. Even when Ben Carter took the seat next to her she did not suspect any contrivance.

As usual she blushed to the roots of her hair – combed and brushed and dressed pleasantly but unpretentiously for the party – and glanced in fright at him, then was relieved to see him half smile, and she curled up her lips tremulously in return. She was wearing a simple dress of cerise-coloured cotton that Amadora had lent her, and it did no harm to her looks or her complexion.

'I didn't expect to see you here then,' lied Ben.

'Nor me you neither,' said Essie, more truthfully, plucking nervously at the shoulder of her dress.

Looking down the table Ross saw that George had been placed next to Mrs Harry Beauchamp of Pengreep. It was a safe pairing: the Beauchamps were unmistakeably county, and Mrs B could chatter with the best. On George's other side was Faith, the eldest of three unmarried Teague sisters, whose youngest sister was the bereaved Ruth Treneglos. Another safe placing: George and Faith had known each other in a casual way for thirty years. Ross counted that he was seven places south-west of George and on the other side. They had nodded on seeing each other, and that was all that was necessary.

He turned to his own dining companions and wondered if Geoffrey Charles was exhibiting an unexpected sense of mischief.

'Lady Harriet,' he said. 'I need not ask you if you are well.'

She was wearing yellow silk tonight, which did not quite suit her.

'Sir Ross,' she said in her husky voice. 'You need not. I am never ill. Are you?'

'Seldom.'

'And you are now leading a retired life?'

'Yes. But occupied.'

'All retired lives are occupied; it is a form of frittering.'

'What is not?' Ross returned. 'Hunting, fighting, cubbing, loving?'

She was silent at this, then said: 'Is Valentine here tonight?'

'I don't think he was invited.'

'Ah. Perhaps as well. Is he ostracized?'

'Not really. He is busy with this enterprise he has begun, shipping goods to Ireland.'

'Legitimate?'

'I have no idea.'

'Diplomatic as ever.'

'I did not know I had that reputation.'

'You do not with George . . . You did not with me the first time we met.'

'First time?'

'You do not remember. We quarrelled over a horse. And the second time we met we quarrelled over a dance.'

Ross examined her thoughtfully for a few moments. 'At the risk of being thought undiplomatic, madam, my memory of these events is quite different.'

They were served with French pâté, brought from Brittany that morning.

Harriet said: 'Pray go on.'

'Quarrel seems rather over-dramatic a word for our encounter at the horse sale. And if there was a substantial difference of opinion it was between myself and George, not between myself and you.'

'It was my horse!'

'Not at all! It only became yours in the end.'

'You are splitting hairs.'

'And as for quarrelling over a dance, Lady Harriet, my memory is that you were trying to teach me the waltz and I was rather a clumsy learner.'

'Quarrel I suppose was meant as a tease. Your first attempts at an entirely new sort of dance were quite admirable. You never stumbled, fell, trod on my toes, kicked my shins, tore my dress or damned my eyes.'

'You have very beautiful eyes,' Ross said, 'and that I would never dare to do.'

Harriet laughed lazily. 'Is there to be a dance tonight, do you know? I see we have the fiddlers. But this great table . . .'

'That other party Geoffrey Charles gave – it must be six years ago – he took up the table, turned it against the back wall, under the window. But it meant breaking the slate floor. Possibly, if the room were cleared of everything else it might be possible to dance round it.'

'I would like to dance around it,' said Harriet. 'Perhaps you will invite me . . .'

Chapter Seven

Philip Prideaux said: 'I am grateful to Geoffrey Charles for arranging the table so that I may have the privilege of sitting next to you, Mrs Carrington. Shall you be staying with your family for some time after the party?'

'Probably until Sunday. I should be back in Penryn on Monday morning . . . Captain Prideaux.'

He adjusted his glasses. 'Yes?'

'We do not know each other very well, but I have been your guest at two concerts and there have been numerous – encounters. In these circumstances, do you think it might be appropriate to stop calling me Mrs Carrington?'

'What else might I call you?' His Adam's apple moved as he swallowed. 'By your first name? Clowance? I should esteem it the highest privilege.'

'I don't believe it is such a privilege as all that, Philip. But in these country districts in which we live I do not feel we need to preserve the formalities of high society.'

'I am honoured indeed! You give me the courage to ask another favour.' She looked at him enquiringly. He smiled at her. 'Allow me on Sunday to escort you home.'

'But shall you not be leaving tomorrow?'

'Geoffrey Charles will not, I'm sure, object to my staying two more nights. However good his servants, there will be much tidying up to do.'

At the other end of the table Essie whispered: 'I cannot begin to guess which fork to use.'

'Nor me neether,' said Ben. 'That young woman opposite is using the little one.'

' 's, I see.'

There was plenty of talk going on around them but none between them. Essie was overawed, Ben tongue-tied, wanting to talk but lacking trivial conversation. He knew what he wanted but he couldn't say it out loud in this company.

'Tes some hot in 'ere,' he adventured.

'I never thought I should come and sit here like this,' Essie said. 'Like a guest. Like a high-up guest. I've the notion that Aunt Demelza have put the mistress up to it, but gracious knows why.'

Ben stared across the table. It seemed to him that Essie had put her finger accidentally on the truth. But she didn't seem to have the least idea in the world about the purpose. As she had just said: 'Gracious knows why.'

He found he was staring far too long at the lady on the opposite side of the table, Miss Daisy Kellow. Daisy smiled at him, as she would smile at any good-looking man of eligible age, and he dropped his gaze in embarrassment. He realized she had not recognized him.

Perhaps others had not. Perhaps the lady on his left had not, Miss Hope Teague, because his beard was shorter than it had ever been before in all his adult life, until it was really a Van Dyke, the corner of the scar just showing. Anyhow, was it likely that Miss Hope, the most desiccated of Ruth's unmarried sisters, would see any resemblance between this trimly dressed if rough-spoken gentleman and the uncommunicative, sullen man who strode past their house, head down against the wind, on his way to work at Wheal Leisure?

At the top of the table Señor de Bertendona sat flanked by his wife: on her right was Geoffrey Charles, with Demelza beside him; on the Señor's left was Amadora, and beyond her Dwight Enys.

'Philip.'

'Yes, Clowance?'

'May I make an enquiry of you? Perhaps it may seem an impertinence, an intrusion upon a – a personal matter which should not concern me . . .'

'I'm sure you may ask anything of me you wish.'

'Well,' said Clowance, 'I wonder why you have just put on those eye glasses?'

Philip's expression changed. He stared in front of him. 'You must know why people wear glasses – it is to see the better.'

'Of course. Is it at short distance or at long that you need them?'

'Short.'

'Yet – excuse me – you were able to see your name on the plate to know where you shall sit.'

'That is not writ very small. Perhaps,' he looked up, 'my wish guided me to the right seat.'

'Oh, come.' She took out her little gold watch. 'What is the time by this?'

'Twenty minutes after four.'

'The face and figures are quite small.'

'Yes, they are quite small.'

The plates were being cleared away and new ones laid for the dessert.

'Sometimes eye glasses, Miss Clowance, serve an extra purpose.'

'Can you instruct me?'

'Of course.' But he made no attempt to do so.

Christopher Havergal said to Demelza: 'Lady Poldark, I have had little opportunity since we arrived of bringing you up to date with happenings in London. Of course Bella has written you regularly, I know, and she will have told you the more important things. Also, since we came home you will have seen much of her.'

'That I have,' said Demelza. 'But it has been a trifle come and go, so to say, with so many people in the house and much talk of this party. I take it you will stay over the New Year?'

'Gladly. Thank you. Then I must return. Bella could stay another week.'

'I should like her to stay.'

'Indeed. So should I. She deserves a holiday. Perhaps it will depend on whether she can find someone to travel with her.'

'Ross can ask around. Friends at his bank are often travelling.'

'How do you think Bella looks?'

'No different. But she *is* different. Some of the girlishness has gone.'

'I know. I'm sorry. But perhaps it would go naturally, in any event. She has developed in personality. She will, I believe, be a great personality in a concert room.'

'I'm sure.'

'She told you, no doubt, about the concert Mrs Pelham gave on her birthday in October. That was a great success. And Mrs Pelham is doing so much for us, she knows many influential people. We had one great disappointment earlier this month. Did she tell you of that?'

'I don't think so.'

'At the birthday dinner party was a man called the Hon. Charles Wynford, who is a great friend of the Prince Regent. He vowed himself greatly impressed with Bella's singing, and he arranged to give a party on the third of December, where she was to be one of three singers, and the Prince Regent had promised to be present.'

'And did he not come?'

'He was laid up with some illness (the newspapers speculate but no one can be sure), and if the old King dies it will even be a matter of some doubt whether the Regent will be well enough to succeed.'

'And who will succeed if he cannot?'

'Prince William.'

'He has not a very good reputation either,' said Demelza.

'Of course the Regent may pull round, but it destroyed our plans, at least for that evening.'

'How old is the old King?'

'Eighty-one or eighty-two. But he is completely blind and mostly insane. It would be vital to Bella's advancement if she were to receive some sort of royal approval . . .'

'She is still very young, Christopher.'

Christopher looked at Demelza and stroked his moustache. 'Yes, there is time. But it was a great opportunity that went by the board. Without seeming to press the point I will continue to seek Wynford's friendship. I do not think he is well to do, and in my banking profession there may come an opportunity to do him a good turn. After all, his impulse to promote Bella was entirely selfless.'

Ben said: 'Your brothers are miners?'

'Haven't got no brothers.'

'Oh, uncles then. There be no work around Illuggan?'

'Precious little.'

'There's little round 'ere. Grace is finished. Only Leisure is still kindly.'

'Thanks be, I say. An' you are manager?'

'More or less. Y'see in big mines there's a mine cap'n and a grass

176

cap'n. Leisure be scarce that big, but my grandfather, Zacky Martin, is manager in charge, but he's oft too sick to do it, so I do both jobs, like.'

'An' Wheal Grace?'

'Sir Ross keep her open. Forty on the pay roll. There's always the hope we maybe strike lucky again. Twas a rare money-maker over ten or more years. Big money. That's 'ow Cap'n Ross can keep open Grace even though of late she's not paying for herself.'

Essie stared suspiciously at the fruit, quartered and peeled, that had appeared on her plate.

'Is it oranges?'

'Reckon so.'

'Don't think I ever tasted one.'

'Try it. Do you good.'

Esther glanced around the table and nervously picked up a spoon and fork.

'D'ye like music?' he asked.

'That's nice, what they're playing now.'

'D'ye like organ music?'

'Dunno as I've ever heard it. D'ye mean like a harmonium? Like they have in some of the big churches?'

'Yes.'

'I've hardly heard anything of it. Why?'

'I built one,' said Ben.

She looked at his dark, forbidding face. 'Sam told me you had done something like that. That's wondrous clever, Mr Carter.'

He shook his head. ''Tis only a knack. An arrangement of pipes. Some folk d'call it a box o' whistles.'

She sensed that now there was something he would like to talk about.

'Sam said you'd built one over your mother's shop.'

'Yes, that be so. But when I moved to me own little cottage I left all that behind and began anew. This one's just finished and it's much betterer than the old one. Pipes are bigger, an' the wind-chest too, and I got me new wooden sliders that make all the difference.'

She hesitated and swallowed, but now was the time if ever, if ever.

'I'd dearly love t'see it, Mr Carter, sometime, maybe if you've the time. Does it play? Can you play tunes on it?'

He looked at her, and his black eyes kindled. 'Oh yes,' he said. 'Oh yes.'

Amadora had taken the nod from Geoffrey Charles, and got to her feet. All rose, and presently the ladies separated themselves out and proceeded to leave the room in chattering twos and threes. The last had hardly swished and rustled out of sight when a man's voice could be heard in the entrance hall raised in amused complaint. Several of the men who were about to resume their seats remained standing.

Valentine came in, followed by a plump, rosy-cheeked man of about his own age. They were both well dressed, but carelessly so. Valentine's cravat needed retying; his companion had lost the top two buttons of his military tunic, and his hair was awry.

'My dear GC,' Valentine said, and took his half-brother's hand. 'I know you thought I was away, but when I came home unexpectedly I felt I could not disappoint you for your party! . . . Have we missed the feast? The ladies are vanished! Never mind, we'll join in a glass of port. Oh . . . do you know Lieutenant Lake? He was my fag at Eton – for one term. We had many adventures together. Eh?' Valentine laughed infectiously. 'David knew Jeremy in Brussels, they were both in the same damn' regiment together. What was it, David?'

'Fifty-second Oxfordshires.'

'Used to gamble together too,' Valentine said. 'David and Jeremy used to gamble together. Eh? Great gambler, Jeremy, by God. Lost a lot, didn't he, David?'

'What?' said Lake. 'I've forgot. Expect he pro-probably did. Everyone seemed to lose. No one won. Is – is Cuby here?'

Valentine said: 'Is Cuby here?'

'Yes.'

'Great gathering this. May I?' He took the vacant chair opposite Paul Kellow and waved David Lake to another. 'My father, Sir George, my godfather, Sir Ross, this is Lieutenant Lake of the Fifty-something Oxfordshires. Went through Waterloo without a damn' scratch. As you did, GC, by God. Takes a clever man to go through a battle like that without a scratch. Though you got a number of scratches before that, GC. Blood and bones, this is good port! Did you run it or buy it?'

'Bought it at a reduced price,' said Geoffrey Charles, 'knowing it had been run.'

Valentine stretched his legs. 'You've a fine selection of the county here, Cousin, I must say. I nearly brought Butto.'

'Butto?'

'My pet monkey. Got him off a lascar in Falmouth Dock a few weeks ago. Twas lonely without Selina, don't you know!' He snorted with laughter. 'Nice cuddly thing. Though not so little and not so cuddly now – he grows apace! My friends make much of him – spoil him rather.'

'A monkey,' said someone. 'That's a trifle queer. What sort of monkey?'

'Damned if I know. Biggish. Scares the women.'

'Should not fancy having a monkey round the house,' said Harry Beauchamp. 'You getting eccentric, Warleggan?'

'Always have been, old boy. Used to pets at school, d'you know. My school anyway. Popsy Portland had a snake, claimed he fed it on mice. Johnny Russell kept an owl that would perch on his head. Nick Waldegrave kept a long-tailed monkey – not at all like Butto, I must say! Well, it all adds to the fun!'

In the meantime Geoffrey Charles had decided to ignore his uninvited guests, and was superintending the clearing of the great table of all except the decanters of port. The band, after a pause for their own refreshment, struck up again.

When the ladies returned most of the men were still sitting over their port, but under discreet persuasion they got up and went about their own affairs while the chairs were swept away and the floor sanded. Groups of armchairs situated at each corner of the room were set out for those who by inclination or expectation were inclined to sit and watch. The room, even with its vast central table, looked much bigger with this arrangement, and it was clear that there would be room enough to dance, though country dances, usually group dances, would not be practicable.

So the evening went pleasantly by, beginning with a minuet, followed by a gavotte and then the ever-popular waltz. At the second gavotte Vyel Vyvyan, who always had an eye for good looks, asked Demelza to dance with him. Having watched them safely launched, Ross went across to ask Lady Harriet. She was talking to Harry Beauchamp, and George was close by, standing hands clasped behind back, watching the dancers with a calculating eye as if weighing up their realizable worth.

Harriet looked at Ross, pretended to fumble in her bag. 'Sir Ross. Let me see, have I got you on my card?'

'It's on your mental card, ma'am. You pledged it between the plums and the cheese.'

Harriet sighed. 'Ah yes. Between the plums and the cheese. I do remember. You'll pardon me, Mr Beauchamp. I shall hope to resume our conversation later.'

When they were on the floor Ross said: 'It hurts me to tear you away from such enlightening company.'

'So it should. I was being instructed in the way the Swiss build cuckoo clocks. But you might have chosen a less tedious dance than this.'

'There's a waltz to follow.'

'I am promised for that.'

'No you are not. Anyway I have possessory rights.'

'Oh, la. I feel faint. Who is that you were nodding to?'

'Your husband.'

'Oh, la, again. You and he are oil and water, are you not? You don't mix. But both of value in their own way.'

Ross smiled grimly, but did not comment.

'Mayhap some day,' she said, 'I can bring your heads together.'

'To bang them?'

'Yes, possibly.'

'We have tried fisticuffs more than once, but the bloodletting has not eased matters.'

'Just exactly what have you got against him?'

'Dance with me till midnight and we might have made a start.'

A loud shout of laughter came from the end of the room, where Valentine was drinking with Christopher Havergal.

Harriet said: 'Why does not George invite your wife to dance?'

'Ask him. In any event she would refuse.'

'Has he done her some hurt?'

'Only . . . well, only that she has been wholly involved in the trouble he has tried to wreak on the Poldarks.'

'Then why do you ask me to dance?'

'Because I like you.'

'That reminds me, when I danced this tedious dance in my girlhood – about forty years ago – the exercise had a more interesting termination. After the last step the partners bowed and kissed.'

'Indeed,' said Ross. 'I have been waiting forty years for the opportunity.'

With Geoffrey Charles's permission but unknown to the rest of the company, Isabella-Rose had stolen up the spiral staircase to the minstrel's gallery and whispered a request for a special kind of waltz that she had danced in London. It was called a *valse à deux temps*, and was a quick six–in-a-measure dance with two steps to each measure. She and Christopher led off, he managing expertly with his false foot; and soon there were others on the floor. In a formal ball it might have been frowned on, but in this pre-Christmas dinner mood everyone took it as an excuse for high jinks.

Ross bent to kiss Harriet, she as willingly gave him her mouth. Then they were off. Surprisingly, it was a success. Grasping her brutally round the waist and holding her close to him, he slid and hopped and swirled, and somehow she kept her feet and avoided his. Someone had fallen down ahead of them, but they swayed past. In the middle of it all Ross was conscious of a voice trilling, a soprano's effortless ability to soar above the common noise. While she was dancing at top speed Bella still had the breath for using her voice in high clear spells. Ross suddenly felt very happy. For the first time since Jeremy's death he knew himself to be *happy*. He had come to the dinner in a wayward eccentric mood, half-rebellious, half-pleasurable. Now suddenly, with this exciting woman in his arms, the beat of the music and the clear pure tones of his daughter's voice soaring at intervals above them all, he knew himself to be happy.

The dance at last came to a stop. Everyone was laughing and trying to get their breath.

Harriet's great dark eyes were darker than ever as she looked up at Ross.

'By God!' she said. 'I thought you were lame.'

'By God!' said Ross. 'I had forgot it!'

They both laughed. People were moving off the floor.

'I must return you to your cuckoo clocks,' Ross said.

'Pray come again,' she said.

'I will.'

*

They had not joined in the dance, but for a while stood together in a corner watching, then they had drifted into the back parlour to drink lemonade. They said nothing, but neither showed any inclination to break away from the other. They were islanded by people of another class. But they were in no way ignored; other guests spoke freely to them; twice Esther excused herself briefly to see Amadora and ask if she could not help with the waiting on. She was smilingly refused.

When she came back the second time Ben said: 'Reckon you got a good mistress, eh? Reckon she must've caught it from the Poldarks.'

'Caught what, Ben?'

'Makin' friends of their servants. Was they like this at Tehidy?'

'Well, no . . . I didn't expect it there.'

'Did you expect it 'ere?'

She gave a little nervous spluttering laugh. 'Well, no. But I suppose I been upped a bit on account of Lady Poldark being my aunt.'

'I see,' said Ben grimly.

She was alerted by his tone. 'I've no wish nor thought to be anything more than what I were born to be. Tis their kindness, not my seeking.'

Ben looked at her carefully. 'I haven't the words, Essie. Not any of the words still. But I've a taking for you, Essie.'

She flushed. 'I'm glad, Ben.'

'You're – glad?'

'I'm glad.'

'Then look, I'll say no more now. D'ye ever get a day off?'

'Half a day.'

'I'll meet ee. Fix a date an' a time an' I'll meet ee. If there's some girl ye'd like to bring with ee – just for form's sake . . .'

Esther took a deep breath. 'I'll come alone.'

Chapter Eight

Four miles seemed a long ride home, but there was no opportunity for private conversation because Dwight and Caroline and the two girls accompanied them halfway until their paths diverged, and Captain Prideaux, though sleeping at Trenwith, had gallantly insisted on escorting Clowance. Cuby partnered Clemency, and they chatted quietly together in the wake of the others. The night was very dark and very quiet. The cloud cover had continued, blanketing out the stars, and they had to be on the constant alert lest one of the horses should stumble on a stone.

It was nearly three a.m. They had been at Trenwith for twelve hours.

When they got home, Matthew Mark was up and alert and waiting to take the horses. Clowance kissed her parents a tired goodnight; there were kisses from the other girls, who were sleeping in Jeremy's old room. Ross and Demelza went into their bedroom together. They had both drunk a lot more than normal.

Ross broke a yawning silence. 'By God, that was a marathon! Never in my life have I seen so many of my friends and neighbours so much the worse for drink. Where was George spending the night?'

'He didn't confide in me. Did not Harriet say?'

'No.'

'No doubt she was too overwhelmed by the attentions you paid her.'

Ross chuckled. 'I have been enjoying myself.'

'So it seems.'

'But very decorously. I was still your loving husband. Mark that. For an hour or two I slipped a trace. I had the Christmas impulse.'

'Was that the Christmas impulse? Astonishing! But I suppose . . .

I suppose, yes, we have been married – in June we shall have been married thirty-two years. It is a long time. So suddenly you exhibit an entirely new mood that I have never ever seen before. Is it really, truly a new mood, kissing flirtatiously every woman in sight and enjoying a lecherous prancing with the wife of your arch-enemy? Dear life, I ask myself is this a *new* mood, or have you been suffering all these years – all these thirty-two dreary years hiding these strange impulses from me?'

'You were not, I thought, above flirting – lecherously, as you call it! – flirting lecherously with Vyel Vyvyan, and your daughter's intended, Christopher Havergal, and Harry Beauchamp, and Lieutenant Lake.'

Demelza spat as if there were something stuck to her tongue. 'I am astonished – quite astonished that you had any attention left to take note of what I was doing! Did you tick my partners off on the fingers of one hand while with the other you fumbled with Harriet's stays? It's – it's an outrage that—'

'What is an outrage?'

'That you should try to shoulder the blame upon me when your behaviour was the gossip of the room. Why I—'

'Blame is the wrong word,' said Ross, 'and I'd call anyone out who tried to prove that there was some other motive in me than the spirit of Christmas—'

'Well, you cannot call *me* out, though I would take a wager that I am as good a shot as you!'

'With paper darts, no doubt—'

'You kissed . . . How many people did you aim *your* paper darts at? You kissed—'

'Yes, I kissed Amadora's mother and Clowance and Morwenna and Amadora herself and Harriet! And – and I should have kissed you twenty times over if I had been able to come near you in the crush.'

'All very well to say that, but—'

'Yes, I say it, I say it. And I have greatly enjoyed the evening, and I hope now we shall get a few hours' sleep. I am for Truro later today.'

Demelza sat on the bed. 'What is she really like?'

'Who?'

'Judas God, you know who.'

'I fancy her stays are laced – *have* to be laced – tighter than yours. But well, if we *must* discuss it at this late hour, she's – I like her. She's a challenge. Do not forget that I did not fight with George all night. Was that not an achievement? Was that not what you most wanted? Peace on earth and good will towards men.'

'And good will towards women? I saw him watching you. I think Harriet will come in for a wigging.'

'I feel sure she will be able to hold her own.'

'When you were prancing with her I could not help but recall all the trouble that sprang from your love for his first wife.'

He sat slowly on the bed beside her. 'God, yes. But that was deeply deeply serious. This was froth. A mischievous impulse. But who put us *together* at the dining table in the first place?'

'Amadora, no doubt, who does not know our history.'

He took her hand. She wriggled to be free and then gave up. He bit each of her fingers gently in turn.

'All very well,' she said.

'I know.'

They were silent for a while. She said: 'That port was not as good as our port.'

He said: 'They talk of midsummer madness. Never of Yuletide madness.'

'Have you made an assignation with her?'

'Merciful Christ! I tell you it was froth.'

'The village will be talking.'

'Let 'em. I'm sick of gossip. I'm sick of this village, though I would not move away from it for all the tea in China. Give me a kiss.'

'Not likely.'

'Have you dried up – after thirty-two years?'

'There are better times to suggest it than after you have been fondling all sorts of other women.'

'Fondle be damned! I'm not Hugh Bodrugan.'

'Come to think of it,' Demelza said, 'there's a growing likeness.'

A brief convulsion of the bed suggested that Ross was either hiccuping or laughing.

'To tell the truth . . .' he began.

'Oh, that will be a nice change!'

'To tell the truth, it occurred to me tonight that there might be some point in smothering a few old feuds. In fifty years the tide will be coming in and going out just as it does now, the blowhole will spout, the wind and the sun will blow and blaze just the same; but we shall all be gone – or nearly all of us. I suppose, if I'd gritted my teeth, I could have gone up to George and grasped his hand.'

'Instead you poured oil on old embers by grasping his wife.'

He put his head on her not very sympathetic shoulder.

'I thought Bella was splendid,' he said.

'So you are converted.'

'That was a brilliant idea at midnight – whose was it, I wonder? – a brilliant idea to play the Floral Dance. At least I danced that with you!'

'You did.'

Just before twelve the trio playing the music had been reinforced by two extra drummers, and as the clock struck, so they had opened with the Floral Dance. In fact it was ideally suited to the limitations of the dance floor, since a procession could be formed around the enormous table, each man with a partner doing a hop and skip three times, followed by an exhilarating triple twirl. Round they had gone and round they had gone to the thud, beat, thud of the big drums. It had gone on and on, on and on for almost twenty minutes, when the music ended in a final *clash*, and everyone stood panting and sweating and smiling and laughing at everyone else.

'A great idea,' said Ross. 'Geoffrey Charles's, I suppose.'

'Yes.'

'Bella does not shout now,' Ross said. 'I'm totally converted. She doesn't *strain*. Her voice is so *clear*.'

'They were little songs, you know. She specially asked not to sing anything which might seem she was showing off her paces.'

'Maybe I like all voices like that, at half-pitch, men's as well as women's. And I loved her dearly for singing that song you first sang in that house when we were first married. Will you sing it for me now?'

'Tomorrow, Ross. Do you think you can get round me so easy?'

'Yes.'

They sleepily undressed.

He said: 'What do you think of Lieutenant Lake?'

'A fit companion for Valentine, maybe.'

'That is not a very good recommendation.'

'He made a great fuss of Cuby. I must ask her. He said in Brussels he was Jeremy's gaming partner.'

'Jeremy left few debts,' said Ross.

186

There was a brief silence.

'I think from something Cuby said the other day she did not quite like David Lake. Perhaps that is the reason. With her brother clinging desperately to his castle and burdened down with racing debts, Cuby does not favour the gaming tables.'

'At least Valentine did not disgrace himself tonight.'

'Except by coming uninvited. I suppose George and Harriet may be staying with him at Trevaunance? It would be the only house in the neighbourhood that had vacant bedrooms.'

Ross thought over the complications of that suggestion. He did not quite like it. Why did he not like it? Had he not emphasized all through the evening that this was the season of good will?

When the two young men returned to Place House David went straight to bed, but Valentine climbed to the attics to see if all was well with Butto.

His story of having 'bought' the young ape from a Lascar was not altogether accurate. (He had thrown the man a shilling.) Just off Arwenack Street in Falmouth, near the church, there was a small square flanked by stone-built cottages with a few broken steps at the end leading up to a sail-maker's yard. Hearing shouts of laughter and shrill screams of annoyance, Valentine had looked in and seen a group of boys aiming stones at a small fat ape, while its presumed owner danced round behind his barrel organ crying for them to stop. The ape was sitting on one of the cottage chimneys, while the owner of the cottage through an attic window was trying to poke the animal off its perch with a broom handle. The man was shouting and swearing at the lads, for some of their stones were hitting the area very near him. The screams were from the ape.

'Here! Stop this! Stop it, I tell you!' Valentine struck one of the boys across the shoulder with his cane, and there was a pause in the stone throwing while the issue hung in the balance. Some of the lads looked as if they might turn their marksmanship on the intruder. But his rich clothes and air of authority gave them pause. Then David Lake came shambling in, and they took to their heels up another narrow alley between the cottages.

The organ grinder was silent and so, except for an occasional whimper, was the ape, who, dug violently in the back by the broom handle, shifted his position to a chimney further along the row.

''E vill kom down,' the Lascar said, showing a lot of subservient teeth. 'Me vill get 'im down.'

He began to dance up and down as excitedly as apparently he expected the ape to do.

'Butto, Butto, 'e is my own animal. I bring 'im from the jungle.'

'Butto,' said Valentine. 'Is that his name? I think I rather fancy him. Butto. Butto. Good boy.'

The animal fixed this new person to use his name with coal-black eyes and seemed to be weighing up the situation.

'Well, then, get him down,' Valentine said harshly. 'See if you can. Let's have a closer look at him.'

It was Valentine who eventually persuaded the animal to come down by offering him a piece of cake, but even then he cowered in a corner, lame and pathetic. He seemed to take a cautious fancy for Valentine, and presently they were in touching distance.

'Look at his feet!' Valentine exclaimed. 'This criminal has been trying to turn him into a dancing bear! Kick him into the harbour, David!'

David made a menacing move towards the Lascar, who dodged away, but stood at the entrance to the alley shouting abuse.

'See,' said Valentine. 'These great feet. They're badly blistered. That's the way they teach a baby bear to dance. Start the music and then stand him on a bed of hot coals. And look at the stick the fellow has been using – sharp and bloodstained. I have a fancy to take this poor creature, this Butto, home.'

'For Gawd's sake,' David said, 'you'd never *get* him home. He's too *big*. You're crazed. You're off your head!'

'Maybe.' But this opposition was just the thing to make Valentine more determined. He sent David off to buy a laundry basket, and while he waited he fed the ape with two more buns and made soothing noises with his lips to calm him down.

It was a nightmare of arms and legs and scratches before the squealing, wriggling weight was pushed into the basket and pressed down fighting until the lid was shut and secure. Then it had to be tied firmly to David's saddle. (Valentine had cunningly argued that David's horse was the more docile.) They left Falmouth, pursued until they were well out of the town by the Lascar shouting that he had been robbed.

Once they reached Place House it had been a question of finding somewhere for the beast to live, and Valentine had allotted him the two back attics. But as he entered them on the night of the ball he realized this could only be very temporary because of the smell. No wonder the maids complained.

He shut the second door behind him and whispered, 'Butto!' Two brilliant eyes at once blinked up at him in the candlelight.

'Butto,' he said again. 'I've brought ee a morsel or two t'eat. Here, my handsome.' He held out half a watermelon that he had crushed open downstairs, and watched Butto relishing the juicy fruit until saliva ran down his jaws. When the animal was grunting and blowing with satisfaction Valentine opened a cupboard – which had not yet had its doors torn off its hinges by Butto – and took out a bottle of salve. With patience and good temper he persuaded Butto to let him put the salve once again on his blistered feet. This he succeeded in doing, receiving one bite (almost a love bite), but satisfied with the recovery. The soles were already hardening.

It was perfectly clear now that if Valentine had adopted Butto, Butto had also adopted Valentine. When the healing cream was put away the ape wanted to curl down with Valentine for the night, but Valentine gave him a couple of love taps on his cheek and slid away to return to the human-occupied part of the house on the floor below.

Chapter Nine

The elderly Paynters continued to live on in the last cottage of Grambler village. They were now both so decrepit that they were incapable of looking after themselves. Indeed they could not possibly have managed but for the kindness of Music and Katie Thomas, who lived in the cottage next to theirs. The Thomases both worked at Place House, Trevaunance, but slept out, and Katie always found time to brush out their hut, wash their ragged clothes, bring them a stew to put to simmer on their Cornish stove until they were ready to eat it. Music brought in coal and kindling wood and fetched water and shopped for them, this last being usually to bring a pint jar of gin from Sally Chill-Off's.

The Paynters accepted their assistance more as a right than as a privilege, grunting and complaining noisily when being so helped. It seemed sometimes that Demelza was more grateful for the help than were the Paynters. She felt a sort of obligation to Jud and Prudie: had they not been servants at Nampara when Ross first brought her home as a starving waif from Redruth fair? If the Thomases had not been to hand the only refuge for the Paynters was the Poor House, and that was hard to contemplate. Demelza might have paid for some woman to go in to live with them and look after them, but even in the poverty of the villages around it was hard to pick on someone to care for such a contentious and dirty couple, especially one who was not as old and dirty herself.

At Christmas she always bore them a number of presents, and the day after the Trenwith party she conscripted Clowance while she was still at home to go with her on this very difficult and overpoweringly smelly visit of mercy and good will. Clowance felt rather the same instinctive obligation towards the ageing couple, but Bella, being so much younger, had escaped from this sentimental weakness and generously allowed the other two to go on their own. Henry had a snivelly cold, and this was a good enough excuse to leave him behind.

It was another dark, still, dry day and the land had a brooding quiet about it that was old and comforting: the year was nearing its end and all passions were spent. Even the gulls sounded tired and lonely.

Because Cuby and Clemency and Noelle were late leaving, it was well on towards evening before the two women set out on their charitable mission. It was already full dark, but the path to Grambler was so well trodden that it did not occur to either of them to bother with a lantern.

On the way there they talked about the party. Clowance said: 'Papa was a mite frivolous last night, was he not?'

'A very large mite,' said Demelza. 'And it was not because of the drink he took. Spirits seem to have but little effect on him.'

'He made the greatest of a fuss of Lady Harriet. And I do not think it displeased her.'

'Nor should it,' said Demelza enigmatically.

'On the south coast, Mama, she has become my best friend. As you know, I think – d'you know, I think it all stems from the day when Music and I saved one of her great boar hounds from a mantrap. She was very kind to Stephen too. But she has gone out of her way again and again to help me since he died. She has even tried matchmaking by introducing Philip Prideaux to me.'

'I'm sure Philip is grateful. Are you?'

'Ha! How well you turn the subject! I was going to say that I hope you did not scold Papa too severely for his misdemeanours.'

'Who said they were misdemeanours?' Demelza asked pleasantly.

Clowance laughed. 'Some wives might have thought so. I am glad if you did not.'

Demelza raised her head and sniffed. 'D'you think it is going to rain? This bonnet does not like getting wet; it tends to crinkle at the edges like a pie crust.'

'Mama, do you think I could be odious and sneak away from the Paynters after, say, ten minutes? They are almost insufferable. And everything stinks so! Would you very much mind?'

'You were never brought up to the smells of poverty, as I was. What shall you do?'

'It isn't poverty that smells so bad, it is dirty unwashed things.

Well, I thought if you did not mind, I'd call in at Fernmore to say goodbye. I think Paul and Mary are still there; and I hardly had a good chance to talk to Daisy last night.'

'She's got a horrid cough. Have a care.'

'I will.'

'Clowance, I do not greatly enjoy seeing your father flirting with some handsome woman, any more than he would take too kindly if I flirted outrageously with some handsome man, as has happened now and then in the past. But we have been together for a very long time, him and me, and except for one dire event on his side, and one dire event on mine – of which you already know much and need have no expectation of hearing more from me now – we have been a veritable Darby and Joan to each other.'

'Who were Darby and Joan?'

'Oh, folk in some old ballad. But mark you, we still feel as much for each other, your father and me, as we have always felt. In our lives, and I'm serious now, we have had *so* much loving, so *very* much loving. It has not staled. It varies from year to year, but it keeps always to a constant pitch of – of being deeply and truly involved. And *desirous*. Against this – if you put this against your father having a frolic on the dance floor with the beautiful second wife of his oldest enemy – this frolic is as important as a ball of fluff.'

'It's lovely to know,' Clowance said, embarrassed now that she had brought up the subject. 'Of course, I have always known. The whole family knows it. I was – sort of joking.'

'I think,' said Demelza judiciously, 'in fact I have come to the knowledge gradual through the years, that your father passes through periods of rebellion, of ambition, of a need for adventure. He is going through such a time now. He would – though he protests he would not – he would dearly like to be entrusted with some mission: like when he went to join the escort of the Queen of Portugal; like being sent to the British Embassy in Paris to report on the Bonaparte feeling in France; like being asked to support or oppose some Bill in Parliament. These moods pass, often they come to naught, but since – since Jeremy died he has been very much at home. Looking after me, he tells folk: but sometimes it's me who's looking after him. Last night he was in the best of spirits ever I have seen him in since – since Waterloo. He said to me last night

192

he felt like kicking over a trace. If a simple noisy flirtation releases something bottled up in him, I shall certainly not complain.'

They were nearly at the Paynters. Clowance squeezed her mother's arm. 'You are a wise woman.'

'No,' said Demelza. 'Just a woman.'

The Paynters accepted their Christmas presents with a fair grace. Clowance had helped to carry them and then, having served her ten minutes, excused herself and set off for Fernmore. Demelza gave Prudie a censored account of the great party. Jud was not deaf, except with the inattentive deafness of old age, and while not interested in what his visitor said, he pursued his own line of thought amid the clouds of smoke he created with his clay pipe.

Eventually, when the parcels were all opened and the vision of last night's party fairly well explored, he tapped his pipe on the edge of the fire grate and said: 'Your maid left some soon. Reckon she soon had enough of we.'

'As you saw,' Demelza said, 'she was bearing presents for the Kellows, and she wanted to see them tonight before she went home.'

Jud sucked his pipe, making a noise like a choked drain. 'Reckon your young don't take no account of we. Why, that Bella-Rose 'asn't been nigh us, not once since she come home wi' her flipperty dandical young man. Reckon she'll be off t'London 'gain afore ye know it.'

'She's staying until the New Year.'

'Reckon she'll come to no good up in that there town. She'd do betterer for herself if she done her scholaring in Truro. I've allus said that, 'aven' I, Prudie?'

'Hold thy clack,' said Prudie. 'Tesn't no business of ourn what the Cap'n and the mistress d' do wi their childer—'

'And that there Clarence,' said Jud. Having wilfully misheard the name at her christening twenty-five years ago, he had ever after been impervious to correction. 'That there Clarence. She don't show 'er age, do 'er? She be mopping wi' some other man now, eh?' He screwed up his eyes and examined Demelza's expression for evidence of guilt or conspiracy.

'Miss Clowance is doing very well on her own,' said Demelza.

'She has been a widow only four years. She is in no haste to marry again. When she wishes to do so no doubt she will tell us.'

So the time wore on, and eventually she decided she had done her duty and could leave.

Prudie, the only moderately mobile of the two, waddled out in Demelza's wake and gratefully pocketed the guinea she usually received privately on these occasions.

So to walk home. Demelza calculated she had been at the Paynters' about an hour, so it would now be around seven of the clock. She wondered whether to make the detour and call in for Clowance, but decided she would rather go straight home to see if Henry had settled after his fretful day. It was pitch black now and even the most familiar path had the odd loose stone. Better to have brought a lantern after all. Although there is usually some light in a Cornish night sky, it can at times be ineffably dark. 'Black as a bloody sack,' as Jud was fond of saying.

Demelza began to think about Harry. With Jeremy taken from them, he was their only son, to whom the inheritance of the baronetcy would eventually pass. One daughter dead, two daughters alive, one son. Much the youngest and probably the last of the Poldarks – unless Amadora's second child should be a son. It was fortunate, Demelza thought, that Henry was such a robust little boy. One had to be careful not to spoil him, and if he had been like Jeremy, an excitable child with endless minor ailments, the pressure would have been great. Even disciplining Harry, in the small ways one has to do with any child, took on a greater significance. Like the heir to the throne. Except that all Harry would inherit was a part-converted farmhouse, a hundred acres of shallow, windswept farming land, a couple of mines, a few external assets which Ross had, almost against his better nature, allowed to aggregate around him, and on one side of the farmhouse a part sandy, part shingly cove and on the other side an unmatched vista of one of the most beautiful beaches in the world.

Henry, she suspected, had somehow come to comprehend that his family looked on him as someone special. He knew when to take liberties, how far he could go with his parents, when to test his will against theirs.

Or am I imagining this? she asked herself. Am I imagining it and has it had no influence on him at all? Was he just one of those people who knew as soon as they saw the light that they were special, and expected, with the greatest charm, to be so regarded?

Thinking of light, she found that as her eyes grew accustomed to the intense darkness after the ochre yellow candle flame in the Paynters' cottage, she could just pick out the familiar delineations of the track.

She reached the church. There was nothing living round here, only the dead. The vicarage was hidden by fir trees. So it was not the best place to hear footsteps.

She still had the animal faculties of her youth, otherwise she would not have detected the faint crunch or separated it from the normal noises of the night. Even then she thought she might be mistaken. The sound came from behind her, and she went on for about twenty paces more before her ears caught it again.

Without interrupting her pace she turned her head and peered behind into the night. The spire of the old church was an extra pyramid of darkness against ink-blue plumes of cloud, but nothing was visible at ground level. Having turned her attention from her walking, she tripped and caught the sole of one shoe more heavily on the ground.

She went on.

This was just moorland, interspersed with a few old diggings and some wind-stunted bushes as the path climbed towards the higher ground where Wheal Maiden had once been. Built out of the fallen stones of the mine was Sam's Meeting House. Until she got to the top she would not be able to see if there was a light in the window. It was a matter of two hundred yards. A little way beyond that was Wheal Grace – not yet entirely closed. Then down to the house. In all not much more than half a mile. No distance. She could do it comfortably in ten minutes. So why hurry? This was probably one of the miners walking to Wheal Grace to take up his evening core. (Except that Grace had very few miners left and the time for changing cores was eight o'clock.)

As a country person accustomed to walking about from place to place in the dark, she would hardly have given two thoughts to there being any danger in being followed. The obvious thing was to stop and let this unknown person catch up with her, and they could go on together. So it would have been with her if a month or two ago Agneta Treneglos had not had her throat cut nearby. And had there not been others, other women attacked?

Rubbish. These things didn't happen on Nampara land, even on the darkest night. She stopped.

She listened and narrowed her eyes to stare behind her. There was no sound now. No untoward sound or movement. Even the light wind had dropped. She waited. Then she went on.

It was a minute or so before she heard the footsteps following.

She stopped again. 'Who's there?'

She detected, or fancied she detected, a man's tall figure. Her heart was thumping now. Perhaps those things did happen, could happen, on Nampara land.

'What do you want?'

There was no answer. Her throat tightened.

'Tell me what you want? Who are you? Say something or you'll spend a night in jail!'

The only answer was a puff of gentle breeze wafting against her cheek. This brought a whiff, a hint of cigar smoke.

She turned and walked on, her pace quickening at every step. When she reached the top of the hill she was breathless, but not from exertion.

There was no light in Sam's chapel.

Sam had told her that he never locked the door. In fifty paces she could reach it.

But if she went inside, there was only the one door. Supposing the person behind her followed her in?

She broke into a run. Having come up to the chapel she fled straight past it. On her right the buildings of Wheal Grace loomed up.

The footsteps were running behind her, catching her up. He was making a sort of noise as he almost came up with her. It was a chuckling noise, or a gobbling. She burst into the engine room of Wheal Grace.

The younger of the two elderly Curnows was there; he worked at Leisure but was gossiping with the Grace engineer, a man called Watford.

They stared at her arrival, then looked alarmed at her white face and laboured breathing.

'Mistress Poldark!' said Curnow. 'What's amiss?'

'I . . . er . . .' Demelza blinked in the lantern light and took a deep breath, and swallowed. 'It is nothing. But – are you free, Tom?'

'Free, ma'am? Yes, ma'am. I just called 'ere on me way 'ome. What be amiss?'

'I – thought someone was following me. I – I'd like you to walk with me just down so far as Nampara.'

'Gladly, ma'am. Now, ma'am? Yes, gladly.'

'And Watford.'

'Yes, ma'am?'

'Have you a spare workman, someone you could spare for an hour?'

'Ais, I reckon.'

'Would you ask him to go over at once to the Kellows and ask him to wait there until he can escort Miss Clowance home. Tell them you are acting on my instructions.'

Chapter Ten

Lieutenant Christopher Havergal took coach for London on the second of January 1820. Before he left he asked Demelza if she could persuade Ross to let him marry Isabella-Rose at Easter. By then Bella would be eighteen. Christopher said that, apart from their love for each other, there were other reasons why their association would be easier if they were married.

As Mrs Pelham's goddaughter – which was the 'relationship' they had agreed on – Bella was in a favoured position, but he, Christopher, lacked any status; and Bella was frequently attracting attentions from young men who presumed too much.

Demelza said: 'I do not think Bella would encourage another young man. She is completely committed to you.'

'Your daughter is a very striking young lady. She does not need to show an interest in some young man for him to show an interest in her.'

Something made Demelza ask: 'Is there one or another particularly?'

He stroked his moustache. 'Five or six, I suspect. But one, yes, one is a slightly greater danger than the rest. You will remember the young Frenchman who visited Mrs Pelham's house when you were in London. Maurice Valéry.'

'Oh? Oh, yes.'

'He has recently been appointed as conductor to the Académie Orchestre de Rouen, and this I think has gone greatly to his head. But there is no doubt he is an accomplished musician, and that attracts Bella.'

Demelza was thoughtful. 'Yes. I know – we all know – that you have been very patient.'

'Mrs Pelham's generosity towards Bella is boundless. Though she

198

clearly is enjoying all she does for us, this does not make it less worthy; but in some ways – soon now – we shall be better on our own. By Easter I shall be able to afford a nice new house for us to live in. Bella's progress as a singer is startling, and it may be good sometime for us to go to Hamburg or Paris, and this we can only do comfortably if we are man and wife.'

Demelza had not told Ross about her scare in the dark, but had had to explain to Clowance why she had sent a miner from Grace to accompany her home. Clowance was indignant that she must not tell her father lest it should 'worry him', but reluctantly promised. While the murderer of Agneta was still at large any follower in the dark had to be taken seriously, whether in fact he was sinister or innocent.

The following day, in the rush of Clowance's departure, with Philip Prideaux to escort her, Demelza began to wonder if she might have dreamed or imagined the whole thing. (She knew of course she had *not*, but wondered how she would have behaved if Agneta had not just been murdered. Would she not have stopped and confronted her follower, and might it not have been Music Thomas with some request to make or a drunken miner on his way home and not wanting to be recognized?)

But did such men smoke cigars?

Was it a cigar? Might it not have been something that Jud smoked, some cheap scented tobacco out of a clay pipe? Pigtail? Or Thick Twist? She had never smoked. She knew well the smell of Ross's tobacco. Could she be sure of any other?

At this, still the darkest time of the year, it was an uncomfortable feeling to have in the back of one's mind, the idea that some evil person might just be lurking. For Heaven's sake, this was a *peaceable* district where everyone knew everyone else, and the biggest crime in a year might amount to the theft of a dozen eggs.

Perhaps it was as well that Clowance had an escort home. Perhaps Bella might be safer in London after all!

On the fifth of January there were signs of a change in the weather: a strong wind blew the heavy cloud away and brought a new shifting canopy of its own, which threatened blistering rain. The sea, which had been talking in its sleep for a day and a half, suddenly woke and frothed at the mouth.

One afternoon Demelza spent an hour in her garden. At this time of year there was little that a storm could hurt, but one or two of the roses had sent up tall shoots which might crack at the root if they swayed about too much. A stick in support would be a good thing. Also that foreign tree from the Carolinas, which Hugh Armitage had brought and they had planted against the protection of the house wall, still clung obstinately to life though making little progress in this unsuitable soil. Its evergreen leaves were like spaniel's ears that flopped about in the wind.

The hour was almost up, and for a while the wind had paused for breath as darkness pended. The last distorted rim of the sun, pale and cold, looked like a great luminous iceberg sinking into the sea. She wrapped the thick string into a ball and moved to go in. As she did so she saw a tall man in black peering at her over the wall. She dropped the string.

'Lady Poldark, excuse me.'

'Who on – oh, Captain Prideaux! I did not expect – to see you again so soon.'

'I trust I did not startle you.'

'I did not, was not quite expecting someone to come on me from the beach side.'

'Is this gate open? May I come in?'

He came in, tall and gaunt, not at present wearing his eye glasses. That perhaps was why she had not instantly recognized him.

He picked up the ball of string, gave it to her. She thanked him.

He said: 'I left my horse on the rough ground by the fence. Excuse this unorthodox arrival. I saw someone in the garden, and thought at first it was just a member of the household.'

'So it was,' she said. 'Will you come in? The wind will soon be picking up again.'

'Thank you. But may I ask if Sir Ross is indoors?'

'Did you want to see him? I believe he is at the mine. If—'

'No, Lady Poldark, I wanted to see you.'

'Oh.' They went in. She noticed he was almost as tall as Ross, had to bend his head in the same places.

In the old parlour he waited for her to sit down, then put his hat on a chair and his cloak over it.

'You must forgive me, Lady Poldark, for a slight subterfuge. I promised Clowance.'

Oh dear, Demelza thought, another suitor.

'What did you promise Clowance?'

'She told me that a man, an unknown man, had followed you home last Sunday evening and that you felt at some risk because of the unfortunate death of Agneta Treneglos. You told Clowance but made her promise not to tell her father because you thought this would worry him unduly. Am I right?'

'You are perfectly right.' So he had not come to declare his love. It made a change.

'But she told me. On the ride home. She said she felt she must tell someone. And she asked me not to give anything away to your husband.'

'Did she ask you to come and see me?'

He found his glasses in a pocket, fiddled with them nervously, put them on. 'Oh, no. Not at all. I wondered if you could kindly tell me exactly how it happened. Where you first noticed that you were being followed, whether you have any idea how this man was dressed, whether anything like it has ever happened to you before.'

Demelza was not quite at ease with Captain Prideaux. She wondered why he was so concerned, why he was personally pursuing the matter.

He heard her story out in silence. 'You believe this man was dressed all in black?'

'I think so. Rather as you are now, Captain Prideaux.'

He smiled coldly. 'But you did not see his face?'

'No. Oh, no.'

'Was he tall or short?'

'Tall. He may have had something across his face.'

'What makes you say that?'

'There was a chink of light coming through the door of the engine house. I could see no face.' She shivered.

'A very distressing experience,' he said, in that stiff voice he sometimes used. 'But why, if I may ask, did you not tell Sir Ross?'

'What could he do? Except worry for me. What can you do, Captain Prideaux?'

'Would you do me the honour of calling me Philip.'

'It's kind of you to take this interest, Philip. Do you think you *can* help?'

'Last year, when I had just returned to Cornwall – oh dear, it will be the year before last – a parlourmaid at Cardew was murdered one night on her way home. It was while I was staying at Cardew that it happened, and out of idle curiosity I went to see the dead woman. She had been stabbed and her throat cut in exactly the same way as Agneta Treneglos.'

Demelza moistened her lips. 'And was there not some other girl killed more recent? Somewhere betwixt Indian Queens and Padstow.'

'Yes, but she was strangled.' Philip glanced up quickly and took off his glasses. 'I remember reading that.'

'And do you feel there may be a connection?'

'Someone has asked me to find out. I tell you this in confidence.'

Demelza took a spill, lighted it at the fire and went to the candlesticks on the sideboard. 'Is it someone round here who has asked you to do this?'

'I'm not at liberty to tell you, Lady Poldark. But I can tell you that this morning I did actually make some progress.'

The third candle was guttering and the flame stayed small.

He said: 'As you know, ma'am, Agneta ran away from home, and no one seemed to have the least idea where she had spent the time. It was four days before the body was found, and Dr Enys said she had probably been dead for about two days. That left two nights unaccounted for, as well as two days. No one had seen her. Isn't that so?'

'I believe tis so.'

'Which suggests to me that she hid for most of the time – or was hidden. Well, I know now where she was.'

Demelza turned. 'You do?'

'She was at Fernmore.'

'Fernmore?' She dropped some candle grease on the mantel-shelf. 'The Kellows? How could that be?'

'I called to see Miss Daisy Kellow and asked her questions. She told me in the end that she thought Miss Treneglos had been there both nights. You will of course remember – though I did not know – that Fernmore was originally occupied by a Dr Choake. It seems that Dr Choake utilized a large shed at the rear of the house for his surgery. Since he left, this shed has been neglected and used only as a lumber room. It should have been kept locked, but was not. From what she found in the shed Miss Kellow could tell that someone had occupied it.'

'But it could have been some tramp.'

'No, there was a comb that Miss Kellow recognized. And other things.'

'Then why did she not tell the coroner at the inquest?'

'She thought it would not make any difference to what had happened.'

Demelza scraped the cooling wax off the mantelshelf. 'And does it?'

'It raises many questions. Did Miss Kellow know of the other girl being there while she was there? I asked her, and she said she had no idea. I asked her if she was a special friend of Agneta, and she replied that she was not.'

'Did you see Daisy's mother and father?'

'No. She said her father was in Redruth and that her mother was not well enough to receive visitors.'

'Her brother and sister-in-law were at the party with her.'

'They have gone home. But I will see Mr Paul Kellow later on. I have met him several times and this will give me an excuse to call.'

There was a pause.

'I think that is Ross now. But he has gone through to the kitchens.'

Philip got up. 'Then I will leave you. This has been a courtesy call, Lady Poldark. Pray give your husband my warm respects.'

Demelza said: 'I wish you well in your quest, Captain – er, Philip. We shall all breathe easier if this mystery is solved . . . It still puzzles me a small matter that you are personally going to so much trouble.'

Philip Prideaux smiled more warmly. 'I do it willingly. Like you, with a number of women probably at risk, I shall breathe easier if the murderer is caught.'

It was not until after he had left that she wondered why she had not mentioned the smell of the cigar.

Ben walked Essie home from his cottage to the gates of Trenwith. The wind was bringing up broken masses of cloud, with the moon behind them in the high January sky. So fast were the clouds moving that the moon might just have been thrown across the sky. Where there were clumps of trees they looked like cloud shadows on the moor. They had skirted Grambler beside the gorse bushes, prickly and stark, stunted hawthorn trees and waving brambles among the skeletal old mine buildings long fallen to waste. Few used this desolate way, and it was a narrow track with only just room to walk abreast without touching. Never quite touching. They had both been brought up in a rough country world where life, under a thin veneer of Wesleyanism, was plain, hard and crude. Sex was as often as not a hearty rough and tumble in the dark, a subject for tittered innuendoes and loud guffaws. Hardly anyone had time or patience for that pretty word romance or for anything that amounted to courtship.

Yet Ben Carter at thirty-one and Esther Carne at nineteen had remained separate from the crowd. Ben because of his long enduring preoccupation with Clowance. Esther, perhaps because she was a little like Rosina Hoblyn had once been, born with an awareness that she was a little too good for the village lads and not good enough for any man with minor claims to gentility.

He had met her at the gates at three; they had walked along the cliffs behind Trenwith while the light lasted and then gone back to his cottage and taken tea with his mother, who had been commanded by Ben to be present. Later he had taken Esther into the back room and explained how his new-built organ worked, and then played pieces of church music and dance music for about half an hour. Jinny had stayed until they left.

Little of anything which might be called flirtatious conversation had passed between them – because of Jinny's presence and because Essie could hardly take the lead. Ben just did not know how; but they had exchanged glances, looks, occasional smiles.

Jinny by this time was stout and grey and in her sixties, still fresh-complexioned and comely, but with a tight set to her mouth which reflected a life of struggle and prideful resistance to misfortune. She had in fact, with an occasional and never-sought gift from Ross, prospered more than most: her little shop, which sold everything from candles to sweets, from cotton to paraffin, had kept the family above water when Whitehead lost his job and while Ben prospected vainly for tin in little sub-surface workings of his own. The great tragedy of Jinny's life, which she had suffered when barely twenty, had been the death of Jim Carter, her first husband. She had never loved any man before or since, her later marriage to Scoble being one simply of liking and convenience. She had become a staunch Wesleyan before Sam turned up, and of later years, with Sam's encouragement, she had played an active part in his church and his Witnessing to the Truth.

She had no objection to the thought of her eldest son marrying, indeed it was high time – long past time, some thought – the only tiny fly in the ointment being that this thin blonde girl was chief nurse to the Poldark baby, and *almost* acting as a companion to the Papist Major Geoffrey Charles had married. To many people in the county Catholicism was a serious menace, something still to be fought and feared like a dread complaint. And even though by some strange mischance the British had for long been fighting on behalf of the Spaniards in Spain, the less one had to do with such folk the better. In their eyes the Pope was close to the Devil, the Scarlet Woman, long allied to Napoleon; and before him to King Philip of Spain. Many brave men – including Jeremy Poldark – had laid down their lives to save their country from the Papists. It was therefore very unsuitable and dangerous for one of them to have married a Poldark and be living in their midst. If – only if – Ben were to marry this Carne girl, he would be well to do it quickly and withdraw her from the evil influence which at present threatened her.

Ben, his mother knew, though a nominal Wesleyan, was not as committed as he should be, and might not feel as strongly as Jinny. It was clearly a sign of his intentions, a sign of his recognition of the proprieties, that he should have invited her to be at his cottage for Esther's first visit. The girl, like all decent girls of her age, was as yet unformed, seemed a little lacking in character – it was quite hard to imagine what her middle-aged son *saw* in her – but that would all change with maturity. Jinny's chief – only real – concern was that she should be encouraged to join the Community and to develop without improper or impure thoughts of incense, of confession, of black-robed priests. (It had been rumoured that such a priest had called at Trenwith and been admitted to the house.)

Before they separated Ben, as if conscious of the importance of this first meeting, said: 'How d'ye like my mother?'

She looked up at him quickly. 'She seem nice. But tis more a question, isn't it, as for how she like me.'

'Mebbe. Mebbe. But twould be good to see you and her gettin' along.'

The path as they approached the gates of Trenwith joined the wider way running downhill towards Pally's Shop. There was a clatter of hooves, and four riders came out of Trenwith, two men and two women. They were talking and laughing, voices raised to make themselves heard above the stamping, prancing feet of their horses.

It was Valentine Warleggan and David Lake. The two women were strangers, and they looked too gaudily dressed for a winter's evening.

'Who's there?' called Valentine, seeing the dark clad couple standing together.

After a moment, 'Ben Carter, Esther Carne,' came the reply.

'What's your business here?'

'Miss Carne live here. I am taking of her 'ome.'

A wisp of cloud moved away from the moon.

'Oh, aye,' said David Lake. 'You are the pretty little blonde thing. I saw you at the party.'

'Hey, hey!' said one of the girls, and laughed loudly. 'You keep your hands to yourself, me old lad. Don't you see they're courting?'

'Oh, it's Ben,' said Valentine. '*The* Ben. Are you courting, Ben?'

'Good evening to you, Mr Warleggan,' said Ben coolly, and took Essie by the arm to lead her past them.

'It's a cold night for courting out of doors,' said Lake with a fat laugh. 'And Cornish hedges are draughty. I've tried 'em!'

'I have no doubt,' said Valentine, 'that he has been showing her his organ.'

There were wild squeals of laughter at this from the women as the quartet moved on.

Essie walked with Ben holding his arm. At the last gibe Ben's grasp on Essie's arm had tightened painfully, but she would not wince or complain. It was the first time this evening he had actually touched her.

He walked her up to the side door. 'Take no notice of such attle,' he said. 'Folk like that needs their mouths washed out.'

'I take no notice,' she said.

He released her arm.

She said: 'D'ye know Katie Thomas?'

'Who?'

'Katie Thomas. Married to Music Thomas.'

'Yes, I know Katie. She's my sister.'

She drew in a breath. '*Sorry*, Ben. I'm sorry. I'm new to these parts.'

'No matter. She's married to that half-wit, isn't she?'

'Oh, Music? He's kind, Ben. And – and Katie is kind.'

'So what of it?'

'You d'know she works for young Mr Warleggan. They both do. She was telling me that the house is near full of strangers – like those two women on they horses. She say – Katie say tis like unto a bawdy house, folk coming and going, and laughing, and drinkin' and gambling. Katie says they've put a table in the big drawing room, and this table has a sort of wheel lying flat on the top and the wheel turns and folk gamble on where a little white ball d'fall.'

'I b'lieve Valentine was cursed at his birth,' muttered Ben. 'He causes trouble wherever he go.'

'He cann't cause trouble for we,' said Essie.

Daring, she stretched across and kissed him on the cheek.

He put his hand to his face. 'Don't do that.'

'. . . Why not?'

'Twould lead to things.'

'Bad things?'

He stirred restlessly. 'Not *bad*, Essie. No, not bad. D'ye know I want to marry you?'

'You haven't said so. You haven't asked me—'

'Well, will ye?'

After taking a breath she said: 'Yes, Ben. I would dearly like to.'

He took her hand. 'Essie, I 'ave strong feelings. I want everything proper and above board. A proper wedding in a church. You in white. I want it to be how I've always wanted it to be. Not snatched at. Not hole in corner. Not like those men jested 'bout. And if I kissed you, fondled you now, mebbe I should not be able to stop.'

She put her hand on his. 'Why don't ye try, Ben? I'm strong. I'll tell you when to stop.'

Chapter Eleven

'Who was that?' Harriet asked as she came in to the hall, to be greeted by her two elderly dogs.

George looked at his muddy wife with disapproval. 'Your friend, Captain Prideaux.'

'I thought it looked like the cut of his jib, but it was too dark to be sure. Did he want me?'

'He did not ask for you. He sent his respects.'

Harriet was bent examining Castor's floppy ear. After a minute she said: 'We picked up a good scent but lost it by the Carnon Stream . . .'

Relations between George and his wife had not been of the warmest since the Trenwith party, though it had not come to an outright quarrel. Harriet, George had long ago concluded, was quite a difficult person to quarrel with. Unless he stormed and shouted about the house she really did not take much notice of him. Sarcasms were not taken up, coldness was ignored. When after the party George had asked her if she had deliberately attempted to insult him by making the greatest of a fuss over Ross Poldark, Harriet had just said: 'No, I thought nothing of it. Why should I? It was a party.' 'It does not even occur to you that that man has been my greatest enemy throughout my entire life? It was a plain affront to me to act as you did.' She had flicked Bargrave with her whip and replied: ' 'Fraid I just take people as I find 'em. Hope this damned rain will hold off.'

Bringing Harriet to battle was the problem. She always seemed to be doing something else at the time, even if it was only brushing her hair. Whatever it was it claimed the larger part of her attention.

The other deterrent to making a major quarrel of the folly at the party was that George was uneasily conscious he cared more not to break up their marriage than she did. If she left him, of course she would lose most of the trappings supplied by his wealth; but he would lose the prestige of being married to a duke's sister. She was not Lady Warleggan, she was Lady Harriet Warleggan, which made all the difference. It put him among the aristocracy of England.

So for weeks he had been cold and often sarcastic, and she, if she even noticed, had taken care to ignore it.

'Why did Philip leave so early? Did you not ask him to supper?'

'I think he will return.'

She looked up enquiringly, then concentrated on Castor's ear.

'He asked permission,' said George, 'to speak to Polmesk.'

'*Who?* Polmesk? You mean our butler?'

'Yes.'

'Whatever for?'

'Now your friend has gone off to see Polmesk's brother at Angorrick Farm.'

At last her attention was engaged. 'You cannot mean it.'

'Ask him when he returns. I think your war hero is turning into a busybody. Not many months ago he called into my bank and wasted my time prating about the dirty condition of the Truro streets. Now apparently we have another scent to pursue.'

'My dear George, this is not April Fool's Day.' Her attention was straying to Castor again. 'I think Henderson should look at him. I don't *think* there is any sign of canker, but . . .'

'I was not suggesting that Captain Prideaux was in need of a veterinary surgeon. Though, come to think of it, a horse pill might set him to rights.'

She looked up again and gave a low chuckle. 'It's agreeable when you show a sense of humour, George. You should do it more often. When we have disentangled Castor's ear from Philip's curiosity, could you explain to me what it is all about?'

'It seems,' said George after a moment, 'that Captain Prideaux has taken it upon himself to enquire more closely into the sudden death of Mary Polmesk, who, as you will recall, worked for us about a year and a half ago, indeed was walking home from here when she was attacked. I fail to see what business it is of young Prideaux's to take any interest in the matter. Busybody, busybody, is what I say. Apparently he is even trying to connect, or trying to find if there are any similarities between, the Polmesk girl's murder and the death of Agneta Treneglos last October!'

Harriet did not snort with disgust, as George had half expected. She said: 'Do you know how I think Agneta died?'

'I have no idea. Nor have you.'

'Hm. It occurred to me when I was on the north coast at Trenwith. Agneta was making a great nuisance of herself. She had become intensely inconvenient to Valentine – and possibly others, we do not know—'

'Are you pretending to think—'

'I'm not pretending anything. But if I were Valentine and Agneta had become impossible in her demands on me, I might pay some out-of-work miner to dispose of her and meanwhile sail across to Ireland so that no one could accuse me of doing it. Had that occurred to you?'

George brooded for a few moments.

'Anything can be imagined by a fanciful imaginative mind. You could well build a case against Prideaux himself.'

'Come, come—'

'Well, why is he going to all this trouble? Where was he when Agneta was killed? He ranges far and wide. We know where he was when the Polmesk girl was murdered. He was here, in the house, enjoying our – *your* – generous hospitality. I know little of the criminal mind, the deranged mind, but it is common knowledge that a murderer is wont to return to his old haunts. He is, we know, still convalescent from his breakdown after Waterloo. His mind could well be sufficiently deranged for him to have developed a grudge against women . . .'

'My dear George, what an ingenious theory! Developing that, he might even have been conducting a shabby little affair with Mary Polmesk and found her presence inconvenient! After all, it was his first visit to us, and he had been with us all of four days. And so now, now, you think he is revisiting the scene of his crime?'

'You may well scoff,' said George. 'I am merely putting forward the theory to show how many theories can exist and each of them as likely to be as true and as untrue as another. I tell you, nobody knows – nobody will ever know.'

Harriet stood up. 'I'll send Treglown for Henderson. One cannot be too sure. Where is Ursula, by the way?'

'At her piano lesson. Mercifully we cannot hear it from here.'

'She is not musical. Why do you persist?'

'Because it is one of the attributes of a young lady's education. Or supposed to be.'

'*I* am not musical,' said Harriet reflectively. 'I lost nothing for being unable to perform.'

'You married that oaf, Carter.'

'A childish folly. Music, I assure you, did not come into it! Lust was the motivating force. That and the fact that I thought him richer than he was.'

'I'm sure you laboured under the second delusion also when you married me.'

'Not at all. You are very rich, George. And none of it inherited. That is an asset, not a social disadvantage. Men who inherit large estates seldom turn them to advantage. Often as not, it dribbles through their fingers. You have the *habit* of making money, and you continue in that habit.'

'Yes,' said George. 'I make the money and you spend it!'

'Precisely. Could there be a better arrangement?'

George sneered to hide a slight sense of gratification.

'I'm told the younger Poldark girl is affianced to that moustached fellow she was with at the party.'

It was the first time he had overtly mentioned the party to Harriet since the journey home.

'So I have heard.'

'Another down-at-heel army officer, eh? They're scattered all over the county now, now that the war is over. Half of 'em are destitute. Your friend Prideaux would be if it were not for his family connections.'

'I'm told Christopher Havergal is not without modest connections, and that he is at present employed with Rothschild's.'

'Did Poldark tell you this while you were making an exhibition of yourself dancing with him?'

'No, we had no breath to talk. I heard it from Polly Codrington, who seems to know these things.'

George turned the guineas in his fob and was silent for a few moments.

'Rothschild's, eh? From my acquaintance with Nathan I should not think that likely to be a sinecure. He will have to sweat for his daily bread.'

Harriet was feeling tactless. 'Polly also says she has heard that

Isabella-Rose is on the verge of making a success of her singing career.'

'Success?' said George. 'That girl? If she tries to sing in London they'll laugh her off the stage.'

Chapter Twelve

When Isabella-Rose returned to London she found a thick yellow sooty fog enveloping the city. It lay upon everything, it penetrated everything, it hid everything. Daylight almost disappeared; lamps were kept permanently on even at midday. The great city was surrounded by lime kilns and brickworks; they were like a besieging army pouring out a gas to asphyxiate the inhabitants. Carts, drays, barrows, coaches, those on horseback, proceeded all at the same snail's pace, cursing and shouting at the shadows which lurched and loomed perilously near them. Flaming torches seemed often to add to the density of the fog. Now and again traffic came to a complete standstill, and one was surrounded by a mass of human beings all impatiently trying to break free on missions of their own. The stink of unwashed humanity mingled with and almost over-powered the smell of rotting vegetation, dead fish, horse and cow droppings and sour milk.

If one blew one's nose the handkerchief came away looking as black as a drain. Everyone, practically everyone, was coughing, and not a few spitting. Influenza was rife, bronchitis and tisick wide-spread. It had never been in Bella's nature to be apprehensive of anything, especially not infection, but with two small engagements to be fulfilled in the first week in February she was naturally keen to keep her voice clear. She had a small but important part in a performance of Byrd's Missa Solemnis at St Martin-in-the-Fields, and the following week she was due to appear on stage – for the first time – in a musical recital before, it was expected, the Duke of Cambridge. Hers again was a small part, but Christopher was strongly of the opinion that, aside from her voice, her personality would help to make an impression.

And then the old King died.

It was shortly before ten on the evening of Saturday the twenty-ninth of January that the news became widely known. He had been so long out of the public eye, blind, deaf, and mentally confused, and his eldest son had been Regent for so long, that one might have supposed that 'Farmer George' was long forgotten. But, because his sons were all so unpopular, particularly the Prince Regent himself, a large part of the public held the old man in high esteem and remembered his earlier days with affection. He had been King of England at least in name for sixty years, and his passing was the end of an era.

The tolling of bells spread the news across the fogbound city, and continued throughout the Sunday. Every bell in a city of a hundred churches spread its wailful message. Churches were full. Parades and processions crowded every available square. Shops were still closed on the Monday, as were theatres and places of entertainment. *The Times* of Monday announced that all theatres would be closed until after the funeral, which would take place on Ash Wednesday – in two weeks' time.

Bella could hardly believe her ill luck. Her appearance in the musical evening before the Duke of Cambridge was an obvious casualty, but surely Byrd's Missa Solemnis would go ahead, since that would be in keeping with the mood of the time? Christopher enquired and was told no. This would in a sense have been regarded as an evening of pleasure; though it was to be held in a church, the public were to be charged admission and that put it in the wrong category. Instead the evening would be devoted to prayers and an address given by the Reverend Dr Ireland, Dean of Westminster.

Bella had only been three times to Dr Fredericks's school since it reassembled: the intense fog and the crowded streets, which had been increasingly rowdy since Christmas, made Christopher and Mrs Pelham dissuade her from going even with an escort. She was not only disappointed but restless. It seemed as if her career had come to a halt and now there was not even the theatre to go to. Sometimes she even found the spoken dramas more exciting than the operas. She loved the melodramas, especially those at the Royal Coburg Theatre and at the Adelphi.

Happily Christopher had an evening planned for the following Thursday. A German Count called Von Badenberg, who had links with the Rothschilds, was in London, and was giving a party at the Pulteney Hotel in Piccadilly. They had a private room to seat twenty. Franz Von Badenberg was a blond young man of about thirty with a big voice, a large moustache which curled over his upper lip, and impending dewlaps which wobbled when he laughed, which he did frequently. Bella at once spotted a tawny-haired young man whom she knew: Maurice Valéry.

In the streets, either from decree or out of a sense of respect, everyone had dressed in dark clothes since the King's death, which itself had been preceded by only a few days by the death of his younger brother, the Duke of Kent, and was shortly followed by news that the Prince Regent, now King George IV, was gravely ill with pneumonia. And everyone coughing, coughing in the raw yellow fog. So this party was a complete relief. Youth, good health, good spirits, wine and food and laughter: they asserted themselves among the gloom in defiance of the gloom, a microcosm of light and warmth in a bereaved city.

'London,' said Von Badenberg in his big voice, 'is now the centre of the world. Socially, financially, politically, since the end of Napoleon it has become dominant over all the other cities of the Continent. It is richer, freer, in manners, in fashion, in social behaviour. There is poverty, of course, but even that is minor compared to the poverty in Europe. Tradespeople are becoming ever more prosperous, the middle classes are coining money, the rich so much that they scarcely know how to spend it. They say that Oxford Street is the longest in Europe. You now have five bridges across the Thames! You folk are lucky to live here. I come from Frankfurt – my father knew Meyer Rothschild – and though it is an important town it rates as a village beside London. All Europe seems by comparison provincial!'

'Very well so far as it goes,' said an older man. 'But London also is the centre of England, and the English provinces are not prosperous. The new towns of the Midlands and the north are decrepit, the workers – where there is work – live on starvation wages. In Glasgow weavers, who once were paid twenty-five shillings a week, now try to subsist on five. And those who have no work starve. The streets of the new towns are silent and empty – unless you chance to walk through them, when you will be accosted by beggars who emerge like spectres from their hovels and claw at your cloak asking for a piece of bread. As you know from Peterloo, violent unrest exists everywhere and is fanned by agitators who seek to achieve what they achieved in France!'

'Well, London itself is none so pretty,' said a lady, fingering her necklace with jewelled hands. 'There are enough beggars in the gutters here – many of 'em discharged soldiers and sailors who fought so brave in the wars – and the gutters themselves choked with every sort of filth imaginable. Every pillar and post is bedaubed with slogans, many of them obscene. And there are marches and counter-marches, and rough and rude crowds everywhere . . .'

Bella had become separated from Christopher, and she noticed that he was eating none of the *bonnes bouches* which were being handed round on trays before supper, but had a glass of white wine in his hand. A little worm of anxiety moved in her.Three times only in their fairly long acquaintance had she seen Christopher drink white wine. Normally he ate and drank no more and no less than the next man. But he seemed to have a weakness for Canary or any Rhenish wine, especially if it was a little sweet, and every now and again the need for it overcame his self-control. Then he would refuse all food and drink glass after glass until he became totally drunk.

They were sitting down to supper now, and she tried to edge towards him, but a middle-aged man, who was called Jasper Brown, took her arm and said: 'Miss Poldark, the Count has asked me to take you in. Would you do me the honour?'

She found that Christopher was on the other of two circular tables, each seating ten, and he had two elegant if middle-aged ladies to flank him. That would not matter, she thought, Christopher had a special charm for older women – perhaps all women – with the intent blue eyes, the military bearing, the drooping blond moustache. He still had the same fascination for her – when he was not drunk.

She had no stern principles about drinking. *She* drank herself: she liked the slightly tipsy feeling when life, always exciting, became still more rosy. Her mother and father drank. *Everyone* drank, most people over-drank. It was not an unusual thing for men to slip under the table and snore till morning.

But it worried and upset her when Christopher proceeded to do just that. Moreover, his was not quite a normal drunkenness. It was not a part of gluttony. On those – mercifully rare – occasions when the mood took him, he would never *touch* food: he just poured wine into himself as if down a drain, as if some devil entered him and commanded him to drink himself insensible.

A few months ago Bella had sat beside a judge at Mrs Pelham's house. The subject of drunkenness came up, and he had defined for her the four legal definitions of the stages: jocose, bellicose, lachrymose, comatose. She never forgot this. But they could not be so ascribed to Christopher. The middle two stages were completely missed out. He had always been a jolly, daredevil young man, and the only change in his nature when drunk was an exaggeration of his normal impulses. He was kind, friendly, loving towards Bella, protective of her person, anxious for her comfort, ready for anything. The second bout that had occurred since she knew him had taken place at the musical party at Mrs Pelham's; the first had been at a Hallowe'en party given by some friends, where he had ridden a bucking horse sidesaddle until he was thrown off, and later, false foot and all, climbed a clock tower to tie a pair of gentleman's stays to a lightning conductor. Bella had been told by Geoffrey Charles of his first meeting with Christopher under the walls of Toulouse, and his chasing and catching a hare with the guns of the enemy trained on him, and she wondered sometimes whether spirituous liquor had been in him then.

After supper Maurice Valéry came to sit beside her. 'Mad'moiselle, I am so happy to see you here.' He spoke fluent English, but it was heavily accented. 'You are so beautiful.'

'Yes, I know,' she answered.

'You know?' He opened his deep-set eyes wide. 'Then it—'

'I meant only that I knew what you were going to say. Because you said it the last time we met.'

'Did I? *Alors*, that is what I *meant*! Is it unforgiven to repeat oneself twice?'

'Not if it is sincerely intended.'

'Why should you doubt it, Mad'moiselle?'

She smiled at him. 'How is your orchestra in Rouen?'

'It prospers mightily. But it is not quite *my* orchestra. I direct it and am given considerable freedom, but there is a committee to oversee. The committee controls the funds which enable us to function, so who holds the purse strings has a high degree of authority.'

'What have you been playing most recently?'

He told her. 'Of course there are some choral performances as well, but all too few. And I and two friends have a proposition to put before the committee that we should produce a series of operas. Why do you not come and see me there?'

'Christopher and I?' Bella said, looking around for Christopher.

After a slight hesitation Maurice said: 'With Christopher? But of course. Is it true that you are shortly to be married?'

'Probably at Easter. We shall go back to my home in Cornwall for that.'

Maurice dabbed his mouth with a lace handkerchief.

'Forgive what may seem an impertinence, Mad'moiselle, but it is sometimes incautious for a professional singer to become attached too soon.'

'Why?'

'Oh, it is so clear to be seen. A woman who has the ambition to become a prima donna assoluta should have – it is almost essential that she should have – a total dedication to her art. For her, love is a dalliance, a light emotional interlude, enabling romance to broaden and deepen her life, while on the other hand a settled domestic existence will only serve to choke and stultify.'

At the next table they were talking about the King's sudden death. 'I have been told,' came Count Von Badenberg's powerful voice, 'that the King just turned his face to the wall and said: "Tom's a-cold", and when his valet touched him he was dead!'

'Who is Tom?' someone asked.

There was a laugh.

Bella said: 'Are you married?'

Maurice smiled. 'No, Mad'moiselle. Oh no. Of course I have *amours*. That is necessary for a balanced life. But music is my marriage. I do not – I *think* I do not have the potential future that you have. To be a prima demands everything that a human being can give. A conductor is one stage lesser in the order – in a sense more important in the musical world, but he does not carry his instrument about in his own body, where it is a precious but fragile possession on which he depends nightly for his reputation, his fame, his total success or failure.'

'How do you know what my potential is?' Bella demanded. 'When have you heard me sing, Monsieur?'

'I have heard you twice. Do you remember going with your tutor,

218

Dr Fredericks, to a convent in Southwark, where some of his pupils performed before an invited audience?'

'Yes, but you—'

'I was there, quite by accident. Then again I called on Dr Fredericks to discuss one of his former pupils, and I heard you singing. I asked who it was, and he told me it was Miss Bella Poldark. Which in fact I had already guessed. Your voice has the rare quality of being unmistakable.'

Von Badenberg was still talking: 'Now the new King is sick almost to death. Eh, well, you would be well quit of all the Hanoverians. Britain would make a pretty republic!'

Bella said: 'Pray excuse me, I must seek Lieutenant Havergal.'

'He is in a little room off the dining room. I will take you to him – in a moment. First . . .'

'First?'

'I invited you to come to Rouen. It is only a provincial town but it is near Paris. If at any time in the future, *any time*, either before or after your marriage to Lieutenant Havergal, you thought to come *alone* to see my town, my orchestra, my theatre, either a visit of two or three days or to stay longer and sing at one of the operas we are planning, pray keep this card – that is my address, and send word to me. It would be a great privilege to escort you, and you shall be escorted home again whenever you choose.'

'Oh, thank you. But I—'

'This is not – what you call it? – superficial; this is serious. I want you, Mam'selle. I need you. I am making my way, and you are making your way. I need your voice and your presence. With them I could get to Paris, and take *you* to Paris. I do not know if you were jesting with me about your looks, but to me you are beautiful, and I long to put you in a new opera called *The Barber of Seville*. I would want you for the principal part, the mezzo part of Rosina. It is an opera that has not yet been seen in France. Will you please consider it?'

Bella looked into his earnest eyes. She felt suddenly hot.

'I – will . . . yes, I'll consider it, Monsieur Valéry. But . . .'

'Pray say no more now. I shall be in London again in early March. Return me your answer then.'

She had been about to move away, but she turned back.

'Monsieur Maurice . . . I do not think you can ask me to make such a decision. I am, as you know – committed. And willingly, happily committed. You have great hopes for my career. Christopher has great hopes for my career. I am – that grateful for your – your admiration and your interest. Perhaps somehow we might *all* get together sometime so that your hopes – and his hopes – can be put to the – put to the trial, the test. I am not ungrateful for your – your warm words, believe me. It is very good to be so – wanted. But I am – have been for a long time – bespoke.'

He smiled. 'You are very gentle. If—'

'No, I am not!'

'At least, you are very young. I am thirty-one. As life goes on one becomes more – more *cynique*. I admire you for your loyalty. But in ten years' time, looking back, you may feel that loyalty is not all.'

The house that Christopher was proposing to buy was in the Green Lane, which ran north parallel with Tottenham Court Road, a little further from Mrs Pelham's than Bella would have liked, but it was pretty, or would be when it was finished, being a smallish terraced house built in the style of Nash. The air, Christopher explained, was fresher up here, and the area was being rapidly developed for that reason.

She had found him last night asleep in a chair in the cloakroom; and he had staggered to his feet and then fallen down before pulling himself up again with Bella's help. Their carriage had been called and Bella had been irritated to have to wait inside the coach while Christopher was helped down the steps of the hotel to join her. As usual he was full of apologies and tender in his concern for her, but she felt his apologies a shade superficial as if he had accidentally trod on her foot in a cotillion.

As they were returning to Mrs Pelham's after visiting the new house, she interrupted him by saying: 'Christopher, have you heard of a man called Rossini?'

'Who? Rossini. I think he's a tenor. An Italian tenor. Why?'

'I'm told he has written an opera.'

'Oh? What is it called?'

'*The Barber of Seville.*'

Christopher stroked his moustache. 'I have heard of it. But I cannot recall where. What is it to you, my pet?'

'Maurice mentioned it last night. He said it was very good.'

'Has it been performed in England?'

'He did not say.'

There was a pause as the carriage rattled over some specially uneven cobbles. 'Bella,' he said, 'my sweet and lovely Bella, was I over-indulgent with the drink last night?'

This was the first time he had ever mentioned it on the following day.

'Yes, you were.'

He studied her face. 'All men do it from time to time, d'you know. It is like a safety valve in these new-fangled steam engines.'

'When you are like that I cannot control you. I cannot really speak to you.'

He looked displeased. 'I doubt if it is as bad as that. One comes to drink substantially in the Army. Perhaps it helps to keep one's courage up.'

She was minded to drop the matter, but some worm of contention in her nature pressed her to go on.

'Why do you not *eat*, Christopher? I mean on such occasions. Most men eat as heavily as they drink. I mean, they do it at the same time. You eat and drink normally at ordinary times. But – but on evenings like last night it is as if a demon is in you and taken away your appetite for food altogether, and leaves only . . .'

'A love of white wine? You are right. So it does. It is very sad, and I am sorry if it distresses you. But it happens but seldom. Maybe it is frustration.'

'Frustration?'

'Perhaps I shall be able to mend my ways after we are married.'

The following day Bella said: 'Dr Fredericks, do you know of a musician called Rossini?'

'Is it that you mean the horn player or his son, Antonio? It will be Antonio, no doubt. He has written several operas. He is a young man of talent. He was, I think, made musical director of the San Carlos Theatre in Naples when he was in his earliest twenties. What have you heard about him?'

'Did he write an opera called *The Barber of Seville*?'

'*Il Barbiere di Siviglia*? He did, yes, indeed. Of course it is a much-used subject, but he rewrote it in a new style. It is the most musically substantial of his works – so far.'

'Has it been performed in England?'

'Yes, here in London at the King's Theatre – oh, three or four years ago. I did not see it, but I read it. Please to tell me what your interest is?'

'I think you have met Maurice Valéry? At my aunt's house? He is the musical director of the theatre in Rouen. He was speaking of this opera on Wednesday evening. He hopes to put it on himself, in France.'

'Does your Monsieur Valéry know Rossini?'

'I don't know. I don't think so. But he thinks highly of the opera.'

'Good. Good.' Dr Fredericks eyed his pupil thoughtfully. 'I do not think it is for you, my little one. It is . . . *opera buffa* – *opéra comique*. You know – light in weight. Had you been thinking of it for yourself at some far, far future date?'

'No,' said Bella.

Book Three

MAURICE

Chapter One

Katie Thomas called to see Demelza. She was profuse in her apologies, but it seemed it was all to do with Mr Valentine's monkey. When he was brought here some months ago he had seemed a frightened thing, chattering, scratching, jumping about, up to all sorts of mischief, but no one really so much minded. Gentry often had strange pets, didn't they. But he was growing and growing – just like some magic pumpkin, as Cook said – mornings you could hear him barking, thumping the walls, and then screaming and coughing just as if he was being tormented. The upstairs maids had not really liked the monkey even when he was small, but now he was growing so big and so hairy twas like a nightmare when come upon sudden like.

'Where does Mr Valentine keep it?' asked Demelza.

'Two rooms at the back of the kitchen, ma'am. They'm just being fitted wi' bars. Last week he broke the windows and climbed over the fence they put up. Maisie, that's one of the maids, was affrighted out of 'er life when she seen 'im running round the cabbage patch!'

It happened to be the evening when the Enyses came over for their monthly supper, so Demelza brought up the subject of Katie's call. She added as she finished: 'I think most of the folk are scared of approaching Ross, so they come to me with their problems.'

'Very proper,' said Ross, 'but I think my influence on Valentine has been greatly exaggerated.'

'I've seen it,' said Dwight.

'What, my influence or the monkey?'

'It's an ape really. Valentine called one morning and asked my advice. The beast had a cold, a rheum, just like you and me. I rode back with him and made out a prescription.'

225

'He's growing fast?' Ross asked.

'Very fast. I don't think I have ever seen the like.'

'And what miracle does Katie expect me to perform?' Ross asked Demelza. 'Since the death of Agneta Valentine and I have scarcely spoken.'

'She wants for you to ask him to keep the monkey in a compound outside.'

'I doubt he'll take notice of anything I say.'

'It is unlikely you could keep him alive there without heating,' Dwight said. 'These apes all come from Africa and are none too hardy in spite of all their fur.'

'Perhaps that is in the minds of the staff,' Caroline said. 'It would certainly be in mine.'

'And to think I always supposed you to be an animal lover,' Dwight said ironically.

'Within limits, yes. I like dogs, especially pugs, spaniels, hounds, terriers, retrievers, bulldogs, beagles, collies; I like badgers and foxes and hares and rabbits and chicken and ducks; I like horses, cows, bulls – less extravagantly – sheep, deer, geese—'

'Very good, very good – '

'Very good. But that does not mean I relish the thought of some hairy beast at large in the village – or at least in a position to be let loose on the village by that dangerously neurotic young man who now lives at Trevaunance.'

Demelza laughed.

'What are you laughing at?' Ross asked.

'At Caroline, of course. It all seemed, suddenly seemed – very funny.'

'I suggest,' said Ross after a moment, 'that funny is all at present it can be. I'm sorry for Katie and the other maids, but unless Valentine *does* let the animal loose on the village there is little or nothing to be done. Certainly for me to call with a protest would be to invite the rude rebuff I'd deserve.'

Dwight said: 'I was reading only yesterday that there are large farms in Mongolia where dogs are bred for their skins. When the dogs are eight months old they are all strangled, skinned, and after being cured the skins sewn together and made into a coat. I believe they fetch about six shillings and sixpence per coat.'

'Sometimes,' Caroline said, 'I wonder how I came to marry you.'

*

226

Clowance had been riding with Philip Prideaux when he asked her to marry him.

A brilliant March day with a light easterly wind made the air cold, but if one got out of the wind, the sun, unfiltered by haze or a heavy atmosphere, was strong and powerfully warming.

They had stopped and dismounted at Helford Passage, where the ferry crossed the Helford River to the village of Helford, but they had no intention of crossing. The ferryman, short of custom, had had to be waved away.

In early March Philip's father had died, and he had been absent two weeks. She had missed him, even the slight abrasiveness that was now a part of their companionship. Two days ago he had called and suggested they should ride together today if the weather kept up.

As they rode he had told her a little about his family. They were country gentlefolk of long ancestry – could trace their ancestry, he said with that touch of arrogance, to Devon and Cornwall before the Norman Conquest. His uncle, the Reverend Charles Prideaux-Brune, occupied the family house at Padstow, his father had been son of a younger brother, but they farmed extensively in Devon. There were villages in Cornwall called Prideaux and Little Prideaux near Luxulyan.

'My uncle,' he said, smiling, 'was ordained, and since the living of Padstow was in his gift, he gave it to himself!'

Philip's father had died of a sudden heart attack. Philip said he would have to return shortly to comfort his mother, but before he did this he specially wanted to ask Clowance if perhaps they might plan a future together.

This much was said before they dismounted. Tethering their horses, they sat on one of the green benches placed along the river bank where one could wait to catch the ferry. On the opposite bank the little town of Helford crouched among its massive shelter of trees. The river gleamed peacock blue and emerald in shafts of the morning sun. Three tiny boats with ochre and scarlet sails were tacking here and there, casting for mackerel and whiting.

Clowance said: 'When the trees are in leaf it's hardly possible to see the town. It might be a church tower sprouting in a forest.'

He flipped some tall grasses back and forth with the end of his riding crop. It had been easy for him so far, words could be spoken out loud, cast into the air, some she might not even have heard.

'Clowance,' he said, 'I have long, as you know, had a deep affection for you. I – trust I have made that clear.'

'Yes,' she said.

'I have hitherto refrained from attempting to take it further for – mainly two reasons. One, I was not sure I had sufficiently recovered from my breakdown to offer myself as a husband and friend. Two, my income was too slight. Now – now my father's sudden and much regretted demise will result in the second objection being removed. I shall not be rich, but I shall have more than a competence. As for the first . . .'

She did not speak, assembling her thoughts and feelings.

He said: 'As for the first, I confess I'm not yet quite the man I was. I cannot get control of my responses to some situation that suddenly presents itself – often too hasty, sometimes regrettable. Nervous tensions appear to build up unawares.'

'Are you suffering nervous tension now?' she asked, with a smile.

Stopped in his tracks, he said: 'Well – er – not, not in the way I had meant—'

'Because I am.'

Her interruption had lightened the mood. He smiled back, though still a little tight-lipped.

'You must,' he said, 'be lonely at times, as I am lonely. Loving companionship is beyond price. I find it quite difficult to smile when I am on my own! There's not much light-heartedness in solitude. Your very presence at my side would, I'm convinced, give me the strength to overcome these nervous tensions. Possibly they will go of their own accord in a year or so. They have already improved – I'm certain that you are capable of dismissing the last of them at the altar!'

One of the boat fishermen threw something into the river and gulls swooped down in a patter of conflicting wings to seize on the prospective food. For a moment the assembly of them looked like a large paper dart fluttering in the boat's wake.

'This,' she said, 'is a – a considered proposal, Philip. Perhaps I need a little time to give you a considered answer.'

'Of course,' he said, 'of course.'

He had put a hand in his jacket pocket to take out his glasses, but only grasped them and released them.

'You see, Philip,' she said, 'it is not perhaps as easy for me as one might suppose. But thank you, thank you for paying me this compliment.'

'What does that mean?'

'It means that I was in love with my husband.'

He pursed his lips. 'And still are?'

'No. *No.* I *was* in love. It's a very complex situation. I – I tell you it's hard to explain.'

'Pray pay me the compliment of trying.'

The two ferrymen were rowing over to Helford, having spotted someone who wanted to cross.

'Sometimes I find it hard to explain to myself! It is all really bound up in feelings that are hard to describe. I can't remember how old I was when I first saw Stephen – about seventeen – but I fell completely and immediately in love with him! We had a long – and once interrupted – courtship before I married him. He was not, Philip, a very admirable man. He had been brought up rough and lived rough all his life until he came ashore from a wreck at Nampara and met Jeremy and the rest of my family. Although I thought – truly believed – during the time when we had quarrelled and he had gone away, that it had all been a girlish passion which had now blown over, I knew instantly, irrevocably, when I saw him again that there was only one man for me, and that there never would be anyone else in quite that way.'

The wind had backed a point or two and was coming round the corner. Within five minutes the river had quickened into life and little wrinkles disturbed its placid surface. Clowance put her hand to her hair and tucked a few errant wisps more securely under her hat.

'I married him and went to live in Penryn and we were very happy. Then, after he had escaped several dangers while he was sailing in one of our ships under letters of marque – in *great* danger of being captured by the French; an incredible escape from being killed by a French gendarme – after all that he was killed in a stupid riding accident. It was too absurd!'

He touched her gloved hand. 'I'm sorry.'

'I am telling this very badly. What I have so far failed to tell you is really the crux of the matter. I will not – cannot – go into details, but before he died, shortly before he died I found that he had lied to me, deliberately lied to me in a matter of great importance. I think for *any* woman it would have been a matter of great importance. And I found myself, found myself when he died, grief-stricken in two quite separate ways!'

'Lady Harriet did mention—'

'Harriet knows nothing of this. No one knows *anything* of this. But it has left me in the strangest way bereft. Bereft of feeling for him. In a sense bereft of feelings for other men.'

'Perhaps we can help each other.'

'Perhaps, Philip. That is what I have to decide. D'you know, I read the other day of a clergyman who had committed suicide because he had lost his faith in God. I have not lost my faith in God. I have lost faith in other human beings! And I have lost trust – completely lost trust in my own feelings, my own judgement!'

She had said more than she had intended and on the way had become as serious as he. They sat there as the cool breeze wafted against their heated faces.

She said: 'I told you Harriet knows nothing of this. But if she did I think she would think me humourless and silly. She *has* deep feelings, but they are always controlled by a sophisticated awareness – awareness that it is fatal to expect perfection either in oneself or in other people.'

'Harriet is a very sophisticated person,' Philip said.

There was a long silence. Then Clowance shivered.

'Shall we try another way home? We can make for Porth Navas and then instead of crossing the creek I know a way across country back to Mawnan Smith.'

Chapter Two

On the twentieth of March Demelza received one of her weekly –
or almost weekly – letters from Isabella-Rose.

Dearest Mama,
Your last letter told me lots of things I have been wanting to
know, but sadly that no one has yet been caught for the
murder of poor Agneta. It must be uncomfortable to feel that
someone is at large and perhaps prowling. Yet what you write
is always like a breath of Nampara: I can smell the sea, feel the
push and pull of the wind, smell the cows in their byre, the
scent of mown hay, hear the crackle of the Welsh coal in the
hearth, and the tap-tap of Papa's pipe on the fire bars.

You may think I am homesick? Well yes, I am. And no, I am
not. I *long* to see you, and in a month I shall be home. But I
love this life too – the *noises* of London, and, phew, the smells!
And the bustle, and the things folk write about and the things
they talk about. It is a great beehive of learning and struggling
and scandal and sophistication. While I long for the purity
and simplicity of Cornwall I relish this big bawdy, booming
city and the challenge that it has for me.

Well, after such a long prologue, now let me tell you the
most important news of the month – it is that Christopher and
I have decided to postpone our marriage until June!

First, our lovely little house, which had been promised for
us at latest by the end of April, is lagging behind, quite
seriously behind, and the builder cannot see it likely to be
ready for occupation before the end of June.

Second, Christopher has been asked by Mr Nathan Rothschild to go to Lisbon to visit the branch of the Bank they have

established there. He will be away seven weeks, and I would love to go with him as his wife, but he must leave on the third of April, which would not permit of the banns being published in time. Christopher is also a little against it because he hears there is a deal of fever in Lisbon and he does not want to put me at risk.

So, dearest Mama, if you can confer with our new vicar, Mr Profitt, is he called? – what an excellent name! – and your dear husband – my beloved father – and suggest one or two dates in late June, I will talk with Chris and see what is the best date for us all. I will write soon to Clowance and Cuby and Sophia and Meliora, and break this brief postponement to them, but if you see any of them in the next week pray warn them that they may inform their seamstress not to be in too great a hurry to cut out the bridesmaids' frocks!

This, I think, will be a big move up for Christopher.

The letter went on for two more pages.

When Demelza showed it to Ross that evening he took what seemed a long time reading it. Then he started to read it again from the beginning.

Demelza interrupted this: 'Well, what do you think of it?'

He fingered his scar. 'I think the lady doth protest too much.'

'What does that mean exactly?'

'She gives us three reasons why the wedding should be postponed.'

'I know. But—'

He said: 'The house is not ready. Hm, valid enough, I suppose. But after so long a wait might they not have taken some other house for three months?'

'Ye-es. Perhaps she did not like the idea. But Christopher will be away . . .'

'True enough. But I always have a suspicion of when there are a variety of reasons for doing or not doing something. Of course it may be taken precisely at its face value. But I should be more inclined to believe the first two reasons if the third were not so thin.'

'You mean . . .?'

'Christopher says there is a deal of fever in Lisbon and does not want to expose her to the risk. Have you ever in your life known

Bella to be deterred from doing something she wants to do because of the risk?'

Demelza listened to Henry stamping his feet. The thumping came from his bedroom, and it sounded like temper.

'There's nothing we can do, Ross.'

'There's nothing we *should* do. Except take it for what it is . . . I wonder if we are in any way to blame . . .'

'Us? Why?'

'I mean, perhaps they have been together too long, have got to know each other too well.'

'How could she marry earlier? She was a child! Still is, in many ways.' Demelza turned. 'Yours is a very cynical view, Ross. Are you saying that two people who want to marry and are not able to they will in the end get to know each other so well that they no longer wish to marry at all?'

He smiled grimly. 'It *could* happen. But in any decent marriage there is the element of lust – call it what you will – that binds the two people together. If that fails they will drift apart – after marriage. But so far as Christopher and Bella are concerned, Bella has been very carefully guarded by Sarah Pelham. I do not wish to speculate as to the physical relationship between Christopher and Bella, how far it has gone, but it cannot have been remotely similar to a loving marital state. It can have staled.'

'Listen to Harry,' said Demelza. 'I must go and stop him.'

'He needs the swish of a cane,' said Ross.

'I know. And we are both too soft-hearted even to threaten him.'

'We do not threaten him, because if you once do that and he defies you you have to carry your threat through.'

The trouble had all really begun about three weeks ago when they were coming out of a tiny shop in Little Swallow Street, where Christopher had just bought a buff yellow and rose silk waistcoat. A young woman waved to him and came across the street.

'Oh, Christopher, my dearest, I have not seen you for days. You was not at Mme Cono's last night.'

She was a doll-like young woman in a reseda green dress, a white foxtail about her throat and a jaunty green hat. Wisps of excessively blonde hair escaped around her ears.

Christopher had not seemed disconcerted. 'I have been busy, Letty. My employer is a hard taskmaster. May I introduce you to Miss Isabella-Rose Poldark? This is Letty Hazel.'

Conversation had followed. Bella nodded and smiled noncommittally and prodded the cobbles gently with her parasol.

'So you are the young Cornish lady who is going to marry Christopher,' said Miss Hazel. 'I wish you both much happiness.'

'Thank you,' said Bella, a little less impersonally, and smiled again.

'When are you to marry?'

'After Easter,' Christopher said.

'Oh, quite soon! We shall miss you at Mme Cono's, Chris. *I* shall miss you. Are you coming tomorrow night? There is to be a party for Captain Crossland.'

'I do not think so. Anyway, Crossland was never a captain. He was never gazetted beyond a lieutenant.'

'These army officers,' said Letty to Bella, and giggled. 'Faith, they are always quarrelling as if the war was not long since over!'

'And some *talk* as if it were not,' said Christopher. 'Well, we must be going, Letty. Pray give my regards to all my friends.'

'I'll tell *all* the girls. Perhaps some of us may come to your wedding if we was invited!'

'It is to be in Cornwall,' he had said. 'Four days' travelling, at the least. But remember me in your thoughts.'

In Dr Fredericks's establishment there was a young man of some fortune studying to be a horn player. His family lived in London and he seemed well acquainted with the modern, fashionable life of the metropolis. He had twice made fairly courteous advances to Bella until she had introduced him to Christopher when he sheered off. Talking to him the following day, she brought up the name of a coffee house called, she believed, Mme Cono's. Had he heard of it?

He looked surprised. 'Cono's. Of course. Though I haven't been there. That is if it is the place I suppose you to mean? But it is not a coffee house. I presume – I trust – your fiancé did not take you there?'

'No . . . oh, no. It was just in conversation. I heard the name several times. Could there be, do you suppose, two such places?'

'Not with that name surely. I believe the owner comes originally from Chile.'

'And what exactly is it?'

'Oh, a form of restaurant, a club with quite an exclusive membership. But in essence it is chiefly known as a house of ill repute. Do you know where it is? Just off Berkeley Street on the left as you approach Piccadilly.'

'Oh,' said Bella. 'I see.'

'I believe the Duke of Cumberland is a member. And Lord Walpole.'

'How interesting.'

'Christopher,' Bella said, out of the blue, as it were, 'where did you meet Letty Hazel?'

'Who?' Christopher asked. 'Oh, Letty. I met her at a friend's house in Twickenham.'

'This month? Last month?'

They had been supping together at an expensive coffee house in Great Jermyn Street. Bella was sometimes allowed out with Christopher if they used Mrs Pelham's coach and coachman to take them to their destination and to bring them back. Tonight, being fine and balmy and the ways assured, they had chosen to walk a little way together. Harris and his coach followed at a discreet distance.

He limped beside her for a few moments in silence.

'Before you met me?'

'What? Oh, Letty. No, not before I *met* you. But *long* before I became betrothed to you.'

'She and I have never met before. You have never brought her to a party I was at.'

'No. I did not think you would mix very well.'

'May I ask why?'

'Because you are a lady and she is not.'

'Why is she not a lady?'

'Oh, Bella. These are troublesome questions. Do you not – can you not guess?'

'I am a young provincial, Christopher. Don't you think you should explain?'

He reflected a moment. He wondered if his betrothed was having him on.

'Let's say she belongs to a circle that I would not wish you to belong to.'

'Do you belong to it?'

'Not really. To some extent, I suppose.'

'We have been together much, Christopher. You have never told me of it. It is – another side to your life.'

'Possibly you will guess it is a part of my life I didn't wish you to know of.'

They turned out into Piccadilly. This was well lighted and paved. There were beggars about, but they did not importune. They stood mainly in the shadows watching the rich go by in their carriages.

He said: 'We are not now far from Pulteney's, where we were last week. Did you like Von Badenberg?'

'He speaks English beautifully.'

'But talks too much, eh?'

'Perhaps.'

He took her arm. 'We'll walk a bit further. Harris can keep us in sight.'

'Yes.'

'Do you know how Piccadilly came by its name? Rothschild was telling me last night. It comes from Piccadill. It is the name of a fastening that holds the collar of a doublet. A draper called Robert Baker made a fortune selling the things and built himself a great house just north of Marylebone Street. That's a couple of hundred years ago.'

They walked in silence. With his false foot he managed amazingly well.

She said: 'Dear Christopher. Was it wise to take me into that area where you might at any time encounter some lady from Mme Cono's?'

He sighed. 'Dear Bella, I have not lived my life without risk. I don't think you need trouble your mind about it, pet.'

After a minute she said: 'Perhaps it is not my mind which is chiefly troubled. There could be – baser instincts.'

He smiled, and his moustache twitched in the attractive way she knew so well. 'I do not believe you have baser instincts, Bella.'

'And you have?'

'But of course.'

'And was I ever to catch sight of these – these baser instincts?'

'I don't think I shall have the need of them once we are married.

I intend to resign from Mme Cono's shortly. Perhaps in a year or so, when we have been happily married for a while, I might have told you of the existence of the club. It will by then have become part of my past life. I am not a saint, Bella. I think I told you that when I first met Geoffrey Charles, when he was my commanding officer in the forty-third Monmouthshires, that I then had a Portuguese mistress who followed me in my wagon train.'

'You did,' said Bella. 'It was part of your past life. I found it infinitely dashing.'

'Well, then?'

'That was your past life, Christopher. This is your present.'

'Which will soon be past.'

A little later, as they drove home in their darkened carriage, she said: 'How long is it, may I ask, since you saw Letty last?'

'Saw her? A week.'

'And before that?'

'Two weeks, three weeks.' He waved an impatient arm. 'Something like that.'

'Very much in the present, then.'

'As you say.'

'No, *you* say. And all the time you were meeting me, encouraging me, kissing me, and I knew nothing of this other life!'

'As I shall continue to do, as far as you are concerned, my pet. My *endless* interest in you and my *temporary* interest in her are two entirely different things. Have done with it, Bella.' There was a hint of steeliness in his voice now. 'Have done with it, my pet. Forget it. It is nothing.'

Bella said after a moment: 'To me it is not nothing.'

He kissed her. He brushed her lips from side to side and whispered: 'Sigh no more, lady, sigh no more. Men were deceivers ever.'

Chapter Three

Ben Carter and Esther Carne were married in the Church of St
Sawle, Grambler with Sawle, on Monday, the seventeenth of April
1820. Sam Carne, Esther's uncle, gave the bride away.

It was a quiet wedding – at the request of them both, but a fair
number of people turned up just the same. Tom and Clotina
Smith, Esther's elder sister and brother-in-law, walked over from
Lanner with Luke, one of Demelza's brothers. And Drake and his
tall, elegant, spectacled wife, Morwenna, and his tall and spectacled
but not so elegant daughter, Loveday, also came. Ross and Demelza
shared their pew with Geoffrey Charles and Amadora, who, having
quite recently given birth to another daughter, Carla, came specially to wish her favourite nursemaid well. Though not yet quite
farewell: Essie had agreed to stay on until such time as she might
become *enceinte* herself.

The engagement had been short but not without incident. The
question of Religion reared its head; both Sam and Jinny in their
respective ways showing their doubts about Essie's apparent liking
for the Catholic religion and their desire – if the marriage *had* to
go ahead – that Essie should be taken out of the sphere of
Amadora's dangerous influence.

They could have wasted their breath and saved a number of
fruitless arguments. Ben had a strong will, a quiet but dynamic
presence, and he knew exactly what he wanted for himself and
what he wanted for Essie, and that was that. Having been introduced to Amadora Poldark more formally than at the Christmas
party, he formed a high opinion of her and, having sounded out
Essie's views previously, decided that she should stay on at Trenwith
as a daily from eight till four, just so long as she wanted and so
long as she was able.

The bride wore the same dress that she had worn to the party, but with some extra lacy decorations and a little inexpensive borrowed jewellery. The bridegroom also made do with the fineries that had been stitched up for him for Christmas, except for a blue tailcoat with brass buttons that Ross had once worn at sea.

Mr Odgers had died in the September, and the ceremony was performed by the Reverend Henry Profitt, who had since been appointed curate in charge, and who was temporarily lodged in rooms in the village while Mrs Odgers tearfully gathered the remnants of her children about her and prepared to move. Profitt, who, as far as Ross could discover, had no more claim to being considered an ordained clergyman than Odgers had, but who came with recommendations from Francis de Dunstanville, was a tall thin man with a stork-like appearance. Caroline said that if there were any fishponds in the district one would be anxious for the safety of the fish.

He was a brisk man; religion to him was a brisk affair. The mills of God moved to a timetable. At least he had the edge on old Mr Odgers in not confusing the marriage and the funeral services and remembering the Christian names of the couple to be joined.

In the end the church was more than half full, for Ben, for all his gruffness and quick temper, was well respected and indeed liked, and Esther, though a foreigner from Illuggan, was a pretty little thing. Several matrons, now with young families of their own, came to see him wed at last and remembered when they would have wanted to be in her shoes.

The vows were taken and the couple moved into the vestry to sign the register. (Ben could manage, but it was 'Esther X, her mark.') Esther had asked Demelza if she would be one of the witnesses, and she followed the others in.

So she was unaware of the commotion that broke out at the back of the church when two or three, intending to go out with bags of rice, exclaimed in wild surprise.

People stopped and hesitated and shoved from behind as others, half out, turned to come back. Then the shouting began.

'Tis a hanimal!'

'Nay, tes the Devil Hiself. My ivers, leave me get *back*!'

'Shut the door. He'm comin' this way!'

Ross, who had not gone into the vestry with Demelza, forced his way down the aisle and reached the church door, which some women were trying vainly to shut. He pulled it open again and two boys, who had been the first to leave the church, shot in.

There were a half-dozen people scattered about the churchyard, but the path to the church was occupied by only one figure. It was a large ape standing part on its hind legs. It was at least four feet tall, with a great cannonball of a head, flattened nose, deep bloodshot eyes, a mat of black hair on its chest and down the outside of its enormous arms. In one hand it carried what looked like a loaf of bread. When it saw Ross it coughed, then barked like a dog and bared its great teeth.

'What in hell is it?' demanded Geoffrey Charles, who had followed Ross out of the church. 'And where in hell has it come from?'

'It's Valentine's ape,' said Ross.

'My God, it must be! I've heard word of it but never seen it until now.'

The beast dropped on its haunches and began to tear what it held in its hands and eat it. Quite clearly it *was* a loaf of bread.

'More importantly,' Ross said, 'where in hell is Valentine?'

'Darned thing must have escaped. The women will never come out of the church with this at large. I've had a lot to do with Frenchmen but nothing to do with apes. Don't even know if they are dangerous.'

'I wouldn't risk it,' said Ross. 'I don't even have a stick. Anything in the church, d'you think?'

He went back. Everyone was standing facing him. Ben and Essie were just coming out of the vestry.

He raised his voice: 'There's a big monkey outside,' he said. 'I think it belongs to Mr Valentine. No one should leave at present because the animal may be dangerous. I'd advise you all to sit down and keep calm. It won't come in here. In the meantime will two of you, Varcoe and Emil Jones – you're both young – take the vestry door and run to the village. Borrow a horse from someone and hurry to Place House, find Mr Warleggan and tell him what has happened.'

While he had been talking, reassured by his tone, three or four of the young lads who had been pushing first to get out and then to get in again, now stepped out a second time and viewed the animal from a cautious distance. The ape had moved a few feet further away and was moodily pulling at one of the headstones. It still looked a savage animal, its lips taut, its fur bristling. It seemed out of breath and gave regular grunts as it tugged at the slate stone.

A few people were looking in now from behind the comparative safety of the churchyard wall. One threw a stone. Then another stone was better aimed and hit the animal on the arm.

It raised itself suddenly to its full height, then beat its breast in a fearful roar. It tugged violently at the slate headstone and this time the slate snapped. The ape picked up the broken piece and hurled it in the direction the stone had come from. Even its great strength could not propel the headstone far enough to hit anyone, but the people scattered at the threat. Trotting on the balls of its feet, it regained the lychgate. The onlookers had fled for their lives. The ape hooted in annoyance and frustration. Then instead of going after them it turned and galloped back towards the church door.

There was a strangled shout as the boys dived back into the church, but two could not get in in time, panicked and ran across the churchyard. The ape pursued them at twice their pace and quickly caught up with one, a boy called Tim Sedden. The boy stood and screamed at the top of his voice. The ape stopped barely a yard away and bared its teeth.

Then there was a whistle. 'Hey there, have you got my little man? Butto. Butto, my old friend.'

It was Valentine astride Nestor. He looked entirely composed and clucked gently to the ape, which cocked its head knowingly at the familiar voice.

'Cousin Ross,' said Valentine, raising his crop in ironical greeting. 'And Geoffrey Charles? Has my little man been disturbing you?'

Butto made a sudden galloping rush at the group of people who had now come out of the church, and they scattered for their lives. One elderly woman stumbled over a gravestone and fell heavily. Butto stopped and stared at her, and she screamed piercingly. The ape plucked at his bottom lip and chattered, while two men, greatly daring, edged nearer until they could help the woman to her feet and drag her out of danger.

Then the ape was off again, leaping up to the windowsill of the church and from there to a vantage point astride the church porch.

'You're frightening him,' said Valentine. 'He is far more frightened of you than you are of him. Butto, Butto. Tutti-frutti, tutti-frutti,

241

tutti-frutti, come down from there, boy, or you'll fall. He's not a great climber,' he said conversationally to Geoffrey Charles, 'but of course he gets around!'

'He is getting around altogether too much,' snapped Geoffrey Charles. 'You see what the women think – they're terrified by the brute. You must find better ways of keeping him under control – that is if you want to keep him at all!'

Valentine laughed. 'I would not lose my Butto for all the world! Now that my wife and child have left me, he is my only companion. Tutti-frutti, tutti-frutti, look what I have for you, boy.' He put a hand in his pouch and took out a parcel. He said to Ross: 'He cannot resist fruitcake.'

'Shoot'n!' came a shout at the back of the crowd. 'Oo's got a gun? Tes a danger to the community!'

'Shoot'n,' others took up the cry. 'Tes a dangerous wild beast. E'd eat our childer! Shoot'n. Shoot'n. Go on, 'Arry, you got a shotgun!'

'Not 'ere I ain't!'

Valentine's answer was to dismount from his horse and walk up to the church porch, making soothing sounds and clucking with his lips almost as if mimicking the ape. Butto looked at him cunningly and extended a long hand. Valentine was just tall enough to pass up the large loaf of cake. The big beast carefully unwrapped it from its paper and stuffed the whole cake in his mouth, grumbling with satisfaction. Great teeth and pink gums and a pink tongue were much in evidence, and the torn paper floating.

'Greedy Butto,' said Valentine. 'It is more genteel to eat it in smaller pieces. However, we shall see.' When Butto had finished and was licking his lips and picking at his teeth, Valentine took another similar packet from his pouch and held it out for the animal to see. Butto stretched out his hand.

'No, no,' said Valentine, 'you must come down. I will give you this when you behave properly.'

After a while Butto got tired of holding out his hand. He withdrew it to scratch.

'Come along,' said Valentine. 'None of this nonsense. Tutti-frutti, tutti-frutti. Down you come.'

The ape stared with cavernous black eyes at the men and women watching the scene. He extended his great arm over the side of the porch again.

'When you come down,' said Valentine, 'then you may ride home.'

There was a lot of chattering and blowing out of lips.

'They will not hurt you,' Valentine said. 'And they had better not try. They are only here to watch.'

A scuttling at the back of the crowd and someone shouted, 'Ere's 'Arry wi' 'is musket!'

'I doubt if twill fire,' said the owner. 'I not used him for two year!'

'Use it now at your peril,' shouted Valentine, and then angrily: 'Butto!'

The ape began to slide down the slate roof and fell to the ground landing on all-fours. Valentine grasped the animal by the fur behind his neck and pulled forward Nestor. Horse looked at ape. They clearly knew each other. Then Valentine said to Geoffrey Charles: 'Give me a hoist.' Presently he was in the saddle and he turned and clucked at Butto, still holding the second parcel of cake in one hand. A moment's hesitation, then Butto took hold of the saddle and in an ungainly lurch pulled himself up and sat himself behind Valentine. Nestor twitched his ears and snorted. But he did not rear or show other distress.

'Good day to you all,' Valentine called and touched his hat. The horse turned awkwardly on the path and then made its way quietly to the lychgate. One or two people laughed nervously as if in a release of tension. As soon as the horse and its two riders turned away towards home everyone in the churchyard began talking at once.

Isabella-Rose was not home for Easter, but she arrived the following Friday. She had found difficulty in picking a travelling companion, she said, and Christopher had taken ship for Lisbon on the day after Good Friday. She seemed just as cheerful as ever, and discussed the postponement of their marriage plans without apparent embarrassment. It would now probably be June, which would give her another term with Dr Fredericks. Christopher thought, and she agreed, that it was time for her to leave his school and move on. The question was where and *how* to move on. Someone offering both some further teaching but mainly performance was what she now needed.

Clowance had not come for Easter either but, hearing that her sister's wedding had been postponed and that she was on her way home, she took a few days off from her 'hobby' as Christopher was inclined to call it and rode over the day after Isabella-Rose arrived. She was therefore present at most of the family conversations and agreed with her mother that Bella seemed perfectly normal, unruffled by the postponement and 'not a bit changed'. But she wondered privately whether Bella was deeper than most people thought.

Demelza wondered exactly the same thing.

Sisters can sometimes confide in each other where a mother and daughter cannot. The two young women walked on the beach in the wayward, windy April sun, the sea's surf rushing and sucking at their feet. They clattered down into Nampara cove. They climbed along the cliffs together. They became young again and slid down the great sandhills. They decided that before Clowance left they should ride over to Place together and see Valentine and make the acquaintance of Butto, the great ape. They laughed and chatted and joked as they had not done since Jeremy died.

(Clowance had a letter in her pocket that she had received just before she left Penryn. She had not brought it to show her mother – still less Bella – but she wanted time to read it again and did not like to leave it lying about the house.)

She asked Bella if she had met Philip Prideaux. Bella said, of course, at the party, and then again when he came to escort Clowance home; but she did not know him well, they had only exchanged a few words. Christopher had talked more to him because of their army history.

'He has asked me to marry him,' Clowance said, surprising herself that it had come out.

'Oh?' And then: 'What did you say?'

'I said I would think it over.'

'And are you?'

'What, thinking it over?'

'No, going to marry him.'

'I don't know. I'm thinking it over.'

'Do you love him?'

'Not the way I did Stephen.'

They thought of this together.

'I suppose there are more ways than one of loving a man,' said Bella.

'Oh, yes. He's . . . eligible.'

'Good-looking.'

'I'm glad you think so. He – says he has money enough.'

'That's not a disadvantage. It would mean you would sell your shipping line.'

'Such as it is, yes.'

'You must be tired of it, Clowance?'

'I am not tired of my independence.'

'Ah . . . That's another matter.'

'You see . . .', the elder girl struggled with her words, 'you see, I *like* Philip. At first, not so. I thought he was – well, certainly not for me. But as time has passed I have grown to like him very much. He is a victim of the war – just as Christopher is – but in a different way. He is – very high-strung, taut – sometimes it seems almost overmastering. But I have helped him – could do more. I – at times we still bicker a little with each other, but it is quickly made up and no longer seems to matter. And his company is stimulating. I lack company in Penryn. Except for Harriet Warleggan and one or two such as she, I have few friends. And most of those have families – interests of their own . . . But at the moment I have an uncomfortable feeling . . .'

'What is that, m'love?' Unusual, the younger girl counselling the older. Bella's time in London had already matured her in a way that gave her the edge of experience over the provincial Clowance.

'I am still – partly in love with Stephen. At the end I almost – almost came to hate him. Yet he is the one I fell in love with at first sight. In a way I know now I am, sort of, remembering a fallen idol. I should forget him. But, when it comes to the physical part of marriage, should I? Should I?'

The clouding sky was miles high today. Bella thought she heard a lark. She said: 'Perhaps we have been brought up too well?'

'How do you mean? Given too much of our own way?'

'No, not that . . . Clowance, I do not wish to shock you, but if your experience was not with just one man, I mean if you had had love affairs with three or four men before your marriage, the attentions of one man, the art of love would not seem so special and you had nothing else, no one else, to compare it with.'

'I think, Bella, you do shock me!'

Bella laughed. 'Well, is it not so? Women are so gravely disadvantaged compared with men. Men have all sorts of experiences before they marry – that is not shocking, nor does it belong only to one class, it is expected of them. They think it is their right!'

Clowance smiled in return. 'That's the way of the world. Alas. Or perhaps alas. You would not have me frolicking with all sorts of young men even before I met Stephen? Should I be better equipped now to take another husband? Would I?'

Bella said: 'Yes.'

They both laughed again.

Clowance said: 'So I am supposed to think you have been living a randy life in London for upwards of a year? Perhaps even with Christopher? Perhaps with someone else? Is that the cause of the delayed marriage?'

'That's clever, Clowance, but you are wrong. But there are other reasons why I am not sorry for the delay. Especially to come down here among my own family and take a few deep breaths. Sometimes one feels – do you feel? – that your own family is better than any other? You grow up to certain standards . . .'

'Don't talk to me about standards! One thing I know for sure, that Philip's standards are higher than Stephen's were. I – have another man who is proposing I shall marry him, and I daresay his standards are even higher than Philip's—'

'*Clowance, who –* '

'But does one marry *standards*? Does Christopher ever deliberately lie to you, Bella? Or would he? Stephen did many times, but, I ask you, does it *matter*?'

Bella patted her sister's hand. 'Yes, I think he may have lied to me. Or – at least – he may not have spoken, when not to speak amounts to a sort of lie. Yes, I think it does matter. But who is this other man? Do tell. Do I know him?'

Clowance shook her head. 'Lips sealed. For the time being, at least. Do not tell Mama!'

'I promise. "Cross me throat and spit to die," as Prudie used to say.'

'Because Mama's perceptions are altogether too sharp. It is so good to have you home, Bella, if only for a short time. You have grown up – so grown up. It would be good if we could stay here all together as a family for just a few months.'

'I know. I know!'

They had come back to the stile which led into the garden of Nampara. A curtain of mist hung over the Black Cliffs at the further end of Hendrawna Beach, most of it caused by spray hitting the tall rocks and drifting before the breeze. There was a heavy swell which reached far out to sea, and a couple of fishing boats from St Ann's had gone scudding back to the safety of the very unsafe harbour. Gulls were riding the swell, lifting high and low as the waves came in; occasionally they took to the air in a flurry of flapping white when a wave unexpectedly spilled its head. No one yet expected rain: that would be tomorrow. The sun was losing its brilliance and hung in the sky like a guinea behind a muslin cloth.

Clowance squinted up at the weather.

'Have you got a watch?'

'No. Not one that goes.'

'It must be an hour since we finished dinner. It wants four hours until dusk. I have a mind to visit Valentine today. What do you think?'

Bella said: 'There are a few of those bananas left that you brought with you.'

'Did you like them?'

'Yes, I did rather.'

'They come every month now to Penryn Quay. Most of them have to be cooked because they're over-ripe. But this bunch was just ripe.'

'The ape – Button, is it?'

'Butto.'

'Butto. We might take a few with us to see if he fancies them.'

Chapter Four

As they came in sight of Place House they had a good view of the workings of Wheal Elizabeth, which almost straddled the bridle path near the house. The headgear had grown considerably this year, but there was still no sign of any fire engine or pumping gear. They were greeted respectfully by the only two miners visible above ground, edged their horses round a monstrous mound of attle, of which many tons had already been tipped or slid down the sloping cliff into the sea.

'It is not a pretty house,' said Bella, as they clattered up the short cobbled drive.

All seemed quiet. A horse whinnied in the stables, and Nero snorted his response. Dismount at the stone step, tether their animals and go up the three steps to the front door. Clowance gave the bell a healthy tug.

They waited. Now they could hear voices, laughter, shouts, before the footsteps in the flagged hall. The door squeaked open. A stocky man in a black coat and a striped apron looked out. Neither of them had seen him before.

'Yus?'

'I hope Mr Valentine is at home,' Clowance said.

The man stared at them, then past them at their tethered horses. 'That depends.'

More footsteps in the hall. The tall, debonair figure of Valentine. But he was not very debonair today. His black lank hair was awry, and someone had spilled wine down his shirt front.

'Clowance! And B-bella! Well, damn me. Well, damn my eyes. Have you come to dinner? We h-have all but finished!'

'At four o'clock,' said Clowance, guessing at the time and smiling. 'You eat late, cousin. Perhaps we may call again—'

'Nay, nay, nay, nay, nay. Come in! Come right in! Come in and meet my friends. All right, Dawson, don't h-hold the damned door like we were in a damned fortress! Well, my grandfather's ghost, this is a surprise! We can offer you a slice or two of goose, and a pot or two of brandywine. Let me greet you!'

He kissed them both on the lips with gusto, breathing spirituous fumes, then took each by the hand and led them towards the big dining room at the back of the hall.

The table was laden with half-eaten food, wine glasses, bottles, crockery; and a half-dozen people were still lolling over the remnants of the feast. The girls recognized only David Lake; Ben Carter would have known two of the women from their encounter some time ago. Two other men. And, at the head of the table, half-crouched, one huge hand clutching the arm of the chair, the other feeding an apple into his mouth, was the great ape they had come to see.

'Why do you not siddown?' Valentine invited. 'Dawson, bring the ladies a couple of extra chairs. And a drink of brandywine. Heigh-ho, me darlings!'

Bella looked at Clowance, who spread her hands slightly in a disclaiming gesture and took the seat she was offered. They were taking in the condition of the room. A tall mirror beside the window was cracked from top to bottom, with a hole halfway down as if a cannonball had shattered it. Two chairs had lost their legs and lolled in drunken partnership beside the fireplace, and some of the wallpaper had been torn.

'But you have not met Butto,' said Valentine, leaning tipsily over them. 'I am sure you will be de-delighted to meet him. Butto, these are my two beautiful cousins. My beau-beau-beautiful cousins.'

'Good day to you,' said Clowance.

Butto snarled in a reasonably good-tempered way.

'We've brought you some bananas,' said Bella, opening the bag she carried. 'I wonder if he would like them.'

'Now, now,' said Valentine, suddenly sharp. 'Quiet, boy. Stay where you are. *Quiet*, boy. There, that's a good fellow. See what your friends have brought you. Ah, ah, don't snatch.'

A banana was passed up. A great hand, the fingers as thick as if wearing winter gloves, was thrust out to accept the gift. The red tongue showed and the great white teeth. The ape shuffled in his chair, a crest of short hair on his forehead began to twitch up and down and with great delicacy he peeled the banana and began to eat it.

There was a roar of applause from round the table. 'So he's seen 'em before!' 'So he knows what they are!' 'Shows where he comes from!' The banana was gone in no time, the jaws ceased to champ and the banana skin was suddenly flung across the table, where it caught one drunken man a slap on the side of the face. Helpless laughter all round. Butto chattered and held out his hand for another. Bella slipped a second banana out and passed it up the table, while careful to conceal that she had two more.

'Do you have him down to all meals?' Clowance asked.

'How pretty you are, cousin. I had almost forgot. You are always hiding yourself in Penryn . . . No, Butto only comes down on special occasions – don't you, boy? – when I have parties. Like this. Butto is the life and soul of any party, as you can well see. Do you know I am teaching him to smoke!'

'Do try again, Val,' shouted David Lake. 'It fair kills me to watch him!'

'No, he's getting too excited. I shall take him upstairs in a few minutes. You have two more b——s?' Valentine whispered to Bella. 'Keep them back. They will be ideal for enticing him to bed. I am running short on fresh fruit at the moment.'

'Val gave him a cigar last month, the first one: I was here,' David Lake shouted. 'Val showed him how to do it – puff, puff, with a spill – then asked Butto to do the same. Butto looked at the cigar – one of our best – then put it in his mouth and *ate* it! I wet myself laughing!'

'As you can see,' Valentine said, 'he's getting the hang of it – just by watching me, but he is a small matter afraid of the burning spill. I must try to get something less flickery. Maybe I could light it myself and pass it over!'

Another man staggered into the room. He was instantly recognizable as Paul Kellow, but it was not quite the Paul the girls knew. Whatever the problems facing him, he had always seemed in perfect control of himself and confident of his ability to deal with any situation that arose. Now he was comprehensively drunk. He lurched into the room, clutching at a chair and a sideboard to remain upright, negotiated his way to an empty chair at the end and hiccuped noisily.

'By God! I have lost most of my entrails!' He gazed blearily up

the table and said: 'I wish I had the cap-capacity—'. He stopped
when he saw the two new arrivals. 'Clowance, Isabelly-Rose, where
– where in purple hell have you come from?'

'They came to dinner,' said Valentine, 'but mistook the time.'

'Isabelly-Rose!' screamed one of the girls, who reminded Bella of
Letty Hazel. 'You are a perfect shriek, Paul, are you not?'

Valentine's attention was drawn to Butto, who had slipped out of
his own chair and was on the prowl. One banana skin still dangled
from his jaws.

'Do you still keep him in the *house*?' Clowance asked Valentine
incredulously.

'No, it was only for the first weeks. When I bought him, sweetheart, I did not know what his full size was going to be. He was no
use upstairs in the attics. D'you remember the panelled ones?'

'No.'

'Well, he removed the panels. He pulled them screeching out of
the wall with his own fingernails.'

'How do the servants cope with this?'

'Oh, most of the old ones have left. I have new ones, like
Dawson. They are tough, not scary-kids like the old – and they
know what to expect.'

'And is Butto not dangerous?'

'Lord bless you, sweetheart, he wouldn't hurt a – a fly. Least
unless the fly annoyed him.'

'So *you* must be careful not to annoy him?'

'He knows I'm his friend. And he knows I'm his master. It is all
a tremendous lark.'

'Do you ever hear from Selina?'

'Only if she is short of money.'

'Do you send her some?'

'No. She should come back to live here.'

'I do not suppose, do you, that she would like to see the house
being used as it is.'

'If she came back she could change it.'

'Do you want her back?'

Valentine stared blearily at his cousin. 'Blood and bones, what
do you *think*? I've had a long-time fancy for her, as you well know.
She should accept my terms!'

'And they are reasonable?'

'*I* think so. I do not sleep with Butto, as you well may imagine! I

251

have these whores in from Truro and Falmouth, but them I could easily dispense with. I never brought any here when she was here! I was not dog-faithful to her, as also you must well know. But what man is? She imp-imp-imposed impossible terms. I have a *right* to my son. He should be brought up *here*, instead of being dragged about the London suburbs at his mother's whim!'

At that moment Butto jumped on the table and walked bow-legged down it, the table creaking under his great weight, crockery and silver flying. He came to a crouching stop and squatted opposite Bella. He patted his mouth with the back of his hand in what looked like a polite yawn and grumbled encouragingly.

'Ah, ah,' said Valentine, 'he has spotted where the bananas come from! Let me have them, Bella. This calls for a little delicate nigoshiashun!'

When Clowance got home again to Penryn she felt the change more than she liked to admit. Ever since Stephen's death she had been lonely, but a toughness and resilience in her nature had enabled her to keep the loneliness at bay. It was just not good enough, she thought, that five years after his death she should miss him more than ever before.

But in a different way. Perhaps, she told herself scornfully, what she was really missing was the loving companionship of a man. (Any man?) Possibly the two proposals of marriage within a month of each other had pointed the issue and thrust her feelings into a new and uneasy depression.

Edward Fitzmaurice had written:

My dear Mrs Carrington, Dear Clowance,

I have decided to write to you and put a proposal before you.

I have started this letter four times and each time it has finished in the fire. So in the end I have come to the conclusion that only the bluntest and most matter-of-fact proposal will do. Be assured that there is nothing matter-of-fact or calculating in my feelings for you.

I love you.

Do you recall when you were staying at Bowood, when I had asked you to marry me, you told me that from the first

moment when you saw Stephen Carrington no other man
would do. Well, may I state that, from the moment I met you
in the Pulteney Hotel at the Duchess of Gordon's Ball, no
other woman but you could give me happiness?

If I have not said this explicitly before it is because in your
presence I stumble over words and cannot assemble my
thoughts. I think, I hope, that you must have sensed part of
this. My attentions cannot have gone unnoticed.

When you married I felt all ways lost – there was nothing
left to hope for. I deeply grieved when I heard your husband
had died, but I made no move, anxious not to fret you with ill-
judged sympathy, and also careful not to open up the wounds
within myself. I had a very wretched year after you refused me.

But that chance, that happy chance of a meeting with you
when you were with Mrs Pelham and others at the opera, tore
away the curtain that I had tried to draw over my mind when
I thought all was lost. Sight of you reaffirmed in my mind all
the memories of you that I had tried to forget. After that I
took the liberty of asking you and Lady Poldark to visit Bowood
again. So far you have not accepted and so far you have not
refused. (Unless you are too tender and do not like to give
offence.)

This year we have not corresponded, and this is not of itself
an invitation to visit us again. It is a plain and unadorned
proposal of marriage. This letter need not immediately be
answered. I pray that you will read it over and over, and then,
and only then, say yea or nay.

I am aware that if by some marvellous chance you should
answer 'yea' I would always rank in your eyes as second to
Stephen Carrington in your heart and in your esteem. To try
to make up a little for that, may I state what else I could offer
by way of a compensation, which I know would be minimal?

I am thirty-three, unmarried and completely unattached.
After one or two light flirtations in my very early twenties, no
woman can claim any lien on me, nor have the right to remind
me of responsiblities. Compared to my brother, who unexpectedly came in for so very much, I am a poor man. But poor is
a relative term; I have more than a competence. I have the
house on my brother's estate that I showed you when you
came to Bowood. I have a roomy apartment in Lansdowne

House at the south-west corner of Berkeley Square: four resident servants there and four in Wiltshire. My brother has other substantial properties in England, and a shooting lodge in Scotland to which I sometimes repair on August the twelfth. I am a Member of Parliament, but unlike my brother I have not yet been in government. I dance – badly, as you know – I ride fairly well, I play whist and poker and backgammon, but none of them to excess, and I gamble with what loose change I have on me. I am a regular theatre and opera-goer. In my place in Wiltshire I plant trees. In politics I am mildly radical, and rejoiced in the abolition of slavery, only regretting that the law is still so often flouted.

(I do not suppose any of this is of the slightest interest to you, but I have to say it.)

Like my brother I took no active part in the war that killed your brother and which engaged so much of your admirable father's time. (I took much longer than Burke to realize what a tyrant Napoleon had become.)

So much for me. Now on to you, dear Clowance. What sort of a life would you lead if you made my cup fill with happiness and married me?

We would live as frugally (within limits) or as extravagantly (within limits) as you chose. You could live mainly in Wiltshire or mainly in London, according to your choice. Something you said once was that you were not happy with your horse's stabling in Penryn. Nero – that is his name. We have ample stabling in Bowood and you could have four or six horses if you wished for galloping over the green downs of Wiltshire. You would have almost as much of your own preferences as you wanted – you know all the important members of my family, and I am certain they would rival each other in trying to spoil you.

I know your addiction for Cornwall, though I have seen it only once – when I came down on a gloomy mission – gloomy because you were not there – for Lady Mount Edgecumbe's funeral.

We could not *live* in Cornwall, but you could visit your parents just as many times a year as you do now. I could come with you when you wanted me, or stay behind if I thought you happier alone. I do not think the society life of London much appeals to you, and I agree it is often affected and starchy. Its hysterical sense of values – or lack of values – is something I find hard to stomach.

Of course, I am to some degree used to that society; but I assure you that you would not be expected to live by its values. We as a family do not, and no one would expect you to.

It is a big decision for you to make, I know. You are not drawn to me by a magnetic sense of love, as you were to Stephen. It is a big step from which, once taken, there is no drawing back. (A friend of mine recently divorced his wife; it took him two years, an Act of Parliament, and ten thousand pounds!)

It is not a step to be taken lightly. I know that you would not ever take it – or me – lightly.

If you find me physically repulsive or you do not like me, then pray return a 'nay', and there it shall rest. If that is not the case then I beseech you to give it the long and serious consideration of your loving heart.

Edward

Chapter Five

Late one summer evening a girl called Jane Heligan was walking back to her home in Marazanvose from the direction of Trispen, where she had been to see her sister, who had just given birth to her second child. Jane Heligan was nineteen, daughter of a miner who had scraped together a few pence to send his younger daughter to a dame school, where she had learned laboriously to read and write. She worked on a farm on Zelah Hill, sometimes read a piece of scripture in Chapel and generally earned rather less than she would as a bal-maiden at Wheal Leisure. She did not worry about this as she was of a happy disposition and looked forward to marrying soon and being able to teach her letters to her children.

There was no proper path from Trispen, so you had to climb hedges, skirt fields and at one point ford the River Allen, which here was little more than a rill as it trickled across the moorland on its way to the town of Truro.

She had just passed St Allen Church, with its scatter of cottages and its inner necklace of tombstones, and was taking the cart track towards Boswellick when a figure stepped out in front of her and barred her way. The late moon had not risen and it was very dark, but with eyes accustomed to that dark she could see it was wearing a black hat and a long black cloak.

She stopped.

He said: 'My pretty,' and showed her a long knife that he carried.

She screamed.

He stretched out a black-gloved hand and clamped it over her face, at the same time pulling her round with his other arm and pinioning her, with the knife glinting.

She was a very strong girl and grasped the arm with the knife. Then she kicked wildly and caught him on the knee cap. So she wrenched herself free and went screaming back towards the hamlet of St Allen. He followed her more than half the way before giving up the chase as the first still-lit cottage window appeared.

In mid-May Isabella-Rose Poldark wrote to her mother.

Dearest, darling Mama,

I hope this finds you in the best of health and spirits. Although it is little more than a week since I returned it already seems like a month since I saw you. Thank you for a perfect holiday.

I have a little shock for you. I hope and trust it will not upset or worry you, for I truly know there is no need for fret or worry or concern. Tomorrow morning I am leaving for France.

Do you remember Monsieur Maurice Valéry? We all met, you'll recall, in Mrs Pelham's house: he was there with Mme Jodie de la Blache, when you were in London to choose a school for me. Almost as soon as I was back in London this time, he called at the school and invited Dr Fredericks to choose three of his most promising pupils to accompany him back to France, where he is director of the Théâtre Nationale in Rouen and where he is shortly going to produce a new Italian opera called *Il Barbiere di Siviglia* in a special new French translation. He asked Dr Fredericks to choose two of his pupils, but specially insisted that the third should be me!

He was only in England for a few days, and it was essential that he should take the three singers back with him. Dr Fredericks made his choice, and I had rather quickly to make up my mind. So I said yes.

It is a wonderful opportunity, for Rouen is the third city in France, and only a day's ride from Paris. This is the first time this opera, which is by a man called Rossini, has been shown in France and if it is a success it may well go on to Paris.

But now is the hardest part! Tomorrow morning at six of the clock I shall steal out of Hatton Garden and take coach with the others for Portsmouth – without telling dearest Mrs Pelham! Mama, what was I to do? I am certain sure that Mrs Pelham would understand this big opportunity which has just come up, and I am certain sure I could persuade her into allowing me to go. But what I am also certain sure – for I have had many opportunities to observe it – is that she takes her 'guardianship' seriously, and she would not, indeed could not, agree to allowing me to go *without your consent* – and how were we to obtain this in time?

Of course I shall leave her a letter even longer than this, and I hope and believe she will forgive me. I am positive that she will come to forgive me this grave discourtesy if *you* are able to let her know that I would have had your consent.

Do not worry. I shall be with others, chiefly the two whom Dr Fredericks has chosen. We are all singers, travelling together. There will be many rehearsals, and then about six performances in a week, then I shall come home. Christopher is not expecting to return from Lisbon until the end of May. Of course I have written to him, and I hope he will be as happy for the future as I am.

Do not worry about money. I have a little saved, and we are promised payment for our time even during rehearsals! Please tell Clowance and Papa and Aunt Caroline and Uncle Dwight. I leave it to you if you wish to tell others, but generally I should prefer you not to say too much until after the first performance!

Mama, cross your fingers for me and wish me God speed!

Your devoted

Bella

It was not in Bella's nature to be a liar, but there had been a few occasions in her life when to adjust the truth had been a great convenience. Things had moved so rapidly during the last two months in her relationship with Christopher, with Maurice Valéry, and with her feelings about her prospects in her profession.

It was not quite as she had told her mother. She was travelling alone with Valéry, and the other two girls whom Maurice had somewhat reluctantly been persuaded by her to invite were to follow in a day or so. There was no guarantee that they would be in the opera – that would be decided during early rehearsals. But their chief purpose was to give an extra air of decorum to Bella's trip. In fact it had all the slightly sinister, heavily romantic air of an elopement, as she stole out of a side door of Mrs Pelham's house, deliberately left unlocked the night before, and in the chill air of a six o'clock dawn, carrying a small bag came out into Hatton Garden, and there was Maurice, head bared, to kiss her fingertips and help her into the green plush carriage he had waiting. They sat each in a corner of the carriage, almost unspeaking as it rattled off over the cobbles on its way to the Lamb & Flag on Cheapside, where they were to take the coach for Portsmouth. Maurice had said in his letter that the larger coach and longer sea voyage to Dieppe were an easier way than to sail Dover to Calais and have the long jolting journey to Rouen across the side roads of France.

Bella had taken some other liberties in her letter to her mother. Valéry had not arrived suddenly at the school looking for singers for his opera; Bella had written to him as soon as she knew Christopher was going to Lisbon, accepting Maurice's offer to her, first made at the Pulteney Hotel party and later repeated twice in letters to her. He was now in England solely in answer to her last letter and solely to pick her up and return in triumph with her to Rouen. She had also implied to her mother that Christopher had been informed of her trip. That was not true. He knew nothing of it, but she told herself it was better, and safer, to wait until she was installed in Rouen and fully embarked on the rehearsals for the opera before writing to him. He was not likely to be pleased. He might indeed be furious. But it seemed probable that she would be safely back in England and able to present him with a fait accompli by the time a fitful wind brought him across Biscay and up the chops of the Channel on his return from Portugal.

She still loved him, she thought. He had grown into her life. And he was Christopher. But besides being the director of a minor theatre in France and passionate about music, Maurice Valéry was a very pretty young man.

'What are you smiling at, *ma chérie?*' Valéry asked her, as the coach began to leave the last suburbs of London behind.

'Oh, nothing important,' Bella said, turning her dimples on him. 'But this is all more than tolerably exciting.'

Maurice sat back, satisfied, and hummed under his breath the theme of a tune called 'Una voce poco fa'.

Bella's smile was of amusement at the recollection of a phrase

Mrs Pelham had used at supper last night. She had said, apropos of some minor scandal among her friends: 'After all, what is sauce for the goose is sauce for the gander.'

Bella thought, perhaps this adventure will be a fiasco, who knows? Perhaps I am being a silly goose. But at least it could be argued that in view of what had already been considered suitable sauce for the gander might be allowable to the goose too.

Jane Heligan, when she was 'meating' the calves on the Zelah Hill farm, was told by Mrs Higgins, the farmer's wife, that 'thur was a gent to see ee.'

Rubbing her hand hastily on her apron, Jane went into the kitchen, where Mrs Higgins with one expressive thumb indicated the parlour. Jane kicked off her sabots, knelt down and brushed her bare feet with a corner of the apron to make sure they carried no deleterious matter into the room in which she had only been twice in four years and which she regarded as the holy of holies.

That there should be such a room showed that the Higginses were moderately prosperous farmers – also that they had no children to clutter up every inch of available space for sleeping.

A tall youngish man, very upright, in a dark cloak. His riding hat and crop were on the table.

'Miss Jane Heligan?' he asked.

'Sur?'

'You are Jane Heligan? My name is Prideaux. Captain Prideaux. I'll not keep you long from your work. I came to ask just a few questions.'

'Sur?'

'About the incident last Tuesday evening when I gather someone attacked you with a knife. Is that correct?'

Jane blinked at the Bible placed on a small round table in the centre of the room.

'Sur? Oh, ais, sur.'

'I am making some enquiries on behalf of the Justices of the Peace. We are trying to discover who this man was. Would you care to sit down and tell me in your own words just what happened?'

Jane glanced round and saw a horsehair armchair, but it did not look inviting. Indeed she had never sat down in this room before.

She continued to stand, rubbing her hands nervously on her apron. She knew she should have taken the apron off before she came in.

'Well?'

She began the tale. There was not much to say, but every now and then he stopped her, asking her to repeat words or sentences that he had not been able to understand because of her rough accent.

'Could you try to describe him a little better? Was he a tall man?'

'Please?'

'Tall. Was he as tall, do you think, as I am?'

She considered this. 'I'd 'ardly think so. Mebbe. Tes 'ard to tell in the dark.'

'He – grappled with you?'

'Oh, ais, sur. Some strong 'e was!'

'Did he – smell of anything? Did his clothes smell of anything? His breath?'

'I can't rightly 'member. Notsino. Mebbe a bit smoky?'

'Wood smoke? Tobacco smoke?'

'I reckon it might've been tobacco.'

'What was the knife like?'

She shuddered. 'Like – like one you d'use in the kitchen to slice bacon. But a bit shorter mebbe.'

'And he spoke to you?'

'Please? . . . Oh, ais. Two, three words like "sweetheart".'

'I thought you told Parson Williams "my sweet".'

'Did I? I don't rightly remember.' Jane looked tearful.

'Pray do not distress yourself. You will perhaps remember several other solitary girls have been attacked in Cornwall in the last eighteen months, and it is not impossible that the same man is responsible. You are, it seems probable, the first – or second – of his victims to have escaped alive. Therefore anything – anything – you can recall of your encounter might be of great value in discovering who he is.' Jane was looking at him wide-eyed. 'Pray take your time. There is no hurry.'

Jane racked her brains.

Philip said: 'Did he look like anyone you know?'

'Oh, no, sur!'

'Did he look like Farmer Higgins or Parson Williams?'

'No, oh no, sur!'

'Do you know anyone who owes you a grudge? I mean, who would wish to hurt you?'

'Nay, sur, for sure not a one!'

'His voice, now. Was it thin or deep? It was a man's voice?'

'Ais, I bla. Mebbe twas a bit 'igh pitch.'

'Did it have a country accent?'

'Please?'

'Like yours, for instance.'

She considered. 'Nay, twas not like mine.'

'Like whose, then?'

'More like yourn, sur. If ee d'know what I mean.'

'Educated?'

'Er – ais, I s'pose.'

'He sounded more like a gent than, say, a miner?'

'Ais, sur.'

'Ah,' said Prideaux. 'That is something a little fresh to go on. Thank you, Jane.' He prepared to leave. 'Nothing else? If you remember anything further I will come back.'

'That cloak,' said Jane, pointing. 'That cloak you'm wearing. Twas like the one he was wearing. I think I tore it a small bit. Meaning no liberty to say so, sur. Beggin' your pardon, sur.'

'But my cloak,' said Philip amiably, 'is not torn. Well, thank you, Jane. You have been . . . helpful.'

Chapter Six

George Warleggan had been with three of his men, Garth and Trembath and Lander, to inspect an apparently nearly spent mine near Gwennap Pit. His three men were being given a tour of the workings while George drank coffee and brandy at grass level with the six active venturers.

South Wheal Tolgus had been producing a good quality of copper for upwards of fifteen years, but the product was deteriorating and profits had been scanty since 1817. George had information (which he automatically distrusted) that there were excellent deposits in various parts of the Tolgus Valley, and he had a hunch that if he could get a footing in this area it might be ripe for expansion when the price of copper picked up again. His bank had advanced the adventurers of South Wheal Tolgus several large amounts of money to enable them to continue operating while the copper was being marketed. The venturers had paid back the earlier advances most promptly while times were good, but had lagged badly behind during the last eighteen months. The financial honeymoon, George felt, was now over and the venturers had to face the facts of life.

The team he had brought over to examine the mine was, he knew, short on expertise so far as the physical extraction of minerals from the ground went, but long on knowledge of matters arising. Hector Trembath, under George's tuition, possessed as good and as devious a legal mind as existed in Cornwall. Frederick Lander knew all there was to know about the financial promises and plights of mining, and indeed, as a consequence of Cary Warleggan's continuing ill health, was beginning to take Cary's place at the rock-hard centre of Warleggan's Bank. Tom Garth was a good knowledgeable all-round sort of man, and, though he had

263

never worked in a mine in his life, he had probably more experience of the blunt end of mining than any of the rest of the quartet.

George talked to the venturers coolly and composedly, aware that his team, whatever they truly found, would see everything and report everything in the worst possible light. His bargaining position was strong and could only be reinforced by their report. He was prepared to save the mine from bankruptcy, but at a price. With Lander's assistance he would be prepared to put forward a package which would enable the mine to continue trading, would allow the adventurers to remain partners in South Wheal Tolgus, but which would vest most of the rights of profit into a company that was itself entirely owned by Warleggan's Bank.

So it proved. The investors, at their wits' end how otherwise to pay the miners' wages at the end of the month or to pay for the coal to keep the pumps working, signed away seven-eighths of their shares. They would remain as adventurers; they would in fact be puppets and do what they were told.

There had been torrential rain over the last few days and on their way home the four horsemen picked their way with care over the greasy track, well satisfied with the day's work.

The land here was much dug over and misused, but gorse had found enough nourishment between the sheds and the ruined walls and the half-filled-in trenches, and had sprouted and was now flowering in a dazzling explosion of yellow, almost bright enough to make one shade one's eyes. As the quartet rode on, hares and rabbits dipped and dodged away from the horses.

They passed Twelveheads and here there was a choice of tracks. Left they would turn and make their way towards Baldhu and then to Truro, which was the direction three of them should take. George, by going straight ahead, would make for Bissoe and thence across the Falmouth–Truro turnpike road on his way to Cardew. Both Garth and Trembath volunteered to accompany him on his way, which was much overgrown, but George refused. It was little more than half an hour's ride to where he should cross the toll road, and he could manage well enough. The days were drawing out and he would be home long before dark.

So the three not unwillingly accepted their dismissal and turned their horses towards the north-east. George rode home in the anaemic sunshine, counting his gains.

Beside him on the right Carnon Stream presently appeared, yellow and in spate. It was a good twenty feet below the road and between them ran a drang or sloping ditch which drained the track, water trickling out of gullets along the road to form a deep water table alongside the stream proper. The stream was noisy as it bubbled among the stones on its banks; birds twittered and a lark sang. Out of the breeze the spring afternoon was very warm.

A pity about Cary, George thought. A thin scarecrow like him; it was strange that he should become dropsical, with a swollen stomach showing through his gown. Water of course could be removed, had been removed, but it had filled up again, just like Carnon Stream, and about the same colour. He had said he would not have it done again, but Behenna was adamant – or else he would die.

But he would die in any case. He'd be eighty-one later this year. We all came to it. Not yet for him, George: the Warleggans were healthy stock, not like some of those effete gentlefolk. He, George, had ailed little if anything in all his sixty years. He had always rather despised ill health, considered it more a mental than a physical weakness. Employees of his were not treated sympathetically when they pleaded illness. Of course people had to *die*, as Cary was no doubt preparing to do. The chief grief of the matter was that it left George so short-handed.

His mother should have had more children so that there might be a nephew to slip into place.

Lander was the man. Lander must clearly be made a partner as soon as Cary passed out of the picture. But George was becoming irritated with Lander, and not purely because of his bad breath. Lander tended to take too much on himself. He took decisions that Cary would and should have taken, and this often without consulting George. He had been slapped down twice and he had not liked it. He must be kept in his place. George had one or two ideas about this. Frederick Lander had little or no money of his own, so a proposition might be put to him – better if Humphry Willyams were to do it, not George – that in order to become a partner, he would have to put down a large sum to establish his place in the bank, and this he would have to borrow, preferably from the Willyams Bank in Plymouth. That way he would be a little hamstrung if he wished to kick up his heels too much.

This thought coincided with his horse, Garry, lurching suddenly and almost unseating him. A very bloated water rat had run out of the straggling bushes right under the horse's hooves.

George tightened rein and over-corrected. The horse's head came up and his right rear hoof slipped in the slimy mud. He staggered, half-corrected himself, then the other hoof slipped too; he panicked and tried to jump back to safety, but instead began to fall. With a total sense of disbelief that out of nowhere, for no good reason at all, he was going to fall, and fall badly, George was pitched down the bank, his horse rolling with him. He came up spitting from the deep water of the drang, clutched at the root of a fallen tree; it came away, and he found himself being carried along by the swirling water.

He was in a pit, standing on a ledge and clinging to the greasy wall of the pit, up to his waist in water while water cascaded into the pit from above, swirled round and round, and sucked itself out on a lower level into some further cavern.

Though he had never been in such a place before, George knew that he was in an old burrow, part of a disused mine, a deep pit dug by prospecting miners of long ago and long since abandoned. The stream when it was in flood overflowed into the old working, and if there had been no outlet this would have quickly filled up, like a giant well perhaps thirty feet deep. That it was not filling up meant that it was draining away further into the old mine, otherwise George could have swum round and round until he drowned. As it was, fortunate chance had provided a floor or a ledge on which he could just kneel and then stand, retching out the water he had swallowed, gasping for breath, pushing back his soaked, scanty grey hair, scrabbling a hand for reassurance against the wall behind him, but afraid to take a step away from it lest what he was marooned on was indeed a ledge and not a solid floor. Where was the water going?

There was no sign of Garry. Whether the horse had not fallen all the way and been able to scramble out, or it had drowned or just bolted he could not tell. It was not his usual horse, Albatross having damaged his fetlock yesterday. Garry was one of Harriet's – he had taken it as it looked a likely beast, solid quarters, middle-aged, not likely to be skittish or unstable. What a mistake, the animal could hardly have behaved worse. When he got home, he would have it shot.

When he got home. *If* he got home. The water, up to his waist, was cold, and soon he would begin to shiver. It wanted at most two hours to dark.

He felt more carefully at the rock behind him. It was not natural rock, having been built to create and support the old mine burrow maybe fifty or sixty years ago on the principle of a Cornish wall. It was firm and solid, the years having helped to knit it together. He was what – twenty feet from the daylight? The water was rushing over the edge in a two-foot-wide flood that had just carried him to the edge and tipped him over. In thrashing and splashing about for his life he had luckily chosen to claw his way and stand up on the other side from the fall of water so that he was not drenched by it as it came down. But there was no way up. Twenty feet was nearly as bad as two hundred feet, if you could not fly.

Would anyone hear him if he shouted? It was unlikely. The Carnon Valley had had a degree of traffic in its heyday, but that was long past. Nowadays there was just the odd cottage that was still lived in. Coming this way this morning he had seen a few miners panning the stream for tin.

It was undignified to shout, but he shouted. The effort caught his breath and he brought up some more water from the stream. The shout ended in a fit of coughing. When his throat was clear he shouted again. In such circumstances one could not afford to stand on one's dignity. The damned river with its fall of water in this pit would surely drown out any human cries.

Was the water half an inch lower where it lapped against his belly? There had been a torrential shower while they were in the mine. A temporary flood. But even if it subsided altogether, what better chance had he of *climbing* out?

He peered again at the wall and picked at it fastidiously with his fingers. It was heavy as Killas stone, the sort of thing used frequently for building houses. He felt in his pockets. There was nothing whatever in any of them that he could use as a tool. Then he put his wet finger into his fob pocket and pulled out one of the two guineas he always kept there. He looked at the wall and chose what he estimated was a vulnerable crack. He began scraping with the gold coin.

He was starting to shiver, and his left ankle was painful to stand on. It was a sprain, no doubt, and would make it more difficult for him to climb the wall. If the wall were even climbable. Could he, with the persistence of a man in peril of his life, make any footholds, any handholds that he could use?

He worked for a long time, making some impression, but unless he could pull one of the smaller stones out there would be no way of lifting his considerable bulk even a few feet out of the water. He stopped for a rest now and then and cupped his hands to shout. The water was definitely subsiding. It was also going dark.

Ross was in Truro for a meeting with his fellow partners in the Cornish Bank when he encountered his lawyer, Mr Barrington Burdett, who told him what had happened.

As Burdett explained, there were rumours and counter-rumours, which he supposed was inevitable when the story related to so influential a member of the town as Mr George Warleggan, but as far as he could tell from the accounts he had heard and sifted through, what had occurred was as follows.

On Tuesday – this was Thursday – Sir George had ridden out to Redruth to visit one of his mines, and when returning on the afternoon of that day along the Carnon Valley his horse had tripped and precipitated himself and his rider into a drang or deep water table bordering the cart track or former road. From there he was unable to climb out and, in view of the desolate area where the accident occurred, he was likely to have died of exposure or starved to death.

Were it not for fortunate chance.

'Which was?'

'When he did not return to Cardew Lady Harriet sent out a search party, which found nothing. However, shortly before midnight his horse found its way home, and in the saddlebag were some documents showing that he had been visiting South Wheal Tolgus. So a further search party was sent out – some say with Lady Harriet leading the way with her two boar hounds. Sir George was discovered about two a.m. on Wednesday morning, and brought home on a stretcher.' Barrington Burdett coughed politely into his fist. 'Here is where the rumour is hard to verify. Some say he is at death's door, some that he is just badly bruised, with a sprained ankle, and suffering from exhaustion.'

This information Ross took with him to the Bank meeting, which nowadays was not held at Pearce's Hotel but in an upper chamber of the Bank at the bottom of Lemon Street.

It was a long time, Ross thought, since that first meeting in 1799, these partners coming together, reforming the old banks and naming it as a new one, the Cornish Bank. It had prospered, being second only in capital to Warleggan's, and first in the county's general esteem. It had prospered and Ross prospered in a small way along with it.

He found they had all heard the news that he had just come by, and it was discussed at length before the actual meeting began. The gravity of George's accident and the degree of his injuries was of economic importance, since George's death, with no apparent heir, even his permanent invalidism, would have a serious effect on the stability of the Cornish Bank's greatest rival in the county, might even precipitate a run on the funds. Of course it was pointed out by the elderly Mr John Rogers, and agreed, that the Warleggan amalgamation with the Devon & Cornwall Bank of Plymouth some years ago had given them a greater resilience and stability. And yet, and yet, Sir George Warleggan, whose personal fortune, which by now must be in the region of £500,000, was by far the biggest shareholder, and although it had originally been put about as an amalgamation between the two banks, George Warleggan had been so much the most dominant and aggressive partner in Warleggan & Willyams that in effect it had almost amounted to a takeover of the Devon & Cornwall Bank by Warleggan's.

Therefore the health and survival of this, one of the most important financiers in the West Country, was of the utmost interest to all in the banking profession.

After the meeting was over it was the custom to dine together about two, either at Pearce's or at the Red Lion. This time Ross excused himself, saying he had another appointment.

He did not have another appointment, but he had come to the conclusion that he would keep one of his own. Throughout the meeting he had been absent-minded, behaving in a rational way to his partners but waging an inward battle with the impulse that had come upon him. After leaving the others he walked slowly to the stables where he had left his horse. He had him saddled, mounted him, clopped slowly along Lemon Street and together they clattered up their first hill on the way to Cardew.

Cardew looked perfectly beautiful in the spring sunshine. The tree-lined drive was startling, with all the green of the newly opened leaves at their most pristine. The hedges on each side were lemon yellow with primroses, and deeper in the woods the early bluebells flashed their kingfisher blue. As horse and rider emerged from the mass of trees into the open spaces before the house, a herd of deer flaunted their antlers as they grazed the parkland.

He dismounted at the steps, looped his reins on the tethering post, went up to the front door. Before he could pull on the bell Lady Harriet Warleggan opened it.

She was wearing a long black skirt over highly polished riding boots, a royal blue tight-fitting jacket, a white muslin blouse, and a jaunty black hat.

'Sir Ross! What a pleasant surprise!'

'A pleasant surprise to me too. To have the door of so splendid a house opened for me by the splendid lady of the house.'

She gave a low husky laugh. 'I saw you coming. Through the window. I said to myself hallucination can go no further! Pray come in. Were you calling to see me?'

Ross went in, bending his head by instinct though this doorway was eight feet high.

'I had thought you might be hunting.'

'Oh, come. Even you rough mining characters from the north coast must know we don't hunt in May!'

He smiled back. 'Riding then. To tell the truth I had forgot it was May.'

'That cannot be the truth either. But let it pass. Riding was correct. I have been out exercising the hounds and had just returned.'

They were still in the hall. The butler put his head round a door, but silently withdrew.

'I come on another mission,' Ross said. 'The fact that you have been out riding suggests that the wild rumours overheard are happily unfounded.'

'You came to ask about George? *You* came to ask about *George*!

That is the biggest surprise of all! But if it is true I must say it is very genteel of you. I have to tell you, my dear Sir Ross, that had you cracked your skull open falling down a mineshaft I should have had the devil's own job persuading George to call and ask after *you*!'

'*Has* he cracked his skull open?'

'No. Oh, no. A broken rib. A sprained ankle. And noticeably knocked about. He is not dead but sleepeth.'

Ross eyed the tall woman speculatively. There was something about her that greatly appealed to him, something sparky, sophisticated, challenging and downright female attractive. How had she ever allowed herself to be joined in holy matrimony to this dry, vindictive, mean-natured banker? For the same reason possibly as his delicate Elizabeth, his very first love, had agreed to marry George all those years ago – for money, and all that money could buy: security, comfort, freedom from responsibility.

She was aware of his look and clearly did not resent it. 'D'you wish to see him?'

He wanted to say 'not particularly' but instead: 'Not if he is sleeping.'

'That I was about to find out. I have been out about three hours. Ellery!' She had just caught him: 'Will you go up and see if Sir George is awake.'

'Yes, m'lady.'

Harriet took off her hat and shook out her hair. 'What's this I hear about your younger daughter?'

'Isabella-Rose? What do you hear?'

'Ursula was saying it is whispered that she has eloped with a Frenchie.'

'Fortunately,' Ross said, 'this rumour is as greatly exaggerated as the extent of George's injuries. With two other girls from her academy she has been chosen to sing in an opera in France. So she has gone there.'

'To Paris?'

'To Rouen.'

'Ah. Never been there. Is this with your approval?'

'I approve of most things Bella does.'

'Indulgent father. I wonder what sort of a husband you would make.'

'Excessively indulgent,' said Ross.

'Pardon, my lady, Sir George is awake and is taking tea.'

'Very well,' said Harriet. 'Then we'll go up.'

'What brought you here?' George demanded. 'Was it to gloat?'

'George,' Harriet said, 'you must not be so curmudgeonly. Sir Ross was just passing and thought to call. Is not that so?'

'Indeed,' said Ross.

George was in bed, propped up by a welter of pillows. His face was puffy and pale. There was a purple bruise on his cheekbone. He looked suddenly old.

'You have a fine place here, George,' said Ross. 'I've been here only once before. I came with my parents when the Lemons had it. I was about nine at the time, so I do not remember it well. But my memory is of a more untidy place, with the grounds much overgrown.'

George grunted. He was very angry with his wife for having brought this man up to see him when he was at such a disadvantage. She should have turned him away like a mendicant.

Harriet said: 'You've finished tea?' To Ross: 'You'll take a glass of wine?'

'I have not come to stay,' Ross said. 'I was passing, as you guess, and came in on impulse.'

'Then you'll take a glass of wine.' Harriet went to the bell pull.

'I knew I should not be welcome here, George,' Ross said, 'at least by you. But I sought to verify . . .'

'If I was dead?' George said. 'Well, you may observe that I am not.'

'Brandy or Canary?' Harriet asked Ross, as the servant appeared.

'Neither, thank you.'

'Brandy,' Harriet said to the servant, and then when the door had closed, 'Now don't, I pray you, become curmudgeonly too. You rode up the drive of your own free will, so you must take the consequences.'

Ross smiled but did not reply. He said to George: 'I do not know how accurate are the accounts I have heard of your accident, but if they are half correct you are indeed lucky to be alive. I know those drangs. If your horse had not been able to find its way home . . .'

'And d'you know,' said Harriet, 'how in fact he was *eventually* found? My two beautiful hounds! They followed back the way Garry had come, and I believe George, standing shivering in the dark pit, first saw two pairs of eyes he did not recognize, whereupon they set up such a coughing and a howling that the lanterns came nearer and nearer and we peered over too, and a ladder was fetched and my husband was brought up, looking, at that time certainly, more dead than alive. I believe never again will George begrudge the best places before the fire for Castor and Pollux!'

Ross could not be sure how far the mockery in Harriet's voice contained a sediment of concern. Possibly George did not see any, for he glared at Harriet, and then grimaced as he moved his injured frame.

'Who is tending on you?' Ross asked, fingering his scar.

'Behenna. And another sawbones from Falmouth called Mather.'

'Not Enys?'

'I have my own medicals without calling for upstart lackeys like Enys.'

'I cannot,' said Ross, 'imagine anyone in their right mind could suppose that Dwight Enys was anyone's lackey.'

'I see the old sparks beginning to fly,' said Harriet. 'Lord have mercy, you are both old men. Ross has much more hair than you have, George, but that is hardly excuse to rekindle a feud.'

The footman returned with the brandy bottle and three glasses. Harriet talked into the taut silence as the liquor was poured.

'You'll take some, George?'

'Pour it out. I will take it when I am alone.'

Ross lifted his glass silently and drank to his hostess.

'Before we quarrel worse, George, there is one other matter which I feel I ought to raise. It concerns Valentine.'

'Valentine is no concern of mine!'

'Of course he is,' Harriet said sharply. 'What have you got to tell us, Ross? What has he been up to now?'

'Earlier today,' Ross said, 'I met Barrington Burdett, who seems to have taken over Harris Pascoe's role of knowing all the news. He told me that John Permewan has been arrested.'

'Who is he?' Harriet asked. 'A scavenger?'

'No. He was not in Truro at the time but in Plymouth. He has been arrested for forgery and for making out false prospectuses for the copper mines. Particularly the United Copper & Zinc Company.

Barrington said there were others mentioned. Valentine was seen much in the company of Permewan towards the end of last year. I trust Wheal Elizabeth is not involved.'

'What is Wheal Elizabeth?' Harriet asked.

'Valentine's mine. The one he started some years ago on the cliff edge very near Place House.'

'Damned young fool,' George said. 'I warned him about Permewan when he called to see me last – that's what? Eighteen months ago!'

'Forgery is a capital offence,' said Harriet thoughtfully.

'Which might persuade Permewan to give away everything and everyone he knows in the hope of having his sentence lightened,' Ross said.

'Well, let him go down, let him suffer,' George said. 'He's his own master and has always claimed to be. He's nothing to me. I've finished with him!'

'He has your name,' said Ross. 'It is an unusual name. You would not want a Warleggan to be in prison, surely?'

George looked at him suspiciously. 'What is it to you? Of course you and Valentine are thick as thieves – always have been.'

'I hardly ever see him.'

Harriet sipped her brandy. 'Had you something specially in mind?'

'I have had little enough time to think. I heard only this morning. One reason I came to see George was to consult with him.'

'Consult with me. What damned impertinence!'

'Your response, then, seeing him struggling in the water, is to say: it's his own fault, let him drown.'

George was about to make a further angry reply, but Harriet silenced him with a gesture. Harriet was the only person on earth who dared to silence George with a gesture. She did it very seldom.

'Ross, contain your own hostility for a moment. If you have *any* thoughts on this matter, pray let us have them.'

'Last month I was shown a prospectus on Wheal Elizabeth. From my own observations – I've passed the mine a couple of times recently – this was clearly a false prospectus. It talks of the erection of a pumping engine. There is no such engine. I spoke to one or two of the miners, and their view of what lodes they have in prospect and those claimed are very different. Even without Permewan's testimony

Valentine is in a very exposed position. Perhaps one may have castles in Spain, but Cornwall is only three or four days' travel for investors living in Lancashire and Yorkshire.'

'*So?*' said George.

'It is difficult to see how Valentine can be helped. I agree with you that this is a mess of his own making. But I was thinking on my way here that Wheal Elizabeth is not without its prospects. Do you remember Hector Chenhalls?'

'Of course.'

'He was one of the astutest prospectors of our generation. I don't know what has happened to him.'

'He went to Australia on some mining business. That was four years ago. I do not think he is back in England.' George had forgotten to snarl.

'Well, after Mr Pope died, he and Unwin Trevaunance approached Mrs Selina Pope, as she then was before she married Valentine, with a view to buying the mining rights of Place House, with particular reference to the area that Wheal Elizabeth was opened to exploit. I advised her to say no.'

George grunted.

Ross finished his brandy. 'I know Valentine had his eye on this piece of land from the early days of his marriage. Clearly his efforts so far have been disappointing. They have opened five levels, but only two are yielding, and then it is indifferent stuff. But it is early days. I don't know how he is operating things, but I imagine his personal knowledge of mining is not great, and, lacking funds to live as extravagantly as he wants to, he is persuading people who know even less of mining than he does that it is the success he would like it to be.'

'By issuing false prospectuses!' said George.

'Exactly.'

'For which, if discovered, he will rightly go to prison.'

'Yes.'

There was silence.

Ross said: 'It occurred to me that if someone came along and offered him a fair sum for the mine he would be happy to sell it.'

'No one would be such a fool.'

'Unless they wished to save Valentine from prison. No investor would proceed against him if they received their investment back in full.'

275

'As I have said, no one would be such a fool.'

Harriet refilled Ross's glass with brandy.

He said: 'Opening any mine is a gamble. Wheal Leisure, it was officially accepted, was played out twenty years ago. Now it provides me and has provided me, for a decade, with a comfortable income. Of course, it is up and down as all mines are, but it has been very profitable.'

He wondered if he was wise to mention the mine, which had been a bone of contention between him and George for years. But the years marched on.

'What I mean,' he said, 'is that several people, better qualified than Valentine, have fancied that site. Should someone buy the mine and continue to work it, it may well repay him tenfold.'

George said aggressively: 'So why do you not do that?'

'I do not have the money.'

'You are a banker like myself,' George said ironically.

'The investment I was asked to put up when invited to be a partner was minimal. It has not greatly increased since.'

'Your partners are very warm fellows. I know most of 'em. Put it to them at your next meeting.'

'Which will be in three months' time. Apart from which, they have not the same interest in Valentine's fate. You are his father. My concern is that he is Elizabeth's son.'

Perhaps that had been even more the wrong thing to say. To mention the unspoken name. There was a cold silence.

'Well, I must be off,' Ross said. 'I am glad you are no worse for your accident.'

'Does Valentine know that someone might get him out of trouble by buying his mine?' asked Harriet.

'I certainly would not think so. I have not seen him for nearly a month, when his ape interfered with a marriage ceremony at the church.'

'Tell me of it.' He did. She laughed.

'Diverting. So you have no idea whether Valentine would consider selling the mine.'

'I think faced with that or prison he would choose to sell. We could drive a hard bargain.'

'We?'

'As George and I seldom agree about anything it would be well to appoint nominees, who must not be just figureheads.'

'And you would put money up for that?'

'George would have to carry the major part. If it came to negotiation, neither he nor I should play a prominent role. There is no need, I think, to decide anything now, but if anything can be done it must be in the next two to three weeks. I'll wish you good day.'

'Harriet,' George said austerely. 'I'll take that brandy now.'

Chapter Seven

The Théâtre Jeanne d'Arc was near the church of that name in the rue Fontenelle. Its exterior was shabby, the area rundown, the architecture of a type popular before the Revolution. But inside the auditorium was cosily plush and conventional of shape, with boxes arranged in ascending semi-circles looking down on the stage and a pit where many could stand. South and east of the Place du Vieux Marché was a warren of tiny, crowded, dirty streets running down to the river. Most of the buildings were drunk with age, leaning away from or towards each other as if for support. Many of them were wood-framed and gabled, with quaint carvings. Ragged children, women on doorsteps, starving mongrels foraging for scraps, noisy wine taverns, the occasional prie-dieu with or without flower stems at its base, shops selling wine, cheese, fruit, vegetables, candles, fresh bread. The smells were predominantly of garlic and open drains.

The rooms that Maurice showed her into were on the edge of this district, her landlady had a moustache and a dirty apron; but Bella did not concern herself with her lodgings – over the past two months Maurice had sent her several scrawled pieces of sheet music which were particularly appealing. Mrs Pelham had heard her playing them and asked what they were. Bella had explained how she had come by them.

'Play them to me again, will you. Or if you have the words, sing them. They are very taking.'

'I can hum them, if that will do. I do not understand all the words, and the second one is not for me.'

She played and half sang 'Una voce poco fa' and 'Ecco vidente en cielo'.

'That is really sweet music,' Mrs Pelham had said. 'But how do you mean, the second one is not for you?'

'I mean,' Bella stammered, 'it – it is really for a tenor to sing.'

'Oh,' Mrs Pelham had said. 'They are from a new opera?'

'It has been on in England, a couple of years ago.'

So far, though, Bella had not read the complete score. On the long, jolting, sickly and again jolting journey from Hatton Garden to Rouen, Maurice had sat beside her, telling her the story of the opera and explaining to her the choices and dilemmas he would encounter with the casting; but she had never seen the music all written down for her to judge and absorb.

Nor had she quite realized how central the part was that Maurice was assigning to her. They ate together the next day at a little bistro near the cathedral in the company of three youngish Frenchmen. One, Jean-Pierre Armande, was to sing opposite her as Count Almaviva. He was tall, blond, with close-set eyes and a flashing smile. Another, called Etienne Lafond, was the oldest of the group and would 'probably' play Don Basilio. He had a thick accent which Bella could hardly understand. In fact, though her French was now fluent – and her Italian coming along – she had to keep her ears at constant stretch to follow the quick patter of the interchange between the four men. The last man was Edmond Largo, the stage manager. They were all courteous to her, and Maurice was careful to bring her into the conversation as often as he could. She caught Jean-Pierre Armande looking at her speculatively during the meal, or more often eyeing her over the rim of his glass; she hoped he was considering her qualities as a singer and not otherwise.

After it was over and the others had gone, she fingered the score. 'I did not think you had chosen so big a part for me, Maurice.'

'You are to be the star!'

'But there are no other women singing important parts. I am surrounded by men!'

'There is Berta, your governess. She has an important role. But have no fear you will be alone. There are musicians, soldiers, notaries, dancers.'

'Shall you give Helen or Polly the part of Berta?'

'No, they are too young. And the Mayor's daughter is playing Berta. It is good to have some local interest!'

She was thoughtful for a minute. Boys were playing in the square outside, their long bare legs flashing in the sun.

'When are they coming?'

'I have not heard.'

'Will they travel on their own?'

'My cousin is returning from London soon.' Maurice's face creased into a wry smile. 'Though I do not think he would be quite the most suitable chaperone!' He called for the *addition*. 'As I assuredly was for you, my Bella.'

'I am not sure my aunt or my mother would think you a suitable chaperone at all!'

He spread his hands. 'What did I do? What have I done except to behave towards you with the utmost respect?'

'Constantly kissing my hands,' said Bella, 'stroking my arms, rubbing your head against mine. Well, I suppose that might be looked upon as good behaviour for a Frenchman.'

'Frenchman, *ma foi*! It is good behaviour of any man companioning a beautiful young girl with a voice like an angel.'

'Please do not forget that this angel can scream.'

'Not in the part,' Maurice said. 'I pray you not in the part.'

He paid the bill.

Bella said: 'Oh, there was an argument between you, chiefly between you and Etienne Lafond, and because of his accent – where does he come from?'

'Burgundy.'

'Because of his accent I could not follow what he was saying. It was about me, was it not? You mentioned soprano.'

'Ah, yes. Ah, yes. He was arguing that *Il Barbiere* was originally written for a soprano, not a mezzo. That is not true: it was originally written for a mezzo, but later I agree it has been keyed higher. Etienne seemed to think that we were playing for a mezzo-soprano out of consideration for you. That is not so – although I do believe you will do better in the lower key. Personally I prefer it.'

She rose, aware that she had drunk too much red wine. (Must not get like Christopher. Imagine on the stage falling flat on your back!)

'I can manage the soprano, if you wish it.'

'I do not wish it.'

'When is the first rehearsal?'

'Perhaps not till next week. Not full, though we can begin the preliminaries tomorrow. Figaro will be here on Friday, but I have

280

got to find a Dr Bartolo. Arturo Fougasse was to have taken it but he has withdrawn. He decided that the part did not suit him!'

They left the restaurant, skirted the roistering boys and walked gently on in the afternoon sunshine. The day was warm, early summer was on them. Bella thought of a time not so long ago when she had walked arm in arm with another young man in Burlington Arcade.

'Tomorrow,' Maurice said, 'we dine with the Mayor. He is not the most intelligent of men, but he is full of good will towards our venture. Think, there has not been an opera put on in Rouen since before the Revolution!'

'Have you not had any pressure on you in this town for a French singer to play Rosina?'

'Not in this town,' said Maurice. 'There is no one in our choir who would be up to it. No one with your presence. No one who can act! Understand that, apart from Nellie Friedel, the Mayor's daughter, no one in any of the leading parts will come from Rouen. The choruses will be largely local people, of course. For the main roles I have gone far afield. Witness yourself!'

'Thank you. And there will be no jealousy?'

'There is always jealousy.'

'But being English – when we were in a bitter war only a few years ago?'

'If there is any prejudice it will soon fade. Have you noticed any so far?'

'No.'

'Set your mind at rest. The French love opera. And opera is cosmopolitan.'

'I shall look forward to when Helen and Polly arrive. Even if they are only in the chorus they will be from England.'

Maurice squeezed her arm gently but did not reply.

Valentine Warleggan had a visitor. He was not exhibited to the muttering Butto but shown into the smaller parlour off the hall, where last year the weeping Agneta had confronted Selina Warleggan.

While waiting the visitor stared out of the tall sash window at the warm buttery sunshine falling on the green and brown and granite cliffs which sheltered Trevaunance Harbour, or what passed for a harbour on this inhospitable coast. The incoming surf made a ring of fine necklaces round the blue throat of the bay.

Valentine came in. His face looked bony in the hard light.

'Captain Prideaux, what a surprise! To what do I owe this honour?'

Philip put on his spectacles. 'Valentine . . . I come to see you on business.'

'Take a glass.' Valentine went to the cupboard and poured two drinks out of a brimming decanter. 'Sit down. I have relatively few guests. And even fewer come uninvited.' This was meant to be pointed.

'I should have written. But it was difficult to explain myself on paper. It seemed better to call.'

Valentine looked the other man over insolently. He pushed back the heavy strand of dark hair that always fell over his brow.

'I imagine you would expect me to say this. But I did not do it.'

Philip peered at him. 'Do what?'

'Kill Agneta.'

'Kill . . . Did you suppose I thought you did?'

'Possibly so. Possibly not. But I am not really a man for knives, d'you know. If I wanted to get rid of someone I'd rather shoot 'em. Knives, however sharp, are nasty sticky things. To kill they have to cut through sinews, muscles, maybe even bone. Blood spurts, viscera spill, the victim struggles, screams, claws, vomits perhaps or urinates. Disgusting! I should not like it at all.'

Philip took a sip of wine, then put the glass down. 'You're mistaken if you think that's why I have called.'

'Well, what a relief . . . My only other speculation is that you may have come about Clowance. Have you come to ask my advice?'

'About what?'

'About wooing her. You must know that I have a way with pretty women. And Clowance – and her baby sister – are a couple of luscious plums. I used to fancy Clowance myself, even though we were – er – related. In those days, of course, she had no eyes for anyone but Stephen Carrington. Now she has no eyes for anyone. Have you tried a little roughness with her? Sometimes girls who spurn gentlemen will respond to the hot breath, the searching hand—'

Philip struck Valentine across the face, knocking the wineglass

282

out of his hand. They stared at each other. Philip's face was livid, Valentine's became red where it had been struck.

Philip bent and picked up the glass. The old overmastering anger had come on him unawares.

'I should apologize. Your humour doesn't appeal to me. But it is your house. We have insulted each other. The normal consequences . . .'

'The normal consequences being a duel?' said Valentine. 'That's military poppycock. Fortunate that glass did not break; it belonged to my Grandmother Chynoweth. It's old. Most of the things they possessed seemed to date from before the Norman Conquest.'

Philip tried to swallow his anger. 'I have apologized. I came on business. My feelings for Clowance and the contemptuous way in which you spoke . . . I beg your pardon again.'

Valentine put the glass back in the cupboard. 'Well, perhaps you should state your business and go.'

Some of the wine was on Valentine's jacket; Philip had only one or two splashes but he was carefully wiping them away.

'Well, yes. I have made a bad beginning, but . . . I don't suppose you have yet heard that a new mining company has been established calling itself the North Coast Mining Company. I am its chairman.'

Valentine rubbed his face. 'What on earth do you know about mining? Next to nothing!'

'I entirely agree. I know only what most sensible people know in this county. In mining you get rich quickly or you get poorer slowly, and the odds are heavily stacked against you. I know next to nothing about mining, but my partners are well informed.'

'Who are they? And what is it you want?'

'I am not in a position to tell you the names of the partners in this company. What does the company want? It is interested in buying the shares in your mine, Wheal Elizabeth.'

Valentine stirred some of the spilt wine with his foot, rubbing it into the carpet.

'Wheal Elizabeth? You must be mentally retarded! Why should I sell what promises to be a gold mine?'

'That's not our information. We understand it has failed in three shafts and the remaining two are unsatisfactory.'

'Ah, but your information is wrong. In our last report you will see—'

'A few idle speculations dressed up to look like facts.'

Silence fell.

Valentine said: 'So why do you want it? If it is of no value to you?'

'We think it has prospects. We think we may be able to develop it.'

Another silence.

'Who are your partners? I shall know soon enough. It's not possible to keep such a secret in Cornwall.'

Philip took his glasses off and put them away. 'The question is whether you *will* know soon enough.'

'What's that intended to mean?'

'You know John Permewan has been arrested in Plymouth.'

'For forgery, I understand.'

'It is strongly supposed that he wrote the latest prospectus on Wheal Elizabeth. In any case your prospectus includes a lot of information that is totally false, and on which you have raised a very substantial sum of money from investors in the north of England. Issuing a false prospectus is fraud. If you were convicted you would go to prison.'

'Indeed,' said Valentine. He looked up, listening. 'How peaceful it is now in the house! I have just moved Butto to his summer residence and he does not at all like it. You must see him before you go. Hark! I can hear him now!'

They listened together to a shrill distant screaming and roaring, which went on for a couple of minutes before the sound was blown away by a gust of wind. 'He thinks he's being punished. Sometimes it's hard to reason with one's pets.'

'Shall I leave you with the proposition to think over for a few days? Though from what I hear there is very little time to lose.'

'Blackmail, in fact. At the risk of provoking you to further violence, I would say I am surprised that Captain Philip Prideaux, an ex-cavalry officer of the highest reputation, should be a party to blackmail!'

'With, I might suggest, a certain amount of benign interest.'

'So-ho. So this – is this some sort of rescue venture that you and your friends are planning?'

'My dear chap, the whole of Truro is buzzing with rumour. We believe it is only days before some of your North Country investors arrive. If a large new mining company has taken the mine over lock, stock and barrel and is ready to repay these investors their investments with some small profit added, they cannot complain. And if they are told that they will receive their money back only if they halt any proceedings they have put in hand . . .'

'Phew! It grows warmer every day. I must go and let Butto out . . .' Valentine went to the window. 'This is all very surprising to me, Captain. And the biggest surprise of all is that you have been put in charge of this venture. Are either of our two local knights shareholders in this concern?'

'Knights?'

'Sir George or Sir Ross. If it were only the latter I should suppose that his heart was sounder than his head and that this was a quixotic but foolish attempt on his part to save a close relative from the consequences of his folly. If it were only the former I should suppose he has had investigations made at dead of night as to the future profitability of Wheal Elizabeth – if he were to get it cheap enough.'

'I am not at liberty to say.'

'But you are here to make me an offer for the mine with a pistol at my head!'

'There may be an element of truth in that. The choice is yours, but it is not a wide one.'

'Indeed not. Always assuming that I am not able to convince my North Country partners that I am an honest man losing their money for them in all good faith!'

'And can you?'

'It remains to be seen. It also remains to be seen what your share company is prepared to offer. No doubt they have sent you along with a knock-down price.'

Philip reached for his glasses and put them on, hooking them carefully behind each ear.

'The figure mentioned to me was seven thousand pounds.'

Valentine laughed loudly. 'If I accepted that I should—. By the time I have settled with my partners and accounted for some general expenses I should have nothing!'

'That was what one of my partners thought possible.'

'And no doubt your other partners opined that nothing was all I deserved.'

'Not in those words. No, not in those words.'

Valentine swung round. 'Well, *mon capitaine*, it will not do. If I go to prison, however distasteful that may be, I shall have the satisfaction of knowing that I have not disposed of my birthright to satisfy a group of sanctimonious robbers. For that is what you are, you and your crew. I wish you good day.'

Philip said: 'Your objection may be a little abated if you know that they would be willing to allow you to retain a quarter share of the mine if that price were paid. It is the feeling of a lawyer in the group that it might be possible to negotiate a settlement with the men you have cheated on those terms. But we cannot promise that. It very much depends upon how revengeful they may feel towards you.'

'Go now,' Valentine said, 'before I set Butto on you.'

Chapter Eight

On one of her visits to see her parents Clowance overtook Ben Carter, who was walking over to Trenwith.

It was the first time they had seen each other since the Christmas party, and Ben flushed slightly and took off his cap.

'Why, Ben, how are you?'

'Nicely, thank ee, Miss Clowance. And how's yourself?'

'Which way are you going?'

'Past Sawle Church, y'know. Towards Trenwith.'

'I'll walk with you as far as the church.' Before he could help her she slid off Nero, looped the reins over one arm and was standing beside him. She smiled as he deferentially stepped back. 'You're married, Ben.'

'Yes, that's true.'

'My mother told me. To that nice girl you were with at the Christmas party.'

'Yes, that's true.'

'She's a cousin of mine, you know. I think that's the relationship. My mother is her aunt.'

They looked at each other.

He said: 'You've picked a handsome day this day for your visit.'

She said: 'Are you happy, Ben?'

'Oh, yes. Oh, yes.'

'Perhaps I ought to say, at last.'

'Well . . . mebbe. It's took a long time, 'asn't it.'

'Perhaps after all this time we should not go into it.'

They began to walk.

'And you, Miss Clowance? – Sorry, I can't ever bring meself to call you Mrs Carrington . . .'

'Why do you not say Clowance? You used to once, you remember.

We have known each other long enough. And after all we are now related.'

He smiled. 'Tis true. Though not mebbe as I once had the – the kick an' sprawl to – to hope for.'

'It was not kick an' sprawl, Ben. There was nothing wrong in feeling the way you felt for me. I just did not – feel that way for you. But I swear it had nothing to do with your being a Carter and me being a Poldark. It – it was just that I fell headlong in love with Stephen Carrington.'

They were in sight of the church.

'It must have been a bitter blow when he died.'

'It was. It was.'

'An' ye've not yet come out of the grief?'

'A little way.'

'Shall you stay on in Penryn? Why not come back and live 'ere, where ye b'long?'

She shrugged.

'Are you going to Trenwith to see Esther?'

'I'm going for to meet 'er. She finishes work at seven each day and I like go meet her and walk her 'ome.'

'She's a lucky girl.'

'I'm a lucky man.'

'Yes . . .'

'I would come with you all the way and meet her again – I hardly saw her at the party – but I left late from Penryn, and my mother will begin to worry, as mothers do.'

'Tes kind of you to stop – Clowance.'

'I very much wanted to. Will you give me a leg-up, please?'

His face was close to hers as he bent to grasp her boot. She kissed him. Then he gave the necessary hoist and she was in the saddle.

'Don't tell Esther,' she said.

He put his hand up to his cheek. 'She would not mind. She d'know how I have long felt . . .'

'Dear Ben,' she said, 'I am happy for you.'

At supper Clowance said: 'I thought Cuby and Noelle would be here.'

'I have not had any word,' Demelza said. 'I expect they will be here tomorrow.'

'I saw Ben on my way. He was going to meet Esther. You were telling me last time that Ben and Esther's wedding was interrupted by the ape, but Harry came in and you never finished the story.'

Demelza finished the story.

'Did it upset them, d'you think?'

Demelza looked at Ross, who said: 'By the time the disturbance began the ceremony was over. They did not like it – it is another black mark for Valentine in Ben's eyes. But they were both too concerned to get away from the church without being pursued by a crowd of rowdy youths. I think in a way Butto was a useful diversion.'

'And Music and Katie are settling in at Trenwith? I did not mention them to Ben.'

'Cousin Geoffrey Charles seems very pleased with them. He says Music has a real gift with horses.'

'Yet he hated Butto . . . Have you seen Butto, Mama?'

'I glimpsed him out of the vestry door.'

They ate in amiable silence.

'Henry is very quiet tonight,' Clowance remarked.

'He was more than normally self-willed,' said Ross. 'I laid a relatively gentle hand upon his sacred person and he did not like it. After a few screams that would have rivalled Bella at her worst he has gone sulking to bed.'

Demelza frowned. 'He said to me: "Papa's a naughty boy. Smack him for me." I promised I would.'

'Any time,' said Ross.

'You have an unruly family, Papa.'

'I can't think where they got it from,' Demelza said.

'Talking of the unruliest of us all,' Clowance said, 'I showed the letter from Bella to Mama while you were out. Pray read it if you wish.'

She passed the letter over, and Ross was silent for a couple of minutes. 'It says very little fresh. Indeed it is much the same as she sent to us. But the more letters she sends the better I am pleased. One feels she still has some conscience.'

'I have had another letter from Mrs Pelham,' Demelza said to Clowance. 'She is inconsolable. She seems to think it is her neglect that is somehow at fault. I took her letter to Caroline, and she is writing to try to reassure her.'

'What does Caroline think of it all?'

'I believe she feels uneasy because it is her aunt. If it were not for that I think she would be quite behind Bella's escapade. Tis in Caroline's nature.'

'It is in mine,' said Clowance.

'And ours,' agreed Ross, 'were it not for a little parental anxiety.'

'Has anyone heard from Christopher?'

Ross shook his head. 'Bella says she has written, but we do not know if he has replied to her or what he has said. I cannot imagine him being pleased.' When no one commented on that he added: 'Bella has been his protégé. It was his idea that she should go to London and become a singer. He was engaged to marry her and they would have been married by now were it not for a – for a disingenuous postponement, apparently by agreement between them. My inner feeling is that there has been a cooling off, even an agreement to a temporary separation. In that case he has no real cause for complaint. Or not much. Did he know there was a likelihood that she might go away with this Frenchman?'

Demelza said: 'A while ago he spoke of wanting to marry Bella to protect her from the attentions of other young men. One of those he mentioned was Maurice Valéry.'

Ross stirred, impatience coming to overshadow the tinge of anxiety.

'Until we have Bella in front of us to answer our questions we shall not know the ins and outs of it. Perhaps not even then.'

'I should not worry about it too much, Mama. Bella has her own life to live. We had many long talks when we were together at Easter, and I was astonished, simply astonished at the way she had matured. Instead of her being my brash little sister it was as if she was almost older than me, different, come to see things in a different way.'

'The way of the world?' Ross asked gently.

'I do not say she had become a part of that world, only that she sort of *understood* it. She might have been a young married woman and I an old maid!'

'That you are certainly not,' said Demelza.

'She was never, never condescending. I only mean that we have

290

now been living different lives, so that the eight years between us no longer existed.'

They rose from the supper table and drifted into the old parlour. Demelza had her glass of port, Ross his brandy, Clowance took an extra glass of wine.

'Why do you not come back and live here?' Ross said. 'We should very much welcome that.'

'Ben suggested the same thing this afternoon.'

'And so?'

Clowance wrestled with unexpected impulses. She was by nature the friendliest of people; only Stephen had brought about situations which had caused her often to think twice before she spoke; and the circumstances of his death, and her discoveries about him at the time of his death, had inhibited her further. But here she was with her mother and father, whom she dearly loved and from whom she had never received anything but kindness and common-sense understanding, in their own home where she had grown up, where everything was familiar and friendly and a part of her old life. Perhaps the wine was helping. She told them of the two marriage proposals she had received.

Ross glanced at Demelza but she had her eyes down, staring deeply into her glass of port.

He said: 'Philip has been courting you long enough and has never been backward in showing his feelings. Edward Fitzmaurice – well, his is a much older suit; but I thought he had asked you to marry him once long ago and you turned him down.'

'He has never given up,' said Demelza without raising her eyes.

Moses, their latest cat, inserted himself round the parlour door and moved slinkily across the room, his tigerish back sinuous in the fading light.

'Well, yes,' said Clowance. 'There it is.'

'Is that a sufficient answer to our suggestion that you should return home to live? That shortly you shall choose between these two gentlemen? Or does it mean that you have chosen?'

'No.'

'But that you might soon?' asked Demelza.

'I ought,' said Clowance. 'I did ought.'

'You did ought,' said her mother. 'That is the sort of grammar I have been trying to live down.'

'It is very expressive,' said Clowance.

Ross said: 'And do you have a taking, the merest sliver of an inclination towards one or t'other?'

'I could marry either or neither. I like them both.'

'Not love them?' said Demelza.

'Not exactly. Not what I – I remember of love.'

It was a sad remark, thought Demelza. Her pretty, blonde, down-to-earth daughter was waiting for someone to sweep her off her feet. As Stephen had in his swashbuckling way. But with good results? She remembered Clowance saying to her soon after Stephen's death with great bitterness in her voice: 'If I ever marry again it will not be for love, it will be for position and money.'

'Well, you cannot marry both,' Demelza said. 'I believe it is against the law. If you marry neither you could always stay just as you are at Penryn. Or, as we said, you can come home. It is a pleasant life here, with little stress these days. Cuby seems to have settled back in Caerhays.'

'She has a child,' said Clowance. She stood up just as Moses was going to jump in her lap. 'I told you – Edward sent me this long letter. I have it upstairs. I'll get it and you can read it.'

She was out of the room, her feet pattered, a door banged, more pattering and she was down again. 'There. Who shall read it first?'

'Your mother. She reads more slowly.'

Demelza made a face at him. 'Does he write with too many loops? Oh, no, this is proper. Oh, I never had such a long love letter in all my life!'

While her mother was reading Clowance slumped on the floor and stretched the cat out on his back. Moses was still young and tended to be nervous and scratchy, but this time he recognized a friend.

When she had finished Demelza made no comment but handed the letter to Ross, who took up a pair of spectacles to read it.

Further silence, except for the cat purring.

'Well,' Ross said, 'he states his case. And states it well. It is not exactly passionate but he purposely did not intend it to be. It is pretty clear that the young man loves you. You have to admire him. He must have the pick of half the aristocratic young ladies of London and the shires, but he has never given you up.'

'I feel flattered, and a weeny bit sorry for him. I would like to make him happy.'

'And Philip?'

'I feel flattered, and a weeny bit sorry for him. I would like to make him happy too.'

They all laughed.

'Do you want an opinion on which of the two we would *like* you to marry?'

'Ross,' said Demelza reprovingly.

'Well,' he defended himself, 'Clowance has paid us the compliment of telling us of her dilemma. The very last thing either you or I should do would be to *press* her to make one choice or the other. Our *opinion* is our own. If she solicits it, she is entitled to treat it as no more than, and no less than, a breath in the wind.'

'Well said, Papa. Mama, what do you think?'

'Let your father say first.'

Ross went round lighting the candles. The sky outside, from being of grey-stretched silk, turned a shade darker as each candle caught and slowly lit the room.

'Philip is a very brave soldier. If there were decorations for bravery he would surely have them all. Like Geoffrey Charles he will always be a little military in his bearing and in his straightforward attitude to life. He is, I am certain, honourable and kind. He has the disadvantage of having had a bad breakdown in the West Indies, and often when I meet him he seems as taut as a wire. He tells you he has a competence and knowing that family it will be fully adequate. They will find him a home in Cornwall – there is one in Penzance now where mainly he makes his home – and even if you do not live at Nampara you will be living the sort of life you love in the county you love. The Prideauxs are a very old family – I think you could make a very good life with him.'

Clowance got up and drew the curtains across, stood with her back to the window looking at her father.

'As for Edward, in this letter he has spelled out the life that you might live with him. That too is very attractive. Although he says he will not be rich, that is, compared to his brother, who came in for so much, Edward will have enough property to live where and how he wants. He has offered you almost a choice of lives. If you keep him to them he will fulfil his promises, I'm sure. You will become Lady Edward Fitzmaurice, but your children will not have titles. Edward took no part in this past war and is a Whig. I think he is quite exceptional in that, although an aristocrat, he has lived a singularly decent and unprofligate life. And that, I can tell you, is highly unusual.'

'Are you recommending him, Papa?'

'I am commending him, not recommending him. I commend them both. Very recently – I have not told you this, Demelza – I have been more associated than usual with Philip Prideaux, and he has impressed me with his – his good sense and grasp of unfamiliar things.'

Moses, deprived of Clowance's ministrations, stood up, straightened up, stretched enormously, pointed his tail and walked towards the door.

Clowance said: 'Was it something to do with mining?'

'Yes. How do you know?'

'Philip had a book about mining finances under his arm when last he called.'

Ross was reading Edward's letter for the second time. When he had finished it, Clowance said: 'Papa has given me his views about my two gentlemen. Not you, Mama. Do you not wish to say anything?'

'I am not sure what to say, my lover. My – my heart says that if you cannot decide between the two of them you had better not to choose either.'

Clowance went across and opened the door for Moses. When Moses, having been offered the means of exit, hesitated on the threshold, she helped him out with her toe.

Ross, after waiting for his wife to say more, said: 'These are both good, decent men.'

'Yes,' said Demelza. 'That is what one has to think on. Maybe I have been spoiled. Many marriages are a great success because there is a – a sort of affectionate companionship which grows with the two people being together. To do without that, to throw away the chance of that, to turn them both down because you have not lost your heart to either one of them is not perhaps a wise thing or even a kind one.'

Clowance said: 'Of course I have to decide for myself. And shall. But I have welcomed your advice, even though there is no guidance in it.'

Demelza swallowed her port. 'I think, if I were you, Clowance, I should try to ask myself one question. If you wish to choose one of these men I should ask myself the one question. Which of these two – Philip or Edward – would you most like to be the father of your children?'

At early morning breakfast, with the sparrows twittering and the sun slanting in, the mood had lifted, had lightened, the tenseness gone. That was not altogether because of the presence of Harry, who had apparently forgotten his bitterness of the night and was as affectionate towards his father as ever, demanding of him that they should go on the beach 'immediate', 'immediate' – it was his new word – to discover the leavings of the dawn tide. It was only after Harry had been temporarily diverted by the promise of the arrival of a litter of piglets to Judy, the old sow, and had disappeared clomping into the kitchen that Clowance asked in what way Philip Prideaux was involved in mining with her father. Had it something to do with Wheal Leisure? Demelza, who had meant to ask Ross about this when they retired to bed last night, but who had been too involved thinking about Clowance's choices, pricked up her ears.

Ross said: 'Two of the banks in Truro wanted to mount a rescue operation for a tin mine we knew to be foundering for lack of capital. For reasons we need not go into, neither bank wished to become publicly involved, so a device was come to whereby a new company should be formed to discharge the debts of the mine and to take it over. We wanted a negotiator – chairman, if you like – we needed a man who would act as independent manager, reporting to the banks, who would remain in the background. We tried to think of someone entirely neutral among the various cross-channels of jealousy and petty politics of the mining world, so we approached Philip Prideaux, and he accepted the position and has done all that was asked of him.'

Demelza said: 'Excuse me if I ask the wrong question, but apart from Fortescue's, which is very small, there are only two big banks in Truro now, The Cornish Bank and Warleggan & Willyams. Did you say they were Truro banks?'

Ross hesitated.

'Yes, it was those two.'

'Working – working together?'

'I – yes – it suited them both.'

'My grandfather's ghost!' said Demelza. 'My dear life and body! My blessed Parliament!'

'Do not be so exuberant,' Ross said. 'It is merely a matter of convenience. George continues to snarl at me whenever we meet. But it so happened that I saw him soon after his accident and circumstances were such that we thought this should be done.'

'What mine are you helping?'

'Wheal Elizabeth. Valentine's mine.'

'Is he in trouble?'

'He could have been.'

Demelza wafted her face with a napkin. 'How is George?'

'I have not seen him for two weeks. He was in bed then.'

'He still is,' said Clowance. 'Harriet says he gets up for dinner and stays up until about six.'

'Did Harriet have a hand in this?' Demelza asked.

'Only in suggesting Philip as a neutral chairman.'

Demelza was thinking over the question of how her husband had come to visit Cardew, to have seen George so soon after his accident. But too many questions might seem too much of a good thing. It would come out soon enough.

'Well,' she said, 'it draws Philip more into our family.'

Chapter Nine

'Heider,' said Maurice, coming off his rostrum, 'can you move over front left as you begin the duet. Your tone blends most beautifully with Jean-Pierre's, but from the auditorium his voice is too much modified by what he has to say to register as it should.'

Sulkily Figaro moved a couple of paces to his left and then two more as Maurice continued to wave at him.

Heider Garcia had been later than the rest to be engaged. As Bella knew, Maurice Valéry had been looking for someone younger, but could not find just what he wanted. There was no real reason why Figaro should be a very young man, except that throughout he behaved like one.

Garcia was an old hand, had been in the opera world for thirty years, and he played in any part that suited his high baritone voice. A relative of the two better-known Garcias, he was a little bit on the way down, and the fact that he accepted a part with a provincial and untried company was proof of this. He felt himself rather above the rest of the cast, and took little notice of Bella except when he had to act and sing with her, which on stage was frequently. There he was co-operative but greedy. He thought himself the centre of the play and tried to make sure of that by the way he sang and acted. Twice already Maurice had taken him aside and explained to him that after all this was Bella's first appearance, she was an amateur seeking to be a professional, poor girl, she (by implication) represented no threat to him and would be eternally grateful for his help. So could he please not try – or appear to try – to crowd her out?

Now Maurice was trying to do the same for Jean-Pierre Armande, who was quite capable if need be of looking after himself. But it was the producer's job to produce the piece as he chose and give his necessary directions in such a way that the members of the cast did not resent them and that they did not come to quarrelling among themselves.

'You are exhausting yourself to death,' Bella said, when eating supper with him later that evening. Today's rehearsal had seemed to go on for ever, Maurice here, there and everywhere, directing, advising, cajoling, tireless and endlessly good-tempered. '*Mon cher*, that is too loud a protest. If it is quietly spoken it is much more *funny*. D'ye see?' 'Jean-Pierre, although it is all in good fun, I want you to *inhabit* the character. You must try to *be* him. When you turn away it must be in *real* despair.' 'Etienne, it does not so much matter *where* they are as *how* they are. Here, may I show you? You are over here and you begin your song. But the *récit* you have before it gives you reason to expect that the ladder is still *there*!'

The dress rehearsal was tomorrow, the opening night on Monday. It was hoped to give at least three performances. After an unfortunate outbreak of summer cholera in the town there had been talk of a postponement, but it was decided to go ahead. Because of this certain areas of the town were out of bounds to the cast until the performances were over.

'I am not exhausted at all,' said Maurice, looking her over. 'On the surface, yes, I puff, I gasp, I sigh, I shout, I tear at my hair, but this is not what is happening *below*. Underneath that is a – a steam engine which drives me on and replenishes my surface energies in sleep.'

'You should take an early night tonight,' Bella said. 'There is so much to do tomorrow.'

'Maybe. But tomorrow is another day. Now we are at last alone I want to know if you have chosen your songs.'

'I think I have. It will partly depend on what you think.'

In the second act of *Il Barbiere di Siviglia* a music lesson takes place. Already in the few performances of the opera which had been given it had become an acknowledged privilege of the star playing Rosina to sing whatever songs she fancied. (After all, it is a music lesson.) In England Mrs Dickons had chosen to sing two of Rossini's own arias taken from his other operas, but elsewhere in Europe other quite unrelated love longs had been chosen.

Maurice had told Bella he thought it a brilliant idea if she would sing in English. At her protests he had said: 'I assure you that there is no feeling against England at all now. The war has been over five years. Napoleon is permanently exiled. I think that if the audience likes your personality – as who could fail to? – and approves of your singing, this will greatly appeal to their good humour and good taste. Have you time to come to my rooms for one hour?'

When Bella had not been able to choose two songs, he had sent his cousin to Paris, and he had returned with some English song-books for her to try out.

'All right,' she said. 'Just for an hour.'

His rooms were on the first floor of a tall lodging house, and contained, of course, the invaluable piano. He sat on a stool beside her while she first played and then sang the pieces she had provisionally chosen.

The first was a late sixteenth-century piece called 'With My Love My Life Has Nestled' by Thomas Morley. The second was Purcell's 'Crown the Altar, Deck the Bay'.

'These are splendid,' Maurice said. 'May I join you?'

He pulled up his stool beside her.

'I'll take the bass, you take the treble.'

'Two hands?'

'Four.'

'We shall get entangled.'

'No matter. One, two, three.'

They began on the Morley piece. It went well. Then they tried 'Crown the Altar' and here his hand tried to touch the same key as hers. They both laughed. She removed her playing an octave up, but he did the same. There was the same contact and the session ended in more laughter.

He kissed her. He said: 'Is this not good? Music and love? It is everything that life has to offer!'

Her left hand played a trill. 'Are you telling me this or asking me this?'

He kissed her again. '*That* is what I am saying. *That* is what I am saying. No more, no less.'

Her right hand played an arpeggio. 'Love, did you say? I thought you did not believe in love?'

'I do not believe in *marriage*, for one is married to music. But perhaps for you I could contemplate even that.'

'What a sacrifice!' she exclaimed. 'How you impress me!'

'What is this that I feel for you but love? It is not just lust. It is not just desire. It is a true – emotion. Bella, you are very wonderful to me.'

She got up, partly to distance herself from the proximity of his person.

'And how long will it last?'

'Love? Last? It will be sublime, like the "Moonlight" Sonata.'

'And then?'

'When one is young it is not *then* that matters. It is *now!*'

'You argue well, Maurice.'

'And persuade, I trust?'

She turned and smiled at him. 'It is two days to the opening performance.'

'They go together!'

'They *may*. But we have so much to do, to think of, to concentrate on.'

'You said they may. Is that a promise?'

'How can you promise with a *may*? I expect it would be very easy for me to slip into an affaire . . .'

'Let me help you.' He came over to her.

She said: 'I heard from Christopher last week.'

His face changed. 'So? At last? What does he say?'

'He thinks I have left him.'

'And have you?'

'I – don't think so.'

'But you are not sure. You are not as sure as when you helped him off the floor of the Pulteney Hotel.'

'I have known him for a long time.'

'And you have been amorous for a long time.'

'Not amorous as you would describe it. But deeply affectionate and – and more.'

'Is he at home now?'

'No, still in Lisbon. Or was when his letter was written. It has taken two weeks to reach me.'

He went back to the piano and played one or two single, thoughtful notes.

She shrugged into her cape. 'Dear Maurice, I think I should go. We have a long day tomorrow. On Monday it is not just my reputation that is at stake, but *yours*. *Much* more yours, for I have no reputation – on the stage – to lose . . . Little of a normal reputation too, I conjecture, among my friends and family at home.'

'Then lose what is left and be free!'

She came up to him and he swirled round, kissed her passionately, lips, neck, eyes, until she was breathless. His hands were gently undoing buttons, but she stopped him.

'Maurice. We cannot be free while this opera is upon us. You cannot be free. I cannot be free. I know it is not the end of the world for either of us. But just now it seems so. You tell me this is a comic opera – that the audience is there to enjoy it – that if the soprano is squeaky they will forgive it, that if the conductor misses a beat and the chorus is ragged and Figaro forgets his lines – as he did last night – and if the Count's guitar is tuned to the wrong pitch – as you say happened at the very first performance – yet the audience will applaud just the same at the end.'

'Not just the same. And not just at the end! This is France!'

'But it has all yet to *happen*! I think it should – should be allowed to happen before we – before we commit ourselves further.'

Maurice decided to smile. 'I have reason to hope?'

'For the success of the opera, yes.'

They kissed again, and there was no lack of emotion on her side.

As they separated she said: 'My elder sister has two men who wish to marry her. But I suspect she cares deeply for neither. It seems that I also have two men who wish to marry me. (Though one of them has reservations about marriage.) At least I have two men who are very fond of me. And I—'

'And you?'

'Unlike Clowance, I am very, very fond of them both.'

'But one of your suitors is here by your side, *ma chérie*. The other is in Lisbon.'

Paul Kellow took his sister Daisy to see Butto.

The animal was still growing, and while of a continuing amiable disposition was now so formidable of appearance that unless Valentine was present he was never let out of his kitchen compound. Even this had had to be reinforced with iron staves let into the ground, lest Butto's huge muscular weight flung against the brick should break the sides open as if they had been hit by a cannonball.

Daisy had been unwell ever since the Christmas party, but it was a warm balmy day with little wind to trouble her, so Paul had brought a spare horse over from Ladock and had helped her to mount it and ride the three miles to Place House.

Daisy, as always, was in high spirits. (It was the only good symptom of her illness.) She cooed delightedly when she saw Butto, who instantly took a liking to her and, though carefully watched by Valentine, allowed himself to be rubbed around the head and ears like a friendly dog.

Valentine, flush with money made from an illegal shipment of a cargo of tin to Rosslare, and a shade relieved, in spite of himself, that he had disposed of his mine at a sensible profit to his well-wishers in the North Cornwall Mining Company – and also at the lifting of the threat of imminent arrest – was back almost to his best, elegantly clad, shiny of hair and healthier of skin. For the last week or two he had had no guests carousing in the house, and therefore less excuse to show off Butto and get drunk in the process. Also he had engaged a couple of extra servants on the proceeds of the prospective sale of Wheal Elizabeth, and they had cleaned the house up, bought new chairs to replace broken ones and cleaned the attics of the pungent stink of Butto. What was going to happen when winter returned he was not sure; possibly some form of heating could be contrived for Butto's present out-door residence. Nothing should induce him to part with the ape.

They took tea – yes, genteel tea – in the larger drawing room. The one remaining guest, David Lake, joined them.

Daisy was much changed, Valentine thought, from the days when rumour had linked her romantically with Jeremy Poldark. His own life had been disjointed in those days – sometimes he was at Trenwith – sometimes at Cardew – sometimes in London. But he remembered her then as a fresh-faced but high-coloured girl with her sister Violet. Violet had long since faded and died, and Daisy had developed prominent cheekbones and a febrile cough, her hair was lacklustre, her shoulders more bony.

After tea he suggested they should walk to the sea and a short way along the cliffs to see the battered wreck of a fishing vessel that had come ashore in the gale of last week and was slowly breaking up. Daisy said she could not manage it. David said: 'I'm lazy too,' and stared down at his increasing belly and laughed. 'You two go if you wish. I'll stay with Daisy, entertain her with stories of your misdemeanours.'

So Valentine and Paul went off alone.

They first discussed the mine. Turning the crisis to his own advantage, Valentine told the story as if he had got the better of this new company led by the inexperienced and gullible Philip Prideaux.

At this Paul said: 'Prideaux. He is in everything. He seems to be meddling in too many county matters.'

'He has recently meddled in mine to good effect. But I owe him no thanks. He has been a figurehead and has made rather a fool of himself – as well as of his employers.'

Paul picked a length or two of grass and sucked them. All this sloping cliff top was covered with heather and gorse. Wildlife abounded. The great black-backed gulls hung and swooped in the gentle wind, on the lookout for a baby rabbit that had strayed from its burrow. Spiders' webs glistened in the sun.

Valentine went on talking, speculating aloud, observing that it was only just over the next hill that Agneta's body had been found, describing some of Butto's latest antics, how he had caught one of the maids by an apron string and pulled and pulled until she let him have the apron and ran screaming into the kitchen. She left the next day, walking back to Camborne whence she had come only the week before.

'You'll not find many maids will stay here,' Paul said.

'We are down to two. But men will do well enough if paid well enough.' Seeing Paul's lowering face Valentine said: 'Daisy likes my ape. She is in very good spirits today. Maybe you will stop and sup with us?'

Paul picked another strand of grass. 'Daisy is dying, just like Violet and Dorrie. But she is of tougher stuff than they were. She'll take some killing.'

Valentine tutted. 'Too bad to have that in the family. Your mother and father are pretty well for their age?'

'My father is a drunken sot. Over the years I have found means to help him. Various means, legal and illegal. He has drunk the money I have made for him . . . My mother is a crouching, creaking old biddy who feels the world has treated her rough. So it has! But she does not have the courage to hit back. She creeps about as if she is afraid a thunderbolt may fall on her. I at least . . .'

'You at least?'

'Did you know – I think I have told you – that when I married

Mary she was a healthy young woman of twenty. Now she is scrofulous like the rest. I suppose I am accursed too. But I have had ways of hitting back!'

'Stephen Carrington in his cups one night hinted at something of the sort.'

'The fracas in Plymouth Dock when Stephen killed the man from the press gang? Yes . . . Later, a matter of – of shall we call it a robbery? Your half-brother – cousin, what you will – he was in that. On the proceeds he was able to buy a commission in the Army and live a high life in Brussels. Stephen financed his shipping firm in Penryn. I – what did I do? – hand-fed my father who, so soon as he had any spare capital, poured it down his throat!'

There was scarcely any sound but the humming of flies and bees. The sea was a metal-blue slate on which two fishing boats scrawled a lazy arc.

'Down there,' said Valentine, pointing. 'It has nearly all gone. You can just see the bows. The *Tresawna* from St Ives. The crew climbed out onto the rocks and when the tide went out they were able to walk round to Trevellas Porth.'

'Mary – my wife – has now lost all her hair,' said Paul, his expression muted. 'She is being fitted for a wig.'

'Good God!'

'I doubt that.'

'This has all happened since Christmas?'

'The disease progresses in fits and starts.'

'Sorry to hear that.'

They walked on.

Paul said: 'D'you ever think those screaming gulls sound like women being tortured? *Please! Please!*'

'Is there some point in your telling me all this, Paul?'

'All what? About the diseases of my womenfolk?'

'And your earlier adventures. I cannot cry for you. We are all masters of our own fate. Or is that too tedious a concept for you?'

'I do not accept the fate that a cruel God has designed for me. I perceive that you are of the same breed.'

'I rather think I am more closely related to Butto. I like to thump my chest and snarl. But within I'm really a peaceable soul.'

'Well, it seems to be fairly common knowledge that you employ a fishing drifter to ferry forbidden goods across to France, and bring back tea and silks and brandies and the like.'

'*Au contraire*, my dear chap. I follow a perfectly commonplace trade with my little brig between Padstow and Rosslare. There is nothing illegal about that.'

Paul smiled thinly. 'Well, no one supposes I am doing anything illegal in *my* commonplace life. If there is a God – or if there is only the Devil – He may know different. I am delighted to shake my fist in His face and spit in it too.' He followed the words with the action, his face temporarily ugly with anger and resentment.

'If you don't believe in God, why are you so angry with Him?'

'Do *you*?'

'I hardly ever think about it. My mother used to make me go to church, to say my prayers. When she died giving birth I stopped all that.'

'And you try to revenge yourself on Him?'

'Not so far as I am aware. I was at constant loggerheads with my father – my titular father – who often treated me like dirt, blew hot and cold, so that I came to hate him. Now I think I rather pity him. And I pity my other father. They have made a pretty mess of their lives and have tried to drag me in . . . Lately I have let them fund me out of a mess of my own making.'

'We are much alike,' said Paul.

'So you have said. I suspect there is one big difference.'

'That is?'

'I was born with an insatiable appetite for pretty women. Ever since puberty I have – this has been my great recreation. Whereas you . . . you give me the impression of not liking women.'

'I hate them.'

Valentine inspected his companion with interest. '*All* of them?'

'A few I can tolerate.'

'And men?'

'I am not interested in them in the way you mean.'

'But you married?'

'Mary was for a while – different. After a short time I did not satisfy her as she would have liked, and she did not satisfy me as *I* would have liked. If she had given me a son it might have been – a sort of solution. Instead she went rotten on me, she became like a worm-eaten apple, tainted, diseased. She would be better dead.'

'Butto would make a good family man,' Valentine said sardonically. 'In a year or two I may take him back to Africa to see if he can find a mate.'

'I wish you luck.'

'Precisely. Now look,' said Valentine, pointing with his stick. 'That cleft is about where they found Agneta.'

Paul shaded his eyes. 'No. It was on the crest beyond that.'

'How do you know?'

'I went with Ben Carter and Constable Purdy to examine the spot the following day. Ben found the body, y'know. I can remember exactly where it was because the ground all around it had been trampled flat by sightseers.'

Book Four

CLOWANCE

Chapter One

In the spring the English Cabinet, having survived a plot to massacre them all – when their heads were to be exhibited on pikes before the Mansion House – had prepared for the lesser embarrassment of arranging for the crowning of the most unpopular monarch in history. Yet no expense was to be spared. New jewels for the crown costing a million pounds sterling, parades, festivities, religious and secular ceremonies in many of the cathedrals of the land. (The Duke of Clarence, the next heir, expressed his opinion to a friend that if eventually he ever were to succeed to the throne there should be 'very little of this stuff and nonsense'.)

Queen Caroline, vulgar, stout, rouged, dyed hair and all, had long since been packed off to Italy, where she had lived an immensely dissolute life of her own; but now she announced that she would return to England and be crowned alongside her husband. The new King was horrified. He had just taken up with a fresh mistress, and wished Caroline to be excluded from the liturgical prayers of the Church, even – possibly – to get a Bill of Divorcement introduced as well.

However, all efforts – and plenty were made – to discourage her were fruitless, and she landed at Dover on the fourth of June. She was dressed in a low-cut bodice of cream Belgian lace, short skirt widely swirling in azure blue, showing fat legs inside tall shiny Hessian boots. To the disappointment of the crowd she had not brought her Italian lover with her, but they did their utmost to make her welcome. Church bells rang and cheering crowds lined the route all the way to London. She might have been the Duke of Wellington fresh from his victory at Waterloo. In London the carriage horses were unharnessed, and she was pulled with great acclaim all the way to Carlton House. Amid the din and tumult of

309

broken windows, ripped-up railings and the explosion of fireworks she was acclaimed Queen of England, whether George or the Cabinet liked it or not.

It was thought by many that acclaim of the Queen by the population sprang not so much from admiration of her sterling qualities as from a desire to show their contempt and dislike for the man who until January had been the Prince Regent.

Weeks of sober meetings began; the Coronation was postponed until the autumn amid endless noisy processions and demonstrations. The Queen went everywhere. During the prolonged negotiations as to her rights, or lack of them, she proceeded each day to Westminster in a coach attended by six footmen in red and gold, while she, deliberately different, wore a black curly wig almost to her shoulders, a hat with white ostrich plumes, a long black clerical cloak. The King could not go out of doors for fear of being stoned and his carriage overturned.

Revolution was in the air. With the present insurgence coming so soon after the Peterloo shootings, then the Cato Street plot to murder the entire Cabinet, there was little else one could expect. Demelza, worrying about the safety of her singing daughter, was almost relieved to feel that she was out of it all and living in the comparative peace of a French country town.

The first performance of *Il Barbiere di Siviglia* in the new French production took place at the Théâtre Jeanne d'Arc four days after Queen Caroline made her triumphant return to England, on Monday the eighth of June 1820. In spite of the summer cholera the production had gone ahead and in the end every seat was taken, and there was a noisy crowd standing in the pit.

Maurice ingeniously had allowed some of the street mendicants to get hold of a few of the very appealing tunes, so that they became known, though not too well known, and would be recognized by the audience and welcomed. Bella, as Rosina, played the young, pretty and flirtatious girl, rich in her own right, who is the ward of Dr Bartolo and has fallen in love with a travelling nobleman called Count Almaviva. Bartolo, intent on marrying his ward himself and anxious to lay his hands on her money, does all he can to prevent the match. Then along comes the strident Figaro, the barber, who only helps to confuse things but somehow eventually furthers the lovers' search for wedded bliss. Plot and counterplot, disguise and deception, concealment and surprise, are all interspersed by platoons of soldiers and itinerant singers, much fine singing, with acting designed to create laughter, until it all ends in frustration for Dr Bartolo and happiness for the lovers.

Although she appeared and lightly used her voice in scene one of the first act, most of Bella's activity was to come and go on the balcony, to take part in recitative and to be demure, flirtatious and distressed by turns. It was not until the second act, and the opera forty minutes advanced, that her testing time came. Then she had to sing 'Una voce poco fa' ('A little voice I heard just now'), and this she shortly had to follow with 'Io sono docile' ('With mild and docile air'), though it is clear by then that she is anything but docile.

Maurice had said: 'You have been preceded by several powerful male voices: tenor, baritone, bass; this is now your turn. By contrast your voice may seem to you too light to impress. Do not regard it so! The audience will have had just a taste of your quality in the first scene. Now begin softly and sweetly. Do not give them your full voice too soon. Remember the part you are playing: reflective, romantic; then later you can become positively vicious – oh the bravura of that later part! It will be magnificent!'

The audience, though there was an undercurrent of unrest, had been well behaved through the first scenes, and when Figaro appeared they were totally enraptured. Bella had been warned by Maurice that Garcia would come doubly alive on the night, and it was so. 'There are some who rehearse well and some who do not. Heider does not; but wait for the night.'

The duet between the Count and Figaro also went well, and then when the curtain came down all was bustle to change the scenery. The first scene had been in the street outside Dr Bartolo's house. Now this façade was split in two and pushed on rollers, part to the left, part to the right, to give sufficient space for his drawing room, nicely furnished and with, prominently displayed, the all-important piano, to be pushed forward to fill the gap. The stage manager, Edmond Largo, was in charge, but all the same Maurice slipped up for two minutes to congratulate everyone on progress so far. He kissed Bella briefly and climbed down the steps to rejoin his orchestra. The audience was getting restive at having to wait so long. As it was, the curtain went up before three of the soldiers who were doubling as stagehands could disappear out of sight. This was greeted by wolf whistles from the pit.

And soon it was time for Bella. Maurice caught her eye and smiled. She launched into her piece, which was written in high *bel canto* style, beginning almost *andante*, then gradually convincing herself that she is badly done to, finally launching into this tirade of defiance. Halfway through she noticed that one of the candle lamps illuminating the stage was smoking. Somehow the sight of it brought to her mind the party at Trenwith – not the latest one, but the one seven years ago when she had sung 'The Barley Mow' and 'Ripe Sparrergrass'. This time, instead of singing to groups of friends clustered in the great hall at Trenwith, she was in a foreign country looking down on a sea of faces, some listening attentively, some staring mouths agape, some scratching, some whispering, some (women) almost hostile. (And the candle, just above her head, still smoking.)

She had a moment of stage fright, her voice faltered for two bars, then picked up again; then she was into the trills and brilliant bravura of the final section. When she finished and the music died away, there was a silence, then a few sporadic claps, then a grumbling noise which she just recognized as applause. She saw Maurice signalling to her, and she began to bow. Three, four, five times, then Maurice raised his baton, the last noise subsided, and the opera was resumed. Now there was much laughter at the conniving of Figaro and Almaviva and at the clever antics of old Dr Bartolo, a lovely duet between Almaviva and Rosina, and then a descent into sheer farce with the arrival of the soldiers (one of whom composedly brought a pair of short steps, stood on them and snuffed the candle).

So at last the long first act was over, and a twenty-minute break to rest and recoup. There could have been a further change of scene, but the action all took place inside Bartolo's house, so a few shifts of the furniture would suffice.

'*Merveilleux!*' whispered Maurice to Bella. 'Better than I had ventured to hope. Those extra rehearsals were immensely worthwhile.'

'*Merde!*' said Bella. '*Je me suis trompée dans ma chanson*. I had caught sight of the candle and—'

'Unimportant!' said Maurice. 'Scarce anyone noticed it. That is the whole truth. Did you not hear the applause?'

'Yes, but I—'

'It is very well, Rosebud. Continue, *je t'en prie.* All is *very well.*'

He was gone with a flash of ruffled tawny hair.

The second act was ready to begin, but disturbances in the pit held the curtain for half a minute. Then Maurice, not waiting for complete silence, struck up.

Much of the extra farce that Maurice had planned was squeezed into this act, but before that came 'the music lesson' about which there had been so much discussion. Figaro, in trying to help the match, has persuaded the tall, ungainly, deep-voiced music teacher, Don Basilio, to pretend to be indisposed, and has replaced him with Count Almaviva disguised as Basilio's assistant. He and Rosina begin the lesson under the stern eye of Dr Bartolo, and Rosina, having recognized her lover under his disguise, is beside herself with joy, and proceeds to sing love songs with Almaviva at the piano.

The second act, as Maurice had said, was rather short, and he had seized on a precedent set in St Petersburg of having the prima donna sing pieces not of Rossini's composition but of her own choosing. There had been three songs then; he had decided on two, following the rondo 'L'inutile precauzione' which sends Bartolo into a doze. Bella began with the Morley song. This simple tune, with no demands upon the singer except sweetness and rotundness of tone at which Bella had learned to excel, had five verses, and was listened to in silence. When it ended there was light applause. Bella found that the backs of her knees were sweating. For the story's sake there had to be a bit of acting, when Bartolo roused himself from sleep and then was lulled off again.

A second English song? Was it wise? Few people here would understand the words. She had a moment to reflect while Bartolo woke a second time, proclaimed his affection for the old tunes and launched into 'Quando mi sei vicina', which received noisy applause. Then, ogling Almaviva, Bella began her second piece, 'Crown the Altar, Deck the Bay'.

The audience liked the song, they appreciated Bella's pure youthful rendering of it, but they had not, she felt, quite taken to her. Halfway through, a single voice from the pit shouted, 'A bas les Anglais!' There was laughter then whistles, but they soon subsided as she negotiated the difficult finale. Much applause, some genuine, some sympathetic. She looked out, bowing, over the sea of faces. It was not quite the applause Figaro had got, or even

Almaviva. In spite of Maurice's reassurance, she knew that her minor hesitancy followed by a few seconds of dry-up had not gone unmarked. Most of the audience was unsophisticated and knew very little about opera, but not all. Some of the people in the boxes were keen judges and went to the opera in Paris, which was not so far away. It was not a serious black mark in their minds, but it was a black mark all the same. 'Una voce poco fa' was her first great chance. She had stumbled. Other lovely arias and duets had come and gone. But this scene was her second big chance, her opportunity to register in the minds and affections of this audience. And it *was* such a perfectly lovely part.

She bowed and bowed again. Maurice was waiting. He was waiting to continue the opera according to Rossini. His baton was in a horizontal position, halfway to being raised.

There was a combative side to Bella. In a sense she was not just competing for the approval of the audience, she was competing against the men with whom she was singing. Apart from Berta, she was almost the only woman. A devil of temptation grew in her. A devil of temptation. She looked at Maurice, who half-smiled back at her. His baton came up an inch.

Bella went to the piano, where Count Almaviva in his thin disguise was waiting for the music to re-start.

She said: 'Jean-Pierre . . . Would you permit me?'

He gaped at her, but she had no time to lose. She edged onto his stool and edged him quickly off it. As he stood up she spread her hands over the piano keys.

She was going to give another encore.

She began to play.

Shades of a time nearly five years ago when, on a shaky old spinet, surrounded and breathed down upon by a score of lusty and probably lustful Polish soldiers, she had played this same tune.

She began to sing.

> 'Allons enfants de la Patrie,
> Le jour de gloire est arrivé.
> Contre nous de la tyrannie,
> L'étendard sanglant est levé.'

It could have gone badly wrong. It had become the song, the patron song, of the revolutionaries, and later of the Bonapartists. It had been the song of war which had now become the national anthem. It might have raised anger, derisive laughter, hoots of contempt, even a scandalized resentment at its introduction into Italian opera. But it did not.

Halfway through the first chorus of 'Aux armes, citoyens' one or two voices from the pit joined in. By the time she began the second verse the whole audience was singing.

> Amour sacré de la Patrie,
> Conduis, soutiens nos bras vengeurs.
> Liberté, liberté chérie,
> Combats avec tes défenseurs;
> Sous nos drapeaux, que la victoire
> Accoure à tes mâles accents;
> Que tes ennemis expirants
> Voient ton triomphe et notre gloire!

Some of the violins had now joined in, and Maurice was gently keeping time with a half-raised baton.

When it came to the end of the second chorus there was pandemonium. Whistles, cheers, stamping, a sea of faces. Bella took her tenth bow; Maurice raised his baton, then lowered it again as the applause would not stop.

At last it began to dry, and the opera was resumed.

When it was over and the cast was taking a final curtain call they were joined by Maurice Valéry. He split the line, one hand in Bella's, the other in Figaro's. As they bowed and smiled he hissed: 'Serpent! Sorceress! Vixen! Tigress! Angel! Witch! Tomboy! Sweetheart! *Je t'adore!*' As they bowed he kissed her hand. '*Tu es adorable!* I love you! No other woman could have had such *effronterie*, such flair! *Je m'enflamme.* You could have destroyed us, but you made us!'

She accepted a big bunch of red roses that was handed to her – obviously from him. 'I – I do not think Signor Rossini would have approved of me.'

'I had invited him.'

'*What?* But he—'

'No. At last he sent back word. But perhaps tomorrow.'

'I do not think I would dare to show my face.'

'That you shall! That you shall!'

When the audience had finally trickled out into the summer rain, the cast and all the helpers sat down to a feast on the stage. Armande, Garcia, Lafond congratulated her – and she eagerly congratulated them, for she had merely, in her view, taken a risk and brought it off. To them was the credit of the main singing and the comedy. Onion soup, chicken legs, fish pies, plovers' eggs, red wine, white wine – everyone was laughing and talking, relieving tensions which had built all evening – quails' eggs, bacon pastries, syllabubs, asparagus tips, jam cakes, white wine, red wine—

When this was all over and people were stretching themselves and yawning and belching and noisily taking their leave, Bella could still not unwind. Maurice put his arm round her. 'Come, *ma chérie*, I will take you home.'

Darkness had only just fallen, but there was a half-moon some-where lightening the mists of rain. They walked arm in arm through the empty streets, through the main square, turned towards the river. They talked about the production, the unexpected twists and turns of a first part-amateur staging when so much, so many little things had gone wrong and so many things had gone beautifully right. Figaro's joyous energy, Don Basilio's comic black hat and strutting walk, Dr Bartolo's agility when it came to making people laugh.

They came to her door.

'A last coffee?' he said.

'Yes. I do not think I shall sleep.'

'We all will in the end. Do you know?'

'What?'

'I think this might run to four performances instead of three.'

They had had two coffees and were lying sprawled in chairs, the tension seeping out of them at last. Yet they were still wide awake. It was a contented silence, a satisfied silence, a replete silence. But when she yawned and looked at him he was looking at her, and she knew that for him his long day was not yet complete. She realized that she wanted what he had to offer her. She knew it must not happen, but she knew that she wanted it to happen. Her con-science, her propriety, were fighting a losing battle.

He moved slowly out of his chair and dropped on one knee in front of her, then the other knee. She watched him take off her shoes.

Neither spoke. He lifted her skirt gently, almost clinically, reached for her garters, pulled them off, then peeled off her stockings. He arranged them in a little pile with the shoes. Then he began to kiss her legs. First left, then right. His strong teeth made little love bites. Then he sat back and stood up and went for a pair of scissors. When he came back he leaned over her and cut the ribbon that held up her petticoat. Then he took her hands and gently pulled until she was leaning forward. He undid the buttons of her dress and kissed the nape of her neck. He lifted her to her feet and slid the dress down, then with his hands round the upper parts of her legs he persuaded her to step out of it. She now had on only a thin white chemise. He kissed her gently all over her face while his hands slipped the straps from her shoulders and she stood before him naked. He did not draw back and look at her body in a way that might have embarrassed her, instead he held her close and cupped each breast in turn and covered them one by one with his mouth. They stepped back gently together almost as if in a dance towards the alcove where the curtained bed lay.

He pulled the curtains back, put his hand round her waist and behind her knees, lifted her in. She lay there, knees drawn up, great eyes fixed on him while he tore off his own clothes as if he hated them.

When they were scattered about the floor and he too was naked he climbed in, parted her legs and gazed down upon her like someone who has found buried treasure.

Two days after that, in the late afternoon, Sir Ross Poldark arrived in Rouen.

Chapter Two

George had made slow progress after his accident, far slower than he was willing to admit. Dr Daniel Behenna bled him repeatedly and spouted a lot of Latin names at him, the Anglo-Saxon translation of which was that he could find no broken bones, fractured liver or punctured lungs: it came down to the fact that the patient was not as young as he used to be and that his middle-aged system had suffered a profound shock from which it was going to take months rather than weeks to recover.

After the first three weeks his carriage took him to the Bank daily, but he did not arrive until eleven and left again at three. Dinner at Cardew was postponed until four p.m., after which he wrote letters in his study and retired about eight, supper being served in his room at nine. He saw little of Harriet, who busied herself about the estate. She was civil and advisory but not noticeably sympathetic.

Of course he received many letters of condolence and sympathy, but these were chiefly from men or families or organizations which were in debt to the Bank and whose solvency rested upon his good will. One letter he received had a motive, but there was nothing ulterior about it. This was from Selina Warleggan.

She knew nothing of his accident, but asked plaintively for financial help. She pointed out, somewhat unneccessarily, that her husband had taken over the fortune that Mr Pope had left her and spent it in foolish ventures into mining and on profligate living, on gaming, and on pursuing other women. But now, though she owned the house she was living in with her cousin and elder stepdaughter, she was deep in debt. The chief reason for this was the expense she had been put to over the recent marriage of her younger stepdaughter Maud. She had married a Mr David Shah, the son of a well-to-do cotton exporter by his English wife. Although the Shahs were Christians they lived in a rather expensive Oriental style, and when it came to the wedding she had felt obligated to spend substantial sums which she could not afford. So she had gone to the moneylenders and was now in considerable trouble on how to repay. As a family they were almost destitute. She appealed to George for help, not merely for herself but for his grandson, who did not deserve to go hungry.

George threw the letter away. Half an hour later he went to the wastepaper basket, persuading himself that he should have burnt it or torn it across so that none of the servants should read it; but when it was in his hands he read it through again and decided instead to file it away for further consideration.

Two days passed. He had another small crisis at the Bank because of Frederick Lander's growing tendency to take substantial decisions on his own judgement.

And then Cary died.

After the funeral, which was arranged for a time when Sir George could attend it, he rode back in the open carriage to Cardew, sitting beside the handsome black-eyed woman with whom he had chosen to spend the second half of his life.

Cary's death had shaken him more than he had expected.

He glanced sideways at Harriet, sitting so straight in her mourning clothes. No wonder she had such a good seat in the saddle.

'It was a fair turnout,' he said.

'Yes.'

'Cary would have been pleased to know he was so esteemed.'

'Or feared.'

'You cannot fear a dead man.'

'You can keep in the good graces of a living one. Who, by the way, was that tall young man standing by the gate? It looked like that lawyer fellow, Hector Trembath.'

'It was.'

'Was he a mourner? He seemed to be taking notes.'

'He was – well, yes, he was taking note of those who came.'

'There you are, you see. I have no doubt he will shortly present you with a black book listing those who did not.'

'I was glad to see Trengrouse there. Also Allen Daniel.'

She did not reply. He would have liked to say a lot more, but hesitated to do so. She had never been his confidante. Not as Elizabeth had been. They had never been so close. He and Harriet *did* talk, but he seldom told her any of his innermost thoughts. Was it true, was it possible, that she knew nothing of the doubts about Valentine's parentage? Surely in the years of their marriage some-one, *someone*, was likely to have whispered the scandal.

Who? All along there had been whispers in the district of Nampara. But apart from that, *was* it widely rumoured? *Did* he believe the whispers had spread as widely as he imagined? Probably no one in Truro knew. Harriet had never been to Nampara.

'I did not tell you, Harriet, but I had a letter last week from Selina.'

'How is she?'

'In desperate straits. Or so she says. No doubt she puts it all on for my benefit.'

'Does she want money?'

'Naturally.'

'Shall you send her some?'

'Would you advise it?'

She laughed. 'Since when have you consulted me on money matters?'

'Perhaps I should more often.'

'Then by all means send her some. I have always seen her as a likely pensioner. But you *have* a son and you *have* a grandson. Dip into your vaults and send her a bag of gold.'

'It would be by banker's draft,' said George automatically. And then: 'This is not a teasing matter.'

'Is money ever that?'

'In your eyes it is never anything else!'

'That is because you are so generous to me.'

He glanced at her to see if she was still joking. He decided she was not.

But he still made no move. Two weeks passed and he did not write. Then he picked up his pen one evening and drafted a letter. Still he did not post it but sent for Hector Trembath. They talked for an hour. Then he redrafted the letter and let it go to the post.

*

Bella was pulling on her stockings when the knock came at her door. She was not expecting a visitor but assumed it was Maurice, who could not keep away.

When she saw who it was she gave a crow of delight.

'Pa-*pa*! Pa-*pa*!'

Ross allowed himself to be embraced, and then gave her a special big bear hug.

'Pa-*pa*! How *lovely*! Oh, I am so delighted! But what a surprise! You are *here*! Are you really *here*? How is it that you are here? It is so lovely!'

'I was passing,' said Ross, 'and thought I would look you up.'

'Oh, Papa! What a joke! But what a pleasure! How did you know? How did you guess? Where have you come from? It is a dream!'

He said: 'I saw the posters when I came into the town. Am I too late?'

'No, it is tonight! And probably tomorrow.'

'Then I shall hope to get a seat.'

'It is sold out. But Maurice will see to that. Is Mama with you?'

'No, she entrusted me with a mission.'

'Oh, *mon Dieu*, I shall not be able to sing if you are listening.'

'I might,' said Ross, 'like to believe that, but I cannot.'

She took his hand and pulled him further into the room. 'Oh, Papa, you know me altogether too well. But all the same—'

'I do not think I have ever understood you completely – not since you became a woman.'

'When was that?'

'About sixteen years ago.'

She laughed delightedly. He could see there was no trace of reserve in her welcome. She poured him a cordial, apologizing for the untidiness of the room, asked when he left Nampara, where was he staying, how everybody was, and exclaimed that everyone here would be delighted and honoured to meet him.

It was five already. In half an hour she would have to leave for the theatre.

'First,' she said, 'I must write a note to Maurice, tell him he must find a seat for you. The little Bourges boy will carry it.'

While she scrawled the message he looked her over. Every time he saw her he saw a change. She wore more make-up than ever before. Her lustrous hair was brushed and tied and pinned, her eyes were bigger, her legs, under a tucked skirt, longer and more to be seen. Her gestures had always been a bit extravagant, now they were a little more elegant, more poised. God's my life, he thought, she is an actress! On the way to becoming a prima donna!

When the message had gone, she made him a cheese sandwich and wolfed one herself.

'What do you all think of me? It was the chance of a lifetime and I took it, but clearly it was not quite proper of me to do so. What *do* you think of me, Papa? And Mama? Was she 'orrible shocked?'

'As parents,' Ross said, after a moment's thought, 'we have always been over-indulgent with all our children. You must know that. You should all have been soundly beaten with a broom handle or worse. But we chose not to and so we reap the whirlwind.'

'You said that Mama had sent you on a mission. Darling Papa, have you come to see me on a mission?'

'Yes. To take you home.'

Bella let out a slow deflated breath. 'Oh. I had thought that.'

'Be of good cheer,' said Ross. 'You are eighteen. My authority is not absolute.'

'But your authority,' Bella said, picking at her finger, 'is not based on – on the broom handle. It is based on love. And that makes it much harder to defy.'

'How long do you have to stay here? When do the performances end?'

'Oh, Thursday. But it has been such a success that Maurice is trying to get a theatre in Paris.'

At that moment the man referred to appeared at the door. He was dressed for the theatre in a black cut-away suit and a black velvet bow tie.

He came in uncertainly, smiled briefly at Bella, bowed with the utmost courtesy to Ross, who also rose, took the Frenchman's hand.

Maurice's normally fluent English deserted him, and after a few exchanges they began to speak in French. Age had not yet bowed Ross's shoulders, and he towered above the young man. The high cheekbones, the pale eyes, the scar – which had come so much to resemble a duelling scar – made him look more formidable than he wished to appear; but a few smiling remarks from him soon eased the situation. Maurice asked if Ross minded sharing the Mayor's box with one or two other distinguished visitors who would be coming tonight. One of them was M. Auguste Pinet, who was a close friend of Rossini and would report back to Rome, where the composer was at present staying. There was a good chance, Maurice said, that the production would move to the Théâtre Gramont in Paris.

'Soon?' asked Ross.

'I hope soon. I – I trust you do not want to take Bella home?'

'I want to take her back to London. She has her peace to make with Mrs Pelham, who believes she was gravely remiss in allowing Bella so much freedom. In fact she seems inconsolable. This – Bella making her peace with her – is not so much a filial duty as a moral one.'

There was a short silence.

'If in a few weeks you can see this production set up in Paris we shall not stand in the way of Bella's returning.'

'*Thank* you, sir,' said Maurice fervently, and glanced at Bella.

It was a glance Ross intercepted. So there *is* something between them, he thought. Not merely music.

By now Bella's choice of songs in the singing lesson had been wholly accepted and there would have been shouts of complaint if she had not sung the 'Marseillaise'. So they would have to risk the disapproval of M. Auguste Pinet. In fact M. Pinet seemed amused by the idea and smilingly congratulated Bella at the end of the performance.

There was no banquet at the end tonight; instead six of them supped at the Couronne. Ross, Bella, Maurice, M. Pinet, Heider Garcia and the Mayor. Ross had a poor accent, but since his sojourn in the country five years before was entirely fluent, so there were no linguistic embarrassments. The newspaper in Rouen was only published weekly, but Maurice had been able to obtain an advance copy of the issue due out the next day, and he read out the review.

It spoke of the opera as an outstanding success. It criticized some clumsy phrases in the French translation and thought that the director had over-emphasized the comic scenes. But it had special praise for Heider Garcia as Figaro and Etienne Lafond as Don Basilio. As for Rosina, this had been the debut of a young English girl, not yet twenty, who had impressed everyone not only by her elegant voice – there had been one or two traces of nerves – but by her stage presence and sheer acting ability.

That seemed a fair enough review, but M. Pinet had brought along two small reviews from the Paris papers, one of which mentioned Bella. 'The soprano part of Rosina was taken by a young British actress who has a remarkable voice, a taking personality and a future, one dares to expect, of exceptional brilliance.'

So they toasted her in good red wine, and when it was over the young couple walked Ross back to his hotel. On the steps he stared after them and saw they were holding hands.

Thursday passed with a trip up the Seine in the morning, local sightseeing in the afternoon, attendance at the theatre in the evening. It was not quite full this time, and this seemed to indicate that the promoters' estimate of potential audiences had been about correct. After all, opera-going was an acquired taste, and most of the inhabitants of Rouen had never seen an opera before.

Friday Bella had agreed to join Ross on the tedious coach journey to Le Havre, but early that morning Maurice brought news that a small paddle steamer drawing barges, *L'Hirondelle*, was leaving at dawn for Le Havre and they would arrive in good time to catch the ship that would take them to England. With their permission he would accompany them on the first stage.

It was a lovely June morning, with only the slightest of breezes, and sailing at a slow, steady beat down the Seine was a very agreeable way to travel. Sometimes it was as if they were stationary and the land on either side was moving. Single-storey cottages loomed slowly up, women carrying pails of water, cows stood ruminatively in pools and shallows bordered by chestnuts, poplars and aspen, young horses galloped, ducks in a stream, a ruined abbey, a quarry, a church attended by clustered houses on a hill.

Bella went below for a few minutes, and Maurice at once took the opportunity of saying: 'Sir, I hold your daughter in the highest esteem.'

Ross inclined his head. 'I'm glad.'

'Indeed, esteem is hardly the word I should use to express my regard for her.'

'Indeed?'

'It is a dual regard, sir. She has, I believe, as *Le Monde* says, a brilliant future as an opera singer. I have seen this almost since the day I met her. Apart from the high quality of her voice, she is *musically* so good. And dramatically so good. She lives the part she is playing.'

Three fishermen in frail dinghies steered themselves lazily out of the way of the paddle steamer.

'The other regard I have for her is of course as a woman. She is entrancing . . . *ravissante*. I have declared my love for her.'

Ross gave the young man a quiet smile. 'I was not unaware that there was something between you.'

'I hope you view that situation – at least without disapproval?'

Ross said: 'She will have told you, of course, that she has already engaged herself to marry Lieutenant Havergal.'

'I believe that undertaking is in abeyance.'

'That may be the feeling on Isabella-Rose's part, but I don't think it is on Havergal's.'

'Have you seen him? He is back from Lisbon?'

'I have *heard* from him. He is back from Lisbon.'

Bella came up the companionway but waved her hand and moved to the bows of the vessel to watch two white horses frisking near the banks of the river.

'I have two daughters,' Ross said. 'Perhaps I should consider myself fortunate that they appear to be so appealing to men. My younger daughter has two eligible suitors, it seems. My elder daughter is a widow of twenty-seven, and she now has two very eligible young men who wish to marry *her*.'

'And will she choose soon?'

'She has already chosen. She told me just before I left home.'

After a moment Maurice said: 'I trust Bella will choose me. Merely on practical grounds I have more to offer. Havergal is a former soldier and is now a banker. I am a conductor and producer, I live and breathe music. Bella does likewise.'

'But perhaps,' Ross said, 'you – your attachment for my daughter, your love for her, does not go as far as marriage?'

'What makes you say that?'

'She told me once – some time ago – that you felt it was a mistake to marry because one has to be married to music.'

Maurice bit his lip. 'That was certainly my belief – until I met Bella. Now . . . if she continues to favour me, then I will be entirely guided by what she wishes – and what you and Lady Poldark wish.'

'Can you wonder what her parents would wish – even in these dissolute days?'

'Er – no. Well, I should be very happy to accept that decision. Bella and I can very well, I believe, be wedded to music and wedded also to each other.'

There was just enough air to get out of the port, and midway across the Channel a light south-easterly breeze picked up. All the same, it was going to be a slow crossing, probably eight to nine hours. Surprisingly there was a considerable swell; it was coming from up-Channel, and the little brig lurched disconcertingly. Bella, who was not the best sailor in the world, insisted on staying on deck, where the fresh air saved her from actual sea-sickness.

Ross sat beside her, dozing a little in the sun while she darned stockings. A pleasant domestic scene. It was quite a while before she said: 'Did Maurice ask you if you would agree to our getting married?'

'In a roundabout way. Well, yes, towards the end of our little talk he did declare his intentions.'

'And what did you say?'

'That you could not marry two men. Any more than Clowance can.'

'Have you seen Christopher?'

'His last letter was – forthright.'

'If we go straight back to London I shall have to meet him.'

'What shall you say?'

'That I am very sorry to have – to have deserted him.'

'Have you – permanently?'

She stirred restlessly. 'I don't know. What is permanent? We have known each other, have had such affection for each other, for so long. Maurice – is new. He is – wonderful, but so wrapped up in his profession. I don't want to hurt either of them!'

'Are you – committed to them in more than affection and the goodnight kiss?'

'To both for more than that! I am not made of stone, Papa!'

'Are you likely to have a child?'

326

There was a long pause. 'I don't think so.'

'But you are not sure?'

'No.'

'Oh.'

'Papa, you are *impossible*!' She stood up indignantly. 'To ask me such questions!'

He took her hand. 'But, Bella, I know it is not *impossible* that you should return me such answers!'

'You – have no right!'

'Who, then, if not I?'

'And now I have returned you the answer you did not wish to hear! And so it will go to Mama, and thence to all the rest of the family!'

'It shall be kept from Henry.'

She put her hand to her face and burst into tears.

'It is not a laughing matter,' she said.

'I am sorry. Believe me, I do not see it as such.'

'You surprised me by asking such a question – the enormity of it! – and then I answered it when I should not have done!'

'But I know you would not have lied to me.'

'That was why it was so unfair to ask!'

Ross thought a moment. 'Yes,' he said, 'I suppose it was.'

She continued to cry, bubbling like a child.

'Let us make a pact, then. We will agree that the question has never been asked nor ever been answered. How about that? I give my word. Will that suffice?'

She half dried up; he handed her a handkerchief; she glanced around in embarrassment to see if anyone had noticed. She began to wipe her face, though tears were still welling. Then she appeared to choke and cough.

'Come, come.' He stood up too and put his arm round her shoulders. 'Do not upset yourself so much.'

She coughed again. 'Well, it is not just that. I have had a sore throat since early this morning. It is nothing, but it catches my breath.'

'All this singing,' he said. 'Not surprising.'

'But it *is* surprising. Singing has never been any strain to me before.'

'Nor did it seem so last night. But don't forget this has been a severe test. So many rehearsals, I'm sure. And the acid test of singing the lead in a full-length opera in an unfamiliar language. No wonder you are over-tired, over-strained. And you have the added complication of having become over-fond of the producer!'

She half smiled as she handed him back his wet handkerchief. 'It may be so . . . but I feel so awful. Delighted as I was to see you, you should – you should not have come. I should have had the task of ending this in my own way, of – of finding my own way back to – to England in my own time . . .'

'Instead you return like a recaptured prisoner being taken back by a jailer?'

'That is not it, Papa. You know I do not look on it that way at all.'

'Perhaps you feel, as Jud once said, if you make your own house you have to lie in it?'

She half giggled – and winced. 'No . . . I don't know. Perhaps you are right.'

'Remember, Bella,' he said, 'you have been a great success. An outstanding success. Everything else will fall into place with a little patience and a little understanding. I am very proud of you.'

'Thank you,' she said.

They docked soon after nine.

'We'll lie at the King's Head,' Ross said. 'The coach leaves at seven tomorrow. Will you have a little supper in your room?'

'Very little,' said Bella. 'I have been eating altogether too much.'

They were wakened at five-thirty. As soon as he was roused Ross went along to Bella's room. She was sitting up. The sun shone in spears across the bedroom floor.

'How are you feeling?'

'I – slept well.'

'Your throat?'

'Still sore. It is nothing.' She coughed. 'Have you broken your fast?'

'Not yet.' He sat on the bed. 'Let me see your tongue.'

'Gladly.' She put it out, pulling a hideous face at him.

He grunted. Then he felt her arm and her forehead. He stood up.

'Bella, we shall go home.'

'Home? Where, to Cornwall?'

'Yes.'

'Oh, I am that pleased! I can defer all my apologies!'

'You have a fever,' he said. 'It is just slight. But I do not trust the sawbones of Portsmouth. Nor even of London. When we get home you will be in the capable hands of Dwight Enys.'

'I'll take a bet with you, Papa. Sixpence. That I am in the best of health by the time I see Nampara.'

'Done,' said Ross. 'I hear there is a coach for Exeter leaving at eight.'

Chapter Three

Lord Edward Fitzmaurice's apartments in Lansdowne House at the south end of Berkeley Square consisted of six spacious rooms, where he was attended by a valet, two maids, a cook and a scullery girl. His windows looked out onto Curzon Street. He had been in London most of the summer Season, but was looking forward to going next week to spend a while with an old schoolfriend, Humphry Astley, in Norfolk. It had been a bright enough early spring and summer, and Edward had dutifully attended the main functions of the Season, taking comfort in the thought that soon he would be breathing the purer air and less ceremonious life of Swaffham.

He was a modest young man who had not been brought up to expect great possessions. Unexpectedly a series of deaths had deposited upon his elder brother a marquisate, the huge estate of Bowood, a hunting lodge in Scotland, great wealth, a seat in the Lords and the possession of two other seats in Parliament for his bestowal.

Edward had officially become his brother Henry's heir in 1809, a matter of much less importance before that date, and he sometimes reflected whimsically that he was rather like the Duke of Clarence, the younger brother of the King. Henry was now laden not merely with great possessions but with great responsibilities, while Edward, five years younger, had no responsibilities at all. Fortunately Henry had been more sensible and assiduous than George IV by entering into a happy marriage and already having two small sons, so the risk of Edward being called to greater eminence was mercifully remote.

Edward had a number of interests: the theatre, the furthering of popular education, architecture in general; and when he sat down that morning to break his fast with fresh salmon and poached eggs, he looked at the letters on the silver tray just placed there by Watson, his valet, supposing most of them to be concerning a speech he had made on the Sunday, in which he had spoken in favour of Catholic emancipation. He turned the pile over with a paperknife, and suddenly his heart lurched, for a letter lay there, the address being in a handwriting that he well knew.

He grabbed the letter and stood up, pushing his chair back, went to the window, tore at the seal, unfolded the letter and began to read. What he read made his hand shake so much that he dropped the letter and he had to slide it out from under a chair, where it had disobligingly floated.

He read it carefully, very carefully, a second time, then he let out a great shout.

Watson, a fat little man, came hastily in. 'Something wrong, my lord?'

'Wrong?' said Edward. 'Wrong? Wrong, wrong, wrong, wrong, wrong, wrong? Heavens above! Oh, my God! I – must think!'

'Your breakfast will be going cold, my lord.'

'Watson, you know that beggar, the one with an arm missing, please take my breakfast down and give it to him. And please give him this guinea.'

'My lord, you know Lady Lansdowne says it is unwise to encourage people to wait at the door—'

'I will explain to Lady Lansdowne. And also I shall need a coach. Oh, my God! Do we have a coach here? If I—. No, that will not do! Our coaches carry a coat of arms. I shall want to hire a *plain sturdy* coach from the Half Moon stables. And six horses ... No, one mustn't be ostentatious! Four horses, for a long trip. Tell them I shall want the carriage for at least two weeks.'

'My lord, you are due to leave for Norfolk on Friday.'

'Yes, well that must go. I will write to Mr Astley. He will understand. Everyone will understand. Oh, my God! Everyone has to! Watson, I shall not need you for at least two weeks. Pray take a holiday and take double pay ...'

'Thank you, my lord. But does that mean you will be travelling alone? Surely—'

'Yes, surely. Oh God, this is tremendous. Oh God, I think I shall explode. Angels of Grace! Is – is my brother in?'

'No, my lord. He is riding in the Row with her ladyship—'

'Well, is *anyone* in? Anyone of my family? I must tell someone of this – this letter from Heaven I have received, or I shall burst!'

'I believe Lady Isabel is in her room—'

Edward took his valet familiarly by the arm. 'I am going to seek her out. But before I go let me enjoin you to step out into this lovely, lovely morning *at once* and make all haste to the Half Moon stables, preferably at the double, and request, nay *demand*, that they should rent me out a stout sturdy four-in-hand with a coachman to drive me down to Cornwall—'

'Where is that, my lord?'

'Never you mind, they will know. And if they do not know they will quickly discover. It is in the far, far west of England, almost toppling over into the Atlantic, and it will take maybe three days of hard driving to get there. Come to think of it, perhaps I shall need another man – I cannot have them going to sleep on the box—'

'Why do you not take Higgins, my lord?'

'Higgins? Higgins?' Edward stared at the fat little man. 'What a supremely helpful chap you are! I don't know how I shall do without you for two weeks. But it *shall* be two weeks, it may be three, or four, or five, or ten. Higgins is just the man. He understands horses, as you alas do not, and he is cooling his heels all day here. Higgins shall come.'

'Very good, my lord.'

Five minutes later, in a large bedroom in the east wing of the house overlooking Berkeley Square, Lady Isabel Fitzmaurice, about to begin her breakfast with a tall glass of orange juice laced with rum, was startled to see her maid look in and say that Lord Edward wished to see her. Behind her, his face transformed from its usual polite lineaments, came her nephew, who gently took the diminutive and scandalized maid by the elbows and lifted her out of the way.

'Aunt Isabel. A divine morning. I come to greet you with some news which has just transformed my life. Allow me to tell you.'

'Patsy,' said Lady Isabel. 'Pass me my trumpet, if you please. Did you say good news, Edward? Pray impart it. I think we all need good news.'

When the trumpet was fixed and Patsy had retreated Edward told his aunt the contents of the letter.

She was silent for a few moments, while he waited to make sure she had heard properly. Her little round face was recollective.

'*I* remember,' she said. 'An entirely charming young lady. She stayed here for a week or so. She used to read to me. Edward, I am so pleased for you.'

'That was not the lady I am going to marry,' he shouted. 'That was her mother.'

'If you speak clearly into the trumpet,' Lady Isabel said, in gentle reproof, 'I can hear perfectly well. There is no need to shout.'

'I am so pleased for myself,' he said. 'I have read her letter six times, and it turns my heart over and over.'

'I do not think I have met her then. But if she is like her mother I know I shall immediately take to her. I remember her telling me about her daughter now. It is very fortunate, a happy stroke, a lovely coincidence that she should have the same name as myself.' She chuckled. 'I trust you will not mistake one of us for the other.'

'Dear aunt.' He patted the hump where her knees raised themselves in the bed. 'The Poldarks have *two* daughters. Isabella-Rose is, I believe, not yet twenty, and is making a name for herself in the opera world. This is Clowance I am going to marry.'

'Clarence?' asked his aunt, making Jud's old mistake. 'Is that not a man's name?'

Long ago Harriet had advised George to put Selina in some house in Cornwall where he could keep an eye on her and his grandson. This advice he had now taken, though he would not give Harriet the satisfaction of telling her so. The guarded invitation – it was almost a direction – was hedged about with stringent conditions; but it seemed that Selina had not hesitated to accept.

It all happened very quickly. He had talked about the prospect to Hector Trembath before he wrote the letter, and unexpectedly a small house belonging to Lord de Dunstanville and almost in the shadow of Tehidy had come vacant. It was a little more on the north coast than George would have chosen, but the rental was low and the place, Trembath reported, was in excellent condition following the sudden death of the tenant, a retired major in the artillery. George told his henchman to close the deal.

By the time he decided to tell Harriet, Selina was already on the way down.

Harriet said: 'Well, why not? So long as she does not hang

around Cardew. She has been badly treated by that son of yours, and for one so rich as you it can be no hardship to make amends.'

'I am not making amends,' George said pettishly. 'She comes only on the understanding that she abides by my conditions.'

'Which are?'

'That I should pay off half her debts, the other half to be found from the sale of her house in Finsbury or wherever it is. That she should live rent-free in the house I provide her with, and that she should subsist on the allowance I shall give her, without plunging into further debt. That her cousin and her unmarried stepdaughter can live with her if they choose. But that she shall not let any of this monthly payment find its way into her husband's hands. That the education of her son shall be entirely at my discretion and under my control.'

'And she has accepted all this?'

'Yes. She is on her way down with her cousin, a Mrs Osworth. The elder stepdaughter is abroad somewhere. (She must have money enough to pay for *that*!) I expect it is all partly a device to enlist my sympathy. Anyway, we shall see . . .'

She thought this over. 'You do dislike Valentine, don't you. I wonder why.'

He hesitated. 'You do not know?'

'I have heard a few scurrilous rumours. Is there any truth in them?'

'I do not know. No one will ever know.'

'But I suppose that poisons your mind against him?'

'It is part of the equation.'

'But if Valentine is . . . suspect, how is little George free of the suspicion?'

George shrugged. 'He is not. But I lack heirs, male heirs, as you have been at pains to point out. I lack relatives bearing the name of Warleggan. You yourself have expressly told me that you will bear me no more children.'

'Yes, that's true,' she said easily. One set of twins is quite enough for me. So? . . .'

He said, broodingly: 'Of one thing I can be sure: Valentine was Elizabeth's son.'

'And that is a consolation? I understand. She was your first love. Your first possession.'

'It makes up a little.'

'And I am here merely to annoy you and to spend your money?'

'If you wish to put that interpretation upon it, you are at liberty to do so.'

She yawned. 'Well, no. Not altogether. Do not forget that I led the rescue party that saved your life.'

'Not to mention your animals,' he commented drily.

'Which are still out walking. It is time they were home.' She looked up at the clock. 'These disagreeable rumours, George, why do you make so much of them? You like to believe you are in good society. Well, I can tell you, in the *best* society hardly anyone can be certain who their father is. You have the morals of a Wesleyan.'

'It is not altogether a question of morals!'

'Well, what is it – possession, jealousy, carrying on the blood? Why do you *dislike* Valentine so much? Whatever the truth of your suspicion, it is not his fault.'

'Oh, I cannot explain it all to you! And do not wish to! Suffice to say that he has always challenged me, thwarted me, sneered at my ambitions for him, held everything I wanted to offer him in supreme contempt!' George scowled out at the bright day, which was beginning to cloud over. 'Perhaps I was not as considerate towards him as I might have been – when he was a child, that is. Conceivably I allowed my suspicion to show.'

'Did you confront Elizabeth?'

'Of course.'

'And she denied it?'

'Of course.' Her memory held his thoughts. 'Of course. Most vehemently. She swore an oath, once. But afterwards I thought she had phrased it in such a way – in such a way . . .'

Harriet sighed. 'I am not surprised that you and Valentine did not see eye to eye. But it is a mountain made out of a molehill. You cannot call Elizabeth up out of her grave to swear to you over again! My advice to you—'. She broke off as footsteps were heard in the hall.

Ursula came in with Castor and Pollux following on separate leads.

'Your pets are growing old, Mama. Pollux could hardly drag his weary legs. It is spitting with rain. Phew, we could do with some! The very fields are dusty. Am I late for tea?'

'Pull the bell.'

Pollux went up to Harriet and laid his great muzzle in her lap, then raised his bloodshot eyes seeking sympathy. Harriet began to stroke his ears.

It was a domestic scene, and George looked on not entirely dissatisfied with the conversation. Harriet still did not know the whole of it, but her sophisticated, cynical common sense was not without its balm.

Ursula said: 'Oh, I saw old Mrs Harris. You know, she is the sister of Char Nanfan who lives in Grambler. She had seen her sister yesterday and she tells her Bella Poldark is home and she is mortal sick.'

'What?' George said, pricking up his ears at news which did not sound well for the Poldarks. 'I thought she was in France.'

'So she was, but her father went after her and brought her back to London. They returned home on Friday.'

'Is it true,' George asked, 'that she eloped with a Frenchman?'

'I expect so. Though I know no more of that. But they say she is serious sick. They have had Dr Enys to see her three times already.'

That morning Clowance received a letter, hand delivered, from her mother.

Dearest Clowance,

You already know of my delight that you have decided whom you shall marry. I believe and pray that you and Edward will be blissfully happy together; and soon no doubt we shall be discussing Wedding Dresses and the like. Have you heard from Edward yet? I wish the Post was faster.

However this is just to tell you that your Father is home again, and Bella with him. They was to have gone to London for a few days first, but on arriving at Portsmouth Bella developed a Fever. It must have been a very trying journey home, and Bella as yet seems no better. Uncle Dwight has been to see her and prescribed Peruvian bark and Melrose water. She seems particular troubled with a sore throat. This, as you will understand, alarms me, as the sister you never saw died of the morbid throat.

They say that there was an epidemic of Summer Cholera in Rouen. Although Uncle Dwight says this is certainly not Cholera he cannot be sure it is not infectious, so he has advised me to send Henry away. So at his invitation I have packed Henry and Mrs Kemp off to the Enyses for the time being.

I believe Bella is a shade better this morning, but I do not think she has ever been ill in her life before and she does not know quite how to deal with it.

Your father says she was wonderful in the Opera, and if he says that it means a lot. And there was a piece in a French paper that praised her highly.

Ever your loving
Mother

Despite her mother's concern for her daughter's saftey when she rode alone – especially while Agneta's murderer remained at large; and there seemed no progress at all in this matter – Clowance decided to go over to Nampara at once. She knew her mother would insist on nursing Bella herself, and that might mean night work, so she could spell the nursing with her mother. She was not quite sure from the tone of the letter how seriously ill Bella was. But it did not sound promising. It was her mother's way to look on the bright side of life. And Dr Enys's suggestion to get Henry out of the way was not a good sign.

Anyway, there was nothing to keep her here. She could have Nero made ready in half an hour and pack an overnight bag. In four hours she would see for herself.

She called a boy who was looking over the sea wall and gave him a penny to deliver a note to the stables. She scribbled another note to be sent to Bunt; then she went upstairs and changed into a riding habit.

She was just looking around for her hat when there was a knock on the front door. Impatiently she went down, hoping it was not the boy from the stables with some excuse for delaying the delivery of Nero.

A man stood there. A big young man. A man whose face she well knew. Her heart missed a beat.

'Edward!' she said.

'Clowance! Did you – have you not been expecting me?'

'I – I wasn't sure. I thought perhaps you would write.'

'I . . . At once. I could not wait. Even so it has taken more than two days.'

She stepped back. 'Please. Please come in.'

He entered and stood there awkwardly. Then he took her hand.

'Clowance. Your letter . . . I could not wait a moment more to come to see you. Your letter filled me – with joy.'

She smiled uncertainly. 'Oh . . . Do sit down, Edward. It is kind of you to say that.'

He was a stranger. He had only ever touched her once or twice before. His jacket smelt of tweed – Scotch tweed probably. *Why* had she changed into her oldest riding habit?

'This is the little cottage I have lived in since Stephen died. It must seem like – like squalor to you.'

'Nowhere is squalor where you are, Clowance.'

A pretty speech. But she hardly knew him. *Why* had she written like that? *What* had got into her?

'*Do* sit down,' she said. 'It is such a surprise. Where is your horse? Only two *days* from London? You must have rid all through the night!'

'I did. But by coach. It is such good weather I thought to ride all the way. But it would have taken twice as long.'

'Private coach?'

'Yes.'

'Can I get you something to drink? You must be exhausted!'

'Thank you, no. I am not in the least exhausted at all. I am merely – merely over-joyous to be here.'

He was sitting awkwardly. She wondered if now he had found her he regretted all the rush. She was only an ordinary young woman, poorly dressed, hair not too tidy, a stain on her boot, living in a tiny cottage. To him she must have a Cornish accent. Perhaps already he not only regretted the rush but the long letter proposing marriage which had prompted her incautious reply. She should have invited him down for a visit for two or three weeks so that they could get to *know* each other, *first*.

He looked at her clothes. 'Were you going riding? Perhaps I have interrupted your day?'

'No! Oh, no, of course not! . . . That is, I was going riding but it was not important. At least—'

He took her hand again and smiled. 'Pray tell me.'

It was probably a way to break the ice, so she told him.

'Isabella-Rose,' he said. 'I first met her about five years ago coming out of Drury Lane with her parents. Are there any more pretty sisters?'

'No, one small brother, that's all . . . Do let me get you something to drink. You – you flatter me coming so quickly.'

'I begrudged every mile.'

She poured him a glass of cordial, and nearly dropped the jug. They laughed together, but nervously.

She said: 'Where is your coach?'

'I left it at an inn called Selley's at the top corner of the town. From there I walked, asking my way. I did not wish to – to arrive too – too prominently.'

'You have a coachman to guard it? One never knows – '

'Two,' Edward said apologetically. 'But look, I cannot keep you if you are going to see your family. Pray continue with your plans, and I will find a place to lie tonight and we can meet again whenever you think suitable.'

'Certainly I cannot do that! When you have come so far and so fast. Edward, I have been thinking.'

They sipped together as he waited. She said: 'Is your coach sturdy?'

'It has had to be. The West Country roads are atrocious.'

'Well, I have been thinking . . . You could take me to Nampara. You know both my parents.'

His angular face lit up. 'I was about to suggest it, but thought that might be a liberty.'

'Surely you must be allowed that liberty. But your horses will be tired.'

'How far is it?'

'You cannot go across county with a coach. You would have to return to Truro and then turn north. It might be twenty miles.'

'They are being fed. After an hour's rest they will not quibble at a further twenty miles.'

'And you?' She looked at him fully for the first time, meeting his direct gaze with her own.

He said: 'This is what I came for.'

There was no point in going in an old riding habit if she were to travel by coach, so she went upstairs to change.

In her bedroom she had another onset of panic. She took off her top clothes and stood a moment in front of the slightly mildewed mirror that she was always intending to replace. Her reflection did not please her. Yet by the terms of the agreement she had promised to engage in with this young stranger downstairs, he would be permitted to come into her room whenever, or almost whenever, he wanted, to observe her in undress, to pull all the rest of the clothes off her, to claim his rights as her husband. Was he entitled to the unparalleled liberties that Stephen had taken? In a sense she felt like a virgin on her wedding night, but this was worse because she knew what could happen. Stephen had been gentle but masterful, rousing her and allowing her to relish the sensation that came from preliminary fondling, and carrying her on to an appetite scarcely less than his own. But Stephen she had known half intimately for years before. This was a *stranger*.

Probably, as she had comforted herself, he too was regretting having come. He was essentially a kind and honourable man. Sometime soon, when they had come to understand each other a little better, she would give him the opportunity to withdraw. If he still felt himself bound she would be at pains to release him. And if that failed, and only if that failed, she would steel herself to tell him that she had made a grave mistake. She felt that she could mate with no man but Stephen.

Probably he would be delighted, relieved; he came from such a different class. She might be gentle born, but it was a rough Cornish gentility. Never in his life had he ever had to do something for himself that a servant could do for him. He had a valet, she knew, who would help him dress. She, until she was fifteen, and greatly to her mother's disapproval, had gone barefoot *all the daylight hours*. How could two such disparate people live together as man and wife? His standards – they must be very different from her own. His friends – did she know any of his friends? Very few. She would be a curiosity to them, a West-Country girl whom they would have to be polite to for his sake.

And the Lansdownes themselves. They seemed a charming family, but they could hardly help but regret if he married so much beneath him. How unfortunate, they would think, that chance encounter at the Duchess of Gordon's Ball.

Nevertheless, when it came to the point, she put on her best day dress, knowing that the apple green suited her hair.

The coach Edward had hired for his journey was quite a curiosity so far west. Four horses instead of the customary two, and painted in a dark reseda green with gold outlines; no name of the carrier or proprietor, which meant that it must be privately owned. A small but respectful crowd had gathered at a distance to watch Mrs Carrington step in, followed by her burly but well-groomed escort.

For the first part of the journey the route was quite straight-forward, simply a return along the turnpike road by which he had come. The trees were at their heaviest overhanging the road, which after climbing a hill or two began to wind its way beside a glinting stream.

It was a commodious coach, and Clowance sat very much in a corner, staring out at the countryside and leaving a twelve-inch space between herself and the man she had agreed to marry. Conversation was polite but sparse, Clowance telling him that the very last part of the journey from just beyond Shortlanesend to Nampara itself would be not nearly as comfortable as this was, not even a turnpike at all, but a well-worn track which could be bumpy and dusty in this dry weather.

Edward was courteously concerned about Isabella-Rose's illness, and Clowance courteously told him what little she knew.

Edward said: 'When your letter came the only member of my family in the house was Aunt Isabel, so I hurried to tell her. She was delighted at the good news.'

'How is she?'

'A little more frail. There was only one drawback to her reception of the news.'

Clowance braced herself. 'What was that?'

'She thought I was going to marry your mother.'

Clowance laughed with him. 'And when she knew the truth?'

'She thought I was going to marry a man called Clarence.'

Clowance laughed again. 'I have never met Aunt Isabel. My mother has spoken often of her. Isn't she the deaf lady?'

'She is . . . Clowance, are you afraid of me?'

She continued to admire the sunlight on the leaves. 'A little.'

'Well,' said Edward, 'I have to tell you that I am a little afraid of you.'

She looked at him to see if he was serious, then away. 'Whyever?'

'Just the same reason. We have known each other so long, but at vast intervals. I have hardly ever more than touched you!'

'I know.'

'When I took your hand today, it was touching something warm and living but belonging to somebody else.'

'Oh, yes.'

'If I touch your face it will also be warm. The essential person of the – the girl I love.'

'Or think you love.'

'There has been no doubt of that in my mind for many years.'

'Yet it has only been a – a surface thing. You could not put it to any sort of test!'

'Nor you of me. You may come to regret that letter you sent me. Perhaps you would like me to forget I have ever received it?'

'Oh, *would* you? If I asked?'

She thought it strange that his thoughts had seemed in general to parallel her own. Yet somewhere at the back of her mind was a touch of pique.

'No,' he said, 'I would not. Not for everything in this world.'

There was a long silence.

He said: 'But now we have time. Time to meet, time to talk, time to come to a loving understanding.'

'Time to put it to the test?' she asked.

He said: 'May I hold your hand?'

Chapter Four

They stopped and dined at Pearce's Hotel in Truro, arrived at Nampara at five, lurched and wobbled perilously down the sloping valley to the house. They did not risk the bridge and Parkin, who was the man who had come with Edward from the Half Moon stables in Berkeley Street, was reluctant to try the ford fifty yards downstream of the bridge. With the dry weather there was little water to worry about, but the big pebbles were in his view too unstable to risk his horses.

By chance Dwight was visiting Bella when they arrived, and Caroline had come with him bringing a few sweetmeats to tempt the sick girl's appetite, so there was a very friendly welcome. Caroline had known Edward for years and kissed them both in congratulation. She at once invited Edward to stay with her and Dwight at Killewarren for a few days. This he gratefully accepted.

Caroline said: 'It's lovely to have people staying. Have you met Sophie and Meliora? They are home from school, and Henry has already assumed full control of them.'

Clowance was shocked at her first sight of Bella. The girl had wasted away, must have lost twenty pounds; her skin was blotchy, she spoke scarcely above a whisper.

She smiled brightly enough, but could only raise her head a few inches off the pillow by way of greeting.

'Clowance!'

'Darling.'

'No kissing – 'fraid.'

'Are you any better?'

'Think so.'

Dwight had said: 'I am starting an iron treatment. Her fever is lower than it was, but it will be touch and go for the next few days.'

'Is it the morbid sore throat? The one that my sister Julia had – died of?'

'Much the same, I'm afraid. The French are beginning to call it *diphtheritis* because of the rough membrane that forms in the throat. Do not forget many survive it. Your mother did.'

'At least I can take some of the work off her. She did not let me know until this morning.'

'She has good help. But the difficulty is to keep her away.'

'I'll see that she gets more rest.'

In the room Clowance said: 'So your opera was a huge success! I'm so very glad!'

Bella's face creased as if a new energy were flooding into it. '*Yes.* Oh, yes!' Then the light went out. 'But I cannot sing now!'

'You will – it will come back.'

Bella coughed, and winced with the pain. 'Did Uncle Dwight say that?'

'Yes . . .'

'It has been nearly a week!'

'D'you remember Mrs Kemp's first lessons in French? *Avec de la patience on arrive à tout.*'

'*Prendre son mal en patience,*' said Bella. 'I fear I have little of it. Nor have I any patience to eat food. Nor much appetite for life.'

'A little while, dearest,' said Clowance, choking a sudden impulse to burst into tears. 'Never fear. In a couple more weeks you will be as right as rain.'

'Did Uncle Dwight say that?'

'. . . Yes.'

When she came out of the room, leaving the nursing to one of the Martins, she found Edward talking to her father and mother.

They looked at her, and she pulled a grieved face. 'I had no idea. You should have written earlier, Mama.'

'I did not want to trouble you. She has become much worse these last two days.'

Ross said: 'Dwight thinks it is coming to the crisis now. It may be tonight.'

Edward said: 'I have come to Cornwall at the worst possible moment for you all. When I received the letter from Clowance I was so delighted that I lost no time in thinking of anything else.'

'Natural enough,' said Ross.

'Caroline Enys, as I expect you know, has invited me to spend a few days with them. That I should be glad to do, but I feel I am entering on – on a family crisis here. You cannot want me here at such an anxious time. A stranger – any stranger – is *de trop*. Yet – I am deeply concerned for Isabella-Rose's recovery. To go back to London would be very hard. If I stay with the Enyses...' He paused.

'I thought you had already agreed to,' Demelza said.

'How far is their house from here?'

'About four miles.'

Edward looked at Clowance for guidance. She said: 'I should not wish you to go back to London.'

'That is really all I want to know. You have asked me to sup here. After it I will leave you until the morning.'

'I think Dwight is coming back here after supper,' said Demelza. 'He may spend the night here. Clowance ... would you like to go to Killewarren and show his driver the way?'

Clowance said: 'I don't think Edward will mind if I say no. If this is likely to be the crisis I must stay up with her. You may not sleep, Mama, but you must lie down. What is the good of me coming if I cannot be allowed to do that?'

Dwight returned at eleven. He had left a draught of white poppy syrup for Demelza, and Ross had stood over her while she swallowed it.

He helped her to bed and sat holding her hand until she went to sleep. After that he took a book and smoked a pipe in the library, where he could not hear Bella coughing. The trouble with many of these old farmhouses was that sound echoed everywhere.

In the bedroom Bella was watched over by Dwight Enys, Jane Gimlett and Clowance. Clowance wanted to be more active, where such minor action was possible, in painting Bella's throat or getting her to sip diluted blackcurrant juice; but Dwight had priority and after a while he passed these duties over to Jane. Clowance wondered if he were trying to keep her at a distance from the closest infection.

It was near the longest day, so darkness only lasted a few hours. Ross had dozed off, but woke slightly chilled in the first ghostly streaks of dawn. He remembered all too well, even though it was thirty years ago, when the dawn had broken at a late hour in the

345

very depths of winter when a gale was raging, and he had roused himself from a similar troubled doze to learn that his first daughter was dead.

The whole picture was abominably reminiscent of that earlier time. The Gimletts were new arrived, young and active; now they were grey-haired and stooping. Dwight Enys was a young doctor, only just qualified. Demelza ... well, she was older but little changed; and, as then, in the centre of it all. In that earlier time she too was ill and had nearly died. This time not so – or not so yet. (Dwight had urged Ross to keep her out of the sickroom; in his experience, he said, a former attack of this dread disease did not make one less likely to catch it again at a later date.)

It was all happening again, Ross told himself, but thirty years later. And then it was black and wild midwinter, now it was high summer and calm seas. And the person at risk was his daughter again, his *youngest* daughter, and she was seventeen years older than Julia was when she had died in this house, tended by the same doctor and the same maid. It could not be. The repetition was obscene.

He got up sharply and went towards the stairs. Slits of grey light coming through curtains warred with the guttering candles, one smoking and another out. Something moved against his legs, Moses wanting to greet the dawn. Ross lifted the latch of the front door and let the cat out, then went up the creaking stairs.

Demelza was still asleep. Evidently Dwight had given her a fair dose of laudanum. He retreated, closing the door behind him and holding the latch with his finger so that it should not click.

A shadow moved on the landing. It was Dwight, just come out of Bella's room. He put his hand on Ross's arm.

'Well?'

'She's sleeping. It is the first natural sleep for a long time.'

Ross listened. All was quiet. 'Is that . . . ?'

'A good sign, yes. Don't build too much on it. But I think the crisis was between two and three a.m. this morning.'

'So you may not have to use your instrument?'

That meant tracheotomy.

'I pray not. I believe not.'

Tears welled into Ross's throat and he tried to swallow them. 'Thank God for that.'

'Amen. I must go now. I have two other cases I should see. I hope to be with you straight after breakfast.'

'Shall I go in?'

'I think not. Two of the Martins are with her and it's better she should not be disturbed. Is there a spare room in the house?'

'Jeremy's.'

'Lie down yourself for a couple of hours. Tell John Gimlett where you are in case of need.'

'Thank you, Dwight.'

Dwight looked down. 'You're still a strong man, Ross. I shall need that arm again.'

'Apologies.' He released Dwight and they crept down the stairs.

Two days later Ross rode over to Wheal Elizabeth at Trevaunance. It was not that there was any urgent need to go, but while Bella had been so ill he had felt unable to stir from the house. Now that there was just a suggestion of convalescence about her, some action outside the confines of the farm and his own mines was a way of releasing his still current anxieties.

The North Coast Mining Company had officially taken possession of Wheal Elizabeth last month, a new mine captain called Trebethick had been appointed, and after a general survey of the present workings three of the current shafts had been abandoned; the other two were to be developed and renamed (for luck) and a third new excavation begun about fifty yards nearer the house. Valentine had been allowed twenty-five per cent of the promised investment, and was the third largest shareholder after Warleggan's Bank and the Cornish Bank.

There had been little time yet to make appreciable progress; a small pumping engine had been ordered, costing £600 from Perran Foundry, and when installed would be used chiefly to drain the new shaft, which was further from the cliff and had less natural drainage. Almost at once Trebethick came out of the purser's shed to greet the unexpected visitor, and almost at once he told Ross that Captain Prideaux was below ground in the Margaret shaft and they could quickly send down for him.

Ross told him not to bother. He was interested in the other shaft, Sunshine, which had been more recently developed from an early adit dug many years ago to drain some long ignored and forgotten excavation. Ross's instinct, grown from long years of dealing with mines, picked on this one as a more promising spot to prospect. It had been Trebethick's first interest when he came to manage the mine.

The work at the moment involved renewing the timber setts, which had largely rotted, then shoring up and capping the roof by joining one sett to another. Lagging boards were also being fitted, so that the miners could explore into the chilly, draughty cavern beyond.

It was an hour later, when he was about to untether his horse, that he saw Captain Prideaux bearing down on him.

They greeted each other cordially and for a few minutes discussed the future welfare of Wheal Elizabeth. Then Philip said: 'I understand your younger daughter has been unwell. I hope it was nothing serious?'

'Afraid it was,' Ross said. 'She is making progress now, but it is not forgone and will take weeks yet.'

'Did she contract this in France?'

'It seems so. But Dr Enys says the infection may have been latent for some time.'

'And Clowance?' Philip asked.

Ross stared out at the pellucid sea, which was as flat as a plate.

'She made her own choice. I'm sorry.'

'It destroyed my hopes.'

'I understand how you must feel.'

'I gather she has known this – this Lord Edward Fitzmaurice for several years.'

'Quite a time. I am not sure how long, but it was well before she married Stephen Carrington.'

'But they met infrequently?'

'Yes . . . Philip, I do not think much advantage will be gained by discussing this with me. I am, as it were, on the outside. I could not see, cannot see, into Clowance's heart.'

'Possibly he could offer her more than I could.'

'That was for her to decide. But if you mean more in a material sense, I think I can speak for Clowance with complete authority in saying it would not have made the slightest difference.'

'I'm sorry. That remark was not worthy of me.'

'She wrote you?'

'Most charmingly, and at length. It did not affect the – the bitter disappointment to me of the message.'

'Of course not. Have you seen her since?'

'No. I understand she is staying at Nampara looking after her sister.'

'Yes. But Lord Edward is also here, staying with the Enyses. Probably it would be better, when you see her again, if you saw her alone.'

Philip inclined his head. 'I agree, though perhaps it is good for the modesty of one's immortal soul that one should meet the man who has been preferred by the girl one loves.'

Ross looked over the sea again. 'My dear chap, I do not believe virtue enters into it at all. The mysteries of physical attraction are an enigma that no one has ever quite solved.'

Just then another tall thin figure approached them.

'Well, well,' said Valentine. 'I was about to go to bed for a snooze when I was told that Wheal Elizabeth had visitors. So I came to greet you – if briefly – before I retire.'

'Bed,' said Ross, 'on such an afternoon?'

'Am just back from Ireland. We was becalmed in the St George's Channel – becalmed! When the Irish Sea is short of wind one wonders what the world is coming to. And I could not sleep in that pesky cabin for the bugs. I have rid all the way home. They tell me Bella is unwell?'

Ross explained. 'How did you know?'

'I breakfasted at Prideaux Place. Cuby was there with Noelle, stopping a few days. She told me they had been advised not to come to Nampara for fear of the infection.'

'I was at Prideaux Place yesterday,' Philip said.

'Did Cuby tell you about John?'

'Her brother? Yes.'

'What about him?' Ross asked.

'She tells me he has fled abroad.'

'Fled?'

'From his creditors. They have been hunting him for weeks.'

'She said nothing of this when she was over last.'

Philip said: 'Perhaps she did not like to worry you and Lady Poldark, as you might feel some responsibility for her welfare.'

'Of course we do! I wish she had told us.'

Valentine stifled a yawn. 'Maybe the greatest responsibility, if one goes back far enough, is mine. You will remember Smelter George had come to an agreement with John Trevanion that I should marry Cuby and in return Cuby and I should live in the Castle and George would pay all John's debts. I never knew all the details or how many t's had to be crossed and i's dotted, but if I know George he would have had it all writ on paper and legally binding.'

Philip was staring at Valentine. 'I know nothing of this at all.'

'Why should you? You were playing soldiers.'

'And what went wrong?'

Valentine laughed. 'I married someone else without my father's permission.'

'That is your present wife? – the one who left you?'

'Just so. I have managed only one wife so far. Though she has partly come back.'

Ross looked his enquiry. 'I have been away two weeks.'

'Selina arrived back two weeks before that, accompanied by my son and a dragon of a cousin. Not, of course, *here*. For some nefarious purposes of his own George has installed her in a little house called Rayle Farm near Tehidy. I have not seen her, nor do I propose to see her. But I am thinking of taking her to law and claiming custody of the child.'

'I must see Cuby,' Ross said, half to himself.

'They too are looking for a smaller home,' Philip said. 'That is, for herself and her mother and her sister and Noelle. I'm hoping my cousin may be able to find something for them. Apparently, now that John has finally given up the fight, there are bailiffs already in the Castle.'

Chapter Five

The following morning, Bella having been persuaded to take a cup of beef tea and been able to keep it down, Clowance felt at liberty to steal a few hours off to pursue her own life. When Edward arrived at eleven she proposed they should walk the length of Hendrawna Beach.

The weather remained set fair, windless, pellucid, warm. Dwight had lent Edward two light blue shirts with open necks, and yesterday Edward had ridden into Truro and had had a pair of cotton breeches stitched up for himself while he sat and waited.

'This is not true Cornish weather,' Clowance told him.

'Maybe it is specially for us.'

They set off, through the gate, across the few yards of stony sand covered with marram grass, onto the soft sand seldom reached by the sea, felt it harden under their feet, then they were on the great three-mile stretch of pale gold, bordered on the left by the sleepy sea and on the right by hairy sandhills that soon grew into black granite cliffs, on the first of which Wheal Leisure muttered and smoked.

For a while they walked in silence. Then she said: 'D'you mind if I take off my shoes?'

'I'll carry them.'

'No. Thank you.'

He said: 'Do you mind if I take *my* shoes off?'

She giggled. 'Not at all.'

She had been able to kick her shoes off and pick them up while standing; he had to unlace his, so squatted on the sand. While he was doing this he recounted to her his visit to Mr Norris the tailor, who seemed to spend all his life with his mouth full of pins.

Then they were off again, squelching into the occasional puddle, talking in a companionable way.

'The sea is a long way out,' he said.

'All right. I'll race you to it.'

She was off before him, fleet of foot, fair hair flying. He set off in pursuit, pounding through the sand which now seemed treacherously soft. He tried to catch her, but her feet just splashed into the creamy curl of surf a second before his.

He caught her by the arm, pulled her laughing and breathless against him. He bent his head and found her face with his lips, began to kiss her. She turned her lips to him.

Presently they waded back to dry sand, began to walk arm in arm, the high sun casting shadows like dogs at their feet.

They were still both a little more out of breath than the chase warranted. This was the first time in all their association that they had ever embraced. Yet they were engaged to be married. It was a courtship in reverse.

A little archipelago of cloud had come up to make the hot sun temporarily less fierce.

He said: 'Those cliffs are growing bigger and blacker as we near them.'

'They *are* called the Dark Cliffs! But you are not very near yet. At least a mile. A mile and a half.'

'Distances are deceptive.'

'Not only distances.'

'What, for instance?' he asked.

'You, for instance.'

'Explain, please.'

'Need I?'

'Yes.'

'Well, I thought you were more formal.'

'Not always.'

'Perhaps it is the sea air.'

'Not just that.'

'What, then?'

'You, for instance,' he said.

She laughed again. She had almost forgotten how to.

'Let's go to the Holy Well. That's less than a mile. Over there. In that cleft where the green comes nearly down to the sea.'

'Why is it holy?'

'It was on the pilgrims' way. I don't know where they were

walking to – it may have been St Ives. But they used to shelter there. It is a sort of wishing well.'

'Good. We'll go. Are secular wishes permitted?'

'I think so.'

When they got there it was not an easy climb, though only about thirty feet. The rocks were jagged, mussel-grown and slippery with vivid seaweed.

'Are your feet sore?'

'No,' he lied.

'I'll lead the way.'

They got up without a mistake and stood on a moss-green platform of rock, with a raised circle of rock in the middle enclosing a small pool. Edward put some fingers in the pool and licked one.

'It is only faintly brackish.'

'Yes, it's a genuine fresh-water well.'

'And how do you make a wish?'

'Drake says – my mother's brother, who is now a boat builder in Looe but lived near Nampara for some years – oh, but it is a long story. Drake says you wet your finger and wish. There is something you have to say – he told me, but I have long forgotten – Oh, *you* . . . !'

Edward had put two of his damp cold fingers on her neck. She thumped him on the chest. He took a step backwards but pulled her with him. He kissed her where her neck was wet and she ruffled his hair, pulling it gently.

He said: 'My wish is to be with you always.'

Bella said: 'My voice . . .'

'Do not think of that yet, my lover,' Demelza said. 'Just be grateful that you are on the mend.'

'It still hurts to cough.'

'Don't talk if you do not wish to.'

'I wish to – a little. I have hardly said anything since I came home!'

'That was not your fault.'

'I wanted to ask you: did you send Papa to Rouen to bring me home?'

'It was not like that. We talked about it and talked about it and then your father said: "I would like to see this opera. It's not every man who has a daughter who, before she is twenty, is playing the lead in a professional musical production in a foreign country." He said: "Why do we not go?"'

'He asked you to go?'

'Yes. And I would dearly have liked to come with him, but I – I am at sea with the language and I felt we must not look like jealous parents come to seize you and return with you to lock you up in Cornwall.'

Bella gave a wry smile. 'I must write to Mrs Pelham so soon as ever I can.'

'You must. But your father did write to her so soon as you were home.'

Bella said: 'Mama, you had this terrible disease – when Julia died – was your voice husky when you recovered?'

'I don't recall.'

'But ever since I can remember your voice is clear in speaking but has a little huskiness when you sing.'

'Has it? Maybe so. But my voice is as nothing compared to yours. Nothing at all. I don't believe you should think one thing would follow on the other like that.'

'How long was it before you were yourself again?'

'Oh, I have forgot. Anyway, it was not at all the same. I had lost Julia. And your father was in danger of arrest for something he did not do. That would make anyone slow to mend!'

Bella settled down into her bed. 'I am a small matter anxious. Where is Papa today?'

'He has gone Padstow to see Cuby. It seems that John Trevanion is in deep water and has fled the country.'

'Oh yes, you did tell me yesterday, but I wasn't greatly attending.'

Prideaux Place was a long castellated mansion situated just above the town of Padstow, with an extensive view over its own deer park to the sea. When Ross reached it and turned his horse up the short drive he found the house en fête. Or as near that degree of jollity as its owner, the Reverend Charles Prideaux-Brune, would sanction. It was the twenty-first birthday of his second daughter, Dorothea, and apart from the Trevanions there were six other guests.

Charles Prideaux-Brune was a man in his early fifties, strongly built, with an incipient paunch, a stern expression but a kindly twinkle in his eye. Dorothea was tiny, slight of figure, pretty in a discreet way, played the piano, the violin, the oboe. She had a number of suitors, two of them present today, but Frances, her mother, was keeping them at bay until she made up her own mind.

Ross had come to see Cuby, privately to counsel and console her, but this cheerful conversational company was not suited to personal exchanges and advice. Noelle, a chubby little girl of four and a half, galloped quickly up and shouted for a kiss. Ross obliged and shook hands with his hosts, whom he knew only slightly, apologizing for his unannounced arrival and explaining that he had heard Cuby was here and wished to see her on a personal matter.

As he was speaking Philip Prideaux, whom Ross had seen only the day before at the mine, came down the stairs, adjusting his glasses and smiling a welcome. Then out of another door, a billiard cue in her hand, Harriet Warleggan.

The Prideaux-Brunes insisted that Ross must stay to supper and spend the night. Ross smilingly dissented and then allowed himself to be persuaded when it became clear that George was not here. He knew that Philip and Harriet were old friends.

Most of them strolled on the terrace in the balmy evening light before supper was taken. Ross was a little put out by the presence of Mrs Bettesworth, Cuby's mother, a lady he had had some dealings with since Jeremy's death, but someone whom he never personally could bring himself to like. It was probably true that she had suffered a great deal coping with a spendthrift husband and then a spendthrift son; it could not have been a happy life attending race meetings at which their horses always seemed to come in fourth, or being dunned by creditors outside your back door while your son talked to the builders and planned some grandiose addition to a mansion which was already too big for them to keep up. But Ross found it hard to warm towards someone who had so strongly supported, indeed, perhaps was the stronger party in urging her pretty daughter to marry into the Warleggan fortune for the sake of the preservation of the family name and the family seat. Whenever Ross saw her she had a faintly injured expression, as if the world and life had dealt with her too harshly.

He did not have an opportunity until Mrs Bettesworth, pleading a headache, had retired early to bed, to get Cuby on her own.

(The kind, gentle Clemency had taken Noelle, protesting, in her wake.)

'Cuby,' he said, 'tell me how it is.'

She looked up at him with her velvety eyes, pulled a face of disquiet.

'John has gone and will not be back until he can clear some of his debt. And that is not very likely. He is, I believe, going to Brussels. We all put together what money we had, to give him a chance of escape and of a few weeks of subsistence there. Perhaps you will pardon me for using some of the allowance you so kindly give me—'

Ross pursed his lips. 'What little I give you—'

'It is not little, my dear—'

'What little I give you is for your maintenance and to help Noelle. But the gift has no conditions. When there is an emergency . . .'

'I think this was an emergency. The bailiffs have taken possession of the house, and some of the furniture has been seized. My mother has laid claim to it, and I hope to go with her on Wednesday to put a stop to such seizures. The servants have all gone, most of them unpaid, the horses and the carriage, even the gardening implements . . .'

'Philip Prideaux told me you were thinking you might have enough to move into a small house somewhere – was it near Bodmin?'

'We went to see it this morning. It has three bedrooms, good water, two nice living rooms, a tiny kitchen, stables. We can manage.'

'Your mother would go with you?'

'I think she would have to.'

'Well, keep in touch with me, please. It might be worth my seeing this house; to look over it; even perhaps take a builder who could go over it for possible faults.'

'That would be very helpful. But I do not like to take up your time. With Bella being so ill, and Clowance and her new fiancé, you will be busy.'

'I see too little of you both.'

'It is my fault; but I have been trying to help my brother keep his head above water.'

Still later he saw Harriet and Philip standing on the terrace deep in conversation. He exchanged a few words with Charles Prideaux-Brune and then, as his host was called away, he saw the other two coming in off the terrace.

Harriet was in a pale lemon-yellow dress ruched at the throat and cuffs. As Philip Prideaux turned away, she looked at Ross ironically.

'Well, Ross, glad to learn your daughter is on the mend.'

'Thank you. It's early days yet, but so far so good.'

'And Clowance is to marry Lord Edward?'

'It seems so.'

'Never met him . . . I tried to make a match for her with Philip Prideaux, but did not know she had other arrows in her quiver.'

They had drifted out onto the terrace again. The last blue streaks of the evening were still showing light over the sea. A cool air wafted across. The trembling stars were growing brighter.

'Nor, I believe, did Clowance. Although Edward had asked her to marry him before she married Stephen Carrington . . . How is George?'

'A little grumpy. He's half well, but prefers not to seek social pleasures yet . . . I hear Caerhays is for sale.'

'I had not heard that, but it is only, I suppose, a question of time. Does George want it?'

'Not now. All those plans, as you know, fell through years ago.'

'I hear he has brought Selina and the child back to Cornwall.'

'Yes, they are near Tehidy. Some farm.'

'Anyway, he went along with me – or *you* persuaded him to go along with me in the formation of the North Coast Mining Company. Does that mean he is hoping to bring Selina and Valentine together again?'

'No, I think one of the conditions he has made is that Selina should not take little Georgie back to his father.'

'Strange.'

'Not very. I believe George does not want his grandson to come under the influence of his sardonic, dissipated father.' Harriet pulled her dress more closely around her.

'Are you cold?'

'No . . . Nothing.'

Ross put his arm round her shoulders. They were not quite like anyone else's shoulders he had ever touched, stronger, broader, but still very feminine.

They stood in silence. A shooting star slid across the sky. Two small boats were heading in for Padstow harbour.

He said: 'I have never been able to understand why you came to marry George.'

'Well,' she said, 'you were not available.'

'I was trying to be serious.'

'How do you know I am not serious?'

He waved his free hand. 'Try again!'

She was silent. 'Can't you guess?'

'No.'

'It must be perfectly obvious to you. I was a moderately attractive widow with no money to speak of.'

'You were a very attractive widow, and there are many rich men in the world.'

'I did not descry them.'

'So you married him for his money?'

'So everyone thinks. And everyone would be right – or partly right.'

'And the other part?'

'You would not believe me.'

'I am open to persuasion.'

A white bird flew silently across the arch of one of the windows behind them. Its shadow fluttered over the part-lighted terrace.

'Is that an omen?'

'That owl? Possibly.'

'A warning. That in this life it is better to live by absolutes, not to live by subtle dealings that no one can understand. Of course I married George for his money.'

'And?'

'And I was physically attracted – sexually attracted to him too . . . not by his looks – though he is not all that bad looking if you take a detached view. Shall we say I am a self-willed woman and relish a challenge. Shall we say that I was sexually attracted to him by the transparent ugliness of his moral character.'

There was a step on the terrace, and they automatically detached themselves from each other by a degree of inches. But it was only a footman.

'Beg pardon, sir – er – my lady. I thought just to keep the moths out.'

'We'll go in,' Ross said, and then added: 'a perverse assesssment.'

'I told you we should live by absolutes.'

'George and I always have,' Ross said. 'With dubious results.'

'Have you and George ever shaken hands?'

'George and I? I don't know. I don't think so.'

As they separated Harriet said: 'Sometime it might be worth the experiment.'

Chapter Six

The following day was very hot, and the faint easterly breeze which rose and fell turned the sandhills even paler. If the breeze strengthened it would presage the end of the fine weather.

Demelza had been feeling unwell but was rather better today. She had had a sore throat, but had tried to ignore it. Ever since Julia died, all through the years, she had suffered from what she called the 'Meggy Dawes' symptoms. If Jeremy had a toothache, some of her own teeth ached in sympathy; if Clowance had a stomach upset, she felt sick too; if Henry took a feverish chill, she sweated likewise. The present symptoms were altogether more serious because Bella was gravely ill, and she, Demelza, had been ill of this complaint thirty years ago. This present sore throat might be a 'Meggy Dawes' copycat symptom, or it might be the real thing. There was no way of being sure. Of course she never told Ross any of this, nor even Dwight either. (Years ago Ross had discovered that this miner's daughter had nervous tensions that exceeded his own.)

So it was a profound relief to be able to swallow this morning without discomfort.

It was a more profound relief to see Bella sitting on a chair by the window, warming her body in the sun.

Demelza decided to celebrate by taking a dip in the sea. Ross was still not back, but Clowance and Edward could be invited to accompany her, and Sophie and Meliora Enys and Henry, all of whom had just come over from Killewarren. Long years ago Demelza had designed a brief tunic for herself and her children which resembled a Greek chiton, being sparse, just decent, and easy to slip into and out of. The men wore cotton drawers, and Edward had been loaned a pair belonging to Ross.

The tide was half in, and the six of them walked abreast across the hot sand. Unusually in Cornwall the air was so warm that the plunge into the cooler sea was not so much a challenge as a delight. None of the Poldark family, except Ross, was a strong swimmer, this because the sea was usually so rough it was not safe to go out of one's depth. Today it was possible to float on one's back barely ten feet from the sand. The baby waves came into being only a few yards out and were scarcely born before they collapsed into a gentle froth. Edward and Clowance went out and out. Demelza kept herself afloat with a quiet breast stroke, cocking an occasional eye far out at the engaged couple, whose heads were together, and then the other way inshore to where the youngsters frolicked.

On this came Ross, who had had a long hot ride from Padstow and had hurried indoors to see Bella, and then had torn off his clothes, throwing them across the bedroom floor, pulled on his short costume and dashed out to join them.

This, thought Demelza, when she saw him, is one of the little peaks of my life. From the intense anxieties of three days ago, now I am high, high. Bella is on the mend – visibly on the mend today. Clowance and Edward have stopped fencing politely with each other, Henry will soon be back home, Ross is here splashing beside me. Hallelujah!

Amid cascades of water flung at them by the Enys girls, with Harry as the ringleader, Ross told Demelza of his meetings at Prideaux Place and of Cuby's plight. He told her he was going with Mrs Bettesworth and Philip Prideaux to meet a group of the more important creditors in Bodmin the next Wednesday to see what could be done to have the bailiffs withdrawn or at least their depredations kept in check. Afterwards they were going to inspect the house near Bodmin which the Trevanions might be able to rent. Philip, it seemed, was bearing no grudge against them because of Clowance and was being very helpful.

Further out, Edward was diving under water trying to catch some flounders. Once or twice he came up with one, but sure enough they wriggled out of his grasp. Clowance laughed until she swallowed some sea water and choked. Edward tried to pat her on the back, and in the course of it they were semi-naked in each other's arms. By weaving their legs gently about they were able to keep afloat.

'I never – want to leave – Cornwall,' he said. 'You've introduced me to Heaven.'

361

'It isn't – always – like this,' she gasped. 'Often it rains for ever. And usually it blows for ever.'

'I can endure that,' he said, 'if I can – have you for ever.'

'Well . . . I promised, didn't I?'

'Rash woman. There's no way out for you now.'

'*I* know,' she said. 'You'll get tired of me – and then reflect, well at least the weather was nice.'

'Can we try?'

'What?'

'Marriage.'

She felt his body stirring against hers. 'I'm considering it.'

'To have and to hold, to love and to cherish?'

'I'm out of my depth,' she said. 'If I don't say yes you might push me under.'

'I'm out of my depth too,' he said.

All the normal activities of Nampara had come to a stop while Bella was ill. Now, as it became clear that she was on the mend and that her impressive vitality was returning with every hour that passed, the routine of life was resumed. Apart from her weekly visit to the Paynters, Demelza often called on the Kellows, mainly to see Daisy, who was chronically but, it seemed, not terminally ill. As her brother had said harshly to Valentine, she was going to take a long time dying.

Clowance went riding with Edward after dinner, so, leaving Bella in the safe charge of Jane Gimlett, Demelza walked over alone to Fernmore.

As she neared the house she glanced up at the sky and saw they had had the best of the day for their bathing. The weather at last was on the change. The wind had not freshened as she had expected, but minute by minute it was becoming a different world. The sun had withdrawn behind a filament of high cloud which looked ominous.

Fernmore, in spite of some claims to gentility, had never really, even in Dr Choake's day, been anything but a large farmhouse. She wondered how it had come to be built, for no land which could optimistically be described as farmland went with it. She must ask Ross sometime.

Dr Choake's day was long over: the eight servants he had

employed had diminished to two, and they recently had left and not been replaced. Mrs Kellow did what housework she could, and Daisy lent a hand when she was able. The garden in front of the house had become a wilderness, some curtains were ragged and there were roof slates missing.

When she reached the door it was opened by Paul, and when she showed her surprise, he said: 'I am looking after the invalid for a day or two. My parents are taking a holiday.'

'Oh?' She stepped in. 'Is Mary with you?'

'No, she's at home and indisposed.'

The house was dark and psychologically chill. At four o'clock on a midsummer afternoon it still had its own shadows. It smelt of cabbage and cigar smoke and mildew. He was standing close beside her, watching her, an open shirt his only concession to the heat; his hair, worn long, was pomaded back.

'Bella?'

'Much, much better.'

'Good. You would not want her to go the way of Jeremy.'

'Jeremy did not die of a fever. He was killed fighting in a war.'

'I put that badly. I meant that Jeremy's death would make the loss of another child even harder to bear.'

'She is not going to die, Paul.'

'That's a relief. D'you know, I still miss him – as you must.'

'As I do.' She was containing an unreasonable anger. But was it unreasonable to resent an attitude which trampled over half-buried griefs?

'Jeremy was my greatest friend,' Paul said. 'He and Stephen Carrington. Strange that I am the only one left.'

'Yes, you were the lucky one.'

'Would you call it lucky? Perhaps so. We avoided the law. Having broken it.'

'I think that is best not brought up now.'

'You know of it? You know what I'm talking about?'

'I know as much as I want to know. So your father and mother are from home? Is it to be a long holiday?'

'You know, Lady Poldark – is that what I must call you? You know, Demelza, mother of my greatest friend, you know I did not fight in any war, not like Jeremy's father, not like Dr Enys, not like this Philip Prideaux, not like Jeremy . . . yet I seem to have become more accustomed to death than any of them. I have only lost two sisters – and Jeremy – and one or two others, but it makes me feel that life is cheap.'

'That could be a great mistake, Paul.'

'You know the way upstairs? She was up late last night, so is taking a rest before supper. Go up, she'll not be asleep.'

Yet when she went upstairs he followed very close behind her, stopped her on the landing.

'Jeremy used to say you had second sight.'

'Oh, no.'

'Well, you have a sort of *in*-sight that does not come entirely from the reason. I would like to talk to you sometime.'

'About?'

'About life – and death.'

'Is that not what we are talking about now?'

Through a window the thin sunlight showed up his sallow face.

He tapped on a door, opened it. 'Daisy, a friend for you.' And left her there.

Daisy said: 'He's broken up with Mary. They seemed so fond of each other a few years ago. Of course she has lost all her looks. But it is not just that. The Temples are very upset. But thank you for coming. Tell me all your news. So Clowance has got her man! Will it be a big wedding? I expect you will all go off to Bowood for it.'

'I know nothing yet,' Demelza said, feeling that the Kellow family had a talent for expressing their thoughts ungracefully. 'Your father and mother. Isn't this sudden? I saw your mother last week and she did not say she was going away.'

'They weren't. But when Paul came last week with the news of the break up of his marriage and said he was coming back home to live for the time being, they seized their opportunity. It should do them a deal of good.'

Daisy's bedroom was untidy, and the greying daylight showed the neglect. A white rambling rose had grown from the flowerbed below, and spindly shoots rested against the panes. However infirm, Demelza would not have tolerated this sloppiness. Surely when there was any wind the tendrils would wave about wildly and tap on the glass. An inch of window was open, but the room was stuffy and airless. The whole house was stuffy and airless and depressing. The family of Kellow, she thought, was ingrown, always expecting more of life than it could provide for them and seldom enterprising enough to do anything for themselves. Since the sale of the coaching business Charlie Kellow had done nothing, and Paul, though helping his father-in-law, had made no extra effort to maintain his wife.

Poor Daisy. She was the only lively one.

Interrupting Daisy's light chatter, Demelza said: 'Does Paul smoke cigars?'

'What? Cigars? Oh yes. Why do you ask?'

'I thought there was a strong smell of cigars downstairs.'

'Oh, all the men were smoking them last night! And Butto!'

'*Butto?*'

'While the old people were away we invited Valentine and David to sup, and they brought Butto, whom I adore. And we were teaching him to smoke a cigar. When Valentine is there Butto is *so* good-tempered! He *smoked* it, copying Valentine in everything until he put the cigar into his mouth the wrong way round! Then it was pandemonium! But even so he only broke two plates and a dish, and that was accidental!'

At least it was something for Daisy to laugh about, though her laugh was interrupted by a fit of coughing.

When it was over Demelza said: 'It must have been jolly. But does cigar smoke not disagree with you?'

'Oh, fiddle, maybe. But many things disagree with me. Including the sight of Dr Enys coming up the path!'

Demelza said: 'I suppose Valentine and Paul have something in common now – they are separated from their wives.'

'If you saw them last night you would not have thought of them as grieving!'

'I hear Selina is back in Cornwall. I hope she and Valentine come together again. How long will your mother and father be away?'

'It is a mite indefinite. They have gone to St Ives, where my mother has a cousin.'

Demelza looked out at the sky. Still darkening, but still no wind. She rubbed her foot along the edge of a rug, then withdrew it as an ant moved rapidly from under the rug and disappeared down a crack in a floorboard.

Casually she said: 'Did Valentine bring his own cigars?'

'I have no idea. Why do you ask?'

'I thought I had recognized the smell. Ross, you know, is content with a pipe.'

Chapter Seven

The next morning Bella received a letter from Maurice.

Amoureuse,

I have been wondering why it is so long and you have not
written to me, and now I hear, *quelle horreur,* that you are ill!!!
I hear it only yesterday from Jodie de la Blache, who has been
in London and has seen Madame Pelham.

She say it is your throat. Pray Heaven it is not your beautiful
singing voice. Please write to me soon to the above address, or
if you are unable pray ask your respected father. If it is only a
line or two, to set my mind at rest.

You will see I am back in Rouen, and not yet hopes for the
opera. The bigger houses in Paris are booked up, and M.
Leboeuf, who owns the Théâtre Gramont, is afraid to take the
risk. I may persuade him later, but his mistress has just left
him, having run through most of his money, so he is at present
bent on retrenchment, or at least the avoidance of risk. He
will bring on some old revival, he says, with a cast of four, then
handpick two stars who are sure to draw the public. Next year,
he says, he will think again.

Meanwhile my beautiful cast is all dispersed, and my *prima
donna assoluta* is five hundred kilometres away in her native
Cornwall, *et tu es malade.* I am most anxious.

Last night at Jodie de la Blache's house in the rue Gambon
I met Signor Rossini! He is very charming and very good-
looking and very jolly. And young! I am thirty-one, as you
know, and I think he is younger. He had had good reports of
my production of *Il Barbiere* from M. Pinet and I feel sure if I
can find the theatre he will help me assemble a cast – or

367

reassemble *the* cast – and he will find means of helping me to fund it. Meeting him was one of the most happy days of my life – only exceeded, I think, by the day I met you.

And that first night of the opera in Rouen! That is supreme!

My darling, please write to me very soon. It will take at least a week to reach me, and until then I shall wait anxiously for news of you. *Tu es adorable.*

Ever,

Maurice

Bella was now able to walk with a stick, and, after reading the letter three times from end to end, she stowed it away in the top drawer among her stockings, where she was reasonably sure it would not be found. She did not know how much her father had told her mother, but he had given his word not to repeat their talk on the ship. She would like it to stay that way, at least for the time being. Now, if she had the stamina, she must at once reply.

Three days later Edward Fitzmaurice returned to London in the dark green coach which, during its enforced stay, first at Nampara and then at Killewarren, had drawn so many interested spectators. With Edward went Clowance as far as Penryn, where he left her to put her shipping company up for sale and make arrangements for her move back to Nampara.

They had agreed to be married in Sawle Church on the first of September. That was in a month, and offered just time – barely but just – to make preparations and for the banns to be called. They would honeymoon at Bowood, where Clowance could meet a selected few of his friends, and then return to Cornwall for a month. Plans beyond that were not yet made. He was beside himself with pleasure and she, early hesitancies nearly gone, had caught the contagion of his excitement.

Ross spent the Wednesday after they left at a meeting of the creditors of John Trevanion, ex-Member of Parliament, ex-High Sheriff of Cornwall; and later he went to inspect the house where temporarily, until the more pressing of the debts had been discharged, Mrs Bettesworth, Miss Clemency Trevanion and Mrs Jeremy Poldark and her daughter could take up residence.

The weather was still dry but gusty and lowering, and although it would be late when he got home Ross decided not to spend another night away.

Which was fortunate because, arriving after one a.m. on the Thursday morning, he slept late and, breakfasting on his own, he was the first to spot a horseman riding down the valley, and recognized his way of sitting an inch or so to the left in his saddle. He took a last gulp of coffee before going to the bridge over the stream to intercept him.

'Christopher.'

The man took off his hat to wipe his brow with the back of his hand. 'My dear Sir Ross. This is well met.'

'I saw you through the window. You did not tell us you were coming. Let me help.'

'Thanks, no.' Lieutenant Christopher Havergal slid out of his saddle, landed awkwardly on his artificial foot, and winced slightly, then extended his hand. 'You live a pesky long way from London, sir. I believe it gets further every time.'

'It does after a certain age, but you are a long way from that. Have you come to see Isabella-Rose?'

'Who else?'

Bella's bedroom looked the other way, out to sea. After a brief glance behind him, Ross said: 'That branch that sticks out; it is left specially for tethering horses. And the grass grows rank round about . . . Come in. Let's have a word in the library before we go further.'

Christopher followed him in. Ross poured two glasses of cordial from a pitcher and brought one over. Christopher took a chair.

'One *sits* endlessly in coaches and on horse, yet at the end of it one's legs are as tired as if one had walked all the way.'

He was little altered. He had changed to a shorter hair and moustache trim last year, but they were still much in evidence. His back was still as erect, his manner as pleasantly worldly.

'How is she?'

Ross told him. It had been a very near thing. She was now much improved and walking about in the house. Now that the summer had turned inclement she only went out, a short trip to the beach, once a day. 'It is early for her to be down yet. What time did you leave Truro?'

'How is her voice?'

'Not right yet. We daily wait for an improvement.'

'I'm longing to see her.'

There was a pause.

Ross said: 'I am not sure about that, Christopher.'

The young man looked his surprise. 'Whyever not? She is surely well enough to receive visitors.'

'Yes, of course. But certain severe illnesses leave the patient in a very taut, high-strung condition. It might be safer to consult her doctor first.'

'But I am engaged to be married to her! But for a hitch at the end I *should* be married to her already! On what possible grounds . . .'

'Did you not quarrel with her?'

'Not at all! I went to Lisbon on an important mission for Rothschild's. When I came back she was gone!'

'She wrote to you?'

'Later, yes. She had chosen to go to Rouen with this French impresario. Admittedly, this did not please me. But it was not grounds for breaking my engagement to her! Nor anything like it!'

Ross had not sat down while they were talking, and he stood with his back to the light looking down at his visitor.

'Christopher; forgive me, but what you are just saying, is that not grounds for us to go carefully about a meeting now? It is essential she shall not be upset. What you are saying to me she might find upsetting. I appreciate how you feel, but we must try to handle this very carefully.'

'Is she in love with Valéry?'

Ross said: 'I am not a party to all her feelings. All I know is that she scored a great success in France. And I know that she has been dangerously sick with white throat fever. I am not here to judge you – or her – or him. My only concern, now that she is recovering, is that she should suffer no setback as a result of an emotional scene that I could have prevented, that I could prevent.'

Christopher stroked his long moustache as if to pacify it.

'Having travelled three hundred miles, am I to be denied a meeting with the young woman I have courted and encouraged for more than five years?'

'No . . . I will have to consult Dr Enys. But you must see my dilemma. We must help each other to think all round this very carefully. I – her mother and I – want only to do what is best for Bella's happiness. When she marries and whom she marries are entirely for her to choose.'

'Has he asked her to marry him?'

'That you must ask her, but not until she is entirely well again—'

'Impresarios like Maurice Valéry do not believe in marriage. And as for those performances in Rouen, I could have got the same sort of engagement for her in England, where she would not have caught this pernicious disease.'

'Dwight – that's our doctor, Dwight Enys – whom I'm sure you have met – will probably call in to see her this afternoon. I would like to get his opinion above any other. But I don't want you to confront Bella before I hear his opinion. Christopher, may I make a suggestion? . . . That you go at once to call on my cousin, Geoffrey Charles Poldark, at Trenwith, which is only, as you know, four miles away. Call on him and explain the position and ask if you may spend the night there. I am sure he will be delighted to have you. Later today, I will come over and see you, at Trenwith. If he has time I will bring Dwight Enys, and we can discuss it together. I haven't seen Demelza this morning, but I will tell her, and maybe she will come with me to see you as well. She has always been very fond of you – as I have. In my mind it is absolutely *vital* that Bella is not suddenly confronted. We must find a way to break it gently.'

Christopher gave an unamused laugh. 'Very well. Let us break it gently, this unexpected arrival of her promised husband.'

Demelza said: 'Christopher, you say you did not quarrel with Bella before you left for Lisbon. What did you talk about the last time you went out with her? Can you remember?'

'Yes. We went to sup at a coffee house in Jermyn Street. Mrs Pelham's coachman, I may say, played the part of a distant chaperone! On the way home we talked about a certain lady whom I knew and she did not know. It was all quite agreeable.'

'Can you please tell me more about this?'

He hesitated, and then told her.

'And you do not think that this may be partly the cause of Bella's feeling of estrangement?'

'I do, and lately I have kicked myself for having been so frank with her. To me it seemed just a simple fact of life. Bella felt different. But it hardly explains what has happened!'

They were sitting in the handsome upstairs drawing room with its panelled walls and big oriel window. Amadora had excused herself, sensing that they wanted to be alone. Ross was coming over with Dwight in a few minutes.

Christopher said: 'It seems to me, if that is the cause, or partly the cause, there is a tremendous disproportion – of reason – of emotion, on Bella's part. I am very sorry it happened and wish to explain myself to her. I tried to that evening, and I thought she understood. I have never been a saint, Lady Poldark, and I never pretended to be to Bella. Indeed, it seemed sometimes as if she rather enjoyed my occasional raffish ways. I fell in love with her when she was fourteen; and she, I believe, fell in love with me. Of course, as you felt at the time, Bella was far too young for a formal engagement. But we never lost touch with each other. We wrote, and now and then by luck or contrivance we were able to meet.'

He got up and began to limp about the room.

'From the first I was convinced she was an exceptional person with a quite exceptional talent. As you know, it was only as a result of my persuasions that it was agreed she should go to London to train. I went with you to make the choice of school, and when she came to London I was always at hand to visit her and advise her if I could. I contrived most of her early concerts; and it became a generally understood thing that we were committed to each other. Then you agreed that she should engage herself to marry me. In all this I think I behaved as a gentleman should.'

He waited. Demelza said: 'Yes, that is true.'

'I was her "sweetheart" in the romantic nature of the word. I kissed her frequently, encouraged her when, as rarely I admit, she became discouraged. But I never took advantage of her eager, romantic, loving personality to be more than a model suitor. Quite so. So I have never been a saint. My life as a soldier made quite sure of that. In the Peninsular campaign I had a Portuguese mistress, who travelled with me everywhere. Bella knew this, and was amused by it. It added a certain flavour to our relatively chaste relationship. You may understand the physical make-up of an impulsive vigorous man better than your daughter. While helping

Bella in every way I could, and while continuing to treat her with the respect due to a young lady, I continued to belong to a club called Mme Cono's, where women of a different calibre were always available. Sometimes I availed myself of what they had to offer. It was a life – or recreation, if you will – that was entirely separate from the life I led with Bella, and it was very unfortunate that the two should have crossed. But this does not mean that when I marry Bella the secondary life I have been leading at the club will continue. On the contrary!'

'Did you tell her this? Did you explain it?'

'Of course!' He hesitated. 'Of course. But now, whatever she may feel for me, she will need comfort and encouragement. I know she will get it from her family but I can add to it – greatly add to it – because in this respect, forgive me, I know her better than they do. For a singer to lose her voice – even if temporarily – it is almost like losing one's *life*! She will feel bereft, crippled, humiliated. I *have* to see her to try to give her back the confidence she has lost. I pray you to consider this.'

'Christopher!' Bella exclaimed, her voice rising above a croak. 'They told me you was here! No, you must not kiss me, I am still infective!'

'Nonsense,' said Christopher. 'You know my moustache kills every germ in the calendar. But you are very *slim*! Well, well, here we are; I have been here already two days of the five I can stay, and they would not let me see you until now, not until Little Red Riding Hood had been warned of the dangers of seeing the Big Bad Wolf. What joy to see you again! Are they treating you well in this hospital?'

'Quite well, thank you.'

'Are you permitted to come for a swim with me? At Christmas it was too cold.'

Bella looked at the raindrops slithering down the windows, and giggled. 'You are late, too late. Last week was *so* hot.'

Christopher took the cork out of a bottle of medicine Dwight Enys had prescribed and sniffed it. 'Is he good, this sawbones? He rather impresses me, I must say, but you cannot expect the best attention in a back-o'-beyond place like this. As soon as you are running around you must come to London.'

After a pause Bella said: 'I am glad to see you, Christopher. We must talk—'

'Of course we must talk when you are better. Meantime, I hear you were a brilliant success in Rouen. I must hear first all about that. I know Dr Fredericks is inclined to dismiss *Il Barbiere di Siviglia* as *opera buffa*, but my instinct is to dismiss *him*. The other day I bumped into Franz Von Badenberg, and he was asking about you. He had seen *The Barber* at the King's when it came over a couple of years ago, and he said it was angelic fun!'

Bella gave him an edited version of what had happened in Rouen, and he stroked his moustache and watched her, his blue eyes never off her face.

At the last she tailed off, and the eager expression faded. 'But my voice, Christopher. My instrument. Has it gone for ever?'

'Of course not. In—'

'It is three weeks. Soon it will be four. Of course I try it out sometimes, just here in my room when nobody is about. The – the lower register is none too bad. But at present the higher notes are impossible. It is not so much that I cannot reach them, it is that they are harsh.'

'But it has improved over the last two weeks?'

'Oh yes, but—'

'Then you are being too impatient, my sweet. What does Dr Enys say?'

'Much what you do. But does he *know*? Does anyone know? My mother had the same disease thirty years ago, and her voice when she sings today is still just a teeny bit husky.'

'I have never noticed it.'

'You would if you were listening to her singing carols! If the high notes of my voice remain husky I shall be of no further use to Signor Rossini or any other operatic composer!'

He took a handkerchief out of his pocket and gently dabbed her face, drying the tears.

Chapter Eight

Valentine rode over to Rayle Farm to see his wife.

Rayle Farm was much more a farmhouse than Fernmore had ever been. It had begun as a smallholding of about a hundred acres, but tin had been discovered on the land and most of it had been despoiled by the scouring and excavations of the tinners. As often happened, the tin prospectors had found what little there was to find, the workings had been abandoned and the mining work had moved elsewhere, leaving a scarred landscape, two small ruined buildings and mounds of attle. The farmhouse looked out on them and it was not an agreeable vista. However, the view from the back was altogether different, there being the massed bank of fir trees, mixed with holly and arbutus, which separated them from the carefully preserved estate of Tehidy.

Valentine reached the front door, could not at first find a tree, so wrapped the reins round a granite pillar about four feet high with an unreadable inscription on it.

Selina's cousin, Henrietta Osworth, came to the door. She was a tall, masculine woman with a wisp of moustache on her lip. (George had hated her on sight, and Valentine, who had met her before, was for once of the same opinion as his putative father.)

He put on his most agreeable smile. 'Henry! Welcome to Cornwall! I thought I'd look in on you to see if you were happily settled.'

'The kitchen chimney smokes,' said Henrietta. 'There is mildew in the parlour and in this district you cannot get any help. Anyway, what do you want?'

'I called to see Selina and little Georgie.'

She barred the way. 'I was told not to let you in.'

'Who said that?'

'Your father. Sir George—'

There was a patter behind her, and a child dressed in a woollen playsuit insinuated himself round Henrietta's powerful legs.

'Dodie! Dodie! Dodie!'

It was the child's pet name for his father. Valentine picked him up, lifted him high, then gave him a great hug. A big man in shirtsleeves and a green apron also appeared and looked at Valentine with hostility.

'Georgie, Georgie, my little man, so you have not forgotten me!'

'Dodie! Dodie!' His tiny hands were stroking his father's face.

'Do you wish this gentleman to be admitted, madam?' said the man in the green apron.

Selina had appeared, her blonde hair scraped back, her cat's eyes unwelcoming. 'Certainly not.'

'Look,' said Valentine, eyeing his wife. 'I am coming in for fifteen minutes. I have a right to see my son, and I have a right to speak to you. If this man tries to stop me I'll break his back.'

'Come along now,' said the servant. 'You 'eard what Madam said.' He took a step forward.

'Wait,' said Selina. She knew what Valentine in one of his rare tempers was capable of. 'Let Mr Warleggan in, Jessop. He may stay for fifteen minutes only. If I ring the bell please come in and throw him out. In the meantime go to the Gales and ask Bert Gales to be on hand to assist you.'

Glowering, Jessop withdrew. In the front parlour Valentine looked round at the green chintz furniture, at the military sketches on the walls. Georgie was holding onto his hand and trying to resist having his other hand held by Henrietta.

Valentine crouched down talking to little George. Then he looked up and said: 'He has made big strides. He talks well for his age. Have you been teaching him yourself?'

'Dodie! Dodie! Dodie!'

'Pray say what you want to say and then leave.'

He took a seat and crossed his legs. Georgie looked at Henrietta resentfully and buried his head in his father's lap. Valentine stroked his son's dark curly hair.

'Why have you come back to Cornwall, Selina?'

'Because I chose to.'

'With my father's encouragement?' When Selina did not answer,

'Then why come and live in a hovel like this? When you could live in a house that once was yours and is a mansion by comparison?'

'I would gladly move in if you would move out.'

There was a pause. Valentine said: 'Henry, will you please leave us for a few minutes? And take Georgie with you. It is not suitable that a child should be present when his parents are quarrelling. I endured that a lot when I was young and swore a child of mine would not be subjected to it.'

Henrietta glanced at him, then looked at Selina.

Selina said: 'Yes, go on, go on. I am not afraid of being alone with this – this man. I will call when I need you.'

Georgie began to whimper when Henrietta picked him up. Presently husband and wife were alone.

'That's better,' Valentine said, stretching his legs. 'Now tell me what arrangement you have made with my father.'

She stared at his long legs, focused on the crooked one, as if by looking at this mild deformity she would strengthen herself to reject everything he said.

'Your father has offered me this house and a monthly allowance provided I have no association with you.'

'Is it generous?'

'Generous enough to live on. Not generous compared to the fortune I brought you on marriage, which you squandered.'

He shrugged. 'That was my misfortune as well as yours. But not all is lost. I have sold the mine at a profit and kept an interest in it. And, not unnaturally, I am fond of young George – as he is of me.'

'That's *your* misfortune.'

'You are not legally entitled to the exclusive custody of my son. If I take this to court, offering you and him a home and a family life, they will find for me.'

'Family life!' she said. 'With whores and drunkards in and out of the house at all hours! With a wild ape rampaging! Your father will bring all his weight against you in that. A man of his standing against a man of your reputation! And he will certainly offer to accept responsibility for little Georgie's upbringing—'

'Ah,' he said. 'I suppose I should have known that was what he was planning. He will gradually take over complete custody of my son and try to bring him up after his own money-grabbing image. Smelter George! Little Smelter Georgie! Really, Selina. I can hardly believe that you should not see through his shoddy devices!'

'Of course I see through them!' she shouted, her delicate face distorted. 'And I welcome them! Compared to the dissolute life you lead! A life of lies and deceit. Do you wish him to grow up like *you*? What a model – what a prospect for a child!'

The clock struck four. Time was pressing. He said: 'There may be something I should have told you long ago. Perhaps you have heard rumours, I don't know. Don't you really know why George hates me so much?'

'I well understand it.'

'Not the depths of it. It is because all these years there has been a suspicion in his soul that I am not his son.'

Selina took out a handkerchief and dabbed her heated face. 'You've hinted at it before – before even we were married. What does it matter?'

'It matters to him.'

'Well, of course it does. And to you if you believe it. But it makes no difference that you betrayed me with half a dozen women, and when the last refused to be thrown over when you tired of her, you killed her or had her killed by some crony. Now you have turned the house into a brothel and a gaming den . . .'

He slowly sat up and put his hands on his knees, staring at her.

'My cronies do not stoop to murder. They come and go at my invitation to liven up a life that I find increasingly dull. At present I am living alone with only David Lake and the ape for company. If you believe I kill the women I make love to, I might kill you, might I not? Do you realize the danger you are in?'

She said: 'You will never be admitted to this house again.'

There was a rattling at the door handle. She went to the door and opened it. Georgie scuttered in.

'Dodie, Dodie, Dodie!'

Valentine gathered him up and looked at him closely.

He said sardonically: 'What a fine lad! I can see him growing up the spitting image of his grandfather.'

When he got back to Place House – it had been a thoughtful ride – Valentine stopped at the mine and spent half an hour viewing the small pumping engine which was in the process of being erected, before he went in, ignoring for the time being Butto's screams of greeting, and found David Lake in one of the back kitchens cleaning his fowling piece. Hanging from a cord were a brace of wild duck, six rabbits and three packs of dried figs.

Noticing Valentine's glance at the last, David said: 'Could not shoot those, so I had to buy 'em from that fellow who comes round.'

Valentine sat on the corner of the table and dangled a leg. 'Trying to curry favour with Butto?'

'Course I am. Wish he liked me as much as he likes you.'

'He tolerates you. But take your time. Pander to his belly and he will like you in the end.'

David peered up the barrel of his gun. 'How was the little woman?'

'Not coming round at all. To think I used to think I loved her.'

'Sure you don't still?'

'Little Georgie was in good form. By God, how he has grown!'

'Did he recognize you?'

'Of course, you fool.'

'One can't take it for granted. Little boys of that age tend to cling to their mamas and to forget the old man if he is not about.'

Valentine chewed the finger of his riding glove. 'How long have you been here, David?'

The other man looked up. 'What, here? In this house? Six or seven months, on and off. Why, are you getting sick of me?'

'No . . . part of the time you are my only companion. But you stay. You do nothing very much. This is a barren corner of England. I wonder what attracts you.'

'Just because it is the life I enjoy leading. By nature I'm slothful. I like the sun and the wind and the sea and the sand and all the smells, of seaweed, of salt water, of gorse bushes, of broom, of rabbits, of dogs, of wild apes, of wild men, of—'

'That will do.'

'If I go back to Leicestershire my father will nag me to read for the bar . . .'

'I thought you already had.'

'More or less. But I prefer the life of dissolute drunken parties given by a dissolute drunken fellow old Etonian who has space in his house and wine in his cellars and makes amusing company. Do you want me to *pay*? Or to *go*?'

'Neither. Calm yourself.'

'I am not agitated. I am only agitated when someone advises me to reduce my diet.'

Valentine said, after a moment: 'It is strange: I eat and drink excessively but never put on an ounce of weight. Every ounce you eat or drink translates itself into fat ... Yet we are both really equally unfit compared – compared, say, to Butto, who continues to have a great belly on him and yet is immensely stronger than we are.'

David said ironically: 'Maybe we should eat nothing but roots and shoots and nuts.'

'Don't know if he is entirely vegetarian,' Valentine said reflectively. 'I saw him the other day catch and eat a thrush.'

'Let's hope he doesn't develop a taste for human flesh.' David took up his gun and hung it from a nail on the wall.

'David.'

'Yes?'

'I have been thinking.'

'So it seems.'

'You may be unfit, but it is not so long since you were a soldier. You're trained. Could you climb a wall?'

'How high?'

'I wondered if you would like to undertake a little adventure with me. Not perhaps yet, but in a while.'

'Say on.'

Valentine picked at a front tooth. 'Would you like to help me with a kidnapping?'

'Kid—? You're joking ... Who?'

'Little George Warleggan.'

'What d'you mean? The baby?'

'The boy, yes.'

'You serious?'

'Smelter George is intent on preventing me from having access to the lad. He intends virtually to adopt him, bring him up in his own image, turn him into a pinch-penny usurer – and Selina is prepared to go along with that. She is playing the complete bitch. I am not prepared to lie down and accept such a terrible fate for the boy. I want custody of him – part of the time or the whole of the time.'

Silence fell. Even Butto had stopped chattering to himself.

David said: 'What's the sentence for kidnapping? Death by hanging, I think.'

'For seizing some young person and demanding a ransom from his parents? I shouldn't be surprised. This is my *own son*, kept from me by force! I have a right to his custody!'

'Could you not first go to the courts?'

'Smelter George carries a lot of weight in the county. With most folks in Truro it's "Yes, Sir George. No, Sir George. Of course, Sir George." My chances would not be that good.'

'So you mean—'

'In the vast stores of your memory, my dear David, accumulated from your extensive studies, you will perhaps have stumbled on an old proverb which says "Possession is nine-tenths of the law." '

'Very droll. You know it was our favourite proverb at Eton. Or at least the practice of the proverb, which practice I assume you expect me to recall. Go on.'

'There is not much to go on about,' said Valentine, 'as yet. I would do nothing yet, in order to lull them into a sense of false security. But plans might I think be made, talked over, considered. There are a variety of ideas which can be given an airing. I want to know if you would be willing to help me.'

'Put that way, how could I refuse?'

Chapter Nine

Edward had said he would like the wedding to be as quiet as possible, and Clowance had fully agreed. But his position in the world forced some extra attention and publicity on them. His brother and sister-in-law had said they would certainly like to come. The finest house in the district was Trenwith, so they were invited to stay there. A dozen of Edward's personal friends could not be left out, and those had to be accommodated. Killewarren was made use of. Valentine, who in his downbeat offhand way seemed pleased with the prospect of his cousin's remarriage, offered accommodation at Place House, but every Poldark in sight thought this an invitation not to be taken up.

During August there was another sound in Nampara, of a girl singing. Bella was trying out her voice. But for the time being some of the lilt had gone. In earlier days Bella's voice had come out unforced, rising from naturally good lungs and strong, clear vocal cords. It had been no effort at all to allow it to emerge in all its fullness and glory. Now she was tentative, sure enough of most of the middle register but less secure as she climbed the scales. Once or twice Demelza heard her stop, cough or clear her throat, and resume.

Once she followed her into her bedroom and found her sitting in front of the mirror, tears streaming. As Demelza came in, Bella turned away from the mirror and grabbed up a handkerchief.

'Oh, my dear,' said Demelza, sympathetic tears already welling. 'You must not grieve. It will come. Look how much you can already sing! Far more than I ever could at my best! Your voice is already beautiful again. Uncle Dwight said it was simply a question of healing.'

'It is eight weeks today since I came home. I now – feel well. I

382

eat well, enough to be regaining my weight. I swim when the weather is good. I ride when it is not. When you will let me I am stitching towards Clowance's trousseau. I read. I play the piano. In most things I am back to normal. But when I try – try what I used to reach on the instrument so easily it – it does not come. *I* am healed. *That* is not healed.'

'Let us wait another month. Then I will come with you to London, and we will see all the voice specialists we can find. All singers must have anxieties from time to time. At your age such an injury – if it is an injury – cannot be permanent.'

Bella sighed, and that too broke halfway. 'Mama, I am terrified. Truly terrified. Since I tasted of that life – it would be too cruel if I were not able to go back to it. It is strange where I got this passion from. Ever since I first saw a play, when you and Papa took me six years ago, I have wanted nothing but to be – be in the theatre. The candlelights, the smell, the face paint, the wigs, the make-believe, they have entranced me. Do not mistake me, dearest Mama, I love my home. I love you and Papa: you have been wonderful to me in every way. I love the sea and the clank of the mine engines, and the wind and the wildness. I love to talk to the folk on the farm, to the bal maidens – the simplicity and the warmth of it all. But London is like a great magnet. I could not believe my good fortune in getting so far, so quickly. Now it would near break my heart to have it so quickly snatched away—'. She choked and recovered again. 'You know I have had many letters from Christopher. I have replied to them all, trying to sound in the best of spirits, but have told him he must not come down again until—'

'He is coming for the wedding!'

'Oh, yes, I had all but forgot that . . . And I have heard three times from Maurice. I have replied telling him precisely what is the trouble and telling him – telling him he must not leave his work and come down here until I am quite cured. Neither of them can possibly be expected to marry a croaking wife—'

'You do not croak at all, my lover. And I know either of them would marry you tomorrow if you would agree to it. But probably you are right in wanting to be more sure of yourself – of your returning gifts – before you go further.'

Bella blew her nose and half-smiled. 'There, it is all over. Now show me – is that the new wedding hat?'

Demelza said: 'I think, I b'lieve you would do better to talk of your worries more – to Papa, to Clowance, to Cuby when she comes. If – if you speak of fears they sometimes grow less the more they are aired. And it may also be better if you was to – to spill more tears.'

'Don't worry,' Bella said. 'I weep myself to sleep every night.'

The heat of the summer, the long sunny spell, had come to an end about St Swithin's Day. The weather had been broken since then: sunshine and showers and gusty winds, mostly from the south-west. Warm in the sun, but generally cool in the wind: chilly for those who came from the inland towns, bracing for those accustomed to it.

But the first of September was worthy of the occasion; none of the heat of June, all the weather changes slowed to a leisurely pace as the wind dropped. Clouds, white-browed and dark-based, decorated the sky, but the sun on its trip across seemed most often to wend its way through them like a ship avoiding rocks, as it looked down at the great family function being enacted at St Sawle with Grambler. The Reverend Henry Profitt officiated; and on this occasion he was assisted by Arthur Skinner, the absentee vicar of St Ann's, who, chancing to be making his annual visit from Bristol – where he lived more comfortably because of the £240 a year that reached him for St Ann's when added to the stipend he received from St Vincent's in Bristol – hearing there was to be a big wedding in the next parish, and that both the bridegroom and the bride's father were 'titled personages', hastily expressed his wish to participate. The bride wore a veil and gown of silver lace, which fluttered becomingly in the gentle breeze, and she carried a bouquet of Harrisii lilies. The three bridesmaids were the Misses Sophie and Meliora Enys and Miss Noelle Poldark, and they were followed by seven ladies in matching dresses: the Hon. Mrs Edwina Hastings, Mrs Patricia Harrison-West, Mrs Jeremy Poldark, Miss Isabella-Rose Poldark, Mrs Geoffrey Charles Poldark, Miss Loveday Carne, and Mrs Ben Carter. (Clowance had specially wanted Ben's wife to take part. They had also invited Emmeline Treneglos, in the hope of healing the rift, but she had not been permitted to accept.)

Inside the church was packed, and at least twenty guests volunteered to stay outside for the service, where they were joined by almost all the villagers of Sawle, Grambler and Mellin, come to see one of their favourite ladies, half-genteel herself, though oft you would hardly notice, being joined in holy matrimony to a real titled gent from up-country.

The problem of where to hold the reception had been difficult to resolve, and in the end, gambling on the weather, they had opted for Nampara. If it had turned wet they might have contrived to feed the guests in the library, with overflows in the parlour and the hall; but after all it was still summer, and it was *their* daughter, and it would be putting too much on little Amadora, who already had two children and was again with child. Geoffrey Charles and Trenwith were already doing their bit by playing host to all the most important guests.

Ross knew Henry, the third Marquess of Lansdowne from numerous meetings in parliament, and Demelza, of course, had spent a week at Bowood, so they could meet at least as old acquaintances. And much was helped by the fact that Ross and Henry Lansdowne greatly admired each other.

The lawn in front of Nampara had been laid for the breakfast feast. It was very perverse of Demelza's memory to cast itself back to the first-ever outdoor party they had given, soon after they were married, to celebrate the christening of their first child, Julia. Then it had been turned into a fiasco by the mistaken arrival of her father, who, fresh from conversion to the Wesleyan faith, had sought to rebuke and redeem them all. *That* could not happen, but the *weather* could turn nasty, as it had then – a strong blustery quarter-gale working itself up into a tantrum – blowing tablecloths about, even relieving Aunt Agatha of her newly curled wig.

Looking round now, one could see how different it all was then. Many people long dead: chiefly Francis and Elizabeth. Now the sun beamed down, food was consumed, toasts drunk – perhaps the only minor embarrassment coming from Sam, who, uninvited, stood up and said a long-winded grace before the breakfast began.

Edward and Clowance were travelling only as far as St Austell tonight, where a cousin of Edward's was going to welcome them, then see them off for Bath next day. When Clowance went up to her bedroom to change, Demelza waited ten minutes, during which time she reckoned that most of the bridesmaids and ladies-in-waiting would have been up there with her, chatting and fussing around her. Then she slipped away for a few minutes to join her. On the way Paul and Daisy Kellow stopped her to say goodbye, since Daisy was now fatigued and needed her bed. Philip Prideaux, who had been invited and had arrived with Cuby and Noelle and Clemency the day before, said he would walk with the Kellows, helping Daisy. But with Demelza's permission he would return.

When Demelza tapped at Clowance's bedroom and was invited in, only Bella remained with her sister, helping her to button the back of the blue silk tight-fitting dress Clowance had had made for her going away. Clowance was looking out of the window and saying something to Bella, but she stopped on seeing her mother and said: 'Thank you, thank you, thank you, my dearest. It has all gone like a blissful dream. I hope you are not too exhausted.'

Demelza shook her head. 'But I shall miss you, miss you – even though you have been living so long in Penryn. I felt there I could always discover you. Now, gracious knows where you will be!'

'Edward wants to buy a house in Cornwall, but I shall not press him until we are more settled. At present he thinks Cornwall too heavenly to leave for long. I would not disagree with that, but I would not want to take advantage of his first enthusiasms.'

Clowance had moved away from the window, naturally drawing Bella after her, Bella protesting that there were still some buttons to fasten. But instead of following them, as Clowance clearly intended, Demelza took their place at the window and gazed down. From this window one could see most of the lawn, dotted with guests drinking and talking. It was a lively colourful scene. Just by the door to the library Ross was talking to Lady Harriet, and they were enjoying a joke. For a few moments Demelza watched her servants – her own and those on loan – discreetly dismantling the tables once they had been stripped of the remnants of the feast. Esther was talking to her husband. Ben had played his part today as her escort, and she had played her part as a lady who by good fortune happened to be his wife. Sometimes as they spoke Essie's eyes strayed to the various servants passing to and fro, as if she felt her proper place was among them, indeed, that she *wanted* to be among them, putting her energies to some use instead of just being a decorative guest. Demelza remembered when she had felt just like that. It had taken years to grow out of the habit of doing something oneself instead of pulling a bell. But this of course was only a one-off for Esther – who was with child – her life would only be genteel when she was drawn into the life at Nampara. Sam was talking to Geoffrey Charles, both smiling at this unfamiliar meeting.

His long 'grace' had satisfied Sam. Morwenna was with Loveday, talking to a young guest who had come with the Lansdownes. A perfect mixture of totally different occupations and classes. No ardent, belligerent convert to Wesleyanism in the person of her father (long dead – God rest his soul – she hoped he had found a suitable pulpit in Heaven).

Clowance, her dress now buttoned, had come up behind Demelza.

'I'm sorry, Mama.'

'What for?'

She indicated the corner where Ross and Harriet were still in conversation.

'I felt I had to invite her, Mama. I told you, she has always been particularly sweet to me – especially after Stephen's death.'

'Indeed. Why not? Of course you had to invite her! I wonder why Sir George refused.'

'Harriet says he is still recovering from his accident and goes out little. And then, there is the old feud—'

'The old feud. Your father tells me that Lady Harriet was at the Prideaux-Brunes when he was there a few weeks ago. On her own.'

'Yes, on her own.'

Demelza ruminated for a few moments. 'Why did you have to say you were sorry about inviting her?'

'Oh, I don't know. I thought – I just thought—'

'Because she was enjoying the company of your father? And because he was enjoying hers?'

'Not really. A bit, I suppose.'

'But we have talked already about it after the Trenwith party. Why should he not like her?'

'Oh, no reason at all. Bella, I think I'll put my shoes on.'

Demelza continued to watch the couple near the library door. Harriet laughed, showing her brilliant teeth.

Demelza said to her daughter: 'Tell me, do you think sometimes that your father has a slight degree of arrogance?'

'Oh yes!' said Clowance. 'Indeed yes!'

'And you, Bella?'

Bella nodded. 'Sort of.'

'Well,' Demelza said. 'Sometimes it seems to me he takes a fancy for a pretty young woman who has – who has his own kind of arrogance. It appeals to him. Like Caroline, for instance. Your Aunt

Caroline, as you have been taught to call her, who, I may say, has long had a fancy for *him*.'

'Aunt Caroline?'

'Who is a very dear woman. *Nice*. So good-hearted. She is the choicest of my friends, my dearest friends . . . Now Harriet, now Harriet I scarcely know. But from all I learn of her I b'lieve she is a very agreeable person too . . . It does not mean a great deal to your father really . . . The young lady whom he would have married if he had had the chance – for all her faults – and I could not like her, for that would have been unnatural – for all her faults could never be accused of arrogance. Nor can I – though perhaps I do not have anything to be arrogant about—'

Clowance said: 'You have the right to be arrogant or anything else you may feel.'

They had broken up below, Ross to enter the house by the library door, Harriet to stroll elegantly towards Philip Prideaux as he returned.

Demelza said: 'Do not, I pray, claim too much for me. I am – just me. I am just happy to be myself . . . and to be your father's wife. I have no wish to be anywhere else than at his side. I also believe that he has no wish to be anywhere except at my side. That will be the way it will be, until I die – until we die. I have only one regret – and that is that time just goes too fast.'

Book Five

BELLA

Chapter One

As the summer wore on the endless quarrelling over the Queen's position and her trial for adultery had gradually ceased to engage the public, and even the government and its opposition began to find it boring. As countless Italian witnesses to her immorality and licentiousness were brought over, the general consensus come to was that she was really no more worthy of admiration than the King. During one of the long sessions in Westminster Hall even the Queen herself was seen to doze, giving rise to Lord Holland's quip that while in her exile she slept with couriers, now she was in England she slept with the Peers.

Indeed, as October came, it was remarked that there was a slight swing back of public opinion in George IV's favour.

Isabella-Rose, accompanied by both her father and her mother, arrived early in the month and found London a reassuringly peaceable place after the riots and upheavals of the previous year. There seemed to be not only an exhaustion of mob violence but an upturn in general trade. Not only were the nobility and the middle classes growing richer, but the working class and the poor were discovering easier times. More work was available and the price of labour was rising. An attempt in Manchester to organize a great rally to commemorate the Peterloo massacre had fizzled out because most of the operatives were at work.

They did not stay with Mrs Pelham, though the rift between her and Bella was quickly resolved and Aunt Sarah was soon engaged in offering her advice as to which specialists to see.

Dr Fredericks was no medical practitioner, but he expressed himself mystified by the failure of his former pupil's vocal cords. He speculated that undue pressure on a young voice might result in temporary failure. (This was clearly intended as a snipe at

Maurice Valéry and Bella's wilful and wanton incursion into the modern operatic world.) Of course, he said, many pupils went through periods of anxiety because of coughs, colds, catarrh, sore throats. They were the common bugbears of the profession, and he could see no reason why Bella should not regain her normal register in six or nine months. He had naturally several specifics in the form of lozenges and tinctures which he could recommend, and Demelza came away carrying two bottles and a cardboard box.

Dr Amos Jennings – a medical doctor this time and a throat specialist – made a more professional and, needless to say, painful examination and declared he could detect one or two scars left on her larynx by the 'white throat' disease. He explained the morbid nature of the complaint, this being characterized by the formation of a false membrane, yellow or greyish in colour, which spread in patches on an ulcerated base in the pharynx or gullet and often extended into the oesophagus. This, when the disease was on the wane, gradually peeled off and disintegrated, but sometimes left behind minute fragments of scar tissue. This was what Miss Poldark was at present suffering from. Regular gargling and washing out the throat with salt water should improve the condition, together with the pills and the throat wash he would prescribe. (These pills made Bella vomit, and the throat wash looked and smelt suspiciously like the Melrose water Dwight had prescribed at the outset.)

Dr Ernest Faber, who had inherited some of Dr Fordyce's practice and had continued his extensive researches into the causes of fevers, detected some muscular failure and was of the opinion that the throat was still infected and might remain chronically so unless heroic treatment were applied. He prescribed aquafortis, to be taken internally three times a day, and a stronger solution of nitric acid to be used twice a day to gargle and wash the throat, in fact to 'burn' out the infection.

They were staying at Ross's old lodgings in George Street in the Adelphi, and each evening Christopher would come to glean the results of their consultations.

It was a somewhat gloomy household, for Bella was feeling sick as a result of the medicines she was taking. On the third evening Ross went out to pay an arranged call on George Canning.

This was the first time the two old friends had met since Canning had lost his eldest son of some wasting disease. It was pleasant to exchange news, and Canning was quick to congratulate Ross on his daughter's marriage to Edward Fitzmaurice. George Canning had never been on the friendly terms that Ross had been with Henry Lansdowne, but he admired the family's integrity and intellect while deploring their Whiggish tendencies.

Canning himself was on the point of resigning from the government, and was in as low a spirit as Ross had ever seen him. In earlier days Canning had been friendly with Queen Caroline, so that in the controversy over her vulgar return he had felt it a measure of his loyalty to support her as best he could. That had alienated him completely from the King, who persisted in believing that soon after Caroline became the Queen she also became Canning's mistress. Now in the latest turn Caroline was being tried for her alleged adultery with her Italian companion Bartolomeo Bergami.

Canning was very uncertain as to his future, but would shortly go to Paris to rejoin his wife and daughter, and thought he would not return unless a Catholic Emancipation Bill should be brought forward in the New Year, in which case he would come over to speak in its favour.

They parted as firmly friendly as ever, but Ross felt a sense of disappointment that this immensely gifted man should seem to be moving into a dead end. Long ago he should have been Prime Minister.

Unknown to Ross, while he pondered the misfortunes of his distinguished friend, a little drama was playing itself out in George Street.

Demelza and Bella had just finished their supper and been joined by Christopher, who listened to the news of their visit to Dr Ernest Faber. They were both uncertain about his prescription of 'an heroic treatment' for the voice, and Christopher was indignant.

'It is as true of voice specialists as a friend of mine said it was over rheumatism: you choose your treatment and then go to the doctor who prescribes it. Every medic has a cure, nobody agrees what it is.'

'I should prefer rheumatism,' said Bella.

'Oh, there are heroic treatments for that too,' said Christopher, 'such as jumping from a bath of hot water into one of cold, and then back again, six times. I'm sure you will disregard Dr Faber. I can think of nothing more likely to irritate the throat than nitric acid.'

'I told Mrs Parkins when we came in,' said Demelza, 'and she said she had had an actress staying here last year and she used some such acid.'

'And did she survive?'

'I suppose so. But I have already advised Bella not to touch the stuff. I'd sooner consult Meggy Dawes.'

'I've smelt it,' said Bella. 'It could be worse.'

There was a tap at the door. Demelza was nearest and opened it.

Mrs Parkins said: 'Excuse me, m'lady, but there be a young man to see Miss Isabella.'

Something conspiratorial about her: Demelza went out into the passage. Three steps lower down was Maurice Valéry.

'Lady Poldark,' he said, advancing and bending to kiss her hand.

She put her other hand to her own lips. 'Monsieur Valéry. Quiet, please. It – it is not convenient—'

'I have come to see Bella. I only heard yesterday that she was in London.'

'Monsieur, unfortunately it is not convenient—'

'Why? Is she not well enough? She wrote me saying she was much better.'

'Yes, she is much better. But Lieutenant Havergal has just come to see her.'

That stopped him in his tracks. 'That is unfortunate. I have been travelling all day, and I must return tomorrow. Her voice – she said it was still troubling her?'

'It is.'

'I went first to Madame Pelham's thinking you would be staying there. I must see her—'

The door opened behind Demelza and Bella looked out.

'Maurice!' she breathed. 'Oh, my God!' She hesitated. Then: 'Pray come in.'

It was a pleasant living room, the one where Demelza specially remembered she had rebuffed Mark Adderley and where she had nursed Ross with the pistol wound in his arm. A long mirror doubled the image of Christopher Havergal looking towards them as they came in.

'Christopher,' she said, determined to head off a first explosion, 'you will know Maurice Valéry. He has just arrived from France and called to see how Bella is.'

Christopher's face was white and taut. 'Then he will not need me to greet him. If you will give me leave, I shall go now and call some other time when Valéry has returned whence he came.'

Bella put her hand up. 'No. You must stay, Christopher. It would upset me greatly if you were to go now. I have been ill and claim that right. Maurice, pray sit down. Have you had anything to eat? To come so far, so quickly. *Tu es gentil.*'

The two men glanced at each other, then away.

'Jodie I met last afternoon and she said she heard you were come to London to see specialists. I – I broke off as quickly as I could. I am – so glad to see you. You are looking paler, but very well. The high notes, they have not yet come?'

Bella told him of her experiences so far, the conflicting advice, the disagreeable lotions. Conversation became haltingly more general, tried to become normal, wandered to accounts of Clowance's wedding. Maurice had met Edward Fitzmaurice once. He said he knew of a Madame Kaletski, who was renowned for her experience with the troubles of opera singers. If the advice Bella received in London was of no avail, she must come to Paris to see her. Apparently she had studied under M. Mesmer, and sought to discover the causes of impediments and how to overcome them.

Christopher said: 'She caught this filthy disease in Rouen. Had she not gone, there would have been no trouble with her voice at all!'

'Christopher!' Bella said. 'That may be true. No one knows. But it's a disease which is widespread. I might have caught it in London. My mother, years ago, caught it in Cornwall. You mustn't *blame* anyone for it.'

'He blames me,' Maurice said, 'because I invited you to come over. Bella, it would tear my heart out if I thought I had destroyed your life – your singing life. You know what I think of your voice. You know what I think of you!'

'I think in a little while you should both *go*,' Demelza said. 'Bella is in full health now, but if you both care for her you should not *quarrel* in front of her. You should not quarrel at all.'

There was a taut silence. Then Bella said: 'Tell me, Maurice, about your own career. Have all my friends in Rouen dispersed? What are you planning to put on now?'

*

It was a fine night, and Ross walked home from the Commons.

He gave a penny each to three beggars who crouched at the corner of George Street and the Strand as he turned down. A half moon gave some shadows to the night, and a knife-grinder still plied his trade by the light of a candle-lit window.

Lower down there was a scuffling, a grunting and shrill laughter as two cloth-capped women, arms folded, were urging two heaving figures to go ahead and split each other's guts. Just enough light for Ross to recognize the figures.

'Havergal! For God's sake! And Valéry! What in Hell are you about . . . ? What on earth's got into you both? . . . Have you been calling?'

Maurice was the first to withdraw, trying to pull his cravat straight. Christopher took a pace to follow him, but Ross barred his way.

'Stop it, I say!' To the two women who were picking their noses and grinning: 'Go on. Off with you! It's all over now. Off you go or I'll call the watch!'

Hissing and spitting at him, they edged further away, then flounced their hips and moved up the street, talking coarsely and loud enough to be overheard.

'This – man – has insulted me,' Maurice said, gathering his breath as he spoke.

'No more than you deserved! Little Frog!'

'*Sale Anglais!* I shall have satisfaction for that!'

'Damned sure you will.' Christopher fingered the bruise on his cheek. 'Sorry, Poldark, this is no business of yours. You just walked in at the wrong moment.'

'I think,' said Ross, 'if you were visiting my daughter, it is very much my business. Kindly explain yourselves.'

They interrupted each other to tell of the coincidence of their joint call, the bickering argument that had gone on in the house; then Lady Poldark had asked Christopher to go, and had retained Maurice for twenty minutes more so that they should not meet outside. But Christopher, fuming, had waited.

'It is now, what, about ten o'clock, is it not so?' Maurice said. 'It will be light at five. I shall be put to it to find seconds, but Hyde Park is not far away. No doubt suitable gentlemen will be found to arrange the contest.'

'I can find two for you,' said Christopher contemptuously. 'At my club. You need not bother about that!'

'Listen to me,' Ross said, his heavier voice having its way. 'There will be no duelling in this matter. It is not to be considered.'

'Bid me leave to contradict—'

'*Listen*,' said Ross. 'Duelling is a criminal offence in this country. You are not in France, Maurice. And Christopher, shame on you! An ex-soldier allowing yourself to meet a civilian—'

'Oh,' said Maurice. 'I know how to use a pistol! Never fear for me. I have had other duels! This outrage must be expiated!'

'I'll shoot with my left hand,' volunteered Christopher. 'Anything for the fun of meeting this creature.'

'You see?' Maurice stood up to Ross. 'You see it must be.'

'I see nothing of the sort! Look . . . there is a tavern by the ferry. Let us go down and settle this over a drink.'

'No,' said Maurice. 'It cannot be laughed away.'

Ross tried to keep cool. 'Let me tell you something. I once fought a duel in Hyde Park. I killed another man. Killing a man in a duel is not like killing a man in a battle. War, in some circumstances, is necessary, killing is a part of war. Duelling, beside that, is evil. It is a form of murder. What do you think Bella would say if she knew?'

'She need not ever know,' said Christopher.

'She would, for I would tell her.'

Maurice spat on the cobbles. 'Ha! What a gentleman!'

'Pray do not insult me. I would not wish to kill a possible son-in-law.'

The knife-grinder's wheel screeched, and sparks flew off the knife he was sharpening.

Ross said, as if thinking out loud: 'So you two gentlemen have been to see my daughter. I presume you both made her proposals of marriage?'

Christopher flexed his right hand as if it was suffering from cramp.

'You know my feelings about that, sir. You know she accepted me, and a house is waiting for her when she agrees to a date. But as you also know she says she will not commit herself to anything—'

'Or anyone,' said Maurice.

' – to anything until she knows whether she is going to regain

her voice. Until then I must wait, and she must accept the unwelcome attentions of itinerant musicians who try to persuade her that
they only can show her the way to success.'

Ross put a very firm restraining hand on Maurice's arm.

'I do not think that is the best way to express the situation,
Christopher. Valéry is a distinguished and talented musician. Bella
went to Rouen of her own volition and made a great success of her
visit. She tells me that there was a certain estrangement between
you just before you left for Lisbon. This experience, or her illness,
seems to have caused her to rethink her life. We must allow her
time. Time to recover her voice or time to become reconciled to its
loss. Therefore you must both wait. Agreed?'

Neither of the young men was pleased with this summary. Bella's
father had the edge. Reluctantly, though clearly reserving their
rights, one nodded, and then the other.

'But,' Ross said, 'there is only one certainty about my daughter's
feelings. If there were a duel between you and one died, can you,
either of you, possibly imagine for one-tenth of a second, that Bella
would marry the victor?'

An unusual silence fell upon the street, as if all the inhabitants
were listening.

'No,' said Christopher, and waited.

'No,' said Maurice.

Chapter Two

On Monday evening the sixteenth of October Elaine Curnow was walking home from Lelant Downs towards her home at Rose-an-Grouse. It was no distance, but on the edge of a piece of woodland she was attacked by a man with a knife and her throat was slit. A plump little widow of forty-two, she did not quite match up to the other victims of the killer who had been at large so long, but the manner of her death seemed to bear his marks. The body was not found until the following morning because it had been dragged about a hundred yards and clumsily disguised among a tangle of gorse. The doctor who examined the body said it was clear she had put up a struggle and might indeed have scratched and clawed and perhaps inflicted injuries on her attacker.

One significant find at the scene of the crime, apart from her carrier bag and neckerchief, was a man's boot. The boot was of black leather and was built up, with a platform sole and heel. The constable and the investigating magistrates from St Erth concluded that the murderer was lame, with one leg a couple of inches shorter than the other. A wide alert was sent out, and in the first twenty-four hours three arrests were made, two old soldiers and a sailor with a wooden leg. But all of them had substantial alibis, and they had to be released. In the next few days a tall, thin ex-army Captain wearing small spectacles called on all the people in any way connected with the victim: her aged father with whom she lived, the innkeeper whom she worked for, her friends at chapel, her brother in St Ives. Mrs Curnow had two sons, but one was in the Navy and stationed at Portsmouth, the other in Australia. Eventually a verdict of 'Murder, by person or persons unknown' was returned, and the district began to settle back into its normal routines. But as the darker evenings crowded in considerable care was taken that women should not walk the barren districts alone. In various parts of Cornwall, where similar crimes had been committed, a sense of unease prevailed. Paul Kellow, back from visiting his parents in St Ives, thought a militia of some sort should be formed.

Edward and Clowance returned from a month's honeymoon, during which they had travelled as far north as Scotland and as far east as Norfolk. Edward had delighted in taking her to meet his friends, and, after an initial shying away from the idea, she found herself rather enjoying it. Edward was so inordinately proud of her that this, while adding to her initial apprehension, seemed to make the actual meetings stimulating and easy. He said to her once: 'D'ye know, I don't feel I need to introduce people to you, I just want to burst in on them and shout, "Look what I've got!"'

'Do you fish much?' Clowance asked.

'Not much. Why?'

'You might feel perhaps the same if you had landed a big trout.'

He thought. 'With shiny scales? Yes, maybe. The most beautiful fish in the pond.'

'I know,' Clowance nodded, 'with a big mouth and fishy eyes.'

'That's just it,' he said. 'That's just it. How did you guess?' And stroked her cheek.

The happy couple returned to Nampara only a few days after a less happy trio returned from London. Bella had seen two more voice specialists and had refused Ross's offer to take her to Paris to consult Maurice's Madame Kaletski. By now Bella was tired of examinations and advice. She was putting a more cheerful face on things for the sake of her parents, but among all the long words and the prescriptions the truth was beginning to appear. *No one knew.* They could hear there was something wrong, but they could only guess why and they hadn't the least idea whether it would come right.

In addition to the professional experts they had also called on Mr Pieter Reumann, the musical director of the King's Theatre whom they had seen on that first visit to consult about teachers. He said: 'It is still good. Not now the best, no . . . Sometimes this happens without an illness to cause it. Young would-be prima donnas do not quite have the tonal development to make the top. They strain, and then the vocal cords lack the resilience to meet the musical demands. Last time, I think, you saw Madame Schneider.'

'Yes. But she is in Rome at present.'

'I know. She might be better able to advise than I.'

Later he said privately to Demelza: 'I do not think her voice will change now. Possibly she tried to do too much too soon. But why not advise her that that great ambition is – finished? She still has a good voice. She could still sing in the little musical plays we put on to complete an evening's programme. I think she can act. Put it to her. Do not let her mope.'

The arrival of Edward and Clowance for a week's stay was a godsend. Bella put her terrible self-destroying despair behind her, and for the first time since her illness contrived to behave like her old extrovert self. The weather was still equable, and one morning Edward plunged in the sea with Ross. Presently the two girls joined them, and finally Demelza, holding Henry's hand.

As the icy water clutched Demelza by her waist and then by her shoulders, she again felt a surge of exhilaration that made her want not merely to gasp but to shout with joy. All might yet be well for Bella, she thought, and Clowance was so obviously excited and happy that it made her own heart sing.

They were soon clustering indoors, drying off by a hot coal fire, talking and laughing, the only outsider, Edward, already a part of the fun.

Later that day, as darkness was falling, and the wind rising, Edward said to Clowance: 'I have never known a family quite like yours.'

'What is wrong with it?'

'Nothing is wrong with it. I just appreciate being a part of its easy, friendly ways. Affectionate without fuss, banter without rudeness, understanding of another's point of view without bickering. You are lucky. My family has many virtues, I am proud of belonging to it, but there are little fences, little hesitations within it that are not unusual – in fact far more common – and I cannot see them in yours.'

'There have been some in ours,' Clowance said, thinking of the strains that her infatuation for Stephen had put on it. 'But on the whole . . .'

Edward said: 'I think having so many servants about makes life in a house slightly less real. And living in a degree of state . . . And London is so artificial. Society on the whole is superficial, rotten. Now that I have a companion in life – and such a companion – I shall stay out of it more.'

'You have responsibilities.'

'Not many, thank Heaven. D'you know what little Henry said to me when we first met?'

'What?'

'It was while he was staying at the Enyses with Mrs Kemp. I came on him rather unexpectedly. He knew I was hoping to marry you. He sized me up and down when he thought I was not looking, then when we were alone he planted himself in front of me and said: "Excuse me, sir, but are you a lord?"'

Clowance laughed. 'What did you say?'

'I think I said " – er, yes." Then he said, "My father is a sir." I said, "Yes, I know that." Then he said, "Is a lord higher than a sir?" So I said, "Yes, but your father deserves his sir." He wanted to know why, so I said, "Well, your father has served his country and I have only inherited my title." So he wanted to know what inherited meant.'

'What an inquisition!'

'I explained that my father was a lord and I came into the title later. So he said, "Did your father deserve his title?" I told him my grandfather probably did. He said, "What did he do?" "Well," I said, "He was in the Cabinet, in the Government." I thought that had satisfied him, but after looking down at his feet he said, "My mama tells me I shall be a sir one day if I behave myself." "So you will," I assured him. "Sir," he said, "I s'pose I shall then be like you." "In what way?" I asked. He replied, "I shall be a sir and have done nothing to deserve it!"'

They both laughed. Edward said: 'I told him that perhaps by then he would have done something to deserve it.'

'What did he say to that?'

'He said, "I don't want to go to London and be in the Government. My sister has just come back from there with her morbid sore throat, and I have been turned out for fear of catching it." I said, "Who told you that?" He said he had overheard Mrs Kemp telling Bone, Dr Enys's servant. "She whispered, so I could only just hear."'

They listened to the waves breaking, lonely and hollow and dark.

'I wish I could do something to help Bella. Do you think if her voice does not properly return that she will get over the disappointment?'

'No,' said Clowance.

Before they left Edward saw the miners building a bonfire out of driftwood and broken pit props. Then he realized it wanted only ten days to November the fifth.

He said to Ross: 'So you celebrate this old anniversary as far west as this?'

'Very much so. This is Wesleyan country, and to celebrate the defeat of the Catholics is always a popular feast.'

'They were a few fanatics, weren't they. Better surely to celebrate the defeat of the Spanish Armada.'

'Oh, they do that as well. And Hallowe'en, which is soon upon us. The Cornish are always looking for some excuse to have a feast.'

'Do they have fireworks?'

'Not many. They have few pennies to spend. As it is, they are wasting firewood which would serve them well in the winter.'

'Have you seen Bengal fire?'

'No.'

'There was a display in Hyde Park to greet the Queen. In the old days they could only produce a bright green, which you will know was used sometimes for signalling. Now they add other substances, chlorate of potash, nitrate of strontia, sulphur, lamp black, magnesium powder, compound of arsenic. One can have all the colours of the rainbow, and quite brilliant. I wonder . . .'

'It would be too expensive altogether. Though there is arsenic aplenty.'

'They welcomed me and crowded into the church,' Edward said. 'I know that was a testimony to the Poldark name, but you have told me the Cornish are suspicious of strangers. They were not suspicious of me. They seemed instantly to welcome me as a friend. I would like to send them some extra fireworks. It must be anonymous. I do not want to seem to be patronizing them, nor do I want to usurp your position of the chief personage of the villages. A selection of Bengal lights could be sent down: there is just time to get them here. If you could deny all knowledge of who had sent them, I should be happy to do that.'

Ross laughed. 'But if I have to deny I am responsible they are sure to search in their memories and quickly come to the right conclusion.'

'That I think will be acceptable. So long as they understand the anonymous donor stays anonymous and is not looking for any thanks.'

They were walking past Wheal Grace, and they turned down the valley towards the house.

Edward said: 'Do you think Isabella-Rose will eventually marry Christopher Havergal?'

'It's hard to say.'

'He called to see us when we were in London.'

'Christopher did? A social call?'

'Not quite. He knows I have interests in the theatre and seemed to believe that I might be able to help Bella.'

'It's too early. She would not want to sing yet.'

'It was not just opera he had in mind. He thought the straight theatre.'

'Oh.' Ross digested the news. 'Does Bella know anything of this?'

'I don't think so. He brought the subject up while Clowance was absent.'

'Did he say what he had in mind?'

'He knows I have a financial interest in a new theatre in London called the Royal Coburg. It was only opened a couple of years ago, and it presents a mixture of farce and overblown melodrama, interspersed now and then with some good stuff – a Shakespeare or a Marlowe. This is just over on the other side of the river. The audience is inclined to be unsophisticated, but the better stuff has done pretty well. I think something is planned for mid-December. Havergal thought if she were introduced to play some minor role it would give her a new incentive in life. He even thinks that such an experience might stimulate her to the extent of restoring her voice to its full health.'

'I'll say this for Christopher – he never loses faith. I agree that it would be an uncommon generous act to do such a thing. But could you arrange something like that?'

'I would think it likely ... I know Frederick McArdle, the producer of the last Shakespeare put on there. He has a reputation for brooking no interference. But the finances of the theatre, like those of all the more famous ones, are not in a healthy state.'

Ross said: 'I would not want you to involve yourself further on our account, but if you can do anything without extra cost to yourself I should be greatly obliged. I understand the musical director of the King's Theatre did say he would be willing to take her on trial.'

November came in cool and draughty. And dark. Every evening seemed to vie with the one before for the earlier lighting of candles and lamps. Valentine moved Butto to his winter quarters, these consisting of the open compound of brick and stone which had been specially built for him and leading to a scullery, where he often slept. Now Valentine had opened the door at the back of the scullery, which led down stone steps to the cellars. This was much warmer, and being under the kitchens benefited by the heat from the cooking that went on just above. The cellars continued on to a wine cellar, a coal cellar, and one where casks of ale were stored. But these were separated from Butto by a locked metal door. Since early September Butto had taken it upon himself to transfer his bed to the cellar. Valentine had come to the conclusion that the ape had a well-developed interest in his own comfort.

Cuby and Clemency and Mrs Bettesworth took up occupancy of the little house near Bodmin and left the Castle empty of anyone except the bailiffs. Philip Prideaux helped with the move. John Trevanion wrote from a house in Antwerp, where he was staying with friends, but gave no hint of a return. Most of his income from rentals in and about Cornwall was seized as soon as paid, and John himself had no prospect of accumulating enough capital to come home and put a brave face on it. It was safer to scrape a pittance together to live off his friends in Belgium than to go to prison in England.

The Bengal lights arrived on the third and were delivered to Will Nanfan, who was an elder of the villages of Sawle with Grambler and a ringleader in the Bonfire Night celebration. He was delighted to receive three large wooden cases. Each coloured powder was packed separately with metal saucers in a smaller box. In his present euphoric mood Edward had included also Roman candles and Catherine wheels and rockets. Nanfan went up to see Ross, who was as enigmatic as he knew how to be, and Will went away briefed with platitudes. Anyway, everyone felt, it was good of someone to send

405

such a munificent gift, and that young lord who had been around here much of the summer and had married Miss Clowance was a handsome proper sort of a boy.

In the old days Guy Fawkes celebrations had been held on the flat ground above Sawle Combe, where the summer fairs with their racing and wrestling competitions took place. Lacking a village green, as nearly all Cornish villages do, this was as near the centre of the straggling community as could be. But in the days of the Napoleonic Wars, when invasion was a constant threat and no celebratory bonfires were permitted, the bonfire, only prepared in readiness to raise an alarm – when they had constantly to be rebuilt because of the wet climate – had been moved much nearer Nampara, on a piece of flat moorland just beyond Wheal Grace. It was the highest place around and could easily be seen from St Ann's Beacon and Trencrom Hall, linking up with a chain around the coast. The bonfires celebrating Trafalgar and Waterloo had been lit here, and since then, because alarm lights to rouse folk to meet an invasion or to inform them of some great feat of arms were no longer necessary, no one had suggested that the fifth of November bonfire should be returned to its former place.

An advantage too was that this was much further from any house or thatched roof which might catch a flying spark. The only place in mild proximity was Sam's new chapel, built out of the fallen granite from Wheal Maiden, but this had a roof of Delabole slate, and the wind was scarcely ever in that direction.

On the third of November also a letter from Christopher for Miss Poldark.

Dearest Bella,

I have some news for you that I trust will give you pleasure. I called on your new brother-in-law about the beginning of last month and in the course of conversation, which needless to say included your career and your illness, he brought up his interest and influence in the Royal Coburg Theatre. You will remember we went to it a couple of times soon after you came to live with Mrs Pelham – it is just across the river by the new bridge. We saw a spectacle and melodrama called *Trial by Battle,* which we both enjoyed. Well, of late, Lord Edward and some of his friends, including the producer Frederick Mc-

Ardle, have been introducing some plays of greater quality and interspersing them among burlesque and ordinary melodrama to see if the audience will accept and appreciate them. There have to be a few alterations in the text of the plays, to evade the law that restricts the plays of Shakespeare to the patent theatres; but apparently they played to almost full houses with *Macbeth* in August, with Frederick McArdle producing. There is now a plan afoot to produce *Romeo and Juliet* for some time in December. Dates not yet settled, nor cast. But they hope to get a young actor called Arthur Scales for Romeo.

Edward has spoken about you to McArdle, and McArdle would be willing to interview you with the idea of offering you one of the smaller speaking parts. What do you think of that? The theatre may not be the most fashionable and the part not a big one, but it would enable you to return to the theatre, and if they like you and you like them this could lead to better things. If your voice fully recovers you can resume your singing career at will. But this can do you no harm professionally and it will get you into the theatrical swim again. As you know, I have always felt you could act and you have a presence which a lot of young women would give their ears for.

If you are willing to come to London at some agreed date in December, I will make no claims upon you that you do not invite, but I will do all in my power to put you back into the world where you truly belong.

And I will come to Cornwall for you.

Christopher

'What shall you do?' Demelza asked.

'Oh, I would go! Without hesitation I would go. But for one thing.'

'What is that?'

'I am fond of Edward. I feel for Clowance. I so long for them to be happy, as I think they will be. But she has married above her. I do not want him to think, or her to think, that almost before they have finished their honeymoon the Poldarks are asking favours of him. Making use of him, in fact.'

'He mentioned the idea to me before they left,' Ross said. 'I don't know him well, but he did not give me the impression that he looked on it that we were taking a liberty – or that Christopher Havergal was presuming on a possible relationship by asking him.'

After a moment Demelza said: 'Clowance is anything but an angel, but at the moment Edward thinks her one. He has also fallen in love with Cornwall, and appears to include all his new relatives in a general sort of affectionate view. At present my feeling is he cannot do enough for us, his only regret that he cannot do more. Look at the great supply of fireworks he has sent to the village! I still understand your sort of reluctance, Bella, to seem to take advantage of a new relationship. But my own feeling in my heart, in my judgement, is that you should take this chance. You agree, Ross?'

'I do. If something comes of it, I believe Edward would take pleasure in feeling he had helped so much.'

Bella gave a little nervous cough. 'My voice is quite satisfactory – I talk just so much as I want and suffer no inconvenience. But I suspect at times I speak a little rough. I wonder if in a play I had to raise my voice in making a long speech it might become husky.'

Ross said: 'Dear Bella, why do you not face that difficulty when you come to it, eh? You do not know what part you will be assigned to play. It seems likely that you may have only few sentences to speak, such as, "Here is the wine, Lady Capulet."'

Demelza said: 'I thought she was called Juliet.'

'So she is. Lady Capulet is her mother.'

'So your father knows all about it!'

'I wish *I* did,' Bella said. 'It is a classic. Do you think Mrs Hemple's Academy might have a copy they could lend me? Do you think if I went in and called on them they might be able to help?'

'There is the library in Truro too,' said Ross, 'where Arthur Solway used to work. We might try them.'

That afternoon, soon after lunch when the rain, which had been threatening all morning with low scurrying coal-edged clouds, was about to begin, Valentine kidnapped little Georgie Warleggan and took him back to Place House, Trevaunance, where he had been born.

*

408

Valentine refused to use the word 'kidnapped'. He claimed that he had simply resumed possession of his own son. Kidnapping one's son was like raping one's wife, a contradiction in terms.

After some prospective visits to examine what might be termed the defences of Rayle Farm, they had established that these would not be difficult to breach. Selina had only three servants and her cousin Henrietta; and Valentine, for all the hard words between them when he made the formal call, had not actually threatened to take the child away from her against her will.

Valentine said to David, 'In times of open warfare surprise is all.'

Usually Henrietta took the child for a walk directly after dinner, while Selina rested. It was noticed that, being no energetic walker herself, Henrietta would frequently allow Georgie to run on ahead and then come back to her. She seemed quite arbitrary as to the direction she took, but they were keen not to snatch the boy under the eyes of those few miners who hacked and picked above ground.

This afternoon the threat of rain was enough to deter Henrietta from stirring far from home, and sure enough they made off behind the house in the direction of the woods surrounding Tehidy. Halfway to the first bank of arbutus trees Henrietta stopped, presumably to get her breath, and Georgie ran on. Presently he was confronted by his father, who tried to stop the squeal of delight the little boy uttered, and gathered him up in his arms, and made, as if it were all a great joke, towards the woods, while David Lake, who was unknown to Henrietta, accosted her and asked her the way to Basset's Cove. After a brief, pleasant conversation David turned away in the direction she pointed and, once out of view, made a quick detour to where they had left their horses, to find Valentine already mounted, with his son in front of him on the saddle, waiting for his friend.

They made for home. The worst of the rain mercifully held off, though for the last five miles it spattered into their faces in vicious spurts before the driving wind.

At Place House preparations had been made to receive the honoured guest. Polly Stevens, née Odgers, at one time a nurse-maid to Valentine himself, had been engaged. Georgie, who at first had seen the joke in this clandestine escape from his mother, had begun to get fretful as the saddle chafed his legs, and when he tottered into the front hall of Place House his eyes were red with rubbing them, and he looked ready to go to sleep. The motherly approach of the ex-clergyman's daughter – who had been anything but motherly when she was young – was enough to soothe his fretfulness, and a bowl of warm bread and milk, fed him by his father, revived him.

Like a fire that has had fresh dry faggots thrown on it, he was suddenly all energy and interest. When he saw Butto he momentarily cringed, seeking his father's protection, so Valentine picked him up, opened the door of the pen and went in.

'Butto,' Valentine said, 'this is my one and only son. Georgie, reach out and touch his muzzle. He could as well eat you as kiss you, but I know that only the second is in his thoughts.'

The little boy began to stroke Butto's great ruff. Butto sneezed as if pepper had been thrown on him, shook his great head, sniffed a couple of times and then put out his gloved hand.

Demelza's occasional attacks of migraine had become much less frequent as her reproductive cycle ceased, but on the morning of the fifth she woke hardly able to get her head off the pillow. It improved by dinnertime, but as darkness fell she decided not to go to the bonfire. The thought of standing about in the chill breeze while men fumbled with flint and tinder or waved torches defiantly to the happy sound of joking and laughter, did not appeal to her as much as it normally would. But being Demelza, who always hated to miss anything more cheerful than a funeral, she said she might walk up a little later. The bonfire was due to be lit at six and the fireworks would begin at seven. Until then she would flick over the pages of the *Spectator*, which Dwight faithfully delivered after he had read it – or even a fashion magazine which Clowance had left behind. Ross was expected to be there to put a torch to the bonfire, but deputed Bella to do it instead, and he said he would companion Demelza until seven, when she might be persuaded to turn out – or not, as the weather promised.

After the downpour last night, which had lasted until midnight, the day had been fine, with only a rare flurry of rain, and even a few rags of sky appearing in faded blue among the grey clouds that for the most part hid it.

That other Poldark – Geoffrey Charles – would be expected at the bonfire; as would the Enys family, minus Caroline. She said: 'They know I love them dearly – why else should I allow my husband to risk his health moving among their dirt and feverish infections – but I can do no good to or for them by standing about watching their squibs.'

Daisy Kellow was not well enough to come out, and Paul had gone to St Ives to bring his parents back. Demelza felt that if she was recovered sufficiently to go to the fire herself she might call in at Fernmore on her way. Edward and Clowance had spent part of their last day with Daisy and Paul, but Demelza had not been for more than three weeks – for reasons that she was disinclined to face.

Most of the servants at Nampara had gone to see the lighting of the bonfire, and just before seven Ross left. Demelza was very comfortable, toasting her feet before the fire. She said: 'I'll come in an hour.'

'If you are not there by eight-thirty,' Ross said, 'I will come back for you.'

'No. Don't bother. I can find it, you know.'

'Just follow the lights,' said Ross. 'But I'll come for you just the same.'

Left to herself, Demelza poured a second glass of port and settled into Drake's rocking chair. Port neither cured nor made worse the light-headedness that followed her migraine, but it was comforting to have it at her elbow, and she adored the taste. It was so pleasant to have the house entirely to oneself. Although usually a gregarious person, she found her privacy so rare that she valued it. Now that Ross was more or less permanently at home, she had almost forgotten the empty periods of her life when she had ached for the sight of him – a long hollow ache that the presence of nobody else, not even her children, could assuage.

With a poker she rearranged the coal on the fire, hitting one piece until it split and burst into a new flame. Good sea coal, recently arrived from Wales. One result of keeping open two moderately successful mines was that one could have the pick when it was delivered at Basset's Cove or in Truro River.

She must have dozed off for a few minutes because she woke still staring into the fire. She looked at the clock by the door. It still wanted five minutes until half-past seven, so Ross had been gone only fifteen minutes.

In a wide range of thoughts before she dozed off her mind had gone fleetingly to Paul and Daisy Kellow and Philip Prideaux. She was very uneasy about Paul. Another woman had died: was it coincidence that Paul had been visiting his parents in St Ives at that time? Was she justified in breathing her suspicions, even breathing them, to Ross on the strength of one of her famous – or infamous – forefeelings and the smell of a cigar? She was a little afraid of Paul; there was something unnatural about him, and something unhealthy about his preoccupation with her. It was not precisely sexual. It was not merely because she was Jeremy's mother. But the two were facts somehow related to the way he looked at her – detached, as if he hardly knew her or she him, yet deeply engaged. His eyes seemed to say that they understood each other's secrets. Two or three times he had wanted to involve her in some personal confession; always she had put him off, not wanting at all to hear what he had to say, sensing that it was to Jeremy's detriment, wanting to hurt her, wanting to penetrate to something in her motherhood, something in her femininity. It was an uneasy situation. She had been relieved when he married and went away. But now he had come back, more or less permanently it seemed, leaving his wife alone to fight her losing battle with tuberculosis, instead looking after his sister, who was herself fighting the same battle.

She had hoped when his parents went away to stay in St Ives that this might herald a move for the entire family.

Nampara was exceptionally quiet. She wondered if there were a single soul left in it except herself. Even old Jack Cobbledick had hobbled out on his two sticks, and they had hoisted him onto a donkey for a ride up the combe. The only sound in the house was the rattle of an upstairs window, in Jeremy's room, and the creak, creak, creak of a door. Which one? She ought to know every sound, but this one she could not identify. Fortunately for the fireworks, the wind had taken off and only a gentle breeze was pushing against that window in Jeremy's room. When Ross left there were even a few smeary stars in the sky.

She should be moving. She stretched her legs towards the fire, luxuriating like a cat in the warmth.

Philip Prideaux had been on her mind of late too. He had only once been to Nampara since Clowance made her choice. Ross had seen him, she knew, and, according to Ross, he was taking his disappointment pretty well. For the last few days he had been staying with Geoffrey Charles and Amadora at Trenwith. She must get them over for supper before he left.

She specially wanted to see him privately in order to impress on him, if that were possible, that Clowance's choice had been entirely her own, without her parents attempting to influence it any way whatever. Ross said he had emphasized this when they met and Philip said he understood. That might be all right so far as Ross was concerned, but Philip might still harbour suspicions about Clowance's mother. Women, most women it had to be said, had an eye to the main chance where their daughters were concerned. In marrying the brother of a marquess Clowance was taking an enormous step up in the world.

The fact that Demelza, herself sprung from nothing, should not try to influence her daughter would be hard to believe. She hoped to make it clear to Philip, when she had the chance, that at an early age she had caught from Ross the doctrine of egalitarianism and had consistently put it into practice in her attitude even towards her own children.

Strange about Jeremy's window. Why should this still rattle? Someone should go up tomorrow and see that it was wedged. She could of course go up tonight. It was only along a dark corridor and up a single flight of stairs in a house of which she had been the mistress for thirty years. She couldn't possibly be scared of ghosts here. She would go into the back kitchen, open the second drawer on the left, and find a collection of various-sized wooden wedges kept precisely for this purpose. Then in the next drawer was a small hammer, and armed with these she could take the candle she was carrying and go into Jeremy's room. Of course when she got there she might find Jeremy, his face pressed against the window, his tunic plastered with Flanders mud, waiting to get in.

Her back hair prickled. What a silly lootal she was! Sitting here all alone half a-tremble because a window rattled and a door creaked.

She wondered if the dead felt the cold. Twice Ross had suggested to her that they might travel to Brussels to see her son's grave; each time she had not taken it up. At first it was all too fresh and raw, now it was a fear of all that killing grief coming upon her again. Upon them both. Out of sight was out of mind. Partly anyway. She knew a stone had been erected. That was enough. But supposing Jeremy was upset by her neglect. Supposing a week ago, on All-Hallows' Eve, he had struggled out of his grave wrappings and begun the long walk back. It would have taken him all of six days. Meggy Dawes had said once that at All-Hallows' Eve the white spines of dead men wriggled out from their graves and tried to return home. Perhaps he had found a horse as dead as himself. He would leave behind him the smell of decay. Would he himself smell or would all the flesh have rotted off the bone?

Something tapped on the window of the parlour.

She leaped up, a slipper off, chair rocking, port glass rolling but not breaking, falling on the rug. Heart thumping, she grabbed a poker, went to the window, pulled back the curtain.

The dark garden, a few last leaves waving in the light breeze. No plant had been allowed to overgrow so that it would be big enough to tap the window. She could not have imagined the tap. Or could she?

The light from the room flooded out into the garden. Henry's small wheelbarrow was upside down with his spade on top of it. A few emaciated hollyhock spikes leaned about drunkenly. They should have been cut off. Nothing else stirred. But the night sky reflected a vivid, startling yellow from over the hill where the Bengal lights had begun.

The clock said a quarter before eight. They had been impatient to start. Well and good. The display would surely last until half-past nine.

She let the curtain fall. She was well enough now. She kicked off her other slipper and pulled on her boots, laced them up, put a scarf over her head and tied it in a bow under her chin. Her cloak was in the hall. She blew out the three candles in the candelabra, retained the single lighted candle on its stick.

Don't hurry. What are you hurrying for? Back to put up the fireguard. Moses was out and would have to stay out until they returned. In any case there were plenty of sheltered spots in the rear of the house, among the farm sheds.

As she went out into the hall, pulling the parlour door to behind her, there was a tap on the front door.

This could not be imagination. Who would want something at this time of night? All the back doors were unlocked, as was this one. One did not have thieves about in these country districts.

She held the candle high, lifted the latch and opened the door. It was Paul Kellow.

Chapter Three

Printed instructions had been included with the Bengal lights and most of the fireworks. Will Nanfan had picked as his helpers those miners who could read, and they had rehearsed it once, so it became quite a well-ordered display. Ben and Esther Carter had been included, rather against Ben's natural inclination, but Essie had persuaded him. In succession the night was lit up by brilliantly dazzling displays of indigo, scarlet, yellow, green, white, purple and azure. The villagers had seen nothing like it before, and while the fire licked its lips after consuming the straw-filled Guy, these brilliancies caused gasps of awe and appreciation.

Most of the gentry had already turned up, Geoffrey Charles and Amadora, with Philip Prideaux and the Enyses. Presently Geoffrey Charles came over to Ross. After commenting on and receiving the explanation for Demelza's absence, he said: 'Have you seen Valentine this week?'

'No.'

'He appears to have seized his small son, who has been in his mother's keeping for the last six months.'

'I'm damned.'

Geoffrey Charles said: 'That's official, I believe. Polly Stevens has been called in to look after the child. I don't know exactly where Selina has been living. Do you?'

'At a place called Rayle Farm near Tehidy. You mean he has the baby at Place? Presumably he did not take his son without her permission . . .'

'Stole the child from under their noses. So I've been told.'

'Confound the fellow,' Ross said. 'You can rely on him only to do one thing – the unexpected. That's no home for a little boy.

Everybody drunk, light women infesting the place, that great ape rampaging.'

'I saw David Lake last week, and he was complaining that life there had become comparatively dull of late. No one would ever expect Valentine to mend his ways, but apparently the place has been cleaned up somewhat. Maybe Valentine has had this in mind and is aiming for a degree of respectability to justify his having Georgie back. I find him quite unfathomable, you know.'

Ross watched a Roman candle send up its coloured stars.

'What will the legal position be?'

'I have no idea.'

'You should have, after all the time you spend at Lincoln's Inn.'

Geoffrey Charles smiled. 'Afraid we deal in wider matters such as international law. It's a fault of the system. No doubt the local judges' clerk would be better informed than I am. I suppose . . .'

Ross waited.

'I suppose . . . well, I suppose in law the father's claim is paramount – that is unless he, the father, has been legally deprived of custody for some obvious malpractice and the wife and grand-father have been granted it instead. As far as I know there has been no such case. You and old George indeed have clubbed together to save Valentine from bankruptcy and maybe prison, so his character is not irredeemable.'

'Who told you that?'

'It is the common gossip of the local inns.'

'Since when have you frequented the local inns?'

The sparkling white of a Catherine wheel showed up Geoffrey Charles's uneven teeth when he smiled.

'I have friends, Ross. I have friends.'

They were in the parlour. The scene had not changed since Demelza had left it three minutes ago. The piece of coal she had split still smoked and flickered behind the firescreen. Clowance's fashion magazine lay open on the table. One of the two snuffed candles in the candelabra still sent up a faint wisp of smoke. The single candle burned, the one in her hand in the candlestick when she opened the door, now it was on the table.

They sat opposite each other at the table. He was wearing a black suit with a white scarf tied like a cravat. His face was expressionless, his eyes malignantly curious. He was wearing built-up shoes.

'That's better,' he said. 'Just a cosy, friendly chat.'

'I was just – going to the bonfire,' she said again.

'Can you get pleasure out of that?'

'Out of what?'

'Watching fireworks.'

'Yes.'

'I can't. You see ... I don't believe it. I don't believe it is happening.'

'Oh, it is.'

'Demelza. You know I have wanted to talk to you for quite a long time. I think you suspect me of something that you are afraid to speak. Isn't that so?'

'Ross will be back soon. He is coming back for me.'

'I saw him up there laughing with his friends. He does not care for you the way I care for you.'

'Paul, you are being very silly.'

'The way I *intend* to care for you, that is.'

'I think that is his step now!'

'No, it is not. Sit down. He is up at the bonfire chatting and laughing with his friends. What do you think of me, Jeremy's mother? Do you suspect me of killing all those women in the county over the last two years? You could not be more wrong. When you heard that my father and mother had taken a holiday in St Ives, did you believe it? Or did you think they were both lying in the cellar, beginning to stink, where I had killed them? Well, you are wrong, Jeremy's mother. I brought them home safe and well this afternoon. They are both much happier for the change.'

Demelza again stirred in her chair, but he instantly moved to stop her if she thought of making for the door.

'You think I kill women? Quite the contrary. I watch them die, but that is another thing. I watch them die of tuberculosis. First Doris. Then Violet. Then Mary – or she soon will – then Daisy, though she will cling on as long as she can. I know who the murderer really is. Don't you?'

She glanced at the clock. Three minutes before eight.

'It is Philip Prideaux. You should guess that! He had a first breakdown in the West Indies, where he murdered a woman. He has been in the vicinity every time a woman has had her throat slit in Cornwall. He was staying at Cardew when the maid there was killed as she was walking home. And he was close by when every one of the others died. Tall, thin, long black coat, pretending to help the justices.'

'It was a man killed by Philip in the West Indies.'

'Ah, that's what he tells you. Don't believe it. He is an intruder. Why should you suspect me when I have lived here all my life?'

The clock had moved three minutes.

Paul said: 'Let me tell you about Jeremy. He organized this robbery on the stagecoach from Plymouth to Truro. No wonder he was a success in the Army. Did you know I dressed up as a woman? To wear their clothes disgusted me even then. And it was all for a woman that it began. He was crazy for Cuby Trevanion. All for a woman . . . Yet when we got away with it he made no use of the money except to buy himself a commission in the Army. Stephen bought his boat business and married Clowance. I used my money better, I used it to bolster my father's coaching business, and to buy a few whores . . .' He raised his head, listening.

'That is Moses, wanting to get in.'

'Moses?'

'Our cat.'

'I don't like cats. If I let him in I should slit his throat.'

All her blood was frozen. She wanted to be sick. Paul said: 'Even cats are preferable to women. Women are abominable.'

'Whores may be.'

'What?'

'You may think some whores are unpleasant.'

'Those I had I could have killed, yes. I could have *ripped* them open. But I did not have a proper knife. I tried once with a pair of scissors, but it didn't work.' He took a long thin knife from under his cloak, slid off the sheath and laid it on the table. 'This is more the sort of thing.'

Demelza stared at it and swallowed.

'So far, Paul, you have told me of the things you hate. Tell me of the things you love.'

'The things I love? Ah, you want to be knowing, don't you. Don't you. Well, you'll know soon enough. One of the things I love is to make a woman scream, and then to stop her screaming. I assure you it is fascinating. There will be such a change in your face when I do what I intend to do to you. At first your face will be contorted with pain, but as you open your mouth for your second scream your lungs will collapse, and soon your face will go all grey and drawn like an old woman and your hair will drag. And as I open you up the greatest moment will be over.'

'Paul—'

'Hush.' He glanced at the clock. 'What time is Jeremy's father coming back?'

'Eight o'clock.'

'You said eight-thirty before. I suppose you are trying to keep me talking.' He frowned, smoothed back his sleek black hair. 'Well, I don't mind. I did not specially want to kill Jeremy's father, but he will be so surprised to see what I have done to Jeremy's mother that it will be a way to catch him unawares . . .'

The fireworks were at their peak. Having first refused to take any part in it, Ben was now enjoying the evening. Essie was at his side when he set off a rocket, and she jumped and gasped when it whooshed out of its bottle. Ross came across to them with a box of Roman candles.

'All well, Essie?'

'Lovely, thank ee, sur.'

Ross said: 'Could I leave you to set these off, Ben? It's time I went to pick up my wife, else she'll miss it all.'

'Is she not well?' Essie asked.

'Only a headache.' He handed the box to Ben, and turned to go. Then he saw a newcomer, someone who had just arrived within the periphery of the lights. Valentine. He was alone. Ross decided to speak with him, and changed his tack. Then he saw Betsy Maria Martin. 'Betsy.'

'Sur?'

'Could you walk down and fetch your mistress. She should be ready by now.'

'Er – yes, sur.' The maid turned to go.

Then Ross saw the disappointment in her face. This was a firework display such as she had never seen before and probably never would again. She couldn't bear to miss it.

'Betsy.'

'Ais, sur?'

'Don't bother. I'll fetch Lady Poldark myself.' A word with Valentine, and then he'd go.

Demelza's migraine had just returned.

Paul said: 'You want to keep me talking. Well, that is what I came for, to talk to you.'

'I . . . I asked what there was in your life that you – really liked.'

'Liked? *Liked? LIKED?* How can I like anything when I cannot *feel* anything! Everything that happens around me I see through a screen. If I used this knife to strip the clothes off you, if I stripped you naked – *Jeremy's mother naked!* – I should not feel anything – no lust, no embarrassment, no excitement. But when I cut your throat and see your blood spurting onto the carpet, then I shall have all the sensation there is in the world! You've no idea, Demelza. It is an engrossing excitement. Do you know what an orgasm is? Well, I shall have an orgasm.'

He smiled at her. 'This – it is like an addiction. It is such a *dominance*. The first time it happened – the time with the scissors – I was quite shocked, shaken. Rather afraid, very surprised – and it only happened because she tried to rob me while I was asleep. That was in a house in Plymouth Dock. But later I came to look back on it and think of it with the sort of pleasure life has never held for me before. And I began to think that all women are whores. After all, if the occasion arose, I might do it again. I asked myself – might I? Then I did. And I did. And I did.'

'I am your friend and neighbour,' Demelza said.

'No, you're Jeremy's mother. But still pretty enough to kill. To destroy. All women are built to be whores, are they not? Their naked shapes are full of disease. My sisters, my wife, my mother. If one cannot remove some of them from the earth, what is the purpose of having been born?'

It was a quarter after eight.

Demelza said: 'Paul why are you telling me this? You could not escape from a murder like you propose . . . Why do you not just go away and forget all you have told me? If I were to tell anyone, you could deny that you had said anything. There is no other person here to have heard it and to confirm what you say . . . But if you will go away I can promise to say naught of what you have told me

. . . In fact I can't believe what you have told me. It is too – too unreal. And don't forget you told me it was Philip Prideaux.'

She had said the wrong thing. 'Oh, but it *is* true. Everything I have told you is true. As you will be discovering for yourself in a few minutes now—'

'But why *tell* me—'

'Because life is so dull if one's achievements are kept secret. I want people to know about me. I am tired of pretending it is someone else—'

'But you tried – at the beginning you tried to put the blame on Philip Prideaux . . . Why should you do that if you want it for yourself—?'

'I was trying the idea out on you. I could see you didn't believe it. I could see that I couldn't escape. So it is giving me real pleasure in explaining to the victim what is going to happen to her and why I am taking pleasure in inflicting pain. Pain is the one reality. Everything else is unreal and tiresome and not worth enduring. You may say I am *inflicting* the pain, not suffering it. But that is just as good. It is all part of the one experience that I can believe in and relish—'

He stopped, listened. A light scratching.

'That cat?'

'He is not outside the front door now. He is . . . is outside the door of this room. Did you leave the front door open?'

Paul picked up the knife. 'If you scream I'll soon stop it.'

He went to the door and lifted the latch. Moses shot in. Paul stabbed at him, but the cat, with a feline sense of self-preservation, swerved his body at the last moment and howled as he reached the fire.

Outside the hall was dark. The only light in the parlour was from the fire and the one candle Demelza had been holding and had put unsteadily back on the table.

Knife poised, Paul kicked the door wide and peered out. The front door was ajar. A cloaked figure stood by the stairs. The knife glinted as Paul took a step into the hall. Then the other figure rushed at him.

Demelza clutched the table for support, her back straight. She was on the point of fainting. The noise in the black hall was tremendous. Furniture falling, hatstand clattering, curtains ripping, two men shouting at each other between grunts and gasps and the conflict of heavy bodies. She felt she must do something, if no more than take up the candle and carry it to the door. But she had not the strength, and if that fell or was pushed from her hands the darkness would be complete.

Yet someone was fighting Paul. Someone was risking his life. If Paul killed him then he would return to kill her. But it had not looked like Ross or anyone she knew.

But suppose it *was* Ross. She had to see. She moved an inch from the table and swayed. She clutched back at it for stability.

The fighting had stopped. A man stood at the door looking in. It was not Paul Kellow. It was Philip Prideaux. He was breathing heavily and one arm hung useless at his side. He had lost his cloak and there was thick blood on his shirt.

He said: 'Are you . . . ?'

Demelza said: 'Where is – where is Paul?'

'Just here. On the floor. I do not think he will – will trouble us for a while. I found a club. In the – the hatstand. I think – I think he has – has injured me.'

There was a cut on his face as well, but it looked more like a scratch than a knife wound.

He came a couple of steps into the room, stopped, peered behind him, then, satisfied, took another step.

He fumbled in his waistcoat pocket and took out his spectacles. They were splintered across and across. He threw them on the floor, where they slithered over to where the cat crouched. Moses spat at them.

'I'll not – need those again,' Philip said.

Then his knees gave way and he quietly, slowly, collapsed at Demelza's feet.

Chapter Four

The splendid fireworks display ended in panic. Ross had delayed only a further five minutes to speak to Valentine, but he was barely halfway home when he was met by Mrs Zacky Martin (who had left the display early to see for Zacky), in a complete lather of horror, to tell him that Lady Poldark was in deep trouble. Mrs Zacky had heard her crying out from the window. Mrs Zacky was sent hurrying back to the fireworks to fetch Dr Enys.

Ross rushed to the house and found it a shambles: Paul Kellow senseless in the hall, Philip Prideaux senseless in the parlour, Demelza clinging to the front door trying to steady herself and weeping like a hurt child.

Into his waiting arms she poured out an incoherent account of protest that barely bore belief. Ross picked her up and carried her into the library, where there was a settee, laid her on it; then, having assured himself that she was not physically injured, and urged violently by her, left her there, went back into the slippery main house and tried to succour Philip and to staunch the flow of blood from his arm.

On this came Dwight, followed shortly by his medical bag brought by Bone, who had run to Killewarren for it. The hall of Nampara was like a charnel house. Eventually, after having eleven stitches in his arm, Philip was half-carried upstairs to Jeremy's old room and was given brandy and hot milk and told to rest. Paul was only just stirring, and Dwight thought his skull might be fractured. He could not at once be taken away and locked up, but Constable Purdy had been found and waited by the side of the young man.

Philip gasped out an explanation to Ross. For some time he had suspected Paul, and had tried to follow him when he had the opportunity. Staying with Geoffrey Charles, he had come with him

424

to the bonfire, and there had seen Paul and had noticed his built-up shoes. When Paul left the fire he had followed him, but had missed him in the dark and thought he had gone home to Fernmore. Only when he reached Fernmore and had not been able to find him had he then gone on to Nampara 'just to check'.

'In time,' said Demelza, 'to save my life.'

Ross ground his teeth. 'God! I was halfway home when I met Mrs Zacky!'

''Tis my own fault if anyone's. I had partly guessed about Paul.'

'*Did* you? Why did you not *tell* me!!!'

'I had so little to go on. Only a few tiny things . . . and – and my instinct, which – which—'

'Which so often *can* be relied on.'

'I didn't *want* to suspect Paul!'

Demelza's wrists and ankles were aching. It was 'a sickness of the bone'. It could not be got rid of by vomiting. Paul. Jeremy's friend. She had never truly liked him. But not this. Not this. Not *this*. She had tried to disbelieve her own suspicions. Not this. Not this. Only a little while ago he had looked at her with his expressionless face and intrusive eyes, and she had been in the direst danger. A sharp knife on her throat, and instead of lying on this settee – and later in her own bed, unharmed, with Ross beside her – she would instead be a corpse, her blood mingling with that of Captain Prideaux in the hall.

Many people came to see her in the library. All expressed shock; all, even Bella and Henry, were gently ushered out. Geoffrey Charles had taken general charge. Ben Carter and two others tried to put the damaged furniture to rights and to mop up the blood. But it was impossible to hide all the horrors.

The knife of a madman.

Later, hours later, Demelza said: 'Ross.'

'What?'

'Why are you shivering?'

'What? I'm not!'

'Yes, you are. Or you were in your sleep.'

'I haven't been to sleep. But, well, yes, in the halfway between waking and sleeping—'

'What?'

'It came to my mind to see exactly what you had gone through. The scene came up in front of me as if in an engraving, you on one side of the table and he on the other – talking to each other, he pouring out the poison of his twisted mind and – and me at that firework display. Why couldn't I *sense* there was danger?'

'Because,' Demelza said, 'we have lived together here all these years, and there never has been any danger like this before.'

He was silent for a while. 'When I first reached you, when I first gathered you up, you screamed at me.'

Did I? Yes, I suppose. I was hysterical.'

'Of course. Now in reflection . . . you screamed at me that I should have come to you instead of talking to Valentine.'

'I tell you. I was hysterical. You muttered something about Valentine. I did not know what I was saying.'

'So I want to explain more clearly now. As I was about to leave, Geoffrey Charles told me that Valentine had just stolen his small son, Georgie, back from his mother. I went to ask him what his scatterbrained plan was. I swear I was not with him three minutes!'

'Well, in the end the milk was not spilt.'

'But I *have* to cry over it. D'you know, when I walked over to speak to him I told Betsy Martin to go down to tell you I was coming. *Then* . . . then I looked at the – at the sheer enjoyment on her face and realized I was asking her to miss the best of the spectacle, something she might never see again, so I *stopped* her, told her not to bother. *Not to bother!* Great God, I might have been condemning you to death!'

'I said before – how could you have known?'

Ross put his hand on hers. 'You asked me what I was shuddering about. *That* was what I was shuddering about!'

'You know,' Demelza said, 'he *had* a twisted mind, Paul did. It was *terrifying*! Is there something that can go wrong with a compass on a ship? Is it a magnetic field or something? Dwight was trying to explain to me once. Well, twas as if Paul's compass has gone wrong. He drives his ship with a compass that's so far off true that he can kill people and yet behave soon after as if nothing unnatural has happened. None of his family suspected anything.'

'Mrs Kellow did, I believe. From what Constable Purdy told me of his interview when he told them at Fernmore. Mrs Kellow confessed that she had known Agneta Treneglos was sheltering in the outhouse the night before she died. And Mr Kellow was, he says, terrified by him.'

'And Daisy?'

'Ah, Daisy, no. She refuses to believe it even now. She says it is all made-up falsehoods. She became hysterical.'

Demelza gave a shiver of discomfort that almost got out of hand. 'It may be I shall have to stand up in a court of law?'

'It depends what other evidence there is. And also how he behaves when they question him. He may decide to make a full confession. In a lot of murderers' minds there is a mountain of pride and conceit. They like others to hear of their misdeeds. He was very open with you.'

'Yes, Ross, but then he did not expect my evidence to go very far!'

'Nor you! God's my life, I am trying not to believe it—!'

After a minute Demelza said: 'Well, this clears Valentine.' She sighed, and tried not to let it become a sob. 'He will be relieved. At least, I think so. Unless he sort of *enjoyed* being suspected. At times he too seems to be steering by a false compass.'

For a few moments it had helped them both to think of something else, at least obliquely away from the intense horror of Paul Kellow. It was now well after two a.m., and in the pitch darkness of the early winter morning they needed each other's presence as if there was something new-found in it. A woman's hand and a man's hand were clasped, a warm breath occasionally moved between them like a communion of two people whose lives might well have been ended six hours ago by the intrusion of a friend who had turned into a monster. Their lives over the last thirty years had not infrequently been in danger, but it had in most cases been a perceived danger, an expected danger, a danger that had been partly anticipated, planned for. This had come so unawares. Demelza had stood on the edge of a cliff and, by the merciful intervention of a relative stranger, she had been pulled back.

But there was no sleep in either of them. Demelza wanted to tell Ross in more detail of her conversation with Paul, in which he seemed to be trying to explain to her his reasons – or unreasons – for killing these women. Self-justification was at the root of it all – and a sort of exploding egoism, as if there were an overwhelming *need* to do these evil things – to prove something, to himself and to the world at large. But she knew if she once began to talk about it to Ross there in the dark she would never be able to stop until she dissolved into a weeping creature shaking from head to foot in a paroxysm she would later come to despise.

They both dozed round about four, and an hour later they were wakened by the cocks crowing. So well attuned were they to this sound that normally it would not have disturbed them.

Bella and Harry were late for breakfast: it turned out last night that Harry had singed a side of his hair on an untrustworthy firework, and before breakfast Bella had taken him into the scullery and clipped away the hair from around his right ear to match what the firework had done to shorten his hair on the left.

Henry explained: 'Bella says I have to match.'

'You were in luck not to burn your ear,' said Demelza, clutching gratefully, unbelievingly, at normality. 'What was it, a cracker?'

'No, a Roman candle. I was poking at it to see why it didn't go off.'

'But it did.'

Harry beamed brightly and nodded. 'That's right.'

'And where was Ellen while this was going on?' Ellen Proctor was paid to keep Henry out of mischief.

Henry waved a hand. 'Oh, talking to Saul Grieves or Fred Smith or Marcus Daniel.'

Demelza glanced at Ross, who smiled and shrugged. 'I said she was too good-looking for a nursemaid.'

So conversation was pleasantly evasive until Harry touched on the tragedy of last night. He was chiefly admiring of the viciousness of the fight.

'A club against a knife! My dear life, I wish I'd seen it. *Jag – whoom. Jag – whoom! Whee – whoo – whee – whoo.* I used to take that on the beach when I was a tacker and throw it for Frobisher. Captain Prideaux must have caught Paul *bonk* on his napper. Where is Captain Prideaux now? I thought he was in Jeremy's room.'

'He was, but your Uncle Dwight wanted to dress his arm properly, so he left here this morning, about one. I must go and call on him, try to thank him.'

Demelza said: 'He was like – like an angel sprung out of the ground.'

The morning passed in a troubled whirl which dealt unrelentingly with the subject they were doing their utmost to put in the back of their minds. Dinner was late and neither Ross nor Demelza had any appetite.

After dinner, when Bella was able to get them alone for a few minutes, she said diffidently: 'I did not have a chance last night to tell you, but the post came about four and I had a letter from

Christopher. Will you want to hear now or would it be easier perhaps this evening when we have more time?'

'Please tell us now,' said Demelza.

'Of course,' said Ross, 'if it is good news.'

'Well, yes, I think so . . .'. Bella felt in her blouse and took out a letter, which already looked as if it had been read many times. Bella's hand was not quite steady and bits of sealing wax fell on the table. 'You won't want to hear everything he has said.'

Demelza said: 'You choose, my dear.'

Bella unfolded the letter, scanned the early part, then said: 'I have been offered a part in *Romeo and Juliet* – but first, before we build too much, it has to be said this depends on an interview. I have to be seen by Mr Frederick McArdle. If he approves of me I am to be offered the part of cover to Mrs Charlotte Bancroft, who is playing Juliet . . .'

After a moment Demelza said: 'Cover?'

'Yes. If Mrs Bancroft were to be taken ill or some other misfortune were to befall her, I should be called upon to take her place. That means I shall have to know her part off word for word and I shall have the opportunity of seeing her act and learning from it. Also . . .'

They waited. She turned over a page of the letter. 'I am also invited – if I pass the test – to play a small speaking part in the play. I am asked to play Balthasar, Romeo's servant, so though the speaking part is quite small I shall be standing beside Romeo on and off all through!'

A pause. Ross said: 'It sounds a good invitation to me. But is not Romeo's servant a man?'

'Yes,' said Bella, and coloured a little. 'You see – as Christopher explains – apart from Juliet, there is *no other speaking part* for a young woman in the whole play. The Nurse and Lady Capulet, and Lady Montague, they are parts for older women. There will be plenty of opportunity in some of the scenes where the Capulets and the Montagues come on to have a young woman about, but none of them have to speak. Of course . . . it is not uncommon for women to play men's parts.'

Demelza said, 'It sounds wonderful. But who is this Mr Frederick McArdle?'

'The producer. It depends on his approval, but Christopher is optimistic that I shall be accepted.'

Ross said: 'Bella will have to study Juliet's part very closely, just *in case*. At the same time she will be acting as Romeo's servant, who is a man. Do you think you can do that, Bella?'

'Oh, yes!'

'When is this to be? Does he say?'

'The date is provisional. If . . .' She stopped.

'If?'

'If it is early December, as he thinks, it would be wonderful if you could both come and see the first performance. Is that being selfish? Will you be able to rid yourselves of this – of the remains of this – of what happened last night in time?'

A pause. 'I would very much like to,' said Demelza. 'I much regret not being to see *The Barber of Seville*.'

Ross said: 'We shall most certainly come.'

Demelza stretched herself and sighed. 'At least it is pleasant to talk of this. Inside – inside I still feel desperate sick.'

Paul Kellow appeared before the magistrates and was remanded in custody until the fifteenth of January. Until then he would be kept at Bodmin prison.

'I do not think he will give any trouble,' Dwight said to Ross. 'I saw him, as you know, before he was taken away. He was quite composed and detached. Of course he must still have been feeling dazed from the blow Prideaux gave him. But he seemed to want to engage me in a discussion as to why the tuberculous bacillus was more prevalent among women than men. I had to tell him that there are no statistics to prove such a theory; but he went on to argue that it was almost certainly because women's bodies were more easily diseased and ready for corruption. He appeared about to imply that killing a few of them was contributing to the wellbeing of society, but Purdy came in and he broke off.'

Ross said: 'What has been his wife's reaction? I have heard nothing of her.'

'I haven't seen her. I know she will not visit him.'

'Do you think she had any suspicion?'

'I doubt it. She may have felt there was something wrong but, like his mother, chose to ignore it. Such men are very clever.'

Ross said: 'Can a man hang if he is so obviously out of his mind?'

'I think so. But when his trial comes up I shall hope to speak for him. Would you object?'

'I'm not sure. On what grounds?'

'He had a blow on the head long years ago. Probably not nearly so severe as the one he received from Prideaux last night. But this he took full on the frontal bone. The one he received on a previous occasion was on the occipital bone, to the left, at the base of the skull, and though there was less obvious damage, this is a much more vulnerable area and more likely to result in a permanent injury.'

'You saw him then?'

'You may or may not know that Stephen Carrington and Paul, before Stephen married Clowance, went off on some rash adventure to Plymouth, buying and selling some boat they had picked up. While in Plymouth Dock they were pressed for the navy, but they made a fight of it and got away. When they returned home they both needed treatment. They came to me.'

'I don't remember anything,' Ross said. 'I expect Clowance would know.'

'Since then, once or twice a year, I suppose, Paul has come to me complaining of headaches, and I've done what I could to help. It's quite possible that the injury he suffered then has had some long-term effect on his behaviour.'

'And you think that if you testify to this, that he may escape the death penalty?'

'No,' Dwight said, 'but there is just a chance. And I think it might be worth making the plea.'

They stared at each other, envisioning it.

Ross said: 'I am not sure if the alternative for him is not even worse. I think if I had to make the choice I should choose the rope.'

They walked on a few paces. 'And how is Philip Prideaux?'

'Oh, he'll keep his arm. But it was a near thing because of the severed artery. You probably saved his life with that tourniquet.'

'Is he back at Trenwith?'

'I shall see him again tonight. But it was a clean cut; there should be no infection.'

'There was no infection,' said Ross grimly, 'for all those women Paul killed.'

*

At the same time Caroline saw Demelza to offer her appalled sympathy. She was almost equally appalled at Demelza's suggestion that they should go together to visit the Kellows.

She said: 'You astonish me, my dear. Although you attend church scarcely more often than I do, you exhibit these Christian impulses which most Christians would hastily repress and turn away from.'

Demelza said: 'I don't know about a Christian impulse. Maybe I am wrong, but there are many folk involved in Paul's misdoings without blame to themselves. Three of them are almost our nearest neighbours. My mind shakes at the thought of what they must be feeling now. Tis beyond imagining that any of them should know anything about this side of Paul's character, and it seemed to me that it would be proper to offer them some comfort.'

Caroline, out of friendship, raised no further objection. In her eyes Paul was a murderer and she questioned whether the family who bred him could avoid all blame. What could a narrowly escaped victim have to say to the mother of such a man?

In the end she might have considered herself proved right, for the visit was not a success. Mrs Kellow was weeping by the fire. Mr Kellow sat at the table drinking brandy out of a nearly empty bottle and mopping his un-wigged head as he constantly broke into a sweat. He had little to say, but Caroline suspected he was trying to unload some of Paul's guilt onto society in general and anyone who called here could only have come to gloat. Daisy had got over her hysteria. Someone must have talked soberly to her and convinced her that there was no way of escaping the grim reality. So now she preferred not to speak of it. The shock had temporarily checked her cough, and she walked about while talking to them with a sort of false gaiety, like a party hostess welcoming unwelcome friends.

Realizing that Caroline had been right, and blaming herself for the ill-judgement, Demelza was about to make an excuse to leave when she was halted by the arrival of Valentine Warleggan and David Lake. They were, they said, on the way to Nampara but had stopped to console Daisy. Valentine, for once, had felt, like Demelza, that it was neighbourly to sympathize with the innocent partners in this outrageous tragedy.

So conversation was maintained for about fifteen minutes more. They tried to discuss the fireworks, Clowance's wedding, the discovery of a small lode of tin in the new shaft at Wheal Elizabeth, Bella's adventure in France, Essie's pregnancy and Ben's outspoken wish for a son. But this was interspersed with little icy silences, which hung in the air like stalactites until they were broken.

The two young men had come on horses, and they walked back with the ladies, trailing their reins, to Nampara.

Demelza said to Valentine: 'You did not bring Georgie?'

'I imagined this wouldn't be quite the fit occasion for childish prattle.' He looked at her assessingly. 'You must have suffered a devilish wicked shock last night.'

'Me? Yes, I did. It will take time—'

'I'm not surprised. What surprises me is that you are about today as if – as if . . .'

'As if nothing had happened?' As he seemed genuinely interested, she went on: 'I am trying to behave as normal in order to try – to try to get it out of my mind. Of course, I can't; but movement, the ordinary business of living—'

'All the same,' he said, 'most women would be in bed for at least two days with the emotional shock.' He screwed up his eyes in a scowl. 'I feel I should have known something was coming, tried to warn somebody – I don't quite know who.'

'You? Why?'

'I've seen a lot of Paul and Daisy this last month. Paul and I have talked together. Things he said. And these last two weeks he has grown ever more quirky.'

'Did he threaten anyone?'

'No. Oh, no. It was just his attitude, particularly towards women . . .'

'Did he speak about me?'

'No.'

'What could you have done?'

'Oh, I know, I know. But Philip did.'

'Only when Paul had committted himself.'

Valentine's frown did not lift. 'Philip, by great good fortune, was close by. I was – close by all the time. Maybe I should have dropped a hint to Ross.'

Nestor whinnied and shook his reins.

'Your horse disagrees,' said Demelza. 'Who is looking after Georgie while you are out'

'Oh, Polly Stevens. Odgers that was.'

'Is he safe from Butto?'

'Butto adores him. Anyway I now employ two men to see he behaves.'

'Is he happy?'

'Who? Butto?'

'You know who I mean.'

'Georgie? Georgie wants his Mama.'

'Does that surprise you?'

Valentine glanced at Demelza walking beside him. 'By God, I'm glad that madman did not get his knife in you. It's a wonder you're not a jelly.'

Demelza said: 'I was at the time.'

Behind them David Lake and Caroline Enys were in conversation. Caroline did not much enjoy walking, being wedded to her horse for all but the shortest journeys. She often complained to Ross that his wife did not know how to conserve her energies.

Valentine said: 'Selina came over this morning, with that harridan of a cousin, Henrietta. I would not let them in. Fortunately little Georgie was out with David. But sometimes he talks and says he wants his Mama.'

'You turned her away?'

'No, I gave her the option to come in – and stay. To return to me, in fact. To occupy her proper place as my wife, in my house, with our child. There is nothing to stop her. Paul has conveniently confessed – or almost confessed – to the murder of Agneta. Selina pretended to suspect me – I doubt if it was ever more than an excuse. I may not tread the primrose path, but I am not the killing kind. Well, that is out of the way now.'

'So she left?'

'With her dragon she left.'

'Did you know your father was away when you seized Georgie?'

'Of course. And pray, dear Cousin, pretty Cousin, can you refrain from referring to Smelter George as my father.'

Demelza thought for a moment. 'Is it not the accepted view? You have his name. Most of the world looks on you as his son.'

'Ah, yes. Ah, yes. But this is in private, between friends.'

Demelza wondered whether on this subject it was appropriate to claim to be able to wipe out all the passions, all the jealousies of thirty years and claim that she and Valentine should share such a secret as being 'between friends'.

It was the longest personal conversation they had had together in some years, and the latent sarcasm usual in his voice was absent. Nor had he ever spoken so forthrightly as when he said how glad he was she had survived the attack. It was her nature to be warm in her relationships, and she wondered if they might move to a better understanding. Perhaps the next time he came to Nampara she would welcome him not as a challenge to the nucleus of her family, but as a friendly addition.

As they reached the house she saw two strange horses tethered and realized that she had forgotten this was the Thursday when Cuby and Noelle came for their regular visit.

It was clear by the time they went in that Mrs Gimlett had given young Mrs Poldark a hasty, stammered account of what had been happening on Bonfire Night. Cuby put her arm round her mother-in-law.

'My dear, it is such a horror! My dear, do say, are you – have you recovered?'

While she cuddled Noelle Demelza gave Cuby some more of the general details, making of Noelle's presence an excuse not to say more. Valentine and David had refused an invitation to go in, so presently they clopped off into the gathering windy dusk. But to replace them Ross and Dwight arrived. Conversation threaded its way between the grim and the normal. Presently Caroline and Dwight left and Henry arrived to greet Noelle with a boyish grin, and Bella came in from the library, where she had been trying out her scales.

Supper came and went. Reluctantly – for it seemed so trivial – Cuby brought them up to date with affairs on the Trevanion front. She ended by saying how helpful Philip Prideaux had been. Was he still in the neighbourhood?

'We saw him this morning,' Demelza said. 'Just to try to thank him.'

'Is it – a grievous wound?'

'He does not behave as if it was,' Ross said. 'When we got to Trenwith he had already come back from Trevaunance, where there is some excitement over Wheal Elizabeth.'

'Excitement? Let's hope it is a pleasant excitement for a change.'

'They have found a pretty lode of tin in Sunshine shaft – which is one new-digged from an old working. They're tunnelling and stoping now; there's a surprising amount of water, which is a good sign, though the engine has been ill placed to work it. We shall see.'

'We might all go over in the morning,' Demelza suggested, Ross's surprise.

In the week that Cuby and Noelle stayed life in the village strained itself to return to normality. The Poldarks at Nampara entertained the Poldarks of Trenwith, including Philip, who contrived to avoid Demelza's suggestions of invalidism by riding about as normal with his arm in a sling. Dwight and Caroline had all of them to sup. They visited the mine twice, renewed acquaintance with Georgie Warleggan, who seemed to be a gregarious child, also prospected Butto's den and watched him walking arm in arm with Valentine and smoking a cigar like an old club man.

Mid-November settled in fine, not such a St Martin's summer as the previous year, but the scant daylight had its fair share of sun, and nights were not cold. There was a plague of late flies, but these were sporadically killed by Henry, who was at the age to massacre, and the rest were for the most part ignored. The sour sad thought of the Kellows at Fernmore was also something to be avoided. The sick feeling in Demelza's solar plexus was gradually working its way out.

On the day before she left for her new small house near Bodmin, Cuby and Demelza galloped along the beach as far as the Holy Well and there dismounted, to sit and talk on the smooth dry rocks just above high watermark while their horses recovered their wind. Over these years of bereavement the women had come to know and understand each other. Noelle had been a common preoccupation and still was a constant subject for discussion and interest. But they did not talk about her today.

After some speculation about the strange malign insanity of Paul Kellow and Demelza's close personal escape, she asked Cuby when she had first met Philip Prideaux.

'It was soon after Waterloo. A lady called the Hon. Mrs Falkirk invited me to a party which was supposed to console the new widows of the war. I would have refused – I wanted only to bury my head and weep – but she had known Jeremy and me in Brussels, and I felt a sort of – of duty. So I went. And Captain Prideaux was there. He was – racked with nerves, wanted to leave early, but I persuaded him to stay by talking to him of Cornwall. So when he came back to Cornwall about three years ago and we met again we became casually friendly.'

Demelza watched a gull standing beside a pool and preening its wings in the elderly sunlight.

'All my life now I shall feel in debt to him. But it is not because of that in any manner at all that prompts me to ask you if you – if you like him?'

'Like him? Most assuredly. During my brother's bankruptcy he has been a real friend to me – to us all.'

The gull cocked a suspicious eye at the tethered horses and waddled off.

Demelza stared out at the sea.

'D'you know – have you noticed how beautiful a swell is when it is moving into the shore on a great beach like this? Often I watch it from the house. The surface of the sea is quite unbroken, and it seems to move more slowly than the wave under it. There's a sort of back-turning of the surface, you see, which makes a great camel-shaped ridge far out and stretches itself smaller and sharper as it comes in, until the fine edge can stand no more and bursts into a lovely white froth of spray.'

'I often watched it at Caerhays,' Cuby said, 'though it is never so fine on the south coast.' She picked up a handful of fine sand and let it trickle through her fingers. 'Do you not like him?'

'Philip? Oh yes. *Very* much.'

'Well, it seems Clowance is very happy with Lord Edward. She certainly deserves better than Stephen Carrington!'

Demelza persevered. 'Forgive me, tis not – it is not proper that I should ask this. But you will understand that I ask it out of love.'

Cuby's dark-fringed hazel eyes were narrowed in the sun. 'You mean, am I – more than fond of Philip? It – it could be, were circumstances different.'

Neither spoke for a while. Cuby said: 'I was remembering only the other day the fifteenth of June five years ago. We were in Brussels, Jeremy and I, spending the evening together. Jeremy had returned the tickets he had been able to get for the Duchess of Richmond's Ball, and we supped quite alone in our favourite little restaurant on the corner of the square. Although it was an anxious

time, it was also a happy one – happy for us because we were so –
so wrapped up in each other. We discussed the coming baby,
although I was then only four months forward, and I said I would
prefer a girl, and he said, well, if we have to wait till Christmas
perhaps we shall call her Noelle. It was all light-hearted, but all
heavy-hearted too. He – he tried to reassure me by telling me how
inaccurate the British musket was. It was a wonder, he said, how it
ever shot anyone. Then we went back to our apartment – you
remember it? – and lay together in the dusk, still talking, still
loving, until there was a tap on the door, and it was Jeremy's orderly
with a message from Sir William de Lancey, the Quartermaster
General, ordering Jeremy to rejoin his company and to leave at
once for – for I think it was Braine-le-Comte. That night. That
moment.

'I helped him pack and dress. There were lonely horns blowing
somewhere outside, and the shrill fifes. We talked as he got ready
to leave. We had planned a little supper party for the following
week. He promised – he promised to be back in good time for that,
"after our little skirmish". My heart was full. But even so, I did not
believe I should never see him again. I *did not*! *I did not*! It was
against nature! It was against our youth! Oh, we should breathe
such a happy sigh of relief when he came home! It had been quite
a fight, but . . . it was all over now. Now we could go on with our
supper party, happy to be together again, happy it was all over, at
least for the time being. When – when he left I put my head against
the door and wept. But it was with tears of sadness and anxiety, not
the deadly tears of bereavement. I knew in my *soul* he would come
back. But he never did. He never, never, never did . . . I still recall
the press of his lips when he left that night . . .'

Demelza had put her hand to her heart. 'Stop. You've said
enough. I should not have asked you—'

Cuby smiled at her through her tears. 'Perhaps you should.
Perhaps, as usual, you see more than most of us. Perhaps you see
that I am lonely. Noelle is a comfort and a joy, yet it seems to me
as she nears her fifth birthday I am becoming more lonely, not less.
At first it is like – like living with low horizons, but each year the
horizons get wider, and now life seems to stretch ahead in a great
empty desert. Do I sound sorry for myself?'

Demelza brushed her hand across her eyes. 'At least tis good that
we can talk.'

'Strangely,' Cuby said, 'life with Jeremy has quite spoiled me for life as a Trevanion. I am fond enough of my mother; I love Clemency; I tolerate John and Augustus. But I am no longer part of the family. I am an alien to their standards. It may do me good to marry again, if the opportunity comes my way, but I do not think it will.'

'It could,' Demelza said.

'To Philip? He had eyes for no one but Clowance. Still has!'

'He could be lonely too.'

'Is loneliness a good foundation for a marriage?'

'Sometimes; affection can grow. Forgive me, I have said enough. Far too much, I reckon. You are right – loneliness is not enough, especially for one so young as you are. I must take care of my own garden.'

Cuby patted her mother-in-law's hand. 'He is quite the hero in this week's paper. There will be many pretty girls waiting to swoon at his touch.'

'I have seen him looking at you,' said Demelza.

'So he should,' said Cuby, 'but he sees, as everyone sees, a sad widow with an orphan child.'

'You must not think of yourself like that. If you think like that you will look like that. You say you are not a Trevanion any more. Well, you are a Poldark.'

'I am still sister of a notorious bankrupt and widow of a brave but penniless soldier. Come, my dearest mother-in-law, let us remount and gallop home. Perhaps that will rid us of our sick fancies.'

Chapter Five

Christopher arrived to collect Bella on the twentieth of November, and they started for London on the following day.

Clowance had sent a warm invitation to Bella to stay in Lansdowne House. Left to make her own decision, Bella had tactfully and affectionately and sweetly refused. She said eventually to Demelza: 'Lord Edward has given me this chance. I cannot, simply *cannot*, accept anything more. I must, must stand on my own feet.' To Demelza's reply that 'only the jealous will care', she had replied: 'I *know*. I cannot help it, Mama. I am so sorry.'

Christopher had said that without some sort of marriage ceremony, which at present Bella had ruled out, they could not occupy together the new house in Green Lane; so, feeling that all their earlier promises to each other were being held in abeyance, he had let the house furnished on a lease of six months. (He was lying. He had sold the house because he needed the money for something else.)

In the end, after thinking of and discarding Mrs Parkin's lodgings in George Street, she had decided to go back to stay with Mrs Pelham. A long and affectionate and apologetic letter had done the trick, and Mrs Pelham, privately glad of the renewed companionship, had agreed to take her for the next two months.

So all was as before. Or almost as before. She went to see Frederick McArdle, who was a black-browed, hard-faced Ulsterman with big hands and clumsy movements, and a high reputation in the theatre.

She also met Joseph Glossop, the present owner of the theatre, who was stout and astute and scrupulously polite. His politeness did not prevent him from eyeing Bella with professional interest, and he was present when McArdle asked her to recite a speech from

440

Act 3 Scene 2, where Juliet hears that Romeo has killed Tybalt, beginning 'O serpent heart hid with a flow'ring face! Did ever dragon keep so fair a cave?'

Helpfully Mr Glossop offered her the pre-marked text, but Bella for two weeks had been soaking herself in Mrs Hemple's school copy and was able to speak it unprompted. When it came to an end, she stopped. 'It is the nurse now. Do you wish me to go on?'

After a brief pause, each man waiting for the other, McArdle said: 'Nay, nay, that is well said. Now, please, just a little passage from Balthasar. "I brought my master news of Juliet's death." Act 5 Scene 3. Just a few lines!'

Bella obliged, slightly roughening her voice to speak it.

'Ver-ry satisfactory. We will be starting with a read through next Monday. I will see Captain Havergal is in-formed.'

When Christopher came to Hatton Garden that evening he said that McArdle had sent a special message by his grandson to the Rothschild Bank saying that he would be prepared to engage Miss Poldark as a standby to Charlotte Bancroft and to take the part of Balthasar in the play itself. For this they were prepared to pay £4 a performance, increased to £15 if by any chance she had to go on for Mrs Bancroft.

Christopher said: 'You have taken the first step, my sweetheart. It is not a king's ransom, but it is a start.'

'I can't wait for it to begin,' Bella said. 'Will you come to the first performance, Aunt?'

'I think so,' said Mrs Pelham. 'I have never been to the Coburg. It is quite respectable, Christopher?'

'Oh, indeed. More so than some of the fashionable theatres, which are overrun with prostitutes. The neighbourhood is poor, but it is being reclaimed by the Waterloo Bridge Company. Clearly it is to their interest to develop the area, as it collects the tolls.'

'One thing I noticed as I came out,' Bella said. 'There was a poster advertising coming productions, and one was called *Two Lovers of Verona*. That is in December too.'

'That is our production,' he said. 'Owing to an obsolete law, only two theatres are allowed to put on Shakespeare: Drury Lane and Covent Garden. They therefore have the pick of actors and possible productions. There is a strong and bitter feeling among all the other theatres – the new ones like the Royal Coburg and the Surrey and the Olympic and the old ones like the Haymarket and King's –

441

that this law cannot last much longer. It will be overthrown by public feeling; but until that happens these other theatres have to find a way round the Patent Law. So sometimes they evade it by setting a Shakespeare play to music, sometimes by altering the title and a few lines here and there.'

'It did not say *Two Lovers of Verona* was by Shakespeare.'

'It will say so on the programme. Everybody knows the truth.'

'You have been to this theatre, Christopher?' Mrs Pelham asked.

'Oh, yes. I took Bella twice last year. Edward Fitzmaurice, as you know, is a patron.'

'I thought it was a lovely theatre,' Bella said. 'Much more modern than – some of the others.'

She had been going to say 'than the theatre in Rouen', but thought it better not to refer to the Théâtre Jeanne d'Arc in the present company.

'I go seldom to the theatre these days,' Mrs Pelham said. 'There is so very little put on but spectacles and performing animals and battle scenes. I don't think it is because I am old that I feel there is this change for the worse.'

'The public is changing,' Christopher said. 'The two Patent Theatres are now so big that they must appeal to a huge audience nightly. Many of the new middle classes don't have much taste but they have the money, and there are not enough of the old aristocracy to fill the great theatres without them. That is why Edward Fitzmaurice and those like him are helping the smaller theatres by putting money into them. A lot of the stuff now on at the Coburg and elsewhere is melodrama – trivial rubbish, but they are trying hard to improve. Glossop has poached McArdle from Drury Lane for this production and probably will entice one or two more of his actors from the patent theatres.'

'One thing, Christopher,' Bella said. 'You must teach me to walk.'

'Walk?'

'Like a man. And sit like one. Have the – the mannerisms of one. After all, we have two good weeks.'

'Oh, gladly,' said Christopher. 'You are a quick mimic.'

'I suppose it is in the tradition,' said Mrs Pelham. 'The best tradition. But it seems all a trifle improper to me.'

*

George said: 'Well, I cannot accept this situation. Though I hold you largely to blame for the dilemmas in which you find yourself. You should have taken better care of the child!'

'How was it possible?' Selina burst out. 'I only have two servants! I can only afford two on what you pay me! Henrietta took him for a walk and they were in waiting!'

'Have you been to Place since then?'

'Of course! At first I did not know what had happened. Then I rode over with Henrietta on the Thursday morning. He would not let me see him!'

'Valentine would not let you see young George? What did he say?'

'That if I came back to Place and resumed my place as a wife I could resume my place as a mother!'

'Why don't you?' Harriet asked.

Selina gave her a look of pure hatred. 'Would you?'

Harriet made a gesture. 'It's a point. You are not me. I did not marry the man. Presumably when you did you were in love with him. Or what passes for love. You found him attractive. He went against his father's strongest wishes in marrying you. So at one time you cared for each other—'

'Wait a minute,' George said, in annoyance, 'it is no good quarrelling. This matter should be viewed all round. Did you go into Place House?'

'As far as the front rooms.'

'How did you find them? Was there – any sign of debauchery – of wild living?'

'You could hardly expect it, could you! This was eleven o'clock in the morning.'

'Were there any other women about?'

'Not that I saw. Perhaps they were still sleeping off the night's drinking.'

'Who is looking after Georgie?'

'A local woman, Polly Stevens.'

'Do you know her?'

'I know her as someone in the village. Valentine informed me that she had been *his* nurse when he was a child.'

'Oh, Polly Stevens. Odgers that was. My wife – my first wife engaged her. So she is a – well, a respectable woman, reasonably reliable. You will understand, Selina, if this comes to a court case, the defence will argue that a father has the prior right to his son. If it could be proved that his father's habit of life was disorderly, that he consorted with harlots, that the house was not fit for a child to be brought up in, then custody might just be granted to the wife. But an ecclesiastical court will take a very lenient view of a man who is being deprived of help and companionship because his wife has left him and will not return. There might well be a counter-petition brought by Valentine for the restitution of his conjugal rights.'

Selina looked more cat-like than ever, and her breast rose and fell. 'That would be utterly disgraceful!'

'Disgraceful it might seem to you. But the law sees the situation with dispassionate eyes.'

After a pause Harriet yawned. 'Go back to him. He did not keep a disorderly house when you were there.'

'Be quiet, Harriet,' George snapped. 'Selina has put herself under my protection. I am trying to see all round it. By stealing his son back Valentine holds the advantage.'

George's statement had pleased Selina. She said: 'We could take him back in the same way.'

George looked up. 'I am not prepared to break the law. I never have on my own behalf, so . . .'

'You will not do it on mine! But *is* it breaking the law? This is a family dispute!'

'You might try financial pressure,' suggested Harriet.

'What makes you say that?' George demanded.

'Because, my dear, it is your custom to see everything through a distorting spyglass – the glass having a mercantile handle and a financial frame.'

This took a little digesting. George was not sure whether his wife meant to be amusing or offensive, but he was not pleased at Harriet's outspokenness in front of another woman.

However, Selina cared nothing for the metaphor. 'Does he owe you money?'

'No.' George had clammed up.

'Philip was telling me that Valentine has made a fortunate strike in his mine,' Harriet said, 'but don't you own that mine?'

'The Bank does. A share of it. As you know.'

'What is the share?'

'Why do you not ask Philip? He knows everything.'

444

'Not everything. Nor have I ever asked him about the composition of this new company. He simply remarked about the find of – of tin, is it – as a reason for his late arrival yesterday.'

'As a matter of fact,' George said, 'Warleggan's Bank owns forty-nine per cent of the shares in Wheal Elizabeth.'

'So,' Selina said, 'you could threaten, if he does not give up Georgie, that you could close the mine.'

George said carefully: 'I have not yet – the Bank has not yet received a report from Trebethick, the mine manager. Prideaux is an amateur, a figurehead put there for a purpose. I would need a full evaluation before even threatening to cut down a promising venture.'

Harriet got up. 'I must go and see to the hounds. My advice to you, Selina, is to return to Valentine. Once you are in the house there could be really little difficulty in leaving again with Georgie under your arm when the opportunity arises.'

Letter from Isabella-Rose Poldark.

Dearest Papa and Mama,

Well, here I am, comfortably settled down in Hatton Garden, daily travelling across the River Thames at Waterloo Bridge and attending at the Royal Coburg Theatre. Incidentally, I asked Mr Glossop how the theatre came by its name, and he told me it is under the patronage of His Serene Highness Prince Leopold of Saxe-Coburg, the husband of our English Princess Charlotte of Wales, who would have been heir to the throne had she lived. I do not think from what has been said that either Prince or Princess went out of their way to make a lot of their patronage, but it does provide a good name for a theatre, and the use of the word 'Royal' gives it special prestige.

The casting is now complete and is as follows:

Me – Balthasar, Romeo's servant. There does not seem much to guide me as to how he has been played in the past, but if Romeo is only about twenty I shall expect to look young too.

Romeo – Arthur Scales. Slim, quite small, darkish hair and a dark chin. A nice young man, I think, speaks the verse well but he could put more fire into his acting. (Perhaps he is saving his best for the night.)

Juliet – Charlotte Bancroft. They say she is twenty-six, but she plays younger. Very slim, elegant, thinks high of herself. Nice voice. (Poached by Mr Glossop from Drury Lane.)

Mercutio – Henry Davidson. He looks a little like a watered-down version of Papa. That, of course, means *very good-looking*! Has the most lovely lines to speak! I wish I could play him! Reputation off the stage for being a great ladies' man.

Tybalt – Fergus Flynn. (Poached from Covent Garden.) A black-haired Irishman. Always joking. Does not seem able to sit still. Fits the villain perfectly. I think I might like him if I did not hate him for killing Mercutio. The fencing is lovely to watch!

You will not want to have a list of all the others, but Lady Montague has a West Country accent, and I find she was born in Launceston! The Nurse tells me she has played the role thirty-six times in four different productions. She is a little like Char Nanfan.

Do you know in the middle of the play (Act 1, Scene 5) they are going to introduce musicians who will hold up the play for about fifteen minutes! Although it is all part of the plan to avoid the law, I have to tell you that I quite *enjoy* it, and I think the audience will too. At the first full rehearsal they played Vivaldi and Mozart, and I was strongly tempted to join in!

Ross said, in amusement: 'Already she writes like an old stager.'

'It sounds as if she is happy,' Demelza said. 'She even mentions singing!'

'But not Christopher or Maurice. I hope they are both lying low.'

'She heard from Maurice before she left. He is deep in some production in Rouen, some pantomime for Christmas. So Christopher has a clear field.'

'D'you know, sometimes I have the strangest premonition that at the end of it all she will suddenly kick up her heels and marry someone entirely different.'

'Twould be hard on Christopher,' Demelza said. 'But for him she might never have done this.'

'Quite true.' Ross began to fill his pipe. 'Isabella-Rose, our domesticated daughter. Milking the cows, meating the calves, gathering the eggs, making butter and cheese. Can you see that in your imagination? For I cannot. She would have exploded on the world somehow. Maybe singing in a local choir until someone else noticed her and invited her to Exeter or Bath. But Christopher took her right to the centre of things.'

'He deserves her.'

'People don't always get their deserts.'

'Do you know more about this than you have told me? Did something more happen in Rouen?'

He took a few breaths to light his pipe, to shake the spill out and throw it into the fire. He did not often lie to Demelza.

'Nothing I have been told of. Quite clearly there was more between her and Maurice than just a normal conductor–soprano relationship. But that was clear to anyone seeing them together. I have no more idea than you whether it is a trivial flirtation or something deeper. Certainly he has proposed marriage – but for that he was late in the field. Apart from a question of "deserts", I rather hope if she takes either she will take Christopher. Maurice does not look as if he would always be a faithful husband.'

'How do we know Christopher would?'

'We don't,' said Ross.

Chapter Six

Next day Ross went to see Ralph Allen Daniell at Trelissick; they had a few business interests in common, including the reverbatory furnaces just outside Truro, and Daniell had been laid up for a month with gout. The main drive of Trelissick emerges halfway up the steep hill leading from King Harry Ferry and on his return, as he came out onto the grass-grown, rutted, pot-holed lane, Ross glanced down and perceived the ferry must just have arrived, for a group of people were toiling up the hill, including one horseman and two pony-drawn traps, all being led up by their owners. Ross saw that the solitary horseman wore one arm in a sling and was instantly recognizable for his black cloak and erect figure.

He stopped, his head on his horse's muzzle. 'Philip! I see you are giving yourself no rest.'

'Sir Ross.' Philip took off his hat. 'I have rest enough. My arm is nearly healed. D'you know your Dwight Enys put eleven or twelve stitches in it, and so delicately that it felt like pinpricks. Your average Army surgeon – and I should know – might as well be a saddler for all the care he takes!'

'You came over on the ferry?'

'Yes, I had cause to go to Menabilly.'

'A long ride.'

'Fairish. How is your wife?'

'Has recovered well, I think. My obligation to you remains.'

'Thank God I was there. I travel a lot for the Duchy and on my own concerns, and I could as well have been on the other side of the county.'

'But you say you suspected Paul Kellow?'

'After a fashion, but of course no proof. As I went round to the sites of the murders and to meet the relatives of those who had died, a vague picture of the murderer came to form itself. A gentleman of thin build, wanting to appear taller and more frightening than he really was, someone at a loose end who could travel about the county as I could, a Cornishman who knew his districts, a man who liked to talk about the murders; three times in my company Paul brought the subject up; Agneta Treneglos slept two nights in the Kellows' shed; the killer seemed to have a special interest in your wife. He had tried to kill her – or tried to frighten her – once before.'

Ross shivered. 'Have you seen him since the night, since he was arrested?'

'No. He is safe in Bodmin. They say he is giving no trouble.'

'You were asked by the Duchy of Cornwall to make some investigations?'

'No, no. By Sir Charles Graves-Sawle, the then Sheriff. He and one or two others were becoming anxious about these unsolved murders and seemed to believe I might be of use. And in the end I suppose I was.'

'God's my life, you were!'

They had passed the steepest part of the hill and paused to mount their horses.

'In fact,' said Philip, 'I lay at Menabilly. William Rashleigh is the new High Sheriff, and after supper last night I gave him – him and others – an account of Paul Kellow's arrest. That was the purpose of my visit.'

'I should expect them to be very appreciative of what you had done.'

'Unduly so. So much of it was good fortune. Especially that I should have been staying with Geoffrey Charles on Bonfire Night!'

'Amen. Shall you continue in this vein?'

'What vein?'

'Taking at least some interest in the law and order of the county.'

'No. Oh, no. I told them so last night.'

Ross looked at the younger man.

'You speak with a certain amount of – well, of vehemence. Did you not enjoy the experience?'

'I certainly felt a real sense of satisfaction at the outcome. But I do not want to develop that attitude of mind.'

'I'm not quite sure what you mean.'

Philip touched his horse and the two men began to move up the lane.

'I sometimes think,' Philip said, 'that maybe I lost Clowance because of it.'

Ross stared. 'Now I certainly do not know what you mean.'

'Well . . . I have spent all my life as a soldier, have I not? I know I ride and stand like a soldier. A soldier, an officer; it is part of his duty to enforce the law. Discipline becomes second nature. This – this pursuit of a murderer, this helping to enforce the law, it is all part and parcel of the same attitude of mind – is it not? Justice. Discipline. Order – these are all a necessary ingredient of life. But there are other ingredients too. There are music and scholarship, laughter, love, the enjoyment of the seasons. Since – since I proposed marriage to Clowance – and especially when she said no – I have thought there is enough of the censorious in my nature, too much discipline, not enough appreciation of the gentler sides of life, and this, although I know she is fond of me, may have been enough to turn the scales against me—'

'Oh, I don't think you should blame yourself—'

'I do not know that it is blame, but it is an awareness that many of these attributes I have listed may not altogether look like attributes to a woman . . . All right, she might still have preferred Edward Fitzmaurice to me; but you will still see that I do not wish to pursue the role of a soldier in civilian life if by doing so I develop those characteristics even further.'

Ross said: 'I follow your meaning now. But I think you are being hard on yourself.'

They reached the main toll road from Falmouth to Truro. This too was grass-grown and rutted, but wider.

'You are not wearing your spectacles, Philip.'

'They were shattered in the struggle with Kellow. I shall not bother to replace them. I think perhaps they were a sort of symbol.'

'Of what?'

'D'you know, since I had that breakdown in the West Indies I have struggled with a very wayward temperament. When I confronted Kellow in your hall and he stabbed me in the arm, and I knew that he intended to kill your wife, I struck him down with joy – and was in a great temptation to go on smashing him about the head until there was no life left in him at all. Perhaps I should have done so, but the fact that I did not was a sort of victory. It is hard to explain to you.'

'I think I understand.'

The two horses ambled along side by side, neither of them in a hurry, and the riders gave them their head.

'Are you still staying with Geoffrey Charles?'

'No. I shall go straight back to Prideaux Place. I shall see how Cuby and Clemency are faring.'

'Cuby was saying how much she owed to your help.'

'It has been a pleasure.'

'I wonder you don't ask her to marry you.'

Philip did not answer.

Ross said: 'I'm sorry. I should not have said that. But it would be another and – I would have thought – most agreeable way of becoming a part of our family.'

'A sort of guard dog?' Philip shook his head angrily, then laughed. 'It is my turn to apologize. It was perhaps meant to be a joke. If so, it was a bad one, an unworthy remark.'

'In suggesting what I did I was not confusing gratitude with friendship.'

'I'm sorry. But no.'

'You do not care for her?'

'Very much. But she would refuse me. And one refusal is enough for any man's self-respect.'

'And why do you think she would refuse you?'

'Because she would inevitably think I was looking on her as second-best.'

'I don't think self-esteem would enter into it. In marrying Jeremy's widow – if that had come to pass – you might have had reason to think that you yourself were being regarded as second-best.'

'You argue well, Sir Ross.'

'In a good cause.'

'Thank you.'

'Do not forget,' Ross said, 'that there are other men about. Cuby is a very attractive young widow. In the eyes of most men, no doubt, she has two serious flaws. She has a child and she has no money.'

'That would make no difference to me,' said Philip, almost

inadvertently. Then he caught Ross's eye and laughed again. 'Shall we change the subject?'

It had been a pleasant enough day, but dusk was not far away. As they neared Truro the first lights were glimmering in the town.

At the top of the long hill Philip said: 'There is one other subject I should raise with you. I have had some doubt about it since we first met today. The group I supped with last night – insofar as there is any modern law in Cornwall, I suppose they represent it. The present Sheriff, William Rashleigh, Charles Graves-Sawle, a Boscawen, a St Aubyn, and so on. In the course of the evening clearly other matters were discussed apart from the capture of Kellow. But what was said there was totally confidential. So for a time I have hesitated . . .'

'Pray do not break your confidentiality on my account.'

'I have strict reservations about becoming a member of your family – at least on the grounds now open – yet I warmly appreciate the wish you have expressed, and I – I should fail . . .'

'Come, come, man, stop wrestling with your conscience! I cannot imagine that anything said between these gentlemen can involve me!'

'Only in an indirect way.' Philip swallowed and pulled his horse to a halt. Ross did likewise.

'Do you know a man called Paulton?'

'No.'

'Vic Paulton. Captain Paulton, as he likes to be known. As you will know, Valentine Warleggan began to employ a small vessel for service between Padstow and Rosslare, and after it was wrecked, and he bought from Clowance the half-finished brig that Carrington had laid down, he engaged this Paulton and another man called Mabe to be in charge of this new vessel. But sometime at the end of last year Valentine quarrelled with the two men and sacked them and resorted, with two other seamen as his crew, to taking the vessel across to Ireland himself. This he has done ever since. It seems that he had caught Paulton and Mabe red-handed in defrauding him of his profits. Had it been a legitimate trade they would have gone to prison, but Valentine could only afford to kick them out and carry on on his own.'

'So?'

'Earlier this year apparently Paulton and Mabe were able to rent a vessel and start up on their own. Last month they were caught in Looe River loading illicit tin. They cast off and made sail, but the coastguard cutter overtook them. Shots were exchanged before they were captured.'

'And they have involved Valentine?'

'You'll know that firing at a coastguard is a hanging matter. They are lodged in Liskeard jail, and Gawen Carew, who was there last night, says they are offering to turn King's Evidence in return for their lives.'

Ross stroked the head of his horse, who was getting restive.

'D'you think the Crown will take the bait?'

'It seems so. You see – you must know – that this is not ordinary smuggling on which three-quarters of the county turns a blind eye. This is a matter of stealing barefaced from the Coinage Hall and from the Counting House, in which many of the gentry have an interest. The name of Warleggan, though somewhat to be feared, is also heartily disliked among many of the older families. The fact that this is Valentine, who lives on the north coast and is, apparently, at odds with his father, does not carry the weight it might. There are many in the county who are quite independent of Warleggan's Bank and who would welcome seeing a criminal of that name brought to book – and on such a charge.'

Ross hesitated. 'I'll come into the town with you – we can stop for a drink before we separate.'

'Gladly.'

The steep cobbled hill was not to the liking of their mounts, but they reached the bottom successfully.

Ross said: 'You leave me with an entirely free hand?'

'Of course.'

'Have you any idea when there may be a move on Valentine?'

'I should not, if I were in his shoes, want to delay more than a week.'

'Delay doing what?'

'Leaving the country. Going to France. Or Belgium, like John Trevanion. To be out of reach for a while. But this of course is not, like John's, a simple bankruptcy. I confess I do not know what I should advise him to do. I am sorry to – to burden you with this information, but I thought you would wish to have it – in the

453

greatest confidence. Please, you must repeat this to no one – except of course to Valentine, if so be as you think fit.'

'I promise.'

'You have saved him once, I know. But this is a very different matter.'

'Let's stop here,' said Ross. 'I would appreciate a drink now.'

When Ross returned to Nampara it was getting on for four and half dark. They had kept dinner for him, and while he chatted to Demelza in the hall he saw a letter addressed to him lying on the only table which had not been battered in the fight.

'Post?' he said.

'No. David Lake brought it. He did not stop or say anything to Gimlett, but it looks like Valentine's handwriting.'

He opened the letter as a bowl of soup was put before him.

Dear Cousin Ross (the letter began)

There is a familiar saying about 'stewing in one's own juice', and after reading these lines you may well decide that that is precisely what you would like me to do in the situation as it has now developed.

In spite of owing a lot of money I am moderately solvent, I am the master in my own home, my son trots at my heels, my great ape bellows his joy whenever he sees me. What have I to complain of? Only that Smelter George is proposing to call to see me tomorrow. Is that not gloom enough to make the sun fall out of the sky?

He says not what he comes for, but one need not be a soothsayer to guess it must concern the custody of Little Georgie. He has taken Selina's side of the quarrel to his heart – nay, pocket – and is determined to wrest possession from me. At his age, when a cautious mercantile eye becomes steadily more cautious, I would guess he would eschew brute force and use some sort of blackmail, i.e. financial, foreclosing on the bills I have out, or even cutting off his own nose to spite his face by closing down Wheal Elizabeth with its promising new shaft waiting to be explored.

So I wondered if you would care to come and take biscuits and Canary with us at about eleven? I would not expect you to take my side, but you might be able to act as arbiter or referee? You could make this the occasion of your weekly visit to Wheal Elizabeth and coincidentally be there when he comes?

Possibly you might not show this letter to Cousin Demelza.

Yours filially,

Valentine

Ross at once showed the letter to Demelza.

She said: 'More soup?'

'No, thank you. I'll just take the lamb pie.'

After he was served she began to arrange some late daisies.

He said: 'I imagine he supposes that you would not want me to go.'

'Do you have any doubts yourself?'

'Not sure.' He contemplated telling her what Philip had told him, but decided he could not.

She said: 'I can think of six reasons why you should not go and only one why you should.'

'And the one?'

'You feel – responsible for him. His life has been warped by George's jealousy, which you gave George good reason to feel.'

'And the six?'

She made a dismissive gesture. 'You must know them all as well as I do. He knows you will not be an arbiter, will take his side against George. He knows you would take anyone's side against George.'

He said: 'Have patience, my love. I have to think this out for myself.'

'Then *think*,' she said. 'Don't *feel*.'

In the morning she said: 'Are you going?'

'Yes.'

'Would it not have been better, then, not to have told me, as Valentine advised?'

'Yes . . . But it would not have been fair to you.'

'Why is it ever fair to me to run yourself into needless trouble and danger?'

'Danger?' Ross said. 'Those days are long past. D'you realize, my love, that in all my association with George, all through the years, we have come to blows but twice, and once also, I believe, two or three of his footmen threw me out of the window. But all that was twenty or more years ago. George is twenty years older. So am I. We snap and snarl when we meet, but nothing more. Why, at the very last meeting earlier this year I called to see *him*! And though we were not friendly we came to an agreement – at *my* suggestion!'

'To get Valentine out of a hole of his own making.'

'Well, yes. He, I admit, is the contact point—'

'The fuse?'

'There's no reason to suppose so. Admittedly George was in bed when I saw him then, and now he is well again maybe he regrets the business association. But there can be little *physical* danger in our meeting, however abusive either of us may become.'

She said: 'I really have nothing against you helping Valentine – if you can. But – but saving Valentine's mine from bankruptcy and him from a debtor's prison – that's one thing, Ross. As to who brings up Valentine's son – that may well be touching the most sensitive spot.'

He looked at her.

'I remember once going to Trenwith when I was likely to be thrown off his land – I think it was when Drake was in trouble. I took old Tholly Tregirls with me, and he carried a musket to protect me. It kept George's servants in their place.'

'I mind it well.'

'Well, this time I think I must see Valentine. There is a greater compulsion than I am at liberty to explain to you. But I am taking another friend with me today. Not for physical protection but for having a cool, collected mind. Someone, I agree, whom George does not greatly care for. But then it will all, I trust, look like a coincidental meeting.'

Her dark eyes went up to his, questing.

He said: 'Dwight has agreed to come.'

*

The next morning was very dark. Just after dawn there was a gleam of ochreous sun, but soon the clouds closed down on the land and the wind blew a fog in, blanketing land and sea. As the daylight strengthened the fog grew thicker, moving in in massive clouds of vapour. The only consolation was that this was not the fuliginous sootiness that Bella was likely to be suffering in London. This came straight from the sea, smelling of the sea. The candles at Nampara stayed lit until ten.

At fifteen minutes past eleven the indistinct figures of three horsemen appeared riding up the short drive to Place House. Valentine had had a half hope that the fog might have kept his visitors away, but, peering down at them from an attic window, he recognized George, the lawyer Hector Trembath, and one of George's creatures called Blencowe. He thought as they dismounted that they looked like three black crows, bred of the fog, birds of ill omen. George had lost a bit of weight, but his shoulders were still heavy. Sight of that bull neck took Valentine back to his childhood.

Little Georgie was up here playing with some building bricks. 'Keep him here for as long as they stay, Polly. Don't let him come down until I ring.'

'No, Mr Valentine.'

'You have buns and biscuits if he should get hungry. I hope to be rid of them well before dinnertime.'

'Yes, Mr Valentine.'

'Oh, my God!'

'What is it, sur?'

Belched out by the fog from over the brow of the land two more figures had appeared, mounted women in this case. Selina Warleggan and Henrietta Osworth.

'They come on in great array,' said Valentine. He helped himself to the brandy. 'Maybe we shall persuade them to take Butto in part exchange.'

'You was always the comic one, Mr Valentine.'

'Where is Mr Lake, do you know?'

'No, sur.'

'Waiting for night and Blucher, I wouldn't be surprised.'

'Dodie, Dodie,' Georgie piped. 'Is Mammy coming today?'

'Don't ee worry, my lover boy. Twill all come right for ee sooner or later. Polly!'

'Sur?'

'Little sir has a mind of his own and can very easy slip away. Make sure he does not.'

'Surely I will, sur.'

At the window but from behind a curtain he watched the slow arrival of the two ladies. The three men waited for them and helped them down. Valentine looked north for sign of Ross, but even the mine was invisible. The eerie beat of the pumping engine could be heard – a mite irregular, he thought. Must point this out to Trebethick.

Knocking on the front door. Valentine had instructed them to be shown into the big parlour at the side of the house. Butto was hooting. The damned ape, Valentine thought, was as good as a guard dog.

Valentine went slowly down the stairs, carrying the brandy bottle and the temporarily empty glass. Butto had been restless these last few weeks, thumping at the wall, pulling things uselessly to pieces. Perhaps he had reached an age when he needed a mate.

'Good day to you, Father.' They were clustered together, all standing by the tall Georgian window. Although Selina was in dark green, the general impression was still of blackness, black jackets and waistcoats, black cravats, black breeches. They might, he thought, have come for a wake.

'You were not put off by the fog?'

'It is sunny on the south coast,' said George curtly. He looked at the bottle in Valentine's hand, the empty glass, the false pleasantness of the sardonic smile. 'You received my letter?'

Valentine said agreeably: 'Yes. Otherwise I should not have been expecting you, should I?'

George's remark had been simply intended as an opening gambit. He bristled at what he took to be the facetiousness of the reply.

'Sit down,' Valentine said, waving the bottle. 'Selina, welcome. Pray take the chair behind you. You must know how comfortable it is. I remember, when you were carrying Georgie, you said it was a support to your back.'

Selina, erect as a guardsman now, took the edge of the seat. 'Where is Georgie?'

'Oh, somewhere about. I'm glad to say he is very well.'

'Your father will have told you—'

'What?'

'That I have come to take Georgie home.'

Valentine smiled. 'He is home.'

'You know what I mean. Home to me.'

'This is your home.'

Valentine had pulled a bell, and one of his servants, a low-browed swart man with a broken nose, came in with a tray.

'Thank you, Humphries. Put the tray down. They may help themselves.' To his visitors: 'It is a good brandy, brought from Ireland only last week. Dawson will be in in a moment with hot chocolate and biscuits if anyone should wish to be more dashing. Ah, here he is. And David Lake too. Come in, David. Pray introduce yourself to anyone who does not yet have the privilege of your acquaintance.'

There was a general movement and nodding.

'Butto is making a racket,' David observed, rubbing his hands and looking chubby and rotund in this chill company. 'You can hardly hear him from here.'

'He wants to join in the fun,' Valentine said. 'He likes new people to meet. But is not always partial to strange horses.'

'This house, as you will observe, Trembath, is a totally unsuitable place in which to bring up an impressionable child. This great ape—'

'Yes, Sir George.'

'Nonsense,' said Valentine. 'Butto is entirely harmless, and indeed dotes on your grandson. As for it being unsuitable for me to own such an animal, I'd point out that your wife, Lady Harriet, keeps two great boar hounds as domestic pets, who roam about the house and among your children as well. And our neighbour, old Hugh Bodrugan of Werry House, has his private menagerie. And think of Lord Byron – Cuby Poldark's cousin, though she makes little of it – Byron keeps a wolf, a bear, a monkey, a parrot and a tame crow. Even your brother-in-law, the Duke of Leeds, has a passion for owls—'

George said: 'And do they keep open house as a brothel?'

'Wouldn't answer for Byron, but—'. Valentine stopped and looked round the room. 'Let's see, who is living here, David? You know the composition of the household as well as I do. Tell Sir George.'

David put up a plump hand and began to count the occupants on his fingers. 'There's you, Valentine. And me. (I like it too much to want to leave.) There's Polly Stevens. There's Georgie. And there's the servants. Does Dawson sleep in? That's five, then: old Mrs Craddock, two tweenies, one parlourmaid, Humphries and Dawson. No, six. Ten, all told.'

'Any whores?'

'No, alas. You gave 'em up about July. Mind you, we had a crashing good time while it lasted. But we turned over another leaf, didn't we, old chap? Or you did. Said you found it boring.'

'So it was,' Valentine agreed. He emptied the brandy bottle into his glass and put the bottle beside two other empty ones on the mantelpiece waiting to be refilled. 'Sex is an odd sort of a kind of a thing. I expect you've all noticed it. All you men have. Including you, Father.'

George glanced straight ahead of him, tapped one of his leggings with his crop, as if he might have liked to lay it about his son.

'In the sexual act,' Valentine said, 'gaining is all. I've thought this – and said this – often before, so there is nothing original in the thought. I had congress with my wife many times before we were married, in fact long before her elderly husband slipped his wind. In those days there was an element of the forbidden, an element of risk in our conjoining. That adds a dash of pepper to the dish. Even now there is a trace of reluctance in her attitude, whether real or feigned, I don't know, which makes her specially attractive to me. Also because she resembles my mother. Would you not say so, Sir George?'

Again George did not speak. Trembath had taken out a pocket-book and was making notes.

'When she walked out on me, carrying away with her my little boy, I hoped she would come back because truly, y'know, she was the woman I always wanted for my wife. As for those girls we invited in from Truro and Redruth – and some even from as far afield as St Austell – their open mouths and open legs were scant attraction. It seemed to me that all they offered was acres of quiescent flesh. God, how in the end they all bored me!'

George said: 'I do not know if you are drunk or not, but this lewd dissertation can only come from the mouth of a rake and a libertine, who, *patently*, is totally unsuitable to act as the father of a child not yet two years of age—'

'I am not acting as the father,' Valentine interrupted. 'I *am* the father! There is no disputed parentage in this case!'

460

George breathed through his nose. 'You are constantly offensive. I can very well understand that your wife, a well-brought-up and respectable woman, should no longer wish to share your house or to share your child—'

There was a tap on the door, and Humphries came up and whispered something to Valentine.

'Of course,' said Valentine. 'What a happy coincidence! Send him in.'

'Very good, sur.' He went back to the door and opened it wider. 'Sir Ross Poldark,' he said as the tall man entered. Humphries went out and shut the door behind him quickly, as if he had left a stick of gunpowder behind.

Chapter Seven

The trouble with Butto was not so much that he wanted a mate –
though no doubt he would soon have felt the need if he knew such
a creature existed – as that he was short of exercise, and of things
to interest and engage his mind. Since his earlier escapes and since
his master had devised a safety pen for him from which he could
not set himself free, he had been given a few devices to occupy
him: a swing, which he had quickly pulled to pieces; an old cannon
ball, which did not fit the muzzle of the even older cannon brought
over from a disused fort near St Ann's; the ten-foot trunks of two
oak trees on which he could sharpen his teeth and his claws; a rill
of water, which emerged mysteriously out of an impenetrable gap
in the brick wall and disappeared as mysteriously into a crack on
the further side. He could not make sufficient use of this last,
though it was convenient if he felt thirsty or needed a splash.

What he enjoyed most was the companionship of Valentine.
They had a vague and uncanny understanding of each other, and
Butto had learned how to drink wine out of a mug, to smoke a fat
cigar, to remember that one end of the cigar was hotter than the
other and that they were not good to eat. He had especially enjoyed
those times when his master had had noisy company to supper; he
enjoyed being the centre of attention and having white animals
with fuzzy hair and long thin arms and shrill voices who laughed at
his antics.

Of late these times had ceased and he could only remember
them vaguely. Nor did he seem to see his master as often. The days
were darkening and cooling and the extension of his territory had
hardly compensated. The place under the earth was warmer and
more comfortable, and he had made his den in the corner where
the least light came in, piling up the straw and the bracken and the

blankets to form a bed raised almost two feet off the ground, soft and mossy and homely. There he was quite content. But there was little to do but pick one's toes and scratch and wait for the next meal.

Meals, of course, were the events of the day. Sometimes his master, especially if he had some special treat in store, would tease him by calling to him through the door without opening it, and there would ensue a conversation between the man, talking to him in a language in which the word 'Butto' was constantly repeated, and the ape, responding with squeaks and grunts and immense roars of impatience and feigned anger until the door was opened and the feast brought in.

Today was disturbing because for the first time for a long time there were many new animals around, stamping and neighing just like the times when he had sat at table with the noisy ones, and peeled yellow fruit and tried to eat the plates as well as the food that was on them.

He thought he was missing something this morning. He wondered what he had done wrong. He had a grievance, and went out into the compound and hooted to be let out. The fog swirled around and muffled his protests. After a few minutes he gave up and snuffled and snarled his way down the steps to his lair. The day was so dark that he thought it might be all spent, and he sat on his bed and chewed a piece of one of his blankets in frustration.

Coughing and whistling, he began to waddle around his cell. There was an old cupboard down here that he had pulled to pieces, and he grabbed up one of the shelves and split it with his fingers into long staves. Behind the cupboard there was the metal door that Butto had tried conclusion with before. He put his flattened nose to the edges of the door, where a faint light showed, and sniffed, at the same time tracing the edge of the door with his fingernails. He leaned against the door. It gave a tiny creak but did not move.

He shoved the door with his great shoulders. It did not yield. There was a smell of food reaching his nostrils. He took the handle of the door and gripped it. With a screech it came away in his hand. He pushed again. Just the same tiny creak. He took a couple of steps backwards and leapt at the door with all his enormous weight. The door flew back on its hinges, and he stumbled through.

Darkness here, but a light above at the top of some steps. Not a yellow light, but pale light. And there was the sound of someone moving about. Another passage on this level, very dark. A smell that he recognized as belonging to that red drink like blood that he was given at the parties. Go down this way.

The passage led to a square cellar, from which dull light was also issuing from a grid. The light showed casks. He went up to one and found a tap, but though he tried to turn it, it made nothing more available to him. He licked a spot or two of red off his fingers, recognized it, snuffled, padded on. Another room black as pitch, rubble under his feet. Pick a piece of it. Taste. Nasty. Piles of it. A grid here too. He backed down, blew through his lips. Blowing the taste away. It was so dark he lost his way, found more stairs. At the top a door. Go up; door on latch, lift catch. Butto looked in. Light here. This was the big room where the people all came to feed. Fog blanketed windows. Table with things on, but not food. Fire smouldering. Butto had cracked that mirror. Box of cigars. He took one out, smelt it, tried the taste, threw it away. Then he thought he remembered how it was done. He scrabbled another out of the box clumsily, broke it in two, got a third and put it in his mouth. Nothing happened. He tried to pick up a piece of the black earth in the fire, the way the man did, but it was too hot to hold and he dropped it in the grate. He sat back on his haunches and scratched his head. Something was wrong. Then with the cigar in his mouth he bent his head towards the fire, let the end make contact with a piece of earth where the black earth was gleaming, and saw the gleam catch onto the edge of the cigar. He took a breath and coughed. But a second breath was better. He drew in smoke. Tasted good. He sat back on his haunches again and enjoyed the triumph of doing what he had done at the big feasts in the house, copying his master. But now he had done it on his own.

A sound in the next room alerted him; someone was moving about. The click, clink of metal, of the sort of metal that so easily broke and splintered. Butto had become able to recognize the footsteps of the human animals who lived in this place, and these sounded like the footsteps of the short fat white one who wore a cloth round its waist with a short split tail at the back. This was not one of the bigger ones who brought his food. This one was older and had a thinner voice, but was connected with food, though not *his* food. This one always stood and stared at him and was always unfriendly; it was afraid of him. He could smell the fear.

Butto stirred. He stirred because usually behind this fat old white one with bushy hair were the two bigger ones with voices as deep as the master's and carrying things which they used on him – though never when the master was there – to make him obey, to drive him back into his tunnel. He did not want to return to his tunnel. Or at least he did not want to meet them and be conquered by them. If the master put him to bed it was always quite different.

He was enjoying his cigar. Just like his master, he was enjoying his cigar. He squatted for a minute or so and puffed away in great content.

A clatter in the next room. Butto started up, grabbed another half-dozen cigars in his left hand and made his retreat. Back to the other door, into the darkness, down the stairs, feel your way past the nobbly black stuff; some of it crumbled under his feet; he stumbled but did not drop the cigars. He took a deep drag at the cigar in his mouth, and to his delight the end glowed brightly and showed him a way past the underground room where the big round casks were stored.

Changing his mind, Butto decided that he would like to go back to his den after all. With the light of the glowing cigar he did not find this difficult. The end of the cigar had grown an inch tip of white on it, and when he stumbled it had all fallen off, and a sort of white dust floated down and stuck to his chest. He picked some of this off, but it did not taste of anything.

He came to the broken door. He pulled it aside with a clatter and dropped three of the cigars. He picked them up and with the two he still held put them on the blanket beside his bed. He sank onto his bed in some triumph. Now, with leisure to spare, he stretched his fat legs and tried to copy what his master had done by drawing in breath and pushing the smoke out through his nose. He had succeeded twice before and everyone had laughed and smacked their paws together.

Ross was late because Dwight at the last moment had been called away, and Ross had walked with him. Frowick Thomas, who was short-sighted, had stumbled in the fog down the old mine well at the back of their cottage and had possibly broken her arm.

Dwight was taking a little extra trouble in binding up the arm and sending for a sling. Ross hung about until Dwight smiled up at him and said: 'You go on, Ross. I'll follow as soon as I can.'

So it was half an hour after eleven when, picking his way precariously along the cliff path, he heard the beat of the Wheal Elizabeth engine and presently observed the buildings of the mine looming out of the fog. There were people moving about here, their voices curiously hollow and detached. By chance Ted Trebethick was in his path and, recognizing him, stayed him another five minutes giving him details of the progress of their find.

'It d'look to me that thur's an amplitude of tinstone available wi' careful planning. Tis of modest grade, but twill more than pay for the working. It minds me of the opening of Wheal Bush, ten year gone when I was working as a tut-man. Same sort of parcels to come 'pon unexpected like. Of course Bush were not near the sea, but I've a fancy we shall make a pretty penny hereabouts . . .'

Ross excused himself, promising that he would be back in an hour and then be happy to spend some time with the manager. Then he went on his way, conscious that the message he had somehow to convey to Valentine took away from the importance of everything else – it even devalued the prospect of his, Ross's, own conflict with his old enemy. It clearly reduced the importance of the tin find. Valentine might emerge triumphant in his contest to keep possession of his son. Money might come to him in unexpected quantity from the mine opened on his doorstep. But it seemed unlikely that he would be able to be there standing on his own doorstep to receive it.

When he heard what was toward, would he run? It was not like him to run. He had an obstinacy, an almost suicidal obduracy, that stiffened him against the dictates of common sense. He could very well try to brazen it out, defy the constables when they came to arrest him, defy the court in which he would eventually have to appear.

And what of Georgie in all this? Whatever happened today there would be no question but that the law would return Georgie to his mother if his father were a convicted felon. And so return the child to George Warleggan's tutelage.

Even if Valentine could be persuaded to flee – and the means found for him to do so – Ross was not sure he was willing to cooperate in any attempt to take Georgie with him. Valentine as a more or less penniless fugitive would not be an ideal father for so young a child.

The cluster of horses by the front entrance told him that the meeting had begun. Pray Heaven it would now be near its end. When the heavy-browed man in the black coat came to take his horse and he was ushered into the house, he at once heard the raised voices and knew he was not too late for the fray.

George was saying something in his most dogmatic voice when Ross was shown in, and at once he broke off his angry dissertation and asked: 'What are you doing here?'

Ross said: 'Calling on a relative. What are you?'

Valentine said: 'Welcome, Cousin. Pray come in. Brandy?'

George said to Valentine: 'Is this some prior arrangement?'

'Sir Ross comes and goes as he pleases. We are nearly neighbours. Did you call at the mine?'

'Yes.'

'Good news, is it not.'

'Good indeed.'

'So perhaps Permewan's prospectuses were not so far adrift after all,' said Valentine, with a grin. 'One could easily overlook that they were geographically misdirected.'

George said: 'When you arrived, Poldark, we were discussing an important family matter which requires immediate attention. If you wish to talk to Valentine about the mine, I suggest you leave us now and call at some later date.'

Valentine said: 'I thought you might be interested in this sudden find, Sir George. After all, your bank now owns half the property.'

'We can talk of it later, when this other matter is settled.'

'Selina.' Ross took the glass of brandy offered him and sipped it. 'I am glad to see you back.'

'I am not back. As you should know.'

'That is a matter we were discussing when you intruded yourself upon us,' George said. 'When you have withdrawn we shall hope to conclude the business quite soon.'

Ross exchanged a glance with Valentine. 'But you say this is a family matter. That is certainly of interest to me.'

'*Why?* Valentine is no relation of yours. Selina is a stranger to you. You are just one of the ever-intrusive Poldarks, claiming some right to cause trouble.'

Hector Trembath was still taking notes. Ross wondered what possible advantage could accrue from taking down pointless abuse.

Valentine said: 'Reverting to the mine for a moment. I have had my eye on the site since long before I married Selina. When we started it I christened it Wheal Elizabeth after my mother. Now it seems, not at all by design but by the purest coincidence, that we all own a part of the mine much in proportion to the amount we owned of my mother. Sir George forty-nine per cent, myself twenty-five per cent, and Sir Ross twenty-six per cent. Don't you think that's quaint, David?'

'If you say so,' David replied uneasily, flicking a glance from one to the other of the two formidable men confronting each other, and waiting for an explosion.

But when the explosion came, it came from outside the room. The door flew open and Dawson burst in.

'Mr Valentine, sur. I b'lieve the 'ouse be afire.'

Butto had managed very well until he had almost smoked the cigar. White powder drifted down from time to time as the cigar got shorter. When the butt'end was beginning to singe his nose he sneezed a couple of times and put the cigar end down while he scrabbled away at the blanket for one of the others he had brought. They had rolled away into the straw, and by the time he fished one out and looked about for a way to smoke it, the smouldering end of the first cigar had connected itself to a deep pile of dry straw and what he saw was not a glowing end that he could bend over and make contact with the way he had done upstairs; all he was confronted with was the flame.

He edged his way to the other end of the bed, but then something nipped his leg and the hair on his chest was singed with a horrible smell. He looked about, to see his den flickering at him.

It was in Butto's nature to be afraid of fire, but under his master's tuition he had come to learn that if it was kept behind bars it did not bite at all. But this was not behind bars. It was beside him on his bed. It smoked and leapt and flickered.

He grunted his alarm and stood up and beat his chest. His big voice trumpeted and roared, and he wanted to escape from what he had done. It would be safely dark in the other cellars and dark in the big room upstairs, where the fire burned behind bars and was not angry.

He fled to the broken metal door, squeezed round it, glared back into his underground lair and saw it with bright hot lights leaping up and down all the way along the wall. And the black smoke made him cough.

He went through the door and with many a grunt and snuffle fumbled his way towards the wine cellar.

The first sign in the house itself had been oily-looking smoke curling idly round the open spaces of the dining room. But Mrs Craddock, who had been outside with one of the tweenies for ten minutes, did not notice it until she returned, when, after a little hesitation, she ran out into the long hall to give the alarm. By then the basement was alight.

They streamed out of the big parlour to find the main house already half full of smoke and a sinister roaring from the direction of the kitchen. Wisps of smoke were curling up the stairs.

Valentine shouted: 'Ross, get everyone out! David, come with me.' He took the first flight of stairs three at a time, coughed at the top and hesitated, and was joined by David.

Three at a time they made the second flight. Polly Stevens opened the door. 'I was just a-coming to see – my dear body!'

Valentine ducked past her into the room, scooped Georgie under one arm and made back for the door. Polly had gone back for something, but David grabbed her and pushed her towards the door. She stumbled as he hustled her along the passage to the main staircase.

As if the whole house had been primed to go up like a bonfire, the flames, fuelled by a cellar half full of straw, and helped by the strong breeze, followed on the heels of the smoke like a pack of wolves. Built in the main of sedimentary killas rock, much wood-work had been used in the interiors of the house and this was not oak but soft wood which in a hundred years had dried and shrunk and was quick to ignite.

They brought Georgie and Polly into the hall, and joined the others in a moist fog outside the house. After the sudden heat the chill was welcome. The horses had taken fright at the outpouring of shouting people, and half of them had broken their reins or uprooted their tethering pegs and were stamping and whinnying in the misty distance.

Ross said to Valentine: 'Are they all out?'

Valentine looked around, counting. 'Yes, I think so.'

Ross glanced at George, who was sitting on the corner of a garden seat struggling into the coat that Blencowe had somehow managed to get him. Georgie, reunited at last, was holding his mother's hand but was calling out: 'Dodie, Dodie!' Cook was patting sooty sparks out of Polly's flimsy dress and telling her how it had all happened.

'Water,' Ross said.

'There's a well at the back but only one bucket. Nearest is the mine. There's water there, but—'

'The miners,' Ross said. 'How many will be above ground, eight, ten? We could form a chain.'

Valentine said: 'Well, they've buckets enough, but—'. Ross was gone.

Once he almost blundered down a side track, but a lift in the fog saved him. By luck the first man he saw was Trebethick, who was standing hand to eyes, peering. In a few words Ross told him, and Trebethick, with a voice that belonged to a male voice choir, was bellowing the alarm and calling on men by name who should be within earshot. Water was gushing out of the adit and there were buckets in the new engine house. Ross shouted that he would go on and pray would they follow, filled a bucket and started off.

The mine had always been far too near the house for Selina's pleasure, but even so it was not adjacent, and Ross soon realized his first idea of having a chain of men passing one bucket to the next would never do. It would need a hundred or more. The best device would be if perhaps thirty men each ran ten yards before passing the bucket and taking an empty one back. Then as he broke through the fog he saw that this was probably too late.

There was no flame to be seen, but the thickest of sulphur-black smoke was pouring in great columns from every chimney, open window and cellar grid. There seemed to be fewer people about. Having tipped his water into the front hall, Ross went up to his old enemy, who was looking shrivelled and elderly.

'Where are the others?'

George jerked his head. 'Round the side.'

Ross ran round. Several men were grouped about a tall window, which he recognized as belonging to the side parlour where they had been meeting. There was a trickle of smoke from the top of this window, which had had the glass smashed. But compared to most of the house it was fairly clear. David Lake, the two male servants, Hector Trembath. As Ross came up they looked at him, but no one spoke.

'What is it?'

Lake shrugged his shoulders. 'I tried to stop him.'

'Who?'

'Valentine.'

'What the devil—?'

'He has gone in to find Butto.'

David said: 'I did my utmost to stop him. But you know what Valentine is like when he makes up his mind. This side of the house is not yet so bad – though personally I wouldn't put a leg over the windowsill.'

'When did he go?'

'Oh, about three minutes ago.'

'Five,' said Hector Trembath.

Ross went to the window and peered in. 'Valentine!' he shouted. '*Valentine!*'

He could see to the other side of the room, could see the glasses on the side tables, and two trays upset where the linen cloths had been snatched to provide primitive breathing masks.

'There's a well at the back of the house somewhere,' Ross said to David, who was just behind him.

'Yes, just round that corner.'

More glass tinkled as Ross stepped into the room.

'Hey, come back!' David shouted.

Ross stepped out again. 'Show me where this well is.'

'Look, don't throw good money after bad. Valentine may be back any time.'

'*The well, man!*'

Ross had grabbed two more linen cloths from the trays. Then he followed Lake round the corner, found the well, worked the handle until the water gushed, soaked the cloths so that they were running with water.

'If you go in,' Lake said, 'I shall have to follow.'

'Don't be a damned fool, man.'

'Then don't *you* be a damned fool! It's suicide!'

As they came round the corner Ross beckoned to the two menservants. 'If I go into this room, as I shall if Mr Valentine does not show up, I order you to prevent Lieutenant Lake from following. Understood?'

They hesitated. 'Yes, sur . . .'

'That is an order. See you obey it.'

Compared to that part of the house over the kitchens, where the dining room had been rapidly involved, this side was yet troubled only by thin spirals of choking fog, though a few ominous sparks seemed to flutter up through the floorboards. He had no knowledge of the design of the house. There must be cellars, but he hadn't the least idea as to their location or extent.

He looked at the moulded ceiling of this room, which still seemed sound, then walked cautiously across to the door, through which ten minutes ago they had all exited.

He opened it and a great *whoof* of heat and smoke greeted him. Some of the wood on the other side of the door was smouldering, but a broken window allowed a wind to come in and temporarily, as well as fanning the flames, it was serving to clear the smoke.

From this hall there was a passageway which led to the rear of the house and presumably the kitchens, and there were four other doors, only one of them ajar. He went towards this, stumbling across a piece of debris which apparently had fallen from the second-floor staircase.

He shouted: '*Valentine! Where are you?*'

There was such a noise in the house that a cry might not be heard. He thought he heard something in the room with the door ajar, and he pushed it open and peered in.

It was the sewing room-cum-music room, where Selina had once berated Katie. A half-completed tapestry on a frame, four chairs around a table and a pack of cards, a harpsichord in the corner with a bowl of faded flowers.

Dark in here from the darkness of the day. Outside you could just see a sapling sycamore bending in the wind. No human being.

He came out, stared round the hall. His retreat would soon be cut off. He tried the next door and found a service room. A kettle was singing on a Cornish hob. Onions tied on a string a bit like washing on a clothes line. A bucket half full of potatoes. A Welsh dresser. A black cat stared at him from beside the hob with sleepy, startled eyes.

He strode to the window, screeched it up, grabbed the cat, which scratched him. He put his head out and dropped the cat six feet to the safety of the gravel path.

So escape was still easy from here. He only had to jump. But where in Heaven and Hell was Valentine? The cloth across his face was dry now and he dampened it again in a jug of milk, retied it, returned to the hall.

Three more doors. He shouted again. From the passage the blackest of the smoke was how issuing A studded green door had been propped open with a wedge. Valentine might well have gone looking for Butto in the kitchens. But could he follow? If Valentine had gone that way he was surely lost.

He entered the dark cavern of the passage. An unlighted candelabra stood on a table in an alcove. Shelves on one side of the passage were lined with ornamental china, some of it broken. The heat was intense and Ross felt a wave of dizziness sweep over him. He steadied himself against one of the shelves and the wood was hot to his touch.

He stopped, trying to get his breath, trying not to cough. His eyes were smarting and running with tears.

He could not get a proper breath. He was suffocating. He could not walk into a furnace.

He stagged back into the hall and a burning lath fell at his feet. He tried to stamp it out, but one of his riding boots began to blister.

'*Valentine!*' he shouted, and choked. There was something that sounded like an answering cry. He turned in its direction, took a few steps, stumbled over a chair and fell, bringing some curtains down on top of him and breaking the fall.

*

Voices near; hands on his ankles, hauling him back, hands under his shoulders, Valentine was kneeling beside him. They were back in the big parlour. 'Father!' he said. 'Father, you should not have followed me. I came out the other way. I found Butto. He's dead.'

Then a hail of plaster rained down on them, followed by one of the supporting beams, then half the ceiling collapsed as they were being dragged out.

Chapter Eight

They took Ross to Trenwith, the nearest of the big houses and about equidistant from the nearest cottage of St Ann's. They made an improvised stretcher of an old door, and he lay on a blanket and covered by a blanket. Amadora, confronted by the emergency, in all ignorance put him in the very bedroom where he had taken Elizabeth against her will twenty-seven or more years ago, and so had started all this trouble, which had gone on so relentlessly and for so long.

Dwight caught up with the procession just as it reached Trenwith, so followed the four men carrying the door upstairs.

They laid him on the same bed and Dwight bent over him. There was a bruise turning blue on his forehead, one shoe had been burned and had fallen off, part of his jacket was in black tatters, there were bruises coming up on his shoulder and arm. But the most alarming symptom was his breathing, noisy and laboured and uncertain.

'Twas the smoke,' said Trebethick. 'At first when we got him out he could not seem to breathe at all. I thought he was a goner. Then twas like a corncrake. We dashed water 'pon him. I hope we done right.'

Dwight was listening to Ross's heart. It was fast but not unsteady. He might have run a mile. Dwight did not at all like the breathing: it resembled that of some of his patients when they were dying: it might go on for hours before it finally ceased. Concussion and shock. The bruise on his forehead was spreading and a trickle of blood oozed.

On the way here Trebethick had told Dwight what had happened, and one of the boys had been sent running to tell Demelza.

Ross gave a huge sigh, and his eyelids fluttered but did not open. Then after a dangerously long pause the breathing began again.

Demelza came riding bareback, a habit she had developed as a girl, slid off the mare, leaving her untethered, was met by Amadora and led swiftly up the stairs. Into the room, and hand to mouth she stared wide-eyed at her husband, then sharply at Dwight, who said: 'My dear, there has been an accident at Place House – a fire, and Ross was caught in it.' He tailed off because he saw Demelza was not listening.

She went to the bed and bent over Ross, peering, deeply peering. A lock of her hair, loosened in the gallop, fell over and touched his injured shoulder. She pulled it out of the way, then looked again at Dwight.

'It is concussion and shock, I believe,' Dwight said. 'The burns are not serious. Bone should be here any minute with bandages and salve. I don't see any signs of internal injuries.'

'Could you?' These were the first words she had spoken since entering.

'Could I? Not altogether. But internal injuries betray symptoms, and I see no such symptoms.'

'Did he fall?'

Dwight looked at Trebethick, who said: 'Not that I know, ma'am. I was not on the spot, d'ye see, but I been told he went back into the house to bring someone else out, and the ceiling gave way over his head.'

There was a long silence, eventually broken by Demelza. 'Were there others – injured?'

Neither man spoke. Then Trebethick said: 'I believe twas the ape that caused it. So Cook said. He broke out of his compound and upset something. There was more than usual folk in the house, but I b'lieve they all – or most – got clear away.'

'Have you seen it, Dwight?'

'Not yet. I've heard of no more casualties, but I met the men carrying Ross and thought this must be my first case.'

Demelza knelt beside the bed. 'Ross!' she whispered. She looked up: 'His eyelids flickered.'

'They have done before. It is a good sign.'

A tap at the door, and Bone put his head round. 'I brought what you asked for, sur.'

'Come in. Demelza, get Amadora to make you some tea or give you a glass of wine. I'll just make Ross as comfortable as I can.'

'I'll help you,' she said. 'I want to stay here.'

Darkness had fallen on the fog before Ross began to come round. Two candles flickered, and a dark slender woman sat before a fire burning low.

He could not at all think who he was, where he was, what time it was. There were items of furniture which he partly recognized, but they seemed to belong to a distant past. He could not understand it at all. His memory knew the brown draped velvet curtains held back by a knotted cord. And there was a gilt-framed mirror over a walnut dressing table. He could picture a face reflected in the mirror. But it was not the face of the woman who crouched before the fire.

It was Elizabeth. Merciful Christ, but Elizabeth had been dead twenty years. Knowledge flooded upon him, memory came back; all of it encompassing the fullest remembrance of today. He sat up and his head opened and shut, and he sank back on the pillow with a gasp of pain.

The dark woman was beside him, staring, staring.

'Demelza,' he said.

'Oh, thank God!'

'Where are we? What time is it?'

'Seven, I think. Or maybe eight.'

'Did someone bring me here – to Trenwith?'

She did not remark his knowledge of something he had just questioned. 'You were dragged from the fire at Place House. Dwight has been.'

He looked down painfully at himself. 'So I see. God! That smoke!'

'Your breathing is better. For a time I—'

'I could do with a drink.'

She hastily crossed the room, took up a cup and a pitcher and brought it back. 'Can you sit up a little? I'm afraid . . .'

He edged himself up by his elbows, grimacing with pain. She pushed the pillow up to support him, and with one forearm round the back of his head helped him to sip the water.

He swallowed two or three mouthfuls and then indicated he had had enough. He began to cough, heavily. Huskily. Then he stopped and half-smiled up into his wife's anxious face. 'I'm all right now.'

'Well . . . better, thank God.'

'It was incredible how quick the fire spread. Is everyone safe?'

'Geoffrey Charles has just gone to be sure. He was away – in Camborne – and so knew nothing about it until he returned for supper about half an hour since. He put his head in the door, but you were still – still sleeping, so he said he would go at once and get the latest news.'

Ross brooded. Then he looked about the room, noticing uneasily that his first impression had been mistaken. This was certainly Elizabeth's old bedroom but the dressing table was not, as he had supposed, the same. The curtains were maroon instead of brown. Perhaps the gilt mirror was here. For the rest he must have had an hallucination.

'I believe that ape started it. When I reached the house – I could hear him screaming – something must have upset him. We were – all assembled in the drawing room when one of the servants burst in to say the house – was on fire. By then, by the time we streamed out into the hall – the – the house was – full of smoke.'

'Try not to talk about it. Just lie still for a while. Or would you like something to eat?'

'Not yet, thank you. Is Valentine injured?'

She hesitated. 'I don't rightly know.'

'Did the others come here? I suppose this is the nearest big house, but the Crown at St Ann's has rooms.'

Outside a cow was lowing in the dark.

Ross said: 'How long before we leave for London?'

She was startled. ''Twas supposed to be tomorrow week, but you will surely not have recovered sufficient.'

'It's hard. I'm trying to relate one thing with another.'

'You surprise me, Ross. Half an hour ago you looked at death's door.'

'I feel none too far away yet. But these feel like superficial burns, and the beam that fell on me was only a glancing blow.'

'We shall have to see. And wait to know what Dwight says.'

He took another drink, and while he held the cup there was a tap at the door. Geoffrey Charles came in, his face very white. He smiled brightly enough at Ross and expressed his joy at the improvement. He was still in his riding clothes.

'The fire is pretty well over now, the house mostly gone. They have saved a few things from the west side, and the stables and the horses are intact. It will be much easier taking a detailed look when tomorrow comes. Lanterns cast as many shadows as they cast light. Ross, you were lucky. They say you went back in again to rescue Valentine.'

'Is he injured?'

'I'm afraid he's dead.'

'He was found in the dining room. The big ape was lying beside him.'

'How can that *be*?' Ross said harshly. 'I went back into the room where we had been meeting. Through the window, of course. Valentine had gone in but five minutes before, looking for Butto. When I got in I heard – or thought I heard – a cry from the hall. I opened the door. The hall was almost impossible – but I went in to see if I could find him – I looked in three rooms and then gave up. On my way back through the hall something fell on me – I was dragged out. Valentine was beside me. He said he had come out through another door. He told me Butto was dead.'

There was a horrible silence. Geoffrey Charles's face was mottled with shock. He said grimly. 'I was not there, of course. I can only go on what I have been told.'

'Who told you?'

'At first just the captain of the mine, Trebethick. But three of the servants were also there, and they did not contradict his version. Apparently about six o'clock George Warleggan and his lawyer friends left to ride home. His daughter-in-law, Selina, is staying at the Crown in St Ann's with her cousin and little George. Apparently there was some dissension because old George wanted them all to return with him, and Selina became hysterical. Then I met Sam.'

'Sam? Our Sam?'

'Yes. His forge is not so far away, you know, and he heard of the fire from some tinker who was passing. It was he, I gather, with two of the miners, who first got into the dining room and found the bodies.'

'The last thing I remember,' Ross whispered, 'before the beam knocked me out – was Valentine kneeling beside me and telling me that Butto was dead, but that *he* had got out by a side door.'

The cow was lowing again in the misty dark.

Geoffrey Charles said: 'Valentine built a sort of den in one of the cellars so that Butto could keep warm in the winter. In the cellar, Cook told me, there were bales of straw and blankets and sacks. Somehow Butto got out and accidentally set fire to his den. Thank God it was not at night.'

Demelza had been very quiet. 'Where is Valentine now?'

'At Sam's insistence they have taken him to the church. Sam has borrowed some candles from the mine and is going to sit with him all night.'

Chapter Nine

'Mama,' said Henry, 'are you and Papa not in love any more?'

Demelza stared down at her child. 'What *do* you mean?'

At this response he stumbled. 'I only – only thought . . .'

Demelza said: 'Your Papa is very sad about your cousin Valentine's death.'

'Yes . . . I 'spect you are too?'

'Of course. We all are.'

'I only thought,' Henry began again, and stopped again.

'That Papa is more so. He and Valentine saw much of each other. After dear Jeremy's death Valentine was more the same age, and your father used to call on him, and Valentine, as you know, came here. Valentine was sometimes quite a difficult young man to deal with—'

'What's difficult?'

'Headstrong. And then Valentine's wife ran away with Baby George and Valentine was left on his own. Because we are sort of cousins and because we are almost neighbours your father felt he should try to help him, and so he became very fond of him. It has been very upsetting for us all.'

'Headstrong,' said Henry. 'That's what you call me sometimes.'

'So you are. But not in the same way. Fortunately.'

'I'm not as bad as Valentine?'

'Oh no. Oh no.'

Henry rubbed one shoe against the other. 'You would not let me keep anything like Butto?'

'I should hope you wouldn't want to.'

'At the – at the inq . . . what do you call it?'

'Inquest.'

'At the inquest Lieutenant Lake said that if he had not

481

gone back in to try to save Butto Valentine would not have lost his life.'

'How do you know? You were not there.'

'Ellen Porter told me.'

'She had no business to.'

'And she said . . .' Henry was suddenly breathless. 'She said, if Papa had not gone back in to try to save Valentine, Papa would not have been hurt.'

'That is true.'

'Ellen says they were both brave men risking their lives for a dumb animal.'

'Perhaps so. But it did no good. One human life wasted, and another grievously near being killed also.'

'Is Papa . . . Will Papa be well enough to go to London next Friday?'

'It has not yet been decided.'

Physically Ross made a remarkable recovery. All the burns were light: three places bandaged and four others to be dabbed with a zinc ointment three times a day. Concussion and suffocation had been the real dangers, and once the smoke had cleared itself from his lungs he was able to breathe normally. The concussion had left him with occasional dizzy spells, but he had been careful not to tell Dwight about them.

His chief sensation was of deep-rooted grief, which mingled with chagrin at Valentine's totally unnecessary death. It was not like losing Jeremy – he was not gut-frozen with despair and loss – he felt more as if he had received a poisonous wound. Ross wondered whether it was just Valentine's frustration and natural recklessness which had goaded him into going back to look for Butto. Maybe everyone had underestimated the tie between the young man and the ape. Affection in Valentine had been rare to show itself, but, just as his attachment for his son had become evident over the last year, perhaps his fatherly instincts had extended to cover the ape-waif he had picked up in Falmouth and come to care for.

Valentine's death had shaken open a whole raft of memories in Ross, memories of Valentine as a child, memories of Elizabeth, conversations they had had, such as their encounter in the church-yard when his frustrated love for her had welled up afresh. All those years ago. Back to thinking of the letter she had written him – kept for years but then destroyed – in which she told him she was going to marry George Warleggan. And her final, still partly unexplained, death in childbirth.

He wondered whether Demelza sensed some of the turmoil he was going through: thoughts, feelings, memories overlaid, suddenly turned over, stirred, no longer entombed. Although Demelza had been half afraid to trust Valentine, his death had shocked her in a new way, and she had drawn away from Ross as if temporarily estranged.

The other great mystery to Ross was his own hallucination – for that was all it could be. When he had fallen in the blazing smoke-filled debris of the hall he had seen Valentine beside him, and Valentine had said, 'I came out the other way. I found Butto. He is dead.' And twice he had called him 'Father'. Twice. In actual fact Valentine by then was apparently already dead, clutching to Butto's hand, as he had been found by Sam and the others when the fire died down.

Some sort of thought transference in the moment of death? A communication, mind to mind? If he, Ross, had not been dragged out by David Lake and others it would have been his last living thought. 'Father.' 'Father.' In his memory he could not recollect Valentine ever having called him that. It was a claim. A greeting. An assertion. Now he could claim no more.

The funeral was tomorrow. Since the fire he had ridden three times to see Selina, and once had seen George. Place House was a ruin. Part of a roof still stood, precariously, waiting for the first gale. Skeletal walls. Recognizable but mainly unusable furniture. Volcanoes of black ash, still smoking. The stables untouched, and a conservatory and some outbuildings. There had been looters picking over the ruins several nights, but little remained to steal except some food and drink. David Lake had taken charge and came over every day from the Crown at St Ann's. The mine had restarted.

As he climbed awkwardly from his horse, Demelza was coming up from Nampara Cove.

She said gently: 'You are riding too much.'

'I think it is over now. I may perhaps need to go to Truro on Wednesday.'

'Have you used your ointment?'

'Not since this morning. It is only this foot that's a mite troublesome.'

'Let me do it for you now.'

'If you have time.'

'Of course I have time!'

They went upstairs to their bedroom, and she helped him draw off the boot and stocking.

'It's swollen,' she said.

'A little, yes.'

'Has Dwight seen it?'

'Not since Sunday. I don't think I need to take too much heed of what he says. Medical men always err on the side of caution.'

She dabbed the swollen foot, and carefully he did not react.

'Lucky it is not your damaged ankle.'

He gazed at her bent head, thick hair curling, now slightly tinted at his request.

'Come to think of it, I might get Barrington Burdett to come over here instead on Wednesday morning. I saw the Cornish Bank today, so it should be only a few documents to sign.'

'I thought you had been to see Selina again.'

'I have. But I rode on into Truro after.'

'Has she changed her mind at all?'

'D'you know, I think – of course we are all shocked, saddened by Valentine's useless death, but in the end the one who will sorrow most – and for longest – will be Selina.'

'D'you think—'

'I suspect her bitterness towards Valentine was almost a surface bitterness. Oh, she felt it truly, no doubt of that, but it was a resentment she wanted *him* to *feel*, not for him to be lost to her for ever.'

Demelza said: 'Some of those that love most can hate most.'

The ointment was put on. 'There. Leave the pad be for a few minutes.'

'It is very cooling.'

She stood up. 'You need to rest for a few days. You are – we are not so young as we used to be. You would be wiser not to go to London.'

'Oh, I shall go to London if it—'

'If it kills you.'

He smiled wryly. 'It will not. I want to see her on the stage again.'

'You have had a bad shock, Ross. A physical shock. And one of bereavement. You have made a quick recovery, but—'

'To tell the truth I would have welcomed a rest these last days, but I was driven on. And you, my dear? You have had a horrible time too.'

'Oh . . . yes. Oh, yes.'

Later that night, when Harry was abed, she said: 'You said this afternoon you was driven on. Why?'

'Why? But I have told you why.'

'Tell me again.'

Ross lit his pipe, his mind listless, unconcentrated. 'Valentine taught the ape to smoke. David Lake says he thinks the fire was started that way. When Butto's body was removed he was clutching a cigar in his hand.'

She stared at his pipe. 'I shall always hate the smell of cigars after – after Paul Kellow.'

Ross drew on the pipe, tossed the spill into the fire. 'I cannot explain more why I have been driven on without touching on painful subjects.'

'Painful who to?'

'To you. The – the parentage of Valentine has been gone into far too often. This tragedy – it has, at least in a sour way – produced a resolution, even though it has all been a sorry, criminally cruel mess. The one remaining source of conflict will be the future of Georgie. Obviously I was as totally opposed as Valentine to his being brought up a Warleggan. So I was prepared to do anything I could to heal the breach between Valentine and Selina. And, if that failed, to support Valentine in his claim to the custody of the boy. When he wrote asking me to go to Place House last Tuesday, you advised me not to go. I could not tell you my extra reason for not taking that advice was because I had promised Philip Prideaux to tell no one that almost any day Valentine might be arrested on a near capital charge. At Philip's suggestion I was going to warn him. Thanks to the ape I never had the chance.'

Demelza stared at the great bruise on her husband's forehead.

'And that is why you have been abroad all these last three days, when you should have been resting?'

'It seemed to me that Valentine's death had completely destroyed my hope of rescuing Georgie from being brought up under George's domination.'

'And you have seen Selina?'

'Three times. David Lake told me of Selina's hysterical grief and that gave me a small hope that something else might be arranged.'

'You went on Friday?'

'Yes. She was back at Rayle Farm by then. Her cousin was with her and little Georgie. She was still badly shocked, hardly able to string two words together.'

Demelza said nothing.

'After dinner she began to calm down, to talk more rationally. You know, she has come to me for advice before.'

'I do. Usually when I was away.'

'One of Selina's stepdaughters has recently married, married well, to an Indian or a half-Indian. Her husband is the son of a rich cotton broker who comes, I think she said, from Bombay. They were married in August, and Selina nearly bankrupted herself to pay for a splendid wedding. In the New Year the married couple are going to Bombay to live for probably two years, so Letitia has offered her stepmother their London house to live in rent-free until they return. Selina has been unable to make up her mind about anything, even before the tragedy of the fire. Both she and her cousin hate the property George has rented for them, and it could be that now she has little Georgie back they might all return to Lisson Grove, where the house is, and settle in there.'

Demelza said: 'I can imagine Selina unable to decide anything, with her son being stolen from her. I can see all that.'

'What can you not see, then?'

'I think you are trying to explain to me, aren't you?'

'Unfortunately there is in all this a financial dimension, and that is what I have been attempting to sort out. Selina is not penniless, but she is hard pushed to live in the style she has been accustomed to. When she appealed to George for help she said she had got into the hands of moneylenders to pay for the expensive wedding. George, I gather, paid off the moneylenders on condition she should come back to Cornwall to live – with other stipulations you know. This Selina would have to pay back to George if she broke her agreement, but she can do this, Mrs Osworth says, with the proceeds of the house they have just sold in Finchley or wherever. With a rent-free house in London she could therefore be out of debt and have the rest of the proceeds to invest or to live on.'

'Will it be enough?'

'No.'

Ross's pipe had gone out while he was talking, but he made no move to relight it.

'You may think I have been too precipitate in trying to come to a set of arrangements before we leave for London; but I was much concerned to build on Selina's suddenly sharp distaste for the house she was living in and to help to work on that and to put in front of her a course of action which George would not be able to discourage her from.'

'Tis all a small matter complicated, but . . . Your concern is all for Georgie and not at all for Selina?'

'Oh God, of course it is! I care nothing for her. You – you must understand how I feel about Georgie?'

'Yes. Yes, I do. And what will Valentine have left? It surely cannot all be debts.'

'I asked Selina, and she says that while Mr Pope was alive he paid an insurance against fire at Place House, but she doubts if Valentine bothered to renew the policy. The mine – this new mine – Wheal Elizabeth is the promising source. You know, of course, that when this new company was formed to take over the mine in order to save Valentine from prosecution, Warleggan & Willyams took forty-nine per cent, the Cornish Bank took twenty-six per cent and twenty-five per cent was left in the possession of Valentine. This rescue operation was undertaken as a speculation which might have involved us in a heavy loss. It now seems more likely to promise a substantial profit. In the exceptional circumstances we are in, I have offered to cede to Selina twenty per cent out of the twenty-six per cent the Cornish Bank now owns, if she will return to London and not accept any money from George. This will mean that she will own forty-five per cent of the venture shares, and if the mine yields as there is hope it will, she should be able to live comfortably on that and maintain her independence.'

Demelza said: 'Surely your partners will not be willing to – to cede – to *give* those extra shares to Selina?'

'No, well, I have to tell you now that they were not too willing to take them up in the first place, so—'

'So—?'

'I took them all myself.'

'You put all . . . you put all your own money in the mine?'

He looked down. 'Yes.'

'And you might have lost – what – two, three thousand pounds of your own money.'

'But I shall not now.'

'A very long time ago, d'you remember, when Julia was a tiny baby, you almost went bankrupt and might have been put in jail for debt, for the lack of three thousand pounds.'

'I remember it well. But we are better off now.'

'How much better off, Ross? You never tell me.'

'That's unfair. Sometimes you don't seem interested.'

'I am always *interested*. But I hear that there has been another lode strike at Leisure – and if I want a new dress I may have one. We were able to give Clowance a lovely wedding. We could pay Bella's tuition fees and other expenses. For the most part I am content with that, to enjoy my life without worrying. But there was a time, a *very long* time when I had to worry every day of my life.'

'I know too well. And now you are going to begin worrying again because I make a three-thousand-pound gift of shares to a pretty young woman who flatters me all ends up whenever we meet. Is that it?'

Demelza took a deep breath. 'Maybe it is not the fear of losing three thousand pounds that worries me the most.'

'I have tied it up legally,' Ross said, deliberately misunderstanding. 'Barrington shall come here on Wednesday to ensure the deal is properly struck. You see how much like George I am become!'

McArdle had called an early dress rehearsal.

Although the first performance was still ten days off, he wanted to see how the production would look. Between themselves he and Mr Glossop had spent hugely in having new sets painted and built. They had done the same for *Macbeth* and it had, he believed, doubled the pleasure – and size – of the audience. It was an age of display: the new playgoer was not content with actors performing before a drop curtain. *Macbeth* had been enacted against the impressive mountain ranges of the Highlands. The big scene in *Romeo and Juliet* was the ballroom of the Capulets, but much attention had been given to the scene in the crypt. The scenery had been delayed from last weekend, when it should have been temporarily tried out on the Sunday. Now it was time to move ahead. Dina Partlett, who played Lady Capulet, boarded just north of Hatton Garden, so she usually called for Bella and they went to the theatre together. This time there was dressing up to do, though most of the costumes had been chosen a week ago.

It was a big auditorium (the gallery alone would take eight hundred people) and today it looked even larger with only five men clustered together in the pit.

The early part of the rehearsal went pretty well. Standing in the background, occasionally exchanging whispered comments with one or other of the cast, Bella allowed her mind to wander over the traumas and paradoxes of her life during the last year. Prima in the *Barber* in Rouen to minor part in *Romeo* six months later. Some loss of vocal agility or laryngeal strength had brought her this low. Yet she was still learning. Dear Maurice had promoted her almost untried to play the lead in an exacting new opera in France. It had been a success. Now, bereft by this complaint of the throat, she was already appearing on the London stage in a Shakespearean role, thanks to Christopher's persistence and Edward's influence. She was starting a second life on the stage. Was the first entirely finished? One morning last week she had slipped away from Mrs Pelham's benevolent custody and called to see Dr Fredericks. She had told him of her new good fortune, and he had been astonished, pleased for her sake, but slightly disapproving that she was appearing on the non-musical stage. Before she left he had tried her again. After she stopped singing he wiped a brief tear from his eye and said: 'My dear, dear Bella, it was *such* a beautiful voice – and *still it is* in the lower registers. It is early days yet. Surely God who gave it you will yet give it you back again! Let us hope and pray . . . In the meantime you are behaving with splendid courage, and I shall try to come and see you on the eighth.'

She had not heard from her parents this week, and she hoped they would be able to come. They were due on the Sunday if all went well.

She had written to Edward, thanking him for using his influence on her behalf. Christopher, of course, she saw every night. He never changed, seemed to have faith in everything she did. He had told her in Cornwall that he had given up his passion for white wine. *Could* one give up a weakness like that? Certainly he had shown no signs since her illness. Last week she had written to Maurice telling him of her 'change of profession'.

In the rehearsal they were coming to the second and more serious bout of swordplay. She edged a foot or two forward; she always enjoyed watching it. Once or twice she had picked up the duelling swords and been allowed to practise with them against Mercutio.

They had now reached the main duelling scene in Act 3, Scene 1. Mercutio had fallen to Tybalt and taken his long farewell. Now Tybalt was about to fall to Romeo. Backwards and forwards they went, to the tinny clatter of the blades. This was what the audience would want to see: a battle royal to raise their blood; this must not look like make-believe.

After a long bout where Tybalt had seemed to get the upper hand, Romeo drove him into a corner; now would come the long thrust which apparently ran Tybalt through the body. This was fairly easy to pretend, but the flailing swords before the *coup de grâce* always carried an element of real danger. On this occasion, perhaps because of the presence of the convincing scenery and dressed for the first time in their Italianate doublet and hose, Fergus Flynn put in one thrust too many. Romeo gave a cry, dropped his sword and stepped back, his face streaming with blood. Then he staggered and fell; women screamed and milled about over him. The protective gutta-percha button of the sword had seared his cheek and gone into his eye.

The funeral of Valentine passed off quietly enough. He had been grudgingly popular in the villages, more so than anyone, certainly the Wesleyans, cared to admit. This was mostly true among the women because he never failed to have a word or a joke for them and to look at all but the ugliest with an acquisitive gaze. He was an eccentric, someone to talk about, gossip over. A few men were glad to be shot of him. As a fisherman from St Ann's said: 'I d'ave more sorrow for Butto than I d'ave for his master.'

Harriet and Ursula came to the church. George sent word that he was unwell. Half a dozen painted ladies arrived in a group from Truro. Andrew Blamey junior, temporarily home from sea, came with his mother, Verity. The Carnes dutifully attended. Ben Carter refused to leave the mine, and Essie went with her mother-in-law. Very few of Valentine's gaming companions, who had eaten and drunk so freely at his board, turned up. Philip Prideaux was there, as was Trebethick with three other miners from Wheal Elizabeth. At the last moment Daisy Kellow came with her father.

If it was not the end of an era, there was a feeling that some element of enduring conflict had gone. A mischievous, abrasive element was no more. Within a very short time two young men had gone, one to a cell in Bodmin prison, another to his grave. And only five years since the much-loved Jeremy had been lost. The villages were the poorer.

Although Place House was in the parish of St Ann's, the absence of a resident curate there and the fact that Valentine's mother was buried at Sawle Church made it the natural churchyard to choose.

Mr Profitt preached a sermon which he must have used several times before because it was based on an all-embracing ignorance of the character of the young man whose obsequies he was conducting. It didn't much matter, Ross thought; the only thing that mattered was that he had lost a son.

So after twenty-six years and three-hundred-and-one days the child born under a black moon fulfilled a destiny which Aunt Agatha, consumed with spleen, had prophesied at his birth.

Chapter Ten

They had to leave at six on the Friday morning to catch the Royal
London Mail in Truro. This service had been in operation for five
years, and they had used it before. It followed the old-established
northern route, cutting out Liskeard and Plymouth, and was generally reliable. On an average trip it took thirty-five hours to travel
from the Red Lion Hotel in Truro, to the Saracen's Head in
London. When they joined the coach they were pleased that for
the first part of the journey they were to be the only inside
passengers. It was a wet day, and Demelza did not fancy the
situation of the seven travellers who were, for economy's sake,
sitting outside. At least it was pleasant for Ross to be able to rest his
burnt foot.

There had been little talk that morning. Perhaps, Demelza
thought, it was because of this drying up of normal conversation
between them that Henry had asked his perceptive question.

She said: 'I'm sleepy. After all we were up at four. Mind if I
doze?'

'Yes. Well, take the opportunity before some stout burghers come
to join us.'

There was silence while the coach swayed and jolted along the
rutted road towards St Austell. After twenty minutes Demelza
opened her eyes and saw Ross staring at her. She gave a little laugh.

'I find I can't now.'

'Nor I.'

This trip was always quite an ordeal. Very soon now, Demelza
thought, they would need to go by coach only as far as Bath and
then take a steam train to London. Not that she fancied that much
either. And she could never think of steam without thinking of
Jeremy.

Ross stretched his other more permanently injured leg. 'Tell me, d'you think I have shrunk?'

'Shrunk?' She looked at his big frame. 'You? Why do you ask?'

'It seems to me that George has shrunk somewhat. I noticed it first when I saw him sitting on the wall by himself after Place House had caught fire.'

'Oh?'

'I remarked it again when I had to go and see him about Valentine's death. He was sitting in Cardew more or less hunched up in a chair, and somehow I thought his bulk had grown less.'

'Why should you think *you* were likely to have grown less?'

'He's only a year older than I am. It crossed my mind.'

'His accident may have aged him.'

'I hope my accident doesn't age me!'

'In future you would be wiser not to get burned in a fire and hit on the head with a falling beam!'

Ross stared at the rain beating on the window. Once last year he had come on this coach and they had travelled with the hurrying rain clouds all the way to London.

'I might say, by the way, that whether George has shrunk a little or not, I shall not underestimate his ability to be just as scheming, vindictive and resentful as ever. The leopard will not change its spots.'

'He is sure to grieve about Valentine's death?'

'Oh yes. But he is more concerned for the child.'

'And in this you have thwarted him.'

'For the time being. Selina may prove extravagant. Or Wheal Elizabeth may prove less kindly than we hope. Always his money will be there as a threat.'

'Which you cannot match.'

'Of course not. Nor would ever try to.'

'Or she might marry again.'

'True enough. She has the looks of a frequent marrier.'

They were going through a wooded valley near Probus. All the trees were dripping and dark.

She said: 'And there is still the mystery of Valentine.'

'Mystery? D'you mean my hallucination?'

'In part. Not altogether.'

For a while the noises around the coach, which had stopped to let two outside passengers down, left them unspeaking. Then, as

493

the coach began to move off, Ross said: 'You know, of course, that my chief reason for going to Place that morning was to pass on Philip Prideaux's warning that Valentine was likely to be arrested for smuggling tin ore out of the country.'

'Yes. I understand that now.'

'Well, at the funeral David Lake told me that Valentine already knew.'

'*What?*'

'A member of the crew of his brig told him he had heard it and that he, the man, was going to leave Cornwall to save his own skin.'

'But that means . . . What does it mean?'

Ross shook his head. 'I've thought about it and thought about it. No one will ever know.'

She dozed at last, until they reached Bodmin. There was a break here for tea and cakes. The fire in the inn was welcome, and she took off her gloves to warm her hands. The tea when it came was scalding, and a new warmth began to creep through her. It was a long lonely stage ahead, across wild moors to Launceston. They would dine at Launceston and sleep at Honiton.

As if his thoughts had not been interrupted, Ross said: 'There's a lot now that will never be known about Valentine.'

'Do you think he . . .'

'What?'

'Well – took his own life?'

Ross shook his head. 'He wasn't the kind . . . But under pressure people do the strangest things – God, I don't know. The knowledge of the complete mess he'd got himself into – the conviction that there was no acceptable way out, it may have made him more obstinately determined to *avoid* it, so that on impulse he took a risk – an extra risk – for the sake of his beloved ape – a risk that he would not otherwise have taken . . .'

Although they shared a bedroom at home they were surrounded by the breathing of their family and the servants. At home, the intrusion of the commonplace inhibited reference to more emotionally charged subjects. Usually the time for personal exchanges was in bed before they went to sleep or early in the morning; but in the last few weeks – it seemed like months – this had not happened. In this coach they were imprisoned alone for at least another hour, and no one to intrude on them with affairs of the mine or the farm.

Demelza said: 'D'you know what Henry asked me the other day? He said: "Are you and Papa not in love any more?"'

Ross smiled, but grimly. 'What did you say?'

'I asked him what he meant. He sort of stumbled over what he wanted to say and then dried up. I said then that his Papa was greatly upset by Valentine's death . . . Of course, I said, we all were, but Papa more so. I tried to explain what was after all the truth, if the part truth, that you had made a special friend of Valentine since Jeremy's death and you had become more attached to each other. Then when Valentine and Selina separated, you tried to support him and give him advice.'

'Harry is a perceptive child. But the perception only goes skin deep.'

'That's not surprising, is it? He seemed to have heard all about the inquest from Ellen Porter.'

'We must dispense with that girl, she ain't reliable. Or maybe we could turn her into a chambermaid, to take some of the work off Betsy Maria.'

'Then he asked me if I thought he could have a pet like Butto.'

'I hope you told him he was fairly surrounded by animals that did not set fire to houses?'

'. . . He *is* perceptive, though, is he not; for a child of eight?'

Ross said: 'If you had been compelled to answer that first question of his, what would you have said?'

She bit her lip. 'I would have said, I suppose, that we still loved each other, but that things had not run too easy between us of late.'

'As bad as that?'

'Well, what would *you* have said?'

'I would have said – no, I could not have explained anything to an eight-year-old. You are right!'

'Supposing he was eighteen years old?'

'That's unfair. All right. I should have said that in my life I've loved only two women. Right? The first married my direst enemy. The second married me. She has been my lover, my companion, my housekeeper, the mother of my children, the – the keeper of my conscience. She is comparable in my eyes to no other woman. I would not be a human being if I had not sometimes developed other sorts of affections, other mild fancies, other but not contrary loyalties. Sometimes they have been unnecessarily strong, especially maybe towards the difficult young man I suspected of being my son. I expect a feeling of guilt came into it too! But following that and building on that supposition I shall continue, whether I wish it or not, to have a strong interest in the fortune of *his* son. It can be no other way, but unless my wife demands that my every interest shall be exclusive to her, then she has all my steadfast support, interest, concern, sympathy, love and loving kindness. If I have in any way neglected my true family these last few weeks I ask their pardon and will try to do better. That do?'

After a minute she said in a low voice: 'I don't know whether to laugh or cry.'

'Why do you want to laugh?'

'Because it was a lovely speech which fetched tears to my eyes but spoken in a light tone that made me wonder if you were being – what is the word? – cynical about it. Are you, Ross?'

He stared at her for a long moment, looking straight into her eyes.

'The answer is no. But you should not need to be told it.'

It was strange, thought Demelza, that while such handsome words should bring a complete reconciliation nearer, a lingering trace of the gap was still there.

McArdle said: 'They think they will save his sight. But he has to spend at least a week in a darkened room. And then, if all goes well, two to three weeks' convalescence.'

Joseph Glossop said: 'Well, that is it, then, isn't it. We either cancel outright or postpone the production until the New Year.'

Rory Smith, the production manager, said: 'We have already sold most of the superior boxes! Curse and damn Flynn to all eternity! He should be barred from the stage!'

'He is Irish,' said Glossop, 'and too excitable. Other producers will take note.'

McArdle was pacing up and down the office. 'I have gone through the people who might replace him. James, who has been cover for him, is far too ugly. I should have thought of that before, but of course one does not foresee a crisis like this! Pity, because he has a good voice and is a good swordsman – but the public would never like him if they were expecting Arthur Scholes.'

'No hopes of Kean?' Smith asked.

'Impossible! You know he is playing Lear at the Garden.'

'Davidge is in America. Cooke?'

'He's over fifty and looks it. Of course, if it were Kean, the audience would swallow anything.'

McArdle stopped with his back to the window, blocking out much of the winter light. 'A *name* is what I want. Or a nobody. If you could invent somebody to provoke the audience so that they would come out of curiosity . . .'

'Have you thought of Musgrove?'

'Eric? He is neither a name nor a nobody. He has come down to playing Lord Montague. He's younger than the rest, I admit. But can you expect Charlotte to pretend she is in love with *him*? It is better to cancel. And safer. I have my reputation to think of.'

'There is one other suggestion which has been put to me,' said Glossop. 'It is an eccentric thought. But it was put to me with a degree of pressure.'

They stared at him expectantly. After all, it was his family who had kept the Royal Coburg open, pumping in subsidies to prevent the theatre going dark.

After considering the other two men, Glossop shook his head. 'I don't know. I don't think so. Give me another twenty-four hours. This time tomorrow we'll come to a decision.'

The coach arrived in London at five p.m. on the Sunday evening. It had been as black as anthracite for an hour, but here there were plenty of lanterns about and many of the streets were newly gas-lit.

Christopher, in his city clothes, met them at the Saracen's Head with a private coach which was to take them to George Street. He conveyed Bella's warm love and greetings, also her apologies: there had been a crisis at the theatre and she was wanted there. Much serious thought had been given to a postponement; finally it had been decided to go ahead, but this meant a succession of extra rehearsals. A second dress rehearsal was fixed for Monday, and the first night of the play was to be Tuesday, as arranged. There would probably be four performances, with the possibility, if it were a great success, of its running into the next week.

'The postponement,' said Demelza, 'does it affect Bella?'

'Yes. Someone was injured in a duel fight, and this has meant a rearrangement of the cast.'

'Bella is playing another part?'

'Yes. But I think she might like to tell you all about it herself.'

'No doubt,' said Ross.

'Your letter about Valentine arrived yesterday. We were all very upset. Have you recovered, sir?'

'Thank you . . . On the whole. Very well.'

'It was the ape that started it?'

'Yes. He died too. He has been buried on the cliffs just above the ruins of the house. I believe Dr Enys has retained some parts of the body for research.'

Demelza shivered. 'I wish he had not done so. I don't know sometimes how Caroline manages with – with dissection taking place in the house.'

'Not in the house, my dear. He uses a part of the stables.'

'And then there was the arrest of Paul Kellow since I was down last? Too much has happened!'

The drive passed quickly, and they were soon unloading at No. 14. Mrs Parkins was there to greet them and help Christopher carry the bags upstairs.

'Would you care to stay and sup with us?' Demelza asked.

'Thank you very kindly, but I want to go back to the theatre, to pick Bella up when they have finished and to take her home.'

'What time will that be?'

'She thought eight or nine.'

'Then we shall not see her until the morning?'

'I am not at all sure. I am not sure even then, with the full dress rehearsal tomorrow. It all depends on McArdle, who is a perfectionist. I trust you will both be understanding. In the crisis. We, of course, never anticipated anything like this.'

'We should be more understanding,' Ross said pleasantly, 'if we knew what the crisis was.'

Christopher straightened his shoulders. 'If that is the case I think, sir, that I *could* take a drink, if you have one.'

Demelza pulled the bell for Mrs Parkins, and presently they were all sipping brandy and nibbling at Madeira cake.

Christopher said: 'I would very much have preferred that she should explain everything to you personally, but I see now that it is impossible for you to find your daughter too busy to see you this evening without a full explanation. And it seems I am the only one here to give it.'

'Does this mean it is bad news?'

'Oh, no! I hope you will be as excited as I am, but – but you may have qualms, have reservations. I don't know.'

'Well, tell us what has happened.'

Christopher explained about the grave accident to Arthur Scholes, the search for a replacement, the fine decision that had to be made between cancellation and postponement.

'In the end,' he said, 'in the end it was up to McArdle and Glossop to come to a final decision. Whether there was any *artistic* solution which would involve them in the least loss. So in the end they came to see Bella and asked if she thought she could play the part.'

Ross said: '*What?*'

Demelza swallowed and said: '*What part?*'

'That of Romeo.'

Chapter Eleven

Christopher said: 'I was not there at the time. I was at my office. It seemed they called her into the manager's room at the theatre and point-blank asked her if she thought she could do it.'

'*My God!*'

'And d'you know they said, they told me, that she replied almost without hesitation. "Yes, of course." '

There was a stunned silence.

'But this,' said Demelza, 'is the main part.'

'Yes, along with Juliet.'

'But she was – what is it? – covering for Juliet! This is the *man's* part!'

'It has sometimes been played by a woman. In fact, I gather, it is one of the great ambitions of our leading actresses to play it. Mrs Acton played it. And Mrs Armitage. I believe Siddons wanted to. She played Hamlet. Bella was to have played a man anyhow, in a small part.'

'It's – *impossible,*' Ross said.

Christopher said: 'You are the only one who has seen Bella on the professional stage. And she played the lead. What was your honest opinion of her?'

'I thought her fine. But she was playing a pretty young heiress . . . She sang beautifully, but this is utterly different! I must say the audience then was enthusiastic, but . . .'

'And that a foreign audience.'

'It is a mass of lines to memorize,' Ross said. 'She must be word perfect.'

'She seems to be. Or nearly. Remember she has been soaking up this play for weeks.'

500

Demelza said: 'But does not Romeo have to fight a duel? He must, from what you have told us!'

'Yes. But you may be sure Fergus Flynn, having disabled one Romeo – and in so doing has done his own acting career a grave disservice – he will make doubly sure he does not become over-realistic again . . . And Bella is a quick learner.'

'What does that mean?'

'Since hearing the news I have been teaching her the basic strokes and lunges. When Wellington spent a winter in Lisbon he organized various sports to keep his troops occupied. I won the fencing prize.'

Ross stood up. 'Were you behind this appointment, Christopher?'

'If you mean did I try to persuade her in either way, certainly not. I was not there when she agreed to play the role. I – I have not sought to dissuade her because I want her to *succeed*. This is an astounding chance. Even a noble failure might do her all the good in the world. Perhaps only I know how deeply she has felt about the loss of her singing voice. She said to me last week that she felt like nothing now – as if she did not properly exist. This extraordinary opportunity – to return not as an extra but to the *centre* of the stage will, I hope and believe, act like a renewal of her life. How could I persuade her *not* to do this?'

Ross looked at Demelza. 'What do you think?'

'I am lost.'

'There must have been some influence at work. I wonder if Edward Fitzmaurice had a hand in it?'

'They are in Norfolk,' Christopher said. 'Bella heard from Clowance yesterday.'

'What sort of a number of folk does the Royal Coburg hold?' Demelza asked.

'Somewhere around fifteen hundred to eighteen hundred.'

Demelza said nothing more, but looked at Ross almost appealingly.

Christopher intercepted the glance. 'There was no way of asking for your approval. She had said yes, and I had no authority to say no. I know it is a tremendous undertaking for her, and it may well not-come off.'

'You say a noble failure might do her good all the same,' said Ross. 'But what if the failure is not noble? It could be the end of her willingness to appear in public. It might kill her confidence completely. You must know how fierce and harsh a crowd can be. This cannot be the most refined of audiences. It draws on a poor district.'

'I do not suppose the audiences at Rouen were highly cultivated.'

'No, they were not. But by the time I saw the production Bella had become their favourite.'

'Pray God it happens here,' said Christopher.

It had not all occurred quite like that, but Christopher felt justified for the time being in lying by omission.

Observing the amount of influence Edward Fitzmaurice had wielded by means of an investment of £500 in the theatre, and thereafter being elected a trustee, Christopher had sold the new house (at a substantial profit) and invested £500 in the Royal Coburg. He had reasoned then that if Bella did well in her small speaking part, his influence as a trustee would help Mr Glossop to think favourably of her for some larger part in the near future. He obviously had had no other thought in mind, but he felt it essential to help Bella to go on climbing the new ladder. He could not bear to think of her as destroyed.

Thereafter had come the accident and, unknown to Bella, he had tackled, first, Mr Glossop alone, secondly Frederick McArdle, and then the two men together. There had been instant resistance, though not a hostile one. McArdle surprisingly had been the more amenable, though still against the idea. 'A woman, a girl, it must be fifteen years or more since Mrs Acton did it. It was not badly received. There's always a special interest in a woman playing a man's part. Shakespeare knew all about that. Doublet and hose, a hint of prurience. Bella has certainly got the looks and the presence. But she's got *no* experience. Ach, no, this is a rough audience. Sorry, Christopher, I think for your lady. I doubt she would entertain it.'

'Ask her.'

'No, it's too great a risk,' said Glossop firmly. 'My family has sunk thousands into this theatre. If this production were an ordinary failure it would involve a considerable loss all round. If it were a fiasco it would ruin the reputation we are trying to build up.'

'I am not without money,' Christopher said. 'I would be willing to advance you a draft for a further five hundred pounds to cover any possible loss on this production. If it is a failure the money can go to expenses that you can't retrieve. If it is a success the draft can go to the purchase of five more shares in the production company.'

Glossop rubbed his fat chin. 'You have great faith in Miss Poldark, Havergal.'

'I have known her a long time.'

'What do you think, McArdle?'

'I've been considering,' the director said. 'I have been looking at ways in which we could make a virtue of necessity, so to speak. That she is a young woman, quite unknown, never before set foot on a London stage, trained as an opera singer, a huge success in Paris. That would bring people in . . . If then it all turned out a dreadful failure they could turn nasty.'

Money had been talking to Mr Glossop. He said: 'Do you think any of the existing cast would resent such premature promotion?'

'Whether they do or not,' McArdle said, 'I'll see that they do not show it.'

Monday it rained all day. Bella was called for still one more rehearsal at the theatre, and they did not see her until after dinner, when Christopher brought her to see them at about five. She was glowing, taut, now and then abruptly silent, thoughtful, her hair shortened and subdued. She was wearing a simple blue dress with a ruffed collar that could well have been adapted for a young man. It was clear that she was thinking herself into the part.

Mother-catlike, Demelza looked her over and wondered if, after the grave illness of the summer, she were not being persuaded to put too great a strain upon her youthful vitality. Even her voice had darkened a little; possibly it was deliberate to go with the assumption of maleness, but would it hold out under the strain of speaking, almost declaiming, before an audience of more than a thousand people?

In spite of these thoughts, it was a lively meeting. She and Christopher appeared to be on the old affectionate terms. What if Maurice were suddenly to turn up?

Tuesday was fine, and the rain had lifted. Bella said she would not see her parents before the opening. She was going to have a quiet morning, a light meal at the theatre. Ross and Demelza were to dine with Mrs Pelham and go on to the theatre at six-thirty. There was to be a light comic play called *Harlequin* first, and *The Two Lovers of Verona* was due to start at seven.

Time dragged; darkness fell; a light rain came down and then cleared. They climbed into Mrs Pelham's carriage and clopped off at a measured pace towards Bella's destiny.

Waterloo Bridge was lit by gas lamps, winking and reflecting off the Thames, which as usual was full of lightermen and looked like an intermittent snake of glow-worms.

So to the theatre. A handsome facade, and it seemed as if the crowd which was to fill the house was still outside. Christopher was waiting for them at the main door and led them to their box. They went in as quietly as possible so as not to disturb the actors already singing and dancing on the gaudy stage. Few others in the pit or in the gallery seemed to mind disturbing or competing with the singers in any way they chose.

'They are going to install gas in the New Year,' Christopher said. 'I'm not sure that I like it: these lamps give off a more mellow light.'

The box was close to the stage, scarcely a man's height above the level of the stage and as far back from it. This was a farce that was being enacted and the crudely painted faces of the actors were there to invite laughter, even derision. They tripped up and fell over each other, women shouted and put out their tongues, the twelve-piece orchestra brayed. The theatre was already more than half full; people were pouring in, pushing and crushing to get a good position.

Demelza thought: 'Why did I ever *let* this happen? I could have stopped it all at the very beginning! Said: "Bella, *no!* This is not for you – it is not for us. We are genteel country folk, provincials, concerned with the seasons and the weather and the ordinary, lovingly commonplace routine of animals and crops and the turning world." Why did I ever let her become mixed up in such brash, trumpery tinsel as this? Why does she have to *expose* herself to the stares and the catcalls of all these Londoners, who work in dark factories and come out in the evening to be entertained with crude jokes and pantomime action? It is Bella who will shortly have to come out on that stage and pretend to be a lovesick young man.

Ross is not *short* of money now. Well enough to go to a theatre to be entertained. But not, *not* to take part! Bella will soon be coming on before this rabble. Dear God, I think I shall faint! If I fainted, could I stop it all?'

The musical was coming to an end. The actors were bowing and the orchestra was rising to a crescendo, and in a moment the curtains fell across the stage and all went dark.

Christopher had given her a programme, but she could not hold her hand steady enough to read it. There was some reference to Miss Bella Poldark in larger print, but she did not *want* to read it. It would only upset her the more.

The curtains parted, and a tall thin man in the black and white evening suit made de rigueur by the dictates of Beau Brummel began to speak into a gradually decreasing hubbub of sound. He appeared to be telling the audience what they already knew – about the nature of Shakespeare's tragedy, the remarkable cast which had been assembled to depict it, a late substitution for the actor playing Romeo because of the unfortunate accident happening to Mr Arthur Scholes, the singular good fortune of the management in securing the services of Mlle Bella Poldark, who, fresh from her triumphs in Paris, had agreed *at short notice* to take over the leading role (pause for applause, which was muted). He must also recommend to their attention the remarkable scenery, which had been specially designed and painted and built for this play alone.

He had talked the audience into semi-silence, and now, after he had bowed and withdrawn through the velvet curtains, there was a brief pregnant pause, then the curtains slowly parted to reveal a busy street in Verona.

Scenery had come to mean a lot to a modern audience, and there was a solid round of clapping and whistles of approval. A score of people were on the stage, walking about, women with their baskets, men strolling and talking, a beggar at a corner, stately steps leading to a porticoed mansion on the left. The costumes too were excellently done, colour generally khaki or brown, but with a slash of yellow or scarlet about a woman's head or throat. A convincing scene. The audience was ready to watch and listen.

They had chosen the beggar to speak the prologue, and presently he climbed to his feet, yawned, smoothed down his ragged jacket and came centre stage to speak.

'Two households, both alike in dignity,
In fair Verona, where we lay our scene . . .'

So the play began, the peaceful scene suddenly rent by a quarrel
between the servants and the relatives of the Montagues and the
Capulets, breaking into a fierce fight with swords and bucklers. A
good deal of practice had gone into the battle and it greatly pleased
the audience. Benvolio, Romeo's friend, tries to stop the quarrel,
but it is fanned into flames again by the fiercely quarrelsome
Tybalt, Juliet's cousin. This further duel is quelled by citizens with
clubs and then by the arrival of Lord and Lady Montague and Lord
and Lady Capulet, and then the Prince of Verona himself, to
threaten death or banishment to anyone who in future dares to
break the peace.

As people begin to disperse, Romeo is discussed by his father
and others. Where is he? What is amiss with him? Onto the largely
emptied stage Romeo strolls to meet Benvolio and explain he is
desperately in love with his cousin Rosaline.

Demelza hardly recognized her daughter. Dressed in scarlet
doublet and hose, hair drawn tightly back and slightly darkened
under a soft scarlet cap, sword at hip. Her voice was lighter than
most of the men's, but heavier than usual, every word clearly but
casually enunciated, as if she spoke the words as she thought them.

'Love is a smoke rais'd with the fume of sighs,
Being purged, a fire sparkling in lovers' eyes;
Being vexed, a sea nourished with lovers' tears.
What is it else? a madness most discreet . . .'

The audience, though still restive, was not, as far as one could
see, put off by Bella's sex. Once the play had moved to the great
scene in the Ballroom, and Romeo, having been persuaded to go
to the Ball masked, has seen Juliet for the first time and, Rosaline
forgot, realizes she is the one and only love of his life, then the
audience began to watch and listen more attentively. It was fortunate that Charlotte Bancroft was three inches shorter. In a light silk
dress with hair falling over her shoulders, there was a sufficient
disparity between them to foster the illusion. What astonished
Demelza almost more than anything was that her daughter spoke

with such confidence and so clearly. One year's elocution at Dr Fredericks' Academy! Although she did not shout, as one or two of the men did, her voice came over clearer than any of the others. And much of it was poetry, to be declaimed. Yet she might have been talking in the kitchen of Nampara.

Then Romeo is recognized by Tybalt and denounced to Lord Capulet, but Lord Capulet pacifies his angry kinsman and refuses to turn Romeo away.

At this stage Demelza somehow lost touch with reality and became involved with the star-crossed lovers, not forgetting life as it was but transported to this new tragedy on the stage.

At the end of the Ballroom scene Christopher excused himself with a whispered apology. Bella had not wanted him to come round at the impending interval, but he said he wanted to gauge Mr Glossop's reaction so far.

'And what is your reaction – so far, Christopher?' Demelza asked.

He hesitated. 'I have a great faith in her, but this beats my expectations.'

When he had gone she felt Ross put his hand over hers. 'So far . . .'

'I'm mazed, Ross. Is this *our* Bella?'

'Well, I saw her in Rouen, but I was not prepared for this.'

'Have they darkened her skin?'

'Just a little about the chin. Very subtly, I may say.'

'The way she stands. And walks! Just like a man!'

'Some men. A hint of swagger, but not overdone. I think she is going to succeed.'

'I'm scared to death.'

'So am I. But of what particularly?'

'The fencing.'

'Ye-es,' Ross said. 'But it is only make-believe.'

'Do not forget the first Romeo.'

The play broke at the end of Act 2 Scene 2, when Romeo, having climbed the wall of the orchard behind the Capulets' mansion, makes contact with Juliet and swears his undying love. There are then the long and famous passages between the two, he mainly in the garden, she on the balcony. Here Bella spoke with real passion, occasionally missing a few words, but conveying her feelings with such vehemence and exaltation that the audience forgot to shuffle and stir, but listened with quiet breath. Charlotte Bancroft, not to be outdone, played her part beautifully as a child just come to an engulfing love. When the curtain came down for the interval there was a burst of applause.

Somehow the interlude was endured. The obligatory musical extract had taken place during the scene at the Ball: singers had come on, and some dancers. This had received more catcalls than either of the plays. When the proper interval arrived there was total confusion both in the gallery and the pit; men and women pushed to get out, others pushed with equal urgency to get in, to improve their seating or their viewing. The ham-sandwich men and the pigs' trotter women and the boys with their trays of whelks did a fine trade.

Presently a church-like bell was rung in the orchestra pit and this, repeated at regular two-minute intervals, presently persuaded the audience that the play was about to resume.

The opening scene was in Friar Laurence's cell, and it began with a long speech by the monk before Romeo entered, which gave extra time for the seething multitude to settle down before the continuation of the story. In the ensuing scene Tybalt, not merely Juliet's cousin but master swordsman, picks a quarrel with Mercutio; they draw and in the swordfight which follows Mercutio is run through and dies a long and painful death. Romeo, who has striven to prevent the first fight, is now driven by grief to challenge Tybalt.

Now comes the crux of the swordplay and the duel between them, the one in which Arthur Scholes had been wounded in the eye. This audience cannot bear with obvious pretence. They must *believe* blood is spilt. In the street bounded by the sun-bright houses of Verona and surrounded more closely by a watching crowd, Romeo and Tybalt fought for their lives. Each evening Christopher had come to plan the contest, feints here and thrusts there, lunges and parries. In seven days he had worked wonders with the appearance of this fight. Even Fergus Flynn was an actor and not a fencer. Christopher had instructed them both, particularly on footwork, in how to stop-hit, how to riposte and parry and give ground at the same time, in the *flèche* and *redoublement*. He had even given them steps to learn so that they should come closer to each other, look in each other's eyes, challenge with strength of arm and then break apart to return to the thrust and parry. An old cart had been brought in so that Bella could dance behind it when apparently she was getting the worst of it. Then she took the offensive and drove Tybalt across the square to the steps up to the Capulets' mansion.

Here she slipped, fell on the second step but cat-like was up before Tybalt could draw his arm back. (This was an accident, Bella swore, but on McArdle's insistence it had to be repeated every night.) Back and forward they fought until, trapping Tybalt into a crude forward rush, point aimed at her, she danced aside and thrust her sword into the left side of his chest. Tybalt was slain.

Benvolio's urgent warnings to Romeo to flee the country while he could were totally lost in the roar of approval from the audience at the brilliant audacity of the fight.

Then on through all the mistakes and tragedies of Romeo's banishment, his short night of passionate love with his wife, their agonized parting, Romeo's utter despair, the schemes of Friar Laurence and the Nurse, contriving to help, Laurence's potion to send Juliet into a death-like trance for forty-two hours, her taking the potion, the discovery by the Nurse and her parents that she had died in the night. Her burial, a further duel in the crypt between Paris, her parents' choice as husband, and a distraught Romeo, who finally, having killed Paris, kills himself, believing Juliet dead – her own recovery to find Romeo's body and resultant suicide.

So to the final words of the Prince of Verona:

> A glooming peace this morning with it brings;
> The sun for sorrow will not show his head;
> Go hence, to have more talk of these sad things.
> Some shall be pardoned and some punished;
> For never was a story of more woe
> Than this of Juliet and her Romeo

and the exiting in silence from the stage of the other actors, leaving the three corpses alone. All clearly was well with the audience. But when the curtains finally fell no one in the production was prepared for the rapturous storm of applause that greeted it.

Chapter Twelve

When the approbation was at its height and the curtain was coming up for the fifth time Demelza burst into tears and for a while could not stop. It was a deeply emotional moment, but life for her had been tense and deeply emotional for more than a month and in ways she had had no reason to anticipate or expect. Little more than five weeks before Paul Kellow had attacked her and she had barely escaped with her life. It was less than two weeks since Valentine had died and Ross might well have died too – in a tragedy of Shakespearean proportions. Later there had been the coolness between herself and Ross, of which a trace still existed. She had become far too involved in the outcome of Bella's first appearance in London, and this astonishing success seemed too good to be true. She cried like a child, and Mrs Pelham put her arm round her shoulders and comforted her at the moment of her daughter's triumph.

They made their way out as best they could, since most of the audience was remaining to see the half-hour spectacle which would conclude the evening. They were eventually joined by Christopher and Bella, she mostly transformed back again into her normal sex and character.

It was a cramped but joyous party that shared the coach (Christopher sitting up beside the coachman). They reached Mrs Pelham's house and went in to take a light supper together; it being well after midnight before they all dispersed.

Demelza expressed a wish to walk home. It was more than a mile, but she said she could not sleep yet and had a wish to unwind. A piece of old moon had risen since they went in, and the streets for the most part were all well lighted and no longer busy. She said: 'I have no fear of footpads. You are so tall you would scare anyone away.'

'What an evening!' said Ross presently. 'I am proud of all my children, but this one exceeds everything else that has ever happened.'

'She was so *quiet* after it!' exclaimed Demelza. 'Over supper. *Much* quieter than usual – you know how *talkative* she usually is. And she ate very little. Just sitting there and smiling and every so often taking a deep, deep breath.'

'She must have been *drained*,' Ross said. 'Apart from the nervous tension and the physical action, the *passion*!'

'I know. And those speeches to Friar – Friar Laurence! How did Bella know how to say it as if she spoke from her own soul – from a *man's* soul?'

'That is talent,' said Ross, 'of the highest order. Perhaps something more.'

A beggar came mumbling up, and Ross gave him a handful of coins. The old man was startled and showed his bad teeth in a joyous grin before retreating into an alley.

'Christopher is on air. He has done so much for her. Teaching her to fight a duel! I was terrified that she would get some disfigurement!'

'And all to do again tomorrow.'

'We *must* go again tomorrow, Ross! Can we get the same box?'

'I don't know if I can stand it. Supposing it did not go so well?'

'We must be there. I expect Christopher can contrive something.'

Ross said: 'I wonder if he has some special influence over Glossop? I overheard them speaking together tonight as we came away, and Glossop said something about how pleased he was that he had yielded to Christopher's pressure.'

'Do you mean . . . Well, pressure could just mean persuasion.'

'Of course. Of course.'

'Do you suppose it was more than that?'

'Mayhap yes. Mayhap no. Both Glossop and McArdle are astute businessmen – and very clever judges of an actor's potential into the bargain.'

'Does it matter?'

'Not really – in the event. Not in the least. When I get the right opportunity I will ask Christopher.'

Demelza stared up at the old moon scrutinizing them between the serried rows of chimney pots. 'I don't think I should do that, Ross.'

'Why not? Have you a special reason?'

'Well, it may be. Christopher has been some *wonderful*. He first got Edward to use his influence to provide Bella with a part. They did that. They gave her a tiny part. But nobody expected this accident to Arthur Scholes! The first was a small favour compared to the favour of taking her out of obscurity to play the lead – the leading *man's* part. Of course – of course they had in the meanwhile seen Bella, seen her in doublet and hose, been impressed with her potential maybe. But it was an *enormous* leap of faith. Would they have been willing to take this huge risk entirely on their own judgement?'

'But that is precisely what I suspect!' Ross said. 'That is why I question what might have been implied by what Glossop said! If Christopher had money enough of his own to propose some financial deal . . .'

'Then if he wishes to keep quiet about it, he should be allowed to. He is playing for high stakes.'

'Bella?'

'I do not know what their relationship is at present. It seems good. More than good. But if she marries him she should not feel she is doing it partly out of gratitude. And neither will he want to feel that gratitude towards him is why she prefers him to Maurice or some other young man that comes along. And I expect after this success there will be young men a-plenty.'

'I wonder if her voice will completely return?'

'It was brilliantly clear-spoken tonight, but deeper. That, I know, was put on. I do not know how she will estimate her success tonight against her appearance in *The Barber*.'

'The audience in France was very enthusiastic.'

Demelza took a trembling happy breath. 'It is wonderful to succeed in two ways. I think – I dare think, Ross, that her personality plays a big part. The audience seems at once to – to *take* to her!'

'It will be more than interesting to see what tomorrow's papers have to say. Critics are much harder to please, and if an audience shouts its approval they will often take a contrary view.'

'When will the papers be out?'

'Early tomorrow. They may not all review it. I have ordered the most important four, and Mrs Pelham's lad will fetch them before breakfast.'

Chapter Thirteen

Excerpt from the *Morning Chronicle*, the ninth of December 1820:

London is renowned for the great fruit and vegetable market in Covent Garden. This is certainly the most famous in England, some would claim in the world. The best fruit available is brought there for our delectation: Strawberries from Sussex, Plums from Worcestershire, Pears from Dorset, Apples from Somerset, Cherries from Kent. But this week the Connoisseurs of our fruit supplies allowed a Peach, apparently brought from that dark and craggy county west of the Tamar, to slip through their fingers and be offered up not in Covent Garden, not even in Drury Lane, but in that relatively unimportant and minor theatre on the other side of the Thames, to be exhibited at one of the first attempts of the Management of the Royal Coburg to break away from their routine of Spectacular and Melodramatic trash; putting on a play called *Two Lovers of Verona*. This Mr William Shakespeare would no doubt recognize as akin to that little piece he once wrote called *Romeo and Juliet*, the name in this case having been changed – and a few other things – to comply with the threadbare and antiquated Law passed in the days of Charles II.

What is this all about? First, but incidentally, it is to congratulate Mr Frederick McArdle and Mr Joseph Glossop on having produced a play which for staging, acting and general excellence would have done credit to either of the patent theatres. But chiefly it is all about a young lady who last night appeared as Romeo in this production. She has, it seems, appeared only once before on a public stage, where she 'starred' in the leading female role in *The Barber of Seville* at the Théâtre Jeanne d'Arc in Paris.

Indeed it has been advertised that Miss Bella Poldark is herself French – a natural distortion, we suppose, on the part of the Management to attract an audience; but in fact she seems to be as English as any full-blooded Cornish maid can be. The reason for her appointment to play such a plum part – a part we may say that is at the apex of the ambitions of most of our leading actresses – is because of an unfortunate accident which happened to Mr Arthur Scholes, scheduled to appear as Romeo, and which caused him to withdraw.

So what do we see? A pretty girl quite out of her depth with her immortal lines and speaking them by rote? And too pretty to be a boy. But stay, are there not pretty boys? In our struggle to accept this subterfuge, we are quite quickly arrested by Miss Poldark's *élan*, her strong voice, the vigour and articulacy with which she utters every word, her sheer presence, which carries us along and presently swamps our disbelief. Not only does she look like a young man, she behaves like one, striding about the stage, leaping here and there with elastic elasticity. And, merciful Heaven, fencing like a master! Miss Charlotte Bancroft makes a charming and pliant Juliet; but in all justice we have to confess where our main interest was focused.

We do not need to urge you to keep an eye on young Miss Poldark. If we are doing our job as critics I fancy a lot more will be written about her in the next decade or so. We personally would like to see her play, say, Portia, or Viola, or even Lady Macbeth! Yet may we enter a formal plea that she should not neglect her ability in taking a man's part. After all, in addition to her other attributes, she has the prettiest legs seen on the stage this century.

The Times of the same date carried a piece recording that

as a replacement for Mr Arthur Scholes, who had been seriously injured in rehearsals, the Management of the Royal Coburg Theatre, Waterloo, has introduced a singular young woman who quite took the house by storm. She created a young Romeo of consummate grace and skill, a fiery young gallant, who fights his duels with the same elegance and conviction as he brings to his poetic, gloriously masculine wooing of Juliet. It is a performance such as we have not seen in this part for many years. As an actress she must be celebrated as the find of the season.

The *Morning Post* headed its piece 'Arrival of an Actress'. It reviewed the play at length, while criticizing the unsatisfactory attempts to evade the Patent Law and prophesying that the management was likely to have to pay a fine for transgressing it. The review went on: 'Few Romeos in London's memory have looked young enough and passionately agile enough to be convincing.' And ended: 'The play's final scenes can only be seen through a mist of tears.'

The *Morning Herald* contained a few comments, the critic probably not having been present, but said: 'At the end the house was raised to the wildest excitement.'

The second performance of *Two Lovers of Verona* went off as successfully as the first. Clearly word of mouth had been favourable, and the pit and the gallery, which had looked full last night, were now compressed to insufferable limits. But the audience suffered them, and this time applauded constantly throughout the play.

Christopher Havergal was almost late for the third performance on the Thursday; he arrived at the theatre half an hour before the curtain was due to rise. When he tapped at the dressing-room door and was told to enter, he found Bella already clad for her part.

'Sorry, sorry, darling.' He kissed her. 'There was a minor crisis at Rothschild's and I could not excuse myself. But what wonderful news!'

'Christopher. I'm glad you're in time. I've been rehearsing this afternoon with Charlotte; just those speeches on the balcony and a few small points. You mean – wonderful news – you mean the letter?'

'Of course I mean the letter, you little silly! Do I not! Do I not!'

She said primly: 'I left it at the door for you.'

'I know you did, darling, and I have brought it with me in supreme triumph.'

'Explain it to me.'

'You don't need any. This speaks superbly for itself. Read it again! Read it out loud if you have the smallest doubts!'

She took the letter from him, shook it out between thumb and forefinger as if there might be some enclosure she had been missing.

'Go on!'

She read:

Dear Miss Poldark,

I wonder if you could call to see me sometime. I would like to discuss with you a prospect I have of producing *Othello* at Covent Garden. The play is scheduled to open on Thursday, January 11. I already have the promise of Mr John Julius Booth to play the name part, and Mr Thomas Cobham to play Iago. If we can come to a satisfactory agreement on conditions and terms, I would be willing to offer you the part of Desdemona. This play will probably go into repertory and run possibly to ten performances. If you would kindly send me word I would make myself available to see you. Might I suggest about twelve noon on any day from Friday next onwards?

Believe me, most faithfully yours,

Charles Kemble

'*Charles* Kemble?' said Bella.

'He is the younger brother. He took over the management of Covent Garden a couple of years ago.'

'Do you think he has been to see this play?'

'You can bet your last guinea on it! He is too experienced to rely on press reviews.'

'I've heard of John Julius Booth, but not of the other man. Is he . . . ?'

'They're both top of the tree, only Kean being way above either of them. It would be a testing time for you. This has been your launch. That would be your first voyage.'

'A shipwreck?'

'Having seen you in this production I would say impossible.'

She showed a trace of dimples as she put a smear of dark stain on her chin.

516

'Unsinkable,' Christopher added, with a touch of humour.

'Oh,' Bella said, 'Mama asked if she might watch an act tonight from behind the scenes. I asked Mr McArdle and he said that he was quite agreeable.'

'Are you?'

'I? Yes, of course. When I get . . . get on I forget who is watching me and from where. But I was thinking – the wings get very crowded. Would you be about if she should need some help?'

'With the greatest pleasure. But I don't believe she will.'

'Well, she might perhaps—'

'Your mother is still a beautiful woman. I don't know if you've noticed that.'

'Of course I have. She is—'

'A lady who looks as attractive as she does is not likely to be jostled against or disregarded. I sometimes wonder . . .'

'What?'

'If you are not an amalgam, a mixture of your father and mother, partaking of the best qualities of both. You have the energy of your mother, the staying power of your father. You're too much like your father to be as pretty as she is. But you are full of her determination and strength. When you stand on the stage you attract attention like – like a magnet with iron filings. And I have always been in love with you from the moment I first saw you in the British Embassy in Paris in eighteen fifteen. Remember?'

She turned her eyes on him. Their conversation when they were alone together was often light-hearted, half-teasing. But she knew when his voice changed.

'Of course I remember,' she said. 'You showed me Josephine's bedroom.'

'So I did,' said Christopher. 'So I did. A simple child you were then. But now . . .'

'Now?'

'Now you are dressed up as a man, acting as a man, behaving like a man. Yet to me this attire, this doublet and hose and shortened hair, this masculine shirt and flat-heeled shoes and deliberately deepened voice: to me they all make you look more outrageously feminine than ever before. You won't let me down, will you?'

'Let you *down*?'

He half-smiled, revealing rarely shown teeth. But it was almost a wolfish smile. 'Bella, you have always bewitched me. I would kill for you!'

'Kill me?'

'*No!* To *get* you!'

Her eyes did not waver. 'Christopher, dearest. You will not have to.'

It had been a fancy of Demelza's that she should view at least one act from the wings. When no objection was raised, she chose to go behind for the ballroom scene in the earlier part of the play.

Her interest, she had told herself, was largely cheerful curiosity. She wanted to watch the scene shifters at work, see how they could transform a stage in a few hasty minutes, how the actors could be trained to assemble and be in exactly the right place when the curtain went up again. In the big scene of the ballroom this should be specially interesting. But when it came to the point she discovered that *all* her attention was centred on her daughter. After all, she was playing the *lead*. How had it come about that Bella, whom she had suckled as a baby, succoured as a little girl, nursed through a few mild childhood ailments and one serious illness earlier this year – how had it come about that she was playing one of Shakespeare's greatest roles in London in front of a concourse of people who now applauded her at the end of every scene? Just as when Julia and Jeremy died it had torn a piece out of her heart, now it seemed to warm, to burn, to stupefy, to enchant her heart that this other child of hers should be elevated and celebrated and almost fêted in this bizarre setting.

She stood amid the crowd in the wings when Bella came from her dressing room, beamed at her mother, kissed her, waited for her cue, changed her expression, then strode out like some power upon the stage – then to watch this whole scene from the side, watched it develop, change, tense up, become more complex, resolve itself. Ten minutes of magic, then Bella came off to more applause, stood in the wings, went out again, returned and took her mother's hand. Demelza could feel the girl was strung up, her nerves taut, breathing deep as if after a race, her whole body, it seemed, in a high even glow. She listened with a charming modesty to whispered congratulations, put her head briefly on her mother's shoulder, then accepted a warm shawl from a dresser and made her way back to the dressing room to prepare for the next scene.

When at the interval Demelza was shown back to the box, Ross said: 'You look as if you have seen a vision.'

'I have.' She settled into her chair, holding tight to her impressions, as if afraid someone might steal them.

Then the curtain went up again, and silence reigned in the box. When the curtain fell Ross said: 'Have you seen who is sitting in the box opposite?'

She looked. 'Heavens! It is Clowance and Edward! Heavens! They were not here when I left!'

'They were late. They sent a note over. Their coach broke a wheel. They wanted it to be a surprise.'

'Oh, how lovely!' She caught Clowance's eye and waved. They waved back.

'Mrs Pelham,' Demelza said. 'I do not know how we can possibly thank you enough for all you have done for Bella.'

'It has been the greatest pleasure, my dear.'

'You are good to say that. But even if it is true, and I trust it is, that does not repay the – the obligation, as you might say.'

They were taking supper together on the following night at Edward Fitzmaurice's apartment in Lansdowne House. The time was already eleven. They had told Bella she could be excused, but she said, rubbish, she would sleep on in the morning. It was just Ross and Demelza, Bella and Christopher, Sarah Pelham, Edward and Clowance.

The newly-weds had come home in haste, having seen a copy of Wednesday's *Times* in Norfolk, and left early to catch a performance of *Two Lovers of Verona* before it came off. When they reached London – late anyway – they found that, owing to the play's success, it was prolonging its run by four performances, the last being next Wednesday.

Demelza continued: 'You being so generous has made all the difference right from the very beginning. By having Bella to stay for so long – compared to what her life would have been like if she had been living in a boarding house! Christopher has been wonderful, but without you none of this might have happened at all!'

Mrs Pelham patted her hand. 'Believe me, it has all been *such* a pleasure.'

'And now,' Demelza said, 'I am planning this Christmas party. It would give us *all such pleasure* – in return. Ross and I and Bella are leaving for home next Thursday. Christopher will come down with Edward and Clowance on Saturday. Dwight and Caroline will certainly join in with their children. Then my daughter-in-law Cuby – who I think you have never met – with my granddaughter, will certainly be there . . .'

Mrs Pelham was still holding Demelza's hand. She gave it a little squeeze.

'You know, my dear, you must know how often Caroline has pressed me to stay with her in Cornwall. I have always pleaded that I belong in city life. I have always said that I have never travelled further west than Staines! It is *true*! *Now*, now, aside from preference, I am too *old* to travel. I am seventy-eight – though pray do not tell my friends! I shall see much more of you in the next few years; you *must* come more to London – with one of your daughters married to a Fitzmaurice and the other destined to be famous on the stage! . . . I think I must pray to be excused the journey and be allowed to look forward to your next visit here.'

Demelza sighed and then smiled. 'For me this will be a very important party. It will be quite small, but I did want *all* my friends, and you, dear Mrs Pelham, I count as one of the dearest.'

Demelza was in fact giving voice to an idea that until then had been no more than a few whispered sentences exchanged between Ross and herself last night. Bella had told her that she would like to come home for Christmas. Ross had booked seats on the Royal London Mail for Thursday because he had a meeting with the lawyers in Truro on the Monday following. Now it fitted in perfectly because Bella could return with them. Christopher could not get away from Rothschild's until Saturday. This suited Edward and Clowance, who were leaving on the Saturday afternoon. Demelza was very flattered that both her daughters wanted to spend Christmas at Nampara. 'One for pleasure, two for joy,' she said to Ross when they heard of Edward and Clowance's intention.

'Will you mind Bella travelling with us, Christopher?' she asked.

'I shall be hard on your heels,' he said. 'And if Bella is engaged to play in *Othello* she will need to be back by the fourth of January at the latest. It will give her two weeks at home.'

'Do you – do you believe that she will get the part?'

Christopher said: 'I always expect the impossible of Bella, and she always exceeds my expectations.'

Three more days of the *Two Lovers of Verona* and then it was all goodbyes to one's fellow actors, to the stagehands, to Frederick McArdle and Joseph Glossop. Bella seemed to be kissed by everyone – only perhaps Henry Davidson, who had played Mercutio, was a little grudging; no doubt he felt that an experienced actor of twenty-eight should have been given preference over an untried girl ten years his junior. And who could blame him? The others were typically theatrical in their warmth. 'I'll be back!' Bella said over and over again. 'And thank you, thank you. I'll be back,' she said to Frederick McArdle. 'I shall expect you,' he replied with equal warmth, while nearby Joseph Glossop smiled benignly, knowing that if she continued as she had begun he would have to compete for her with people like Charles Kemble, who would have the greater pull.

It was a rush to catch the mail coach on the Thursday, for it left at seven-thirty and Bella was rubbing the sleep out of her eyes as she climbed aboard. There were two other inside passengers, so personal conversation was not possible. But Ross had heard Basingstoke given as their destination, so perhaps with luck no one else would join it there.

For a little while after leaving London and going through the brickworks and the market gardens Ross stared out and felt a slow malaise creeping upon him: it was the malaise connected with Valentine's death, and while he had been in London, particularly while caught up in the delights of his daughter's success, he had been free of it. Now, for once, he did not relish returning home and resuming the responsibilities of the life he had left behind. The useless, pointless loss of Valentine hung about him like a threadbare coat which was waiting to be put on again. The strange hallucination he had suffered when about to be dragged back from the burning house still plagued him in moments just waking or near sleeping.

He must, he knew, never allow it ever again to come between him and Demelza. He shared totally her exuberance over Bella's astonishing success. But Demelza had acute perceptions. He must hide all darker thoughts from her. He must put on a brave face, a good-tempered face, which *should* not be difficult because the happy face was the *true* one; there should be no need to pretend feelings which his common sense told him were entirely genuine.

He thought again of George, and then of Harriet. Perhaps her influence had helped to tone down George's jealousies, his malevolences. Why had she ever married him? She had attempted to explain that evening they had met at Prideaux Place. They had been talking about absolutes, and she had said: 'Of course I married George for his money. But something else besides. I was physically attracted – sexually attracted by him – not by his looks – though he is not all that bad looking. Shall we say I am a self-willed woman and relish challenge?'

There she had paused for a moment and added: 'Let us say that I was sexually attracted to him by the transparent ugliness of his moral character.'

It was a sentence Ross would not forget. Although half-humorous in intent, it showed a deep insight into her nature. It explained a lot.

In the coach he thought of his liking for Harriet. It was truly a physical – a sexual – attraction. But the sexual appeal was short of lust, the liking not near enough to love. He knew that but for the existence of George they could become fast friends.

It stood to reason that George would still contrive, or make the attempt, to gain control, custody, influence over little Georgie. But limping to the theatre across the bridge one day it had occurred to Ross to think that maybe his own fears had been exaggerated. Even if somehow in the years ahead George contrived to exercise control or influence over Georgie, it need not follow that he would be able to re-create the boy after his own image. George had made earnest attempts to make friends and acolytes of two young men, Valentine and Geoffrey Charles, and they had both ended up by hating him.

After Basingstoke their luck held and no one else joined the coach inside. It had been a substantial dinner, if stodgy, and once they were off again Bella went to sleep, making up for an accumulation of short nights.

Near Andover they were halted because of a broken trace, and Bella woke up, smiled sleepy-eyed at them both, and took to reading a thin green book, on the spine of which Demelza was able to discern, in small gold letters, *Othello*.

Presently she put the book down. Demelza said: 'You haven't told us much about your interview.'

'With Mr Kemble? I'm sorry. I gave Christopher all the details, and then when you came in I just sort of told you the outcome. After that it has been all rush, rush. *Sorry.*'

'Did you like him?'

'Oh, yes. He's an actor, of course. An actor-manager. Very charming and agreeable, light-hearted. The only moment when he was not light-hearted was when we spoke about money. He offered me three hundred pounds for the ten performances. Christopher had told me to ask five hundred pounds. Mr Kemble was very shocked, hinted at my inexperience, the risks they were taking, spoke of something he called "overheads". He gave me a glass of lemonade. Then he said he had heard I could sing, had sung in opera. I told him what had happened. He excused himself and went out to consult someone else. When he came back he said the most the theatre could offer was four hundred pounds, so I accepted that.'

The coach rattled disconcertingly. Demelza let out a deep breath. 'At this rate, you will soon be rich, my lover.'

'Well, it is very nice to earn so much. But Mr Kemble is quite right. I *am* inexperienced. I am learning something new every day. Dr Fredericks, I know now, was *such* a good teacher.'

'Working with high talent,' Ross said. Bella dimpled. 'Christopher did not go with you to see Mr Kemble?'

'I asked him to. He said he thought I ought not to shelter behind him. He did not think I ought to seem to be his protégé.'

Ross nodded approval. 'Which in a sense you are. How *did* you come to fence so well?'

She smiled again. 'Every morning before he left for the bank he came to Mrs Pelham's and we fenced for an hour. Then there were evenings too. As you say, I am his protégé.'

'Are you going to marry him?' Demelza asked suddenly.

'Yes.' The reply came without hesitation.

'Oh, I'm *glad,*' Demelza said.

'You have a date?' Ross asked.

'No. It seems that he had to sell the house he bought for us earlier this year. He is a bit mysterious about such things . . . But he's – very clever, I am sure he will arrange something else.'

Ross said: 'I remember it was thought when he joined Rothschild's that he might not make much progress because he was not a Jew. But the Jews are never above recognizing a man of parts when they find one.'

It had hardly stopped raining while they were in London, and the trip to Cornwall was no exception. This led to pools of mud on the road, the horses struggling against a wet wind, and inevitable delays. Demelza speculated that the Lansdowne coach leaving London two days later might eventually catch up.

When they reached Yeovil it was late, and they were content to take a light supper and stumble off to bed. But when dawn came and a lifting of the clouds presaged a clearer day, Demelza was bright-eyed with plans for the Christmas party. Nampara was very uncommodious, but she was determined this time to house all her visitors, not depend upon the generosity of the Enyses or the Geoffrey Charleses. On a sheet of paper and with a black crayon she had purloined from somewhere, she drew up a sleeping plan. Edward and Clowance should have the larger of the two new bedrooms over the library, Cuby and Noelle should have the next one. After that it was not so easy. Bella should have her own bedroom, Christopher could take Jeremy's, Henry for a night or two would perhaps be found a bed in his parents' room. As for Philip Prideaux . . .

'You are going to ask him?' Bella said.

'If he will come.'

'He must come. He saved your life.'

'He may feel uncomfortable if Clowance is there.'

'So may she, but they will get over it.'

Demelza said: 'There is that back bedroom over the kitchen. There is a deal of lumber in it. We could have it cleared out, buy a new bed – specially long for him – and new cretonne curtains.'

'We shall have barely a week,' said Ross.

'Bella and I can go into Truro on Monday. That man Jenkins has a yard near the old Cavalry Barracks. He makes furniture.'

After a few more jogging miles Bella said: 'Cuby has been seeing much of Philip Prideaux, from what I hear. Do you think sometime they might hit it off?'

Ross looked at Demelza, and they both laughed.

'Is that funny?' Bella asked. 'I merely thought . . .'

'What do you mean by "hit it off"?' Ross said.

'Well . . . read it as you will. I thought possibly they might even marry.'

'The only reason that what you said strikes us as funny is that the same thought has occurred to us *both* – but individually.'

'Well, that is good, isn't it? If three Poldarks are of the same mind, who can stand before them?'

'Don't forget,' Ross said, 'that we are not dealing with Poldarks.'

Demelza said: 'Don't forget also that because this idea has occurred to us all separately, that it may have been the thought of others too. It is not hard to see it, see the suitability. She is – is the widow of an army officer killed at Waterloo. He is a cavalry officer who has had his nerves grievously harmed by the same battle. He is unattached. She is unattached. They are seeing a lot of each other. But – but if too many folk put two and two together, this may come to be known between Cuby and Philip and produce a wrong feeling, a contrarious feeling which might bar it from coming to pass. And even if that is not so, there is a lot to be overcome. She will not want to appear in his eyes as second best to Clowance. He will not want to appear in her eyes as second best to – to – to Jeremy.'

'A pity,' said Bella, after a moment. She gave a little trill of song. 'For I am in a match-making mood.'

'Tell me, Bella,' Demelza said. 'How ever did you come to remember all those lines? I think you were good at school, but not quite brilliant.'

'It wasn't that hard. It is easier to remember something that interests you. And there's a sort of rhythm to it. You learn it all a small matter like music. You could almost sing it.'

'But you did not. There was nothing sing-song about it.'

'That was not quite what I meant.' Bella rubbed her fingers over a suddenly furrowed forehead. 'D'you know what I often thought of when I was playing Romeo? I thought of Jeremy.'

'Jeremy?'

'I used to admire him so much, sometimes I used to copy him, what he said, the way he walked, his – his own elaborate view of things! After all, he was my hero, my eldest brother. So when I came to play Romeo I said to myself, "You're not just Romeo – you're Jeremy too!"'

'Jeremy too,' said Ross. 'Well . . .'

'Also – also of Romeo and Juliet I thought of Jeremy and Cuby. No one could have felt more for a girl than he did for Cuby. And in the end I believe she for him. And that too had a sad ending . . .'

The rain had stopped, but great clouds swollen and pendulous as cows' udders drifted overhead; the whole landscape dripped. Isabella-Rose had a gift for sleeping during travel and she was curled up again in her corner of the coach, breathing peacefully and by now so used to the lurching and jogging that she was undisturbed by it.

Ross looked across at his daughter from time to time and was overcome with wonderment that in that slim, well-formed, sturdy body, that fair-skinned, firmly etched, attractive face, that brain altogether hidden from view, that all these features should in some way contain and contribute to what was a unique talent not given to lesser men or women. Whatever her attempts to explain it away to her parents, this was uncontrovertibly so.

She had sung or hummed a little once or twice today. It had hardly been heard since her illness of the summer – not spontaneous singing, that was. In June everything had been concentrated on one end; in December suddenly quite another. A crowning incongruity.

Was that ability returning? Would she one day become a prima of the opera as well as of the stage? He wondered if her prospective marriage to Christopher would be a success. Under his light-hearted happy-go-lucky manner there was a steely determination, a dedication to match her own.

As he looked at her he could not know that she would never sing opera again; singing for pleasure, yes, in character on the stage, yes, in a singularly sweet tone and reasonably effortless range, but the power and reliability in the top notes had gone for ever. Nor could he know, nor could she know, that she would quickly become the most popular English actress of two generations. A constant stream of successes would follow *Othello*: *The Country Wife*, *The Merchant of Venice*, *Love for Love*, *The Plain Dealer*, *Twelfth Night*. Prints, paintings, engravings would be sold in shops, and her face was to become one of the best known in London. And she was to be fêted and praised by the rich and famous: Wellington, Palmerston, Hazlitt, Coleridge, Southey, Wordsworth.

She knew nothing of this now. She had been dreaming that Dr Fredericks and Madame Lotti Schneider were giving her a cup of chocolate and persuading her that *Romeo and Juliet* set to music would be perfect for her to undertake with her new voice. 'It is an entirely different transcription,' Dr Fredericks, his cravat awry as usual, was saying. 'It is only when Romeo dies that Juliet has to sing top C and that can be taken over by the flute! No one will detect anything amiss.' 'But,' she was saying, 'I play Romeo and I cannot sing *baritone*!'

She woke suddenly at an extra lurch and saw with relief her mother and father in their respective corners and normality holding sway over nightmare. Her mother was asleep, her father fingering the pages of a book but making only a half-hearted attempt to read it.

'Papa,' she said in a low voice.

He looked up, smiled, glanced warningly at his wife.

'Do you think it will wake Mama if we talk?'

'I don't think so.'

'How are your injuries after the fire? I know you do not mention them.'

'Very light.'

'That great bruise on your forehead.'

'It has mended much. In another week it will be gone.'

'And the burn on your foot?'

'Seems to be healing in spite of the walking I have done. Give that another week too.'

She looked at him carefully. 'Nothing else?'

'Nothing else.' He did not mention the occasional dizziness.

She settled back. 'It must have been a tragic time. Can you tell me a little more about Valentine's death?'

He told her exactly how it had happened but omitted the hallucination he had suffered. She asked a few questions, but to Ross's relief did not bring up the subject of Valentine's parentage. He hoped to God she was young enough to have escaped the whispers.

'And Sir George?' she presently said.

Ross answered this too.

She said: 'When I was about ten I was always *terrified* by him and by his name, and the awful feud you had. I was always terrified that you and Sir George would come to blows sometime, that maybe you and he would fight out a terrible duel somewhere, perhaps on the cliffs, and only one of you coming back alive. I would picture you both with flailing swords or smoking pistols. I was really affrighted, and used to worry.'

Ross mused a moment. 'Yes, perhaps that would have been the straightforward way out of it all. But did it not occur to you that this might be unfair to Sir George? I am distinctly the better shot.'

'Oh, yes! But then, you never know. Your foot might have slipped on a stone. It's . . .'

'It's what?' Ross asked, smiling.

'You – you can't trust life, can you? The good side does not always win.'

'A cynical view for one aged ten,' he observed.

'Well, there it is. That's how I used to feel. I don't suppose, from what you say of him, it can happen now, can it?'

'I don't imagine so.'

'Thank goodness for that.'

The coach rattled on into the darkening afternoon, over the deserted moors.

Ross said: 'Did you feel real anger once or twice in the play? You seemed to.'

'What d'you mean, Papa? Real anger?'

'Well, you had shown much love. In the early scenes. If I had seen you expressing such love in real life I should have readily believed it. But anger. I think specially in – would it be a scene in the third act? – where you were in Friar Laurence's cell telling of your anger and frustration and despair that all was lost between you and Juliet, you expressed that with such reality that I thought, I have never seen her face like this! I do not think I have ever seen you angry – certainly not with face contorted and pulling at your hair and such distress. Where did it come from?'

She thought for a moment, hand reminiscently touching her hair.

'I have lost my voice.'

'Ah. Oh. I'm sorry. I'm sorry, Bella. I had not thought.'

'Oh, I love to act,' Bella said. 'It is – enthralling. It is the next

528

best thing. But most of all I want to *sing*. It comes out of myself. To have a voice and not to be able to use it as one wants to, it – it seems a sort of injustice.'

'It may yet come back.'

'I have a feeling . . .' She stirred in her corner. The afternoon light made her profile look pale. 'Papa, I am sure you have known injustice and have not felt willing to lie down against it.'

'Yes,' said Ross, 'there have been times.'

'Many times,' said Demelza.

'You are awake?'

'Yes. I have heard most of your conversation. Please go on. It is so pleasantly cosy sitting here listening to what you say.'

Darkness had almost fallen, but the lamp had not been lit in the interior. The coach smelt of camphor and dust. The air was stale. One of the windows was down by a couple of inches and admitted a thin current of air as refreshing as a tonic. Bella had been dozing again, dreaming again. She drew in a full breath of it, clearing her mind of disturbing fancies.

Then she saw ahead of them a bulk of land with lights twinkling on it. At the top of the rising ground a steep edge of cliff was etched against the sky. Lights showed it to be a building.

'Where are we?' she asked.

'Just coming into Launceston,' said Ross.

'No? Is this . . . Have we passed Polson Bridge?'

'No, just coming to it.'

'Oh . . .' She hesitated. 'Papa, could you, could you ask the coachman to stop the coach after we have gone over the bridge?'

He looked puzzled. 'Stop the coach? Whatever for?'

'I – want to get out.'

He said: 'You will be at the White Hart in ten minutes.'

'No, it is not for *that* reason!'

Ross looked at his wife, whose expression he could hardly read in the half-dark. She made a deprecating gesture.

'I'd like to, Papa. This is the bridge *now*!'

'Oh, very well.' He tapped on the little roof door, and when it opened he conveyed his message.

As he had tipped well, his request was at once obeyed. Four muffled figures travelling on the outside watched with interest as the young lady was helped down by the second coachman and went slipping off into the dusk. They saw her bend down and seem to sniff at her hands. Then she came back. The outside light of the coach showed up her satisfied expression. She was carrying what looked like some crumbled pieces of damp black earth.

As she climbed in, the door was shut behind her and she offered her cupped hands to her parents with one of her brilliant all-embracing smiles that seemed to encompass the whole world.

'Cornish earth!' she said. 'Smell it! It's quite different! We're home!'